S

Leave Love Alone is a magnificent drama that delves into the world of the Rodriquez family as they encounter joy, betrayal, deception, and hope on their road to redemption. Ms. Thompson explores the rich Afro-Puerto Rican and Black cultures by tackling a story that crosses generations and oceans. We experience the intensity of first love and the passion that it yields to the dissolve of true love because of a failure to communicate; the loss of children because of stubborn stances and the abuse of love gone bad; the triumph of perseverance and faith in what is so when we surrender and just Leave Love Alone. We learn that love rises to the occasion rewarding us with the ecstasy of joy and pain, the wisdom gained following the challenges of experience and the gift of love itself as the gift and the giver. Leave Love Alone is about the journey from heaven to hell and back as experienced by one family as they struggle to find their way home.

Ms. Thompson will surprise you with her gift of storytelling and the depth of insight she possesses regarding the human mental and emotional psyche. You will fall in love with some and others you will dislike with great disdain.

This mountainous body of work will hold your interest and keep you guessing while soothing your soul, have you rooting and cheering on the champions and pulling for the underdog. You may even want to get in the ring and box a few rounds out with a couple of these characters. However, why you are evoked or moved to respond is strictly personal. One thing is for certain; you will be moved, touched, and inspired

LEAVE LOVE ALONE

Viola G. Maxwell-Thompson

Silky,

Thank you so much for your support! I really appreciate your love!

All the best,

Viola G. Maxwell-Thompson

9-21-19

LEAVE LOVE ALONE

LEAVE LOVE ALONE

For information, address M2NPublishing.com,
40 East 9th Street, 1204, Chicago IL 60605,

www.M2NPublishing.com

Kai EL' Zabar, Editor
David Smallwood, Associate/Technical Editor
Renne Rhae, Cover Design
Steven M. Johnson, Book Design & Layout

Library of Congress Cataloging-in-Publishing Data

Maxwell-Thompson, Viola
Leave Love Alone: a novel / Viola Maxwell-Thompson

p. cm
ISBN 978-0-692-12022-4

1. United States of America

First Published in the United States of America by M2NPublishing.com
for Viola Maxwell-Thompson

Dedication

This book is dedicated to my mother, Lillian Johnson Maxwell, who lived to be 99 years old and always encouraged me to "Go for it!". And to my father, Daniel E. Maxwell, who taught me to see what wasn't there and believe in what could be.

Acknowledgement

I am so thankful and humbled to have had this opportunity to publish a book. I have been writing stories since I was a teenager but never imagined that one day my thoughts would result in a novel. I thank my husband, James E. Thompson, for pushing me beyond my comfort zone. He read my first draft and said, "You have a great story here." He then proceeded to share his enthusiasm with the woman who helped me mature my skills from being a story teller to a writer, Kai EL' Zabar. Kai mentored and counseled me on the fine art of becoming a writer, and she changed my world forever. Through her expertise, support and guidance, I found my literary voice. Brittany Thompson, my sweet daughter, encouraged me to push forward through this journey and applauded my many milestones along the way. My sister, Gloria Maxwell, who passed away shortly after completion of the first draft, taught me about point of view shifts and loved me so much that there wasn't anything I didn't think I could accomplish. Lastly, I want to thank and acknowledge my loving family members who hold a special place in my life and journey: my sister, Linda Maxwell, and her daughter, Ayodele; and my God Sisters, Cindy Thomas and Margaret McKoy. And to "my sistas", Mercedes Barre, Stephanie Hill, Julie McNeil, Carla Ogunrinde, and Kim Williams, your inspiration and appreciation for my love of writing helped me cross the finish line!

 VII

Chapter One

Lifting his body just enough to see the clock on the dresser, he noted it was only eleven-o-clock. He returned to staring at the ceiling, unable to sleep but with no recourse for accelerating time forward to morning. He felt like this most nights, lately. There was this uncontrollable anxiety that would take over Luis J's mind as the thoughts of the day's activities hotwired every nerve cell in his brain and denied him any possibility of finding peace.

He kicked the covers off his legs, allowing the air from the cracked window beside his bed to flow across them, and then he exhaled. It was always hot in his room, but worse at night because of its proximity to the kitchen. Though his mother was a great cook, her meals almost always involved the oven and the heat would settle in his room and then linger there, waiting to embrace his body.

Luis J glanced over at the outline of his younger brother Robert resting comfortably. He wondered why Robert was never affected in the same way. Every night, Robert's head would hit the pillow and he would barely stir until dawn. Oh how Luis longed for those nights when he, too, would be lulled into a restful sleep filled with comforting dreams.

He hadn't experienced that since his older brother Carlos moved out and his mother rearranged the sleeping accommodations, putting Robert in his room and giving his sister Chell her own space.

When they moved into this place five years ago, it was too small for them then, but after the divorce it was all his mother could afford. She had purchased twin beds for all of them because that's all that would fit in the room when accompanied by a dresser and a chair.

Thankfully, at least they weren't bunk beds. He had some friends who shared those horrific experiences at 6'5" tall. Unfortunately though, with his recent growth spurt, even this bed no longer accommodated his 6'3" frame and that, too, contributed to his restlessness.

He turned from his back to his side, trying to find the right position, but there wasn't one. He lay there searching his brain to determine the source of tonight's anxiety but couldn't tie it to a specific event.

He threw his legs out of the bed and sat up, firmly planting his feet on the floor. He just had to get out of the room and get some fresh air. He pulled on his jeans and slid a tee shirt over his head. Grabbing his pack of cigarettes and lighter, he gently turned the knob, opened his bedroom door and waited.

He noted that the lights in the living room and kitchen were off, but he still needed to confirm that everyone was asleep. When he didn't hear anything, he leaned his head forward. Looking to the right, past his sister Chell's room, he saw that the door to his mother and David's room was closed and the light was out. With that confirmation, Luis J headed for the front door.

About halfway there, he cursed, raised his foot and shook it to minimize the pain. He had stepped on one of Robert's toys that was still on the floor instead of in the toy chest where it belonged. He remembered how it was when he was growing up; he and Carlos were never allowed to leave toys on the floor.

But then, his parents were still together and his mother stayed home. Now, she worked and she seemed to be less strict with Robert's behaviors. Luis J wondered if it was because she was older now or if she was just too tired to enforce the rules.

Then, on top of that, there was his stepfather, David. He was overly forgiving of and catering to Robert's dramatic performances. Perhaps he felt he had to be given his role of step-father. Luis J really didn't know, but he could clearly see the signs of a spoiled child lying on the floor and it pissed him off.

This and so many other things ran through his mind. His restlessness kept his mind in and out of random thoughts that came and went. He needed to catch hold of one thing and let everything else go if he was ever going to calm down enough to fall asleep.

Luis J was the second oldest son of Luis Rodriquez, and Diane Johnson, now Anderson. He was named after his father even though he was not the eldest boy. Luis Rodriquez didn't really feel the necessity to stand on ceremony about the first-born son.

But when Diane held her second child in her arms, she admired his every feature. She looked into his big hazel-brown eyes and at the curvature of his face and it was like her husband was staring back at her. She kissed his forehead and whispered, "Mommy loves you Luis J."

That resemblance never faded. His short, wavy black hair, bedroom eyes and thick brows were encased in a creamy brown skin complexion. The older he became, the more often he mimicked some of his father's mannerisms as well.

Six months ago, Luis J turned seventeen and was now a junior at Benjamin High School. He was the starting guard for the Blue Demons and team captain. Although he favored his father, his body type resembled his mother's side of the family.

He was tall and lean, which gave him an unexpected advantage on the basketball court. His opponents often underestimated his agility and speed, so his jump shots and layups were dead on. He averaged about twelve to fifteen points per game and was already on the radar of a number of college scouts.

He was the perfect blend of Latino and Black, genes that the girls found very attractive. And, like most seventeen year olds, Luis J enjoyed the attention.

Quietly unlocking the deadbolt, he stepped out onto the apartment building's balcony. It was basically a long hallway that every apartment shared and led to the elevators located at the end of the hall. About four feet in front of the apartment door was a ledge that overlooked the courtyard.

Walking to it, he leaned over to check out the activity below. There was very little movement, a few people entering the building and two guys sitting on the bench smoking. The night air felt good as it settled around him. The chill of autumn was moving in and he shivered slightly. Placing the cigarette between his lips, he lit it and inhaled, hoping the mere act of breathing in the tobacco would short circuit the restlessness he'd been battling for the past hour.

After about the third drag, he could begin to feel a calmness seeping into his body. It started somewhere near the impression the toy had left and traveled up his legs to his groin. He didn't understand why smoking brought this comfort, but he was thankful for it every time. He glanced at the time on his cell and wondered how much longer he had before his mother joined him.

It didn't matter that she knew he found some solace from the chill in the air and the still of the night. It didn't matter that he was suffocating in that room with his little brother. She would find her way onto that balcony and invade his thoughts.

Just the memory of his last confrontation with her a few nights ago was already starting to reignite his anxiety. He felt like he was always under her microscope. She was watching and questioning his every move and decision. It was clear she wanted him to do things her way, whether it was right for him or not.

Obviously, she didn't understand the needs of a man. If she did, maybe Carlos wouldn't have moved out before his high school graduation. Hell, maybe his dad would still be living with them, too.

Then he heard it, the voice.

"Luis J, are you out here smoking again? You told me you were cutting back, trying to get to just two cigarettes a day. Are you still adhering to that?"

As she waited for his response she noticed he wasn't even dressed properly to be outside. "For God's sakes, why don't you have on some shoes and a jacket? Are you trying to get sick? You know that when you get sick, Robert catches it. Are you listening to me?" She was getting annoyed with him because he hadn't even turned to face her, let alone respond to her inquiries.

Luis J snapped the ashes off the edge of the cigarette and watched them fall to the ground before turning to face her. When he did, he noted that even in her bathrobe and with a makeup free face, she was a very attractive 5'7" tall woman. She was forty-five but clearly did not look her age. Even with her work schedule and other responsibilities, she still managed to fit in exercise a few days a week and made a point of watching her diet.

She had shoulder length, naturally silky, wavy black hair that she often fixed to depict her emotions. When her authority was being threatened or she was angry and felt powerless, it was pulled back into a ponytail. When it was flowing and loose, all was generally in balance in her life. Luis J noticed that it was in a bun tonight and wasn't quite sure what that meant.

"I'm sticking with the promise. This is only my second cigarette for the day," he said, ever so respectfully. "Mami, you know how hot it gets in that room and it makes it hard for me to fall sleep. And I told you that smoking helps ease my nerves. I'm sorry if my coming out here woke you."

Diane looked at her son, a little irritated to say the least, and admonished him. "Frankly, Luis J, you shouldn't be smoking at all. I hate that you even started that horrible habit. Lord knows it's no good for you. I can't even wrap my head around how it could be easing your nerves. And you keep telling me you're serious about basketball, but for the life of me I can't see why you don't see that smoking is completely contradictory to that statement."

"Mami, I am cutting back," Luis J retorted. "Besides, it's not like I'm doing drugs or drinking. Why can't I have this one bad habit? Everyone has something, don't they? I see you enjoying a glass of wine almost every night."

This was exactly what he was talking about. Here she was again blowing things out of proportion. She didn't have a clue about what he was experiencing, what he was struggling with. All she cared about was him following her rules, even if she wasn't following them herself.

"Ummm, smart mouth. But I'll give you a little leeway tonight. Put that cigarette out and then come inside," she said, pointing at it as it burned between his fingers. She looked at the facial hair and broadness of his shoulders and sometimes found it hard to believe how quickly he was growing up. It seemed like just yesterday that he and Carlos were playing in the living room, wrestling the way little boys do.

The truth was, Carlos was the reason Luis J started smoking in the first place. Luis J idolized him and wanted to be just like him, so there he stood puffing away. When she first learned he was smoking, it broke her heart. She had read tons of literature about teenage smoking when Carlos first started. She already knew of its addictiveness among adults but learned that it was even worse with teenagers and therefore very difficult to quit.

She also knew how it could negatively affect a growing child. She first tried reasoning with Luis J, explaining what was happening to his body. For every explanation she gave, he gave a reason why it wouldn't affect him that way.

Then she began threatening to eliminate his privileges but because of basketball practice and the games, she wasn't able to hold him to those restrictions. So, here she stood with the only option she had left: reminding him of her displeasure with his actions. Above all else, Luis J did not like to disappoint his mother and she clung to the hope that one day that would help him give up this habit.

Softening her tone a little, she said, "It's getting late. You need to get some rest. I saw on the schedule that you have a practice game tomorrow. Come on honey, let's go inside."

Luis J stood his ground and took full advantage of her tenderness saying, "I'll put the cigarette out but I need a little more fresh air. I'll be in shortly. Alright?"

Diane twisted her mouth in displeasure but she was tired so she made herself satisfied that at least he said he would put out the cigarette. She reentered the apartment and on the way back to her bedroom, stopped to check on her baby.

Diane had given birth to four children. The oldest, Carlos, was nineteen, the youngest, Robert, was seven and Michelle was almost sixteen. Her children were from the love she had shared with her first husband. They had been married for about eleven years before he broke her heart and they ultimately went their separate ways.

Now, she was married to David Anderson. He was a hardworking, easygoing man who was willing to be at her side to help raise well-rounded, healthy children in spite of the divorce. He was there for all of them and had opened his heart to each of her children as though they were his own.

He also was a man whom she felt truly understood and supported her, and that meant everything to Diane after experiencing the extreme disappointment and betrayal of her first husband.

She found her baby Robert fast asleep, the covers kicked off his body. It was hot in this room, she understood that. But she didn't understand this anxiety thing Luis J kept talking about. She bent down and rearranged Robert's body so she could cover his legs. She didn't want him to catch a chill from the night air since the window was open.

She placed her hand on Robert's back and rubbed it gently. He didn't even stir. He had no idea that she was there. That's the thing about children, you have to be there for them whether they know it or not.

Her next stop was Chell's room. Instead of opening the door, she just paused to listen for any indication that her daughter was still on the computer. Relieved that all was quiet and she didn't have to exert her authority with that child, too, she continued down the hall to her bedroom, never glancing back.

Entering the room, she found David still asleep, the television watching him. Before climbing back into bed though, she waited to hear Luis J return to his room. As much as she hated that either of her sons smoked, Luis J was right, at least it wasn't hard drugs and alcohol.

The past few years of raising them, especially Carlos, had taught her to choose her battles carefully and strategically. She glanced at the clock and listened attentively. She had heard him when he opened his bedroom door and then the front door. She didn't miss much when it came to her children. And she knew now that he still hadn't come in.

She was truly hoping that Luis J would not force her hand because if he did, he wouldn't like the outcome. She would give him another five minutes before rejoining him outside. 'Did he really think that she didn't know that he had relit the cigarette and finished it, despite what he had said to me?' she wondered.

As she reached for her robe again, she heard the front door open and close, giving her the "all clear" to rejoin her husband in bed. He stirred slightly as she snuggled her now cold body against his warm one. He moved a little and grunted softly as his body reacted to her cold touch before settling back into a sound sleep.

He hated it when she did that when he was awake but she couldn't help it. His body was always warm and it was the fastest way to warm up her feet. Once that part of her body was warm, it would quickly spread to the rest of her body. And soon after that, she would fall into a deep sleep.

As Luis J sat on his bed, some calmness in his body now from the cigarette, his mind started drifting and landed on thoughts of Dany. The more he thought about her, the more he longed for her touch. Confident that his mother was asleep by now, he put on his Converses, grabbed his Blue Demon's jacket and eased out once again, gently locking the front door.

He felt in his pocket for his bus pass, crossed the street and headed toward the corner. The screen on his cellphone now read eleven forty-five; the number fourteen bus would be there in about ten minutes. Thirty minutes to her house and he could still be back home by two. As he stood on the corner, he looked up at the apartment's windows. The house was still dark, except for the flickering of light from David and his mother's TV.

'Adults are so contradictory,' he thought. He was always being reminded to turn off the lights and to be conscious of the electric bill but every night that TV watched David and his mother sleep. All his friends said that their parents did the same thing.

Then just like that, his mind was in the moment. He knew that if his mother discovered he'd left, he would never hear the end of it, but he also couldn't spend another night like the last two. The ease he had experienced from the cigarette had worn off and now there was only one thing that would bring him comfort.

He didn't really know what was going on but lately he needed to release himself at least every other day. Sharing a room with his little brother didn't provide him with any privacy but even if it did, he usually preferred having it happen as the result of being inside of a girl. Tonight, he wanted the girl to be Dany.

He watched the bus approaching, and he thought, 'Right on time.' Things were getting off to a good start.

As Luis J bent his head down slightly to board, he observed a change in the driver's posture. He sat more erect in the seat, demonstrating his command of the vehicle and all the space around it. He even gripped the wheel tighter, making the muscles in his arms protrude through his uniform.

Luis J smiled to himself as he thought, 'I can bench press 250 pounds, so your muscles don't scare me. But trust me, I'm not on this bus to mess with you or any of your passengers. I'm only planning to wrestle with my sweet Dany tonight.'

As they made eye contact, the driver cleared his throat and said, "Let me see that pass again. It looks expired."

Luis J didn't say anything because he didn't want to give the driver a reason to put him off the bus. Instead, he showed him the pass, again, and waited for confirmation to board. The driver waved him on and he headed to the back of the bus to sit.

Propping his foot up on the seat in front of him, he opened the window so he could feel the night air against his face and once again began to relax. He looked around the bus to see who else was going along for this journey.

There was a woman, probably his grandmother's age, sitting in the very first seat, clutching her purse and avoiding eye contact with everyone. Next was a man with greying hair who was sitting near the back exit door. He had on work boots that were covered in cement and his jeans in mud. He was having difficulty keeping his eyes open and Luis J watched as his head kept snapping back.

The final rider was in his mid-twenties and sitting directly opposite Luis J. He was mumbling to himself and fidgeting in his seat. Now it was Luis J's turn to avoid eye contact in the event this man had some mental issues. So he began looking out the window.

There were a number of boarded up stores along Pitkin Avenue. Over the past year, there had been a lot of changes in the neighborhood. He had overheard his mother and David talking about it and saying it was an indication of a soft economy. He couldn't recall the term he had learned in his economics class but they were right.

He remembered when they first moved into the neighborhood, there had been a movie theater, designer discount clothing stores and even an arcade. Now, the only one remaining was the arcade, which was where his buddies usually hung out on Friday afternoons. Sometimes they played games but mostly it was a "hook up" spot and the girls who hung out there knew that.

The bus slowed to allow another passenger to board and then picked up its speed again. They were making good time, which would allow even more for him to spend with Dany. He started thinking about the last time they were together. She was so soft and always smelled so good.

He began to feel his manhood rising in anticipation and then it struck him. "Damn it," he said, under his breath. He had forgotten to grab a condom from his backpack. He slid his hand into his jean pocket hoping one might be there, but no luck. He then wondered if he had left one with her the last time they were together. They usually used two but he remembered that their last time was cut short by her nosy sister.

He couldn't remember but one thing he knew for sure, he had to be with her tonight. As much as he didn't like the way pulling out made him feel, if she didn't have one that's what he would do.

He was finally at her stop. He exited the bus, crossed the street and stood near the entrance of the brownstone building, gazing up at the windows to her apartment. He nodded as some guy walked by, not really taking his eyes off the windows, but making sure that the guy didn't pose a threat.

He was searching for some validation that it was okay to call her, that her mother was indeed at work tonight like Dany had told him at school. The lights were off in all the front rooms, but they were on in Dany's. He wondered if she was feeling the same anxiety he was, waiting for his phone call. So he dialed her and she picked up right away.

"Hey, Baby. What's going on? Another rough night?" she asked, in a whisper.

"Yeah, as a matter of fact. Look out the window. I'm downstairs. Can I come up?"

He saw her silhouette behind the curtain before it moved and then returned to its original position. Then he heard her say, "L, it's late. Why didn't you call or text me first? Now really isn't a good time."

Dany was the only person to call him L. Everyone else said Luis J. She picked that nickname because she wanted her own connection with him. And the way she said it was always very inviting and almost always gave him a hard on.

"I don't know. I just had to get out of there and I wanted to see you. Besides, I knew we had to wait until your Mom was at work. Come on, baby, don't dis me. Let me in."

"Fine, I'll let you in, but you should've called first. You have to be quiet though because Steph wasn't sleep the last time and she's been blackmailing me ever since."

"Are you kidding? She heard us? I told you that you make too much noise," he said playfully.

"This isn't funny."

"Hey baby, I'm sorry. You know that thirteen-year-old sister of yours is a little gangster. You need to straighten her out."

"Whatever…Come on, and be quiet Luis J. I mean it so she won't know. And when you get up here, don't even knock on the door."

Dany ended the call and moved to the front door to wait for Luis J. She was getting used to lying to her mother and sister about things so she and L could spend time together. She was crazy about him but knew that sneaking him in like this was taking a huge risk.

Her little sister would do or say anything to avoid their mother's anger. And quite frankly, so would she. Her mother had an incredible temper and it didn't take much to set her off. And once that happened, she was a mean woman who had no issues with resorting to physical violence. But all of that didn't matter right now. Her sweetie was on his way.

Luis J ended the call and opened the door. The hallway was long, dark and smelled like fried chicken. The smell nudged his hunger pains since he hadn't really eaten since lunch. Basketball practice ran over and by the time he got home everything had been put away. His mother had been in one of her you're-grown-and-can-fend-for-yourself moods, and wouldn't warm up anything for him. He couldn't even get Chell to do it for him. So he just made a turkey sandwich, drank a soda and ate some chips. It was hardly enough given the calories he had burned off during practice but he too was trying to prove a point: that playing ball took a lot of energy so he needed someone to care for him when he got home.

But his mother wasn't falling for that and had stood her ground. Well, if he was lucky, the smell was coming from Dany's or maybe she had some leftovers. Her mother was a decent cook, even if she was mean as hell. The last two steps brought him to the third floor. Her apartment was behind the staircase, and when he turned, there she was standing in the doorway.

As he approached, he admired her Beyoncé-like thighs, which were a result of her interest in dance and her cheerleading, the fingertip curls that caressed her face, and that warm smile. Again, he felt his manhood coming to attention and he had to have her.

Without saying a word, he reached his arm around her small waist and pulled her body into him. Her 5'5" frame required him to lean down and her to stand on tip toe but they were used to that position and fell comfortably into it. Still standing in the hallway, his lips pressed against hers gently at first and then more passionately as his tongue parted them. He moved his hand down to rub her ass, but she began pulling away, quietly. She pressed her finger to her lips to remind him to be quiet and motioned for him to come inside.

The only light in the room was from a nightlight kept near the doorway to the kitchen. He allowed himself to be navigated through the living room and down the short hallway to her room. He had done it so many times before he could have easily been the leader. But, for the moment, he let her be in control. She paused outside her door and looked down the hallway toward Steph's room. They both stood there quietly, making sure there wasn't any noise or movement coming from behind her door. They moved on when Dany was sure that her sister was really asleep.

After closing the door to her room behind them, Dany motioned for him to sit down on the bed. It was a full size mattress and he felt envious at times that she had so much bed for such a petite frame. Her iPod was docked in the iHome and was playing random songs. The genre was hip-hop from the late 80s.

Once again, his eyes were drawn to her body and he now admired her ass as she rolled the dial looking for the right selection. Yeah, there it was, Toni Braxton. They both liked listening to music from that period but Toni's voice was soft and sexy, just like Dany's.

As Luis J sat there, the melody playing with his mind, he took time to look around the room as if he wanted to ensure she was still his woman and no one else had been in the room or in her.

He noticed the new posters she had mounted on the wall of Usher and Omarion. He knew she liked Usher's music and so did he, but he was pretty sure their half-dressed bodies were really why the posters were up there. Because he shared his room with his baby brother, he couldn't put up the kind of posters he wanted, the kind that would surely make Dany blush.

"What's up with that? Shouldn't you have my poster up there?" he asked, pointing to the guys attached to her wall over her desk.

"L, please, keep your voice down," she said, gently, reminding him of the impending trouble before continuing. "You know how I feel about you…besides, last time I checked, you didn't have a poster. But I got you!" she said, with that sexy voice.

He reached out and tried to pull her toward him saying, "Are you sure about that?" She giggled and managed to elude his grasp. Then without warning she pulled her tee shirt over her head revealing her firm, round, brown breasts and tight abs. He thought to himself, 'Man, my baby is HOT!'

He watched as she removed each piece of her clothing except her panties and then he pulled back the bed covers, motioned for her to lie down and slipped out of his clothes. Climbing into the bed and pulling her to him, it wasn't long before they were kissing, hugging and connecting in a way that would ignite a smoldering flame. He was about to enter her when she stopped him.

"L, where's your cover?"

Still kissing her lips, he muttered, "Dany, baby, I didn't bring one."

"Umm, slow down. What?"

"I was in a hurry to get here. I thought I had one on me, but I don't. Didn't I leave one here?" he asked, eyes still closed and in the zone.

"No, and even if you did, I would have thrown it out; that kind of craziness I don't need. You know how my mother is, she sees everything. She found the pack of cigarettes you left in my purse and I had to tell her they belonged to my uncle. She has been on me ever since. She swears I'm up to something. If she found out about us sleeping together, she would kill me. So, now what?"

"Dany, baby, please I really need you tonight," he mumbled, pleading with her and continuing to rub her breasts to keep her aroused.

"L, what's going on? First you call me from the corner, it's obvious what you want, and then you don't even bring a glove. And worse you didn't even bother to give me a heads up before we started. I don't want to get pregnant and I'm pretty sure you don't want that either. So why are you talking like it's no biggie to do this with no cover?"

"I don't even need to answer that. You know what I want. I want you. And no I don't want you to get pregnant but come on girl, I need you. I need to feel your warmth, your excitement. I can't explain what I'm feeling; I just know that I want to be here with you."

Dany cautioned her next words but she was stimulated, too, so she suggested, "Maybe we could do something else? I really am afraid to try it without the cover. If I get pregnant I can't even imagine having to tell my mother."

"Something else like what, Dany? Don't you trust me, baby? You know that I won't do anything purposefully to hurt you. I promise you I won't get you pregnant. I'll pull out in time. Come on. Come on."

He pulled her back into his arms and kissed her on her forehead, her cheeks, everywhere but her mouth. And she let him. "Where were we?"

She said nothing but he could tell from the way she was responding that she still felt apprehensive. Still, he had to have her. He had to release this tension so he could rest. He didn't think it was the same for women, but Dany liked making love with him because he took the time to make sure she was ready for him.

As promised, just before he came, he pulled out. His semen shot out onto her stomach. He had to be careful not to get it on her sheets, which was requiring way more control than he wanted. But damn she had felt so good it really wasn't his fault.

Once she cleaned up, she lay in his arms. He didn't engage her in conversation so it wasn't long before he could hear her breathing getting heavier and he knew she had drifted off to sleep.

And he felt relieved, finally. He always felt calmer after being with Dany, and not always just from the physical connection. Even in their heated moments, her eyes, her face, calmed him. The clock on the iHome read one-thirty. He calculated that he could stay another thirty minutes and still get home long before David got up. He laid back and got comfortable.

"Luis J, Luis J, what are you doing here? Ohh, Danielle, you're going to be in so much trouble."

He felt someone's hand on his shoulder shaking him lightly. The voice sounded familiar but it didn't make sense. He rolled over to see Steph standing on the side of the bed and his heart started racing. He looked over at Dany, sound asleep.

'Yeah that lovin' had been good. She's still knocked out,' he thought, smiling proudly. But all of that was now crashing down as he responded to Steph, "Oh shit! What time is it?"

"Five-thirty. Oh-h-h, did you spend the night? Danielle, Mama's gonna kill you."

"Steph, leave the room so I can get up. And don't say anything to your mother."

"Why shouldn't I? Did you guys make out?" she asked, throwing questions out one after the other. "Is that your underwear? And why are they off?"

"Look, I hear you like to extort people, so I'll make it worth your while. Now would you just get out?"

She strolled to the foot of the bed and then giggled as she closed the door. Steph was manipulative and a real pain in the ass. She had learned two rules early on: self-preservation and secrets can make you a lot of money. She and Dany were complete opposites so Luis J guessed she was learning this behavior from her mother. Steph was always looking for a way to make the best out of someone else's bad situation and he realized they had just handed her a golden ticket.

Luis J bent down and whispered with his warm breath against Dany's ear, "Dany, Danielle, wake up."

She stirred slightly then awoke suddenly when he touched her shoulder. "What's wrong? Oh shit, what time is it?" She looked at him, shaking her head because she knew it was early morning and they were in trouble.

"It's five-thirty and unfortunately, Steph just woke me up," Luis J said.

When she comprehended those words, there was no longer room in her head for grogginess or confusion. "Oh man, L, are you kidding me? My mother will be here any minute and she can't find you anywhere near this building. And on top of that, you're telling me Steph knows? This is bad, really bad."

Dany began looking for her clothes, anything to put on that would hide her activities of the night and allow her to see him out as quickly as possible.

"Don't worry about Steph, I'll take care of her before I leave, but I gotta go, now," he said, zipping his pants and grabbing his jacket.

"Are you gonna be okay? What time does your mom get up?" she asked, even though she knew Mrs. Anderson was nothing like her mother.

"Oh, in about twenty minutes; but at least David has already left so I won't have to deal with his lectures. It's probably gonna be a bad morning…but last night was great! You're so good baby, so good," he said, rubbing his groin.

She smiled as he blew her a kiss but she was still feeling very anxious about the situation. She wanted him out of the apartment and far away from the building.

"See you in school," he said. When he opened the door to her room, he found Steph standing in the hallway between Dany's room and the front door.

"You were saying?" she asked, her hand extended and her fingers wiggling.

"Here's twenty dollars to hold you. I'll give Dany some more at school later this week." He was glad he would be receiving his allowance on Saturday.

"I hope you know my silence is gonna cost you a lot more than this," she said, snapping the bill between her hands.

He half expected her to take out a marker to make sure it wasn't counterfeit.

"Didn't I just say I'd give Dany more this week? Steph, I'm not playing with you. Keep your mouth shut. You don't want me on your bad side," he warned her in a firm voice. The voice of a man.

She put the bill in the pocket of her bathrobe and headed to her room.

He knew this was going to cost him at least another twenty dollars just to keep her in check. As he exited the building, the morning air greeted him and felt almost as crisp as the night's.

He noted what a difference the time made as there was much more activity on the street: cars, buses, bikes, people rushing to work and returning home from the night shift. The noise level was raised about 1,000 decibels and the movement was purposeful. As he waited on the corner for the bus in front of Dany's building, he caught a glimpse of her mom's car sitting at the light. He quickly turned his back and lifted the collar of his jacket to shield his features from her. He thought to himself, 'With any luck, she would just think he was one of the neighborhood guys.' After all, she had no reason to think otherwise.

When the light changed, she drove past him, headed toward the parking lot adjacent to the building. He breathed a sigh of relief because she didn't stop to confront him. He moved to the curb ready to quickly board the bus as soon as it stopped.

As the bus sped down the street, he tried to recall how he had overslept. The last thing he remembered was listening to Dany's breathing, thinking how he'd lay there for thirty more minutes, enjoying the warmth of her body.

Obviously, the restlessness of the previous nights had finally caught up with him. Lucky for him, though, buses ran express that time of morning, so the entire trip took him about ten minutes. He spent that time rehearsing his explanation.

At his stop he exited from the rear of the bus, which placed him closer to his apartment building. He knew every second counted. Walking past the apartment doors, he took note of how noisy it was in all the apartments as the families were beginning their morning routines. He could smell coffee coming from Mr. Joe's home and bacon from Ms. Annie's. That pattern continued until he reached his door.

He stood there for a minute because it was still quiet. By now, his mother should be up, the TV should be on in the living room playing the news and coffee should be brewing. But he didn't hear or smell a thing.

Pulling his keys from his jeans pocket, he turned the tumbler carefully so as not to disturb the silence. But, the force of the door swinging open nearly threw him off balance. There in the doorway stood David. He was dressed for work in a white shirt and blue-stripped tie, but for some reason, he was still home. 'What the hell?' Luis J thought. 'Why is he still here?'

But instead of asking any questions, he just nodded, "Morning," acting as though all was fine and attempting to move past David into the house. David's body didn't yield a pathway. Instead, he repositioned it directly into Luis J's way.

"Mornin' David. Heading to work?" Luis J asked, not really expecting an answer but creating room for some level of interaction so he could get to his room and then the shower. He could still smell Dany's scent on himself and he didn't want anyone else to be exposed to their intimacy.

David was 6'3", 235 pounds, with broad shoulders. He was pretty fit and demanded his respect in the house. Luis J had seen him go up against Carlos a few times before he eventually moved out. Recently, Luis J and David had been having their challenges, but Luis J still respected him and wasn't looking to cause a rift between them.

David had come into their lives about six years ago and married his mother about five years ago. It had been a difficult time for everyone as their mother's emotions were all over the place leading up to and after the divorce.

Sometimes she would be sad, crying in her room behind closed doors, other times really mad at their father for leaving them all alone.

At the time of the divorce, Carlos was thirteen, Luis J was eleven, Chell was nine and Robert was one.

But when David came into their lives and began caring for them, their mother often felt compelled to remind them how much he truly loved her and how good he had been to all of them.

Usually, those statements would send Carlos into a defensive mode about their father and that fueled the tension between David and Carlos from the moment David moved into the house and lasted until the day Carlos moved out.

Luis J was still waiting for some kind of verbal response but what he received instead was an even more rigid stance. The kind of stance that exuded, 'I'm really pissed right now.' So, Luis J responded with, "Well, I'm going to get ready for school. If I can just squeeze by you."

"Man – and I use that term loosely – what the hell is your problem?" David asked.

"Nothing. Why?"

"Luis J, stop. I'm not that old that I can't remember being seventeen and sneaking out of the house."

"Oh, naw man. I woke up early and stepped out for some fresh air and a smoke. I figured you had already left so when you opened the door, you startled me. That's all there is to it. So, if you'll excuse me."

As Luis J attempted to move pass David once again, David grabbed the material of Luis J's shirt in his right hand, pulled him into the apartment and closed the door with his left. He then opened his palm and used it to pin his stepson against the living room wall.

Because David was so swift with his move, Luis J was caught completely off guard and his body began moving into a defensive stance. His leg bumped into the lamp table near the doorway and knocked his mother's Soap Opera Digest magazines to the floor. The lamp also rocked back and forth before finally settling back to its position in the middle of the table.

"David, what's up, man? Let go of me!" Luis J shouted, losing his cool. But David's hand was planted firmly against his chest, limiting his movement and Luis J stayed pinned to that wall.

"Let go of you! Let go of you? Who the hell do you think you're talking to? You don't tell me what to do or not do!"

"Man, what are you so mad about?" Luis J asked, annoyed and embarrassed that he didn't see this coming.

"Try this on for starters. What's in your pocket?"

"My pocket?" Luis J asked, puzzled, wondering what he could possibly have in his pocket that would elicit such a response from David. Drugs, condoms, what?

"I know you heard me."

"My cigarettes and a bus pass. Why?"

"What else?"

"David, what's up with these games while you have me pinned against the wall? Let me go, man." The pressure behind David's hand on Luis J's chest was starting to hurt but he would never give David the satisfaction of knowing that.

"What else?" David asked again, now closing his fingers back into a clasp around Luis J's shirt. 'This boy is really getting on my nerves,' he thought.

Luis J really didn't know what David was talking about, so he reached into his left pocket where he found his cigarettes and bus pass, like he had said. Next, he reached into his right pocket, nothing there. The last place to search was his back pockets and the content of those pockets caused him to curse.

Now, he remembered. His mother had asked him to move the car to the other side of the street right after dinner so she wouldn't get a parking ticket. It was a street cleaning day. Unfortunately, the key was still in his pocket. He hadn't even felt it.

This was an issue for David because his job was way across town and he never, ever took public transportation, even though they lived in New York City. He always hated it, stating it was a waste of his time and unpredictable. Luis J heard his mother say once that public transportation couldn't be any more unpredictable than traffic and they all laughed, except David.

"David, I'm sorry. I forgot I had the key. Really I didn't remember that it was in my pocket."

"You forgot? That's your explanation? If you had put it back where it belonged when you came back, this would not have happened. You are so full of yourself and you think you're slick."

Luis J smirked, thinking, 'You think I'm the one who's full of himself? I take public transportation every day.' But instead he said, "David, I didn't take the key on purpose and I wasn't just driving the car, if that's what you think. Now, will you get off me?"

"Where were you, Luis J?" David asked, not removing his hold.

"I already told you."

"And I obviously don't believe you if I'm asking you again, now do I? So do you really want to stick with that?"

Luis J didn't answer David's question quickly enough, so he pulled him away from the wall and then slammed him back against it. The pain shot down Luis J's shoulder blade and stopped at the tip of his fingers. Instinctively Luis J's fist flew into the air.

"Don't even think about it. I'm warning you," David stated in a firm, authoritative voice. "Don't give me a reason to hurt you, boy."

Reluctantly, Luis J unclenched his fists and let his hands fall and as he did the pain started to subside. He didn't want to fight with this man but he also had no clue what answer he was searching for.

Luis J heard a door open and then footsteps coming down the hallway toward the living room. Based on the swiftness with which the body was moving, he knew it was his mother. He turned his eyes away from David and toward his mother who was standing just in the archway, but he didn't say anything.

Diane looked up at her son, who was staring back at her as he did when he wanted her help and as much as she hated to admit it, he looked just like his father when he had asked for forgiveness.

Luis J waited for her to say something.

She cleared her throat and demanding quietly, said, "David, please honey, what are you doing? Let him go."

That was her power play, her secret weapon, to always show composure. It made the rest of them look out of control.

She had used it on his father, too, and Luis J remembered how it had infuriated him. It affected David just as much, if not more, but he somehow managed to answer her calmly enough.

"Diane, I'm not hurting him, but I wish I could knock some sense into his head, because he needs his ass kicked right about now."

Diane fully entered the room and took a seat opposite the two of them on the couch but she did not take her eyes off her son. She hoped that her calmness and presence in the room would have an influence over her husband.

When David didn't move, she called out to him, again, "David."

He began to loosen his grip; but never took his eyes off Luis J. He finally let him go and took one step backward. Luis J felt eased, maybe even a little bold. David didn't miss that hormonal change and began retracing his steps back toward Luis J.

Diane motioned for her son to sit down near her. This whole scene was making her very nervous and reminded her of David's confrontations with Carlos. Those did not end well at all. They never came to blows but that was because Carlos was calmer. But this son standing in front of her didn't like being bullied.

Luis J moved passed David and sat on the edge of the loveseat near his mother. He knew he was about to get lectured for inconveniencing David.

David walked around to the front of the loveseat, but remained in close proximity to Luis J, standing in front of him with his back to his wife. His eyes still on Luis J, he now asked, "Diane, ask your son where he was. See if he's going to disrespect you, too, with his lies."

"David, why are you blowing this out of proportion? I told you I didn't realize the key was in my pocket. I already apologized. What else can I say?"

"Luis J, answer my doggone question. Or would you like for me to tell you who just called?"

Luis J watched his mother's eyes move from his face to David's back. She clutched her robe near and Luis J wondered which emotion would present itself first.

"What's going on? Luis J?" Diane asked in a demanding tone, slowly articulating each word. She hadn't seen any marks on him so she didn't think he had been in a car accident. 'What on earth had happened?' she wondered.

"Alright, I did leave during the night. I couldn't sleep, so I took a bus ride. I must have fallen asleep and when I woke up I was at the end of the line. I had to wait a while for the return..."

Luis J's response was interrupted as he felt pain shooting across his cheek and down his neck. His head snapped back from the impact just like the man who was sleeping on the bus. Once again, his defensive posture kicked in and he leaped from his seat, ready to return the blow. He would aim for the chin first and then the chest.

"Luis J, no!" Diane jumped up and positioned herself between her husband and her son. David was trying to reach around her to grab a hold of the boy. The whole time, he was talking.

"I've never raised my hand to you since I've been with your mother. I've always told you what I expected from you and what you would get in return. I thought we could make this work, but I won't tolerate lies in this house. I had hoped it wouldn't come to this with you, but I see now that I'm going to have to straighten your ass out, right here, right now. Something your father didn't stick around long enough to do."

"David, stop it, there's no need to bring his father into this. Stop right now! Calm down, please, you'll wake Robert and Chell. You know how easily Robert gets upset. Whatever it is, Luis J will tell us."

Diane stood her ground, facing her husband and trying to grab his flailing arms. She turned her head over her shoulder to look at her son, her eyes pleading for him to say something that would bring this to an end. They both knew that David could easily overpower Luis J's slender frame and she feared for her son.

Luis J was still trying to figure out what David knew. Who could have called him? Did someone see him leave the apartment last night? Did someone see him this morning? Oh shit, Dany's mother must have recognized him. Fine, he had to be cool. Who else did he know who lived over in that neighborhood?

"Luis J, we're waiting," Diane said, pleading with him.

As Luis J opened his mouth to start, David interrupted him, moving from Diane's grasp and once again invading Luis J's space before saying, "Gloria Webber called, that's who. She's Danielle's mother, his girlfriend. Guess whose son she saw in front of her building at five forty-five this morning, apparently waiting for the bus?"

He phrased the question for Diane to answer, but continued glaring at Luis J. "She goes on to tell me that when she gets upstairs, her daughters are awake, still in their bedclothes, and she thinks Danielle was forced to have sex. Now, my educated guess is this BOY was at her house last night, trying to be a MAN. Ms. Webber was hysterical and asked what kind of a son was I raising? Well, now, isn't that a good question?" David exclaimed, slamming his fist on the coffee table. "But I wanted to hear what Luis J had to say so I asked him where had he been when he walked in the door. And he lied. Plain and simple, he lied."

Luis J thought to himself, 'Damn it, this is bad.' He looked at his mother but she was looking down. He didn't know why Ms. Webber had said forced, though. There wasn't anything forced in their interaction.

"Let me explain," Luis J offered.

"Oh, now you want to explain. Guess what, it's too late because we already know everything," David said.

Diane looked at her son now with disbelief. She had listened to ensure he had come in off the balcony, but apparently he had deceived her too. "Luis J, after I warned you to go to bed last night, please tell me this isn't true. You and that girl are having sex? Isn't she like sixteen? She's so young. So are you for that matter. Were you really over there for God's sake?"

"I just told you he was. I wouldn't lie about that," David said, now annoyed that Diane was trying to give him a way out.

"I know but I'm just trying to understand why, David," Diane responded before returning her comments to her son. "You're about to ruin your whole life. Did you really force her to have sex with you?"

"Mami, please, I'm not stupid. No. She agreed and we were careful."

David just looked at him with disgust and shook his head.

"Careful? What does careful mean? Did you use a condom like we talked about?" Diane asked.

After a pause, and feeling embarrassed about having this conversation with his mother again, Luis J responded, "Not exactly."

"How in the hell is having unprotected sex in these days and times careful?" David asked.

"Luis J, how many times have we talked about this? You know the risks. How many times have you done this with her?" his mother asked him.

"Done what?"

"Oh, there's that smart mouth. Don't you know that your mother and I are trying to do what's best for you, give you a chance to grow up and become a man? But I've told you before about that mouth of yours. Now stop avoiding the question and answer it. We already know we aren't going to like your response."

"You wanna try and slap me again? Go ahead and try; you've probably been waiting to do it for years, but it won't change things. You aren't my father. And you never will be."

"Man, for that I should kick your ass on GP. I may not be your biological father, but I have been here for you as a father. I'm sorry you feel that way, but if that is how you feel, then you won't have a father who is involved with your life," David snapped back.

There was so much this boy didn't know about his father, so much Diane had kept from them, but David had tried his best to help raise someone else's teenage boys and it hadn't been easy.

Luis J sat there really frustrated. David was not his father and quite honestly he didn't feel like he needed one. He had managed for the past six years without his father in his life and things were just great. He hadn't done anything wrong and here David was busting his chops just because he had been out for a few hours last night. It wasn't like he was running the streets or clubbing. He had just spent some time with his girl.

"Stop it! Both of you need to clear your heads. David, why don't you go on to work? I know you'll be stuck in traffic and probably late, but you should at least get going. Besides, Luis J needs to get ready for school now anyway. Let's let time help all of us think about what needs to be done. We can talk more tonight after dinner."

"You think it's that simple? That I can just go off to work like nothing has happened? I told you before that there's only room for one man in this house and that's me. Carlos didn't understand that but I need to make damn sure Luis J does. Do you get that Diane?"

"I know. Yes I get it, but we aren't going to resolve this right now. I'm just as upset as you are," Diane offered, as she began pulling her hair back. She checked her wrist for a ponytail holder but there wasn't one there. Instead, she just kept pulling it back and letting it go.

"Oh, but I beg to differ, we can most certainly resolve it, right now," David retorted.

"How do you propose to do that when you're so angry? Please, I don't want this to get blown out of proportion," Diane pleaded.

"Blown out of proportion? Diane, do you hear yourself? Well one thing is clear, you and your son seem to agree that I've blown this out of proportion. Unbelievable! Un-freaking believable!"

"Luis J, go get ready for school and leave me and David alone," Diane demanded, her patience a little short with both of them right now.

Not to be undercut by her, David added, "Luis J, you're to come straight home after school. Got it?" He hoped he was getting through to this boy. He was not going to tolerate anything short of complete respect.

Luis J looked away from David, rose from the couch and said, "Yeah, I got it." He left them standing there, entered his room and shut the door behind him. Robert stirred but didn't open his eyes. Luis J could still hear his mother and David talking. He thought to himself, 'Boy is this some shit.' He reached for his cell phone to call Dany. After the third ring he heard a voice.

"Hello. Who is this? Is this Luis J?"

"Yes, Ms. Webber, may I speak to Danielle?"

"Luis J, you disrespect my house and the first thing you say to me is can you speak to Danielle? How dare you?!"

There was that word again. 'Why were adults so obsessed with that disrespect word?' he wondered. During the silence he was able to hear what sounded like sobbing and assumed it was Dany. He just wanted to speak to her to know that she was alright.

So he humbly said, "Ms. Webber, you're right and I apologize for my actions. But I don't disrespect your home and certainly not your daughter. I care for her. I was actually calling to see if she was alright."

"You care for her? How's coming over here in the middle of the night to have sex showing respect for someone? Let me tell you something – stay the hell away from her from now on! Do not go near her. Do not call her. Do we understand each other?" she yelled into the phone. Then it went dead.

She had hung up. All he could do now was wait to see Dany at school. After lying down for about an hour, he showered and dressed, packed his backpack and headed to the kitchen. Robert and Chell were at the table eating Cheerios. With all that had happened that morning, his mother obviously didn't have time to cook breakfast, so cold cereal and milk would have to suffice.

Chell looked at Luis J and then their mother. Obviously she had overheard some or all of their "discussion" that morning and was looking to see how her older brother was fairing.

To break the tension, Luis J asked, "Hey, you guys ready?"

Diane continued packing Robert's lunch box as she expressed her frustration with Luis J, saying, "Yes, they're ready and you need to hurry up or they'll be late. And Luis J, don't forget, right after your practice game, you better be here."

"I know, Mami," Luis J mumbled, as he grabbed Robert's backpack and his hand with Chell following closely behind him.

The hallway and yard noise had increased greatly as children of all ages headed for the bus stop. They had exited the building before Chell said teasingly, "Ooooh your ass is grass!"

"Shut up and watch your mouth before I have to hurt you. I told you about cursing anyway. It sounds nasty coming from you," Luis J said.

Ignoring his reprimand, she continued, "I heard David this morning. Hell, the whole ninth floor did. I can't believe how mad he was."

"Daddy was mad? Why was Daddy mad?" Robert asked.

Luis J gently punched Chell's arm. Now she had Robert feeling compelled to get into the discussion when he had clearly slept through it all. Robert started calling David Daddy when he was about two. At first Luis J hated it, but he realized that David was the only father Robert knew. He had never spent any time with their biological father the way the rest of them had.

"Chell talks too much, Robert. David and I had a disagreement this morning. That's all."

"What is a dis-a-gr-mint?" Robert asked.

"They had words, except David had more," Chell snickered.

Michelle Rodriquez's wit was just like their father's and Luis J usually loved going up against it but not this morning. She was almost sixteen going on twenty and he recently recognized how much she had grown over the past few years, mentally and physically.

She was named after their mother's sister, Michelle, so they called her Chell for short. She was pretty too. She even had features like her namesake, but her skin color and hair texture were more like their grandmother's. Their father's mother's lineage was from Spain and her hair was curly and black. Chell's hair was long, naturally curly and thick. It was easy to comb until it got wet.

Yes, she was starting to really fill out and that was now Luis J's signal to keep a closer eye on her because the guys in the neighborhood, hell anywhere, would certainly be sniffing after her and he wasn't having that for his baby sister.

He shot her a glance that he was pretty sure she recognized as 'Don't test me,' so she darted off to stand in line with her friends. He finished walking Robert to the bus stop where his school bus picked him up and handed him his backpack.

"See you later, Luis J."

"Yea, little man. You got it," Luis J responded before heading to his bus.

Chapter Two

When he walked onto the schoolyard, he found Maine, Steve and John sitting on the bench.

"Hey. What's up?" Luis J shook their hands and snapped fingers in their normal way of greeting one another.

"You got it," Maine replied.

"Man, Rodriquez, you look like shit warmed over. Had a rough night?" John asked.

"Naw, man. He and Danielle must've been into it," Steve replied, snickering.

"What the hell does that mean?" Luis J asked. Did the whole city know about his rendezvous?

"Like you don't know what I mean. Why you hit her like that, man? That was not even cool," Steve continued.

"Hit her. Hit who? What the hell are you talking about?"

"I saw Danielle on the bus this morning. She had a welt across her face. She looked bad. I asked her what happened and she said you guys had a fight and you hit her."

"What the…? That's bullshit. Steve, why you lie so much, man?" Luis J said, punching the air in front of Steve's chest.

"I'm not lying, man. That's what she said. She looks really bad. Besides, Danielle's a nice girl, why would she lie about that?"

"I'm not saying she did but I swear to you I did not hit her. But I'm pretty sure I know who did."

"Luis J, man, my bad if you didn't hit her, but somebody sure did and it ain't pretty. When you do find out and you need to whup some ass, let us know, we got your back."

"Yeah, that won't be necessary, but thanks. Look, I gotta bounce. I'll catch up with you guys later," Luis J said, turning away from them and heading toward the building. As he walked away, he could hear Steve repeating how bad Dany had looked.

The first bell rang just as he entered the hallway of her homeroom class. When he turned the corner, he saw her standing in front of the room with Sharon, one of her cheerleading friends. As he approached them, Sharon moved to block his path to Dany.

"Can I help you Luis J?" Sharon asked, rhetorically.

"Girl, move," Luis J stated. He wasn't in the mood for her melodrama.

"Why, so you can beat on Dany some more?"

"I didn't hit...Look, would you please just step aside? Dany and I need to talk," he asked, attempting to sidestep her. The action reminded him of his confrontation just a few short hours ago with David.

"My girl doesn't want to talk to you, Mr. Big Shot, so get lost," she said, flicking her hand in his face.

"Sharon you need to move. Don't fuck with me. Not today. Besides, Dany can speak for herself. Dany?"

"Luis J obviously doesn't hear well. Let's go Danielle," Sharon said, grabbing Dany's arm and guiding her towards homeroom.

"Danielle, wait."

When she finally turned toward him, Luis J could see her face for the first time. Her cheek was bruised and swollen and she had a welt just below her left eye.

"Dany, damn, what the hell happened to you? I didn't know. Please, can we talk, just for a minute?"

She stopped, looked at her L, her eyes tearing up and said, "Go to hell!" She turned and ran into her homeroom leaving him standing in the hallway.

He couldn't believe what he had just seen and even more so what he had just heard. Why would Dany lie about what happened and blame him? Why wouldn't she talk to him? Her mother wasn't there watching them now. That woman must really be a witch. Dany hadn't lied about that. Now Steph's actions made sense. She would sell Dany out in a minute to protect herself.

The final bell rang and Luis J was nowhere near his homeroom. He took off at a rapid trot down the hallway. He was hoping that his teacher would be engrossed in the results of the week's football games and on the internet checking rushing yards and team standings and not even notice him. But with his luck this morning, it was unlikely.

However, when he arrived, that's exactly what was occurring. The whole room was abuzz discussing the scores, quarterback ratings and yardage stats. Luis J eased into the conversation as if he had been there all along and drew very little attention to himself.

He spent the rest of the day in a daze, lost in his imagination and self-pity. Dany managed to avoid him; but some of his classmates and members of the b'ball team would not let him forget what he had been accused of and the rumors were spreading rapidly. Most of them were being blown out of proportion, but that's what usually happened with the topic of the day. And it made him chuckle when he remembered what David had said, "Well, it's clear that you and your son agree that I've blown this out of proportion!" But clearly his 'proportion' didn't even compare to what was being said at school.

The only person Luis J hadn't talked to or heard from was Coach. He was pretty sure the rumors had found their way to his office so it was just a question of when and how Coach would bring it to him for clarification. Luckily, he had the truth on his side so he wasn't too concerned. But Coach was not one for drama and certainly not drama involving his team captain. Thankfully, the game had been cancelled for the day so he wouldn't have to deal with Coach until tomorrow.

But when school let out, instead of going directly home Luis J stopped by the arcade to work off some steam. Most of the people there were from a rival school so he could blend in and not have to talk about any of the BS he had left behind in the hallways of Benjamin.

When Luis J finally made it home, everyone else was already there. David was sitting in front of the TV watching the news and Chell was helping their mother finish cooking. Luis J prepared himself for another hot night, literally and figuratively. He nodded good evening and headed straight for his room.

Just as he got to the doorway, the house phone rang. Chell was the first person to answer it, as usual, and Luis J heard her say, "Hello. Yea, he's here. Is this Dany? Hey, girl. How are you?"

'So, she's finally ready to talk,' Luis J thought. "Chell, give me the phone."

"Hold on," Chell said to Dany and then she held the phone in the palm of her hand for him to come and get it.

Luis J knew he didn't want to talk in the living room where he would have an audience, so he said, "I'll take it in here." He closed the door, lifted the handset and waited for Chell to hang up.

"I got it," he yelled out. He had told her about eavesdropping on his personal calls and this was no exception. He could tell she still hadn't hung up so he cracked the door ready to jump on her only to see David holding the receiver instead. "David, I got it," he repeated, not feeling like dealing with him either right now.

"David, can you help me, please?" he heard his mother ask from the kitchen. David turned slowly, pressing the off button as he moved and joined his wife in the kitchen.

Closing the door to his room and sitting on the bed, Luis J began, "Dany?"

"Yea."

"What the hell was today all about?"

"I'm sorry, L. I was hurt and embarrassed and I didn't think the story would spread like that."

"Dany, we both know that's bullshit. You know how Benjamin is. How could you not know? You've been there for three years, too. So, was it your mother who told you to say that I hit you or did you make up that story on your own? Either way, don't you know we have to stick together? And on top of that, what you said can cost me my position as captain. I've told you before that Coach doesn't play around with shit like this. Hell, he could even put me off the team if he believes this lie."

All Luis J could think about was how quickly this could escalate and he could find himself benched or worse and even become ineligible for the college draft. He had been waiting to showcase his talents to the scouts since he joined the team three years ago.

But Coach didn't play around with any abuse to girls, especially ones on the cheerleading squad. And as the team captain, the expectations for him were even higher. He remembered when he got the position, Coach made it clear what it meant and there was NO room for misinterpretation.

He had said, "Luis J, perception is everything so keep it clean. What people believe about you can make you or break you. I don't normally allow juniors to be the captain, but the team voted for you and I won't go against their wishes. Don't make me regret that decision."

And now Luis J found himself having to navigate through this shit, working to minimize the fallout and he hadn't even done anything to deserve it. The silence on the other end of the phone brought his attention back to the call and he felt that maybe he was being too hard on her. So he continued with, "Are you alright? That's what I really wanted to know. Are you in a lot of pain? Tell me what happened."

"Yea, my cheekbone is really sore, but I've been using warm compresses on it since I got home." She paused for a moment to touch it and see if the degree of pain had lessened any. It hadn't, but she continued, "My mom came in right after you left. Steph and I were standing in the kitchen arguing about how much more money she wanted from us and really didn't hear her enter. She overheard part of our conversation and confronted us. She told me she saw you on the street. She recognized the Blue Demons' jacket. She threatened to break our necks if we didn't tell her what was going on. Steph isn't the badass with her that she is with us, so she started spilling her guts, as usual.

"My mom went straight to my room, saw the sheets messed up and went ballistic. She started looking around and found my underwear in the covers at the foot of the bed. I didn't know what to say, L. She slapped me and called me a whore. She said that she didn't go to work every day for me to lay on my back whoring.

"She threatened to send me away to my aunt's house in the south and so much more. Too much to repeat right now. It was bad. I was so upset that I started crying. That made it worse because she said I was crying like a baby but screwing like an adult. Then she got the belt and started beating me. It hurt so bad that after the third blow, I tried to block her arm and the buckle bounced back and hit me in the face. She only stopped because I screamed. I guess she thought the neighbors might hear.

"Then she headed for Steph, accusing her of being in cahoots with me. She even asked her if she was sleeping with you, too. Isn't that sick? I don't know why she thinks so little of us. But she didn't even have to touch Steph before she told it all, everything she knew, and sealed my fate."

Dany couldn't continue anymore. Tears were welling up in her eyes and she bit her lip. Her mother had been more uncontrollable than she had ever been and for the first time, Dany had actually feared her.

"Baby, I'm sorry. It's all my fault for falling asleep," Luis J offered sympathetically. "I really meant to leave, but you meant more to me than a Quik-trip service. I don't care what your mother says, I do care about you. I hope you know that. So I guess after she was done going after you, she turned her venom toward me. She called here and told David I was over there and that I forced you to have sex. Did you tell her that?"

Dany didn't say anything and after a few seconds of silence, Luis J noted it to memory before continuing with, "Anyway, David was waiting for me when I got home. When he told me what happened, I called you."

"I know. I heard what my mom said to you. She wouldn't let me talk to you. When she got off the phone, she told me that I had to end things with you. L, we have to stop seeing each other."

"What? Girl, that's not happening."

"Yes, it is. I just can't take the chance of someone seeing us and telling my Mom. She's making me take a pregnancy test in a few weeks just in case. But if she found out we were still seeing each other, she would ship me out of town for sure."

"Baby, slow down. Let me talk to her. I know I can explain how I feel about you and make her understand. Besides, except for last night, we have mostly been careful. I know I pulled out in time, though, so I don't think you're pregnant. She's just trippin'."

"L, you're not listening to me. She beat the crap out of me. I don't ever want her to go off on me like that again. I really care about you, and I know you care about me, but I'm the one who has to live here. I've told you about my mother's temper and this morning was worse than it's ever been. You saw my face. I never should have let you come in, but I'm responsible for that. I knew the risk.

"But my defenses are down when I'm with you and I can't trust myself. I really shouldn't have agreed to sleep with you without a cover, either. You shouldn't have even started with me without telling me that first. But it's done now. I've just been praying all day that you pulled out in time and I'm not pregnant."

After a pause, she continued, "So if you really care about me, you'll accept this and leave me alone. You're so special and I love hanging with you, but I can't take another beating like that. I won't. I just wanted to tell you that I'm okay and sorry about the lie. I hope everything works out for you at home and with Coach."

"Dany, I can handle home, but you've got to come clean at school. It's my reputation on the line. This could screw up my future. Let's start there and then we can figure out the rest of it as long as we stick together. I promise."

"I'll have to think about what I can do about school. I really didn't mean to cause any complications for you. Like I said, I was embarrassed, but there can be no more me and you. Sticking together is not an option. Take care of yourself, L. Bye…"

He sat with the phone in his hand in complete disbelief. He and Dany had been seeing each other for two years. She was more than a girlfriend to him.

They had met after one of the basketball games his freshman year. She was trying out for the cheerleading squad and was hanging around afterwards to watch the game. She was with a group of girls when the team came out of the locker room but she was hanging back, away from the crowd.

That innocence and shyness made her stand out even more to him than the ones on the front row trying to get his attention. He smiled and winked at her and she returned the greeting. He admired how cute she was in that short skirt, narrow waist, big, brownish eyes and beautiful smile. He liked that she was not an “easy” girl and her innocence intrigued him.

She eventually told him that she had kept her distance from the guys on the team because of the reputation most of them held and she had assumed that he was just like them. Additionally, she was a little apprehensive about the age difference. He was a year older than she was even though they were in the same grade. She had skipped second grade and academics were still clearly a focus for her as she was sporting a 3.6 GPA.

As they came to know each other, they discovered that they shared a lot of similar interests. Math was their favorite subject and they enjoyed sci-fi movies. They found it easy to talk to each other so they would for hours some evenings, especially when Luis J was having trouble with his mother. He had really enjoyed Dany’s presence in his life.

It wasn’t until about four months ago that their innocent fooling around crossed over into an intimate encounter. It was a hot summer night and Dany was wearing really short shorts and a thin, short-waisted shirt that showed off her belly button. Luis J was sitting on the column in front of her apartment and she was standing in front of him. They were desperately trying to catch a cool breeze.

She was standing in between his legs with her back to him, rubbing against his thighs, as she often did to tease him. But that night she kissed him differently. It was definitely more inviting. When she leaned back, she looked into his eyes and asked him if he was ready. His first thought was, 'Hell, yeah,' but instead he asked her if she was. He knew he would be her first and he had always told her he wouldn't pressure her into being with him.

Unlike Dany, Luis J had been sexually active since he was fourteen. It started about two years after his mother and David had married. Even while he was dating Dany, he had continued to be sexually active with other girls, but they all knew he had someone else who was special.

The ones who knew that Dany was his girl also knew that they were never to tell her about his relationship with them or he would shut them down. Most of the girls didn't want it to end because Luis J was different than the other guys on the team. Luis J always treated them with kindness.

So that night he waited for her response, hoping she really was as ready as she seemed. He knew it would make their bond with each other even greater. The next words out of her mouth were, "Let's go." She didn't have to tell him twice.

Her mother and sister were out of town so they could take their time. He slowly removed her clothes, being very deliberate with each action. He had touched her breasts before and even rubbed the inside of her thighs but tonight he was going to make her first time special. He took care to make sure her body was equally as ready to receive him as she was desirous of him. He was very gentle with her but he enjoyed her too.

After that night, they met at least once a week, and each time the sex got better as she became more relaxed and in-tune with her body and his rhythm. They made good love together and he was getting aroused just thinking about it.

He put the house phone down and picked up his cell. Her picture was his screen saver. In one stupid move, he had torpedoed their bond. Luis J was furious. He would have paced in the room if it were bigger. He had to get out of there.

When he opened the bedroom door there everyone was, staring at him. That's exactly what he was talkin' about. Everybody was always in his business. He needed some privacy, so he grabbed his jacket from the back of the couch and headed for the front door.

"Where the hell do you think you're going?" David asked, interrupting the silence.

"Mami, Daddy said a bad word!" Robert yelled.

"Out. I need some fresh air," Luis J responded, ready to back up his words if necessary.

"You aren't going anywhere," David replied.

"David, give me a break. I'm gonna stand on the balcony and have a cigarette. And before you say anything Mami, it's only my third one today."

"Luis J, don't touch that doorknob. I'm not playing with you boy!" David exclaimed.

"Luis J, it's time for dinner!" Chell shouted, much louder than she needed to. She too could tell the tension was escalating and she didn't want to see anything happen to Luis J. She hadn't let on but she had heard the entire exchange between them that morning, including the sound of a slap. She knew her brother wouldn't stand for that again.

Luis J felt like he was about to explode. He had to get out of the house. David was always talking about how he was the "ideal" father, but when he had the opportunity to take up for him with Mrs. Webber, he didn't.

So why not? David should have told her that she was full of shit, that his son wouldn't force himself on anybody. But instead of doing that, he got all bent out of shape about the doggone car key. Incredible.

When Luis J heard his mother clear her throat, he stopped his forward momentum and headed back to his room. He knew what that meant and he wasn't in the mood to add her wrath to the mix. He picked up his cell phone and dialed Carlos' number. He hoped that he would be available. He had to talk to someone who understood him.

"Hola."

"Carlos, you busy?"

"Hey lil' bro. No. Qué pasó?"

"Shit, I'm so sick of David and his damn rules."

"Wait, hold on." Luis J could hear the TV and voices in the background. He wondered if Carmine was over there.

"K, I'm back."

"You got company?"

"Carmine's here. Before you start, how are Chell, Robert and Mami?"

"They're all fine. Chell's a pain in the ass, as usual."

"I don't want to hear about how she's being a pain in your ass because you spoiled her and I told you to be careful with giving her so much shit."

"Well, that's not exactly what happened, but what you should be talking about is her body. Did you see her the last time you were over here? She's really filling out. She's getting hot, if you know what I mean."

"Yeah, I know what you mean about her. I did notice that the last time I was over there. Mira, since I'm not there, you gotta keep those boys off her ass. You hear me?"

"Yea, I'm watching out for her."

"You better be. So, what's going on?" he asked, satisfied that he had covered the critical topics.

"Man, I screwed up." Luis J told his older brother most of the details and waited for his support.

"And…"

Clearly that was not the response he was expecting, so Luis J said, "Whatever. I'm not going to tolerate David acting like he's my father. He wouldn't even let me go out on the fricking balcony for a cigarette just now. That's just stupid, man. Like I don't have the common sense to know that I can't leave the house with them watching my every move."

"You don't get any sympathy from me about that Luis J. I've told you a hundred times that if you're serious about ball you better cut those sticks out of your life."

"Lo, really, you're bringing that up now? Besides, dude, you smoke. Ah forget it. Anyway, all I know is David better not slap me again."

"Hold up. He hit you?"

"Hell…are you listening to me? Yes."

"Where was Mami?"

"Standing right there."

"What did she do?"

"Nothing, until it looked like we were gonna fight. Then she stepped in front of me just as I was about to swing on him."

"Luis J, you have a temper and a smart ass mouth, always have, but he really doesn't have the right to hit you. You need to talk to Mami."

"For what, Carlos, she won't do anything. She didn't do anything when you and David were at it. She just goes along with everything he says."

"My situation was different and I had somewhere to go when I moved out. You don't have that option, so I suggest you talk to her. You need to tell her how you feel and get her to see that David hitting on you is NOT acceptable. I won't stand for it."

After he calmed down a little, he asked, "So, what's going on with Dany?"

Luis J felt good that Carlos had his back. That's what he needed to know if it came to anything...although, he wasn't sure why moving in with him wasn't being considered as an option. So, he'd have to circle back to that one later.

"We broke up tonight about fifteen minutes ago. She dropped me man. She told me that she's really afraid of her Mom and doesn't want to risk getting her ass kicked again. But it still burns. I really feel her, Lo."

"Yeah, man, I hear you. But honestly I think you guys were getting way too serious anyway. You need to be focused for basketball season. You have a lot riding on this year. I know I don't need to ask this question, but I will. You guys have been smart, right?"

"For the most part. I didn't have a condom last night."

"Man, Luis J, bro, come on. What have I told you about that shit?"

"I got that. I did the right thing."

"We'll see, now, won't we? Mira, you gotta control that. If it's not right, you know what to do. Especially now since you're going to be out there swinging in the wind. These chicas will be all over you. We don't need any roadblocks between you, ball and college. Comprendes?"

"I know. That's not what I'm worried about. I'm just frustrated and tired of this place. I need to get out of here and away from David. He's revved up and ready to kick my ass and I'm not going down like that. I can tell you that for sure."

"You do need to get out of there because you guys sound like you're sitting on top of a bomb. Why don't you see if Mami will allow you to come by tomorrow evening and spend the weekend? That should give him and you some time to calm down and cool off."

"For real? You don't have to work? That would be perfect."

"I'm off this weekend so if she's okay with it, I'll pick you up around 5:30. No te preocupes, bro."

Carlos always ended his conversation with "not to worry" even when things weren't cool. It was a saying he had picked up from someone. Luis J never found out who, but it suited him.

Luis J was appreciative of his big brother's wisdom. He always had a way of seeing a path out of situations. He was level-headed and much more mature than most other people his age. His mother used to say, "Carlos has been here before. He's an old spirit." Carlos and Luis J used to just laugh at her because they thought she could see or hear spirits somehow. They didn't really understand what she meant.

Carlos looked more like their father's side of the family. He was only 5'7" – the same height as their mother – only with a stocky build. He had to work out more than Luis J so he would look fit and buffed. Carlos was very sharp academically. He even graduated from high school a semester early. He had received academic scholarships from several schools, but hadn't enrolled in any.

Luis J never understood why and whenever he asked Carlos about it, he wouldn't get a straight answer. Luis J eventually learned to leave it alone and instead just enjoyed having his brother around a little longer. His advice, when Luis J chose to listen to it, was insightful and helpful and he appreciated it. Now that he didn't live with them anymore, it was less frequent.

Carlos and David never really got along from the very beginning because Carlos never seemed to understand or accept why his mother re-married, especially so soon after her divorce, and to someone who was nothing like their father.

As a result, Carlos never let David in or allowed a relationship to develop. The bickering started over minor things like chores and then escalated to Carlos' comings and goings and school. Luis J wasn't clear about what was brewing but he used to listen to Carlos complaining at night once they went to bed. The drawn lines were not budging and the tension was mounting until the Friday evening that Carlos and David entered their final round. When they did, it ended with Carlos moving out.

He was seventeen at the time, didn't have a steady income so Luis J wondered where he was going. It became clear when he heard his mother on the phone talking to his father.

"Luis, what the hell is going on? I did not give Carlos permission to live with you and certainly not that thing you are living with. You know how I feel about her. I told you a long time ago about that."

Luis J could tell his mother's fuse was burning down to the powder and an explosion was inevitable. That thing she was referring to was Maria, their father's girlfriend. Luis J didn't know all of the backstory, but at some point, Maria was no longer a friend of the family and now held the title of number one enemy.

But to their mother's dismay, she lost the battle and Carlos lived with their father and Maria for a year, until he finished high school, found a job and got his own place.

Without warning and bringing him back to the present, the door cracked. Chell had been sent to tell him that David and their mother were waiting for him. Luis J noticed that she looked a little nervous, so as he passed her, he pulled on her hair and gave her a wink. She then took Robert's hand and they went toward the bathroom. It was time for his bath and apparently Chell had been given that assignment tonight.

His mother motioned for him to come into the kitchen. He saw that she looked drained. The aroma from dinner awakened Luis J's stomach, but he ignored it for now. If he had an appetite left after the firing squad was finished, he would eat.

He pulled out the kitchen chair and sat down without being instructed to. He was trying to minimize the number of commands he had to obey.

"Luis J, we have agreed that you'll stop seeing Danielle and apologize to her mother. Additionally, you will be grounded for a month. After school you will come home and there will be no weekend activities." David paused as if he were giving Luis J time to recognize who was wearing the pants in this house.

This was just enough time for Luis J to voice his complete disagreement with their position but instead of addressing David, he directed his questions to his mother, saying, "First of all, who is we, Mami? Did you discuss this with Papi? Secondly, I thought we were going to talk after dinner. I didn't realize this was a sentencing. I'm not Robert.

"And just so you know, Dany and I have already broken up. She called just to let me know that she was fine because her Mother beat the sh…crap out of her. The woman that you want me to apologize to, beat her, and left a welt on her face. Then she forced Dany to say I hit her. And for the record, I have already apologized to Mrs. Webber, even though she didn't deserve it, but she didn't accept it."

Attempting to regain the focus of Luis J's attention, David said, "I'm sorry Dany was beaten but you set that in motion with your actions. So in some regards, you are acting like a seven-year-old."

Continuing to ignore David and hoping to get under his skin, Luis J did not shift his gaze when he asked, "Mami, can we talk about this? You haven't really heard my side of the story and everything that has happened since this morning."

"No. Your chance to talk was this morning," David interjected. "You elected to play the nut role. So we, your mother and I, who are here and responsible for you, chose this course of action," David replied, matter-of-factly.

"David, no disrespect intended, man, but I was talking to my mother. I know she can answer for herself. And as for your course of action; it's crap. Basketball practice has started and I can't miss any practices, I'm team captain. Mami knows this even if you don't. And any punishment has to start Monday because Carlos wants me to spend the weekend with him."

There seemed to be a pause of silence that was sucking the air out of the room until David finally said, "Are you hearing us? First, this is not up for discussion and any violation will result in your ass being put out. Secondly, I don't care about what Carlos wants. He does not direct any traffic for anybody living in this house," David stated, re-asserting his position of authority. 'Obviously this boy still doesn't realize I mean it when I say there is only one man living under this roof,' he thought.

"David…let's not go too far," his mother finally said. "Basketball has to be an exception and honestly, I think it would be good for him to spend some time away from this house. Both of you need to settle down and I don't see that happening with him here right now."

It was clearly for the best since David was hell bent on proving the point that he's the man in this house. She understood that, but she did not want this point made at her son's expense or detriment.

"Diane, would you stop giving in to him?" David implored. "We talked about this, we agreed on the punishment." He was listening to the words coming out of his wife's mouth, but didn't recognize any of them. They were not at all what the two of them had discussed and agreed to. What was wrong with her?

"I know, but we can wait until after the weekend; maybe some time with Carlos will be good for him."

"I doubt it," David commented. For all they knew, Carlos was egging Luis J on and creating this tension in their home.

Luis J assumed that David was probably remembering one of his previous arguments with Carlos but said anyway, "See David, that's what I'm talking about. You don't get it. Even though this morning you said that you've been seventeen, you don't act like you remember what it's like. And you certainly don't know what it's like to have a stepfather who wants to prove that 'he's the man.'"

Before David could respond, Diane interrupted Luis J, saying very sternly, "That's enough, Luis J. I don't need or want you to try to explain my actions." Turning her attention back to David, she said, "David, we cannot interfere with his basketball season. It's the one thing he can focus on and this is a crucial year. It's part of his future."

Exasperated, David said, "Oh, woman, what do you want from me?" He pushed himself away from the table, rose up and walked to their room. He was no longer willing to play this game with them. Neither of them.

When the bedroom door closed, Luis J began, "Mami, thanks. I think he forgets…"

"Shut up, Luis J. You're working on my last nerve. I love that man. He's been good to me, to us, at a time when your father turned his back on us. He deserves your respect."

"I've heard all this before. And in case you've forgotten, I have respected him. That's why this is not all about me. You have got to see that." Luis J had to stop her before she started idolizing David to him again. He really couldn't tolerate it tonight.

"Then act like it. And what do you mean it's not all about you? I will not let you come between us."

"And what about him coming between you and me? You don't even give me the benefit of the doubt anymore. You just stood there and let him hit me. He doesn't have any right to touch me. No wonder Carlos left."

"Luis J, I didn't interfere with him hitting you because you deserved it. We have told you time and time again not to disrespect us and you know I do not condone lying to me. Besides, you don't know the whole story regarding Carlos, so leave that alone. You better be concerned about your situation."

After a few minutes of silence, she asked, "Do you think Danielle's pregnant?"

"No."

"Really, why not?"

"We only did it once without protection."

"It only takes once. I should know." Diane rose from the table and left Luis J sitting there. When she reached her bedroom, she paused for a moment as she wondered what was on the other side of the door. She steadied herself, opened the door and then closed it behind her.

Luis J wanted to ask her what that meant, but he knew that was probably not a good idea at this time. Besides, she had agreed to let him get out of the house for the weekend and that was what he really needed.

Luis J looked in the refrigerator and took out a couple of pieces of fried chicken. He loved his mother's fried chicken. She told him it was an old southern recipe she learned from her mother. They had spent a few summers with their grandmother when he was about six or seven, but Luis J didn't remember smelling or eating any food as good as his mother's cooking. He placed three pieces on a paper plate and put them into the microwave. While it cooked, he stepped out onto the balcony and lit a cigarette. He thought to himself, 'What a helluva day it had turned out to be. Who would have thought that it would have ended like this?'

He had felt so good leaving Dany this morning, looking forward to seeing her at school. Their lovemaking had been awesome. He had taught her how to please him and she really knew how. Their chemistry had been perfected through their time spent together. But it was more than that. He never used her. She was like an investment. He had actually spent time cultivating a relationship with her. Now, they were over. How did that happen?

Chapter Three

Luis J cut classes on Friday because he wasn't in the mood for or ready to deal with any more questions or accusations. The only concern he had was that he would miss practice and wondered what Coach would think about his rationale. So he told Coach a little white lie about his absence being a result of his brother's health.

He didn't like lying to Coach Watson and didn't do it often but he did take note of Coach's brief remarks. Luis J could only assume that Coach had heard something about Dany's accusations. The whole thing with her had unfolded so quickly that his primary concern had been for her wellbeing.

But when the dust settled, what had that action really earned him? The last thing he wanted was for Coach to start doubting him, his commitment to the game or come to the conclusion that he didn't deserve the position of captain. Luis J had worked hard for that title and he didn't have any plans to let anyone take it away from him.

He could see why some guys stayed out of committed relationships during the season. It could really mess with your head, and if your head was screwed, your game was off. The one on the court and the one off.

Still, as he played the games at the arcade, killing time, his mind kept wandering back to Dany. He wondered how she was feeling. He opened his phone to send a text message to her and saw instead that he had one.

It was from Cassie. It read, "Wanna get 2 gether?" Cassie was one of his Quik-trip girls. She was a senior at another school and they had met at Maine's birthday party about four months ago. He wondered if she somehow knew he had cut classes.

Without putting too much thought into it, he hit her back with, "Why not?" They agreed to meet at her place, which was on his way home from the arcade anyway. Their relationship was straight up about the service lane. He knew why she had texted him and she knew why he had responded. There was nothing else to it. They were willing to fulfill each other's desires. Their conversations usually amounted to: what you been up to; seen the latest movie; do you have one or do I need to get one?

Luis J probably saw Cassie a couple of times a month, usually when Dany's mother was working the day shift and they couldn't hook up at night. Cassie's mother didn't have any rules and that gave her the freedom she needed to get with him.

"So, what's going on with you and Danielle?" Cassie asked, as she reached to put back on her robe.

'Oh here we go,' he thought. 'The word is out.' But it was not a conversation he was going to have with her. "I've told you before, that topic is off limits," Luis J replied, with a finite tone in his voice.

"I know. But it's just that I heard about some trouble between the two of you. I was just wondering if you were still together, and what that means for us."

"Cassie, there is no us, so it's none of your business. Besides, I came over here didn't I?"

"Alright, Luis J, I just asked."

Irritated because she was forcing him to acknowledge the pain in his gut when he had come over here to forget about it, he rose from the bed and said, "I gotta go."

"You could stay a little longer if you want. That was good but it could be even better."

His body was tempted, but his mind was ready to go. Carlos would be picking him up and he did not want to be late for that so he said, "Maybe next time."

"So, will we be seeing each other more often, now?" Cassie asked, while sitting on the side of the bed, watching him dress and playing with her hair.

He looked at her and wondered where her head could possibly be. He continued dressing without answering her question. When he reached for the door handle to exit her room, she asked the question again.

"Ask me again, and this will have been our last time together," Luis J replied, closing the door behind him. Cassie was getting a little attached and that was dangerous. The last thing he needed was to be tangled up with her, especially since he didn't have any feelings for her in that way.

He had told her when they first hooked up that there was only one girl he was in a "relationship" with and that was Dany. She often teased him that he was truly a passionate man and that he needed a more mature woman than Danielle. When she started with those comments, he usually shut her up by threatening to find a mature woman, elsewhere. Hell, she was no woman either.

When he got home, no one was there. He felt relieved; it wasn't often he had the house to himself. He put on the stereo and jumped in the shower. The water felt good on his body. He had definitely had a workout with Cassie and now the heat felt good on his muscles. He had to admit, she was pretty good. She knew how to work her body on him and he usually got an immediate release without having to work too hard to please her. If Dany really was "off limits" for a while, he would definitely have to see more of someone.

Leaving the bathroom, he bumped right into Chell, who was headed to her room.

"You're home early," Chell noted. She had heard the shower when she entered the apartment and wondered who it was. She was usually the first one home and had about an hour or so before their mother arrived with Robert. It was her time to make her own choices without parental intervention.

Pulling the towel tighter around his lower body, he said, "I didn't have practice today."

"Really? Stacie just told me her brother was at practice."

"Yea, well, some people, like Roger, need to practice all the time. Your brother is hotter than that," he said, a smile covering his face as he thought about Roger's skills. He was a senior who played forward, but his layups and rebound percentages were dismal given the two or three additional inches he had on Luis J.

Rolling her eyes at him and perching her mouth, she said, "Think a lot of yourself, do you? Anyway, can I come to your next game?"

"I'm not sure. Why? When did you develop an interest in my game?"

"I've always liked basketball and last time I looked, it wasn't a team of one," she said, tagging him back.

"Funny. I never said it was and that's exactly why I don't want you there in the bleachers by yourself or hanging around waiting for me to come out. Maybe you can come one day when Carlos can accompany you and then take you home once the game is over."

Chell scrunched up her nose and rolled her eyes again before saying, "You mean like a chaperone? Luis J, you realize I'm almost sixteen, right?"

"I know, Shortie," he said, thinking to himself, 'That's exactly why I don't want you hanging around waiting for me.' It seemed like every day there was something changing about her. Her body was slammin' physically and she was starting to wear clothes that accentuated the curves. He wondered if their mother was noticing this and if so, why wasn't she reining her in?

Chell didn't understand how boys were at his age. She had no clue that they would lie and tell her what she wanted to hear to get what they wanted; any boy with a pulse and eyes would want to get between those thighs. It was that testosterone that led them to the honey. It was what had led him to Cassie's that afternoon.

He did not want Chell to become free with her body like Cassie. And, he did not want Chell exposed to some of those guys on his team, and definitely not without supervision. They would not resist the temptation even though they knew she was his sister.

"Then why aren't you acting like it? I know how to handle myself. I have to do it every day."

"Why? Is someone bothering you?" Luis J asked, leaping into big brother protective mode.

"No. I'm just saying that I know how to shut boys down."

"Oh. Right. Look, I'll check with Carlos this weekend and see what his schedule looks like. I'll let you know. But right now, I need to get dressed," he said, shuffling past her.

After he finished packing for the weekend, Luis J laid across the bed and eventually dozed off. The sound of the TV in the living room and a low chatter seeped into his dreams and gently awakened him. He sat up and saw that he had about thirty minutes before his ride arrived, so he joined the family in the living room.

David looked up from the paper but didn't say anything. His mother was in the kitchen cooking, Robert was playing on the floor near David, and Chell was sitting at the table doing homework.

"So you finally woke up? Chell told me you were home when she got here. Why didn't you go to practice?" Diane asked.

"I wasn't feeling that well so I just came home. What's for dinner?" Luis J responded, looking to shift the focus of the conversation.

"See? I told you not to stand out there without shoes and a jacket on. Come here and let me see if you have a fever," Diane directed, hoping that he wasn't sick because Robert would have to sleep in her room to keep him from getting sick and that would mess with her weekend plans. She and David usually had their most intimate times on the weekends, and Robert's presence would put an end to that.

"Mami, I'm fine. I don't have a fever. I was just tired," Luis J replied, grabbing a chicken wing off the serving tray. "Stop worrying."

"It's my job to worry about my children," she said, smacking his hand just before it cleared her airspace. "Are you packed?"

Before Luis J could respond, Robert asked, "Where're you going, Luis J?"

"Yea, I'm packed. To see Carlos," he managed to reply while smacking on the chicken. It was good, and if he thought he could get away with it, he would grab another piece.

"Can I go?"

"Not this time."

"Why not? Daddy, can I go with Luis J to see Carlos?"

"No, son. But don't worry, we'll do something fun with Mommie and Chell this weekend," David offered, hoping to provide comfort to his little man.

Robert, obviously disappointed, climbed into David's lap. David hugged him and let him lean against his chest. The knock at the door interrupted the caring moment between father and son and Robert leaped from his lap to open the door for his big brother.

Carlos entered and greeted everyone. A caring tone was directed toward them as he said their names until he got to David. It was now polite and distant. Then, turning to his brother, he said, "So, man, you ready?"

"You bet, let's go."

"Why don't you guys stay for dinner?" Diane suggested. She hadn't seen Carlos in about two weeks and she wanted time with him to catch up. He looked alright from her quick observation but she knew Carlos and he was good at protecting her from any potential hurt.

"Thanks, Mami, but we need to go," Carlos said, kissing her on the cheek. "Maybe next time," he offered, when he saw the disappointment on her face.

"I'm holding you to that. Now, I know I don't need to remind you guys to be careful. I love both of you."

"No te preocupes," Carlos responded, before motioning to Luis J that it was time to leave.

As they walked to Carlos' car, the two of them reflected on the strained interaction between Carlos and David and now David and Luis J. It was clear that David had drawn a line in the sand and all of them, including their mother, were on the other side. Luis J had witnessed some tension between them over the last few days. Carlos pointed out the obvious, though, saying, "Mami still rules man, I told you, just ask her." They both laughed as the car sped toward the beltway with reggae music blaring from the speakers.

Luis J exclaimed above the music, "Free at last. Free at last! So what are we doing tonight?"

"Maria invited us to dinner. Hungry?"

Sucking on his tongue to find a lingering taste of the chicken, he said, "Starving. If you didn't have issues with David, we could have eaten at home. But I'm not sure I'm feeling the Maria and Papi thing." He was already in hot water with his mother; this betrayal would put him on a whole other playing field.

"What do you mean?"

"Man, are you crazy? Mami doesn't see your comings and goings, but she has her eyes on me 24/7. If I spend time with them she'll go all nut case on me. Besides Lo, I thought you and I were going to kick it? I really wanted to just hang with you," Luis J said, with emphasis on you.

"We are, but we have to eat, don't we? And Maria is a great cook. She has already planned to cook a few dishes to reintroduce you to your heritage. I know it's been awhile. No te preocupes, lil' bro'."

"Whatever you say Carlos, but Mami can NOT find out about this. I mean it. I have to live there, you don't." And the minute those words flowed from his mouth, his head flooded with the memory of Dany saying something similar about having to live with her mother, who he was now convinced was the mother from Hell. He got it! Still, it didn't change his desire for Dany. But he couldn't think about that right now.

Carlos just shrugged it off and before long the brothers were back to talking about basketball, school and Carlos' job as they headed toward their destination.

Their father had bought a house in Queens about a year after the divorce. They didn't get to visit him there because their mother wouldn't allow it. Instead, their father always had to come to their apartment to visit.

When Carlos lived with Papi, he would share with Luis J what the home was like. "It's kinda big," he said. "It has three bedrooms, a garage and a basketball hoop in the back yard. Papi installed it hoping that one day he would have the chance to play with us."

When they pulled into the yard, Luis J tried to remember when he had last seen his father. It had been years. As they sat there, with the engine still running and Carlos gathering some bags from the back seat, Luis J wondered if his father was already home, how he would look and if he even knew of Luis J's visit or if he had been tricked into this reunion, too?

When they approached the front door, Carlos knocked three times and then used his key to enter. Luis J didn't know he still had a key to their home and he found himself feeling a hint of envy.

Throwing the door open revealed the silhouette of a woman standing at the end of the hallway and Carlos said, "Maria, estamos aquí."

"Hi, sweetie, vengan. Come in," she said, smoothing out her dress as she waited for the boys to come into the house.

Carlos walked up to Maria and planted a kiss on her cheek. Luis J was a little slower to approach her. He hadn't seen her for about six years; his mother had seen to that. But there he was now, in her house standing in front of her with a mess at home. The light from the living room lamp was shining behind her, creating a sharper image of her features.

Luis J took a moment to let his eyes take her in from head to toe. She looked hot in her red sweater dress that hugged her body. She was about 5'4", with long, dark, curly hair and light brown eyes that blended in with the light brown hue of her skin. She looked like she worked out because he could see the muscles in her arms. When his gaze returned to her face, he saw she was smiling as she studied his features. Feeling a little embarrassed, he looked away. He knew immediately that he should not have been looking at her in that way. She was his father's woman.

Maria helped him recover by saying, "And look who we have here. Luis J, baby, you're trying to get as fine as your father. Come a little closer and give me a hug."

Luis J slowly moved forward and leaned down to give her the hug she had requested. It reminded him of the awkwardness he and Dany first experienced. He lingered for a moment in her embrace, smelling her perfume. As he felt his body responding, and not sure if it was due to her touch or his thoughts of Dany, he pulled away and said, "It's nice to see you, Maria. Is my father here?"

"No, baby, not yet, but he's on his way. Come in. Sit down. Can I get you a soda? Carlos, do you want a cerveza?"

"Of course, but I'll get it." As he moved toward the kitchen, Carlos said in a melodic tone, "Maria, it smells good in here. What'd you cook?"

"Just something I thought Luis J might enjoy. I made bacalao guisado and some flan for dessert," she said, speaking directly to Luis J.

"Has Carlos told you how much he and your father love my cooking?" She watched him shake his head and it reminded her of Luis. It was uncanny given how much she used to think Carlos favored him. "So, Luis J, sit down; tell me what's been going on," she continued, sitting on the couch and patting the seat next to her.

"Not much. Basketball season starts next week. And I'm looking forward to hanging with my brother this weekend. I know he'll have a few pointers for me before the season kicks off. That's always good."

Luis J was glad she had thrown in a question about what he was up to so he didn't have to respond to her question about the cooking. He had no idea what those dishes she had mentioned were and didn't dare admit it, at least not in front of Carlos. He sat on the couch, but not in the area where she had patted, leaving a neutral zone between them.

"How's that girl you were going out with? Carlos told me about her."

"Dany? She's fine, but we're taking a break from each other for a while."

Reading his body language and the look on his face, she said, "Why do I get the feeling it wasn't your idea?"

"Maria, bad subject. Leave it," Carlos chimed in, returning from the kitchen. He knew how relentless Maria could be and he had to stop her from drilling Luis J. He handed his brother a Pepsi and then popped his beer before taking a seat in the chair opposite them.

Holding up the beer, he said, "Medalia Light? What's up with that?"

"Your father said he needed to watch his calories," she said, snickering as she recalled the dialogue. He didn't think he was working out enough and that his usual drinking pleasure, cognac, was adding a few too many calories. She didn't quite understand how light beer was a better choice since he mostly drank the cognac but she played along with it. Besides, from where she was sitting, he looked just fine.

But Carlos' attempt to keep her from prying into Luis J's relationship only worked on the surface; she would most certainly get to the bottom of Diane's issues with her son's girlfriend before the night was over.

But for now, she continued with, "So tell me, how are David, Robert and Chell? And your mother, of course? I really want Robert and Chell to come over and spend time with us, like you're doing tonight."

"Uh, they're fine," Luis J answered, addressing only the first of her questions. They all knew it would be a cold day in Hell before Robert and Chell would be allowed to step foot on the street in front of this house, let alone inside. And since Maria knew that, too, he wondered why she even said that.

"Except for the fact that David is flexing his muscles these days," Carlos added and then immediately regretted opening that can of worms.

Shifting in her seat to face him, she asked, "What do you mean, Carlos?"

"Never mind," Carlos said quickly. He was still so mad at David for hitting Luis J that it slipped out and that was not information they wanted Maria to have.

Just as Maria was about to push forward with her interrogation, she heard the front door open and close and she called out, "Hey, baby. Welcome home. Guess who's here for dinner?"

Placing the keys on the table in the hallway, Luis responded with, "I saw Carlos' car when I drove up and I can smell the food."

"I know, but he has a guest with him, Poppie. Come on in. Hurry up!" Maria said, smiling. She couldn't wait to see the expression on his face. She knew he would be surprised and pleased. When Carlos had called her last night to tell her about his plans, she convinced him to come over and bring Luis J. Luis would surely be appreciative of her actions to bring them together.

As Luis entered the room, Carlos rose and said, "Cómo estás, Papi? It's Luis J. I brought him over to see you." He watched and waited for his father's reaction.

A huge smile broke across Luis' face and he sat his briefcase down before saying, "Carlos, Carlos, thank you!" Extending his arms, Luis said, "Come here, mijo, and let me take a look at you. The sun shines on me today."

Luis J stood and walked towards his father. He was shorter than Luis J by about three or four inches, but you couldn't tell by the way he carried himself. He had broad shoulders and was very fit. Luis J now wondered also why his father was drinking light beer. Considering their physiques, Luis J surmised that his father and Maria probably worked out together or at least encouraged each other.

Continuing his observations, Luis J saw that his father now had a mustache and his hair was cut short exposing his natural waves. It was almost like looking into a mirror and seeing an older version of himself. Even their lips had the same shape.

Luis grabbed his son and hugged him. With his eyes closed, he said, "Ay Dios mío. Maria, look at my son, my namesake. What a man he is becoming." Letting him go so he could take it all in, he finally asked, smiling, "How have you been? How's school? How's basketball? I have a hundred questions for you."

"I'm good, Papi. School's good and the season starts next week." He had imagined for years what it would be like to see his father again. But he never thought Papi would be this happy to see him.

"That's good. Well rounded like I dreamed you would be. Let me know when you have your first game. I would like to be there, if you don't mind."

"Papi, you know I'd love to have you there, but …"

Luis J didn't even have to finish the sentence. Diane was already creeping into his moment with his son. "Son, no need to say it. I understand and I will handle that. That gym is a big enough place that she doesn't have to run into me. You just let me know when," Luis offered, more as a directive than a request.

Luis J smiled to himself as he admired his father's control. He was commanding his space like Luis J did when people were bullying him.

They continued talking for a while, enjoying each other's company while Maria finished preparing dinner. Carlos barely interjected into the conversation. He knew that they needed to reacquaint themselves and he was prepared to give them all the time they required. He felt so good that he was the reason this reunion was occurring, despite his mother.

Luis J talked about how much Robert and Chell were growing up, school and football stats. It wasn't until the topic of how things were really going at home that the conversation started heading south.

Once again, Carlos found it hard to hold his tongue and blurted out information about the confrontation with David, and why Luis J was spending the weekend with him instead of at home. Luis J had not planned on sharing any of that with his father. And calling his brother's name, he tried to stop him, but it was already out in the atmosphere.

Luis leaned forward to gather the full story and said, "Luis J, qué pasó?"

"It's fine, Papi. I'm handling it," Luis J answered quickly, trying to diffuse things before they gathered momentum.

"Before or after he hit you?" Carlos added.

Luis' soft, smiling face now turned to a frown as he inspected his son, looking for any signs of abuse. When he was satisfied there weren't any, he asked, "So, what happened, I ask again?"

Lowering his voice slightly to minimize the effect, Luis J started, "I was with Dany, my girlfriend, and stayed out too late. I honestly forgot I had the car key in my pocket and when I returned home, David was still there because he couldn't get to work. One thing led to another and he slapped me."

"Where was your mother while he was hitting my son? How often has this happened?" Luis asked, not trying to camouflage his anger and resentment at all.

"Papi, really, it's no big deal. Mami intervened and then they grounded me for like a month except for basketball practice and games. It was the first – and believe me – the only time he hit me. But I really don't want to talk about it. I got away from there this weekend so I could put it behind me."

Maria strolled out of the kitchen carrying her baby's cognac and sat down next to him. 'So that's what they were trying to hide from me,' she thought. Not wanting to pass up this opportunity to share her opinion, she blurted out, "David shouldn't be hitting him, Luis. It isn't right and she shouldn't allow it either. He's not their father. He started that stuff with Carlos and he had to get out of there. Now he thinks he can get away with doing it to Luis J? We're not going to stand for it. I'm glad you said something Carlos, looking out for your brother."

Although she was right, Luis said, "Maria, stay out of it. I'll handle this." Then he turned his attention back to his son and asked, "Were you being disrespectful to him or your mother?"

"No, Papi. I mean not really. I had already apologized to him and everything, but things got blown way out of proportion and he lost his cool. He blows up like that sometimes, especially if Mami doesn't agree with him about something. But he's never hit me before, or any of us for that matter. Look, like I said, I really just want to enjoy this visit with you and the weekend. Can we just do that?"

But this was not sitting well with Luis. He and Carlos had talked about similar confrontations before he finally asked to move in. Teenage boys could be a handful and he was sure it was being complicated by the fact that he wasn't their biological father.

But Diane needed to get a handle on it because where Carlos would walk away, Luis could see that this son would not. "I'm going to call your mother. I need to talk to her about this because David has to be able to parent without bringing physical actions into it."

"Papi, you can't do that. Mami doesn't know I'm over here. She'll be furious with both of us," Luis J said, looking at Carlos.

"He's right, Papi," Carlos added, reluctantly. He had talked many times to his father about reclaiming his fatherly rights but he had been reluctant. This situation would have been the perfect entry point but they all knew Luis J was right. It would cause even more friction for him at home.

"Fine, I understand, but if it ever happens again, David WILL answer to me. And that's no threat, it's a guarantee."

After a few minutes of silence, Maria began talking as if Carlos and Luis J were no longer present. "Luis, it's music to my ears to hear that you're finally willing to go up against David and take your rightful place as father to your children. Thank goodness you're finally ready to put

Diane in her place and make her remove those barriers that are keeping you from them. After all, they are your kids, not David's. Maybe we could start with something like we did tonight and have Chell and Robert over for dinner on the weekend."

Luis was sipping on his cognac and trying to come to terms with his feelings. He was disappointed that Diane had allowed that man to slap his son, but he also knew that boys had to have boundaries drawn for them and Luis J was certainly at that age.

He didn't need Maria rubbing salt in the wounds with ideas that he didn't have any hope of acting upon. So he said, "Maria, would you please just stop talking." He drained the glass and then said, "If dinner's ready, let's eat."

Maria rose disgustedly from her seat and headed to the kitchen. She was appalled that he spoke to her the way one would address a child. But she didn't want to ruin the evening so she held her tongue.

The fish stew was spicy and was served over a bed of rice. Luis J had been feeling apprehensive about the meal, but to his relief, it was tasty and he ate until he was full. The dinner conversation shifted back to basketball, team stats and college recommendations, which was a relief for Luis J.

After dinner they convened in the backyard to shoot some hoops and work off dessert. Luis J's moves gave him an advantage and he beat them two games to one, even when they double-teamed him. Tired and sweaty, Luis sat on the porch and marveled over Luis J's prowess with the ball. He had missed so much of his son's growth these past years. Years he could never regain.

Around nine-thirty, Carlos and Luis J headed back to Brooklyn, chatting about the evening. "He's a good man, Luis J. We were never given a chance to see that once David came on the scene. Papi would love the chance to get to know you. I hope you saw that tonight. You should let him."

"What about Mami? You know she'll never let me do that, or Chell or Robert either."

"You know what, she may not have a choice any more. I hate to hear Robert call David 'Daddy'. He needs to know his real father. So do you and Chell. You deserve to know him, to have him in your life. Mami's always making situations more difficult than they need to be. It's her way or bust."

Luis J and Carlos hadn't talked about this topic for about a year, but Luis J hadn't seen Carlos this angry before. Luis J wondered why it was such a strong feeling now.

"Well, you know Mami," Luis J said, "But you can't question David's love for us, though. He has been there through it all. He's never hit me before, but I know why he did it. He doesn't like me having an opinion and pushing back on him. It probably reminded him of his arguments with you."

"Yeah, well, that's still no reason to hit you. And the reason Papi wasn't there for us is all Mami's doing. She's the one who wouldn't allow him to come around or call after the divorce. He tried, many times.

"You know how she was always saying we didn't have any money? Well, that's because she would return the checks Papi sent her every month. He clearly didn't understand why. He knew she had to be struggling with us four kids, but she would never even give him any explanation. So he finally gave up on that and instead opened a savings account for each of us. He gave me mine when I turned eighteen and graduated from high school."

Luis J was shocked. All the times they had to eat the same leftovers for a week and he had to get clothes and sneakers from a second-hand store, she was denying his father's help? His father had been trying to provide for them when their mother had said he didn't care.

Now his emotions were shifting to mirror Carlos' and he wondered why she hated his father so much. She was wrong to deny them their father when he had wanted to be in their lives, but worse was that she lied about it. Still, as his father had said earlier, that was between them.

Chapter Four

David and Diane sat on the couch watching television and enjoying a glass of wine. Robert and Chell were settled for the night and she could finally relax. She had wondered a few times during the evening how her sons were, but she didn't dare call Carlos. She didn't want to start an argument or make them think that she didn't trust them. Besides, she was confident she would find out all about their activities when Luis J came home on Sunday. He would be overly eager to share how happy he was to be with his big brother and away from home.

David was being quiet and she wondered if he was still holding a grudge. Last night he had warned her about letting Luis J come between them. He ran down that whole litany of how he loved Luis J but would not tolerate being disrespected or lied to.

She found herself reminding him that Luis J didn't respond to threats and he had to handle him with reasoning. He had been like that all his life. But she also knew on some level that David was right. She had no intentions of raising children who lied to her or didn't remember the order of hierarchy in her home.

But his reaction to her comments was a tight jaw and the response, "Diane, he needs to be reeled in and held on a tight leash or else you're going to have a buck wild young male to deal with."

The phone ringing sounded like a bell for her thoughts to retreat to their corners and she complied before grabbing the receiver on the second ring.

"Hello," she said, softly, not wanting to wake Robert.

"Diane?"

"Yes. Who is this?" Diane asked, hesitantly. There was something uncomfortably familiar about the voice.

"Maria, of course."

Diane was silent, wondering what this woman wanted at this time of night. She felt a knot slowly forming just from hearing her name and her voice. There could only be one reason for her call, so she waited and braced herself to hear what had happened to Luis.

"Are you there? Diane?"

"Yes. What do you want?"

"I just wanted to tell you we enjoyed dinner tonight."

"I'm sorry. What are you talking about?"

"We enjoyed dinner tonight," Maria repeated. Preparing for the blow, she added more detail. "Luis, Carlos, Luis J and I. You should have seen us. I cooked them a dinner to reintroduce Luis J to his culture and boy did he really enjoy my cooking. But not as much as he loved being with his father."

Maria paused, wishing she could see the look on Diane's face. She wanted the images to settle in before continuing. "You see, I told you I would have Luis J soon. I knew you would drive him away, just like you did the other two men in your life, and he came right to my arms."

Diane was steaming now and didn't hold back any sentiment. She screamed, "Heffa, are you crazy? You don't have anything better to do than make up shit? There's no way my sons were over there. Why are you calling here anyway? Do you know what time of night it is? I'm so sick of your shit. I don't know what the hell you think you're doing, but I know you're up to something!"

"Diane, I'm not lying," Maria said coolly. "How would I have known Carlos and Luis J were together tonight if they hadn't come over here? Do you want me to tell you what he was wearing? Trust me, they were here and they'll be back. You can bet your sweet, boring life on it."

"Damn it Maria. You have my husband, why can't you just leave me and my sons alone?" Diane's voice escalated after each word as all of the memories associated with why her first marriage failed came flooding back.

"Oooh, I hope David isn't lying next to you because if I were him, I would be pretty pissed right about now. Oh, and Luis said that David better keep his hands off his son. Three down, two to go."

"Maria, listen to me very carefully. Stay the hell away from my children. Do you hear me? I swear you better stay away from my sons or I'm going to really put a hurtin' on you. And don't ever call here again unless you're on your death bed!"

"Bye, chica."

Diane slammed the phone back into the cradle before saying, "Did you hear who that was? I can't believe that bitch called here, David. She really has a lot of nerve."

Diane reached up, pulled the holder out of her hair, took both hands to pull it back into a ponytail and then replaced the holder before continuing. "She wanted to let me know Carlos and Luis J had dinner with her and Luis. She was rubbing my nose in Luis J's betrayal. Like father like son, I suppose."

When David didn't respond or react to her ranting, she realized that he must have heard her slip about Luis, but without addressing that, she said, "David, did you hear what I just said? That was Maria."

"Yes, I heard you." And he paused with a mischievous grin spread across his lips. "So what do you want me to do? Shouldn't you be talking to your husband? I heard you, alright. I heard you refer to Luis as your husband. Is that how you still think of him?"

"Of course not, don't be ridiculous. Honey, I love you. I'm married to you, aren't I? It was a response to the context in which she was speaking. She said, and I quote, 'I told you I would have Luis J soon. I knew you would drive him away, just like you did the other two men in your life, and he came right to my arms.' Maria brought up a lot of old baggage, baby, and I just reacted."

This explanation didn't make David feel any differently about what he had just heard his wife say. She was pretty clear and it bothered him. "Diane I want to be here for you. God knows I love you. And I in no way condone Maria's behavior. You should know that by now. She's insecure. She's not married to Luis, for whatever reason, but you have moved on and remarried. You're happy and she knows it. I'm sure Luis J reminded her of that tonight. But maybe you're the one that needs to be reminded that you're married to a strong, handsome, successful younger man."

David ended the sentence with a warm, inviting smile on his face. Diane couldn't help but smile back at him. She knew he was really trying to make things right even though she had been setting things on tilt between them.

David continued, "Through her eyes, you've still beat her at her game. Don't you get it? But I also think it is way beyond time for you to throw out the old baggage. You know she's trying to get a rise out of you and you never disappoint her. Why is that?"

"I hate her!" Diane exclaimed. The knot in her stomach was expanding into other parts of her body and she pulled the hair holder out again and replaced it.

David watched her actions carefully before saying, "For what, Diane? Showing you that Luis wasn't committed to your marriage? Enabling us to be together and raise your kids in a loving home? Or do you hate her because she has Luis and you're still not over him?"

Before she could respond, the phone rang again. David reached for it because he was not going to allow any more interference in their night. After listening for a moment, he said, "No, you may not speak to Diane. Maria has already caused enough turmoil for one evening in our home and Diane isn't taking any more calls this evening."

David held fast to the receiver and cleared his throat before saying, "Excuse me? Luis, you lost the privilege to have a say in how the children are disciplined when you had your fling. Now, I will discipline my children however and whenever I see fit and I will not call you and ask you for anything. Especially permission. Are we clear?" David returned the phone to the cradle, not allowing a response and returned to his seat.

Noticing that his body was more rigid, Diane asked, "David, what did Luis say?"

"Leave it alone, Diane. I handled it." He picked up the glass and drained the wine, but then added, "Now, are you going to let me manage my home, take care of you and the children or not? You can't have it both ways. You can't say, 'David, I don't ever want to talk to or see Luis again. We don't need him in our lives. I don't want anything from him.' and have me take you seriously and then switch up.

"Just like you did with Luis J yesterday. I am a man Diane, your man, and I will not be treated like some teenage boy. Remember that." He leaned against the back of the couch, his frustration with her mounting, and began flipping channels.

Diane was beside herself. She couldn't believe he wasn't going to divulge the details of the conversation. She wanted to know why Luis had allowed Maria to call her and what he thought about David hitting Luis J. She looked at David for some indication he would give in but there was nothing there. So she rose and headed to the bedroom.

Sitting on her side of the bed, she tried to wrap her head around what was happening. How on earth did that woman have that much nerve to call her home? How could Luis J betray her the same way Carlos had? Well, perhaps David was right about that one bit of advice, not to allow Luis J to spend time with Carlos. She wondered if Luis was involved in the scheme to get Luis J over there. Could it be that after all these years he was once again trying to cause trouble for her, David and the kids? If so, why now? What had changed? What had given him the confidence to go behind her back and make plans to be with Luis J?

Well, she was determined that she would get to the bottom of this betrayal and then put an end to it. All of it. Tomorrow, SHE would go over to his house and remind them both to stay the hell out of their lives.

It was eight years ago when Maria had steamrolled into Diane's life. Luis was a professor at Long Island University (LIU) in the graduate school's business department. He was on a fast track to a tenured position. He loved his job, which was evidenced by the commitment he had to the students and their education. As an advisor to the first year graduate students, he worked with each of them to design a curriculum that would enable them to achieve their long-term goals. Some were pursuing doctorate degrees, others were working towards getting hired into a company's management program. He felt as though their success was reflective of his career accomplishments so he was fully committed to each of them. And this didn't go unnoticed by the other faculty members, students or the administration.

At the end of the day, he would sometimes share stories about his "star" performers with Diane. One evening, the story was about Maria

Diaz. At first, the interaction between them was purely student and teacher and then advisor.

He would tell Diane how Maria would struggle with her English Literature professor and wanted his advice. The professor had a problem with her writing style and the topics she often selected. He didn't feel she was performing up to her potential.

As Diane listened to the various stories about Maria, she could tell that Luis was genuinely trying to help her, but his tone also told her how flattered he was by Maria's attention. Over time, Diane learned that Maria was from an area near Luis' hometown outside of San Juan, Puerto Rico, and this, too, was a connection they shared.

Maria would prepare meals for him to share with his family – dishes that Diane had never learned to prepare, but allowed his children to experience that part of their culture. Occasionally, Maria would stop by on the weekends and spend time with the children, since she didn't have any family in New York. Diane began to notice a special connection growing between Maria and Carlos. He was nine and already showing a thirst for knowledge about his Latino heritage. He would ask his father to tell him, in Spanish, stories about what it was like growing up in Puerto Rico.

Carlos was always an inquisitive child and when he was old enough to understand he was from two different ethnicities, he yearned to learn more about the one to which he wasn't as exposed. So, Maria would also talk to Carlos about their country, the beaches, the music and the history, and Carlos was like a sponge, looking forward to her every visit.

Diane didn't really mind because she was learning about her husband's country, as well. She had hoped that one day they would all be able to go as a family and spend time in Puerto Rico with Luis' family. She knew it was important that her children knew both sides of their heritage. She also knew that she had to improve her level of speaking. She just wasn't sure when because of their financial situation.

Luis and Diane had been arguing about their financial soundness and future plans long before Maria entered the picture. When Chell was five, Diane was ready to go back to work, but Luis still wanted her to stay home. They were rapidly outgrowing the apartment and Diane felt that buying a house was long overdue.

She had dreamed of moving into a home in the suburbs, closer to Luis' school, and with a yard for the children to play outdoors. The tension between them about their debt, lack of privacy at home, and her desire to return to the workplace was affecting their ability to have "fun" with each other, the way they used to enjoy just being with one another.

As a result, Luis would look for activities that would keep him away from home in the evenings as long as possible. He would attend evening seminars or just offer to teach a few extra classes.

Diane's frustration with everything was getting the best of her, so she elected to do something about it. She read the wanted ads and found a few interesting positions. She interviewed and secured a job at Chase Bank in their Operations department. She was suited for the position because of her degree in finance and the previous jobs she had held during college.

Her original plan had been to get her MBA and work for one of the major financial mega brokers on Wall Street like Dean Witter or Goldman Sachs. Three children later, that all seemed like a distant dream. However, she hoped that at least working in the industry would help set her apart from her younger competition once she did obtain her masters degree.

The evening she told Luis about it, she honestly thought he would be proud of her, but that wasn't the emotion he portrayed. Instead, they argued all night and into the morning about her betrayal and everything else that had been dividing them. It wasn't until that night that Diane realized how much they had really drifted apart over the years. They were no longer working to achieve their goals together.

She tried to explain to him how much she needed the job to begin to redefine her life and keep her career from falling any further behind. Her college peers were all well established in their careers and getting major promotions to Corporate Vice Presidents and Partners at law firms.

She was even careful to compare herself to the ones who had children, too. Granted, none of them had as many as she did and they all elected to just take the standard two months of maternity leave, but they had all launched their post-graduate activities at the same time.

Diane wanted him to hear about her conversations with them and how they were changing. Every time they talked, all she had to contribute to the conversation was something about the children's accomplishments or Luis'. She didn't know if she imagined it or if it was actually happening, but the frequency of the calls from her college peers were becoming farther in between and shorter in duration every time.

Then there was her mother, who was always asking when she was going to enroll in graduate school and get her degree. She was constantly reminding Diane of her disappointment and displeasure with her life choices. But in contrast, Diane hadn't shared any of those conversations with Luis. She didn't feel like revisiting it with him. As much as she had tried to explain her relationship with her mother, he just couldn't understand the hold she seemed to have over his wife.

But even with all of her explanations, Luis stood his ground. He wanted her to stop comparing herself to women who thought it was alright for their children to be raised in daycare centers. He wasn't asking her to completely abandon her dreams, just stay home with Chell another year or two. This sacrifice had been well worth the investment into the development of each of their children.

Diane loved Luis very much, but she refused to give in to him on this issue. She had spent weeks finding the perfect daycare center that had an environment that would complement Chell's education and take care of her until Diane could pick her up. And, the position in Operations wasn't too demanding; she was going to be home by five o'clock every day. It would give her plenty of time to continue raising Carlos and Luis J, cook and clean. Luis would never even know the difference.

She was determined to prove that it would work, so she accepted the job. But instead of things working out the way she had planned, the interaction between them worsened. Diane tried all kinds of creative approaches that should have worked, but Luis could be very stubborn, a little old-fashioned, very Puerto Rican machismo, and equally determined to prove his point.

As a result, their interactions became routine and mostly centered on taking care of the children. Their breakdown in communication caused Diane even more anxiety and she worried about their relationship's deterioration. Her mother had told her that an unhappy home bred dysfunctional children and straying spouses. Diane didn't want either of those to happen to her family so she suggested counseling to him one evening as he sat in his chair, drinking cognac.

He had responded, "Diane, what do we need counseling for? The answer is simple and you know what you have to do."

Four more months went by and nothing had improved. Christmas was approaching and the university was having their annual holiday party for the faculty, their guests and the graduate students. Since Luis was still vying for a tenured position, he had to attend. It was another opportunity to interact with the board and his superiors.

Given where they were in their interactions, he told Diane he was planning to go alone, but she begged him to take her. She reminded him of the magic of the holiday season. Christmas was her favorite holiday and they used to have so much fun looking for a tree, decorating it, driving around Long Island to look at the decorated homes and secretly buying gifts for the kids. She always felt it was a magical time. She watched him smile as he, too, recalled the memories and so he agreed to have her accompany him.

As she dressed and applied her makeup, she hoped the spirit of the season and the glamour of the affair would be a catalyst to change the direction of their relationship. She wore a black, strapless dress, which accented her long lean body. Her hair was worn down with soft curls that fell gently around her face as the night progressed. She knew how good she looked in that dress and that, too, was why Luis had acquiesced. She hoped that he would also be open to the possibilities. He was usually the one to remind her that the glass was half full.

Diane felt hopeful as they entered the room, arm in arm. She admired the beautiful Christmas decorations and the ambiance created by the soft lighting and the music playing in the background. She had no idea that this night would be her first indication that something was seriously wrong in her relationship outside of them.

As Diane stood by the bar, she closed her eyes and began inhaling the calmness that filled the room. She wished she could box it and take it with her to set free and fill her home with peace and tranquillity. When she reopened them, she caught a glimpse of Luis talking to Maria. It appeared as though Maria was really upset, as her hand was on her hip and her eyes were fixated on his face. Luis was shifting from one foot to another and rubbing his temple as though he had a headache, which usually meant he was annoyed.

Clearly Diane needed to take some of her calmness to the other side of the room and share it. She picked up her drink and sashayed over to join them. As she approached, Maria looked up and Diane observed that the usual warmth toward her was no longer there. Diane dismissed it, assuming she had had a bad day. Luis' back was to Diane so he didn't see her approaching.

As she got closer, she thought she heard him say, "I tried to talk her out of it, but I couldn't." Diane instinctively slid her arm into his and smiled at Maria. He turned with surprise caught on his face. Diane noticed there were also beads of sweat on his brow. Luis shot a glance at Maria, a glance that was troubling to Diane. He usually only had that look and sweat on his brow when he was either arguing with her or was extremely annoyed. It was the look he gave his wife and his kids. She had never seen him do that to anyone with whom he didn't have a close relationship.

"Diane, Maria and I were just talking about her internship."

"Yes, Diane…among other things," Maria chimed in. "I'm surprised to see you because Luis told me you wouldn't be joining him tonight."

"Well, it's a little complicated, but I'm so glad I did. Everything is so beautiful and so romantic." Diane squeezed Luis' arm tighter and moved even closer.

Luis' frown became even more pronounced after Maria's statement and he muttered, "Well, Maria, please excuse us. I'll talk to you tomorrow."

"It was good to see you, Maria. Take care." They turned and began walking away. "Is everything alright with her?" Diane asked. She was used to seeing Maria teasing him about one thing or another and for the life of her she couldn't understand why someone as pretty as she was would come to an event like this alone.

"What?"

"I was just asking because she seemed really mad or upset. Is she having man troubles? Something must have her busy because she hasn't even been by the house lately," Diane said, as that observation suddenly dawned on her.

"Ah, she's okay. I'm going to meet with her tomorrow. I told her to focus more on her studies." After panning the room, Luis picked their next stop. "There's Steve and his wife. Let's go say hello."

"Wait a minute." Diane stopped, causing his forward movement to yield to the hold she had on him. She looked at her husband and admired his features. He was so handsome. She felt a flurry in her stomach, a feeling she was very familiar with when thinking about her man. The same feeling she had experienced the first day they met.

"I meant what I said about being glad to be here, on your arm, talking to you. It feels so right, Luis. You know I love you and I miss us."

He looked at his wife, searching those big brown eyes for a glimmer of hope for their future. He replied, "I never stopped loving you either." And then he kissed her, passionately. Lingering in each other's arms and wanting to savor the feelings, they changed their original plans. They stopped by to say hello to Steve and a few others on the board and then headed for home.

When they arrived there, they could still feel the magic of the evening between them. The kids were fast asleep so they retired to their bedroom. Luis grabbed a bottle of red wine for them to enjoy. He began removing her dress slowly, careful not to tear it where it cinched her waistline and highlighted the curves of her bottom. He could still smell her perfume. It was Chloe, one of his favorites. He had admired how she looked, her full breasts and sexy walk, all evening. Those stiletto pumps had pushed her butt up and all but said, "Come take me."

Luis couldn't wait to get her undressed. He had always enjoyed making love to Diane but assumed that tonight things would continue to be status quo, as they had been for the past few months. But instead they were about to make love and he was going to make it memorable for her.

He was always very attentive, touching her in new places that one would think he would have already found after eleven years of marriage.

But somehow she inspired adventure, and new discoveries were always thrilling with her. It was probably because she suppressed so much of herself that even she had no idea of the range of her sexual capacity.

They climaxed together and he had to use his mouth to cover hers to stifle her moans so as not to disturb the kids. She felt so good to him. He really had missed her. He wondered if she realized how much she had missed being with him.

Luis rolled onto his back and reached for her. She found her spot on his chest, fitting there as though it were made especially for her. They both were feeling like they were starting anew.

"Baby, why can't it be like this all the time? Can't we find our way back to each other?" Diane asked, rubbing the hair on his chest.

"We can, Di. You have to stop being so headstrong. You're trying to prove a point with this job. Why can't you just quit it? That's all it would take and we could be back to how it used to be."

Without moving her head but feeling the intensity in his words and wondering if he would soon shift and make her get up, she pleaded with him, "Luis, baby, can't you even try to understand?"

"No. Can't you? I'm your husband, baby. I want to take care of you and our children just a little longer. I think it's best for them. Why are you making this so difficult?"

And just like that the magic was over. He shifted and she lifted her head. Nothing had changed and they were at an impasse just as before. She rolled over and pretended to go to sleep. After a while, his breathing told her that he had succumbed to the evening's activities. But all she could do was lay there, quietly, fighting back tears until she finally dozed off.

The next morning when she opened the drawer to get her toothbrush, she saw it. She had forgotten to use her diaphragm. She tried not to panic and searched her brain to recall the date. December twenty-third. Her last cycle was on the sixth. She was right in the middle of her ovulation week. She thought to herself, 'This can't be happening. I can't get pregnant. Not now, not when we are at odds with each other.' And then she thought, 'The stress I've been under will probably prevent that union.'

Luis walked in and she slammed the drawer shut. He looked at her to assess what was wrong but didn't ask. He wasn't in the mood this morning. He had a long day ahead of him so he turned on the water and climbed into the shower.

Two weeks after New Year's Day, Diane's cycle was late and she knew she was pregnant. She had been regular every month of her life, except for three times before then. She sat in the bathroom looking in the mirror and wondered: how she was going to tell her husband; what would she say to him; what would he say to her?

Things had returned to being strained between them since the Christmas party. They hadn't been intimate with each other since then either. As a matter of fact, he seemed to be out more: weekends, evenings and on his days off. She had to plead with him to spend more time with the kids so she could get a break.

Now it would seem, they would have something else to confront. She wanted to wait and be sure because maybe being late was just from the stress in her life right now.

The next morning, the blue on the stick stared back at her, confirming her gut instincts. She sat down in front of the sink and began crying. Carlos knocked on the door to see if she was alright. Once she reassured him, the kids all left for school. Diane couldn't face going to work, so she called in sick and stayed in bed. She alternated between crying and sleeping throughout the day.

Luis came home around two in the afternoon and was surprised to find his wife there and in bed. She wasn't sure how to answer his questions about what was wrong and whether she was sick. She wasn't sure if this was the right time to tell him.

He finally sat on the bed and touching her arm, asked, "Di, what's wrong? You look tired, drained almost."

She loved to hear him call her that. It was always so endearing. She wondered if maybe her condition would make things better between them. She still didn't respond, though. She didn't know how. The tears began to well up in her eyes. 'Why couldn't she just say it?' she wondered.

Luis moved his hand to her face and caressed her cheek. "Did something happen? Talk to me."

"I'm…not feeling well."

"I figured that since you're in bed in the middle of the afternoon. But what's wrong? Do you need to go to the hospital?"

"No."

"Then what?"

"I'm pregnant."

He was silent for a minute and then leaned closer to her as if to make sure he was hearing things clearly. "What did you say?"

"I'm pregnant. I didn't use my diaphragm that night of the Christmas party. I forgot. I was so caught up in the moment and the attention. But I took the test this morning and confirmed it. I'm probably about five or six weeks."

She searched his face to see if she could get any indication of what he was feeling or thinking. The darkness in the room made it difficult to tell. The only light came from the TV. General Hospital was on and Monica Quartermaine was complaining to Allen about something. Diane remained quiet; afraid to say anything else.

Luis looked at her and then he smiled. All he said was, "A gift from God." He hugged her and told her to rest.

She apprehensively allowed herself to think, 'Maybe he was right.'

When she awoke, the TV was still on but the volume had been turned down very low. The room was even darker. She laid there for a minute waiting for her eyes to adjust. In the front of the house somewhere, she could hear Luis' voice. After a while she could tell he was on the phone.

She thought she heard him say, "No. I can't, not tonight. Di's not feeling well and I need to help with the kids. Look, you just don't understand. Something's changed. I'll see you tomorrow. I have to go now."

"Luis." She waited to see if he had heard her.

He walked into the room and came to the side of the bed. "Oh, you're awake. How did you sleep?"

"Good...I heard you on the phone. Who was that?"

"Joe, he's in the Continuing Education department. He wanted some help with a program he's developing for his summer session. I told him I needed to be here tonight. Anyway, how are you feeling?"

"Tired. What time is it?"

"About five-thirty."

"Oh, my God, I have to make dinner," she said, throwing the covers back.

"No, you don't. The kids are fine. Pizza is coming and you need to stay right there. I told the kids and they're excited. We've been given another chance, Di."

"You told the kids already?"

"Yes. They were worried about you, especially Carlos. He told me you were crying this morning. I wanted them to know things would be alright. Also, I made an appointment with your doctor for you, next week. I'll take you. Let me get you some juice. The doctor's office said to keep you hydrated."

He kissed her on the forehead and walked out. Was she dreaming? Could this pregnancy really be making that much of a difference?

As the months passed, Luis and Diane seemed to be getting closer again. He was more attentive and they were communicating better. She noticed that his weekend outings and late nights at the office were less frequent and their romance and passion were returning. She was starting to feel like maybe things were really getting better between them.

That June, Chase Bank hired David Anderson to work in Diane's department. When she told them she wouldn't be returning after the baby was born, they named David as her successor. He was a bright young man who had recently relocated from Chicago.

They worked very well together and enjoyed each other's company in the office and over lunch. He was very funny, extremely kind, and sensitive, yet possessed a very strong alpha male personality. She found herself able to talk to him about anything. Him being "easy on the eyes" was an added benefit. Over time she had come to value their friendship. She didn't realize at the time how much she would eventually come to depend on him.

It was raining one Saturday afternoon and Luis had taken the kids out to their favorite kids place, Leaps and Bounds, to give Diane some peace and quiet. She had considered that thoughtful of him and welcomed the alone time.

This pregnancy was much more difficult than the others she had experienced. After performing some tests, the doctors informed them that they were having another boy and that Diane needed to get plenty of rest and avoid stress, especially for the last six weeks.

So she quit work earlier than originally planned and began following the doctors' directions. Luis was very determined to do his part to help her adhere to the instructions and taking the kids out for the day was an example.

Diane sat down and was about to put up her feet so she could finish reading a novel when the doorbell rang. She started to ignore it because she didn't want to converse with anyone soliciting anything. But after the second ring, she went against her first mind and rose to answer the door. It took her a few minutes to get out of the chair, and the bell rang again. When she finally reached the door, she leaned against it and asked, "Who is it?"

"Maria."

"Maria. Maria who?"

"Maria Diaz, Diane."

"Oh, Maria, one second." She hadn't seen her since the Christmas party and Luis hadn't mentioned much about her other than she was busy with her final course work before graduation. Diane unlocked the door and opened it. Maria was standing there in a raincoat, drenched from head to toe.

"Oh, my goodness; come in, you're soaked," Diane said, with genuine hospitality.

Maria stood there for a moment looking at Diane and then down at her stomach before entering.

"I'm sorry it took me so long to answer the door. I'm not getting around very fast these days. Please, rest your coat. Can I get you anything? A towel?" Diane asked, wanting to provide her some comfort.

"No, thanks," Maria responded, sitting down on the couch after hanging her coat on the rack by the door.

"Was Luis expecting you? He isn't here. He took the kids out so I could have some quiet time," Diane shared, smiling.

"I know."

"Oh, really? Then I'm confused. If you knew he wasn't here, why did you come by?"

"I came because I knew he wasn't here and I wanted to talk to you."

All of a sudden, Diane began to feel uncomfortable. She began shifting in the chair and she could feel the baby starting to move around in response to her thoughts. 'How did she know Luis was not here for sure and why would she come specifically to see me? Her involvement with the family has always been mostly with Luis and the children.'

Maria continued, "There are some things you should know."

Diane didn't say anything. She continued to keep her thoughts clear. 'Things I should know? Where is she going with this? Why is she looking so menacing?'

"About Luis," Maria continued.

About Luis? That was it; Diane was not going to let her continue. She could feel her heart beginning to race. Woman's intuition, perhaps, told her to stop Maria.

"Maria, I'm sorry. I'm not feeling well. This pregnancy has been a difficult one for me and I need to get some rest. Maybe you could come back another day."

Diane pushed against the back of the chair to steady herself before heading toward the door. But Maria didn't move from her position on the couch.

"No, Diane, I'm not leaving until I've said what I've come here to say. Luis doesn't want to hurt you, especially because of your condition, but this really needs to be dealt with."

"Maria, you do not come in my house telling me what to do. I asked you to leave nicely, now I am telling you politely." Diane opened the door and turned toward Maria. "Please, you really need to leave now. I really am not feeling well."

"Di…"

She couldn't believe her ears. Maria just called her "Di." How did she know about that? "What did you call me?"

"Di," Maria repeated. "Luis often calls you that."

"Okay, look Maria, you really have to go." Her heart was really racing now and coinciding with that, there was a pain building in her lower back. Diane placed her hand naturally on her stomach and began rubbing her baby. She took the other and began massaging her tailbone. It reminded her of the discomfort that accompanied a Braxton Hicks contraction, but this was much more intense. She hoped that by rubbing her stomach, she would calm down the baby inside and let him know there was nothing to fear.

Maria stood up, but didn't move toward the door. She watched Diane rubbing her stomach and then continued, "Luis and I are in love. We have been for months. He was planning to leave you when you let yourself get pregnant. He's waiting for you to have the baby before he asks you for a divorce. You have him convinced that you're so fragile right now. But I wanted to make sure you didn't try anything else, once you have that baby.

"He told me how you seduced him after the Christmas party that I was supposed to attend with him, and that's how this baby was conceived. He hadn't slept with you in months and the one time he does, you manage to forget to use your diaphragm? How convenient, wouldn't you agree? Well, we have plans and you are going to stop interfering with them. Understand?"

Diane was so dumbstruck that she couldn't move. Her hand tightened around the knob as she used it to steady herself. Her head was throbbing. 'This can't be happening. Why is she lying about my husband?'

"You liar. Get out of my house," she demanded.

"I'm not lying, Diane, and you know it. We've been lovers for over a year."

"No. Stop it. Stop it right now! Do you hear me?" She grabbed her back again as another pain shot up her spine. It was almost paralyzing her the same way as Maria's words.

"Di..."

"Stop calling me that!"

"Alright, Diane, you must have known, suspected something. As passionate as Luis is, you had to know he would find someone if you denied him. And I was there."

"Damn it, Maria, he's my husband. We've been married for twelve years. Luis has never been unfaithful to me. Never! I don't believe you. How could you even think of it? We let you into our home and shared our children."

The tears began rolling down Diane's face. Somewhere inside, she suspected that Maria was telling the truth. Diane released the doorknob as Maria walked over to her and before Diane knew it, and without planning it, she slapped her so hard that Maria swayed. And Diane's water broke.

She doubled over in pain and screamed. At just that moment, the children appeared in the doorway, followed by Luis, who froze in his tracks, trying to absorb what was unfolding before him.

"It's Maria. Hi, Maria," Chell shouted, running to hug her.

Diane couldn't stand up and tears were flowing freely down her cheeks. Luis looked at his wife and saw the puddle, then looked at Maria.

"Carlos, call 911 and take your brother and sister to our room," Luis said sternly.

"Papi, what's wrong?" Carlos asked, as he reached for the phone.

"Just do as I say. Tell them to send an ambulance. Mami's in labor. Hurry up, and do it from our room."

"Di, everything's going to be okay," Luis said, as he grabbed her around the waist and helped her lie down on the couch.

She couldn't say anything to him – partially because of the pain, but mostly because she was emotionally numb.

Turning to Maria, Luis seethed, "What the hell are you doing here?"

"You know why I'm here, Poppie. Di – excuse me – Diane and I have been talking."

"Talking? Talking about what? What the hell happened to her?"

Diane noticed that he didn't wait for an answer as to what they were discussing. This was the confirmation she did not want that Maria was telling the truth, or some version of it.

'How could he?' she thought. "Carlos, Carlos baby, come here," Diane called out for her oldest son. She needed him now.

"Di, I'm right here. What do you need?" Luis said, returning to his wife's side.

She was lying on the couch in excruciating pain, but when he reached for her, she instinctively pushed him away. "No, don't touch me. Take your whore and get out."

"Diane, wait. I'll explain everything to you, but not right now. We have to worry about the baby. You're in labor."

"Yes, I am, thanks to your whore. Carlos, come here."

Carlos entered the room and stood by his mother's side. He could see blood on her clothes and was really worried.

"Did you call the ambulance?" Luis asked his son, trying to distract him from the images.

"Yes Papi," he answered, not taking his eyes off his mother. They had come back to the house early because his father had forgotten his wallet. Now Carlos wondered if his mother was dying.

"Then go back to your room," Luis directed, wanting to spare his son from the sight, and more importantly, any dialogue that might occur between the women.

"But Mami…"

"Go, I said. Now!"

"Luis, get her out of my house!" Diane screamed with another contraction.

"Maria, go home," he directed her.

"But Luis, I did this for us."

"You did not do this for us. You did this for you. Just leave! Go! We'll talk later."

Those were the last words Diane remembered hearing, "We'll talk later," as she lost consciousness.

When she woke up in the hospital, she looked around trying to get her bearings. Her eyes finally landed on Luis, asleep in the chair near her bed. She ached all over. She instinctively started rubbing her stomach but to her shock it was flat.

"Luis. Luis, where's my baby?" she screamed, fear overcoming her.

He stirred and then sat up. "Hey, baby."

"Where's my son? Oh my God, is he alright?"

"He's fine, honey. He's okay. He's small, but he's a fighter, like his mother. He's in the neo-natal ICU. They said he's about five weeks premature, but the doctors feel he'll be alright."

She tried to move, to put as much distance as possible between herself and this man she had called husband and lover for years, but her body ached from the surgery. The only muscles she could move comfortably were her eyes, so she closed them, shutting him out. But when she did, images of her son lying in an incubator connected to tubes and wires and all alone, made tears well up in her eyes and slowly fall down her cheeks.

"Did you hear me, Di? He's going to be okay."

She was barely able to mumble, saying, "No thanks to you. Why are you here anyway? As if you care about me, or any of us for that matter." Her lip was quivering and her eyes remained closed.

"Would you please open your eyes and look at me?" Once she did, he plowed forward, desperate to have her listen to him. "I do care, Di. I love you."

"Oh, please. Do you even know what that means?"

"Yes. You taught me what it means." When all he saw was her cold, bloodshot eyes staring back at him, he stopped those thoughts and switched to, "Look, you must be exhausted. We really shouldn't try to have this conversation now. Get some rest so you can get stronger and we can go see our son. We'll talk about this once you come home. They had to do a Caesarean, so you're going to be sore for a while. But don't worry; I'm going to take care of you."

Diane wanted to scream, from the pain that was concentrated in her abdomen as much as from Luis' subtle concern for the pain in her heart. But she didn't have the energy. Instead she just lay there, with the morphine pumping until it lulled her into a deep sleep.

Diane was released after a couple of days with a list of dos and don'ts. She had to be careful with her stitches in order to heal properly and avoid infection. And no more morphine. She wanted to be healed and ready for Robert's arrival to their home. She was especially concerned about being able to breastfeed. She had breastfed all her children and she didn't want Robert to be an exception. It's a very important bonding connection between mother and child, not to mention all the natural benefits to both of them. For Robert it meant proper immunity protection from diseases. She would never be able to forgive Luis if she couldn't breastfeed her son.

Robert had to stay in neo-natal ICU for care and observation. It would be at least a month before he would arrive home. Luis would bring Diane to the hospital daily to spend time with him. They were going through the motions, pretending there wasn't a boulder between them. Diane accepted this state of interaction because she really didn't have the energy to confront anything more and she needed him right now.

Luis went out of his way to be supportive, taking a few weeks off from work and trying to anticipate her every need. If he was still seeing

Maria, he was being very careful about it. But Diane had made up her mind that she no longer cared because he had broken them. She could never trust him again, let alone love him. And on top of all that, she had almost lost her baby because he had brought Maria into their lives.

One afternoon, after Luis had returned to work, the phone rang. Diane hesitated. She wasn't used to receiving many calls during the day and Maria's unexpected knock at her door had cracked the foundation of her marriage. But to her relief and pleasure, it was David Anderson.

"Diane, how are you, and the baby? Everyone here was wondering how you were so I took a chance I might catch you."

Diane had called him once she had been released from the hospital to share that she had given birth. Their conversation was brief. Now, in the quiet of the afternoon, she took time to talk to her friend.

"We're good. Robert is getting stronger every day. He may be home in a week or so. I'm glad you called. It's good to hear your voice."

"That's great news about Robert. I'll let the team know."

He listened to the other end of the line, expecting her to go on about how cute he was, but when he didn't hear anything, he said, "Diane, how are you really? You sound, I don't know, kinda down."

The softness in his voice reminded her of Luis and the caring way he used to be with her. It made the tears start again. She had missed talking and laughing with David and her broken heart needed his friendship now.

Hearing her sniffling, he chose his next words carefully to provide a bridge for her to reach him. "Diane, what's wrong? Let me help."

"Oh David. I'm a wreck. My marriage is a mess. Luis is having an affair." There, she said it. She inhaled and exhaled deeply and then continued, "This is the first time I have said it out loud. I haven't been able to talk to anyone about it. I'm so numb. I can't believe how he has ruined our life together."

The door was opened, the bricks were laid and she walked right over to David. They talked for about two hours. Mostly David just listened, which is what she needed. It was nearly time for the children to come home so she thanked him and apologized for venting all of this with him.

"Diane, don't be silly. I'll always be here for you." And with that, he was gone and she began preparing dinner with a clearer head.

That evening when Luis came home, Diane told him she was ready to talk. She sat on the bed and he pulled up a chair to sit in front of her.

"May I start?" he asked.

She looked into his eyes and noticed pain that she hadn't seen before. She owed him that much, so she nodded and he started.

"First of all, Diane, you must know how much I love you."

She sucked her teeth and turned her head away from him, more out of pride than anger. And also because she believed him, but she didn't understand how he could cheat on her if that were really true.

"No, damn it; don't doubt that for one minute. Don't turn away from me. I would do anything for you, and I love our kids and the life we have shared. But, when you defied me and returned to work, it really seemed like we were heading in two different directions. We weren't communicating in any way and I felt threatened by your actions. I felt like you were saying I couldn't provide for you and our children.

"You know where I come from. In my culture the man is the provider, as old fashioned as it may seem. No ifs, ands or buts. Plain and simple, period. That's what defines a man. But you made it clear that you wanted a house and the only way you thought we could get it was if you helped out financially. I'm a proud Afro-Puerto Rican man, you know that, but your actions were saying otherwise. Baby, you knew who I was when we married."

"So, now this is my fault?"

"No, but I am saying that it's our fault. It's our fault because we didn't listen or hear what each other needed. It's our fault for not working harder to get through the issues. And it's my fault for looking to someone else to help make me feel good about myself again because I wasn't getting that from you."

"I see. So, when did it happen and where?"

"That's not important."

"Bullshit. She told me you have been lovers for over a year. Is that true? How could you? I let her in my home, shared my children and treated her like family. How stupid of me? A whole year…that's why she stopped coming around, isn't it?"

He looked down and said, "I guess. The further you and I drifted apart, the easier it became for me to convince myself it was okay. I never meant to hurt you, though. It was never about you. I know that now. And you are hardly stupid Di, just trusting – one of your endearing qualities. What I did with her had nothing to do with my love for you and the children."

"Really? You never meant to hurt me and you really find my trusting you to be endearing? Well Luis, she said you were planning to divorce me until I got pregnant. Then you were going to wait until after Robert was born. Did you tell her that?"

"No."

"You didn't? Then why does she think that? Was that to keep her available for your booty calls?"

"She wanted me to leave you. She had some crazy idea that we would get married and we would get joint custody of the kids. Maria's Puerto Rican, too, and she knows how much my family means to me. I NEVER told her I was going to leave you. Then when you got pregnant, I really felt it was a sign from God that we were meant to be together. I told her that our affair was over and we couldn't see each other anymore."

"Did you stop?"

"Sort of."

"Sort of! What the hell does that mean? You either stopped fucking her or you didn't. Which is it?"

"It means it was self preservation sex. I didn't see her as frequently but I couldn't completely stop seeing her. She threatened to tell the university's board of trustees if I did. Even though our affair didn't start until the semester after I taught her, the board would not have cared. Diane, I was up for a tenured position; you know that. I couldn't let her destroy that because that would affect our family's wellbeing and our dreams."

"I see. So you kept seeing her, all during my pregnancy? While I thought we were working on this marriage, you were having sex with both of us? While I was thinking maybe, just maybe, we had a chance?"

Again, he lowered his head, but this time in shame.

"Occasionally. But I knew that if I could get tenured, the board would have a harder time firing me and we would finally have the extra money we needed to buy the house you wanted. The house you deserve. I was planning to end it with her once that happened. She must have figured that out and gone with her Plan B, to tell you to ensure our marriage's demise. I am so sorry, Di but clearly she doesn't know what we have, what we mean to each other."

"I'm sorry too, Luis, because quite honestly, her plan worked like a charm. You betrayed me. How many times did you leave her bed and come get into ours? How many times did you fuck her and then come home to screw me? You took a sledgehammer to our vows, our love for each other and this family. And, on top of that, because you brought that woman into our lives, I almost lost Robert. How am I ever supposed to forgive you for any of that?"

Luis was sick. He never slept with both of them in the same night, but it really wasn't going to matter to Diane. She felt betrayed and her pride would now be the obstacle standing between them. But he had to reach her somehow. He did not want to lose his family over a fling.

"What do you want me to do? What do you want me to say? Can't you forgive me this one mistake? Marriages have to be stronger than this. They have to weather all kinds of storms and obstacles. Diane, don't just throw us away."

Insensitive to Luis' plea, Diane addressed him as if she was devoid of all emotion, saying, "I didn't throw us away, Luis. You did."

She paused, refusing to allow feelings to come to the surface and then continued, "Please pack your things and leave here tonight. I want you out of my house and out of our lives. The way I feel right now, I could never trust you again. I gave you everything. I put you first. I have loved you for so long, I can't remember what it feels like not to, but I guess I will find out."

"No. I'm not giving up on us. Diane, damn it, please don't do this. I don't love her. I don't want her. I want you. I want us and our family. I'm not leaving."

In a cold, steely voice, Diane asked, "Do you want your sons to see the police escort you out of here? Go! Go to Maria. Start a new life with her…but you better know what you've gotten yourself into Luis because she doesn't really care about you or our children. She's devious and conniving and it looks like she's got you all confused. Or, what's the other phrase for it?"

Those words hit him hard, but that was hardly the case. He was not whipped and Maria would never in a million years be the next Mrs. Rodriquez. She wasn't the marrying kind. He knew exactly what and who she was. He had been caught between a rock and a hard place because of the tenure status. Had that not been the case, he and Diane would be sitting there enjoying the newest addition to their family.

"Di, that's ridiculous. Baby, please." Still not accepting what his wife was telling him, Luis pleaded one more time, "Don't do this; don't do something you'll regret. Don't let her win. Please don't make me go."

He didn't understand. Maria had already won. "Just get out will you? And do not call me Di, ever again. Not ever! Just go. When I come out Luis, I want you gone. Don't bother to spend time packing. I'll send you your things. Just leave Maria's address on the dresser."

She got up from the bed, leaving him behind, and slammed and locked the bathroom door behind her. She refused to let him see her cry, again. When she came out of the bathroom, Luis was gone.

After that night, he pursued Diane for three months trying to talk to her, and demonstrate how much he loved her and the children. But Diane had gone ice cold on him and refused to listen or care about what he was doing or not doing. He called to share the news that he did get tenured and he swore, again, that things were completely over between him and Maria.

But Diane was not moved. 'Too little, too late,' she thought. Besides, she was now a single parent with a newborn and three other children to care for. So she redirected her attention to them and focused on the career that she hoped she would be starting one day soon. She couldn't, she wouldn't waste any more energy on him.

The phone rang one evening, about three months later, and it was Maria. Diane hadn't seen or spoken to her since her surprise visit.

"I just called to tell you that Luis and I are back together. I knew he would come back to me."

Diane just hung up the phone. She managed a small smile as she savored Maria's words. So he had left her at least; that much was true.

But he had let her back in his life and that was not good because now Diane would never take him back.

Luis was planning to come by and see the kids the next day and that evening, after Maria's call, she made up her mind that it would be his last visit. She told him then that it would be a cold day in Hell before she would let Maria be involved in raising her children and since he had re-opened the door and let that wench back in, Diane's door to her children was now closed.

Several years had passed and Diane had upheld that proclamation and tomorrow, she would go and see Luis and remind him, and Maria, of that once again. What bothered her most was that Maria was a conniving little witch, just like Diane had told Luis before he left, and she couldn't understand why Luis did not see that.

This made her so angry all over again and did every time she thought about it. She just couldn't understand it. And Carlos, like his father, had fallen for that sorry-ass act of hers, too. She knew that Carlos had taken Luis J there without telling him beforehand.

She thought for a second that she would wait to see if Luis J would tell her on Sunday night when he returned home. She thought he would have more insight because he was actually the one more like her. But it didn't matter because he'd find out she already knew about the betrayal soon enough, once she gave Luis and Maria a piece of her mind.

Carlos' apartment was a one-bedroom unit in Brooklyn. It was sparsely furnished, with a sleeper sofa, bed, dresser and a small non-descript table near the window for eating when he wasn't sitting in front of the TV. The "kitchen" was more like a small kitchenette, like most apartments in East New York. It had the bare minimums: sink, refrigerator and stove, which were all visible from the living room area.

Whenever Luis J visited his brother, he slept on the couch, which was hardly long enough to accommodate his frame. But Luis J didn't care because at least he was away from home. When he visited, it was always about that – getting away from his mother, David, Robert and Chell – that whole family dynamic.

He needed his own space and the fact that neither David nor his mother got that baffled him. His mother should know that sharing a bedroom with his baby brother really cramped his flow – stopped it, in fact. If they didn't want him to have sex, then he'd have to pull into the self-serve. And so, where and when was he supposed to do that?

Luis J was awakened that morning to loud music and a blast of cold air. "Damn, Lo, turn the music down and what are you trying to do with that cold air? Rough night last night after all that grinding?" Luis J asked, smirking.

When he rolled over onto his back he was surprised to see Carmine. 'Lo is surely going to kill me,' he thought. "Oh, hey Carmine, sorry about that. How was your evening?"

He instinctively pulled the cover up to his mid-section because he couldn't remember if he had slept in his briefs or au natural. After all, he didn't want to be disrespectful to his brother's girl. At the same time, he was hoping the question he asked would distract her from his comment.

"Humph. So is that why you guys are sleeping so late? What, exactly, did you do?" she asked, looking around the room at the mess they had created in that short period of time. She had just cleaned the place the night before in anticipation of spending the weekend with Carlos. Now, Luis J was sprawled on the couch and had already infringed on one of her two nights with her man.

Scowling at him, she wondered what time he would be leaving. If she had her way, he'd already be dressed and walking out the door. She was standing over him, hand on her hip and weight on one leg as she stared at him with an accusatory expression on her face, awaiting his response.

So he offered, "Carmine, I hope that this is not an interrogation because I left my mother at home. But just to satisfy you, we saw our father and then caught a movie. I think we're going to some party tonight. You coming with us?"

"Cómo?" she blurted out. She couldn't believe her ears. He did not just say they were going out tonight, too. Carlos was really pushing her to the edge right now.

Luis J paused for a moment trying to remember what that meant. His Spanish was really rusty. "Uh, Carlos was probably gonna tell you later. My bad."

"Really? She put up her hand to stop any further dialogue from him and headed toward Carlos' room, pitching an additional directive over her shoulder, "It's almost noon and you guys need to get up anyway."

Luis J thought to himself, 'She's right, I really screwed up. But, who does she think she's talking to?' He didn't take that crap from anybody and he wasn't about to take it from her. "Carmine, like I said, I left my mother at home. I don't need you to tell me when to get up or what to do. And please don't wave your hand in my face. I know you're Carlos' girl and he might be okay with that, but not me."

She rolled her eyes and walked into Carlos' room, closing the door behind her even though she knew Luis J would still be able to hear their conversation. Quite frankly, she hoped he would listen to every word she had to say and maybe change his mind and leave. He didn't have to go home but he didn't have to stay with Carlos either.

When she turned to face Carlos, she found him sitting up in bed with a big grin on his face. This infuriated Carmine even more. "What the hell is so funny?" she asked, with that "I'm not happy" tone when she spoke. "Carlos, qué pasó?"

"What's going on is under this cover, chica. Come join me," he beckoned in his bedroom voice and patted the bed next to where he lay.

He used this voice when he wanted her or if he was trying to calm her down. Today, he was using it for the latter. He had heard the exchange between her and Luis J and now had to be on the defensive. He was going to have to remind Luis J to keep his mouth shut when they hung out. He was always bragging about how discreet he was with his women, but in one minute he had lit Carmine's fuse. And with Carmine, it didn't take much.

"No. What is this about you and Luis J hanging out tonight, too?" Carmine asked, maintaining her position by the door. She couldn't get close to him because he always knew what to say and how to touch her to get her into his bed.

"Baby, Luis J is having some issues at home. He and David aren't doing well. I told you he was spending the weekend," he said, talking softly now, still trying to stamp out the fuse before it reached its destination.

"No. You only said Friday night. What about our plans? Even if he is spending the weekend here it doesn't mean you have to babysit him. We could still go out tonight, just the two of us."

"I know, Carmine, but my brother needs a break and I want to be there for him. I'll make it up to you."

"When Carlos? You only have one weekend off a month," she said, sucking her teeth and placing her hand on her hip.

"Then let's not waste this morning arguing. Come here."

She still didn't move. She could feel herself wanting to curl up in his arms but that wouldn't get her what she wanted. She didn't just want a few minutes, she wanted the whole day.

"No, Lo, I'm really disappointed. Last month, Maria and your father needed something. You ended up spending the weekend over there to help your father install whatever. Remember, how mad I was about that? And you promised me that we would be together this weekend. You said nothing would get in the way. And now it's Luis J. What's next?" She pouted her lip, hoping this would have an effect on him. It usually did and she wanted him to feel guilty and kick Luis J to the curb.

"Carmine, next month, I promise. Now bring me a kiss."

"Bese mi asno, Carlos."

"I would if you would bring it over here. Come feel how much I missed you last night," he said, rubbing his manhood and smiling at her. She was really playing hard to get and he wondered if he was going to lose this time. He hoped not because one, he would have to be in major make-up mode and two, now he really did want her.

The conversation stopped, so Luis J assumed Carlos had won. He sat up, pulled on his jeans and proceeded to close the windows. From his point of view it seemed like Carlos put up with too much with Carmine. He had been around her a few times and on almost every occasion she exhibited this possessive behavior.

It reminded him of Cassie. That's why he was always keeping Cassie in check. Luis J could never be with someone like Carmine because she didn't get the message. It seemed like the more you tried to get her in line, the more she acted out. He wondered what Carlos found attractive about that.

'Yeah, she's cute but, not for all that shit,' he thought as he walked back to the MP3 player and turned down the Latin sounds that were playing. He was hungry but figured they would eat once Carmine left, hopefully soon. He grabbed Carlos' cigarettes off the table and had just finished lighting a stick when the bedroom door opened and then slammed.

He smiled to himself, thinking, 'Well, I know my brother can last longer than that.' But Luis J didn't say anything to Carmine. He just watched her pick up her purse and head for the door. Based on her behavior, he guessed Carlos really hadn't pleased her.

"I'm out. Have fun with your brother." Not giving him time to respond, she slammed the apartment door shut behind her.

Luis J walked to Carlos' bedroom door and opened it. "Hey man, what's going on?"

"Oh, she's in one of her moods. No te preocupes, lil' bro'." Carlos had pulled out his "A" game, but Carmine had not budged from that sour position. As far as she was concerned, he had ruined her day, week, month and she was fed up.

Carlos could never understand why things were either one extreme or the other with her. He had dated Carmine for about a year, but sometimes it felt like five. He was tired of all the energy it required and had recently concluded that he was going to end it with her. There were too many other women out there to be with one that was so high-maintenance.

"I'm not worrying, but man your woman always brings the drama."

"Whatever. Hungry?"

"Good and hungry," Luis J replied, reminding him of his grandfather who said that all the time. He said it was a southern phrase and it always made Luis J laugh when he heard it. He welcomed that lightheartedness this morning in light of all the craziness he was trying to leave behind him.

"So let's go grab something to eat, and then we can run around. I have to stop by Papi's. I left my hair brush over there last night."

"Man, we can buy another hair brush for the gas it will cost to get back over there. I'm just sayin'. You're joking right?"

Carlos kept his hair cut close and brushed it for five minutes every morning to get it the way he liked it. This process created wavy ridges in his hair and he liked the look. He started wearing this style when he was about fourteen because he got tired of his mother fusing at him every morning about combing his hair. It wasn't that long but the texture made it often look like it wasn't combed and it frustrated him because he had combed it. So one weekend, he went to the barbershop and cut it real close to his scalp. He had tried all kinds of brushes to get the effect he wanted but there was only one he really liked. He would use the backup one for now but he had to get that brush.

From where Luis J sat, he thought his brother's hair looked fine but he was not about to contradict him. He knew all too well about Carlos and that brush. So instead he asked, "Are we still going to the set?"

"You bet. I know there will be some fine chicas there," he replied, remembering the crowd from a few nights ago. "By the way, you really need to brush up on your Spanish, bro. When I stayed with Papi and Maria, they would only talk to me in Spanish and it all came back to me. I love it and Maria said I even have the Puerto Rican accent. Oh, and dancing...," Carlos continued, moving his feet back and forth in a salsa rhythm and turning around as though he were dancing with someone.

"We would salsa every Saturday night. Maria and Papi have some pretty smooth moves. But I've perfected my shit, as you'll see tonight. If Maria's home when we get there, I'll give you a sneak preview." He was still swaying to the music, back and forth and spinning with his imaginary partner. "You know, this all feels so natural to me. I sometimes wish I could live over there."

"That's kewl (cool) man," Luis J said, feeling a little envious of Carlos' connection with that part of their culture and the time he had spent with their father. It seemed like he had become more grounded. He wished he had that. "Mami doesn't really speak it anymore because David doesn't know it. Chell and I do sometimes; she's taking it in school now, but it's more conversational for her, not natural like your flow or like ours was when Papi was there. And Robert, forget it. He never even learned the basics. Papi wasn't there to speak it to him like he did with us. He doesn't even know he's half Puerto Rican."

"Yeah, well, I can't control what happens over there but if you start spending more time with me and Papi, you'll get better. You've got to practice it with people who speak it. Then you can help Chell speak more naturally."

"Man, what were you and Carmine doing in here? Your brain is mush. You know our mother will never let me spend that much time with Papi. If she knew I was there last night, I would be grounded for a year."

"We'll see about that." Carlos had seen first-hand how much his father had enjoyed being with them and if he knew anything about his father, he knew that he would fight to have time with Luis J, Chell and Robert now. Finishing his thought, he said, "Anyway I'm going to shower so we can get out of here. I hope you have some money with you. I don't plan to carry you all weekend."

"Yeah, I got money." This made Luis J think about Dany. He had received his allowance from his mother and had originally thought he would be giving it to Steph. He was really missing Dany. They were supposed to go to the movies this weekend.

He wanted to call or text her to let her know what he was feeling, but he thought he'd better wait until her mom and Steph would be out of the house. They usually shopped on Saturday around two and would be gone for at least two hours, which was when he and Dany sometimes hooked up. Damn, he was missing that girl. He had just been with Cassie, and that was the thing with Cassie – it was all about the sex; with Dany it was so much more.

On their way to Papi's, a lot of thoughts roamed around Luis J's mind. He settled on one for now and asked, "Carlos, what really happened between Mami and Papi?"

Carlos shifted in the seat and glanced in the mirror as if he were checking the traffic. He needed time to think about how to answer his brother's question. His father had told him most of the story about six months ago, but Carlos wasn't sure how much Luis J was ready to hear. Luis J and their father were just beginning to reconnect and he didn't want to impact anything before it even got off the ground.

"I don't know all the details, but I do know there is more to the story than Mami told us. In fact she didn't really tell us anything. I mean some stuff that goes on between a man and a woman is just that, between a man and a woman. Only they really know what happened. But, I do know that Maria was involved and that there are three versions to the story."

Luis J listened attentively as his brother filled in some gaps, then said, "So, Papi had an affair with Maria that started before Mami got pregnant with Robert. That explains a lot about some of Mami's anger. Man, Papi is supposed to know how not to get caught. What's up with that? Where was his 'A' game?"

Shaking his head from side to side, Carlos said, "Only you would think of that, Luis J. Papi should not have had an affair. He was married."

"Hey man, I'm a player. All men worth their weight in balls are players. Women just don't get it. I think it's a conspiracy created by the…what's that group called from the medieval times?"

"What? What are you talking about? Oh never mind. Anyway, Mami refused to forgive him. He tried everything. He even broke it off with Maria, but she wouldn't give him another chance. Papi says he did everything he could think of, exhausted his imagination. He even bent over backwards to woo her, man, but Mami wouldn't budge."

"Yeah, we're all stubborn like that," Luis J said.

"Well their stubbornness is how we got to this. I remember some of the story, Luis J. We had been out with Papi, and when we came back home to get his wallet, Maria was there with Mami and she was going into labor. Papi had told me to call the ambulance but then Mami calls for me to come be with her even though Papi was right there by her. I'm not certain but I think that Maria had upset Mami and caused her to go into premature labor.

"Then one day long after they had split, Papi stops by the house to pick us up and Mami tells him to kiss us goodbye. That was the last time he was allowed to see us until after Mami married David. Papi came by to wish her well and to plead for a chance to see us, to be a part of our lives."

"I sort of remember that. I remember feeling awkward with him being there because I thought he didn't want us anymore."

"I know. That's what Mami led us to think and believe, but it wasn't true. She and David took Robert, but left us in the apartment with Papi. He was devastated by that because he said Robert was 'The Gift from God' meant to heal their marriage. But he was still glad to be able to spend time with you, Chell and me. That was the day he said to hell with the promise he had made to Mami to stay out of our lives. He felt he had the right to be a father to us, so he filed for joint custody.

"Mami went ballistic. You know how women get about their children. Well, I guess you don't. But anyway, she felt that he was trying to hurt her again just because he wanted to be a father to us. She also just knew Maria was behind it all trying to cause trouble, so she hired a good female attorney who was out for blood. Papi's blood. They were prepared to make things really ugly, you know, bringing up Papi's affair and everything. Papi knew you and I would be hurt most by it all, so he agreed to back off. He hoped that as we got older, we would look for him and maybe give him a chance to be involved in our lives.

"When I called to tell him I was moving out of the house, he asked me where I was going. I had talked to a friend and was going to crash at his place, but Papi insisted that I come live with him. He was worried that I wouldn't finish high school or might get into some bad stuff. I knew it would piss off Mami, so I said yes. Papi was so happy and it was the best thing I could have done at the time. Now, you have a chance to get to know him better, too. I hope you take advantage of that."

Luis J had heard Carlos and he got it, yet he had to ask, "But how can you be so nice to Maria? She's the reason we lost our family in the first place."

"Because you know what got me most?" Carlos asked. "It was Mami's total disregard for us. It was all about her, always about her. She never thought about how not having Papi in our lives would impact us, especially you and me. It was always about how Papi had hurt her. But Papi pulled out of a custody battle because of us. As for Maria, I know her type."

Carlos paused when he glanced at Luis J and saw his eyebrow raised. "What? Do you think I'm stupid? Hey, I'm a player, too, but I know in my heart that Maria could not have done anything to break up Mami and Papi if something wasn't already wrong. But I also know how Maria treats me, and she made me feel welcome. I think she really loves Papi. Besides, Papi said he was as much to blame as Maria, so how could I be mad at her and not him?"

"But man, of course she's going to make you feel welcomed. What choice does she have if she wants to stay on Papi's good side?"

"Well she could have had a hissy fit, like Carmine," he tossed back and then burst into laughter, joined by Luis J.

"Good point. So why haven't they gotten married?"

"I don't know. I can't really tell how Papi feels about her except that he's into her sexually." Carlos reflected on how affectionate his parents used to be. His dad would tickle his mother or place his arms around her waist and hold her close. When he was living with him and Maria, he never saw that kind of affection between them, but he would hear them moaning at night. Almost every night.

"Well I know how I feel about Dany. And I have chicks on the side and they mean nothing to me compared to Dany. I'd marry Dany in a heartbeat if I were grown and able to afford it. So it only means that Papi is not in love with her."

"Damn, Luis J that's heavy. You are serious about Dany, aren't you? But you better not do anything stupid. You gotta take care of business first." He paused to let that sink in. Then he continued, "You may be right about Papi. I know how it feels to be with someone you really like and have them torn away from you."

Luis J was just about to inquire more about that comment when they were both distracted by the car they saw parked in front of their father's house. They looked at each other and then back at the car. It was their mother's. Neither of them said anything. Luis J got a sick feeling in the pit of his stomach. He wondered why she was there. How on earth did she know they were stopping by? Did he say earlier that she would ground him for a year? Once she saw him in Papi's house, she would ground him for the rest of his life instead.

"What do you want to do?"

"I gotta get my brush."

"Mami, or the brush?"

Chapter Five

Diane had confirmed with David the night before that he would stay home with Robert as she had errands to run. Chell was going to meet some friends and go to a movie. Diane had given her the "dos and don'ts" the night before so that was taken care of, too. Diane didn't want anything to derail her schedule or her plans.

She was up early and in the salon chair by seven-thirty. She wanted to look flawless, especially if Maria happened to be there. Ninety minutes later, she was heading to the grocery store for a few staple items. By eleven, she was on her way to Luis'. She hadn't slept well because she spent most of the night thinking about the confrontation. She wanted to say just the right words to convey her message. She had created two scripts: one for Maria and one for Luis.

She drove up and sat in front of his house for a minute. In her haste, she hadn't considered that he might not even be home. It was a gray, rainy day, which matched her mood. If she were at home, she would be snuggled tight in bed watching a western. She glanced at the house and could see a light flickering from a room near the back and wondered if Luis had remembered that about her.

His ranch house was mostly brick. It sat in a cul-de-sac near the back of the subdivision. She assumed he chose the location because it wasn't far from LIU. It had a nicely-landscaped yard, which was enclosed with a fence. The emotion that overwhelmed her at that moment was disappointment. This was supposed to be their home.

As she sat there, she could imagine Robert playing in the yard, safe and happy. Chell would be outside talking on the phone but watching out for her little brother. Everyone would have their own room and she wouldn't have to listen to Luis J complaining about his privacy and the heat. Luis would be tenured and finally making decent money, the money they had earned. She wouldn't be in all this debt now and almost living from paycheck to paycheck trying to recover from the bills she'd made when they divorced. And most of all, her mother would be proud of her. She would finally be a homeowner. Hell, she might even have her degree by now.

There was a loud clap of thunder and it shattered her dreams the same way Luis had done with Maria. "Damn it, Luis, why did you steal all of my dreams from me?" she said out loud, as though he were sitting in the car with her.

She stopped to check her reflection in the car's mirror. Her crisp white shirt tied at the waist over a black camisole slightly exposed just enough to tease the lookers. Her jeans were a cigarette cut and hugged her ample hips and shapely butt. Her outfit was enhanced by Calvin Klein "boss lady" black pumps. Her hair was free flowing, the way Luis had loved it. 'Great,' she thought.

Diane was ready to catch him defenseless and off guard. Slowly she climbed out of the car, now sufficiently armed mentally, and headed for the door. Once there, she paused, hoping that Maria was out. It would be easier if she were. As much as she wanted to give Maria a piece of her mind, she really just wanted to have this conversation with Luis.

She rang the doorbell and held her breath waiting to see who would open the door. From inside, she heard Luis' deep voice say, "One minute." Relieved, she could breathe once again. At least he was there, even if Maria was, too. She touched her hair, hoping it was holding up with all the moisture in the air. This was definitely ponytail weather, but she wanted to look her best. She had to. When the door finally opened, there stood Luis, statuesque as always.

"Di?" Luis said, surprised to see his ex.

"Luis," she responded, steadfast and in charge. She had told him not to call her that anymore but she had to admit it still gave her that tingly feeling down below. She gently shook her head to remind herself why she was there and waited for an invitation to come in. Surely he wasn't going to make her stand outside, unless of course Maria was there.

Luis didn't know what to do or say, so he just stood there and shifted his weight from one foot to the other. Finally, he said, "I'm sorry, come in."

She was familiar with his expression of perplexity and she knew she had him where she wanted him. Once she cleared the doorway, she stepped to the side to allow him to show her the way. Even though Carlos had lived there, she had never come to visit. When they entered the living room, the corner of her lip turned up slightly. It was not decorated anything like Luis' taste. There were bright colors in the hallway and even brighter yellows and greens in the living room.

She flinched. It was so unlike him. He had always given input on the décor of the homes they had shared and their schemes were mellow and warm. This had to be Maria's taste, LOUD. There were pictures of the kids on the wall that were from about six months ago. Clearly Carlos had been supplying his father with photos without her permission. How could Carlos still be betraying her? Obviously, Maria's sneaky ways were rubbing off on her son.

There were also clippings from Luis J's games as recent as a year ago. Diane wondered if Luis had been attending them. She hadn't been able to because of her work schedule. Perhaps she needed to make a point to show up to one. Continuing to survey the house, she saw a foyer that had two doorways leading from the living room and she assumed they led to the bedrooms.

'My son lived here a year, under this roof with that woman, and I have no idea under what conditions,' she thought, sighing now that she was inside. At least he had been warm and comfortable. But Diane was determined that Carlos would be the only one of her children who had that experience and exposure to Maria.

"Have a seat. It's good to see you. Wow, you look great! Can I get you something, water, wine, cognac? It is after noon," he said smiling, hoping to break the tension. He watched as she took a seat but she didn't respond, so he continued rambling. "How are the kids?"

Luis was still in a daze. Was she really standing in the middle of his living room? He coyly admired how well she looked. She had been taking care of herself. She even looked happy behind that scowl and he was thankful for that. But he knew she was there because of Maria's call and Luis J's visit, so he prepared himself for her tongue.

"Yes, I would like some water," Diane said, choosing to answer only one of his questions. As he moved to get the water from a room in the back, she discretely eyed him. She hadn't seen Luis in three years, but he looked fit, and the graying at the temples made him look even more distinguished. He returned with a bottle and handed it to her before sitting down so they would be facing one another.

She took a sip and gave him a little more information. "Well, you already know how Luis J is...the others are fine." Taking another sip before placing the bottle on the coffee table in front of her, she quietly asked, "Are we alone?"

"Yes. Maria won't be here for about an hour." Seizing the chance to create some space, he offered, "I'm sorry about her call to you last night. She did it without my knowledge or encouragement. Did David tell you I called too? I was hoping to speak to you and apologize for her actions."

"Yes, of course he did. David doesn't keep secrets from me or tell lies."

'Here it comes,' Luis thought. He recognized the venom but he didn't have to take it the way he used to because they weren't married anymore. He didn't owe her that level of understanding, so he waited to see where she was going next.

She knew that was a hit below the belt and began keeping score. Diane, one. She continued, "Luis, I came here to remind you of your promise regarding my children."

"Our children, Diane."

Ignoring his interruption, she proceeded, "You said you would honor my terms and stay out of their lives as long as you were with her. You agreed they would be hurt by a nasty custody battle and it would be better for them to grow up in one home versus switching back and forth. Now, all of a sudden, she's calling my home late at night, disturbing my husband and me, to tell me about the dinner you all planned with Luis J. Behind my back and certainly without my consent. What the hell is going on?"

"Diane, yes, I agreed to honor your terms and I stayed away even though it hurt me and quite frankly, it hurt the kids even more. It literally tore my heart out when Carlos shared with me his perception of why I was not involved in their lives. I continued to stay away and not intervene. But I never promised that I would turn away from them if they came to me. And how you could make such a demand is still baffling to me. Why I agreed is even more. But you did and I went along. But why did you perpetuate this lie to my kids that I'm some deadbeat dad who doesn't care about them or love them? How could that be what's best for them?"

"I figured you weren't going to be around and I refused to have them sitting by the door waiting for you to come and visit when your calendar had an opening."

"Diane, you know that I would never have treated my kids that way. I would never want Chell to feel abandoned by her father. That's not healthy for a young girl. And it certainly isn't the behavior we want our boys to emulate. It is not how my father raised me. So, when Carlos came to me because he needed somewhere to stay, I welcomed him with open arms. He knows he can come here anytime. That interaction with him began restoring my heart."

He stopped to remember the moments from the night before and said, "You know, most women complain that their children's father disappears and they have to track them down to try to secure some form of child support and interaction. Those women would give anything for a man who really wants to have a presence in their children's lives. A man like me, who tried to assist you financially but you refused. You elected to suffer and make our kids suffer just to make a point. And all for what, Diane?"

Diane was losing ground. He was clearly ahead now two to one, so she had to strike back. "You have the nerve to ask me why? You know damn well why. I will never let my children be around Maria and quite frankly I don't see why you think it's alright. Especially Robert; she could have killed him because of her selfish-ass tactic. So don't ask me why.

"I thought you had left her and I was starting to reconsider our separation. Then out of the blue she calls to tell me that you were back together, gloating over her so-called victory."

"What? She called you back then? Damn, now it all makes sense, that sudden change in your behavior and in the direction I thought we were going." He wondered why she had turned cold as ice toward him all of a sudden.

"And that's when and why you closed me out, isn't it? Oh Di, you always did strike back with a vengeance when you were hurt instead of sharing what was on your mind. If you had told me, I could have addressed it with Maria. We may have ended up on a completely different path." He sighed, shaking his head before continuing, "Well, that's water under the bridge now. All I can say is, I apologize. It seems like I am always saying I'm sorry to you when it comes to Maria. But one thing that hasn't happened yet – you have never acknowledged your role in our relationship's demise."

"Acknowledge what? How did I contribute to our demise?"

"Because you didn't trust me and believe in us. You let Maria manipulate your feelings, you believed her over me, you took her word over mine, the word of a 'conniving witch.' Isn't that what you called her? But you let her drive a sledgehammer between us to split us apart. It takes two to make or break a marriage."

"Well in our case it took three, and the two of you broke the relationship, not me."

"Diane, after all these years, I can't believe you're still clinging to that delusion. We were having problems before Maria ever came into the picture. She just preyed upon them. I let her in, true. That was my fault, but she never would have been able to penetrate our marriage had you not shut me out."

Diane couldn't believe how he was maneuvering the conversation so that she had to be on the defensive. She had come over to his house to regain the upper hand but she hadn't expected *this* Luis. He was scoring points against her and she didn't like it, so she interrupted him by saying, "Actually, you're right. It's been a long time, Luis, and I didn't come here to rehash the past, but to make sure that it will not be repeated. And I'm not just talking about you and Maria."

"Diane, I'm not exactly sure what you're talking about, but let me share this. Luis J came by with Carlos last night, and I was as surprised to see him here as you were when you found out. I didn't know they hadn't cleared it with you first. I guess I should have asked, but apparently Carlos had planned it and I was so grateful he did. It was good to see my son, to hug him, to talk to him, to be a father to him once again. We talked and laughed and my heart ached just a little less. I'm not going to apologize for that.

"I told Luis J the same thing I told Carlos, that he's welcome here, anytime. And I mean that, so please don't punish him for it or prevent him from coming if he asks. He is almost eighteen. He has his own mind. It's clear he's becoming a young man and we have to treat him like one. And Diane, you've got to stop possessing them. Men don't like feeling smothered. Let them make up their own minds or you will run them away from you."

Diane rolled her eyes and said, "Why do I get the feeling that you're saying this whole mess is my fault? So I smothered you and you ran into Maria's arms? Well, understand this, I will not lose Luis J the way I have lost Carlos because he's not as vulnerable to his feelings. You filled Carlos' head with lies and now he and I barely have a relationship. He and David don't have one at all and I hate that. I won't have you turn Luis J against us, too."

"Diane, you know that I'm not doing that and we both know why Carlos doesn't have a relationship with David and why his relationship with you is strained. You are so good at making up these crazy scenarios in your head. I chose you. I married you. You are the mother of my children. I would never talk negatively about you to our children, especially our sons, so why do you do that about me?

"I pray that one day they marry a loyal, loving woman like you. But you can't place blame for your relationship with Carlos at my feet. No one can turn your children away from you but you. Can't you see with all your efforts to make me the villain in their eyes, now that they are older, they're seeing right through it? We were raising our sons to be independent thinkers. I'm grateful to you for continuing that in my absence, but you can't stop nurturing that now because that thinking may differ from what your choices are for them. Carlos felt that he had to choose sides, but I didn't draw a line in the sand."

"You must have said something to him because I find it funny that he ended up siding with you."

"I don't want him on either side. Our children have two parents who love them equally; they shouldn't have to choose between us. We shouldn't make them. Carlos found it easier to talk to me. He simply recognized that there were two different views about how we should participate in their lives and he embraced the one that was less combative. However, I continued to encourage him to work things out with you and David."

"My children have been making new memories with me and David. He's the only father Robert knows and the only father I want him to know. Maria almost killed him. I keep reminding you of that fact. I will not allow you or her to interfere with Robert's relationship with David."

She knew that comment would help her gain some ground. She had kept Luis completely out of Robert's life and that had to be killing him to have his son not even know him.

"Diane, it's time to let your anger go. It's not becoming of you, it's not good for the kids, and it can't be healthy for your marriage. I know Maria and I hurt you deeply. I will take that guilt to my grave, but somehow we must move beyond what's happened. It was not intentional. But I've told you all that before. I'm not saying I want to replace the relationship they have with David, I'm just asking you not to shut me out as their father anymore."

'Now he's lecturing me on how to save my marriage? If he had that knowledge, we would still be married,' she thought, then panicked for a moment as she wondered if he and Maria had tied the knot and he hadn't told her. She quickly checked his finger to see if it bore a ring. She was relieved to see it didn't.

Now fuming inside, Diane still maintained her outer composure and spoke in a deliberate delivery, articulating her words as if they were poisonous arrows. "I will never forgive you for stealing my dreams from me. Never. And I will never have my children spend one minute with Maria. Never. Not even one second. I don't like her. I told you I don't trust her. How dare she come to my home and mesmerize my children like the pied piper? Then she seduced you with opened legs. It's funny that with all her conniving, she hasn't gotten you to marry her or gotten pregnant. It must be you who's holding back…I wonder, umm.

"Why don't you give her a child of her own so she can stop fixating on mine? Is she barren or something?" she asked softly, dipping the last arrow in the sweetest poison as she aimed it directly at his heart.

Angry now, Luis asked, "Diane, why the hell did you come here? What were you hoping to get out of this conversation?"

'There, that's the reaction I was looking for. Now, let's see if I can score the game point,' she thought, wallowing in her victory. "I came here because I wanted to remind you of your promise. I came here to tell that homewrecker to stop calling me. I don't have any business with her and there damn sure isn't anything I want to hear from her. I pray that I can forgive you, but I will never forget how you handled the situation when I had gone into labor because of her.

"You should have put her out of our house when you saw her and saw my condition. You knew she was up to no good. Her presence was not well-meaning. She hadn't called an ambulance and it never occurred to you that her being there was stressing me out? I almost lost our gift from God because of that snake bitch and you.

"No, I'm just fine with my memories. You're the one that needs to adjust the delusion – the woman that you're sleeping with almost cost you your baby son. She wanted to kill him because she thought you'd leave me if there was no baby!" Diane shouted, as all her rage came tumbling out.

She got up to put on her coat. She had finally released the thoughts about him, Maria and that day that had been bottled up inside of her for years.

"Diane, you have been holding that inside for a long time. I hope you feel some sense of relief now and can move on. Rest assured, I will reflect on our conversation today and I will make sure Maria does not bother you anymore. But I also encourage you to think really hard about some of the observations and comments I shared with you today as well. I meant every word."

Diane walked slowly towards the door, with those words hanging in the air. As she reached for the knob, to her surprise it opened and there stood Luis J and Carlos.

"Mami, what are you doing here?" Carlos asked, trying to assess her mood. He could tell from the look on his father's face that this was not an expected visit.

"The question, Carlos, is what is Luis J doing here? You told me you guys were spending the weekend at your place. This is pretty far from there. You know damn well how I feel about this," Diane said, eyes squinted and eyebrows lowered. Both boys knew what that meant and she was waiting for a response.

"Mami, we just stopped by to get Carlos' brush. You know how he is about that brush," Luis J offered, with a chuckle. He felt he needed to let her know that this wasn't his idea and based on the tone in her voice and the look on her face, she was seconds away from killing their plans and making him go home with her. That was the last thing he wanted.

He had suggested to Carlos that maybe he should stay in the car, crouched in the back seat, but Carlos insisted that there was nothing to worry about. But Carlos had been away from home too long. Peering from the back seat of the car would have been a perfect location for him right now.

Next, Luis J's eyes shifted to his father who was standing behind his mother in the hallway. Without changing his focal point, Luis J asked her in a soft voice, "Are you alright?" She still hadn't told them why she was there and what on earth she was so mad about. He hoped it was more than just about running into him at his father's.

"I'm fine. I was just leaving and I want you to do the same. So, you can leave now with Carlos or you can leave now with me." Turning to Carlos she added, "These trips over here were not part of our agreement, Carlos."

Luis J did not have time to respond because his father interjected first, "Diane, I told David to keep his hands off my children last night and I meant it. I will not tolerate him using his hands on my sons."

Luis J froze in his tracks. When had his father talked to David? Had he called the house after he and Carlos left? Why had he done that when Luis J had been clear that his mother could not know he was over there? Now he understood it all and surmised that this was not good for him.

Diane held up her hand to Luis as she walked past her sons and left the door open behind her. She had lost the game. Not because Luis had beaten her but because her sons were betraying her. She sat with the car idling just long enough to see Luis J exit and get back into Carlos' car.

'That arrogant son of a...who does he think he is? I will fight him on this, every step of the way. I will not allow him to have access to my children,' Diane concluded. When Carlos' car finally passed her, she sped off behind them, headed home.

When she walked in, David looked up from cleaning the remains left from Robert's afternoon snack on the kitchen counter and Robert, who was still sitting at the table playing with his action figures, smiled at her. She bent down and kissed Robert on the head before putting the bags down. She then hugged David, lingering in the strength of his arms and refueling her emotional cup. Luis and her sons had drained it. David was so good to her. He had fed Robert and Chell, straightened up and was now in tune with her needs.

He didn't even ask her why she was lingering in his arms. She could feel his body responding to her touch and that made her feel even stronger. He couldn't resist her. She was enough for him. He didn't need some chick on the side to make him feel whole; all he needed was her. If Robert had not been there, they would have made love.

"What's wrong Sweetie, no blue ribbon bargain days at Macy's?" he asked, smiling. He always teased her about her shopping prowess. She could find a bargain any day of the week. When she didn't respond, he shifted to compliments. "Your hair looks nice. Robert, doesn't Mommy's hair look nice?"

Robert looked up from his world, for a brief moment, yawned and nodded. She was thankful it wasn't up to him to cheer her up.

"Thanks. Can we talk? Robert, please go to our room and watch TV while Daddy and I talk."

"Okay, Mommie." He picked up Hulk and Superman and headed for their room, leaving behind two other action figures.

She watched him walk away from them and noticed that he, too, was starting to favor Luis more and more. She sat down at the kitchen table and wondered where her genes were in that pool? She hoped they would think more like her because they were definitely his children.

She poured a glass of water and began, "I've been thinking a lot about Luis and Maria's calls last night. I'm concerned that Luis is plotting something that will surely be trouble again, something to do with custody of the kids. I will not allow our children to be around that woman."

"Why do you think that, all of a sudden?" David asked. "You told me what she said and you didn't mention anything like that. I know I didn't share Luis' comments with you, but he never insinuated anything like that either when I talked to him. So where is this coming from?"

"It's just a feeling I have. I know how Luis thinks and you know we can't trust that witch, Maria. You saw what happened when Carlos moved in with them; they started filling his head with lies about me and you. Now Luis J is their next target and they're using Carlos to do it. Next thing we know, there will be secret rendezvous with Chell and Robert. What are we going to do, David? I'm scared."

He led her to the couch and held her hand until her tears subsided. He didn't like her comment about knowing Luis. What did she think she knew, exactly? He had told her last night that he would take care of things, but here she sat all torn up about it, again. He was getting tired of all the drama this week. That's why he had told her he would stay home today. He was mentally exhausted from the fight with Luis J, the tension Carlos brought to the house with his visit and now the Luis and Maria show.

"Didn't I tell you last night I would take care of you and this family? Stop worrying. I'll see what I can find out and determine the best course of action. But first you have to calm down and not blow things out of proportion."

They looked at each other and burst into laughter. Then Diane said, smiling, "Seems like a lot of that's been going on lately."

"It has. God, I wish I could make love to you right now and make you forget about all this shit. Tonight, baby, just hold on until tonight."

They sat hugged up in silence after that for a little while. David reflected in deep thought, holding her close. Then without words he kissed her on the cheek before rising from the sofa to check on Robert.

Diane brushed aside the voice that said she should tell her husband of her visit to Luis' house because that action was a violation of what David had asked her to do, to let him be the man and handle it. But David didn't know them the way she did. She had to confront this head on.

Besides, she knew he'd put two and two together and then accuse her of going to get her hair done for Luis, which was true, but not to flirt with him. She just wanted Luis to know that she was still looking good, living good and happy, especially if Maria had been there. She just wanted to be on top of her game. She wondered what Maria looked like these days. Luis sure did look good. No, she didn't have any regrets about going. None at all.

Chapter Six

The boys stood there for a minute after their mother walked out, not knowing what to say. They elected to stay out of it. The tension still lingered in the room and in their father's body. His energy was very different today than it had been the night before. But Luis J didn't have any sympathy for him. If he had called the house and started this tumultuous exchange, he was surely getting what he deserved.

Carlos found the brush on the coffee table, shared a few words with his father and then they left. He hoped that Maria would be back soon to bring his father some comfort. He knew all too well how his mother could get under his father's skin and drive him crazy. He had seen it many times when she got into one of those defensive moods. He could tell in just that short time she was in rare form. It would take his father hours to calm down after that exchange and he wasn't even privy to the discussion. The brothers drove to their next destination in silence.

Luis closed and locked the door behind them and walked back into the living room. He poured himself a cognac and turned on some Santana. He had just sat in his chair when he heard the key in the door.

"Hey, Papi, I'm back. How's your day going?"

Maria paused in her tracks when she saw the frown on his face and glass in his hand. It was only two-thirty in the afternoon. Luis never drank that early. She sat the bags down by the door, walked over to him and asked caringly, "What's going on? Did something happen?"

"I had an unexpected visitor today," he responded, a mixture of emotions still battling within.

"Really, who?" Maria asked, as she glanced around the room to see if the house was presentable. Rubbing his back, she could feel the tension in his neck and shoulders and before he answered, she knew who it was. Only one person could suck the air out of him like this. But Maria hadn't expected Diane to react to the call in this way.

"Diane."

"What the hell did she want? She has a lot of nerve coming over here, uninvited." At least she hoped Luis had not invited her while she was out.

Luis looked at her and shook his head. Did she really just have the nerve to say that? "She came to talk to me about my children."

With hands on her hips, Maria asked, "What did she say? Obviously not what you hoped."

He drained the liquid from the glass and refilled it, pouring a glass for Maria as well. He took another sip before responding, "No. She's standing by her original position. She doesn't want me in their lives. Your phone call last night infuriated her. You hit her very hard with the news that Luis J was here. But that was your intent all along, wasn't it? You may have just ruined my chances to connect with my son.

"God knows, you should have stayed out of it like I asked you to, Maria. We've had this discussion before. I've told you that I'm in charge of what I do and don't do with my children. You are not involved. Yet you always manage to go fuck things up.

"You called her back then, after Robert was born, and told her we were back together. Why? To upset her more? To make sure that she'd never forgive me? Just what was your motive Maria?"

"I don't know what you're talking about."

"Yes, you do. But that's done. So now, right now, your actions do matter. So I'm telling you now, stay out of my affairs regarding my children and do not call Diane under any circumstances. Not even if I'm on my deathbed. I mean it, Maria, do not call her. Because of that call last night, she thinks we're scheming to poison Luis J's mind against her."

"Are you kidding me? That chick is so paranoid but somehow right now, I'm the bad guy? She's the one plotting and scheming, not me. Yeah, I called her, but it wasn't to set her off. If Luis J was here, it was because he wanted to be, just like Carlos two years ago. She's trying to run their lives and they're seeing right through her bullshit.

"How dare she try to lay this guilt trip on you, let alone blame me? She's the one who's poisoning your children against you."

"Maria you just don't get it, do you? Or is this all part of your sick game? I asked you, no, I told you last night to stay out of it. But you defied me. Why did you call her? You knew how she would react. I told you if you ever pulled another stunt like the one that almost cost us Robert's life, this relationship would be over. Did you think I was kidding?"

Luis was angry about the whole situation, but right now he was directing all of his anger towards the woman standing in front of him. The master manipulator. One minute she was providing him physical comfort and the next she was killing him.

"Luis…"

"Maria, I can't hear you, I can't hear anything you're saying right now. I am so pissed," Luis said between clenched teeth. "And I'm sick of your excuses for doing exactly what I tell you not to do where Diane and my kids are concerned. Last night with my sons made me realize how much I've given up and I won't sacrifice anymore. I told her that I wasn't trying to interfere with their relationship with David; I just want one with them as well."

"And you should. I've said that all along. So why won't you let me help you? I love you."

"If you do, then don't interfere. Diane will never forget the role you played in all of this and she's not about to let you get the upper hand. She doesn't want you around the kids. And to top it off, the boys walked in while she was here. You should have seen that interaction. It was the final hand grenade you built to hurt her, but in fact, you hurt everyone else in the interim. You fucked up last night with that call and I don't like it.

"Goddamnit woman! You're so full of what you think, what you want, that you don't really give a damn about me. True you want me, yeah you want me, you lust for me but do you really love me? You lust me Maria but lust never holds a man and woman together, love does, true love does, and if there is passion plus love then lust is a marvelous thing. But you better get out of my way of expressing my love for my children to my children. I mean it. I'm not going to tell you again. No more warnings, no more being nice. Stay out of my business with Diane and our children."

Maria had been standing in front of him during this conversation, but now she moved away and sat on the couch, displeased with his position on the subject. He was really pissing her off and she clearly didn't understand why this man allowed that woman to have so much control over his emotions.

Perhaps she was underestimating Diane. It had been easy to manipulate her before, but maybe her marriage to David had given her more confidence. Maria made a note that she would need to reevaluate the game. She began replaying Luis' recall of the conversation in her head and stopped when she got to the part that said, "I told her…"

"Luis, what was David's position during this conversation?"

"David didn't come with her. She was alone."

"Really? Now why was that?" After a brief pause, the wheels in Maria's head started turning and she leaned forward. "Poppie, let's get married. It'll strengthen our position if it comes to a custody battle if we can show that we can provide a stable home for the kids as well."

"I've told you Maria, I'm not ready for that. Besides, that will only make things worse. Lest you forget, you were the other woman, and the courts will not be lenient towards the adulterous father who then married the culprit that almost caused his unborn child's death. Besides, I want to settle this outside of the courtroom and I honestly think I can. Today she said something I had never thought about that would be really damaging in a court case."

"What lie was that?"

"She suggested that your intentions were to kill Robert. You saw her water break and yet you didn't call an ambulance. Why? You knew our house, so it wasn't like you didn't know where the phone was. You had a cellphone, too, so why didn't you call?" Luis watched as Maria squirmed in the chair. Could she really have been that calculating?

"Luis, that's a sick lie. I was in shock. I didn't know what to do at that moment, but I was about to help her when you came in."

"Well, she warned me that I better think about the woman that I'm with…and I'm thinking about it." When Luis saw that Maria was not going to say anything else, he had his answer. Then he added, "So leave her alone. No phone calls, no surprise visits, no interactions with her at all."

Luis didn't see a need to say anything else and the look on his face should have been clear to her that the subject was over.

"Fine."

"No, promise me. Repeat, I will not make any contact with Diane or the children."

"Luis, I said fine!"

"That's not good enough."

"You will not cajole me, Luis, I said fine. Look, I am a grown woman, not a child. I understand English perfectly well." She placed her glass down and headed toward the bedroom, but just before she got to the door, he called out after her.

"Maria."

She turned, waiting to see what else he felt he had to say.

"If I ever find out that there's any truth to the story about Robert, there won't be any place in this world for you to hide."

She didn't respond, just continued into the room, closing the door behind her. Her lack of response bothered Luis. He shook his head as he truly wondered now just how calculating Maria could be and just how far she would go.

Maria was always looking for the next move on the chessboard. That was one of the things that had attracted him to her. She kept him guessing about what would happen next and the humdrum in his marriage at the time made that very appealing. He had been really proud of her when she graduated with honors. He knew he had contributed to her academic success. Currently, she held a position as lead account executive managing the Latino division at the Lee Cohn Wolf marketing firm, and her future looked promising.

Maria was also very driven and could do anything once her mind was set. She took matters into her own hands. That drive, coupled with her funny, witty and very sexy air, had intoxicated him. She really knew how to satisfy him in the bedroom, too.

It was different from Diane. Maria had a sensual, sultry, somber sex appeal that got Luis' passion flowing. But with Diane, it was more than that. She had been his soul mate and when they divorced, his whole world spun off kilter. He missed his children and the connection he shared with the love of his life. He had told Diane that Maria would never be Mrs. Rodriquez but what he didn't tell her was why. Maria had her purpose but she wasn't his future. The truth of the matter was he could never marry Maria, for he was still very much in love with Diane.

Today had confirmed it. Damn, Diane had looked good and she had worn her hair the way he liked it – free and wind-blown. He leaned back on the chair and closed his eyes. He wanted to keep that memory of her for as long as possible.

7 CHAPTER SEVEN

Luis J waited until the last possible minute to come home Sunday night. It was about eleven-thirty when Carlos dropped him off and, thankfully, everyone was asleep. As he showered and dressed for bed, he reflected on the weekend and how much he had enjoyed the time he had spent with Carlos and his father. Unfortunately, he and Carlos hadn't been able to kick it together as much as they wanted to during the weekends because of school, Carlos' job, ball, and of course, their mother. But this weekend, they shot hoops, danced salsa at the club and just had a really good time. They talked a lot about their father, Dany, Carmine, and just girls in general.

The only topic they didn't dwell on was his issues at home. Luis J was surprised when he learned that his mother had not been forthcoming with them about their father's departure from their lives. In fact, Luis J was relieved to know that his father's door was open, anytime, and as long as his mother didn't find out, he planned to take advantage of the offer. It would give him another outlet from the house and David. And, his father had put David in his place. That was good ammunition for him to have the next time David came at him.

The time away had actually made returning home tolerable. He no longer felt like a rat backed into a corner. He could think clearer now that new options had presented themselves. Papi had his back.

He had called and sent text messages to Dany several times during the weekend, even within the last hour, but she never responded. He didn't sweat it too much because he knew he would see her at school.

Stepping out of the shower, he dried his feet enough not to make a trail from the bathroom to his room. He was hoping the wetness would give his body some comfort in that hot room. He had slept on Carlos' couch all weekend, feet hanging off the end, but he didn't care because the room had felt like it was three times the size of his.

'What I wouldn't give for Carlos to rent a two bedroom that we could share. Hell, I would sleep on the floor to get out of here. Anything would be better than this.' Those were his last thoughts as he drifted off to sleep.

As soon as Luis J entered his homeroom, the teacher raised his head from the scores long enough to tell him to go to the principal's office. Luis J inquired several times as to why, but the teacher was clearly annoyed with this interruption so his questions fell on deaf ears. As he headed for the door, he could hear people snickering. He turned to glare in the direction only to see Goober, one of his teammates, whispering to some girl. Convinced it had nothing to do with him, he continued on his way.

He had made it a practice to avoid doing things that resulted in meetings involving the administration. And, he had been quite successful at it since eighth grade. He couldn't imagine what this was in reference to unless…'No! No! No! Not Dany's black eye,' he thought. 'Tell me this isn't happening.'

He entered the office and stopped at the secretary's desk to check in. The administrator never looked up from his desk or the volume of paperwork lying on it when he asked for his name.

"Luis Rodriquez, Jr."

Still without looking up, the administrator pointed to a chair in the corner. Luis J sat down and waited. After about fifteen minutes and well into first period, the principal's door opened and Dany and Ms. Webber emerged. Dany's face was still bruised and she had been crying. Luis J stood up and moved toward her, but Ms. Webber stepped in front of her blocking his attempt.

"Dany?" he said softly, moving sideways to catch her eye and hoping his voice would give her some comfort. He wanted to hold her, let her know how much he missed her, but her mother's response cut through the air and pressed him against the wall like David had the other morning.

"Don't say a word to her," Ms. Webber said, as she grabbed Dany by the arm and led her out of the office.

Luis J's eyes followed them. He saw Dany look back just before the door closed behind her. She was mouthing something but the tight hinges cut off the words from her lips the same way Ms. Webber had done to his.

He knew this wasn't going to be a comfortable meeting with the principal. And next he would have to face Coach. "Luis Rodriquez Jr., you may come in," the principal stated, firmly.

Luis J turned around to find Principal Moore standing in the doorway of his office. He grabbed his things, walked into the office, closed the door behind him and took a seat, saying, "Mr. Moore, what is going on here?"

"Luis, you saw Danielle and Ms. Webber leaving my office. They were in to see me about a very serious matter they brought to my attention. It is my understanding that you have been dating Danielle Webber. Is that true?" His tone was aligned with the authority he held and respect he demanded from his students.

"Yes, we're dating."

"Is it also true you were at her home when her mother was not there last week Wednesday?"

"What?"

"I am sure you understood the question," he said, pronouncing each word very succinctly. All the students noticed he never used contractions and sometimes would make fun of him. They said it reminded them of Data from the Star Trek TV series.

"Yes. I was there."

"Luis Jr., Ms. Webber told me you and Danielle got into a fight and you beat her up, pretty badly I might add."

"That's a lie, Sir."

"Really? They showed the school nurse and me the bruises on her arms and the welt on her face. This is totally unacceptable behavior for the students of this school. I will not tolerate it," Mr. Moore stated.

He had been the school's principal for the last ten years and was very proud of his record thus far. He held very high standards for his students, faculty and administration, and no one was going to tarnish that, especially given that he was one year away from retirement.

"Wait a minute, Mr. Moore. I didn't hit Dany. I've never touched her. We've been dating for almost two years and I've never laid a hand on her."

"Danielle stood right there, young man, and told me you beat her because she would not have sex with you; that you felt like you had waited long enough. She also claims you ultimately raped her."

Luis J sat back in the chair and thought to himself, 'What the f-, this is some shit!' But he remained calm and said, "Mr. Moore, I swear to you, I did not hit her, let alone rape her. Ms. Webber called my parents the morning following my visit. Did she mention that? She also spoke to me that day. She never mentioned anything about rape because I didn't rape Dany. We did have sex, but it was consensual. I swear!"

"Maybe you did, maybe you did not, but I have to take this allegation seriously just the same. I know, for the most part, that you are a good student; I have your records right here. However, I have to follow the protocol. I have to suspend you from school for a period of two weeks and you are off the basketball team this year."

All composure left his body then and Luis J jumped out of the chair. "You have got to be kidding me! I didn't beat her – her mother did when she found out we had slept together; but it wasn't rape. You can ask Dany's sister, Stephanie. She saw me leave that morning and Dany was fine. Her mother is just trying to punish me. Besides, like I said, she never mentioned that Dany was beaten or raped to my parents when she discussed everything else with them that morning. She's just a vindictive liar."

"Luis Jr., sit down." Raising his eyebrows, but not the level of his voice, he pointed to the seat.

Luis J remained standing, towering over the already short Mr. Moore.

Principal Moore pointed to the seat again, with the frown becoming even more pronounced. Luis J returned to his seat and Mr. Moore continued, "I find it hard to believe Ms. Webber would fabricate that kind of story, but it does not matter. This school cannot condone your behavior."

And he flipped him off with his hand. "So get your things and go home. We will be contacting your parents regarding the next steps."

Luis J was only partially listening to him by now. He couldn't believe Dany would lie like that. He had to talk to her. But first he responded, "What behavior? Are you kidding? You have judged me based on what an angry, bitter woman said without even hearing my side of the story or conducting any research. What kind of mother is she that she would force her daughter to lie on me? Dany's afraid of her mother, that's what's going on here.

"Dany called me at home last Thursday evening. My sister answered the phone and everyone heard her say, 'Hi Dany,' before I picked up. She called to tell me that we had to break up because she was afraid of her mother. Would someone who was raped call the rapist to talk? No,

I can't accept this. I'm not going down like this. She's messing with my life and my basketball future. No way."

"Luis Jr., I am listening to these additional points and I am sympathetic to your situation. But even if I do believe you, I must follow the procedure set by the superintendent's office, especially if I am to help you at all. In the meantime, I need you to do as I ask. May I also suggest you not try to contact Danielle? Her mother alluded to criminal charges. You need to accept that this whole situation is very serious." Principal Moore did want to help this young man but he had to consider the ramifications to the school and his career.

"Criminal charges? That woman is something else, Mr. Moore. She's up to something and I don't know what, but I'm the target. As much as I hate to say this, my parents need to know this as soon as possible."

"Yes, I agree."

"May I talk to Coach?"

"Not now. I want you off the school premises in order to stay on par with the process. Besides, he is already aware of the situation and he is the one who said you would not be allowed to continue playing this year."

"Coach said that? He didn't even ask to talk to me?" Luis J was now even more disappointed.

"Luis Jr., understand that he cannot. He, none of us, can appear to side with you. The coach was shocked and actually said that he did not believe it. He said he had seen you and Danielle together and assumed that you were sexually active with her. As men, we know these things. Anyway, he said that you were one of his stars, but you must see this from our side. It is very hard to believe a parent would lie about a thing as serious as this. As you have said, 'What kind of mother would do that?' But Danielle supported everything her mother said and that is where our challenge lies.

"Danielle has been an excellent student and has never had any behavior issues and neither have you, which makes this very complicated – it's your word against hers and her mother's. So, for now, you must go. There is a security guard waiting outside to escort you off the grounds. Do not make this any more difficult for yourself. We will be contacting your parents later this afternoon, as I have already said."

Then Mr. Moore stood up from his desk and said, "Luis Jr., for God's sake, I hope that you get this cleared up and can resume your education."

Luis J thought to himself, 'You damn straight about that.' When he got outside, he looked at his watch. It was about nine. His mother was at work and so was Carlos. He didn't know his father's schedule but he thought he would at least try him at home. He answered on the third ring.

"Papi, it's me, Luis J."

"Mijo, why are you calling me when you should be in school? What's going on?"

"It's a long story. Can I meet you somewhere?"

"Where are you now?"

"Outside the school. I just got suspended," Luis J said, thoroughly disgusted.

After a pause, Luis said, "Listen, I was just on my way to the Brooklyn College campus off Flatbush Avenue. I have a ten o'clock class. After that, I'll meet you for lunch, at noon. Can you get to the Bread Co., on Flatbush near Avenue H?"

"I'll find it. Thanks." His mind was racing. In a few short minutes, the comfort he gained from the weekend was completely destroyed. He knew Dany's mother had a temper, but he had no idea she was this vindictive and a vicious liar. Now he understood where Steph learned her ways. Luis J wondered when Dany would stand up to her mother.

She had to now, so he could prove his innocence.

During the train ride to the campus, he replayed the conversation with Mr. Moore in his head over and over again with the same outcome; he was suspended for two weeks.

Luis J was sitting in the restaurant having a Pepsi when his father walked in. Luis removed his chocolate cashmere overcoat and sat down. He looked at his son, observing his face and body language, to grasp what had happened to get him suspended. He didn't see any cuts or bruises so he ruled out fighting. "Luis J, tell me what's happened?"

Luis J recounted the entire discussion with the principal and told him exactly what had really happened. They were interrupted by the waitress coming to take their orders, and they ordered quickly so they could continue the conversation.

"This is ridiculous. Are you sure it was consensual, that you didn't get carried away with the moment? I can remember being seventeen you know."

"Papi, you have to believe me. Besides, that was not our first time; we've been hooking up since August."

"Have you talked to her?"

"Not since last Thursday when she called to apologize about lying about her black eye and to break up with me because she doesn't want another beating from her mother. Papi, who does that? I mean beat their own child like that? And force them to lie. She knows it can destroy my future."

"Obviously a troubled woman. Don't have any more contact with Dany or her mother. Let me think for a minute. Have you called your mother yet?"

"No, are you kidding? She's going to kill me."

"Let me call a friend of mine. He's an attorney and I think we may need one. I can't leave campus right now, I have another class this afternoon, but when I finish, I'll take you home and together we'll talk to your mother. We both know she's going to be furious."

Luis J didn't respond. His father was totally underestimating her reaction. Luis began rubbing his temple trying to outline the immediate next steps. "Eat your lunch and then come back to campus with me. You can do your homework in my office. You have your books, right?"

Luis J nodded and began eating. His father barely touched his food while he made a few phone calls. Luis J hadn't been to the campus since his father was tenured. As they passed by groups of students, a number of them acknowledged his father. It was clear Papi was popular and Luis J felt proud when he was introduced as his son. Papi's office had books everywhere. It almost looked like he was the student instead of the teacher. Several of them had sticky notes on the covers.

As he looked around the room, his eyes settled on pictures of them on his desk. There was a space between the last one and the lamp. Luis J wondered if it used to be one of his mother. And there was no image of Maria. Once his father gave him logistical information, he headed off to his class. Luis J thumbed through some of the books on his father's desk instead of his textbooks as his mind tried to absorb the events of the morning. Besides, he wasn't in the mood to do homework and he now had two weeks to work on his assignment. He was pretty sure that all he needed was a few minutes alone with Dany. He was sure he could get her to tell the truth and straighten this whole thing out.

When Luis returned to the office, he found his son asleep on the couch. His class had run over and then a few of the students had questions about the assignment, causing him to be about thirty minutes later than planned. He smiled at his son as he remembered being that age and how easy it was to grab a nap almost anywhere. He also smiled because he had seen his son three times in the last four days and it was like drinking from a cup of love. He only wished the circumstances for this visit were different, but even with things being what they were, he was happy to be there for his son.

He nudged Luis J and said, "I want to call your mother and let her know I'm coming over. Get ready." Luis watched his son sit up and rub his eyes like he did when he was a little boy.

"Are you sure that's a good idea?" he finally managed to say.

"Yes. I don't want to just show up unannounced." He had had enough wrath from Diane due to those surprise visits to last him a lifetime. Waiting for Luis J to get ready, he used the phone in his office. On the third ring, someone answered.

"Chell? It's…is your mother there?"

"Yes." After a pause, she asked, "Who's this?"

The hesitation in her response made him wonder if she recognized his voice, so he said, "Your father."

"Papi? Really? Hi, how are you?" Chell inquired, beaming from ear to ear. She hadn't talked to her father in years, but she still recognized his voice and the way he called her name.

"I couldn't tell if you knew it was me. I'm fine, sweetheart. How are you? What's going on with you?" But before she could respond, Luis could hear the irritation in Diane's voice in the background and knew their conversation would be over long before it had a chance to start.

"Give me the phone," Diane demanded.

"Mami, he was calling to speak to you...so what are you mad about? Papi, I have to go now. Bye," Chell managed to say before Diane snatched the phone from her hand.

"Luis, what the hell are you doing calling here?"

"Diane, I didn't mean any harm. It's Luis J."

"What about him?"

"He's here with me, in my office."

"What? Why? What's happened? Let me speak to him."

"He's fine, but there was some trouble at school. He's been on campus with me all afternoon. I didn't want you to worry. I'm going to bring him home and we can sit down and talk."

"What's this about, Luis? Chell told me the school had called but didn't leave a message with her. So why wasn't he at school and why didn't he go to practice? And why didn't he call me?"

"All good questions. We're on our way over there and he'll explain everything to you. We'll be there within the hour if the traffic isn't too bad. Don't worry."

"You know I'm worried. What mother wouldn't be? This better not be one of your ploys. I'll see you both when you get here."

On the way, Luis took this opportunity to continue getting to know his son. They both felt a little uncomfortable with the situation because they hadn't talked one on one with each other in several years. There was so much Luis had missed in his son's life that he wasn't sure where to begin and Luis J wasn't sure what to share with his father. So they both just kept the conversation to what was going on with him today.

They talked about Dany, her mother and, of course, the common question: had they been careful? This question frustrated Luis J because all the previous times he had been careful, and this one time that he wasn't was the one under a microscope.

Luis J's cellphone rang and his father noticed the change in his body language. Luis J didn't talk much; he mostly listened. When the call ended, he said it was his basketball coach.

Luis J had been anxious to talk to Coach about cutting him from the team, but Coach was not willing or able to discuss it over the phone. Luis J was frustrated because of the coach's position. Coach's only comment was, "You know the rules, zero tolerance. What example would I set not cutting you and you're the team captain? But Luis J, I believe in you. Get this mess cleared up and then we can revisit my decision." After the call, Papi and Luis J rode the rest of the way in silence.

Chapter Eight

Diane stood in the kitchen still holding on to the phone. She wondered what Luis was up to now. She barely heard her daughter's chatter about being happy to talk to her father and how he sounded happy to hear her voice and questioning why she was tripping about his phone call. 'God you would think I was the worst mother in the world to let these children tell the story,' Diane thought.

"How about you let the food stop your mouth? I need you to finish up because you and Robert are going to Mrs. Davis' house," she told Chell.

"Mami, why? Isn't Papi coming over? I want to see him. Besides, her daughter Mimi gets on my nerves."

Diane had already given Chell instructions, so she ignored her questions and proceeded to call Sarah Davis. When they first moved into the building, Diane found out that Sarah was a stay-at-home mom and operated a daycare out of her apartment. So when Diane was running late from work and the boys were busy with after-school activities, Sarah would watch Chell. This was a huge relief for Diane to know that Sarah would always be home and could watch out for her daughter and sometimes even for her sons.

Once tonight's arrangements were finalized, Diane motioned for David to join her in the bedroom, where she brought him up to speed regarding her conversation with Luis.

"That's all he said?"

"Yes."

"So why are you sending the kids to Sarah's?"

"I don't want them here when he arrives. Did you see how excited Chell was? I won't allow it."

"Diane, Luis is her father. It's not like she never knew him. Of course she would be excited to talk to him…and even more to see him."

"No. You're her father. You've been there for her, for all of us. Not him."

"Because you wouldn't allow him to."

"David, we've talked about this a hundred times already. You should know by now how I feel about Luis' involvement in their lives. I can't believe you're saying this to me today. Oh, forget it," she said, walking out of their bedroom.

Chell was standing in the hallway with Robert. They were ready to go and Diane motioned for her to get moving. As they walked to the door, she reminded Chell to finish her homework and told both of them to be on their best behavior.

Once they were on their way, she started straightening up the kitchen. She had to stay busy to keep her mind from imagining the worst and to keep her anxiety from building any higher. Her hair was still down and she ignored the urge to pull it back. At least not yet.

David and Diane were now sitting on the couch, but they weren't engaging with each other. He hadn't said a word to her since she left him in the bedroom and if he wasn't going to support her she didn't want to hear anything from him anyway.

When the door opened, Diane leaped from her seat and examined her son from head to toe as he entered the room. She was looking to see if there were any physical injuries on him. Luis was standing behind him. Diane motioned for him to come in and close the door.

She watched him look around the room and knew he was examining her home the way she had done his, but he was also looking for his other children. She smiled to herself as she had denied him of that special treat.

David finally broke the silence, "Luis."

"David, Diane. How are you?" Luis responded, shifting from one leg to the other.

"Fine, considering. Now, what is this all about?" Diane asked, her eyes focused on her son, who was motionless.

"May we sit down, Diane, before he begins?"

She directed her eyes back to Luis and said, "Where are my manners? Thank you for bringing him home. David and I can handle it from here."

"Diane, wait until you hear what he has to say. He's going to need all of us to support him," Luis suggested.

"He doesn't need you," Diane shot back.

"Diane." David grabbed her arm and directed her to sit down. He then motioned for Luis to have a seat.

Luis J sat on the arm of the chair where his father was sitting to stay out of his mother's reach…until she turned her head to the side, which meant, "If you don't get your narrow behind off the arm of that chair I will smack you into next week." So he slid into the seat next to his father.

Luis glanced around the room again and this action was met with a declaration.

"They're not here," Diane exclaimed, thinking, 'I got you. As long as I am able, I will keep those two away from you forever.'

Luis exhaled. She had to know he was hoping to, even looking forward to, seeing his children, but she hated him so much that she had denied him of this one opportunity. 'How on earth was he ever going to work through this with her?' he wondered.

"Luis J, we're waiting. We don't have all night. What's going on?"

He began his story and several times Diane closed her eyes, fighting back tears. When he finished, she looked directly at her son and shouted, "How could you be so stupid?"

"Di."

"Don't 'Di' me! Just like you, these boys don't know how to keep their dick in their pants. First you, then Carlos, now this. Why are you all trying to make my life so difficult?"

"Diane, this isn't about me and you or Carlos. Luis J needs us to focus on him and this situation. We need to figure out what to do."

"Papi has already called a lawyer," Luis J offered, not knowing how this would be received by his mother, but hoping it would calm her down just a little.

"Actually, what I did was call Tony. You remember him Diane? We went to school together. Anyway, he's a criminal attorney. I just wanted to get some initial legal advice."

"David, what are we going to do? This could ruin his whole life," Diane asked, ignoring Luis' attempt to score brownie points with his son and get her to take a stroll down memory lane.

"First of all, Ms. Webber never said anything about Dany being beaten up by Luis J when she called that morning; clearly she was the one doing the hitting and lying. She did say, however, that she thought Danielle had been forced to have sex. What did the attorney say, Luis?" David asked.

"That's good information to have. My friend suggested we secure an attorney who specializes in date rape among teens. He recommends that none of us contact the Webbers; that may push her to seek legal action. Especially you, Luis J – don't call Danielle, don't go near her. Understand?" Luis said affirmatively. "And that's an order."

Diane was not pleased that Luis had just stepped into the role of father to Luis J, but she saw how their son responded to him. It was very different than if those words had been coming from David. This bothered her, but for now she only cared that Luis J did what was best. So if he listened to his father, good, she wasn't going to interfere with that.

They continued talking for about an hour and laid out exactly what the next steps would be and everyone's role. Diane hoped that Luis J was beginning to realize how serious this situation had become. Luis' phone rang and he excused himself as he answered it. From the silence in the room, everyone assumed it was Maria. While he talked, he watched Diane to see her reaction. He had only answered it because he assumed it was Tony, but as soon as he heard Maria's voice, he stepped away from them to have a little privacy. He kept the conversation brief and then returned to his seat.

"It must be time for you to go," she said, scrunching up her nose in disgust, with acid dripping in her tone. "Thank you for bringing Luis J. home. David and I can manage from here."

"Diane, I need to help Luis J with this. Don't shut me out."

Just then the door flew open and Robert came running in, in tears and calling out for his father. Diane watched Luis as he turned toward the voice to find his youngest son standing five feet away from him. Luis turned to offer Robert comfort, extending his arms only to watch him run into David's.

Diane reveled in this action and Luis' reaction as he lowered his arms and sat back down. The door barely closed when it was re-opened by Chell.

"Mami, I'm sorry. I told him you would come get us when it was time to come home, but he just ran out, crying."

Now, Diane was concerned. She knew Chell's reaction to seeing Luis would be completely different. 'Dammit, just once I wish that boy would listen to Chell,' Diane's thoughts screamed before she took the tie off her wrist and pulled her hair back into a ponytail.

As soon as Chell's eyes landed on her father, a smile as wide as Diane's frown broke out onto her face. "Papi!" she screamed, running into his arms before Diane could do or say anything.

The very idea that Luis J, Carlos and Robert looked so much like Luis was undeniable and made David sick that his wife had to look at her ex's face daily, just as he did. It was uncomfortable. Robert, who was tucked safely in David's arms, said, "Daddy, who's that man? He looks like Luis J."

"He's just a friend of the family," Diane answered, making sure David, nor anyone else had a chance to offer any explanations.

"Why did Chell call him Daddy? My friend Antonio calls his daddy Papi."

"Chell, take Robert to your room and close the door," Diane ordered.

"But, Mami…," Chell objected, still in her father's arms, tucked equally as safe as Robert.

"Now!" Diane shouted. She had to pull her child back to reality and get Robert out of the room before he started with the fifty questions.

"Fine." She sucked her teeth, pulled slowly away from her father's comfort and took Robert by the hand.

"See you later?" she tossed back toward her father, smiling.

Luis smiled affectionately back at his daughter. He wished he could say yes, but based on Diane's response, it wouldn't happen any time soon. Luis thought Chell was gorgeous. The pictures hadn't done her any justice. She lit up the room with her smile. He batted his eyes to fight back a tear. Chell glared at her mother and then stormed away.

"Diane…"

"Don't start with me, Luis. I thought you were leaving anyway. It's getting late and we need to put our children to bed."

"Look, I can be here tomorrow around four to review where we are. Is that a good time for everyone?"

"The time is good, but I don't think you need to actually come over. Why don't you just call?" David suggested, as he moved to open the door.

"Sure David, no problem. I'll call around four then," Luis replied, extremely disappointed by Diane's actions.

Diane was relieved Luis was accepting his place as she watched him put on his coat. And she also had some satisfaction in knowing that she still had the upper hand. As he walked to the door, she noticed that his shoulders weren't the same level they were when he had arrived. He was clearly in pain. As these thoughts and images settled with her, she wasn't sure how they made her feel but she just shrugged it away. She had given him a little taste of the recent pain she had suffered because of Maria.

David reiterated, "Yes, four is perfect. We'll look for your call. Thanks again Luis," David said, sincerely. He was thankful that Luis was leaving and this would allow Diane's pressure to be decompressed.

Chapter Nine

It had started raining and there was still traffic on the BQE expressway. It would probably take Luis an hour to drive home. He called Maria to tell her he was on his way. The conversation was brief. He had not mentioned where he had been or where he was coming from. He wasn't in the mood to go into it with her over the phone.

The timing of her call had been terrible and sent Diane into that protective, biting mood again. He inserted a seventies tape and settled back in the car seat. 'Things could really go bad for my son if we aren't able to get on top of these allegations,' he heard his mind say.

His mother used to tell him that he had to be careful of his actions because one bad one could impact his whole life and alter its entire course. Even with this warning from her, it still had happened to him, to Carlos, and now it was happening to Luis J.

Diane was right about his sons being like him. They were all highly sexed males, but it didn't mean that they weren't disciplined. Discipline had to be taught. Sometimes it took a woman to tame your urges. He had never cheated on Maria since they'd been together after his marriage dissolved. He didn't need to and it really wasn't who he was.

As the next song started, "Always Together" by the Dells, it brought up a memory he hadn't allowed himself to explore in quite some time. Tonight, he allowed these memories to take over and the present day was wiped away with every stroke of the wiper blade.

Luis was in graduate school at Georgia when he met Diane. It was an unusually cold winter day in Atlanta. There had been a light dusting of snow the night before so most of the classes had been cancelled; Atlanta wasn't used to that kind of weather.

Luis was tutoring a group of undergraduate students who were struggling with their Poli-Sci courses. This was one of his income streams and he was able to help most of the students turn their grades around. At least the ones who put in an effort. He was just leaving the lab when he saw her walking down the hall with a sheet of paper in her hands and his eyes fixated on her.

She was beautiful, with shoulder-length brown wavy hair that seemed to flow from her medium-brown coppertone complexion. She had a perfect figure. She was wearing a mini-skirt and working it without even trying to give him a full view of her long legs. They were sculptured and firm and carried her body effortlessly.

As she came closer, their eyes met and she smiled. 'What a mesmerizing face,' he had thought. 'You could get lost in those deep brown eyes.'

"May I help you find someone?" Luis asked, without taking his eyes off of her face.

"Yes, please, if you don't mind. I'm looking for Dr. Maxwell's office, the chair of the Business department." She had been looking for this office for twenty minutes and her feet were starting to hurt in her "cute" boots. Her aunt used to tell her all the time, "Honey, it hurts to be beautiful, but it's worth it." Today, she questioned that.

"Certainly. I am very well acquainted with who he is. It may be easier for me to escort you – that is, if you don't mind?" he smiled, giving her back the control.

"It's not necessary; you can just point me in the right direction. Hopefully, accurate directions with a short cut. I've been misdirected quite a bit this afternoon," Diane said earnestly.

"Really, it's no problem. I'm Luis Rodriquez," Luis said, as he extended his hand. "I'm a graduate student here. I've navigated this building for almost two years. Please, allow me."

"Okay, sure. It's nice to meet you. I'm Diane," she said, extending her hand.

"The pleasure is mine, Diane. Are you a student here?" he asked, shaking her hand. Her skin was as soft as he had imagined. It made him wonder what the rest of her body felt like. When she started pulling her hand away, he snapped back to reality, releasing it and pointing in the direction to start their journey. He didn't want her to think he was creepy or make her feel uneasy.

"No. I'm a senior at Emory but I'm applying to the graduate program here."

"I see. What are you studying?"

"Finance."

"Nice. Where else are you applying?"

She hesitated a moment before responding. She was starting to feel a little concerned. He seemed like a gentleman enough, but her mother had warned her about things not always appearing as they seemed.

"A few schools up north and Northwestern, in Evanston, Illinois."

"Well, I'm sure you have heard that we have the best MBA program here, but then, I'm just a little biased."

She smiled and when she did, her whole face lit up. But Luis noticed a hint of frailty or reserve. He wondered if something had happened in her life to make her seem so guarded. They continued down the hall sharing idle chitchat until they stopped in front of the chair's door.

"Here we are. If you don't mind my asking, would you care to join me for coffee after your appointment? I could share some insight about the school. Perhaps a perspective you haven't heard yet."

"That's very nice, but I wouldn't want to take any more of your time." Now she really wondered if he was up to something. Perhaps he had been following her when she was walking around before and knew she was lost. She started looking around to see if anyone else was in the hallway or within her shouting distance.

"I'm actually done with classes and tutoring today and I treat myself to one free afternoon a week. It just so happens to be today. You would make one very overworked graduate student very happy."

Unsure of what might happen with this stranger if she declined his request, Diane said, "I guess I can do that. I should be finished by four. Is there a campus coffee shop nearby?" She knew she had to pick somewhere public, just in case. She asked about a coffee shop because she had already passed it when she was walking around the building. So this was actually a test.

"Yes, in this building, actually on the street level floor. It's called Joe's," Luis responded. "Do you want me to meet you back here at Dr. Maxwell's office?"

She smiled and thought, 'Okay, he passed.' "No. Let's just meet at the coffee shop. I'm sure I can find it. Thanks for walking me to the chair's office."

There's that smile again. He matched it and said, "You're quite welcome."

From that moment, he knew there was something special about her and he was determined to get to know her. They met up as planned and he learned that she liked her coffee black with a little sugar. It wasn't long before they were talking as though they had been friends for years.

Diane was born and raised in D.C. She was the youngest of three girls and was very close to her sisters. She had selected Emory because she wanted to leave D.C., broaden her experiences and put some distance between her and her mom. Her mother had been a bit controlling and she felt she would be stifled if she went to a school in D.C.

She also liked the south. She had visited North Carolina every summer until she was sixteen, as her parents would send the three of them to their grandparents' farm to keep them off the streets and out of trouble. So she knew she could be comfortable in the south.

Luis noticed how she played with the ends of her hair when she got a little nervous, but it was appealing and sexy as hell to him. She told him that her college experience had been fun. She had a 3.75 GPA and was looking forward to graduation, but with mixed emotions. She had made some great friends in school and they were about to scatter around the country. Some were headed for law school, others med, and a few were getting their Mrs.

Luis laughed at that. He liked her sense of humor. Diane explained that one of her friends from Emory and now at Georgia knew she wanted to get an MBA and had suggested their program. So here she was.

Luis then shared some of his story with her. He was born and raised outside of San Juan, Puerto Rico in a town called Loiza. He was the oldest of five and as it turns out, the only one to get a graduate-level education. Luis had made his first visit to Atlanta his junior year.

He and some friends drove up from the University of Florida, Miami, for a concert at Georgia Tech during spring break. He liked the feel of the city and the accomplishments that were being made. He had researched the program and the curriculum in the history department, and he talked to the students to get a sense of the faculty. When all the questions were answered, he finalized his plans, applied, was accepted, and moved to Georgia. He was on time to graduate in May and planned to look for a teaching position in the area.

Luis told her how much he had enjoyed meeting her and how he would like to see her again. Once again, the frailty appeared in Diane. He couldn't put his finger on it, but something was there. "Coffee again, this shop in a week?" He wanted to spend his next free afternoon with her.

She smiled and then actually laughed out loud before she said, "Sure."

He didn't think what he had said was that funny, but he laughed along with her. He watched from Joe's window as she walked to the bus stop. "Always Together" was playing on the radio and he knew then that they would be. Six months later, very much in love, they were married.

Luis couldn't find a teaching position in the area as planned, however. He was late starting the interview process because of the wedding plans, so by the time he submitted his applications, all of the entry-level positions had been filled. They both knew he had to work since Diane would be in school, so Luis started contacting people in his network.

His personality and people skills enabled him to make friends very easily and he had the support of a number of faculty members. Two months after Diane started classes, Luis was offered a position at Baruck College in New York City. One of his frat brothers knew the Dean and had put in a good word for him. Everything else he had found was only part-time, so after talking it over, they packed up and headed to New York.

Relocating interrupted her graduate school plans, but she figured she would just apply at a school in New York. Once they were settled, she took a job in operations at a bank, while she contemplated to which graduate school she should transfer.

However, at the beginning of every semester, there always seemed to be a reason why she couldn't start. Spring semester, her father took ill and she needed to help her mom care for him. The following fall, with the move and the price of living in New York, they were low on funds and the grant she had applied for had been awarded to someone else because of her delayed start. And the final reason, she became pregnant with Carlos. They were very excited about this addition to their family and agreed that she would stay at home with him until he was school age.

Carlos, named after Luis' father, was such a calm baby. It had been a family tradition on his mother Alexa's side to name the first-born son after the paternal grandfather. Luis was glad that Diane supported this request. So was his mother when she met her first grandson.

Carlos rarely cried and was very inquisitive about his world from the moment he was born. When he began walking at ten months, Luis' mother warned them it was because he was making room for the next child. It was an old wives' tale that when babies walked early, it was because they had to get out of the mother's lap to accommodate the one on the way. Luis and Diane weren't planning to have another baby anytime soon so they just chuckled when she told them the story.

They were so very happy. Luis had two solid years under his belt so he started looking for a tenured track position. He found one at LIU and they knew he was on his way. Diane was very proud of her husband and made herself content raising their son. He was the second love of her life.

Shortly after Carlos celebrated his first birthday, they found out Diane was pregnant again. She had been having trouble taking the pill after Carlos was born so the doctor changed her birth control method to the diaphragm. Luis had a hard time getting used to it and often asked her to just leave it out. When she was ovulating, he would just make sure he pulled out. Obviously, she had miscalculated or he had misfired.

Either way, she was about to have her second child. Luis was excited and couldn't wait to share the news with the family and to tell his mother she was right.

Diane was feeling a little overwhelmed, though. She wasn't feeling very attractive as she hadn't lost all of the weight from the first pregnancy. She also was nauseous every morning, much longer than she had been with Carlos. The doctor gave her some tips for minimizing it but it continued throughout the whole pregnancy. This made it difficult to rest and she became very irritable and uncomfortable.

She was so ready to give birth when the time finally came. But even this experience was different. She had a lot of back pain leading up to the eighth month and she didn't know why. When she had her next ultrasound, they found that he had done a late turn and was now breech.

Diane was horrified. She wondered if it had to do with her thoughts during pregnancy of just wanting it to be over. But Luis comforted her and reassured her that he would be there every step of the way and their son would be fine. Diane was in labor for twenty hours. The doctor wanted to see if he could turn him and avoid surgery. She felt that this was better, too, unless her son's life was at risk.

She was hooked up to every machine they had in the hospital and was in isolation because they didn't want to expose her to any germs. Luis felt helpless but stood by her side throughout. He helped her focus and breathe and finally their son was laid in her arms.

Diane's mother often told her that every child was different and that was certainly the case with Luis J. He was colicky, which they found was aggravated by certain formulas. He did not sleep more than two hours at a time and was six months old before he slept through the night.

This took its toll on Diane, as Carlos was clearly in the terrible twos stage and getting into everything. Carlos adored his younger brother, though. He was often eager to sit next to Diane when she fed Luis J and loved it when she read aloud to them. Once Luis J started to walk, the two of them were inseparable.

When Luis J turned three, Diane began to take some night classes in an effort to prepare to reenter the workforce. She began to look forward to working again and finally finishing her degree. But with the confirmation of her third pregnancy, she realized, yet again, that her dreams were to be put on hold.

Luis hadn't realized the effect this was having on Diane. He didn't notice it was taking away the essence of who she was, outside of wife and mother. Her life had turned into reading baby books, watching *Sesame Street* and changing diapers. Even her conversations with her husband were about the kids. She missed talking to adults. She missed the intellectual interaction and stimulus from being around adults and being in school.

And then there was her mother, Margaret. She was frequently asking Diane about going back to school, telling her about her sisters' accomplishments, and reminding her that there were other legal methods of birth control available to her.

In Diane's mind, she was basically telling her that she was a failure and lacked focus and ambition. It was this constant desire to please her mother that caused a lot of inner turmoil for Diane. Luis suspected this pressure was the cause of some of Diane's frailty, and ultimately some of the challenges they had experienced as a couple. Now he understood, but it was obviously way too late.

Luis pulled into the yard and could see the light on in the bedroom. He entered the house, dropped the keys on the table and poured a cognac. Eventually, he was greeted by Maria in the living room, dressed in one of her "secrets." Sheer as it was, he could see all of her as she came over to him and pressed her lips and body into his. He could feel his body responding hungrily but his mind wasn't there. He eased away from her and sat on the couch.

"Poppie, what's wrong, not your color?" Maria asked, turning around to give him a full view.

"No, honey, you look great, as always," he responded, even though he was no longer even looking at her. Maria had a beautiful body and knew how to use it. She worked out and ate well and looked as good today as she did when he first met her. But that wasn't what he thought he wanted right now.

"If it isn't the color, then it must be the style. Maybe nothing would be more to your liking?" She began removing her strap in a slow seductive strip tease. Turning his attention away from her, Luis blurted out, "Luis J was suspended from school today and banned from playing basketball this season. That's bad because this is the year that scouts make their preliminary searches. And, criminal charges may be filed against him for assault and battery, and rape. That's how my day began before nine this morning."

Maria put the striptease on pause to listen to him. They sat on the couch next to each other. He explained to her how this happened and how he had met with Diane and David to figure out what to do.

"Luis, Dios mío. I'm so sorry. How's he taking it?" she asked, as she reached for his hand to comfort him. He didn't really know his son's personality or how he handled difficult situations, so he really didn't know how Luis J was taking it. He was going on gut instinct and hoped he was right.

"I'm not really sure. He's trying to be strong for Diane, but I think he's really scared. He's a good kid and doesn't deserve this. This is a perfect example of why I should have been allowed to be a part of his life. I needed to talk to my boys about being men, the responsibilities that come with manhood."

They sat quietly for a while, Luis drinking his cognac and Maria rubbing his leg. Next, he told her about his experience seeing Chell and Robert. As he relived it, he began staring off and not really listening to Maria's comments. It had really bothered him that Robert called David, "Daddy". He knew he hadn't been in his son's life, but he never imagined Diane wouldn't tell him the truth of his lineage, never show him a picture of his father.

"What?" he finally asked, aware that Maria was saying something.

"I said, what did you talk about with Chell and Robert? I'm sure they were happy to see you."

"Chell was. She hugged me. Maria, you should see how much she's grown. She's turning into a beautiful young lady. She looks just like Diane." He paused to recall the feeling he had when he hugged her. "Unfortunately, we didn't have a chance to really talk, it was time for bed."

"What about Robert?" Maria asked, ignoring the comment about Chell being beautiful just like Diane. She hoped, for Chell's sake, she didn't look anything or act anything like Diane.

"Robert doesn't know who I am. That hurt the most. He came in and called out, 'Daddy.' I thought by some miracle he recognized me, but he was talking to David. He thinks David is his father just like Diane wants him to, really to punish me for you."

"Oh Poppie, I don't know what to say."

"They looked so close. He asked David who I was. I promised Diane I would stay away, not interfere, but I didn't think that she wouldn't tell Robert that I was his father. You should have seen him. He's small, but he has long legs. He's going to be built just like my father eventually, tall and lean. He heard Chell call me Papi and asked why she was calling me Daddy…he connected the dots, Maria. He's smart, too."

"Who does she think she is? She has no right to betray you this way. I know you told me to stay out of it, but I just hate how she's using your children to hurt you, Poppie. One day this is all going to blow up in Diane's face."

Maria thought to herself that someone needed to stop Diane from doing that, to give her a taste of her own vindictiveness, and Maria knew just how. She took a deep breath, thrusting her heavy, heaving breasts forward into Luis and said, "How can I help?"

"I honestly don't know. Can you take my mind off of all that has happened today? Know of any good movies on tonight that I can just get lost in?"

"I have something even better. Let's make our own movie." She extended her hand and said in her sexy kitten voice, "Come to bed with me, Poppie."

And he was done. He followed her into the bedroom. Maria had a way of taking him into fantasyland and tonight that was what he needed, to forget all about his worries and disappointments. She lit candles, refilled his drink and turned on music.

She knew how much he enjoyed jazz, so she played "Flamenco Sketches" by Miles Davis to set the mood. She also had a bottle of champagne chilling. He sat on the edge of the bed and she kneeled in front of him. They began kissing, gently at first and then with more passion. He slid her straps down from her shoulders and began rubbing her breasts, feeling her nipples under his thumb respond to his caresses. She unbuttoned his shirt and removed it. As he lay back on the bed, she climbed on top of him, letting her legs straddle his torso. He could feel his body responding to her touch, anticipating the pleasure that was ahead.

Maria loosened his belt buckle and unzipped his pants. She leaned forward to kiss Luis as he slid off his pants and undergarments.

When she began massaging his manhood, he flipped her over and began kissing her, his tongue parting her lips. He used his fingers to feel her wetness and readiness to accept him. He slid inside and with each movement he became harder. The passion inside of her drew him deeper and deeper.

"Ohhh, Poppie!"

He stretched out her arms and closed his fingers around hers. As he felt the release about to happen, she slowed her rhythm and shifted. Miles' "Someday My Prince Will Come Along" was playing softly in the background. He went with the flow, following her lead. She pushed against him and he rolled onto his back. She climbed on top and reinserted him. Once he was snuggly inside, she started moving to the rhythm that Miles was laying down. He held her around the waist and with each movement, he felt a tingling sensation all over his body. From her moans, he could tell they were both close.

"Come with me, Poppie. Come with me."

Her words kicked him over the edge and he felt everything rush from his body. The more she contracted, the more he exploded. When she stopped contracting and moaning, she leaned forward to lay on his chest. He could feel her heart beat slowing and he tried to slow his breathing to match hers. He was dozing off when he heard her whisper, "I love you, Luis."

He pulled her to his side, put his arms around her and whispered, "I know you do." That was all he remembered until morning.

Chapter Ten

When the alarm rang at 5:00 a.m. as it did every day, Luis J's first reaction was to leap out of bed to get ready for school. But today he just rolled over undisturbed and turned off the alarm. Why had he even set it in the first place? Robert was fast asleep; he didn't need to get up for another hour and Mami always helped him. Luis J could hear voices in the kitchen and smelled the hypnotic aroma of coffee. At the table, David and his mother were drinking out of their "his and her" mugs, all loved up with that morning after look on their faces. It almost made Luis J's stomach turn thinking about his mother being intimate. But he did wonder. His mother was fine, a very pretty woman. But you just couldn't see it half the time because she was so busy being stern. Whereas Maria was all right, nice body, attractive and she knew how to play with her sexiness.

"Good morning," he greeted them both and asked his mother for a cup of coffee. She didn't usually encourage it, but this morning she handed him one. He didn't know why she made a big deal about it. He drank a cup almost every day on his way to school anyway. But it was yet another thing she wanted to control. As he waited for it to cool, he looked at his mother and wondered what she was feeling about the suspension.

Luis J turned to face them both and said, “David, Mami, thank you for supporting me in all of this and thank you for allowing Papi to be here with me.”

“You’re welcome, Luis J. You know your mother and I only want to do what’s best for you. You have your whole life ahead of you and something like this could really set you back. This is why we worry about you. You’re still young and naïve about life. You don’t really know about people. Everyone’s not nice.

“Like Ms. Webber, we have to figure out her motivation. We don’t always have the right answers, but we’re doing our best. Most importantly though, no matter what our differences may be, know that we are here for you Luis J and we will get this mess resolved.”

“I know, and I haven’t said this recently, but I appreciate it. Ms. Webber is a piece of work. Dany says that she was never right after her husband left.” He shifted his gaze towards his mother as he realized she was in some ways acting like Dany’s mom. After a brief awkward silence, he asked, “Aren’t you guys going to work?”

“No, I’m going to the school to meet with Mr. Moore. David is going to get in contact with a lawyer.”

“Can I go see Principal Moore with you? I have to make him believe I’m innocent.” Luis J had a few more points to make and he also wanted to stop by and see Coach.

“I don’t think that would be a good idea. The school administration has made it clear that you are not to step a foot onto the campus. Besides, you may not have raped Dany, but you are far from innocent. You were at her house without adult permission or supervision when you should have been home. Not to mention that you had unprotected sex. No, you need to stay here and hit the books.”

Luis J just hung his head and stared into his coffee. Diane continued, “You don’t want to get too far behind. I’m going to get some information about the public school procedures and I plan to ask Mr. Moore for some guidance around the classwork you'll be missing."

As if oblivious, Luis J asked, "I think Carlos is off today. May I go over there?" He waited for both of them to go off on a tirade, but to his surprise his mother deferred to David.

David spoke sternly like Luis had the night before, wanting to illicit the same obedient response, "Only if you promise to stay at Carlos' apartment. Take your schoolbooks. It's probably better for you to not be alone; that just may keep you out of trouble. I don't want you guys running all over the city, though. Also, you need to be home before four. Your father will be calling then."

Based on Luis J's facial expression and Diane's abdicating to him, he started to feel like he had reclaimed control and that things were finally getting back to normal.

Now that was the David Luis J knew, so he nodded his head in agreement, finished drinking the rest of his coffee in silence and excused himself.

After ten o'clock, Luis J called Carlos. He hoped he would be awake by now and would allow him to come by. When Carlos heard the request from his younger brother, he welcomed him. He had to work the night shift, but having Luis J over for a while would be fun.

When Luis J arrived and settled in, he began his story. He ran down the whole deal to Carlos. He had told the story so many times, it felt like he was telling a story about someone else. Each person had a slightly different reaction.

"Let's go; her house, now," was Carlos' reaction. "I'm going to kick that woman's ass with terror. She's not going to ruin my brother's reputation or future."

"Hey, slow down, man. Don't think I haven't wanted to do that, but everyone, including Mami and Papi, says I can't go over there."

"But man, what's up with your girl? I thought she liked you. She did give it to you, didn't she? I mean you didn't take it, did you?"

"No, it was all consensual. But I can't even call Dany – no contact, no nothing man, so I can't even get an explanation. I just want to ask her what you asked me, 'WHY?' Anyway, Mami went to school today to meet with Principal Moore to get more information about this shit and of course to get my course work for the next two weeks. David is meeting with a lawyer this morning and we'll go from there."

"This is bullshit, man."

"You're telling me. But you know me; I'm Luis J, son of Luis, brother of Carlos. We're lovers, man. It's in our DNA. Women beg us. So it killed me at first to think that Dany had sided with her mother and basically conspired against me. But I get that she's stuck between a rock and a hard place. Where's she gonna go? Her mother is all she has. Not like us. We have each other and now I have Papi. Her mother has kicked her ass and threatened her and she has to stay there. She told me so herself. So it is what it is."

Luis J took a moment to push down the pain that was rising and continued, "The good news is Papi got to see Chell last night. They really seemed to connect. Of course, Robert had no idea who he was. You should've seen Papi; it killed him, man. Stabbed him right in the heart.

"See, Robert came in saying, 'Daddy, Daddy' and naturally Papi thought he had recognized him when he was really talking to David, and Robert ran into his arms past Papi. It was painful man, and I swear I could see a smile in Mami's eyes. But Papi was smooth man, real smooth. He wasn't going to let her or David see him sweat."

Carlos didn't respond, he just lit a cigarette. Luis J wanted one, but wasn't in the mood for a lecture. Instead he grabbed a stick of gum. He smiled because he had only started smoking because he thought it made Carlos look so cool.

"One thing though. During our discussion last night, Mami said something that confused me, regarding you."

"And what was that?" Carlos asked, inhaling deeply and blowing circles with the smoke as he exhaled, tilting his head back as if he was the least bit concerned.

"She alluded to some mistake involving you. What was she talking about?"

"She brought that up? What did she say?" Carlos was surprised. It must have meant that his mother was really upset. She had sworn him to secrecy despite the countless times he pleaded with her to let him tell Luis J.

"That was about it. She said you and Papi, and now me, were ruining her life because we couldn't keep our dicks in our pants. I now know what Papi's indiscretion is, I know mine, but what's yours?"

"She actually said that? She really said dick? I would have loved to have been there just to hear her say dicks." Then he laughed before asking, "Do you think she and David still do it?"

"Oh come on Carlos man, I'm not thinking about that," he said, chuckling to himself at how just that morning, he had thought about that very thing. Then he moved on and addressed Carlos' other question. "Yeah man, she said it and her tone was nothing nice."

"Oh man, I'm not talking about or thinking about her like that; I'm just saying Mami's fine. You ever look at her hips, butt, long legs, little waistline and firm breasts that still sit up – and that's after four babies. What was she like when Papi met her? I get why he fell in love is all I'm saying. I look for women built like Mami."

Luis J looked at his brother and refused to go off on a tangent, so he asked again, "But like I said, what was your mess up?"

This time, Carlos inhaled and stared off into space thinking about Luisa. She and Carlos had met in eighth grade when her parents moved to Brooklyn from Puerto Rico. She was taking a pre-psychology class and had to write a paper about young males who were the product of a divorced family. She asked Carlos if he would be "one of her subjects." He was actually very flattered that she had selected him. She was so pretty and he had admired her from afar for almost a year.

He didn't have the same confidence of Luis J in that way. His confidence came from his intellectual prowess even though he was a great athlete, as well. So he agreed to be one of Luisa's "subjects," and the rest is history.

The report required her to ask him questions about his parents, his siblings and most importantly, his feelings about his parents' divorce. Carlos found himself opening up to her more than he had with anyone about the resentment he felt toward his mother and how he actually blamed her for the distance between him and his father. It was the first time he had actually admitted it to himself.

Luisa found his willingness to open up to her attractive. She wanted to help him in some way. Carlos' passion and openness influenced her decision in their freshman year to become a child psychologist and help children of divorced parents. Interviewing her classmates and writing her paper ignited her passion for a career in psychology even more.

They didn't start dating until they were sixteen and sophomores. It wasn't long before they were completely inseparable.

After the research was completed and she received an A on her paper, Carlos told her that now she was indebted to him. He told her that she was required to go to the movies and eat ice cream with him every Friday for the next three weeks as payment. She laughed at how he thought he had to bribe her and accepted his invitation. It was not long before they became more than two friends going to the movies.

Eventually they would find time to be together every day after school and most weekends. Carlos was technically a virgin, he had not been sexually active yet; personal hand jobs didn't count. It was not because he hadn't had opportunities. In fact, he had always been hit on by older girls and some women, too, because he acted way more mature than his age and people often thought he was in his twenties.

But he had talked to older males and friends his age who had been active and felt that most of those girls had too much drama, before and definitely after. Girls just seem to want too much from a man, too much attention. He didn't have time for that nonsense. But Luisa was different; she was level-headed, smart, fun to be around, and not demanding or controlling. Yeah, she was special and he appreciated that.

Luisa's parents were not impressed or pleased with Carlos, nor did they like the amount of time the two were spending together. They felt that he would ultimately be trouble for their only child. One of the reasons they had left Puerto Rico was to get her away from the many distractions that existed there and to give her more opportunities in life. In Puerto Rico it was sometimes the norm for young people to grow up, marry, and start a family at a very early age. They had moved to the USA so that Luisa could take advantage of the educational opportunities and not be pressured to accept the old ways.

Six months into their sexual relationship, Luisa confirmed that she was pregnant.

"I can't have an abortion, Carlos. My beliefs will not allow that. I have to inform my parents and you'll have to tell yours."

As Carlos thought about Luisa, he could hear the melodic cadence of her Spanish as she told him tenderly yet adamantly that she would not have an abortion.

"Luisa, I'll abide by whatever you want to do." He assumed this meant they would have to marry because he was very familiar with her family's cultural background.

"You would agree to do that? What about school?"

"We'll figure it out. We're in this together Luisa, you didn't get pregnant by yourself. I know your parents will want me to marry you, so I will."

That had made Luisa smile. "Carlos that's why I love you; you're so sweet. It's really brave of you. And I'd like that, but you must marry me because you want to, not because my parents think it is right. My father will not be happy with me, either way."

Carlos hugged her and whispered gently upon her forehead, "I want to."

They agreed they would tell her parents first, so that Friday evening they waited at her home until her parents arrived from work and settled in before they started. They stood hand in hand as Luisa announced her pregnancy to her parents and waited. Mr. Morales leaped from his seat to attack Carlos, who was caught off guard. But Luisa had moved in front of Carlos, causing her father to push her down. Carlos turned away from her father and helped her back on her feet, asking, "Are you okay?" Satisfied that she was fine, he turned his attention back to Mr. Morales who had started yelling at Luisa.

"You ungrateful little whore. You have disgraced the family and for that you must leave this house."

"Mr. Morales, sir, I am prepared to marry Luisa. I want to – I want to do the right thing. And she's not a whore. You're wrong."

"Really, and what exactly do you have to offer her? Do you have a job? How about a high school diploma? You want to do the right thing? The right thing would have been to leave her a virgin! Now you have disgraced her. And just how do you propose to take care of her? You have no skills, no college degree. So where does that leave an unmarried woman with child? In my country, she is disgraced, as is our family."

"It's true I don't have a full time job yet, but I will ask for more hours from my after school job, sir, and I still plan to graduate from high school. I can actually finish a semester early, which will then allow me to work full time. But she's your daughter carrying your grandchild. And we are sorry that it's not what you planned for her, but we will do right by this."

"And what of Luisa's schooling? Will she be able to continue? No! She will have to take care of your sniveling, spoiled brat baby!"

Carlos could not believe his ears. The man was mean and unyielding; it reminded him very much of his own mother.

"Papi, I will only have one semester to finish once the baby is born and we will figure out a time for me to complete my studies. Right, Carlos?"

"And then what, you live in a low rent slum apartment for the rest of your life? Is this what we came to the United States for? You disgust me. I knew this boy would ruin you. I told your mother that this would happen. Well, you have your own family now, so you need to do right by her and take responsibility for your actions. I don't know why you think you are good enough for my Luisa."

He threw his hands up and walked out of the room, leaving them sitting there. Her mother did not say anything, as that was customary. She rose from the chair and followed her husband.

"Luisa?"

"No, it's okay. I expected that," she said, as she wiped away the tears. Carlos admired her resiliency and offered a hug of support.

It was six-thirty now and the next stop was his home. His mother and David would be there by now. When the young couple arrived, the two of them were there, comfortably seated, laughing and talking. Luis

J hadn't come home yet, Chell was in her room doing homework, and Robert was on the floor playing.

"Good evening, Carlos. Luisa, right? How are you?" David offered, looking away from his wife and towards them.

Carlos didn't bother to answer, but rather spoke directly to Diane. "Mami, we need to talk to you."

David instinctively knew something was up because that's how Carlos handled things of importance. He excluded him by directing his conversation to Diane. So he shifted his body forward and braced himself, taking Diane's hand.

"Is everything alright?" Diane asked. Then she looked at Carlos, deep into her son's eyes, and saw that the child was no longer there. Staring back at her was a man looking like Luis and it unnerved her. If she had been a weaker woman she would have come undone.

"Luisa is pregnant," Carlos quietly blurted out, wasting no time. The words hung in the air longer this time than they did at Mr. Morales'. Carlos waited for his mother's response. David was the first person to say anything. He looked at them, observing each to confirm the situation, then cleared his throat and asked, "Carlos, are you guys sure?"

"Yes, and we're going to get married. We just told her parents and now we are here to tell you."

"Married?" David chuckled, in that corporate sneer that put down the uneducated. "Are you kidding me? You guys are way too young to get married. Besides, you both are bright and are supposed to be headed to college, preparing for your future. I'm sure this isn't what your parents had in mind for you, Luisa. It certainly isn't what we have in mind for Carlos."

"But that doesn't matter now. I mean not right now. We will continue school. Luisa can continue school until she has the baby. Luisa is pregnant and I have to do the right thing. I want to."

It was Diane who spoke next. “Carlos, how long have you guys known about this? Have you thought it through? What will you do for money, for goodness sakes? Where will you live? This apartment is way too small for another person and a newborn. David and I are working hard to make ends meet. This was not part of the plan.”

“Don’t worry about that, Mami, I wasn’t planning on bringing her here. I will provide for Luisa and my child.”

“Carlos, we need to talk about other options,” Diane continued, pulling her hair back into a ponytail. Carlos watched as she did this. She was nervous and frail. She was shifting gears. She was going into “Cold Corporate” mode. CC, as he and Luis J referred to it. That’s when she shuts down all emotion, empathy or compassion. He wondered what exactly had happened to the warm, loving mother he had adored as a child. He knew they were in for a long conversation. He just hoped it wouldn’t be one-sided.

“Luisa said that she can’t consider any other options and I want to support her.”

“Can’t or won’t?” Diane asked in an insensitive, accusatory tone.

“Mrs. Anderson, I respect your position, please accept mine. I will not have an abortion. I believe this is a sign from God and I will not eliminate it like it is a mistake.”

‘Oh my God, what is up with these Puerto Ricans and this sign from God mess when it comes to babies? Must be the Catholic guilt they harbor,’ Diane thought. But choosing not to go there, instead she said, “I’m not saying that you should, but you could give the child up for adoption.”

“No. We’re going to get married and raise this child together,” Carlos interjected.

“Carlos, that requires consent from your parents and I don’t, I won’t, give it.”

"Mami, Luisa's parents will give theirs. You can't be serious."

"Really? Well, two wrongs don't make a right. There is no way, do you hear me? I will never give my consent."

Luisa began crying and Carlos became very angry. Then he looked at Diane and asked, "Would you have aborted or given Robert up for adoption just because the circumstances weren't perfect with you and Papi?"

"What did you just say to me? This is hardly the same. Your father and I were married," Diane shot back, now with venom in her voice.

Carlos knew he had touched a nerve and it was best to take Luisa home now. He was willing to take this to another level, but he didn't want to subject Luisa to his mother's sharp tongue or his retorts.

"Carlos, it seems you've been talking too much about my business, things that do not concern you or anyone else."

"Mami, you've got to be crazy if you think that the whole thing with you and Papi doesn't concern us, because it did. It still does. But you don't get it. I'm going to take Luisa home. She doesn't need any more stress this evening."

He looked at David, who actually agreed with Carlos but said nothing. He refused to look at his mother and thought, 'No wonder Papi left her; she's mean and cold.' Then he returned his attention to Luisa and in Spanish said, "Let's go."

The entire ride back to Luisa's home, she cried and he tried to comfort her, but to no avail. He promised her that this wasn't over and he would fight for her and their child. Reluctantly he had to drop her off at her parents, which made him feel worse, but where else could he have taken her? He could have gone to Papi's, but he didn't want to subject her to anything else. He kissed her lovingly before she closed the door.

When Carlos returned home, as expected, his mother was waiting for him and they continued their argument until he could no longer find the words to express himself. But he knew that no child of his was going to be put up for adoption. David intervened several times whenever Carlos' voice escalated to a point that he felt was disrespectful.

"Mami, I'm not a child anymore; I'm having one."

Diane had dug her heels in and refused to hear her son. She heard the words, but she didn't really hear him, so she responded, "Not if I have anything to say about it. This conversation is over."

Carlos was determined to get her to see his perspective. After all, it was her grandchild she was talking about as though it were a non-entity or annoyance in her life. The argument continued throughout the weekend and Carlos looked into other alternatives.

He wasn't getting any support from David, but that was no surprise. After all, David was not his father. He always leaned in favor of Diane's position because he felt he had to in order to keep the peace. He thought that maybe his father could convince his mother where he, thus far, had been unable to.

Diane didn't know that Carlos and her ex were in contact with one another. If she had known, they were both certain that she would not have approved or allowed it.

Carlos had gone to his father's campus one afternoon about four months earlier and waited outside his office until he returned. Carlos wasn't sure why he had reached out to his father that day. Maybe it was curiosity about his father's absence in his life, or maybe it was the need for a male presence in his life that David was never able to fill.

Luis was shocked but happy to see his first born. They went to the campus Choc' Full of Nuts coffee shop to talk. It was awkward at first, but after a while they found they were both able to fill a void that had been missing from their lives since Luis had been banned by Diane. So, Carlos was hoping his father could help him with this dilemma from a father's perspective.

Luis listened attentively until Carlos finished the story. He weighed the pros and cons as he thought about his words to follow. He wanted very much to be what his son needed him to be then, but it was a very delicate situation. So he began with a few questions.

"So you have settled on marriage? Are you sure this is best for both of you? You know it's not going to be easy, mijo. The real question is do you love each other?"

"Papi, I'm not sure. I care about her, a lot, but love, I'm not sure. I just know that I feel that this is the right thing to do."

"Well, I believe that love can heal a lot, but not everything. You must address this in your heart. I can't tell you what to do; that would make me like your mother. So what do you really want from me?"

"Your permission."

"Carlos, that's easy. I give you permission to be a man and choose. But I don't have legal guardianship of you. I really can't, legally, sign anything granting you permission."

"Could you talk to Mami? She's not listening or hearing me and I just don't want to fight with her anymore."

Luis understood where Carlos was coming from. He had been there. When Diane made up her mind, she shut out all other reason. "Son, I would like to, and yes I could, but honestly, I don't think it would help you. If anything, I think it would make things worse. She's still angry with me for ruining her perfect world and the life she thinks we were supposed to have together."

"But Papi, she has a new life. She's married to David. Why does she have to be so difficult? I hate her."

"No, don't you say that. I know she can be hard. But tough love can help mold a good person. It hasn't been easy for her. You don't really know what went on between your mother and me. It's very complicated. She's trying her best to do what she believes is best for you.

"I don't really believe that getting married is the best solution for you guys, but I respect your choice because I recognize you as a young man. Unfortunately, she still sees you as her boy, her baby and she can't let go. Worse, I haven't been involved in your life and I can't say if I were in your mother's shoes that I wouldn't feel the same way she does. Can you try to see it from her perspective?"

"No. Not now, not ever. And you do know. You told me the truth. You agree with Mami that we should not get married, but you're willing to let me make my own choices. That is the difference. She wants to control me. Thanks Papi, really, thanks."

Carlos left his father and stopped by Luisa's on his way home. Mr. Morales answered the door only to inform him that since he was not going to marry his daughter and restore her honor, they had sent her back to Puerto Rico to live with her abuela and have the child.

"Sir, what are you talking about? I never said I wasn't going to marry Luisa, just the opposite. It was just last Friday that we talked, today is Wednesday."

"Well I never had any intention of letting you marry my Luisa. Once we knew that she was pregnant, I bought her ticket back to Puerto Rico. It is best that you leave and forget about her and the baby. Do not try to contact her."

"I don't understand Mr. Morales, I offered to accept my responsibility for Luisa and our child and you disregard my actions and dismiss me. Why?"

"Your father is not a true Puerto Rican like we are. He's from there, but he's not one. You may not understand that, but he does, and because of that you will never be good enough for my daughter. Go home and never come here again."

Carlos stood on the porch in the rain, feeling helpless. Shut out and shut down. Not only the words, but the tone of distaste, arrogance and hatred spewed from Mr. Morales like acid, eating at his heart and burning a hole. For a second, Carlos wondered if he had been hit by a truck. The pain lingered and he wondered why this man despised him so. He had lost his girl and his child and there wasn't anything he could do about it.

He looked through the window and saw Luisa's mother crying in the chair. Carlos watched as her father looked down at his wife and then dismissed her from the room.

For weeks, Carlos tried calling her home hoping to reach her mother, who it seemed would be more amicable. He called Luisa's cell, but it was no longer active. He tried inquiring at school, anything he could think of to try and find her location, but nothing worked.

During this time, Carlos barely said two words to his mother; he blamed her for this circumstance. In fact, he found himself talking to his father more often and stopping by his home to share his feelings.

Finally, he asked his father what had continued to haunt him. "Papi, what did Mr. Morales mean when he said you are not really Puerto Rican?"

"He said that to you?" Luis' voice was calm, but controlled, for still waters run deep and Mr. Morales had struck a chord that did not bode well with him. That fool had messed with his son's head.

"Yes and he said that because of that I would never be good enough for Luisa."

"First of all, I am a real Puerto Rican. Puerto Rico is where I was born, as were both my parents and their parents. It is our nationality, not our race. Just like America is made up of many nationalities, races and ethnicities, so is Puerto Rico. That ignorant fool is prejudiced." Papi used this opportunity to impart some additional wise words, "Don't ever doubt your heritage or feel that you are lesser than anyone else on this planet. Afro Cuban, Afro Puerto Rican, Afro American etc, we all come from Africa, it's just different influences, different cultures and languages. You are to be proud of who you are, who your ancestors are, on both sides of your lineage. You must grow up to be the man that I expect you to be and that my father expected me to be. And now that you have a child on the way, you must instill this pride in him or her. Comprendes?"

"Si, Papi." After a brief moment, he continued, "Papi, there is so much I can learn from you. I have stayed with Mami because I didn't think or know I had an option. I really don't have a relationship with her or David right now. Would it be too much to ask if I can stay with you and Maria? I will pull my own weight. I already have a job and would be happy to contribute to the finances. I will be finishing school in a couple of months. Once I graduate, I'll get my own place."

"And what about college?"

"I'm not feeling that right now. I'm going to work for a while and try to find Luisa. I want to be there for my child. I don't ever want him or her to feel abandoned."

"You may stay here if your mother agrees, but you have to finish school and stay focused. Agreed?"

Carlos did not ask his mother, instead he told her he was moving in with his father. He explained that he thought it best as they had met an impasse in their communication and it could only get worse. David convinced her that it was probably best for everyone as the friction in the home was mounting and also starting to affect Luis J's behavior. Carlos moved out and ended up living with his father and Maria for a year. This allowed him to save money for a trip to Puerto Rico to see Luisa and to take a few classes at night.

After Carlos finished relating his tale, all Luis J could say was, "Damn man – all this and I had no clue. I just thought that you and David weren't getting along. I knew that Mami was upset all the time, but thought it was because of your relationship with David, when all the while it was Mami. I even remember David saying that he thought it was best for you to go. So maybe he does have balls man, he didn't side with Mami on that one."

"Naw, he didn't. There were times when David was cool. He just fell in love with Mami and honestly I believe he loves her more than she loves him. You don't ever want to be in a situation like that, but it's even worse when she's got children who all look like her ex. The ex she is still in love with, by the way."

"What, you're whack man. Mami hates Papi."

"Does she?"

Luis J ignored the question and asked one of his own, "So, what did she have?"

"A boy: five pounds, eight ounces. He looks a lot like Robert when Robert was little. His name is Carlos Deandre Rodriquez, Jr. He's nineteen months now."

"Man, why didn't you tell me? I thought we were tight. How could you keep something like that from me?"

"Mami made me swear not to tell you. She thought that it would make you follow in my footsteps, you know, like the cigarettes."

"It figures. That wasn't cool, but belated congrats, man. Hey, that means I'm an uncle. This is too deep. I mean my nephew doesn't even know us man. That's some crazy shit and you know it. Now I get why you don't like to come around. Man, I love Mami, but she doesn't make it easy. How can she do this, always talking about family this and family that with David and yet she keeps us from our real family?"

Carlos went to his bedroom and returned with a picture he had received from Luisa of his son. It was a framed picture of a baby about six weeks old who very much favored their little brother, Robert.

"So, now what?"

"I don't know. I'm still saving up for a trip to Puerto Rico either this fall or early winter. I hope to at least be able to meet my son. He'll be almost two years old. I'm going to try to convince Luisa to at least let me share custody."

"She must have feelings for you still; she gave him your name and sent you a picture."

"I guess. I think that's why Papi and I bonded when I went to live with him. I realized that, in many ways, we were experiencing the same sense of loss."

"Yeah, I can see that and both situations are because of Mami. You know, I miss that Mami we used to know. What happened to her man? She just seems so cold all the time now."

"You too?"

"Yeah, but, Carlos, you're almost twenty now. You don't need permission anymore. Why don't you fly over there, bring them back and get married?"

"First of all, I have a decent job at FedEx making alright money, but I need to go back to school so that I can earn a salary that can take care of a family. And this place is way too small for more than two people. Secondly, I don't really know if I love Luisa. I care about her; she's the only woman that touched me like she did. I know that, but I never had a serious relationship before her. At one time I thought I loved her, but I just don't know if I know what love is. I can't ask her to marry me and create an environment that wouldn't be healthy for my son. I won't do that to him or to Luisa, for that matter."

As Luis J listened to his brother saying those words, he heard great pride in his voice. But he could also hear the pain Carlos was feeling. Luis J accepted that life could really deal you a jacked-up hand sometimes, with very few options.

"That's why I said you and Dany needed a break from each other. You are too young to be dating someone exclusively, and so is she." The far away look returned to Carlos' face.

The two brothers sat and talked about Luisa, Carmine, Dany and their parents until it was time for Luis J to go home. Hearing Carlos' story made Luis J have greater respect for the insight regarding Dany he had shared with him and for that, he thanked him. When he left, he promised to keep Carlos updated on things.

On the ride home, Luis J found himself anxious about the outcome of his mother's meeting with Principal Moore and David's with the lawyer. Entering the apartment and seeing the two of them sitting at the table, he felt a sick feeling in the pit of his stomach. Luis J did not waste any time asking for an update.

"We were just debriefing," David said, looking at his watch. "We have about ten minutes before Luis' call. Sit down."

It was like a directive from a drill sergeant and Luis J was not sure he liked the sound of it. His mother started with her visit to the principal. She told them how open Mr. Moore was and that he allowed her to give him an historical overview. She hoped that it helped to plant a seed of doubt in the story. He informed her that all of Luis J's teachers would be sending them the coursework they would be covering over the two-week period. He also said that if they could get Ms. Webber to reverse her accusations, Luis J could be reinstated to the team this season and they would remove the suspension from his record. This would all be contingent upon Ms. Webber putting this in writing for their files.

The news gave some level of comfort to Luis J. He felt really confident that they could get Dany and maybe even Ms. Webber to retract their statements. Next, he prepared himself to hear about David's conversation with the attorney.

"This guy is good and is an expert in this area of law. I gave him a complete run down of the events. He feels your academic performance, clean police record, your position as team captain and our family unit are all positive factors. It will be important to get testimony from teachers, your coach, and others who have known you for years. However, it boils down to an adult's word and Danielle's against yours.

"Her mother didn't take her to the hospital, so there's no rape kit to enter into evidence. The attorney's going to have to get someone to corroborate your story, maybe a neighbor who heard the beating. Or maybe he can convince Danielle or Stephanie to contradict their mother's story. I don't think it will be hard once they take the stand and swear under oath to tell the truth, the whole truth and nothing but the truth. Something about that has a way of persuading people.

"He may need to show a history of violence in their family. He said it was not going to be easy because if he pushes too hard, Ms. Webber may act on her threat to file charges. We want to avoid that if at all possible, although there are pros and cons to that happening, too. The pros would be sworn affidavits, subpoenas, etc. I'm sure we all know the cons. He still doesn't want any contact with the family." David looked directly at Luis J. "He's planning to gather some information from you and the school and then he'll pay Ms. Webber a visit."

"She has got to see how much she's ruining my life. I have to be exonerated and I want the truth to be told. I want my record clean. I've earned it. I don't drink, I don't do drugs, don't gang bang, and I don't beat up on females. My mother and father taught me that. That's the only thing I will accept," Luis J proclaimed.

"Luis J, do you see how you're affecting Danielle's life? What if she's pregnant? Can you imagine becoming a father at this age? What about Danielle becoming a mother? What about her dreams for college, a career? You have to recognize your role in all of this. This isn't happening to you, it's happening because of you, because of your lack of assessing the impact of your choices and their consequences," Diane told him.

Luis J felt that his mother just didn't understand. This was happening to him. Danielle was causing these problems for him. She knew he was innocent and refused to stand up for him. He would never do something like that to her.

David observed his wife and then spoke, "Diane, Luis J's right. I know that he may have been wrong for going out that night…"

"You're damn right he was wrong. I specifically told him to go to bed."

"Yes, but he didn't. He went to see the girl he likes, they had sex, but I do not believe he raped her or beat her. You were here when her mother called, she never mentioned Danielle having been beaten. And you were here when Dany called the next day to speak to Luis J. What rape victim would call her rapist?"

The phone rang before Luis J had a chance to respond to his mother's comment. But he was digging David for speaking up on his behalf and nodded at him. Diane answered the phone and based on her conversation, Luis J could tell she was talking to his father. She then handed the phone to him.

"How are you holding up, mijo?"

Luis J was touched to hear his father address him that way. It was the kind of support he needed right now, especially in light of his mother's opinion of his actions.

"Alright, I suppose. I can't believe this is happening to me," he stated, ignoring his mother's reaction to that statement. "Papi, do you think we can work this out?"

"I'm not sure, Luis J, but you can be sure I'll do everything in my power to help you." After a pause, he continued, "Would you like to spend the weekend with me, if your mother and David are okay with it?"

"Sure, that would be cool."

"Let me ask her. Now take care and call me if you need anything, anything at all."

Luis J handed the phone to his mother and listened to her side of the story. "No, Luis. We have it covered." After a pause, she continued, "That won't be necessary either. David and I can handle it." Then her tone changed as she said, "Don't you mean visit with 'us'? Well the answer is no. Luis, this is a punishment for him, not a vacation. He doesn't get a break from it. He needs to learn now that we are accountable for our actions. I really need to go, it's almost dinner time."

When she returned the phone to the cradle, Luis J asked if he could go, even though he already knew the answer. His mother made it very clear that that was not an option now or in the future just by the way she looked at him.

"You just don't want me to go because Maria is there. Mami, get over it. You and Papi are divorced. He has a right to be with someone, just like you. At least he didn't rush to marry her, the way you did David."

"How dare you talk to me that way? You have no idea what has happened in my life or between your father and me. You're not going and that's final. Now get out of my sight."

"Fine. But I do know that this isn't all Papi's fault. And guess what, you don't know all that's happened between me and Dany, for the record," Luis J asserted.

"Boy, I will knock the crap out of you. Say something else."

Luis J knew he needed to back down so he headed to his room and closed the door.

David chimed in, "Diane, you're going to drive him right into Luis and Maria's arms if you don't let up. He's scared and he needs as much support as he can get. Why not let him see his father?"

Diane couldn't believe David was saying the same thing to her that Maria had taunted her about on the phone. Could it be her actions were going to do what she feared most? No, this wasn't happening because of her actions, it was happening to her and her children because of Luis and Maria.

"David, you really don't understand."

"Then explain it to me, instead of shutting me out. Tell me what I don't understand because I think I do understand. You're the one who doesn't get it."

"I can't explain it to you."

"Well, that's unfortunate because that's what life partners are supposed to be able to do. Lately, all you've done is the opposite and quite honestly, I'm tired of it." He headed for the door.

"Where are you going?"

"Out. I'll be home late so don't hold dinner for me."

Diane watched the door close behind her husband and shook her head. Why did men always feel that walking out was the answer to everything? She poured herself a glass of pinot noir and picked up one of the latest issues of her soap opera digest magazines to distract her from all that was wrong with her life. She had about ten minutes before dinner would be ready.

David walked to their car and stood there for a minute to absorb his thoughts and feelings. Diane used to talk to him about everything. They were able to find common ground on most topics. But these last few months she appeared to be changing right in front of his eyes and he had no clue how to help her. He wanted his wife back, the warm, loving, sexy and vulnerable woman who was passionate and strong, but never cold and unyielding. She was turning into ice and he felt the chill. He didn't like it and would not accept it much longer. It seemed like a good time to go see his brother, Marvin, who lived across town.

David's family had warned him about marrying her; he had never been married before and he would be responsible for a ready-made family with a woman who had only recently divorced. Then there was the age difference, though that had actually made him proud. He had attracted a woman ten years older than he was and who was smart and beautiful. But his family felt it was all a recipe for failure.

David had dismissed their warnings because, above all else, he loved Diane. He loved her smile, her humor, her wit and the way she had of looking at you and seeing your soul. He was well aware of the problems she had had in her marriage and felt as though Luis' loss was his gain.

Her children were great and he knew he would grow to love them. Robert really felt like his son, as he had been there in the early stages of the boy's life. And when Robert called him Daddy the first time, it made it all real to him. He had a family. The only thing he was waiting for now was the day she told him that she was pregnant. He had hoped they wouldn't have to wait long, but she kept saying the time wasn't right.

Things were hard for them at first as Diane refused any financial support from Luis and it was a while before she wanted to return to work, but they managed to make ends meet and seemed to grow closer with every challenge. He hadn't agreed with Diane's position to keep the kids away from their father because he always knew that she'd regret it later, and they'd already seen the outcome with Carlos and now Luis J. It wouldn't be long before Chell's curiosity led her there, either. And Robert, what if he ever needed something for medical reasons that only his father could give him, like a kidney or something?

The point was that Diane's stubbornness could blind her, but David didn't want to take on that argument. He had hoped that with enough time in her new life, she would eventually allow her children to embrace their father.

But it had been five years since they married and nothing had changed. At times, she seemed unhappier than ever and she wouldn't let him in. At the next exit, he got off, turned around, and headed back home. He knew leaving would not solve anything.

When David got back to the house, he found Diane in the bedroom with a wine glass in hand watching television and curled up in nothing but an oversized shirt. She seemed calmer, for which he was thankful, but she didn't acknowledge him when he entered the room or sat on the bed until he reached for the remote to turn the television down.

"Diane, may we talk?"

"I thought you had determined there was nothing to talk to me about."

"Diane, don't make this hard. I just needed some air and I thought you could use a few minutes, too." He watched as she finally picked up the remote and muted the TV.

"Look, I'm sorry for making a stressful situation even harder for you. It was not my intention. I wanted to provide another perspective. I want you to know that you can always count on me. As long as we work together, we can get through this. Remember, we have already been through a lot and we're still one."

When he paused, she asked, "Are you finished?"

"Yes," he responded, waiting for her response.

Diane picked up the remote, unmuted the TV and resumed watching it. This infuriated David. He glared at Diane until she looked at him. He took the remote from her hand and slammed it against the wall. The batteries flew out and rolled in two different directions. She jumped, surprised by this rather violent action, while David hoped she realized he would not tolerate her bullshit. He was not going to allow her to minimize him. She was acting like a spoiled-ass brat. What the hell was wrong with her? He watched as her physical response was to turn her back to him and turn out the light. That was probably best for both of them.

David stood there for a moment, staring at her back before removing his clothes and climbing into bed. He could not help but feel some sort of connection with Luis. He wondered if Diane had become cold towards him and cut herself off in the same manner. And if she did, no matter that she thought she was right, it was selfish and self-righteous. No man can put up with that for long.

He did not condone Luis' behavior, but it was true he had not been there and he really didn't know what had happened between them; he only knew what she had told him. Now knowing her as well as he did, he realized that she was blinded by her own sense of righteousness. She always felt that what was done was done to her, just as she had accused her son Luis J of thinking tonight.

'Oh Diane, Diane, come back to me sweet, sweet Diane,' David prayed as he felt the coldness of her back to him.

Chapter Eleven

A week had gone by and today, the attorney was meeting with Danielle's mother. Luis J and Diane were going to join Luis at the attorney's office that afternoon.

Luis was sitting on one of those big, brown, button leather couches waiting for Luis J and Diane to arrive. He was wondering if those couches were mass produced for attorneys' offices when his attention was interrupted by Luis J, who entered the room. Luis rose and embraced his son and then they both sat down.

"Whatever he says, just listen and then we'll figure out where we go from there. Stay calm," Luis said, cautioning his son, whom he remembered used to have a short fuse at times.

"I'll try. Thanks for being here Papi, I really appreciate it."

"Where else would I be?"

The doors of the waiting room opened again and they turned their heads towards the entrance assuming it was Diane. But to Luis' surprise, it was Maria walking toward them, dressed not entirely inappropriately, but certainly distracting for those who had business on their mind. He stood as she approached the chair and instinctively leaned inward to kiss her cheek.

"Hey, Poppie, Luis J."

"Maria, what are you doing here?" Luis asked, perturbed.

"I came to support my stepson and of course you, my love," Maria said to Luis, but directed her gaze toward Luis J.

"That's really sweet of you, but I don't think it's a good idea."

"Why not? Luis J, do you mind that I'm here?" Maria asked, just itching for a fight. But she knew there was nothing Luis hated more than a public scene, so she waited patiently for the other shoe to drop. She knew that she was pushing it, but she did not like the idea that Diane had the upper hand right now. She was here to ensure Diane knew that she was very much still in the game.

But before Luis J could part his lips, his father had answered, "It's not up to him. We talked about this and I asked you to stay out of it. Now, please, leave. I'll meet you later. I appreciate the gesture, but it's not a good idea."

"Why? Because Diane won't like it? Why do you care? She divorced you, remember?"

Luis took Maria by the arm and led her away from his son, through the doors and into the hallway. "Maria, don't do this. Not here, not now, not in front of my son. He has a lot on his mind and he needs his parents focused on him, not fighting each other over you. And your mind games are running their limit. Please abide by my wishes and go home. Actually, I don't care where you go, but just leave from here."

"Alright, Poppie, I'll be waiting at home for you and we can pick up where we left off last night." She placed her arms around his neck and kissed him passionately. Luis was surprised by her quick shift, but was thankful that she was complying.

Without warning, a chilling voice cut through his calmness. "If you're too busy to be here, leave. Your presence isn't necessary. I knew this was a mistake." Diane released her venom and then walked past them, never acknowledging Maria. But she thought, 'Inappropriately dressed as usual.'

Luis responded, "Maria was just leaving," but Diane was already entering the lawyer's office. Luis' face flushed with anger. This is exactly what he had wanted to avoid and apparently what Maria wanted.

"Honestly, Maria, do you realize how difficult you're making things for me? You can't be that dense. Now, get the hell out of here."

She wanted to stay and keep reminding Diane of her presence, but she had gotten what she came for; Diane had seen her with Luis, so she could leave as he asked. She conceded.

Luis reentered the waiting area, but it was now empty. When he inquired at the receptionist's desk, she rose and escorted him to the conference room, where Luis J and Diane were already seated.

"Mami, I thought you said he left?"

"Luis J, it looked like he had more important things on his mind. I thought he had left."

He just looked at his mother annoyed because he knew that she had probably told Papi to leave because of Maria. 'Damn, Papi's got two crazy women in his life,' he thought. Rule number 1: Get a nice girl as a wife and a crazy woman to freak with. What was his father thinking? They were both crazy!

"Of course not, Luis J. My place is here, and your mother knows that," he shot back, glaring at Diane, who refused to acknowledge his presence or make eye contact with him.

"Are we all here or are we still waiting for Mr. Anderson?" the lawyer asked as he entered the conference room.

"We're here. Unfortunately, Mr. Anderson will not be joining us," Diane answered. When Luis realized she was not going to introduce him, he introduced himself. "I'm Luis Rodriquez, Sr., Luis Jr.'s father."

"My pleasure. J.R. Lawson." They shook hands and the attorney pointed for him to take a seat next to Luis J. "Let's get started. I have spent the past week gathering information from several sources and I met with Ms. Webber today, as you know. She was extremely defensive and not cooperative at first. After about an hour of firing questions at her, she agreed to withdraw her claim and not file any legal charges. She realized that there are too many loopholes in her story. It just would not hold up in court. In addition, she has not followed the proper procedures for a rape and beating claim. She didn't take her daughter to the hospital and she didn't file a police report. There is no legal evidence. The ultimate straw that broke the camel's back was when I threatened to conduct lie detector tests on her and her two daughters."

"Thank heaven," Diane sighed.

"Excuse me, but why do you suppose she thought she could get away with it?" Luis asked. "Didn't she realize that she was potentially jeopardizing Luis J's future and potentially her daughter's future as well?"

"Mr. Rodriquez, to be truthful, I think she saw it as an opportunity to get some money. But she realized today that she had nothing, so she relinquished."

"Will she put it in writing? The school principal said we had to have it in writing," Diane insisted.

"Yes. But before you get too excited, there are some stipulations."

"And what might they be?" Diane asked, with a little less relief in her tone.

"One, Luis Jr. is not to see, talk to or interact with Danielle at all from this day forward. Two, if Danielle is pregnant, you will pay for an abortion and all costs, including a tutor for any time she might miss from school."

"Did she say she would completely absolve me of these allegations?" Luis J asked.

"Yes. Once I draw up the papers, we'll be all set. I also need to warn you, though, that during my investigation, I found a few other potential landmines. Apparently, there are other girls in the school who have admitted to sleeping with you, and I want to tell you that you need to be very careful. You need to make sure the sex you are having is consensual, age appropriate, and never abusive, or you'll find yourself right back here and not so lucky the next time," said Mr. Lawson.

Diane pushed back from her chair and began pacing the room.

"Which girls?" Luis J asked. He wondered who had dropped a dime on him. They were supposed to keep their mouths shut. He definitely didn't want Dany to find out about this even if they weren't together anymore.

"I know that is not the first question that came to your mind! What the hell is wrong with you?" Diane shouted. "I don't even recognize you any longer. My head is spinning right now. I can't believe what I'm hearing."

Diane moved to stand over her son. "Have you lost your mind? How many other girls is he talking about?" she asked, before slapping him upside his head.

"I'm sorry. I assumed you knew," the attorney offered.

"You too? Well, I didn't. This is the first I've heard of this. I'm finding out I don't know my son at all."

"Mami...," Luis J began, rubbing the area where she had smacked him.

"No, don't say one word to me."

"May we talk as a family for a minute?" Luis asked the attorney.

"Sure, just tell my receptionist when you're ready to reconvene."

After Mr. Lawson left, Luis looked at his son. "First things first, her proposal. Do we all agree?"

"I guess."

"Not exactly the response I was expecting, but I'll let it go for now. Diane?"

"Yes."

"As for these other girls, we're going to have a LONG discussion about that. You better pray they don't elect to pursue any action against you," Luis warned his son.

"First, that's ridiculous! I have always had protected, consensual sex and Dany is the youngest one, so the age thing doesn't apply to me. And the only time I had unprotected sex was that night with her, and I pulled out. She's not pregnant. Trust me."

"Boy, I could beat your ass right now. You think you know so much and you know nothing!" Diane stopped herself from saying anything further, but she was seething inside.

Luis J turned to his father and said, "Papi, will you please explain to her that I am a young man with needs? It's hormonal and I can't help it. My needs build up and I try to control it. But that's what happened the night I went to see Dany. Truth. I had been suppressing it. But really Mami, you act like it's unnatural."

Luis empathized with his alpha male, handsome son and understood his pain. This is exactly why his sons needed him. He was right. Diane had no idea what it's like to be a growing young man or what it took to raise one. He began by saying, "Diane you may want to consider that he is coming of age. His hormones are exploding. And it's true he can't control the buildup, which makes a man highly aroused. And then sports further exacerbates the situation by releasing pheromones that elevate the sexual desire."

"What are you saying?"

"I'm trying to help you understand his situation. You can talk to David about this, too; he'll tell you the same thing, but you have to accept that your son is going to be sexually active. But he needs to have that talk with a man about control, redirection and discipline."

"And you think that I will let him talk to you? What do you know about control, redirection and discipline?"

"Mami, Papi's right. Coach talked to the team about it because he didn't want any of us to get in trouble."

"Yes, but you still did, didn't you?"

"Diane, let's not argue about this here. Let's talk about it later."

Luis and Diane finalized their discussion with the attorney and planned to execute everything on Friday. They added a clause that Ms. Webber and Danielle could never discuss the terms of the agreement with anyone; doing so would violate the contract and they would, in turn, file charges against her. The lawyer didn't think this would be an issue. He was to take the notarized, signed letter to the principal and Luis J would be able to go back to school and hopefully rejoin the basketball team.

Diane had some errands to run so she agreed to let Luis take Luis J home because it was convenient for her. During the ride, Luis chose to take this time to ask his son about his sexual activity. He wanted to make sure he understood the law regarding statutory rape and then asked if he thought it was going to be a problem.

"Son, although you're underage now, when your birthday comes you will be considered an adult, legally. That means any girl under 18 you have sex with is considered a minor and therefore any act of sex with her could count as statutory rape."

Luis J assured his father that he had not violated that law and would not. Luis could only hope that he was right. "And one more thing mijo, you aren't smoking pot or anything else are you?"

"Come on now, Papi, I'm an athlete, a serious athlete. Besides I have to pee in a cup before every practice and before every game. Coach's rules." Then he raised a fist to his father, who raised his in a ritual as their knuckles touched.

When Diane entered the house, it was quiet. David was sitting in the dark, an empty bottle of Bud Light on the table, another on the floor and a half-full one in his hand. The smell of it lingered in the air. Robert, dressed for bed, was asleep on the couch. David watched as she entered the room. Diane approached him and touched his shoulder, awaiting a response.

"Is everything settled?" he asked.

"Yes. The attorney will take care of everything in time for Luis J to start school on Monday and hopefully resume basketball. Were there any calls?"

Looking down at the table, he seemed to be deep in thought. "Just one; it was for me," he mumbled, as he placed the bottle on the table, rose from the chair and moved toward the limp body on the couch. Robert's arms clutched David's neck and his legs wrapped around his father's frame.

She thought that was an interesting way to answer her question, but she didn't say anything else. Instead, she watched David carry Robert to his room and lay him down, kissing him gently on his forehead. Closing the door behind him, he told Diane they needed to talk. Motioning for her to go outside, he picked up the car keys.

There was a chill in the air and Diane wished she had grabbed her coat. She paused near the doorway to catch her breath, absorb the events of the day, and allow the eve of the door to shield some of the wind.

"Do we really need to go for a ride? I have had a long day and could really just stand and talk. Would you mind?"

"I just don't want us to be interrupted," David stated.

"I understand. What do you want to talk about?" she asked, rubbing her arms to generate some warmth.

"Diane, I love you, but I have some serious concerns about where we're going and how we're going to get there, as a family and more specifically as a couple."

"I know. Things have been difficult around here lately, but you have to know that I love you, too, and it's going to get better."

"Is it? How is it going to get better? Do we even agree on what the issues are?"

"Of course we do."

"I'm not so sure. This is what I mean. I don't think so. We aren't agreeing on much these days but as usual, you have a different perspective and all the answers. So you tell me, Diane, what are the issues?"

Diane heard the frustration in his tone and sarcasm in his words. She didn't address his actions of throwing the remote the other night, but it had bothered her. So she chose her words carefully.

"First of all, there's Luis J. He has to learn to control his impulsive and irresponsible behavior. I just found out that he has been very sexually active this past year, and I don't mean with just Dany. Today I learned that there were several other girls, and Lord knows what other problems lay ahead for us because of that. Secondly, Luis' recent interest in our children. Thirdly, you and I need more quiet time with each other," she concluded, lowering her voice and leaning in close to him.

Placing his hands upon her shoulders and preventing her from getting closer, he looked into her eyes. "What else?"

"That's it, baby. Things aren't that bad."

"Yes, Diane, they are. Trust, honesty and faith in one another are things we used to have, but we don't seem to anymore."

"What are you talking about? I have complete trust and faith in you, in us."

"Do you? Do you trust that I want what's best for you and this family?"

"Yes, I do."

"Where were you two weeks ago Saturday?"

"I don't remember, running errands I guess, as usual."

He smiled and allowed one hand to drop from her shoulder, while the other touched her face. "I know you went to see Luis."

"Who told you that?"

"Who do you think, Diane? Maria called here tonight to make sure I knew that my wife went to visit her ex-husband, at his house, without me. And don't misunderstand me; the problem I have is that YOU didn't tell me, not that you went. You didn't have a feeling that day about Luis starting trouble. He told you what he was planning to do. But you presented it to me as your intuition. And even tonight, instead of admitting it, you asked who told me. I'm not your fool, Diane, and I'm not going to let you play me."

"I couldn't tell you. I didn't think you would understand how I felt. I was afraid that you would try to talk me out of going to see him."

"Even if I did, you would have gone anyway. That's BS, Diane. You could have told me you were going over there, but you chose not to. I could have gone with you. Damn it, I should have gone with you. Even if you didn't tell me before, why didn't you tell me afterwards? So, I have to wonder, is something else going on here?"

"What are you talking about?"

"Oh, now you don't have answers? You had your hair done when you came in. I even complimented you on it. Is something going on with the two of you?"

"Are you crazy? No, absolutely, not! You saw how we went at each other when he came by here with Luis J. I'm sorry if I did or said anything to make you think that." As she said the last word, she couldn't hold back the tears any longer.

"Diane, I'm asking you. What's going on? I can't help if you don't let me in. You used to be able to tell me anything. When did that change? Why did that change?"

"David, you're so wrong about this. Luis is poisoning Luis J about us, just like he did with Carlos, like he would love to do with all of our children. As if he hasn't hurt me enough already."

As if he didn't hear her last words, David asked, "Diane, are you still in love with Luis?"

She could see the vein pulsating in his neck and the stiffness in his body. It reminded her of how he looked when he confronted Luis J that morning.

"No! I hate him. He killed my love when he cheated on me and almost made me lose my baby."

"Well, I have to tell you, I won't let him come in between us. What I'm trying to figure out is, will you help me keep that from happening?"

"David, I just don't want to feel this pain anymore."

She stepped forward, hoping he would place his arms around her, hold her close. He finally did and her trembling subsided. They stood there for a few minutes while Diane wiped the tears from her eyes. Neither of them said anything else as they reentered the apartment. David returned to his spot on the couch and Diane headed to the bedroom, but not before she picked up the two empty bottles and dropped them off in the kitchen. She was exhausted and hoped that she could put this night, the week, everything that had come between her and David lately behind her, including her husband's accusations.

But more than anything, she had plenty to be upset about; she was pissed that Maria had called her house again and this time to talk to her husband. That conniving wench was always a step ahead of her and that had to change.

Chapter Twelve

When Luis J finally returned to school, the interaction with his classmates was a little strained. The rumors about what happened were filling the halls and locker room and questions were being shot at him from every direction. However, he couldn't share anything about it, so he kept to himself a lot, keeping his mouth shut. After a couple of days when the story lost its traction, the interest also waned and everyone was on to the next hot topic, allowing Luis J to get back to normal.

Luis J met with Coach after class and shared the full story with him, including how they were able to resolve everything. He wanted to clear the air between them but even more, he wanted to understand why Coach acted so quickly and benched him.

"Luis J, I'm an administrator of this school and had to be a responsible leader. I had to be concerned about the welfare of the team and the impact on the school's image. You know that I respect you. That's why you're the captain as a junior. I never thought you were guilty and I'm thankful that everything has been settled. But I know that while you think that you did nothing wrong because you had consensual sex, you did go out on a school night unannounced and unprepared. You manipulated the girl's emotions knowing how she felt about you. You were in her mother's house without permission, unsupervised.

"What if she had gotten pregnant? That's your future right there, man – hump time and baby diapers! What if her mother had come home and found you? Technically, she could have shot you and said you raped her daughter. Because she did say that…and if she had shot you dead, well it would have been her word and her daughters' word against a dead man. You see what I'm talking about? Your actions put you in circumstances that were avoidable. You have to be more mindful of what you do on and off the court. If you continue sleeping around without being selective and smart about your choices, you are going to really get into something that you may not be able to negotiate your way out of.

"Danielle is a sweet girl. I can't say the same for some of the others I've seen you with. And Luis J, make no mistake about it – if we find ourselves here again, I won't care about the outcome, I will remove you from this team permanently."

Luis J thought about what Coach said as he dressed for practice. He would prove to him that he was worthy of being reinstated when he got on the court. Courtside, Luis J was known as Smooth J because of his style. His agility and poise were like a dancer's, fluid and rhythmic. He was one of the highest scoring players on the team. By the time he returned to school, the season had started and the team was on a winning streak. It was their first tournament game and his father and Carlos came to watch and support him. The team won again that night and their record was now five and one.

Luis J was finally starting to feel like his life was stabilizing, although, he missed hooking up with Dany after the games. Before the incident, she'd be waiting for him, looking like a delicious chocolate sundae in her cheerleader outfit. It always made him want to kiss her, taste her sweetness in his mouth. At first he thought he might be weird, but then he realized that it was normal when you really liked someone like he did Dany.

He loved her smell, a combination of scents. Her natural body scent, her sweat, the perfume and the musk that she gave off during their sexual intercourse turned him on as much as the taste of her sweet and salty at the same time.

But he was pretty sure she wouldn't be there tonight. He had watched her every now and then during the time outs and at half time. Her face barely showed any more signs of the beating and he was thankful for that. When he opened the locker room door, the only people waiting to greet him were his father and Carlos. No David and no Mami.

"Good game, L. You looked good on the court. I was proud of you. Impressive skills."

"Thanks, Papi. I feel this is the year we go all the way and take State. The whole team is on."

"Yeah, it was good, but you still need to work on those layups," Carlos said, keeping Luis J in line and reminding him that he was still perfecting his game. "Remember what I told you? Use your size against them. We need to do some more drills. You were a little slow getting down the court a few times. Were you getting distracted by something… or someone? Remember, we don't have time for that."

"Papi, this man is never satisfied," Luis J said.

"Whatever. Here today, history tomorrow, lil' bro'."

Luis chuckled and said, "Carlos has always been able to ground you, Luis J. But, for the record, I was really impressed and so was your brother." He finished his comment by hitting Carlos on the back before asking Luis J, "So when will the scouts come out?"

"In two weeks, right after Thanksgiving. I'll have to make sure I don't eat too much of Mami's cooking or it will be hard to move it down the court." The three of them laughed and high-fived. "I'm hoping you both will be there," Luis J said.

"Let me know which days and I'll work it out with your mother."

Luis J wondered why his father thought he had to make arrangements with his mother. She never came to the games anyway and wouldn't even know if his father was there, like tonight. But he didn't ask. Instead, he waited for Carlos' response.

"You know I would, without a doubt, but it's not possible this time."

"Why not, working?" Luis asked.

"No. I'll be out of town."

"Out of town? Where you goin'?" Luis J asked.

"To San Juan. I'm leaving the day after Thanksgiving. I'm going to see Luisa and my son. Before you say anything, Papi, I have been thinking about this for quite some time and I know what I must do. The timing is perfect because the season slows down a bit at FedEx during Thanksgiving and picks up the second week of December. I have to take responsibility for the life I created and I must do whatever it takes to make that happen."

"But I thought you didn't know where she was?" Luis J interjected.

"I didn't, but I told her mother of my intentions and she broke down and gave me Luisa's address."

"For real?" Luis J replied.

"Yep, I'm going. Papi, do you think NaNa would let me stay with her?"

"Of course, mijo. I'll call her tomorrow and arrange everything. I wish that you had told me earlier."

"I know Papi, but I didn't exclude you; I just had to work through it on my own."

Luis had learned over the past two years that his son was very level-headed. He approached everything with a plan, so he knew that Carlos was set, but he thought he would ask anyway. "I understand. What about financially?"

"Thanks for the offer, but I got this. It's a big step, but I waited until I was ready before taking it."

"So how long will you be there?" Luis J hit him again. They had spent all that time together these past few days and Carlos hadn't said a word about having contacted Luisa's mother or that he had already made plans to go.

"I was able to get a few days off because I'm working the holiday, so that Friday counts as my Thanksgiving weekend. I switched my days off with another guy, so I have Monday and Tuesday off, plus a personal day. I get back the following Thursday, so it's seven days, one week, altogether."

"Son, you make me happy. I know how important this is to you. It's important that you see your son, to meet and bond with him. But I hope you are prepared to accept the responsibility of providing for and parenting him. That child has a life in Puerto Rico and feels safe. The worst thing you can do to him is upset his surroundings.

"I ask you to take this slowly and if you have any doubts, then you should wait and not do this now. Don't be selfish and just go see him to make yourself feel better. Either you're going to be a part of his life or not. So you've got to choose wisely."

"Papi, I know that and I promise you I'm ready. I haven't told Mami yet, but I will when I drop Luis J off tonight."

"Yikes, I wouldn't want to be in your shoes for that conversation!" Luis J said. "But you'll have some time to get your thoughts together because she won't be home until about ten. She and David have a counseling session tonight."

At least he was ahead of his mother in this chain of conversation concerning Luisa. That made Carlos feel a little better.

Luis J's words drew Luis's attention away from Carlos for the moment and he asked, "A counseling session? Marriage counseling? When did that start?"

"I don't know. About two weeks ago, I think. Mami said they've been having some problems and needed someone to talk to."

"Is it helping?" Papi continued.

Luis J's phone vibrated with a text from Cassie. He knew he couldn't get away to see her tonight so he just ignored it. He hoped that he wouldn't regret that choice later once he was home and in the bed. He began to wonder about the time, if he had enough of it to run by and see her. Then he thought about what Coach had said and he opted to just go home.

"What? I don't know. They're not bugging me since they are focusing on each other, and that makes me happy. But anyway, Carlos, you ready?"

"Yeah, you guys should get going. I'm sure you have homework. Carlos, again, if I can help in anyway, let me know. Luis J, great game." They hugged and went their separate ways.

When Carlos and Luis J walked through the door, they found Chell on the phone and Robert dead asleep. Chell kissed her oldest brother, flipped Luis J the finger, and then went to her room to continue her conversation. Carlos grabbed something to eat from the refrigerator and then sat on the couch to watch TV while Luis J started his homework at the kitchen table. Around ten o'clock, their mother and David walked in and were surprised to see Carlos sitting there.

Diane's heart skipped a beat. 'Now what?' she thought. She removed her coat, patted Luis J on the shoulder, did a quick scan to make sure Robert was in bed and then sat down next to her eldest.

"How was your game?" David asked, as he looked in the refrigerator. He hoped they hadn't eaten all of the leftovers.

"Great. We won again. Only lost one game," Luis J responded, trying to determine his mother's mood and how Carlos' announcement would land when lobbed in the air.

"You should've seen him. He was on fire. He's still developing it, but the boy's got skills; after all, who taught him?" Carlos laughed and Luis J just half smiled. Both had thought it best not to mention that their father was at the game.

"Nice. Congratulations, Luis J. Anyway, Honey, it's good to see you, but you don't usually stay when you drop Luis J off, so what's up?"

"I wanted to let you know that I'm going to see my son."

Diane looked quickly at Luis J to see if he was paying attention to the conversation. He, unfortunately, was looking right at her.

Carlos, seeing her reaction, continued, "Luis J already knows about Luisa and my son."

"You told him? Who gave you permission?" Why would Carlos tell him when she was very clear that he was not to discuss that secret with anyone in this house, or outside of it for that matter?

"First, you stimulated his interest two weeks ago when you said that he was following Papi's and my footsteps because we couldn't keep our dicks in our pants. Second, I'm not a child anymore and neither is he. You don't get to tell me what I can share or talk about or to whom. I make my own choices now, right or wrong. Anyway, Luis J put two and two together and asked me. I didn't want to lie to him; our relationship means more to me than that, so I told him. Besides, in light of all of his problems, I felt the truth might keep him from repeating my mistake."

"Really? Well, he's still living under my roof and answers to me so you should have asked me about it first. Anyway, what's going on with your son? Do you need some money or something?"

"I just wanted you to know that I'm going to Puerto Rico to talk to Luisa about a shared custody arrangement. You wouldn't allow us to be together before but we are both of age now and I don't need your permission anymore. You and her parents no longer have jurisdiction over what we do. Besides, Luisa isn't trying to keep me away from my son, like you did to us with Papi."

"Watch your mouth, Carlos," Diane warned him.

David left the kitchen and perched on the edge of the sofa arm next to Diane. Taking her hand he said, "Let's hear him out."

"That's it. I wanted you to hear it from me. I'm leaving next week. I've already missed almost two years of my son's growth and development. I won't miss anymore. No one is going to stop me from taking this trip and reconnecting with my son."

"How did you find out where she was living?" Diane asked, her voice a little calmer now even though her thoughts were racing.

"Does it matter? I just did. I'm leaving the day after Thanksgiving."

"That's right around the corner. How long have you been planning this? Where will you stay? You don't know anything about Puerto Rico. Who will look out for you?"

"Mami, don't you see a man standing in front of you? I've made arrangements for the trip. I'm fluent in Spanish and remember, we have family there."

"Sweetheart, I know you think you have thought this through, but I'm sure there are tons of things you haven't considered. Why don't you wait until we can help you get a lawyer? I don't know anything about that place…"

Carlos smirked and said, "Mami, that place, as you refer to it, is where Papi was born and raised. It's where NaNa lives and at the moment, my son and his mother. Why do you think we will need a lawyer? That was the path you took. I won't need to go down like that. Luisa and I had a great relationship before this all happened. We could talk about anything. I'm confident we will do what is best for our son. I had hoped you would respect my decision, but you always have to take control or you don't feel right and therefore, you can't support it. Even if you don't agree with it, you could just wish me well, like Papi did. Anyway, I won't argue with you about this."

"Carlos, you better remember to keep your place. You're talking to your mother," David said, still holding Diane's hand and sensing her tension.

Luis J was worried about where the conversation was heading. Carlos was not going to take any crap from David. To his relief, Carlos' tone remained even as he continued addressing his response to their mother.

"Mami, I'm not trying to be disrespectful, but honestly, I don't need your permission or your suggestions. If I did, I would have asked you beforehand. I didn't. I just wanted to let you know out of respect. And now I have. It's getting late, so I better go."

Diane looked at her oldest son and her natural protective instincts were driving her reaction. He just didn't get it, but one day he would. "Carlos, I just don't want anything to happen to you. And I know that you have a tendency to jump into things, trying to do what's right by someone without thinking it through. You could get started on a path that will ruin your life."

Luis J noticed his mother's voice was also much calmer. He was pretty sure she didn't want David and Carlos to get into it either. But if it came to that, Luis J would definitely have his brother's back.

"Ugh, haven't you learned yet that you can't control my life, or any of our lives for that matter? You wouldn't let me marry Luisa because it would spoil the plans you had for me. Your plans for me? What about my plans? Well, newsflash, look at me, Mami. I didn't go to college for several reasons, but one of them was just because I knew that's what you wanted me to do. You wouldn't allow me to manage my life, and that included setting a path for my girlfriend and my child, so I made the one choice that would defy you another way.

"So I stand before you as a high school graduate, working at FedEx. Don't get me wrong, there's nothing wrong with that. The pay is decent, but I'm not satisfied with where my life is going. I'm finished reacting to you. It's time for me to do something about my life and my child's. This is my first step."

"Carlos, I think you've said enough for one night. Maybe you should leave, as you said," David stated, now standing up. He couldn't understand why these boys were testing him so much lately, but he was getting tired of it.

Carlos rose, nodded at his brother, and headed toward the door. Once he put on his coat, he turned toward his mother and said, "I hope one day you'll understand. If you would prefer, I won't come for Thanksgiving."

"Don't be silly, Lo, of course she wants you to be here," Luis J chimed in before his mother or David could respond.

"No te preocupes, bro. Good night."

Diane had a sick feeling in the pit of her stomach as she walked to her bedroom and sat on the edge of the bed. When David entered the room he sat next to her and asked, "Do you want to talk? Are you going to be alright?"

How was she supposed to answer that question? She was losing control of everything and felt helpless.

"Diane?"

"I'm fine, considering. Why can't he see that this is a bad idea? He said it himself, that his choice to not go to college hasn't made him happy and he doesn't know where his life is going. He has no idea how difficult this is going to be."

"Diane you have to learn to let a man be a man. I think he was saying that this step is the first toward the future he's taking control of. It's clear that he loved Luisa, but you and her parents prohibited them from being together. That altered his plans for the future, as did this child. So maybe he doesn't know the cost, but it's his choice. You have to let go and let him be a man."

Diane rolled her eyes at David. What did he know? He hasn't had to parent teenage boys. Not really. "I should have known you would side with him, with anyone except me."

"Diane you are so wrong, so selfish and self-centered. Everything is not about you. Do I have to remind you who you sound like? I mean, do you honestly feel that way?"

Not addressing the first question, Diane answered the second, "Yes, I do. Every time a resolution has to be made lately, especially concerning the children, I find you on the other side of the line. Why is that?"

"Why do you always have to draw a line, Diane? Can't you see that your children are growing up? You talk about your mother being controlling and smothering and how much you hated that…"

"Yeah, and?"

"Then why are you treating them the same way she treats you? You need to let go a little. You teach your children, then you let them stand on their own two feet; see what they're made of and just be there when they fall to help them up."

"I am who I am, but I'm NOTHING like my mother. If you can't deal with all of my issues, just say so and get out."

"Damn it, Diane, I'm really sick of this shit. You haven't heard a word I just said because you're stuck on what you think I've done. Don't make that statement lightly because I will comply. So do you really want me out?"

"Is that what YOU want?"

"I told you before it isn't, but I do know we can't go on like this," David said, sighing. "I agreed to go to therapy because you thought it would help. I'm not seeing any difference. Are you? You have to be willing to change or no amount of therapy will help."

"Do whatever you want, David, I'm tired of all of this, too."

There was a knock at the door and Diane knew it was Luis J. He had heard their voices escalate and came to check on her. Diane reassured her son that she was fine and instructed him to finish his homework in his room. She felt good to know that he was still looking out for her, the same way Carlos used to. Once she closed the door, her eyes began welling up. As the tears began flowing, she looked at David and said, "I don't even know how long he'll be gone."

"Because, as usual, you were focused on the wrong thing: how this impacts you."

"I'll tell you what I don't need is a lecture and what I do need is a husband who stands by me."

"Right or wrong, no matter what?"

"Yes, right or wrong."

"You know, you should try your own advice. Don't you get it? That's what Carlos wanted from you."

"Don't compare me to Carlos, he's barely grown."

He shook his head and smiled. "Yes, but he is grown; barely or not, he's grown. I'm sorry to disappoint you, but I can't bid you your wish. I went along with 'your way' when we got married and it has done nothing but create a toxic environment for all of us.

"You shut Luis out of their lives because he made a mistake. He betrayed you seven years ago, not his children, and you're still punishing him. And worse, you're punishing the children, too. The only reason I'm pointing this out to you is so you can see that all that anger and resentment is impacting you in so many ways, especially your ability to make good decisions about your children, your life, and us."

"Here's a decision for you. I don't need your help anymore."

"Diane, you better watch what you say to me. You can only push me so far."

"Or what? I know you aren't threatening me? David, I don't care what you do."

David looked at her and smirked, "Yeah, right. You know what Diane, I really don't need this shit. You want me out, I'm out."

She watched him walk that powerful sexy deliberate walk as he exited their room and made a call on his cellphone. She was in need of some caring – it always helped to soothe her, but even that was out of the question now. She could see from her position on the bed that Luis J was still at the table doing homework even though she had told him to go to his room. She was so tired of the men in her life not listening to her. She knew that he had positioned himself to listen and keep watch over her. In that way he and Carlos were very much like their father – protective.

She slammed the door and headed to the bathroom for a long, hot shower. The water felt so good on her body. She wished it would wash away all the hurt she was feeling. Carlos was so defiant and spiteful now that she sometimes didn't recognize him. The warm soft towel felt good and she was relieved to see that David had not returned to their room. She didn't want to argue with him anymore so hopefully he would just sleep on the couch.

Outside, the night breeze felt good to David as he stood on the balcony. He waited for his brother, Marvin, to return his call. He had left a voicemail message just minutes before. When Marvin returned his call, David took a few minutes to share his latest marital challenges. He then asked Marvin if he could crash with him for a few days. He genuinely hoped that's all it would take for Diane to calm down and for him to be able to return to his home. Marvin, of course, gave him the green light. As David sat with the phone in his hand, he knew that even though he had told Diane he was leaving, it wouldn't be tonight. He didn't want Robert to wake up in the morning and not find him so he made plans to leave the next afternoon. This would also give him time to tell the kids that he was leaving and why. He wasn't going to leave it up to Diane to represent his side of the story, not based on her history of handling these things.

After talking to Marvin, David remained on the balcony rehashing their session with the counselor. He wasn't convinced that being apart was the best thing for them right now, but he also knew that staying together was certainly not healthy for him or the kids. Diane was another story. He was beginning to think that she thrived on this sort of confusion. He was getting more and more frustrated with her.

As the chill in the air increased, David returned inside. He grabbed a Coors and sat on the couch. Luis J had apparently gone to his room and the house was now very quiet. Tomorrow night, he would be sitting on someone else's couch.

David awoke, still fully dressed, to the smell of bacon cooking and the clatter of pots and pans. Sitting up, he saw Chell in the kitchen and Robert sitting at the table with a smile planted softly on his face.

"Morning, Daddy."

"Good morning, my boy. Chell, what're you cooking? It smells good."

"Thank you, Daddy. I mean David."

David noticed the look of surprise on his stepdaughter's face. He was surprised, too, but wanted to quickly let her know that he liked the new title. "Chell, you can call me Daddy if you like. I like how it sounds."

Diane had shared with him that Chell sometimes envied Robert's ability to call him Daddy and that she didn't feel she could. He hoped that maybe she would start now. That would complete his family. How ironic though that it would be happening on the day he was moving out.

Smiling, she asked, "Are you hungry?"

"As a tiger. Is your mother up?"

"She left about an hour ago."

"Where did she go?"

"I don't know. She told me to cook something for Robert and that she would be back by noon."

David looked at his watch. It was ten-thirty. "What about Luis J?"

"He's still sleeping, of course."

David chuckled. That boy would sleep the day away if they allowed him to. "I'm going to shower and dress. If Luis J comes out before I do, ask him not to leave. I need to talk to you guys."

David wondered where Diane had gone when she knew they needed to talk to the kids this morning. He wasn't worried about Luis J, but he wasn't sure how Chell would react and he was really concerned about Robert. What or who was more important than this conversation? If he didn't know better, he'd bet that she had purposely planned to be out just to spite him…and he wasn't sure that he knew better.

Breakfast was very good, almost as good as Diane's cooking. Chell's pancakes, scrambled eggs and bacon showed off her culinary skills. She had learned well from Diane. But David noticed that lately Chell was really taking on a lot of responsibility for such a young girl. Before he left today, he would talk to Diane about that. It wasn't fair that she manage all the chores just because Luis J was on the basketball team.

"Daddy, can you take me to the mall this afternoon?" Chell asked, while rinsing the dishes in the sink and placing them in the dishwasher.

"I'm sure we can work it out, but I need to talk to you guys first."

David picked up Robert from the chair, sat down and placed Robert on his lap before continuing. "I was trying to wait for your mother to get back before talking to you, but it's getting late and it'll be time for Robert's nap soon."

Luis J had wandered in from his room only to get the tail end of the conversation. His ears perked up, but he didn't say anything. He grabbed some bacon, pancakes and scrambled eggs before taking a seat at the table to eat.

David continued, "Your mother and I love you guys more than anything, nothing will ever change that. But sometimes grownups have a breakdown in communication and when that happens, it makes it hard for them to be together. That's what's happening between me and your mother."

"Are you getting a divorce?"

"No, Chell, we aren't getting a divorce. I love your mother and she loves me. We just need some time apart to sort things out so that we can come together and be civil. Right now we can't hear each other. I'm going to stay with Uncle Marvin for a little while."

"You're leaving us, just like Papi," Chell said, her voice lowering as tears began falling down her cheek.

"No, Chell, I'm not. This is very different. I will come see you every day and we can do things together on the weekends. It won't be for long, I promise."

"Chell, why are you crying?" Robert asked. "Daddy can't hear Mommie right now and she can't hear him so he's going away until they get better. That's all."

"That's not all. He's leaving us."

"No, baby, I'm not leaving you. I would never do that. It's like Robert said, I'm going away until we can do a better job listening to each other. Right now we're just talking at each other."

"Luis J, isn't that what you said Papi told us?" Chell asked.

David did not give Luis J time to respond. "Chell, this situation is completely different. I'll be back. I'll call you or see you guys every day."

"Can I go with you?" Robert whined, tears beginning to build in his eyes, too.

"No, not this time Robert," David said, hugging him. He then directed his comments to Luis J. "I need to know you will help your Mother with everything while I'm gone. She needs you to be strong and responsible."

"Sure, I'll do what I need to. But what's wrong with her? Is it Carlos?"

Just then Diane walked in and Robert leaped from his father's lap and ran to confront his mother.

"Mommie, Daddy's going away and I can't go with him because he can't hear you and you can't hear him. Why?" He was now completely in tears and reaching up for his mother's comforting embrace.

Diane bent down and picked him up. "Luis J, take Chell and Robert outside so David and I can talk."

"This affects all of us, Mami. Why shouldn't we stay?" Luis J asked.

"Because I determine what does and doesn't involve you and this conversation has nothing to do with you."

Luis J didn't say anything else. He took Robert from her arms and the three of them prepared to leave. David watched them get ready and was in complete disagreement with Diane. Luis J was right, this very much affected them, especially Robert, who was now sucking his thumb. They should be allowed to stay. David could not understand why Diane couldn't see that.

Once they were out of the apartment, Diane said, "You couldn't wait until I got back to tell them you were leaving?"

"You have some nerve. You left without saying a word to me. Where did you go?"

"I had some errands to run," she shot back, taking a seat at the table.

"That doesn't tell me where you went."

"What does it matter, David?"

"It matters because you're my wife and I asked you." David hoped Diane could tell this wasn't a joke to him. The last time she left on a Saturday morning, it was to go to see Luis.

"I went to the cleaners to drop off some clothes and then to the gym. They have a cycle class on Saturdays that I like to take and haven't in a long time. I went to work off some tension. Is that okay with you?" she asked, giving him that look. She was pretty sure he knew what she meant. When he didn't answer, she added, "I knew you had slept on the sofa, but I didn't know you had really decided to leave, so why would I have stayed?"

"The way you talked to me last night didn't really leave me a choice. You told me to go. In so many words you said that you no longer need me. I'm going to stay with Marvin. I told you last night that we aren't working. But I don't want to punish the kids so I told them I'd call or come by every day and we could do things together on the weekend, as a family."

"Oh, you needn't feel obligated; they're used to fathers running…"

"Don't you dare finish that sentence. Damn it, Diane, do you just look for things to say to piss me off? That's hitting below the belt and so wrong. I'm not Luis. Hell, Luis didn't run off either. I love those kids as if they were my own. I've never hurt you, but you're treating me like the enemy and I'll be damned if I'll allow that. This is what you do best. You get on the offensive and attack just to keep from feeling. Keep it up and you will run me away. I was just giving us some space. But this, this is what pushes a man away for good."

"When are you leaving?"

"This afternoon, after I take Chell to the mall."

"She can't go."

"Why not?"

"I need her to watch Robert."

"Why can't you watch him? Where are you going now?"

"I'm not going anywhere. I just need some down time."

"Then let Luis J watch him. Chell cooked breakfast this morning. She needs time to be a child."

"She's a child every day. I don't want her spending money at the mall right now. Besides, she has a project due on Monday and I don't want her up all night tomorrow working on it."

Completely frustrated, David said, "I'll call you tonight." He honestly couldn't believe it had come to this. He had vowed to love and protect Diane, but she was making it extremely difficult. He remembered how she had leaned on him when she found out about Luis' affair. She was so vulnerable yet she had opened up and allowed him to be her rock. It made him feel good to have someone so beautiful need him.

He wondered now if she had found someone else to be that for her. Was she now telling this new person all of her feelings about this husband? It was easier to start over than to go through the fire. 'No, she wouldn't do that,' he thought. He stopped his mind from wandering and concluded that she just needed some time to deal with all these issues, alone, and then she would welcome him back into her life. He'd give her a couple of weeks.

Chapter Thirteen

Thanksgiving was Diane's favorite holiday but this one started off completely wrong. David was supposed to be there by nine to watch the parade with Robert but he didn't arrive until a little after noon. Every year Robert watched the parade with his father, culminating in seeing Santa Claus and launching the Christmas season. Robert began crying exactly at eleven o'clock and didn't stop until his father opened the door at twelve-ten.

Diane knew that Robert's reaction to the parade was exacerbated by the separation. He was not adjusting to it well at all. Every evening he found some reason to delay going to bed, causing Diane to raise her voice and threaten a spanking. The least little disappointment he experienced resulted in a temper tantrum that reminded everyone of his terrible twos.

By the time David arrived, Diane was beyond frustration and she pounced on him with both feet. She opened the door, still holding Robert and trying to quiet him. Before David was able to put a foot in the door, she said to him, "Take him."

David reached for Robert and pulled him out of her arms. He began with an apology really meant for Diane, but he directed it to Robert saying, "Robert, I'm so sorry. The traffic coming from Uncle Marvin's was so bad. There was an accident and they had to close the highway.

By the time I was able to get off to take the side streets, I had been sitting still for over two hours. Do you understand? Can you forgive me?"

Robert didn't respond, he just buried his head into his father's chest, but his sobbing was starting to subside. David hugged him even tighter, looking at Diane to see if she was going to accept his explanation and apology, too.

She turned away, refusing to give him an inch, and returned to the kitchen to continue preparing dinner. With each slice of the knife into the onions and then green peppers, she hoped she could release some of her tension.

Thanksgiving dinner was a time when she got to be the daughter to her mother she always wanted to be. It was a family tradition that she continued in her marriage to Luis. She always prepared the same meal: oven roasted stuffed turkey, candied sweet potatoes that filled the room with such an enticing aroma, dinner rolls, wild rice, collard greens, and last but not least, cranberry sauce made from fresh cranberries. The kids and Luis loved her cooking, as did David, and it was one time each year the spirit of love and family filled every part of their home.

She looked over at David and her son, who was now feeling better and telling David about the parade, and sighed. She was relieved that he finally seemed to have fully recovered from his traumatic morning. Diane shook her head from side to side, annoyed by her son's exaggerated behavior before returning her attention to the cutting board. She was now working on the button mushrooms. All of the ingredients had to be cut just right to keep the stuffing from being too crunchy.

Once Robert climbed out of his father's lap and began watching cartoons, David joined Diane in the kitchen to offer his assistance, but she gave him a cold shoulder. He offered a few comments about looking forward to enjoying her cooking but her mind drifted to different times.

She was remembering her first Thanksgiving without Luis. She had asked him not to come over or call as further punishment for his actions and betrayal. What she hadn't anticipated was Chell, Luis J and Carlos' moping around the entire day, leaping for the phone every time it rang. She had gone out of her way to try to fill the void of his absence during the day and at the dinner table, but to her disappointment, there was nothing she could do to replace the love and affection of their father. She vowed that evening after the food had been put away and the house was quiet that she and her children would never spend another Thanksgiving feeling that empty and alone.

By two, everything was ready, right on schedule as she had planned, except for the dessert. She had miscalculated how much brown sugar she needed for the sweet potatoes and was now short a few cups for the apple pie. It was Carlos' favorite and he had made a special request for it.

When Carlos arrived around three, Diane asked him and Luis J to go to the store. It had started raining so she couldn't send Chell and she wouldn't ask David – to give him any sense that she had forgiven him. An hour later, the door finally opened and her sons came in laughing and carrying the bag. It was soaking wet. Diane was beside herself. Didn't they know what happened to wet sugar?

"What the hell took you so long?" she hissed, steaming.

The laugher stopped and Luis J handed her the bag saying defensively, "Were we gone that long? We didn't know you needed it right away. Sorry."

"That's not an answer to my question. Where were you?"

"We stopped by the center and shot some hoops on the court. Honestly, we didn't know you were waiting for us to bring it right back. You could have said come right back, I need it," Carlos responded.

Diane used to admire how Carlos always ran interference for Luis J. He had done it when they broke something or weren't following her instructions. Today, she didn't care about the reason; she was just annoyed with all of the men in the house.

"That's because both of you are so selfish and inconsiderate. I didn't raise either of you to be that way."

"Diane, come on, it's not that serious," David interjected.

"How can you say that this isn't serious? Because it took them so long, we won't be able to eat until six. What makes any of you think I want to be cooking all day? I asked you to do one simple thing and you couldn't even do that. You stood here last week talking about how you are a man – well your actions today were like a boy's. Would you make your son wait for his formula while you shot hoops?"

Luis J's eyes shifted from his mother to Carlos, not sure how he would respond and where this would ultimately lead. Sitting on the couch, Chell also turned to see what would happen next. Carlos was about to respond, but David said, "Diane, stop it. Don't take this out on them when we both know you're mad at me."

"I'm not taking anything out on them. I'm disciplining their actions. I just wish someone would consider my feelings for a change."

"You're making it hard to do that, but tell us how can we help. You don't have to do this all on your own," David continued.

"Oh, forget it. The whole day is ruined." Diane threw the towel into the sink and stormed out of the kitchen.

Luis J and Carlos left the kitchen so they could talk. "What's going on with her now? Honestly, I would get out of here but I know you would be the one to catch hell," Carlos said.

"It started when Robert started crying, cried for an hour, and David got here late. She's barely said two words to any of us."

"Seriously? Why does everything have to be such a big deal with her? Did you hear what she said to me, as if I would do something like that to my son? I wish I had just gone to Papi's."

"You can say that again. I hope she calms down soon." Luis J thought about what the rest of the evening would entail if she didn't. Then he shifted the subject, "So are you ready for your trip?"

"Sí. I leave tomorrow morning. Got my passport and ticket and I'm packed and ready-to-go, man. I'm excited, but a little nervous, too."

"You do know you don't need a passport, right? Anyway, I wish I could go with you, especially now."

"I know. Next trip. I have a feeling I'll be going back and forth quite often if this all works out. Bro, here's a set of keys I had made for you to my place. Can you go by there and check on things for me while I'm gone?"

"No, shit? Yes, yes of course!" Luis J said, grinning from ear to ear.

Carlos hadn't seen that much twinkle in his eyes for a long time. "Now, look, no parties and shit. I don't want people going through all my things."

"Can I take someone by there, though? That would be so awesome."

"Don't mess up my place, man, or I'm gonna kick your ass."

"Don't worry; you won't even know I was there."

Carlos looked around Luis J's bedroom, clothes on the chair, books on the floor, and shook his head. "I doubt that."

They continued talking until David asked everyone to come into the kitchen. He wanted to figure out what was required to finish the meal. Chell told them the only item remaining was the pie, but she didn't remember how to make it. She had watched her mother do it before, but still hadn't actually been given the chance to do it on her own.

So David sent Carlos to the store, again, to purchase an apple pie and ice cream as a substitute. He also asked him to purchase a floral arrangement that had some daisies in it for Diane. After about an hour, everything was finished and nicely displayed on the table. David took the flowers and handed them to a reluctant Diane, stole a kiss on her cheek, and announced that dinner was ready. He then walked away.

When she entered the kitchen, the candles were lit, Christmas music was playing, and everyone was standing around the table waiting for her. The scene brought tears to her eyes and should have made all the events of the day miniscule compared to this moment, but she couldn't sweep them aside.

She was very disappointed by David's leaving her and the fact that she could be staring at her second failed marriage. It didn't matter that she had told him to leave. She was still pissed about Robert's crying all morning, and the boys' hour-long trip to the grocery store. And, she didn't really want Carlos to go to Puerto Rico and probably end up being saddled with a wife and child. She had hoped her children would have better experiences with their lives, but so far, it was not shaping up that way. For goodness sakes, she was already a grandmother and she wasn't even fifty yet. She had put it out of her mind when Luisa left, but now Carlos was about to make it a reality for her all over again.

Following her cue, the family basically ate in silence with the exception of appreciative chewing sounds and Robert's occasional comments. Everyone took their lead from Diane and she was not willing or able to engage anyone at this point.

Feeling fed up, Carlos broke the silence finally. "Mami, I was hoping to spend a pleasant evening laughing and talking with my family today. It is unfortunate you felt the need to be so angry; you set the tone for everyone. I hope you can snap out of it. But anyway, my flight leaves early tomorrow morning. I'll help clean up and then I have to go. I'll give you guys a call when I get to NaNa's and get settled." He got up and cleared his plate then began putting food away.

"Carlos, don't bother. Chell and Luis J can handle it. You can go ahead and leave now, so you're ready for this trip. Call me as soon as you get to NaNa's house, not once you get settled."

"I will. Are you sure you don't want me to help? I really hate to leave all of this for Luis J and Chell …"

"Carlos, it's okay man, really," David interjected. "I'll stay and help clean up and then I'll get Robert ready for bed. Thanks guys for pitching in and making it a really nice Thanksgiving dinner. Your mother is not angry with you. She's just had a long day."

That was the last thing Diane heard as she rose from the table, taking her glass of wine and returning to the bedroom.

CHAPTER FOURTEEN

Carlos rose at 5:30 am to make sure that he had everything he needed for his trip, especially his brush. He had packed days ago but spent a few minutes that morning double checking the contents to ensure that he had everything. With suitcase in hand, he stood by the door and took one final sweep of the apartment. He hoped that his brother would take care of his place. With that final thought, Carlos closed and locked the door and headed to the street.

Black Friday was always crazy in his neighborhood as people rushed to catch the early bird specials. It was now almost seven and the line was already wrapped around the block for the clothing store on the corner. He saw some people exiting a cab and rushed to grab it. As the driver sped down Conduit Blvd., weaving in between the cars, Carlos tried to come to grips with his emotions.

He was about to leave home for the very first time, but more importantly, he was about to meet his son. His heart raced at the thought of the life he had created but had never seen. He shifted around in the seat, impatiently waiting to get to Kennedy airport. The cab driver was complaining about the crowds on the roadway and how although it was one of his best fare days, he hated how the normal pushing and shoving seemed to be amplified on this day.

Carlos was aware of his comments but wasn't really engaged in the conversation. He was reflecting on his own conversation with his father last evening after returning home from his mother's. Papi had wished him well and given him words of encouragement that he knew he could rely on during the trip. Carlos had wondered how his father felt spending another Thanksgiving without his children. He couldn't imagine. The last two years had killed Carlos inside over a son whom he had never met, and he was hoping never to spend another holiday away from his son again.

To his relief, the airport was not crowded. That would enable him to breeze through security and have time to relax before the flight. He assumed that most people had traveled on Wednesday and were now feeling like stuffed pigs the morning after their Thanksgiving feasts. When he got to the gate, there weren't many people waiting for the flight and he hoped that meant he would be able to stretch out on the plane.

Once he was settled in his seat and they were airborne, Carlos began listening to his favorite genre on the airplane radio and thumbed through the magazine he found in the backseat compartment under his tray. The plane was mostly empty, so Carlos did have the luxury of stretching out across all three seats in his row; he spread his things out so he could enjoy the flight.

The attendants were very attentive to him since they didn't have many people to cater to and they enjoyed Carlos' wit. One of them was flirting with him and gave him a beer, even though they were pretty sure he wasn't quite twenty-one. When he wasn't chatting with them, he was reading a Grisham book or working a crossword puzzle. After a couple of hours, his eyelids grew heavy and before long, he dozed off. The next thing he knew, the attendant was waking him to prepare for landing.

As soon as Carlos stepped out of the plane, the warm air greeted him on the jetway, embracing his body as if to say, "Welcome to San Juan." His immediate reaction was to begin shedding clothes. It was thirty-five degrees in New York when he left and it felt like it was eighty-five here. As he walked to the baggage claim area, he noticed how old the airport looked compared to JFK. As he passed the stores, he saw various shades of people and it reminded him of his family.

At the end of the hallway, near the baggage claim area, stood NaNa and Tía. He hadn't seen NaNa in over three years but she still looked the same. Her hair was pulled back in a ponytail like his mother's, but not as severe. A smile appeared on NaNa's face and she embraced him the same way as the air. They spoke to him solely in Spanish as they greeted him and asked about the family.

Tía was his father's youngest sister. Her given name was Angie, but all of her nieces and nephews called her Tía. She felt it was more endearing. Tía was short and had a tight build, similar to Maria. Her complexion was fair like her mother's and she had straight black hair cut short in a style that framed her face. But he could easily see how she and his father favored each other. She looked beautiful and had an air of confidence about her as she spoke and carried herself. Next, it was Tía's turn to kiss Carlos and welcome him to San Juan.

"You look so much like your father and it warms my heart," she said. "And, mijo, listen to your Spanish! I'm impressed not only with your speaking, but I love your accent. You sound like you were born and raised here. And to think, this is in spite of your mother's lack of interest in it."

NaNa expressed her displeasure with Tía's criticism of Diane by frowning at her. The look reminded Carlos of his father's glare. He smiled and nodded at NaNa to let her know that he understood. "It's true NaNa, my mother does shy away from what is unfamiliar."

Tía continued chatting with him in Spanish as they collected his luggage and headed to her car. It was parked near the doorway in a no parking zone and standing next to it was an officer with a pad in hand.

"Oh no, you are about to get a ticket," Carlos said, slipping back into English. Living in Brooklyn, you had to take great precaution to avoid being ticketed and towed for parking violations. But it looked like she hadn't even tried to park legally.

"Not me, sweetie. He's a friend of mine. He allows me to park here whenever I have to pick up or drop off someone. It saves me time and money." As she approached the officer, Tía placed her hand in the center of his back, confirming a level of familiarity.

"Hey, Angie, will I see you later tonight?" he asked, opening her door.

"Oh Juan, I'm not sure. My nephew just arrived. But I'll call you. Thanks for watching the car." She winked at him as she got into the driver's seat and then blew him a kiss once he closed her door. It was quite obvious she, too, was a flirt.

As they drove, Carlos took note of his surroundings. The city was more developed than he had imagined; the streets were like a mini New York. He saw city project buildings just on the outskirts of town, which reminded him of Spanish Harlem. Some of the balconies had clothes hanging on the rails drying in the air and the curtains were red and white. There were also cars in the yards with hoods up while the owners worked to try to get a few more miles out of them. The traffic going into the city was heavy and Tía told him those were the people getting a jump start on their weekend activities.

She and NaNa pointed out Isla Verde, where they have cockfights on the weekends, and the five-star hotels located along the coast of the Atlantic Ocean. They told him about the various attractions either in or along the way to Old San Juan. They shared stories about a few of the well-known attractions like the old fort, the rain forest, and the Normandie Hotel, shaped like an ocean liner. Unfortunately, they were all in the opposite direction, but Tía promised to show him around when and if he had the time. They were clear why he was there and that was the priority of this trip.

NaNa still lived in Loiza, right on the ocean in the countryside. Her home was moderately sized and cozy. Of the three bedrooms, Tía's was near the front door and NaNa's was in the back of the house. Uncle Bobby was the only other child of NaNa's who lived in Puerto Rico, but he had an apartment in the city.

NaNa took Carlos' hand and told him, "You're at home. Take a few minutes to get settled before dinner. Let us know if you need anything."

Carlos was staying in the room where his father slept whenever he visited, and inside, there were pictures of Carlos and his siblings. The only child who was not displayed was Robert. Just another reminder to Carlos of the importance of this trip that was long overdue. He called to tell his mother that he had arrived safely, but she wasn't home. In a way, he was relieved given how she had acted yesterday.

Chell told him that Luis J was planning to spend the weekend in his apartment. Carlos wasn't sure how he felt about that, but knew that he had given him permission to visit, so all he could do was hope for the best or kick his ass when he got back. Papi was not home either but Maria said she would relay Carlos' message and wished him luck again.

Carlos couldn't wait for dinner. His grandmother made abrazo with seafood and sweet plantains. Abrazo was like a soup or stew with rice, vegetables and meat. NaNa liked seafood so she almost always made hers that way. Carlos loved his grandmother's cooking, which was flavored with a lot of spices. While Maria's cooking was very close and he had enjoyed it a lot when he lived there, it was not NaNa's.

After dinner, NaNa and Tía invited Carlos to join them on the back porch, with the sounds of the ocean's waves in the background. They sipped on a shot of Bacardi rum while Carlos drank a Medalla. Carlos shared his plans with them in more detail, reiterating that he was going to take things one day at a time.

He had asked Luisa's mother to tell her of his trip and hoped that Luisa would be receptive. He appreciated NaNa's reminder that patience was important and so was listening. They sat in silence a while longer and then NaNa said she was turning in for the night.

Once her mother was in her room, Tía said, "So, I'm headed into town. Would you like to come?"

"Not tonight; I need to call Luisa and see what time I can stop by. Once I do that, I'm going to turn in early. Besides, if you're going to hook up with, what's his name, Juan, I'd be a third wheel." Chuckling, he added, "Rain check?"

"Sure," she said, smiling. She hadn't made up her mind yet if Juan was going to entertain her or someone else. "Hey, leave me a note so I know what time you want to go over there in the morning."

Carlos thanked her and went into the house to call Luisa. The phone seemed to ring fifty times, but he knew it was only the third ring when it was finally answered.

"Hola."

"Luisa?"

"Sí?"

"Luisa, it's me, Carlos!" There was silence on the other end.

"Luisa, are you there?"

"Sí. Yes, hi Carlos. How are you?"

"Not bad. Didn't your mother tell you I would be calling?"

"No, but my NaNa did. Where are you? Are you here now?"

"Yes, I'm in Loiza at my abuela's. How are you and our son?"

"We're good, but I have to be honest with you, I'm surprised you're here."

"I imagine you are, but I am and we need to talk. May I come see you tomorrow?"

"I guess. CJ gets up early, so if you want you can come around eight."

"No te preocupes, I'll be there. It's good to hear your voice."

"You still say that?" she said, smiling. "You, too."

"Oh, I better get your address!"

"Your NaNa knows."

"She does?"

"Yes, she does. Hasta mañana."

Carlos returned to the porch to sit a little longer, smoke a cigarette, and drain what was left of his beer. Tía had left already, so he took this time just to chill. It was quiet except for the songs of the night crickets. He was so relaxed he felt himself dozing off, so he rose and headed to his room.

He placed the gifts he had brought for Luisa and CJ on the dresser so he wouldn't forget them. Once undressed, he laid on the bed under the fan, trying to adjust to the humidity and rehearsing what he would say to the mother of his child, until fatigue finally overcame him and he drifted off to sleep.

The morning awoke him, filling his lungs with ocean air and the smell of fish frying. Carlos had left the windows open and could hear the waves rolling onto the shore. His senses were overwhelmed with everything and he loved how good it made him feel. His body was tingling and he felt alive. He could get used to waking up to this every morning. But he had to get back to New York and get on with his life, so he didn't linger over breakfast and was showered, dressed and ready to go see Luisa and his son by seven-thirty.

As he rode in the car with the windows down, he continued to observe what a beautiful land Puerto Rico was. There were street vendors already out, working to make their earnings for the day. The food smelled amazing, making his mouth water; he wished they had time to stop and allow him to experience his heritage. Tía told him the vendors were cooking plantains, fish and pork. He vowed to make time to eat some before he left.

Carlos found himself wishing that Luis J could have come with him. 'This is what he needs to experience to give him a sense of who he is and where he comes from,' he thought. It felt good to see the land where his father and grandfather were born. His pride in his heritage grew even deeper than he ever imagined. The rhythm of the music and the language drew him in years ago and now he understood why. He was one with this ethnicity, with this part of his culture, and now he could share this experience with his own son and talk about it with his father.

They arrived at Luisa's grandparents' house, where the front yard was small but neat; the grass was well-groomed and decorated with a few toys strewn here and there. Obviously, a child lived here, his child, Carlos knew.

Tía was running to meet someone, so she just dropped Carlos off and sped away. As he walked to the door, he suddenly became unsure of how this would unfold. Would his son take to him? Would Luisa be open to shared custody? So many questions and scenarios flooded his mind. As he was standing in front of the door collecting his thoughts, it opened. There stood an elderly woman with a head full of gray hair. She was slightly overweight, about 5'3" in height, and she bore a strong resemblance to Luisa.

She, in turn, examined the young man standing in front of her and immediately knew who he was. Luisa had described his features quite accurately, but the resemblance to the carbon copy little boy who had been running around her house for the past two years was remarkable. The genes were very strong in the Rodriquez family. The facial features were very distinctive and undeniable, and they clearly weren't diluted in her great-grandchild.

Responding now to his smile, the woman at the door said, "Carlos, buenos días! Come in. Luisa's been waiting for you. I'm her abuela, Maria. You can call me NaNa M."

She turned her head slightly and called out for Luisa before continuing, "It's a pleasure to meet the father of my great-grandson. Please, come in. I was just on my way out, but make yourself at home."

Luisa appeared slightly behind her abuela and beckoned for him to follow her. As he did, he admired how amazing she still looked. It had been more than two years since they had last seen each other, and if he didn't know she had had a baby, he couldn't tell from her firm body. But there was now a maturity about her that hadn't existed at this level before. Clearly, she was a woman now. Carlos had no doubts about this trip and was now more than ever ready to finally meet his son.

"Have a seat. I'll get CJ," she said, feeling a little nervous about how this interaction would unfold.

"Luisa, wait before you get him, please, let's talk a minute. First of all, thank you for allowing me to see both of you. Secondly, I'm sorry for any pain you experienced as a result of all of this. I want you to know that I never abandoned you. When I came back to your house your father told me that I was not worthy of you and that he had sent you off and would not tell me where or how to contact you. In fact, he told me to never contact you again. It has caused me great suffering and I can only imagine what you must have felt and believed."

"Carlos, I should have known that you still cared. When I asked my father, he told me that after he had given you the number here, they hadn't seen or heard from you. He cancelled my cell phone and reminded me that my abuela was living on a fixed income, so I shouldn't use her phone to call the States. When you didn't call, I assumed you had made your choice and were going to go on with your life. After CJ was born, I mailed the picture to my mom and asked her to get it to you."

"She did. But your father lied. I asked him, I begged him, for your number or an address, but he refused to give it to me. All of this, Luisa, was out of our control. They had the power to keep us apart then. But it's finally over," he sighed, feeling relieved. "Oh, I almost forgot. I brought you something."

"You didn't have to, but thank you." She took the box from him and opened it. It was a necklace with her birthstone in the center. She removed it and turned for him to place it around her neck. "It's very nice. Thank you," she said, rubbing it as it lay against her chest.

"Carlos, as you said, it's over now. And, honestly, as your mother said, we were probably too young to really know what was best then. But life has been good. You have a beautiful son and he's smart, just like us. Sit tight and I'll go get him."

As she carried CJ in her arms back toward the living room, she noted Carlos' features. He had more facial hair now and had buffed up a little. He was hotter than she had remembered. She thought about how they used to sit and talk for hours. She had missed that so much. When she had learned of his plans to come, she had the biggest case of butterflies. After two years of hearing nothing, she had assumed her father was right and he didn't care, but here he was. That was the only gift she needed from him.

Carlos was trying to be patient as he awaited her return. When he finally saw her, she was holding CJ in her arms. He was squirming around, trying to get down. Tears came to Carlos' eyes as he reached for his son. CJ smiled and extended his arms back at Carlos, as though he already knew his father.

"Carlos, here's your son," Luisa said, allowing CJ to leave her arms.

"CJ, soy tu papá. Recuerdes? Te voy a mostrar fotos. Siempre te dije que iba a venir."

"PP," CJ replied, trying to imitate his mother while touching Carlos' face.

"Sí, mijo, Papi," Carlos said, holding him securely in his arms before turning to Luisa. "Baby, you told him I was coming? You showed him pictures of me? Thank you, Luisa. He feels so good in my arms. I didn't realize how much I loved him, until now. I'll never let him go. He looks so much like my father and Luis J now. It's amazing. At first he looked like Robert." Speechless and in search for words, Carlos paused and then asked, "Has he eaten?"

"Yeah, about an hour ago," Luisa laughed. "And yes he looks like your family. Everybody who sees him says, 'He must look like his father because we don't see any resemblance to you.' I never met your dad, but I can see Luis J and you in him. He has your temperament though. He's fine until he gets hungry," she said, laughing.

"Funny! Jokes so early in the morning!? I want to spend as much time as possible with him. Can we go to the beach or a park nearby? I don't have a car and really haven't quite figured out my way around anyway, but I want to take him out."

"Sure. Let me pack some things for him. Just like you, he loves the beach. There's one not too far from here."

Carlos reluctantly put him down so he could offer his help to Luisa. She declined and told him to play with CJ instead. CJ sat on the floor and played with his toys, handing different ones to his father as if to introduce Carlos to his world. Luisa watched Carlos give CJ the gift he had bought for him; it was a small basketball and hoop and a brush. A smaller version of the brush he used.

She heard Carlos say to him, "I know you're too young for this, but Papi wants you to have dreams. And I want you to learn early how to brush your hair. You will have some nice waves if you start early."

Luisa packed a bag for CJ and one for the two of them. They walked a little ways down the road, past a few homes, and found a path that led to the beach. CJ walked for a while before his legs got tired. He turned to Carlos and stretched out his arms. Instinctively, Carlos picked up his son and carried him effortlessly. They found a quiet spot on the beach, placed a blanket down, and let CJ play with his toys while they talked.

"So, Luisa, how are you, really? Tell me, talk to me. What's going on?"

"I'm okay, Carlos, really. I finished high school down here and I have a job at the Registrar's Office at the University of Puerto Rico in San Juan. I'm also taking classes there at night. My grandparents watch CJ for me. They have been very supportive. How about you?"

"I've been lost, quite honestly. When my mother refused to allow us to marry, I moved out. I went to stay with my father and his girlfriend. I graduated with a strong GPA, 3.8, but I never applied to any schools even though they recruited me. I could have gone anywhere, even attended my Dad's university, but I felt like a part of my life was missing and nothing seemed right to me. Truth be told, my mother had emasculated me. So I reacted by not going to school because that's what she wanted me to do.

"I took a job at FedEx, and before you say anything, I know that was not the plan, but they pay pretty well, they have decent benefits and I have the opportunity to move up. Anyway, I got my own place. I knew I would find you one day so I started saving for this trip."

"We're glad you're here. I'm so happy to see you. You're looking good," she said playfully, punching the muscle in his arm. "How's your family? Is Luis J still playing ball?"

"They're all fine. I rekindled my relationship with my father before you left because I consulted with him after my mom wouldn't support our request to get married. It's really strong now. Luis J is really good with his b-ball. He just might be good enough to go pro someday. Although, you know, I have to keep him grounded. My younger siblings are growing up and my mother, well, she hasn't changed."

He took a moment to imagine this before continuing, "So, tell me about my son. What does he like to do? What is his favorite food?" After a brief pause, he sympathetically asked, "How was the pregnancy for you? I wish I could have been here to help you through it all. I feel like I have a thousand questions."

"That's because knowing you, you probably do," she said, smiling. "You've-we've missed a lot in each other's lives. The pregnancy was uneventful. I gained a little weight, but it was mostly the baby. He was a big boy, so the delivery was very painful. But it was worth every bit of the pain when they placed him in my arms. I looked at his face and saw you. I missed you so much. I was so sad that you weren't there with me to share the experience. But every time I looked at him, you looked back at me and I found comfort in that.

"He's a good boy. He's twenty-one months old now. I can hardly believe it sometimes. He's growing up so fast. He picks up things quickly. We have got to be careful once he starts talking. He's very even-tempered, a lot like you. He rarely cries now, but everyone is warning me about the terrible twos, so that might change. He doesn't say much yet, but it won't be long now. I can tell he is going to have a lot to say once he starts. I love him so much. He hugs me and there's no feeling on earth that compares to how it makes me feel. Until I think about how I used to feel in your arms."

The consciousness of Carlos' pain returned. He had missed so much and he had wanted to be there for all of it. No woman should go through something like this without the support of a good man. He wondered now if she had filled that void in her life to help her then and now, like his mother had done. He dreaded asking the question but he needed to know what he was up against.

"Thank you for sharing that with me. Time is going by quickly. So…I have to ask, since I wasn't here…was someone else helping you through this? Is there anyone else in your life now?"

"That's a pretty personal question, don't you think?" Luisa replied.

"Yes, but I would still like an answer. I mean, don't we have it like that? Besides, I won't have my son calling anyone else Papi the way Robert does with David."

The waves were creating their own melody in the background and people were starting to venture out onto the beach; some were fishing, others just enjoying the view. Carlos wasn't sure what he would do with her response, but this was now his reality.

Luisa had seen a few guys, but she knew that wasn't what he was asking, so she responded, "No, there isn't anyone special. And I would never allow CJ to do that anyway. So now that you know my situation, what about you? Are you in a serious relationship with anyone?"

Now it was Carlos' turn to ease her fears. "I was dating someone, you know that's what men do…but she really was a placeholder. She knew I wasn't into her like she was into me, so I broke it off. We weren't headed in the same direction anyway."

"Good answer. I would hate for CJ to see his mother beat on his father," Luisa said, laughing.

He loved to see that smile and the way she threw her head back when she laughed. He was glad he could still make her laugh. They sat, talked and laughed for hours. CJ fell asleep in his father's arms and they talked some more.

Around four in the afternoon, Luisa suggested they head back to her home. CJ was exhausted, but Carlos had more energy than he had had in months. He stayed and they had dinner together and then he prepared his son for bed. CJ handed his favorite book to Carlos, which was in Spanish. CJ laughed when Carlos pretended to need help from Luisa with some of the words. Carlos kissed CJ goodnight and told him he would be back tomorrow.

Everything Luisa had said about his son was spot on. She had done a great job raising him, in spite of his absence. He was loved and that's what babies needed; that made them feel secure. He wondered now if that's why Robert bonded so much with David. Well, Carlos would make sure that he was the one adding to CJ's love and security, no one else. "Thank you, Luisa, again. Today was wonderful. If it's not too much to ask, may I come back tomorrow?"

"We go to church every Sunday at nine. We'll be home by eleven-thirty. You're welcome to join us for church if you can get a ride. Otherwise, you can come here around noon."

"I won't be able to get a ride because NaNa goes to church around the same time. I'll ask Tía if she can drop me off around noon on her way to work. Think of something else we can do."

"I will, but not outside. It's too hot."

"Really? I was so enjoying our time together I didn't even notice the heat. Good night, Luisa."

Luisa shook her head and, kissing the palm of her hand, blew him a goodnight kiss as he got into Tía's car. When Carlos and Tía returned to the house, NaNa was sitting on the porch reading a book. She wanted to hear all about his day and his first experience with his son. Tía brought him a cold one before joining them on the porch. Carlos couldn't stop talking about it. He relived every aspect of the day, smiling about the times CJ held them a captive audience and tried to explain how complete he felt when holding CJ in his arms.

"Carlos, you remind me a lot of your grandfather. He was the love of my life and a very determined man. He would set his mind to something and no one could talk him out of it. That's a good trait, but it has to be balanced. Not to be confused with stubbornness, which can blind you. Make sure you take this slowly. The two of you have a lot to discuss and you will need to make choices that are right for everyone involved, especially your son."

"I will, NaNa. I don't know what will be the outcome at the end of this trip, but I know that I will no longer be absent in my son's life. He needs me in his life and I need him in mine."

"I understand that and I'm not saying that you shouldn't. I'm just saying that your son has been living here for almost two years with his great-grandparents and he doesn't know you or New York or your parents. As a matter of fact, he doesn't know Luisa's parents, either. They haven't even been here to see her."

"How do you know that?"

"Because Luisa and I see each other frequently and she told me. She reached out to me with the help of her grandparents once she had the baby and wanted me to know that I could be a part of CJ's life, if I wanted. I have spent quite a bit of time with him and her. She is a beautiful young lady and very intelligent. I can see why you two were together. You have similar interests."

Carlos didn't know how he felt about this revelation. He had been looking for them and wondering how they were coping and now he was finding out that NaNa had known where they were since CJ was born.

"NaNa, I don't understand. Why didn't you tell me? You know I've been looking for her, for my son." Carlos recalled Luisa's comment and thought to himself, 'So that's what Luisa meant the other night when she said, 'Your Nana knows.'

"I couldn't mijo; it wasn't my place. The two of you needed to work that out, and I knew you would if it was meant to be. It warmed my heart when you called to tell me of your plans. I share this with you now so that you know I will help you in any way I can and that you have an ear, anytime."

NaNa was right. It wasn't her place to interfere. After a brief moment, he said, "NaNa, I'm glad that you have been a part of my son's life when I wasn't allowed to be." They talked for a little longer before Carlos confirmed his plans for Sunday and turned in. He wanted to be rested and full of energy for his CJ.

The next morning, Carlos joined NaNa at church and to his surprise, he saw Luisa, NaNa M and CJ sitting in the pew. They all sat together, with CJ sitting snuggly and safely between Luisa and Carlos.

After church, Luisa came by to pick up Carlos from his NaNa's. When they arrived, CJ released Luisa's hand and ran right into NaNa's arms, giving her a kiss. Carlos smiled at this scene and then reached for his son, ready for his turn. But to his disappointment, CJ pulled back, remaining securely in NaNa's arms. Carlos was surprised by this action after all the time they had spent together yesterday and just an hour ago.

Luisa noticed CJ's reaction and moved to stand next to Carlos. She hugged and kissed Carlos on the cheek as if to remind CJ of who Carlos was to them. But CJ remained in NaNa's arms until it was time for them to leave.

Once Luisa placed CJ into his car seat, it wasn't long before he fell asleep. "Carlos, don't take his reaction personally. He gets cranky when he's tired and he loves being held by a woman. I guess he's starting early. Besides, he knows her."

Carlos chuckled and remembered the conversation with NaNa. This was what she was referring to, having patience. He responded with, "It's alright. I understand. So, where are we going today?"

"I thought we could drive around downtown and you can see the sights and learn about some of the history. On Sundays there's a market where they have a lot of nice artwork to see and purchase. Does Chell still like art? I remember how much time we used to spend at the art museum. Do you still go?"

"No, I haven't been since you left and yes, Chell still likes it."

"Around lunch time, we'll go to this park for children that I take CJ to sometimes. Oh, look, see that fort over there? That's where the soldiers would fight off the pirates who tried to invade the island; the Spanish fought off the U.S. and the U.S. fought off Germany in World War II. You can actually see part of the enemy artillery which pierced the wall from one of those battles. And those lookout towers are accessible too. Maybe we can go one day while you're here, if there's time." There was a sadness in her tone because she realized the day would come when Carlos would have to leave.

"We'll make time, if that's what you want to do. But let's not worry about that now. Let's stay in the moment and enjoy all that it has to offer."

Luisa looked at Carlos with so much love, remembering why she had fallen for him what now seemed so long ago. She spoke softly, "Yes, you're right, the moment is now."

As they continued driving around, Luisa pointed out other historical landmarks like the cathedrals, the world's smallest house and the home of the first female governor. They found a parking space near the children's park. It was built as a tribute to the governor because she felt that the children were the leaders of tomorrow and wanted to give them a space to use their imaginations and enjoy life.

They let CJ play in the sandbox and pushed him in the swings. After a while, they sat on the park bench and fed him a pudding snack. It gave Carlos the opportunity to ask, "Did you breastfeed?"

She laughed, "Are you kidding? My grandmother wouldn't have it any other way. I still have milk. He gets a little at night now and sometimes in the morning."

"A man after my own heart," Carlos said, through laughter. But it made him remember her sweetness and long for some now.

"Really? Did you just say that?" she asked, smirking.

Placing CJ in the stroller, they walked down the narrow streets toward the market. The houses in this area were all narrow and the exteriors preserved. The government would not allow the exterior to be altered and even mandated what colors they could be painted. Some of the doorways were open as they passed and Carlos noticed the courtyards were enormous. Luisa told him that the houses were large on the inside and quite ornate. She had a few friends from school who lived in the area.

Carlos observed that the artwork in the square was really unique. The patterns and colors were often bright and bold, representative of the heritage. It was just like the research he had done in ninth grade. He purchased a few items he thought Chell would like and a small vase for his mother.

Next, they walked to the African museum. As they viewed the scenes and read the narratives, Carlos learned even more about the Africans' journey to Puerto Rico and understood just how strong the miscegenation of the races really was.

He smiled when he read how the African drumbeat permeated throughout the Latino music and the hip movements were visible in the salsa and merengue dances. By the time they left the museum, they couldn't believe it was already five. They were the last visitors and the curators were ready to go.

"Are you busy tonight?" Luisa asked.

"No. Qué pasa?"

"Some Sundays they have music along the waterfront and tonight is one of those nights. A lot of people come out and mingle, some even dance. I thought you might like it. There are street vendors, too, who make pinchos – they're like pork kabobs – and piragua, which is a shaved ice dessert, and we wash it down with coquito to help it digest!"

Papi had made coquito for him one evening. It was very rich, almost like the homemade eggnog his mother made from her father's Jamaican heritage. It was sometimes spiced with rum. Papi would drink it as an after-dinner drink during the holidays. But it really had a mean punch! He would let them stick their finger in it before putting them to bed. He could still remember how he loved those evenings.

"Sounds like fun. But what about CJ, won't it be too late for him?"

"My abuela will keep him, if you want to go."

"Sure, that would be nice."

By the time they returned to the pier that evening, it was really crowded. The ages of the people there ranged from five to seventy-five. Music was blaring and there were groups dancing while others were talking and laughing. It was a time for reconnecting with one another, and that is what he and Luisa were trying to do. They sat on a park bench in silence for a while, viewing the crowd.

"I have really had fun with you and CJ. Thank you for doing such a great job raising him."

"He's really not a difficult child. I have seen some ill-behaved kids." Luisa smiled as she thought of some of her cousins.

"How are things with your parents, now that you have had CJ?" Carlos asked.

"My mother talks to my abuela pretty regularly, but I haven't had much to say to either of them since they only have negative things to say to me. I have disgraced my father and he will never accept me into his home or life again."

Carlos placed his arms around her and pulled her to him, saying, "I'm so sorry, but you can put all of that behind you now. You can get your support from me."

She didn't resist and moving closer to him, she placed her head on his shoulder. It was an act that brought both of them great comfort.

"Don't be sorry. I have no regrets about us Carlos, only that my parents are missing the joy of their grandson. I love our son. He is a blessing from God and reminds me of the love we shared."

"Shared?"

"I didn't think present tense was appropriate. Is it?"

Carlos lifted her head by the chin and kissed her passionately, without warning, and she allowed him to. He pulled back when he heard someone calling his name.

"Carlos, qué pasa man? I thought that was you, although it was hard to see your face since it was buried in hers."

"Tío Bobby! Nada. Qué pasa?" Carlos rose from the bench, clasped hands and embraced his uncle. Carlos had not seen him for several years, but Bobby's features hadn't changed and the Rodriquez genes were strong. He was about 5'7", medium complexion and physically fit. His build was similar to Papi's, but he was shorter. It reminded Carlos of the contrast between him and Luis J's build.

"Drop that uncle shit, man; you're way too old to call me that. Angie told me you were here. I was hoping to get a chance to see you. So, is this your girl?"

"This is Luisa, the mother of my son."

"Sweet! It's nice to meet you," Bobby said, kissing the back of her hand. "So what are you guys doing later? I'm on my way to my girl's place."

"We hadn't really talked about it," Carlos responded.

"Yeah, well, I know my mother and she isn't going to allow you to be together there, if you know what I mean." He nudged Carlos and winked at him. "I stay in town if you decide you want some alone time or just wanna chill."

"Thanks, man, but we're cool," Carlos shot back, somewhat embarrassed by his uncle's assumption. He also wondered what Luisa thought of the exchange. When he glanced at her she was watching the dancers but he noticed she was blushing.

"Alright, your call, but take my number in case you change your mind. After all, she's beautiful and I know your genes. Speaking of, how's the family? I owe your dad a call."

"Everyone's well."

"Great. Will we have a chance to kick it before you leave?"

"I don't know; I'm only here for a few more days and my son is my priority."

"Got it. I'm easy. Just let me know. Hasta luego! I'll catch you later."

Luisa and Carlos chuckled as Bobby strolled away. As he passed groups in the square, he would stop and chat for a short while. His popularity also reminded Carlos of Luis J. As Carlos watched him fade out of sight, he thought, 'There was definitely truth in Bobby's statement.' All of his feelings for Luisa were returning.

They salsa danced a little and Luisa was impressed with Carlos' moves. He was pretty impressed with hers, too. She had been practicing since she left New York. They bought some of the food she had mentioned and washed it down with soda. She wasn't drinking since she was still breast feeding, but Carlos wasn't about to pass up the opportunity to have some coquito. It went down smoothly, just like Papi's. He was feeling real good, but it was getting late, so they headed back to NaNa's home.

Carlos wasn't able to spend as much time on Monday with Luisa and CJ because of her job and classes. But she arranged to pick him up on her way home so he could feed CJ and get him ready for bed. That evening they sat on Luisa's porch and talked about each other's day. He had taken a tour of the fort and spent the day walking around the town. She had her favorite schedule on Mondays, English Literature and Organizational Psychology.

Tuesday they followed the same routine except that night, Carlos asked Luisa if he could take her out to dinner once they put CJ to bed. They chose a restaurant near her home since he still didn't have transportation and they didn't want to be out too late. She took him to one of her favorite spots that had more good food and nice music. Carlos was feeling the effect of all this food and knew that tomorrow his morning would start with a run on the beach.

After they ate, they walked to the beach, hand in hand, laughing, talking, teasing each other and catching up. The air at night cooled off the remnants of the day's heat. It had been eighty-five to ninety degrees since he arrived.

Carlos found that he loved being on the ocean, especially at night. The moonlight was so bright it provided them with a clear path to the beach and enabled him to admire her features even in the dark of the night. She was still the beautiful young girl he adored from afar. She stood with her back to the beach and the stars in the sky framed her face. The stars were brighter and the sky clearer than he had ever seen them in New York City.

Carlos wanted, needed, to share his feelings with Luisa and he hoped she was feeling the same way. "Luisa, I've been thinking how these past few days have been wonderful and I don't want it to end."

"I know. I'm so glad that CJ took to you. I knew he would. I think he really knows you're his father. It's going to be hard on him when you leave. Me, too, honestly."

Without hesitation, he replied, "Why does it have to be? Two years ago, I asked you to marry me and you said yes. Unfortunately, my mother didn't approve. And your parents shipped you off. I don't need her approval now, but I do need my son. And your parents have shut you out of their life, but you don't need their approval either."

"Carlos..."

"No, hear me out. I came down here intending to ask you if we could work out some kind of joint custody arrangement. But after spending this time with our son and you, I realize that I want more. Being with you has rekindled all the emotions that I had suppressed just to cope. What I didn't know until now is that it is love that I feel for you. I want us to be together."

He paused and then continued, "Now, I know how you are; you want the details and you don't do things without a plan. I have some money saved and I'm planning to enroll in college this spring. I received word of a promotion to evening manager on my job right before I left and in addition to a twenty-five percent salary increase, this position will reimburse me for any job-related courses I take. I'll have to take business management courses even though you know my first love. But this is a means to an end. I will, eventually, follow in my father's footsteps and teach. Anyway, Luisa, do you understand what I'm saying? We can figure out the rest of the details together. I just know that I want us to be together and raise our son. It's going to be challenging, I know, but we can do it if we work together."

"You said you loved me, but...are you in love with me?" Luisa asked, apprehensive about his response.

Confused by her question because he thought that he had just told her he loved her, Carlos said, "I didn't realize how much until I saw you again and especially watched you with CJ. I know that my life hasn't been the same without you in it these past two years. I accept that you may not feel the same way, but I'll be patient and work hard to win your heart, again."

"I heard you Carlos, you said that you love me. I love my parents, I love our son, but a couple that has to face what we're looking at has to also be in love. So are you in love with me, Carlos?"

"Why are you asking me that?"

"I'm saying that my research about divorced families showed that it was usually because the parents lacked real stamina that they got divorced. They loved each other and were in heat with each other, but the glue of being in love was missing."

"Right, your research. I remember the paper. Luisa, come back to the States with me and marry me. I will spend my lifetime demonstrating my love, and showing you what being in love with you feels like."

"That wasn't a question. Aren't proposals supposed to be in the form of a question?" she asked, chuckling.

"Right. I was getting around to that. Luisa, will you and CJ marry me?"

"You're so silly. Yes!"

"Seriously?"

"Si. It's what I've always wanted. I was wondering what was taking you so long to ask me again. After all, you've been here what, three, four days?"

He kissed her and found her mouth warm and inviting. He now wished Bobby's offer from the other night was an option for tonight. When their lips parted, to his surprise and pleasure, she asked him to come back to her house and spend the night.

"My grandparents are a lot more open minded about these things, which is a little backwards, but they don't live by all the same old traditions as my father and his family. Besides, we already have a son, what's the worst that could happen now?"

"Luisa, if we're going to do this, we have to be careful. I mean if we're going to be adults, parents to our son, we can't be reckless or careless. No more surprise babies. For now, one is enough."

"You're right. It's just been so long. I haven't been with anyone since you."

"Really?"

"Really. And I want to be with you. Besides, when we wake up tomorrow, I won't have to go anywhere. I don't have class or work on Wednesdays so we can discuss just how we can make this work."

They walked back to her home, Carlos' arm around her shoulder, claiming to shield her from the coolness in the air, but really he was holding her close so he wouldn't risk losing her ever again. He called NaNa to tell her that he would be staying over there. NaNa hesitated and then said, "Carlos I don't feel that's appropriate, but I won't interfere. You are a man. But let me remind you, don't do anything foolish."

Carlos knew exactly what she meant and he had no intentions of making another baby. When he entered Luisa's room, he found her already under the sheets with a big grin on her face. He removed his clothing and joined her. Her innocence reminded him of their first time together. As much as he hated to break the beauty of the moment he had to ask, "What kind of birth control are you using?"

Luisa smiled and answered, "I told you I haven't been with anyone since I was with you so I haven't had a need for birth control, but my grandmother taught me how to follow my body and know when I'm ovulating. It's the only time a woman can conceive. It's what they patterned the pill after. So there are seven days a month I cannot participate in sexual intercourse. Your timing is perfect! We're good."

Carlos smiled and said, "So Puerto Rico has been good for you. Come here." He pulled her into his arms and began preparing her body to take him. He made love to Luisa with great passion and desire.

Afterwards, he lay next to her, while his son lay sleeping in a nearby room. He closed his eyes, content, and they fell asleep, embracing each other.

The next morning Carlos was awakened by the smell of fried plantain, sausage and eggs. It was eight and Luisa told him she had been up for about an hour. CJ was sitting in his high chair playing with his blocks and watching TV. Carlos picked him up and gave him a hug. He smiled as he thought to himself that this is what it would be like when they got back to NY; they would live together and raise their son as husband and wife. CJ and Luisa would know how much he loved them and was in love with them, always.

Over breakfast they discussed and mapped out their plans. Luisa had already checked online and found a reasonable student fare. She also told him that she would have to go to her school and see what needed to be done to transfer credits and take her final exams. Carlos elected to tell NaNa and his family alone, but they would talk to her grandparents together.

Carlos watched Luisa drive off with CJ in his car seat in the back before he joined NaNa on the porch. She was still sitting there having her morning coffee and reading the paper.

"Buenos Días. Welcome back."

"Buenos Días, NaNa. How was your evening?"

"I should be asking you that question." She patted the seat next to her for him to join her. Once he sat down, she continued, "So, what's going on with my grandson? I didn't say anything last night, but I hope you know what you're doing."

"NaNa, I know that you mean well. And you are right to be concerned, but I carried myself like an adult man. Neither of us is ready for more children right now."

NaNa sighed with relief, "So you were careful?"

Carlos smiled at his grandmother and with great joy, he answered, "Come on, NaNa." Then he continued, "More importantly, I proposed to Luisa last night and she accepted. We are going to get married. They are going to come back to New York with me. Before you ask, we have discussed the pros and cons and we are well aware of the challenges we will face." He paused and looked at her for approval. "I hope that we have your blessings."

"Son of my son, what you have are my prayers that the two of you will be good parents to that little boy and that you will be the man that I expect you to be, that your parents expect you to be, to that woman. Carlos, please don't upset that child's life if you aren't serious about this. I know last night stirred up physical emotions for you, but you can't build a relationship on that. You will be taking on a lot of responsibility. I know you say that you've thought it through, but as a young person, you have no idea of the road you're about to travel."

"Perhaps not completely, but NaNa, I have thought a lot about this for the past two years. I never should've let Mami keep us apart. I should have been down here as soon as I found out where she was staying. I won't let anyone stand in our way now. And what I do know is that I do not want my son to experience what I have, especially when I want to be in his life. I am willing to make that sacrifice and more."

NaNa smiled, stood up in front of her grandson and looked down at him. She placed her hand on his cheek and said, "Well then, you have my blessings. Have you talked to your parents yet?"

"No. But Papi and I talked about this possibility before I left. He doesn't approve of me doing anything rash, but he allows me to make up my own mind and then respects my decision. I plan to call Papi and tell him. As for my mother, she'll find out once we return. She gets no say in this at all and I don't want to hear any complaints or concerns she has before we get back to New York."

"I understand your reluctance to talk to your mother, but that's who she is, your mother. She only has your best interest at heart. You're about to find out how that works now that you are going to care for your son. It's not all black and white."

"Oh NaNa, you and Papi are more than kind when it comes to Mami. I have heard Papi say that over and over. And as much as I'd like to believe that, I know that's not all of it.

"She's still bitter about the divorce and continues to punish Papi, even though she remarried. It's not about my well being, Luis J's, Chell's or Robert's, trust me; it's all about her, even though she has fooled herself into believing that it's about us. I have seen through that crap of hers for some time now. Excuse my French. And yes, I love Mami, but she will not influence the choices in my life ever again."

"Wow, you just said a mouthful, mijo. I think that you will do well as a parent. But do be patient with your mother. She was very much in love with your father. I thought they would be together forever, like your grandfather and me. But my son hurt her badly after she bore him four children and sacrificed her dreams. It affects a woman in a way that you will never know because you don't bear the child and can't feel hurt like a woman. So even though much of what you say may be true, she still means well. Remember that."

"Okay NaNa, I promise I will. And I want you to know that I appreciate you. Thank you again for letting me stay here and for being a part of my son's life when I was not. You represented the Rodriquez family well." He stood facing her and kissed her on the cheek before going into the house to call his father.

When Carlos shared the news with his father, to his great pleasure and relief, he received the support he was looking for. His father, anxious to meet his grandson, offered to meet them at the airport. But

Carlos declined, not wanting his father to have to deal with the rush hour traffic. But he did agree to go straight to Papi's first.

The conversation with Luisa's grandparents was non-combative. They, too, said they would pray for them and their happiness. Carlos and Luisa spent the next two days continuing to reconnect with each other while planning and catching up on all that had been missed between them. They both vowed that never again would they be apart.

The night before their departure they were up very late, packing Luisa and CJ's things. Their flight was scheduled to leave around noon and they were exhausted when their heads finally hit the pillow. Once again they found themselves in one another's arms making love, and Carlos was so happy and relieved to know that his relationship with Luisa was meant to be.

The next morning, CJ's baby talk and chattering had the cadence of ultimate excitement. It was as though he knew he was going on a long trip. Since Tía had to work, NaNa and Tío Bobby took them to the airport and wished them well. NaNa said a prayer over them before they entered the security line. Carlos thanked NaNa once again for everything and kissed her goodbye.

Bobby winked and gave him a thumbs up. Then he grabbed his nephew and hugged him, saying, "Don't stay away so long, nephew. Visit us more often so that we can see the young one grow up…and you, too, for that matter. Although, you're well on your way. I'm proud of you. And tell that brother of mine he's long overdue for a trip home."

The return flight seemed even longer than the flight to Puerto Rico, and Carlos wasn't sure if it was because of his anxiety or anticipation of what lie ahead or something as simple as the wind current going against them. Upon arrival at John F. Kennedy International, they collected their luggage and headed to the cab stand. It was cold and raining, a big difference from the sunshine they left in Puerto Rico.

He had Luisa take CJ and get into the cab while he helped the driver load the luggage. When he finally crawled into the back seat, he was soaked. Luisa and CJ made fun of him dripping all over the seat. The two of them settled back as the driver sped away from the curb and down the highway toward Papi's. CJ was exhausted and fell asleep snuggly and safely between them in his car seat before the cab made it to the Brooklyn Queens Expressway. Carlos leaned in front of the car seat and Luisa met him halfway and he kissed her.

"Welcome home my love," he said. He saw her mouth open but couldn't hear her reply because of the sound of tires screeching and horns blowing.

Chapter Fifteen

Maria had cooked dinner and they were awaiting Carlos' arrival. He had called from the airport over two hours ago. It was still raining, so Luis figured they were probably detained by the traffic.

"Maybe they couldn't get a cab. Or maybe they went to his apartment first. I'll call and see," Maria offered, trying to ease Luis' mind. Just as she reached for the phone, the doorbell rang. She smiled and changed direction to open the door.

Luis could hear voices, but knew right away it wasn't his son's. As the conversation continued and no one came into the room, Luis rose and headed towards the door. When he got there, he found two police officers in conversation with Maria.

"What's going on?"

"Are you Mr. Rodriquez?"

"Yes."

"Sir, I'm Officer Harrison from the New York State Troopers Highway Patrol. There's been a very serious car accident. We believe it involved your son, Carlos Rodriquez. We got your address from the taxi dispatcher. Is that your son's name?"

"Yes. What happened? Is he alright?"

"Their taxi was hit by a truck on the Brooklyn Queens Expressway.

They were taken to Kings County Hospital's ER. We're here to escort you there. Can you follow us or do you need a ride?"

"Damn it, I asked you if he was alright?" Luis asked again, losing his cool and his composure.

"Sir, I'm not able to answer that question. I do know that he was conscious when the ambulance left the scene."

"Then why were you dispatched here? I thought that only happened when there was a fatality. Oh my God, is my grandson alright?"

"Your grandson is alive. However, I'm sorry to tell you that the female companion traveling with your son died at the scene."

Luis' heart sank. He could hardly believe his ears. How could this have happened? Why? He grabbed his coat and keys and headed out the door. Maria was right behind him. He instinctively reached for her hand and they rushed to the car. He trailed the officers, trying not to let his mind get ahead of what he knew was reality.

There was still a lot of traffic and the rain was coming down very hard. He called Diane's cell instead of the house phone to avoid having to share any of this with the kids, but she didn't answer. When he called the house, Luis J informed him she was out. He left a message for her to call as soon as possible.

Luis and Maria entered the hospital and stopped at the registration desk. The woman sitting there held a comforting look as she awaited the inevitable questions about this person's loved one. Luis managed to say his son's name with as much strength as he had to push through the moment. They were directed to the second bank of elevators and took one to the fifth floor. Little to no words were exchanged between them. When the elevator stopped, they walked right to the nurse's station on the south end of the floor.

"Excuse me, I'm Luis Rodriquez. My son, Carlos Rodriquez, has been admitted."

"One moment," the nurse replied, looking at the computer and then walking away from them.

They stood at the desk, unsure of what they were waiting for or where she had gone, but with no other recourse than to wait. With each passing moment, Luis' anxiety continued to build. He was about to approach another nurse on the other side of the station when another law enforcement representative approached. He had on an overcoat which was opened just enough for Luis to see a slightly stained light blue shirt and tie. His walk was purposeful and face stern.

"Mr. Rodriquez, I'm Detective Muñoz. Will you come with me? I have a few questions to ask you."

"No, not until someone gives me an update regarding my son. I want to know where he is and an update on his condition."

The detective cleared his throat and offered what he could. "I know this must be very overwhelming. I'm so sorry. The nurse shared with me that he's in surgery but a doctor will be meeting with you in the room over there." He stopped and pointed for affect. "While we wait for the doctor, I just need to get some information from you. We were asked to come to the hospital because there was a fatality at the scene of the accident. Otherwise, these questions would wait. I know you have a son in surgery and it must be difficult to have to answer my questions, but I trust you understand the urgency."

When Luis didn't move, the detective repeated, "Sir, please." Pointing in the direction of the room, again.

"Alright. Forgive me. It's just hard to focus on anything other than my son."

"I can only imagine. Unfortunately, I have had my share of these conversations with parents and loved ones. I'm glad you're not alone."

The floor was quiet except for the occasional beeping of machines. Visiting hours were almost over so very few non-hospital personnel remained on the floor. Luis and Maria followed the detective to the room. It was sparse. There was a table with seating for four, a couch with worn seating cushions, a half-empty water cooler, and a coffee burner. The carafe of coffee didn't smell fresh at all and probably had been there for hours. All signs of a room that had way too much use as people awaited news of their friends and family.

Detective Muñoz pulled out one of the chairs to allow Maria to sit and then he sat, waiting for Luis to join them. When he didn't, Muñoz started, "As I said, I just have a few questions so that we can finish filing the report for our investigation and then I'll leave you alone."

Luis pulled out the chair and took a seat.

"Thank you sir. So, may I begin with, where was your son coming from?"

"Puerto Rico. His flight landed around four-thirty."

"Who was traveling with him?"

"His girlfriend, Luisa Morales, and their child, my grandson, Carlos Rodriquez, Jr." This was the first time those words rolled off his tongue and now he wondered if this little boy's life would be ended too soon. So he asked,"Where is he by the way, my grandson? Do you have any information about him?"

Before Detective Muñoz could respond, the door opened and a physician joined them in the room. They all waited to see if he was the doctor treating Carlos.

"Mr. Rodriquez?" he asked, anxiously.

"Yes, I'm Mr. Rodriquez."

Detective Muñoz closed his note pad. "Please, go ahead. We can continue once you've received answers to your questions," Muñoz said, before rising and excusing himself. Once he did, the doctor took the seat he vacated. Luis observed how young the doctor looked and figured he was probably an intern sent to give the family an update.

"Mr. Rodriquez, I know that you have been waiting. I'm sorry."

"Yes, what's going on with my son and grandson? I haven't been able to get any information since I arrived."

"Yes, of course. My name is Dr. Stuart. I was on call in the emergency room when they were brought in. Your grandson is going to be alright. It is a miracle. His parent's bodies cushioned him and thankfully he was in a car seat. It could have been much worse. Your grandson is in Pediatrics, which is on the third floor. We're monitoring him closely, but it seems he's resilient, no signs of internal injuries. He is of course traumatized and so we had to sedate him."

The doctor paused to allow Mr. Rodriquez to embrace this good news. Then he lowered his voice and tone before continuing. "Your son, Carlos, is in surgery. He sustained very extensive internal injuries to his organs and has lost a lot of blood. There was also head trauma on impact." Once again he stopped, but this time to allow Mr. Rodriquez to transition his emotional state.

"What are you saying?"

"I'm saying that the prognosis for your son is not good. He has a twenty percent chance of surviving if we're able to stop all the bleeding. We're not sure if he's going to make it."

"Ay Dios mío. No."

Maria reached out her hand to touch Luis' arm and provide him some comfort and support.

"What can I do? You said he's lost a lot of blood, we're the same type. Let me donate some. Perhaps he needs a specialist."

"We have all the blood we need. It's really that his injuries are very critical, Mr. Rodriquez. The surgeons are doing all that they can in an effort to save his life. He's young and healthy but so much damage has been done. It's very extensive."

"There have to be other options."

"I'm very sorry."

"This can't be happening." Luis shook his head. He couldn't really be standing here listening to this doctor tell him his son was dying.

"I need to get back to the ER, but I promise you we will keep you posted. The surgeon will be down to see you as soon as they stabilize him."

Luis had his head buried in his hands fighting to hold back the tears as the doctor placed a comforting pat on his back and then walked out of the room. Luis was speechless and his brain was numb. When he finally looked up, his eyes met the detective's, who had rejoined them in the room. Luis couldn't imagine answering any questions right now so he searched Maria's face for answers. But the tears rolling down her cheeks didn't offer any comfort. He had never let anyone see him cry but tonight tears flowed down his cheeks.

"Papi, I'm so sorry. We'll pray and Carlos will be alright. I know he will pull through, he's so much like you, and he will pull through."

Luis felt himself starting to hyperventilate and said, "I need some fresh air and I have to reach Diane. I have to get out of here."

Muñoz moved to the side as Luis approached the door. To Luis' relief, Muñoz opened the door for him and stated, "If I have your permission, I can ask her the remaining questions."

Luis nodded before letting the door close behind him. Standing outside of the emergency room doors, he watched the ambulances coming and going. It seemed like they were bringing someone in every few minutes. One of them had brought his son to the hospital and now he was fighting for his life. He shed a few more tears and then gaining his composure, called Diane at home again. This time she answered.

"Diane?"

"Yes, Luis, what do you want?" Diane asked, with the usual annoyance in her tone.

"Didn't you get my message?"

"Yes, and I called you back but it went straight to voicemail. What do you want?" she asked again, but softer than before as she heard something strange in his voice. It was an uneasiness that now worried her a little. Luis J was in his room so she knew it wasn't about him.

Luis paused for a moment as he tried to find the right words and calmed himself so that he sounded clear. How was he going to tell her? He first needed to confirm that she wouldn't be receiving this news alone so he asked, "Is David there?"

"No. Why? I don't have time for this Luis, what is it?"

"Please Diane, not now! Then ask Luis J to pick up. Can you just do that? Please!"

"Did you call to talk to Luis J or did you call to talk to me? Why all this cloak and dagger?"

"Diane, please, just once, please don't fight with me on this," he demanded, before his voice cracked.

Diane was not accustomed to Luis being so direct, so she said, "Okay." There was definitely something going on so she called to her son to pick up the extension. They were both silent as they waited for confirmation that Luis J was on the call. Diane was about to call him again when Luis J spoke, "Yeah, what's up?"

"I wanted to talk to both of you. There's been an accident."

"Luis, what kind of accident? Did something happen to you?"

Luis began telling the story, to the best of his ability, hoping that he was conveying the seriousness of the accident, but not revealing all of the information he had or the emotion he felt.

"What hospital?" Diane asked.

"Kings County, fifth floor."

"Mami, I'm coming with you."

"No Luis J. You need to stay with Chell and Robert. We'll call you as soon as we have any more information."

By the time Luis finished, he heard the door slam. "Check and see if your mother hung up the phone. You need to keep the line clear. When will David be home?"

"He's moved out, but I'll try his cell. Papi, this is crazy. Carlos just sent me a text from the airport. Have you seen him?"

"No, I've only talked to the doctor. They're doing all that they can. And son, it is serious."

"Papi, what should I do, I mean what should I tell Chell?"

"Just be positive son, pray. But don't tell Chell anything yet. I'll call you back once I've talked to the doctors again. I need for you to handle this well. Can you do that?"

"Yes, sure."

"Alright, mijo, I need to run. I love you." Luis realized he had not said those words to his son in a long time. Tonight would change that from now on.

Luis returned to the small room, feeling completely helpless as he sat there waiting for Di or the doctor. Muñoz had apparently gotten enough of the information he needed for now and had left the hospital, leaving his prayers for the family. Luis wasn't one to show any weakness, but this situation had really hit him hard and he couldn't seem to find his center of gravity. When he went back to the nurse's station to see if there was an update, he saw Di walking down the hallway. She looked at him but couldn't find any words, so she turned to the nurse sitting at the desk and asked for information.

"Di, please, let me talk to you first," Luis said, reaching for her.

"No." She moved, eluding his touch. She knew if he touched her, she would break down. She had to find out what was happening with her son. "I want to see my son."

Luis continued, retracting his hand, "You can't, not yet."

Turning toward him, Diane fired questions at him frantically. "Why not? Where is he? What happened?"

"I tried to tell you over the phone that he is in surgery due to the seriousness of his injuries." He used these words to preface what he was about to share in detail.

Diane seemed to hang onto Luis' every word. He was saying them but clearly he must be talking about someone else. The words still didn't make it real to him either. As he finished telling her about Luisa and Carlos Jr., she now reached for him and the frailty he recognized when he first met her revealed itself behind the iron mask she had worn for so long now.

He caught her just before she hit the floor. The nurse came around to assist and another grabbed a wheel chair to place her into. As one wheeled her into an empty room, the other paged the doctor on call and began asking Luis what, if anything, he knew about her health. Once the nurse gathered as much information as she could, she left Luis in the hallway and joined the other nurse who was attending to Diane.

Luis prayed that Diane was alright. He couldn't handle another medical emergency. He wasn't aware of any problems she was having, but she was old enough to have had a stroke. No, he was pretty sure she had just fainted. He would have done the same thing if she were telling him the story for the first time. It was all just too much for anyone to grasp. He waited in the hallway now for another doctor to give him an update.

When Maria returned with two cups of coffee, she found Luis talking to the nurse. She walked close enough to learn that Diane had arrived. Maria could only imagine what Diane must be feeling and, for the first time ever, empathized with her pain. She wondered if Diane was visiting with Carlos as she handed Luis the coffee.

The nurse motioned for them to join the doctor in the room. When they did, he said, "Basically, she fainted, which is normal in situations like this. We'll continue to monitor her. I've ordered a mild sedative, just in case, but I don't anticipate any further problems requiring hospitalization. You should probably let us know of any allergies or medical issues just to be safe."

Luis nodded and informed them that she was allergic to strawberries but no pharmaceutical drugs that he was aware of. The doctor noted the allergy and turning, sped off down the hallway, probably rushing to respond to his next page.

Luis moved closer to the bed, leaving Maria near the doorway. Diane looked so peaceful lying there but he knew that this was only a result of the medication, which was now flowing through her veins. Soon that would wear off and together they would have to face the long night that lie ahead of them. Luis pulled up a chair and sat beside her. He began gently rubbing her forehead, wishing he could make her feel better. He would trade places with his son in a heartbeat. He would do anything to spare Diane this trauma.

Maria stood observing her lover caress the woman with whom he'd had four children as if they were still married. After their divorce she knew that he wasn't happy about it or the estranged relationship with his kids, but it had never occurred to her that he might still love her that way.

But just then she saw it. There was this gentleness, a deeply felt love was pouring out of him as he sat by her side caring for her. How did she miss that? And it hit her in the pit of her stomach. All of this was just too much. She didn't even have the strength to protest or run interference. Maria knew that she was many things, but she couldn't compete with the impending loss of a child. She'd have to accept the intimacy between Diane and Luis, so she walked away.

After a while, Diane started to come around. Luis removed his hand from her forehead and took her hand instead. She tried to sit up, but when his grip tightened he felt her body relax.

"Luis. Where am I? What happened? Did I faint?"

"You did. You're in the hospital. They examined you, then gave you a mild sedative."

"What happened to Carlos? Was he driving? Where was he headed? How did it happen?"

She fired the questions at him because she felt he was withholding information from her that would enable her to make some sense out of this. Carlos had gone there to meet his son, not bring him back. What were they all doing here? 'Yet again, Luisa is ruining his life,' she thought.

"Shhh now, relax. Answers to those questions can't change what's happened. We need to be prayerful. Besides, I don't know all of the details, just what I've told you. He was already in the operating room when I got here."

"How is Luisa? How is the boy? Where are they? I need to know Luis." How could she stop interrogating him? There were so many gaps.

Again, the rapid fire of questions, but this set revealed that Diane didn't remember that he had already told her of their fate.

"This is a lot for you to abs orb all at once. Why don't you just relax for a minute? Can I get you something to drink?"

"I don't want anything to drink. Where are they?"

Ignoring the tone in her voice, Luis responded, "Carlos Jr., CJ they call him, he's in Pediatrics. He's doing just fine. They're monitoring him."

"And Luisa?"

"She didn't make it, Diane. Her body took the brunt of the impact."

"Oh, my God. No! This is horrible. This just can't be! Not now! Not now! What were they doing here? Carlos never said anything about bringing them back." Tears were now forming in her eyes.

"Carlos called me yesterday and told me that they were returning with him. He was planning to marry Luisa and raise their son together. He was so happy." The memories of the conversation brought a smile to Luis' face, but it didn't last as the reality of the truck smashed those dreams.

"He called you from Puerto Rico to tell you? Why didn't he call me?"

"I don't know. He was probably trying to watch NaNa's phone bill."

Luis could tell that his answer didn't ease her sadness and disappointment. She had created that distance between them and now she would surely regret it. Luis turned toward the sound of the footsteps to see Maria once again standing in the doorway. He nodded at her to let her know that Diane was fine. He felt he should go to Maria since she had been there to comfort him all evening, but tonight Diane needed him and honestly, he needed her. He hoped Maria would understand. It was their firstborn and grandson that was their focus. When he turned back to face the doorway, Maria was no longer there.

"Luis, please, please don't leave me. I'm scared," Diane pleaded softly in almost a whisper. In her face and intonation, at that moment, was the young woman he met who was searching for Dr. Maxwell's office. The gentle, caring, fragile woman with whom he fell madly in love.

"I won't, Diane. I'll be right here, I promise."

It seemed like hours had gone by and still no word from the operating team. Diane had dozed off again, so Luis covered her and headed toward the nurse's station. Maria was drinking another cup of coffee, sitting in the waiting area just off the hallway. She approached him and they hugged each other. He lingered in her arms for a moment. He really appreciated that she was there and providing him some comfort. He wondered several times why David hadn't arrived yet. Luis thought about calling Luis J, but he still didn't have anything more to tell them, so he waited.

When he and Maria approached the nurse's station, the nurse told them she had just been given an update. They were moving Carlos to ICU and the doctor would be down to talk to them in a few minutes. She left them standing there and went to check on Diane to give her the news as well. Luis finally could breathe a little better now that Carlos was out of surgery. 'This has to be a good sign,' was his first thought.

Turning to Maria, Luis asked, "Would you mind calling Luis J to see if he has reached David yet? If not, tell him to keep trying. If he asks you about anything, tell him I'll call him back within the hour. Please don't tell him about Luisa or the extent of Carlos' injuries." He kissed her on the cheek and she hugged him again.

Maria walked toward the elevator to go to the lobby. As she waited for it, she watched as Diane was being held by the nurse, and then took her place beside Luis. He put his arm around her waist and the three of them headed to the family consultation room to meet the doctor. The elevator door closed and Maria sighed.

When Luis and Diane entered the room, a doctor was already there seated at the table, thumbing through medical records. Diane moved closer to Luis and he instinctively tightened his hold on her as they introduced themselves to the doctor.

This doctor was of a medium height and build. He looked very tired. His shoulders were a little rounded and his lip was tight. He still had on his surgical cap, which was dark blue with white strips. Diane wondered if it was a special order, perhaps his lucky cap, and it had served him well while he attended to her son. She couldn't tell how old he was, but the greying temples told her he was experienced and this was comforting.

"Good evening. I'm Dr. Paul Hunter. I was one of your son's surgeons. I know you have been waiting a long time for an update. I'm sorry it took so long. As I believe you have been told, your son's injuries were quite extensive. He was pinned in the car for thirty minutes before they could even get to him. He suffered massive internal injuries, crushed ribs and damage to his major organs, causing internal bleeding. We had to remove his spleen. He has a severely punctured lung, spinal damage and severe head trauma. He lost a lot of blood before we even began the surgery."

Dr. Hunter stopped as though he was allowing the words to pervade their minds and enable them to imagine the impact of these types of injuries.

Diane began crying again. There wasn't much space left between their bodies but Luis pulled her even closer. He was trying to comfort her, protect her, and prepare her for what he felt was coming next. The prognosis was not good.

"Is he going to live?" Luis asked, his eyes closed, anticipating the doctor's response.

When the doctor didn't respond, Diane chimed in, "Doctor?" She wanted to make sure that he had heard the question, not that he was taking this long to answer it for another reason.

Dr. Hunter exhaled and then responded, "We did everything we could, but the injuries are just too all-encompassing. There's no way to tell. Miracles do happen. But if you want my professional opinion, I don't think he will make it through the night."

Diane screamed and buried her face into Luis' chest. His body muffled her screams and kept his from erupting.

The doctor continued, "We have moved him into ICU so you can be with him. He's not conscious but he may still be able to hear you. There's a lot we don't know about these types of injuries. You can go up there whenever you are ready. I'm so sorry I couldn't bring you better news."

"I asked the other doctor about a specialist," Luis said. "You said you had to remove his spleen. Would a specialist help? What else can be done for our son?" It was now Luis' turn to rapid fire questions.

"Mr. Rodriquez, there isn't anything else that can be done. We worked on him for three hours. There wasn't anything more we could do. We could not stop the bleeding or relieve enough of the pressure on his brain. With this much trauma, his organs have already started shutting down. All we can do now is make him comfortable."

"Is he in any pain?" Diane mumbled between her sobs.

"No, Mrs. Rodriquez, absolutely not. Again, I am so sorry for your loss."

Diane lifted her head for a moment to look at the doctor. She managed to whisper, "Thank you." Throughout her movements, though, Luis did not loosen his hold. Tears continued to fall softly down her cheeks and a few down his.

He found himself only capable of nodding his head to add his appreciation to this man who had worked so hard trying to save his son's life.

"How much time do we have?" Diane barely whispered after standing to head to ICU.

"We're not sure, maybe a few hours."

Diane gasped before she collapsed again. The air was sucked out of her and she was no longer able to stand. Luis caught her this time and spoke softly, "Di, honey, I'm here. We'll go see him together."

She didn't respond; she just remained in his arms. As the doctor moved towards her, Luis said, "She'll be alright." Once the doctor confirmed that for himself, he departed.

When Maria returned to the room and witnessed the embrace, she knew there was bad news lingering in the air. "What can I do?"

"Would you mind going to the house for the kids? They need to say goodbye."

Diane wanted to protest but even she had to admit that tonight, she needed Maria's help because her husband was nowhere to be found and Diane needed to know that the rest of her children would be safe. So she remained silent.

Once Maria left, Diane slowly moved away from Luis and waited for him to guide her next move. She needed his strength. She wanted him to take control. They stood in the conference room without saying a word. When Luis was ready, he took her hand and they exited the room. The nurse led them to the ICU area in silence. She escorted them into the room where Carlos lay. Before leaving, she placed her hand on Luis' back and rubbed it gently. There really weren't any words needed.

Luis and Diane didn't say anything to each other either. They just stood there allowing themselves time to absorb the magnitude of their surroundings. The sounds from the machines were almost deafening, and there, in the bed, lay their son. His body looked so small compared to all of the equipment around him. His eyes were closed and he was very still. Luis found himself watching the monitor to confirm that he was still alive because he knew Carlos was not able to breathe on his own. Luis touched Carlos' hand and leaned over and kissed his forehead.

For the second time that evening, Luis felt completely helpless; there wasn't anything he could do to help his child, his firstborn.

Luis looked toward the ceiling and silently prayed for a miracle. He recalled when Carlos first entered the world and thought of all the things he had planned for his son. Luis had anticipated graduations, a wedding and children. He would take him exploring and introduce him to the wonders of the world. They would talk politics and laugh about life. Nowhere in his dreams and hopes for his son did he imagine this.

"Oh, my poor baby, why has this happened to you? Can you hear me baby? It's Mami and Papi. We're here with you, by your side. Can you hear me? We love you and I'm so sorry for all the pain I've caused you. I hope you can forgive me. I really thought I was looking out for your well being. Oh my God, what have I done? I'm sorry, I'm sorry, I'm so sorry, Carlos," Diane confessed through muffled words choked in her throat by tears that strangled her voice.

Luis listened to Diane use the word, we. It had been years since Luis heard that from her. Why did it have to be something so tragic like this to bring them together around their children? All those years, wasted. Why? Why had he cheated on Diane? That single decision stripped him of his family and his time to watch them grow up. Stripped him of his ability to parent his children, be a father to his sons and teach them what it meant to be a man. No matter how he failed her before, he would be there for her now.

"Di, Carlos loves you and he understands what you did. His recent actions were a result of the maturity and compassion you helped to instill in him. Carlos, mijo, I'm very proud of the man you turned out to be, very proud."

They stood there holding each other, afraid that if one moved, both would fall. Diane's sobs continued uncontrollably. Luis wondered what he could say to her or her to him to make any sense out of this and knew that this was not going to be an easy journey. So they just stood there in silence, watching the monitors that told them Carlos was still clinging to life.

"Mr. and Mrs. Rodriquez, I'm sorry to bother you, but your grandson is in Pediatrics. He's awake and crying quite a bit. Would one of you like to go down there? He's in a strange place, and with no mother or father or familiar face nearby. He needs some assurance."

They looked at each other, acknowledging that neither of them had ever seen their grandson.

"I'll go," Diane responded.

"Why don't we go together, Di?"

"But I don't want to leave Carlos alone."

"He's not alone, the angels are watching over him. Besides, I'm sure he would want us to meet his son together."

When they exited the ICU room, they found Luis J and Chell standing there waiting for them. Diane noticed how frightened Chell looked and could relate to the worry that covered Luis J's face, too. She searched for words to comfort her children. They had not had to deal with death before and both parents knew that this would hit them very hard, especially Luis J.

Diane took Chell's hand and they sat down in the hallway to begin her attempt to make sense of what made no sense. Together they told their children what had happened and that Carlos was not going to live. Chell screamed, pulled away from her mother, and lunged into her father's arms. Luis J sat on the other side of his mother, motionless, as though a knife had just pierced his heart.

"No. Carlos is going to be fine. This is bull. My brother is not going to die. Carlos and I are getting together this weekend. I'm gonna run drills with him. I want to see him. I'll make him wake up. That doctor is wrong!" Luis J shouted, deliriously.

"Luis J, I'll take you in to see him, but you must calm down. Chell, are you ready?" asked Luis, calm and grounded at this point for his children.

"No. I want to stay here with Mami. Mami, don't cry."

"Alright, honey, let me know when you're ready. We'll have to help each other through this. Diane, please wait for me."

She nodded, wiping the tears away because she didn't want Chell to worry about her. They put their arms around one another and hugged tightly as Papi and Luis J headed to the room.

Luis J's pace slowed as the distance between him and the bed decreased. He stopped about two feet away from Carlos' body. He was just close enough to see the lifelessness in his brother and to acknowledge there wasn't anything that he could do, but not close enough to touch Carlos. "Papi, no! Carlos, wake up! Get up man! Come on, get up!"

"Luis J, please. Talk to him. Let him know how strong you can be for him and for his son. You're an uncle now."

"I can't. I can't do this, man! I can't be here, Papi, I'm sorry." Luis J turned and ran out.

"Luis J, honey, come back," Diane called after her son as he bolted past her and headed for the stairway. He kept going, not responding to his mother's voice and pushing the door open.

"Diane, let me go get him; you need to stay here," Maria offered. She had been standing there observing the whole scene and felt out of place. She didn't know what to say or do to help any of them, so she was just standing there with her arms folded.

Diane didn't respond, but instead Luis said, "Thanks, Maria. Where's Robert?"

"We took him to David's brother's house; they said that was where David was staying. Luis J told me how to get there. I didn't think you wanted him here or that the hospital would allow it given his age."

"Was David there?" Luis asked. He still couldn't understand why this man was not standing beside Di.

"No. Luis J told Marvin what was going on. But let me try to catch Luis J before he gets too far. You can call me if you need me."

Luis nodded with approval, then checked with Chell to see if she was ready to visit Carlos. She wasn't, so instead Diane and Luis took her to the Pediatric floor. When they approached the bed and CJ looked at them, they stopped in their tracks. The resemblance to Carlos was uncanny. It was like they had rolled back the clock to Carlos at that age. There was no denying this child. He was definitely a Rodriquez.

Diane walked over to him and stretched out her arms to pick him up. She had to be careful because they still had him on an IV. She wasn't prepared for the response she received though because he pulled away and kept crying.

"Hello, CJ. I'm your grandmother and this is your grandfather."

"And I'm your Auntie Chell."

Luis and Diane smiled at each other before Diane asked, "Are they sure he's out of the woods?"

"Yes, Di. They said he's fine. I'm sure he's just confused."

"Can he talk?" Chell asked, playing with his toes and trying to make him settle down.

"I don't think so. Besides, Carlos said they only speak Spanish to him."

Papi began speaking to CJ in Spanish and told him that he was safe and that they were Carlos' parents, his grandparents. He told him that everything was going to be fine. The sound of his voice and the familiarity of the language seemed to comfort CJ and he reached for Luis. He picked him up and hugged him.

"Luis, what are we going to do? He has no idea what has happened. He's in a strange place with a strange language being spoken around him and no one familiar that he knows, especially his mother. I can imagine how he must be feeling." Diane reached out to him again and this time, he let her pick him up. She began singing to him, softly, and rocking him back and forth.

"I know. We're going to do exactly what you are doing now – love him, like Carlos would want us to do, and keep him safe."

Diane kept singing and rocking him, moving to sit in the chair near the crib. She gave him the bottle that was next to the bed and cuddled him like she was breastfeeding him. He drank the formula and played with her finger until he finished the bottle and then dozed off.

"How long does he have to stay in here?" Chell whispered.

"I'm not sure but we'll find out," Papi replied.

"Papi, I want to see Carlos now."

"Good. We'll all go together."

Diane placed CJ's limp body back into the crib and they exited the room.

"Excuse me, sir, are you this boy's grandfather and the father to the patient in the accident?"

"Yes."

"I'm the ambulance attendant. I was on the scene. I'm so sorry about the young lady. How are your son and the boy?"

"The baby is good. My son is not…" The remaining words were choked by his head or his tongue, he didn't know which, but they were not allowed to escape his mouth.

The attendant shook his head. "I am sorry. I just wanted to tell you, when I arrived on the scene he was conscious. He told me his name and the name of his son. He must have sensed something about his injuries and he asked me to give you and your wife a message."

"Really? Our son left us a message?" Diane asked, not correcting the title she had been given over and over throughout the evening.

"Yes. He said to tell you he loved you both and he wanted to make you proud."

"He did. He absolutely did," Luis said.

"He also said that if he didn't make it, he wanted the two of you to raise his son together, that his son would need both of you. He knew his wife didn't make it. He said that you taught him the importance of raising a child with both parents. Lastly, he said to tell his brothers and sister to be strong and carry him in their hearts."

Diane embraced the attendant and thanked him for the message. "And thank you for providing him comfort when he needed it the most."

"I wish I could have done more," he said, as he walked away.

As Diane's mind thought about her son's message, she became conscious of a knot forming in her stomach. How on earth was she going to raise Carlos' son with Luis? Only hours ago that was an impossibility in her mind and now she found herself wondering what role all of them would have in this outcome, especially Maria. She had been helpful with the kids and didn't cause any scenes, but she was a long way from being viewed as a member of the family. Not even an extended member.

Why couldn't life be simpler? Her first son lay dying from a car accident because he went to Puerto Rico to see Luisa and his son who were there because two years ago she refused to give permission for their marriage. She wanted to scream and inside she did. Her pain raged throughout her body and she felt like she was going to explode. It reminded her of the warnings you see near oxygen tanks to refrain from smoking. She was that volatile. It was not her fault entirely, she could rationalize that, but deeply within the rationale, she knew that her hand was in it. That it was something she'd have to live with every day for the rest of her life.

When they returned to the ICU, the nurse was by Carlos' bed checking his vitals. Chell walked up to his bed and began rubbing his arm. Tears flowed effortlessly from her soul, pouring out the love she had for her oldest brother. He had cared for and loved her in his special way. He was always gentle yet firm with her. Their relationship was not like the one she had with Luis J, who played with her and rarely ever said no to her wants. His was truly like a big brother, protective.

"I love you, Carlos, so much. I'm going to miss you. Your son is very handsome. I'll take care of him like you took care of me. I promise," she said, through tear-stained words. Chell stood on her tiptoes and laid her head on his chest, and then kissed his heart. When she rose, she turned and left the room.

Diane could do nothing. Suddenly she felt suspended in time, an observer of what was happening in front and around her. She opened her mouth but nothing came out. Luis took the lead and filled the room with his words, giving her time to reassess her thoughts and reconcile her feelings.

"Carlos, we're here. I'm here, mijo, son of my soul, my spirit, my first born. Yes, we got your message. The ambulance driver relayed it to me and your mother. We will, as you requested, raise your son together. We'll tell him all about you and Luisa and love him every day. We just saw him. He's beautiful and strong, so much like you at that age. I know that made you smile when you saw him. Your mother rocked him to sleep the same way she did with you at that age. She even sang to him."

He looked for some sign that his son was able to hear him. He continued, "I pray that you can hear us. What a brave man you are. I'm glad that you listened to your heart and saw the future in time to send us that message. I will share that with CJ, too. Yes, I will tell him that you loved him so much that you sent a message to us to love him as we love you. And we love you, son. You can rest now." Luis closed his soliloquy and kept his son's hand in his own. He felt the warmth, the blood flowing through his veins and knew that soon those organs would shut down, his heart would stop and his body would grow cold. He wanted to remember the warmth of his son.

Still in suspension, Diane leaned over and kissed Carlos on the cheek. Lingering close, she studied his face as she had when he first entered the world and was given to her, only now his eyes were not looking back at her. She began crying again while rubbing his forehead, hoping to give him some sense of comfort.

"I love you, Carlos, with all my heart," she mumbled, then she let out a loud scream, drowning out the sound of the machines and releasing her pain before saying, "Good night, my sweetheart."

Just as she shifted her position to be next to Luis once again, the monitor alarm sounded off. It was as if it felt compelled to compete with her scream. Diane jumped and Luis just closed his eyes. Their eldest son was gone, yet he held on to his son's hand; the warmth was still there. When he finally opened his eyes, the nurse was standing next to the monitor and Diane was now holding Carlos' other hand. Diane looked at Luis, and he at her. When the nurse turned off the alarm, Luis released Carlos' hand and reached for Diane, who also let go of Carlos; holding her, together they found comfort in each other's arms.

Luis wished they could be like this. He wished this closeness could last forever, but with Diane, there was no way of knowing what the future would hold. For all he knew, tomorrow things would return to being cold as ice. So, he remained in this place, in each other's arms, for as long as she would allow it. When she finally shifted and then moved, he knew it was time to release his tight hold.

When they exited the room, Luis' arm still around Diane, they found David comforting Chell and listening to her every word. David looked up and took in the scene – Luis' arm around his wife. He moved from Chell and approached Diane.

"I don't know what to say Diane, Luis. How is he?" he asked, lowering his voice, anticipating the response.

"He's gone."

David reached for Diane, to take the place he should have had all evening. She moved into his arms and began weeping again, silently.

"Papi?"

He didn't feel the need to answer, but instead opened his arms so he could now embrace his daughter. It was midnight.

Chapter Sixteen

16

Luis J didn't stop until he found himself on the street. He couldn't breathe when he was in the room and there was a tightness building in his chest. But now, he felt a little relief. His mind tried to return to the image of his brother lying in that bed, but he refused to absorb what was happening upstairs. Not now, not ever. He would not say goodbye to his brother, not until they were old and gray. Carlos wouldn't leave him.

"Luis J, wait, slow down will you?" Maria said, slightly panting.

He turned to see her coming toward him. He could see that she was out of breath and wondered how long she had been following after him. But he was not going back inside that hospital; he didn't care what she said or what message she was bringing from his father.

"Leave me alone, Maria, please."

"I just came to be with you, that's all." After a pause she asked, "Wanna go for a walk?"

"No. I have to get the hell out of here." He could feel the tightness intensifying.

"Where do you want to go?"

"Carlos' apartment."

"Is that a good idea?"

"You asked me where I wanted to go. That's where I am going."

"Alright, Luis J. But, it's late. I'll drive you."

"I really just want to be alone."

She touched his arm and turned him toward her. "I'm hurting, too. We don't have to talk, just let me be with you."

Of course she would want to leave, there was no place for Maria in this pain that was being shared by his mother and father. So, without responding, he followed her to the car and they drove the few miles to Carlos' in silence. But no matter how many miles they were putting between him and the hospital, he couldn't stop his mind from replaying the image of Carlos and the machines.

He was lying so still and barely breathing. It was as though he had already left his body. He couldn't help but wonder if that was really going to be the last time he would see his brother alive? He shut his eyes tightly, fighting back the burning sensation that preceded tears.

Luis J unlocked the door and entered the apartment. He still had the key Carlos had entrusted with him. When he had locked the door last night, he knew it would be the last time before he had to relinquish the key. He remembered thinking that he wished he didn't have to give it back. Now, it would seem, that wish might be coming true even though that wasn't at all what he meant.

Maria followed him into the living room and he stood there for a moment to allow his eyes to adjust. All of the lights were off except for in the kitchen, the way Carlos liked it. Luis J inhaled deeply and could smell Carlos in the apartment, especially in the living room, and realized that eventually that would no longer be. All visible or sensual signs of Carlos would cease to exist. And the very thought pained him more.

"Want something to eat?" Maria asked, now standing in front of the refrigerator looking to see what Carlos had for them to consume.

"No. But I will take a beer."

Maria hesitated for a moment, then appreciating his emotional state, removed two Bud Lights and handed one to Luis J. She laughed and commented, "Carlos loved his culture, but he is a true American when it comes to his beer." They both laughed briefly and Luis J opened his bottle and took a swig. It was cold and went down smoothly.

"Obviously not your first one," Maria commented, watching him effortlessly gulp it down.

Luis J didn't respond, but instead took another swallow. He was not looking for a lecture. He hadn't had more than a drink or two from Carlos' bottle before, but he assumed two or three would do the trick. He just wanted to dull his senses.

Maria wandered over to the window and looked out, as though she were waiting to see Carlos drive up. Turning back toward Luis J, she looked around the place and then said, "This is my first time here. It's small, but it suits him."

When he didn't comment, she saw he was still guzzling the beer. She felt the need to say something else to ease his sadness, so she offered, "You know he loved you, Luis J? He was proud of you, too. He would often tell your Dad and me…"

"Hold up! Don't do that."

"Do what?"

"Talk about him in the past tense. He isn't dead."

"You're right. I'm sorry. I didn't mean to infer that he was." She turned back toward the window. Her words weren't helping him, not the way he needed.

Luis J drained the last of the beer and grabbed another. He wasn't feeling that sensation yet, even though he had downed it pretty quickly. So he set out to find something stronger. He remembered seeing half a bottle of Tequila under the sink a few weeks ago. Bending down to see if it was still there, he pulled the bottle from under the sink by its neck. He took one of the shot glasses off the counter top and poured his first glass. He had watched Carlos sprinkle salt on his hand and suck on a slice of lime while enjoying an occasional shot. But this glass was not about enjoyment so he closed his eyes, put it to his lips, and then took it all, in one clean motion. It really burned as it went down, causing him to shake his head and open his mouth to ease the sensation. He was pretty sure a couple of these would help him find the numbness he was seeking. He poured another, chasing the first with a swig of beer.

Maria knew exactly what he was trying to do and that it would not ease his pain. She walked over to him and stretched out her hand to take the shot glass from him. He handed it to her and in that moment, she chose to join him. He watched her head go back and the liquid disappear.

His eyes followed her chin, neck…but she didn't flinch at all. His hand touched hers as he reached for the glass. But when she didn't release it, he poured another and again watched it disappear. She then placed the glass in the sink as if to make a statement. Ignoring it, Luis J picked up the glass and poured his second shot. She stood in front of him and watched him drink it.

"Feeling better now?" Maria asked.

"Not yet," he said, drinking some more beer.

"Come. Sit down on the couch with me for a second. You remind me so much of your father. You have his sense of sarcasm. I often wondered which one of you was more like him when he was your age."

She had observed Carlos when he was living with them, but she didn't see as much of Luis in him the way she did with Luis J. It made her wonder if Luis J relieved stress the same way as his father. She walked over to the couch and waited for him to join her.

Luis J poured a third before leaving the kitchen. After she sat down, he looked down at her before eventually sitting next to her. She was dressed as she was the last time he had seen her, provocatively. It was just enough to entice the observer and cause them to ponder the softness of her skin. Her cell phone rang and he realized he hadn't heard a word she had just said.

Maria sat there as still as a mouse as she listened. She then extended her hand to give Luis J the phone, but he refused to take it from her. Instead he rose and walked to the window. There was only one reason for a call and as long as he didn't talk to his father, it wasn't real. He heard Maria switch to Spanish just before she closed the door to the bathroom. It reminded him of his conversation with Carlos, scolding him for not practicing his language skills.

Luis J really didn't understand much of what Maria was saying and honestly, he really didn't want to try. He drank the tequila and chased it with the rest of the beer. He put the glass and bottle on the window ledge and kept staring out the window.

The next thing he felt was Maria's arms around his waist. He could feel her warm breasts pressed against his back, matching the warmth he was now feeling from the alcohol. He moved, hoping that it would make her give him back his personal space, but she remained in the position, clinging to him.

He turned around and faced her, but she shifted her weight and arms to maintain her grip. She was stronger than her frame suggested, and now he was starting to finally feel the effect of the alcohol. She placed her head on Luis J's chest as though she were listening to make sure his heart kept beating. Her comfort felt good to him and he found himself putting his arms around her. She moved her body closer into him, allowing him to inhale her perfume and feel her hair sensually against his face.

Luis J felt his body responding naturally to this comfort and, embarrassed, tried to pull away. This made her hold on tighter. His arousal came easy, as he always used sex to take himself out of his funk. This was clearly one of those times.

"Do you trust me?" she whispered.

He wasn't sure how to answer her question. He wasn't sure what she meant. Maybe she was alluding to a massage, but he knew he wanted to release his tension, he wanted to make love. He needed Dany. Once again, tears were threatening to flow, so he closed his eyes tightly and nodded yes.

"Then, just for tonight, let me help you through this pain."

At first, he wasn't sure he had heard her clearly, but it soon became obvious as she lifted her head and began kissing his chest. Luis J thought no further. Allowing the fog of his high to navigate him, he leaned down and kissed her mouth, instinctively parting her lips with his tongue. She moaned. He felt his body becoming even more aroused. He hadn't been with anyone for a few days and right now, he needed the release. He didn't think past who she was and what it would mean, only that she was a female who could help him through the abyss he felt. He wanted her passion to remove the emptiness and the sadness he was feeling.

For a moment, somewhere deep in his mind, under the alcohol, he considered stopping because he knew it was wrong, but he couldn't. He didn't want to, and neither did she. She removed his shirt and began kissing him all over his chest, careful not to miss a spot.

Maria wrapped one leg around him and then slowly both legs as he cupped her butt and slid her into place. He then carried her into the bedroom, still kissing her warm mouth. He slid her skirt up the rest of the way and pulled her panties down. He had done these quickies so many times, it was like he was on autopilot. But this was different. She was much more sensual. Maria sensed Luis J's inexperience. He was lusty and young but he had lots to learn and she would teach him a thing or two that only a grown-ass woman could. She was so moist already. She was in control of his actions and was actually guiding his dick inside of her. He wasn't used to this, but he liked it. It made him even harder and desirous of her.

When he entered her, he had to control his movement to keep from coming too quickly. With each movement, he was drawn deeper inside of her, thrusting harder and harder. Now, he was just trying to release the tension that wrestled with his inner peace. The way she moved and moaned caused him to climax quickly. Feeling all of the tightness leave his body, he rolled onto his back, lying next to her. He couldn't tell if he had satisfied Maria, but he was pretty sure that wasn't her goal. The combination of the sexual release and the alcohol lulled him quickly into a deep sleep.

Chapter Seventeen

When Luis spoke to Maria earlier, he was relieved that she had found Luis J and drove him to Carlos' apartment. It was a way for him to be closer to his brother and hopefully, bring him some comfort. Diane didn't object and was relieved to know that he wasn't in the streets so late at night.

Luis had told Maria that he would be staying at the hospital with CJ. The child had lost his mother and father and was in a strange place. The last thing Luis wanted was for his grandson to be afraid or alone. But he also knew CJ could give him the comfort he craved that night, as well. Diane and Chell had gone home with David, and CJ was the only one left to provide him that unconditional love.

Diane was motionless and silent the entire ride home. Chell somehow was able to fall asleep. Diane found herself envying the innocence of a child. Luis had managed to contact his mother, who talked to Luisa's grandparents, who called Luisa's parents. So when the hospital told them that they had spoken to Luisa's parents, they felt that they had contacted everyone impacted. Diane was too numb to call her family and there wasn't anything they could do for her or Carlos now anyway. It could wait until morning.

When they entered their home, Diane went to her room and sat on the edge of the bed, unable to move. Robert was still at Marvin's house. David was sitting with Chell, talking to her about the evening and helping her begin to come to terms with the loss. Diane felt like she was dreaming but knew that sleep was nowhere in her near future. After a few minutes, David came in with a glass of red wine. She usually drank red at night as it was warm and soothing. She took it but didn't want any. She sat it on the nightstand.

Observing this, David asked, "Can I get you something else?"

"Can you bring my son back?" she asked, rhetorically, without sass or attitude. She wasn't really expecting an answer. Then she began her Diane thing: "Where were you tonight? We tried to reach you all evening."

"I went for drinks with some of the guys and then we went to shoot some pool. I left my cell in the car. I should've been there with you, holding you, helping you."

"Well, I wasn't alone." She knew those words would cut deep. She was in pain and all she wanted to do was share it.

"I'm glad Luis was there. You should never have to face something like this alone."

She lay back on the bed and tears rolled down her cheeks. She was thinking, 'A parent shouldn't have to face something like that at all.'

David lay down next to her. When she didn't retreat, he reached for her. She crawled into his arms like a child would do to their parent after scraping a knee. He held her close and secure, gently rubbing her back. They laid there in the dark until he finally heard her breathing get heavy and he knew that the weight of the day had finally won.

When Luis J awoke, he was in Carlos' bed, barely covered by a sheet. His head was a little foggy. He looked around the room and called out to Maria, but there was no response. He got up from the bed and slipped into his jeans that were still on the floor. The door to the bedroom was partially closed, blocking his view of the apartment. He pushed it open and looked around. The tequila bottle was still open on the counter top but the empty beer bottles had been placed in the trash can and the shot glass was in the sink.

His shirt was still on the floor by the window; he picked it up and put it back on. He sat on the couch trying to remember what was real and what he had imagined or dreamed. But the smell of sex was on him for real and there was no denying that. He returned to the bedroom to see what he could confirm and found Maria's earring in the bed. After putting it on the dresser, he showered and then headed for home. He knew his mother would be there and probably mad he hadn't come home. But then again, she hadn't called.

When he arrived, his mother was in the kitchen with David and his father.

"Luis J, there you are. Are you alright?"

"Yeah."

"Did you sleep well?" his mother asked.

"Not really."

"Luis J, we're all feeling the impact of this tragedy. Your mother most of all. Are you really alright?" Papi asked.

"Just great. And why do you think she's feeling this most of all?" Luis J asked, sarcastically.

"Luis J, just sit down and talk to us."

"About what exactly, Papi?"

"How you're feeling, for starters." Luis had feared this would be his son's reaction to the loss. When Diane called and told him Luis J hadn't returned yet, Luis had left the hospital around seven to go home and freshen up. He then headed to Diane's to be there when Luis J eventually returned home.

All Luis J could think of in response was, 'I feel like shit.' He had lost his brother last night, he didn't get to tell him goodbye, and to top it off, he slept with his father's live-in girlfriend in his dead brother's bed. What else could he say; that about summed it up.

"Papi, I know you mean well, but I really am not in the mood to talk right now. Can you give me some time and some space?" He wasn't sure what that looked like as he didn't know how he would ever get over this.

"Luis J, I understand how you feel, but you can't run from this," Diane said, trying to get her son to face his pain. She knew the sooner he was able to do that, the sooner he would start to heal.

"Isn't that funny, Mami, coming from you? I hope you realize that this is your fault. If you hadn't interfered in Carlos' life over and over again, he would be here instead of lying in a morgue. You kept him from getting married back then and sent his life down this path. You destroy everything you touch: Papi, Carlos, David. Well, not me!"

He noticed that his mother stood perfectly still at first, but then her bottom lip began quivering and she slowly lowered herself into a chair. The words obviously affected her and Luis J wanted them to. He wanted her to accept her responsibility in this horrible outcome, this tragedy that took his brother from him. He hoped she was really listening and feeling one-tenth of the pain he was experiencing.

"Luis J, stop it, right now! This isn't your mother's fault. This isn't anyone's fault. This is God's will. The next words out of your mouth better be, 'I'm sorry.'"

"Papi, how can you defend her after all she's done to you? Just take a look around you. None of us are happy and it's all because of her. You aren't allowed to be with your kids. Robert calls David, 'daddy.' How will Robert ever understand all this when he gets older? David isn't living here anymore. Carlos never knew his son until a week ago. His son will never get to know him. And worst of all, she's just as miserable as the rest of us. She doesn't deserve an apology."

"Luis J, not another word! Do you hear me?" his father stated, in an effort to regain control of the dynamics in the room. 'Although Luis J's comments were factually true this was not the time and he was not the person to share these observations with Diane. It was too soon. She wasn't ready,' Luis surmised.

Diane interrupted, "No, Luis, it's alright. He's right, this is my fault. I admitted it to myself last night. I deserve that." Diane managed to utter these words before leaving the kitchen to find solace in her bedroom.

"You have no right talking to your mother that way," David interjected. He could empathize with Luis J right now, but he would not tolerate any bullshit from him.

"So now you have an opinion? You moved out, didn't you? Besides, that's how I feel, and deep down inside, both of you know I'm right. If you were men, you'd face it and start from there. How both of you let her get away with all she does is beyond me. She's been running her game, wreaking havoc on all of us. She's been a train wreck ready to happen for a long time. And guess what? This is not the first accident, just the one that woke us all up at Carlos' expense!"

David spoke first, feeling that he had to defend Diane and his territory. "Luis J, I don't really care what you think you know about our situation, but I do know this, there's only room in this house for one man. It seems like I have had to remind you a hundred times over the past few weeks about your place in this house. Perhaps you should go to your room and just check yourself."

"Whatever..."

Luis opted to stay out of this exchange. It gave him a glimpse into why David had rolled up on his son last month. He can't say now that he blamed him for calling Luis J down, but he could have done it without hitting him. Luis had his own thoughts about Luis J's comments and would share them with his son later.

Luis J left the kitchen and went to his room. He started going through his things, preparing to leave. David would never let him have a place in this house, regardless of whether he was living there or not. His mind was wandering and random thoughts were jumbling altogether.

He was going to Carlos' and would stay there for the rest of the month. The rent was paid so why not? He'd pack up Carlos' things and use this time to figure out his options because living under this roof was no longer one.

Then, another issue bore its way to the front of his mind. How did he go all the way with Maria? He was so angry after Papi called and her arms were so inviting and comforting. It was the one thing that physically calmed him down and kept him from punching something or someone.

But now that it was done, what and how the hell was he ever going to tell Papi? It would surely ruin his relationship with Maria and put the brakes on any new father and son relationship they were starting. But didn't his father deserve to know? Luis J would certainly want to know if Danielle had been unfaithful to him. But hell, it wasn't really his fault. Maria had made the first move. Even if they told Papi, once he calmed down, he'd tell Mami and she'd kill Maria for sure. No, it would be better to keep this secret.

With that resolved, he made his move to leave the house. As David said, there wasn't room for another man and that included him, too, because his mother was in control of this house – or at least that's the message she always conveyed. David was no longer in the kitchen, but Papi was now sitting on the couch. He looked at Luis J and the bag he was carrying.

"Going somewhere?" he asked, with an 'I'm tired of your shit, young man,' look on his face.

Luis J chose his words carefully so as not to push his father's patience any further. "Papi, you heard David. Even though he isn't living here, he's still sweating me and treating me like a kid with a time out. I may have said some things inappropriately, but it didn't warrant that kind of response. That's why I can't stay here. Not now. I want out."

"Since when did this become about what you want versus what's best for everyone? David is the man of this house, whether he's living here or not. And you have to respect that. When you don't, that's when and why he will check you. Since you don't have a way to take care of yourself yet, you need to be here. Besides, Robert, Chell and your mother need you. You all will have to be there for each other. Isn't that what Carlos would want you to do? He would want you to step up and be a man."

"I can't help them right now. Not until I'm able to sort some things out." He looked around the room to avoid his father's stare. He remembered that stare when they were kids and most of the time after it, his father had the last word.

Luis looked at his son and noticed it seemed he had aged overnight. He was not the same kid who was on the basketball court a few weeks ago. Events like this can be sobering. So instead of meeting him with authority, he offered him words of comfort. "I can appreciate that. Carlos' passing will affect all of us in different ways; it already has." He paused for a moment to reflect on Diane's reactions last night and how easily defeated she was earlier today when met with Luis J's tongue lashing. "Why don't you come and stay with Maria and me for a few days?"

"No! I mean, that doesn't solve the problem. I really just want to be by myself. I was thinking that I could stay at Carlos', at least through the end of this month. I know he's already paid the rent because he told me he paid it in advance since he was going on the trip and you never know ..." Luis J's voice trailed off as he wondered if Carlos somehow knew this was going to be his fate.

Shaking that off, he continued, "I can even drive his car to school until the holiday break since public transportation isn't really convenient from there." Luis J waited to see what thoughts were formulating in his father's mind.

"I don't know Luis J. That's a pretty big responsibility. You've never lived by yourself, without proper supervision."

"I won't need much. I'm telling you, I really need this. I can't stay here with Mami right now and she probably feels the same way about me being here no matter how much I apologize. Besides I'm the only person who knows what to do with Carlos' things. He wouldn't want Mami going through his stuff."

Listening intently to what his son was really saying, he responded, "Let me talk to your mother and David, but you need to sit tight for now. We need to discuss the arrangements and what to do about CJ."

Luis J didn't want anything to do with the discussion, but he had made some headway with his father so he didn't want to push his luck.

They sat and talked about the arrangements for what seemed like hours. They would bury Carlos in Puerto Rico in a week on Saturday. They would all go, except Robert. Diane was concerned about how Robert would react to her emotional condition the day she would have to bury her son. David agreed with her assessment and offered to stay home with him.

Luis understood Diane's rationale, but as unrealistic as his thoughts were, he was looking forward to introducing all of his children to their heritage, even if it had to be done covertly with Robert. He wanted something good to come of Carlos' death. Now, he would have to settle for two out of the three.

Luis J could not contribute anything to the conversation but knew that his father expected him to be there. So he sat and listened. A few times, he found himself thinking about Maria and wanting to call her. He wondered how she was feeling. He wondered what she had said when she saw his father.

Luis and Diane announced that they were going to stop by Luisa's parents' home to share their funeral plans and start the conversation regarding custody of CJ before going back to the hospital.

"Now, for a final topic," Luis stated. "Luis J would like to spend a couple of weeks at Carlos' apartment. I know this is putting a lot of responsibility on him, but I think he's ready to handle it. I believe it will help him have some closure while he packs his brother's things. I'll also stop by there periodically to check on him. What do you think?"

"I'll defer to Diane," David responded. He felt Luis J was a powder keg right now and with everyone's nerves on edge, it probably wasn't a bad idea. David was also concerned that since he wasn't living in the home at the moment, he couldn't run interference between Luis J and Diane. And based on their last exchange, he was sure Luis J would be gearing up and smelling himself.

"Fine, yes, someone will need to pack Carlos' things." Her tone told them that she was still feeling the effects of Luis J's words, and now Luis J was starting to regret his bluntness. But he knew there was truth in what he had said and that someone needed to say it. The only reason she wasn't saying anything else was that she knew it, too!

"Alright, then that's settled. We can drop him off at the apartment on our way to Luisa's parents' home. Luis J, when you get there, check and see what's needed, food, toiletries, etc. and we'll drop them off when I bring Diane back home. Please don't lose focus on why we are allowing you to do this," Papi concluded.

Luis J was relieved and grateful that his father had spoken on his behalf. Finally, someone understood what he needed.

The discussion was over. They all began dispersing. Luis J wished his anger and sadness would disperse like that. When he returned to the apartment, the emptiness really set in. He turned on the TV to watch the sports channel while drinking another Bud Light. Once he drained the bottle, he removed all the evidence of his drinking before his parents' return. He did a quick inventory and left a message on his father's phone. He kept it simple, things like soup, milk and frozen dinners. Since Papi would be out for a while, he thought that now would be a good time to call Maria. He wondered how she was feeling the morning after. She picked up after the third ring.

"Maria, it's Luis J, can we talk for a minute?"

"Sure, mijo. How are you feeling?"

"Hey, don't refer to me like that."

"You're right. That does sound weird after what happened last night."

"Exactly. I'm managing, considering all that's happened. I'm at Carlos'. I'm gonna stay here for a while. What's going on with you?"

"Nothing. Just paying some bills."

"About last night…"

"Last night you needed a friend and I was that friend. Nothing else needs to be said."

"But, what about Papi? This will kill him."

"Which is why we're not going to tell him. No good will come out of that discussion, so we'll just forget it ever happened. Agreed?"

"But what if he finds out?"

"How on earth would he?"

"I don't know. You left your earring over here."

She touched her earlobe to find that her left earring was missing. It was only costume jewelry, so she responded with, "Just throw it out. If you don't tell him, he'll never know. Trust me, this is the best way."

"For real, Maria? You sound like you know all about how to handle this. What's up with that?"

"What are you implying Luis J? I told you, I was there for you last night, that's all."

"I'm just sayin'. I mean are you really alright with this, cause I'm not. I'm sick inside. I had to look at Papi today like nothing had happened and it was weird. I just think it's a bad idea not to tell him."

"Look, you said so yourself, it would kill him. Besides, what good would come of it? Everyone is already in a world of hurt over Carlos. Do you really want to get your mother riled up over this? She would use this to cause so much trouble for you."

"What you really mean is my mother would use it to cause trouble for you. Don't think I don't know that you realize this would end your relationship with my father. He would put you out of his house for sure. And honestly, maybe that would be best for him. I don't want him to marry a woman who isn't faithful to him. I mean, what kind of woman sleeps with her boyfriend's son?"

Maria rolled her eyes. She would have slapped him if he had been standing in front of her. "You weren't complaining or questioning that last night when you put your dick inside me. What kind of son sleeps with his father's girlfriend?"

"You're right. I didn't stop, but I should have. I can see why you were able to come in between my parents back then. You are very seductive." Luis J felt his manhood rising from just thinking about last night. Her touch, her skin and the way she moved her body, her scent.

Yep, he understood why his father was under her spell…but what they did last night was still wrong.

Maria was surprised by Luis J's perception. He was one of the first men to get behind the curtain so quickly. This intrigued her about him, but right now she had to remain focused on the problem at hand. Aware of the need to shift gears, she changed her tone and became more feminine, less offensive, and began to reel him in.

"Look, Luis J, we both stepped over a line last night that we would never have if it hadn't been for the alcohol and losing Carlos. I was just trying to comfort you and honestly, myself. It was clearly what we both needed. I have never been unfaithful to your father and never will again. He and I have been building a strong bond and will probably get married next year. I'm asking you not to get in the way of that."

When he didn't respond, she started choosing her next words even more carefully.

"Luis J?"

"Maria, I don't know if you're telling me the truth or not, but I'm going to keep my mouth shut. Not because of some dream you have of marrying my father, but because I don't want to dishonor Carlos' death with a lot of drama, and that's exactly what we would have if I told my dad. I owe him that much. But I will tell you this, you can't build a meaningful relationship on top of secrets and lies. One day, it's going to come out and you'll see then that I was right. I just hope that it won't completely destroy my relationship with my father when it does. We were starting to build one because of Carlos." He didn't feel the need to hear a response from Maria so he ended the call.

Maria, left holding the receiver, could not believe that Luis J had just summed her up that quickly. He may be more of a challenge than she thought. She would have to keep her pulse on that young man. Guilt can be a dangerous thing when dealing with secrets.

Luis J hated what he had done and about keeping it from his father, but for now it seemed the best way to go. There was a code that men didn't cross and he was way over the line and in foul trouble. And now he had discovered who Maria really was and how she played her cards. His mother had figured that out a long time ago and she was dead on.

He found himself needing to be with someone so he called Cassie. She was home for the evening and he told her he would stop by in a couple of hours. He hoped his parents would be gone by then.

18 Chapter Eighteen

Luis had called Luisa's parents to request a meeting and they agreed to meet briefly. Luis wasn't sure how he felt about meeting with the man who had questioned their heritage, a man who had told his son that he'd never be good enough for his Luisa. Mr. Morales' actions and comments made him as equally responsible for their demise as Diane, truth be told. Luis and Diane sat in the Morales' living room, not sure where or how to start.

Breaking the silence, Luis began, "May God help ease your pain as you accept your daughter's loss. We completely understand what you're going through."

"Do you?" asked Mr. Morales, with a slight frown on his face.

"Of course, yes. Must we remind you we lost our son, too? This has been a hurtful, unbelievable tragedy for us, as well."

"And well it should be. If your son had not gotten our baby pregnant in the first place, none of this would have happened." Mr. Morales was sitting, but now he stood up. "I begged her to stay away from him. If she had, she would be in college now, making something of herself, instead of being a disgraced single parent. And then he still couldn't leave well enough alone. He had to follow her to Puerto Rico, upset her life again and ultimately cause her death."

He took off his glasses and dabbed his eyes with a handkerchief before continuing. "I really don't know why you came here. What is it that you want?"

"Did you really just lay all of this at my son's feet? He didn't create the baby by himself. They were in this together. And you are hardly in a position to stand on top of some mountain and point down at the rest of us. You need to shoulder the blame for what happened to them too."

Luis could feel his Latin blood beginning to boil and sat back in the chair to create some space between him and his feelings before continuing. "Look, it's easy to talk about all the 'what ifs' and 'what should have beens.' Don't think we haven't done that all night. But the reality of the situation is, our children, God rest their souls, loved each other. Perhaps if you had recognized that back then, instead of deciding that our son was not good enough for Luisa, all of this would have ended differently."

Diane was amazed by what she was hearing and interrupted, "What? I didn't know that Carlos' character was ever a question. I thought that they felt what I felt, that they were too young to enter into a marriage, let alone have a child. What are you talking about?"

"Oh Diane, if you only knew the half of it. Mr. Morales would have accepted the marriage except he felt that Carlos' "breeding" wasn't up to par. He preferred to punish his daughter for selecting someone he didn't feel was, as he put it, truly Puerto Rican. But my ancestors are Puerto Rican, I am Puerto Rican, and so was my son. Thank God Mrs. Morales didn't share the same sentiment as you. She recognized how much they loved each other and that your views were antiquated."

Luis turned to Mrs. Morales and said, "Thank you for telling Carlos how to locate Luisa and his son. Your kindness for him allowed our grandson the opportunity to get to know his father, although briefly. For that, you will be blessed."

Mr. Morales looked at his wife with betrayal in his eyes and was about to put her back into her place, when she spoke for the first time of the enduring heartbreak she suffered over the years from losing her daughter.

"Gracias, Mr. Rodriquez. I extend my prayers to you and your family, too. I should have spoken up then and defended my daughter, but instead I followed the old ways. It's laughable to think that we had come here so that Luisa could become a modern woman and when she behaved as one, we shut her down and threw her into the past. I knew that they were in love from the beginning. I thought the world of Carlos. He was always a gentleman and was so brave the night they came to us. You would be proud to know that he went head to head with my husband. He told him, 'I will marry Luisa and we will raise our child together and we will finish school.'

"I believed him and knew that he meant it. I just wanted you to know that. But I didn't have the strength to speak up then. So when he contacted me I was happy to share Luisa's information and I prayed that he would get in touch with her. My parents, sister and your mother have been there for my daughter and grandchild all this time because they know better than we do. They know that blood is thicker than water and you have to embrace your children, even when they make mistakes."

Luis' eyes welled up and he nodded in appreciation of Mrs. Morales' words. He cleared his throat and looked at Mr. Morales, who had shut down. "We all made the best decisions we could at the time with the information we had. We thought we were doing what was best. But my son did not want his son to grow up without him. I admire and applaud him for that. Unfortunately, his time, their time, was cut way too short but their blessing was left here for us. Now, we need to discuss the custody and care of their child, our grandson."

Finally Mr. Morales found strength to speak again. "We're going to cremate our daughter and send her ashes to Puerto Rico. We want a private ceremony, family only."

Luis understood the insinuation. "We can respect that. We're taking Carlos to Puerto Rico, too. We will be laying him to rest next to my father."

Mr. Morales continued, "As for the child, my wife and I cannot take custody of him. We are too old to have to start over raising a child. Besides, he will be a constant reminder of what we've lost. My wife would like to see him occasionally until we move back to Puerto Rico, if you approve. We will be leaving here within the next three to six months."

Diane could hardly believe what she was hearing. She and Luis had assumed Luisa's parents would want some sort of joint custody relationship, but clearly not this. Luis was surprised as well, but given how this man had lived his life, Luis didn't want that negative influence or those beliefs imposed on his grandson. But just to be sure, he asked, "Are you absolutely sure? I know this is a very major decision to make so soon after your loss."

"We're sure. And if you aren't able to care for him either, we will send him back to Puerto Rico to stay with my wife's family. They love him and want him to feel safe. This might be easiest for him, to be in familiar surroundings."

"Our son's dying wish was for us to care for his son, to raise him. We would never consider abandoning his wish. He looks so much like Carlos, we love that little boy already. Don't you feel the connection to your daughter?" Diane questioned.

"I have never met him. My wife has seen pictures of him and Luisa and as she said, she would like to see him if you will allow that. And although I understand your point about my role in their demise, it doesn't alter the facts. My daughter has disgraced me and my family name. I would like her to rest in peace and close that chapter in my life. Let us know if we need to sign anything to relinquish our rights to the child. One of you may bring him to Luisa's ceremony if you think it's appropriate given his age. I honestly don't know if it is best for him or not."

Diane looked at Mrs. Morales. Tears were streaming down her face and she was shaking her head from side to side. She was muttering words in Spanish, but Diane couldn't make them out until she saw her kiss the cross that hung around her neck and knew she was praying.

"Mrs. Morales, you may see CJ anytime you want. I'll give you my number and address. I would love for you to be a part of his life." Diane offered these words hoping it would bring her some comfort.

Mrs. Morales hesitated, looked at Diane and then Luis. Lowering her eyes, she responded, "I have shared my view. However, I am still married to my husband and we practice the old way. His decision is the final one for our family. I will see CJ while I am here, and when you visit Puerto Rico, if you bring him, I will see him then. Each time, I will tell him of his mother and how much she loved and sacrificed for him in her very young life. So thank you for allowing me the chance to do that. But I will not have a place in his life beyond that."

Diane's heart ached for her. She knew how much that woman's pain was flowing through her body. She understood how much she was missing her baby girl and would love to embrace the only living connection to her daughter. When Mrs. Morales came to visit, Diane would make it clear that she would always be welcomed in their grandson's life.

Luis and Diane finished discussing the specifics of the arrangements and exchanged all of the necessary contact information before heading to the hospital. The doctors were going to keep CJ one more day and they wanted to check on him.

As Diane held CJ in her arms, rocking him and kissing him repeatedly, she reflected on their conversation with Mr. and Mrs. Morales.

"Can you believe that?" Diane asked.

"I can understand their anger and disappointment about their daughter, but I could never turn my back on any child, especially my own," Luis replied. Diane's words didn't settle well with him. It was like the pot calling the kettle black. So he just sat quietly after that.

But the words did remind Diane of what Luis J had said to her earlier. 'No, Luis, you couldn't,' she thought. But that was exactly what she had made him do all these years and what she had forced upon Carlos. Luis J was right. With his limited seventeen-year-old wisdom, he was right about this.

Diane had been trying to control her children's lives, all of them, including Robert's. She was trying to make the best choices for them based on her rules, guidelines and expectations, and she was also hellbent on punishing Luis for his indiscretions. But now that the dust was settling, all she had actually done was cause pain for all of them, including herself.

Diane saw the pensive look on Luis' face and knew there wasn't anything she could say that would offer him any comfort or attempt to provide any insight regarding the judgement she had enforced all these years. Instead, she just continued to hold her grandson tightly to offer her love and affection and hopefully to find some absolution in his arms.

Chapter Nineteen

A week had passed, but to the Rodriquez family it felt like months. There was a lot to do to prepare for the trip to San Juan, but everyone seemed to be just going through the motions. Maria had elected not to go and even though Diane didn't know why, it was a huge relief for her.

Diane felt it really was a family affair and, after all, Maria and Luis weren't married. At least not yet. Diane's family was planning to arrive the day before the funeral. Luis' middle brother, Antonio and sister, Mary, who both lived in Chicago, were also planning to attend. They were set to arrive two days before the funeral.

Mary was ten years younger than Luis and at times he felt more like her father. He was honored when she asked him to give her away at her wedding three years ago. She now had two children both under the age of three and this kept her from traveling as often as she used to. So, Mary and Luis could never seem to coordinate their schedules to meet in San Juan, Chicago or New York. Instead, they stayed connected through monthly phone calls. He was looking forward to seeing his baby sister, even if it wasn't for the best of reasons.

In contrast, Luis' relationship with his brother Antonio was strained and had been for years. Antonio was two years younger than Luis, the same age difference between his sons, but unfortunately, they had never shared that same bond as Carlos and Luis J.

Luis didn't understand what had caused the distance between them and tried to connect with his younger brother on several levels: sports, girls, and even school. Sadly, nothing ever gained any traction, so he eventually accepted their state of interaction and found his close, brotherly relationships through his friendships.

Antonio left Puerto Rico the year their baby brother, Bobby, was born. He was eighteen and with Luis away at college, their father was now riding him to get some focus and direction in his life. Antonio hadn't even finished high school and told them he had no intentions of following in his older brother's footsteps and trying to get into college. Instead, he had a knack for fixing things and would pick up odd jobs around the neighborhood.

Their father, Luisandro, found this disappointing because he knew that even with his skills, his son would need formal training to be able to be a self-sufficient man. And then there was the crowd he was hanging out with. They had been getting into and out of trouble throughout high school. Now that they didn't have at least that structure of school, they were surely to get into some serious trouble and Luisandro wanted more for his son. So, Luisandro did what many had done before him to save their children; he sent him to family. His sister, Camilla, lived in Chicago and was willing to take him. She and her husband had never had any children so they welcomed Antonio with open arms.

Camilla's husband, Steve, taught him two skills: electrical wiring and carpentry. Antonio picked them up quickly. Steve said he was a natural. Within six months, Antonio landed a job with the Ross Construction Company, one of the major firms in the Chicagoland area. They were typically awarded construction projects in downtown Chicago, responsible for revitalizing the South Loop area.

But Antonio had two bad habits: he drank too much and he liked to gamble. This combination of two bad habits kept him living from paycheck to paycheck and put a strain on all of his relationships. Neither of his wives was willing to stay with him. He lost two marriages because these habits kept them from getting ahead no matter how hard they worked.

Antonio had one son, his namesake, with his first wife. That boy was now twenty and also lived in Chicago. Unfortunately, the stories about him were equally disappointing; he seemed to be following in his father's footsteps and hitting the bottle as well.

No matter how much Antonio drank, though, he always made it to work on time. He needed the money to support his habits and he was one of the most gifted carpenters at the company. The job paid him well, but there were many times when there still wasn't enough money to pay the rent and take care of his responsibilities, so this became a bone of contention between the brothers.

Whenever Antonio was about to be evicted from his apartment, he would call someone in the family to come to his rescue. It was usually his mother, but sometimes he didn't care where the green came from, as long as it came.

This recurring scenario perplexed Luis. At that time, he and Diane had two children, lived in NYC on only one income, and he and his wife were able to make ends meet. It wasn't easy, but Diane was a planner and she had them on a tight budget. He finally asked his mother if she had any insight and that's when he learned about his brother's addictions. She had shared how concerned she and their father were about Antonio's alcoholism. He had begun drinking at 16 and now that he was 24, it was getting even worse.

After that revelation, Luis could easily connect the dots. He called his brother and offered to help him find some professional help, but Antonio would not admit he had a problem. Instead, Antonio would try to lay a guilt trip on Luis, telling him that he was more interested in giving away the money to some stranger to fix a problem that didn't exist instead of helping him keep a roof over his nephew's head. After all, it was Luis who had the degrees and fancy job.

But Luis refused to fall into the "my life sucks" trap, so he offered to pay the rent directly to the landlord. As Luis anticipated though, Antonio had tons of reasons why that wasn't an option. So, Luis stopped taking his calls and encouraged his mother to follow suit. He wanted Antonio to learn to stand on his own two feet and deal with his addictions. It was way past time for him to be the man their father had raised them to be.

NaNa struggled with this advice, for she didn't want Antonio's desperation to escalate to a point of dangerous or criminal actions. And she didn't want to put her grandson at risk either. Therefore, every month, she would send Antonio some money and Antonio never refused it.

But, for this trip, Luis had to put all of that aside so he could draw his strength from his family to bury his son. He would, however, keep an eye on Antonio because he also wasn't going to accept any bullshit from him.

Diane and Luis had hired an attorney to work with child protective services to award them temporary guardianship while the permanent guardianship specifics were finalized. The temporary placement would allow CJ to live in Diane's home and for him to travel with them.

When CJ came home from the hospital, the first few nights were terrible. He cried for Luisa nonstop. Diane tried to comfort him, relying on her maternal instincts, but her inability to speak Spanish to him and all of the newness fueled his insecurities.

Diane was also pretty sure he could sense the void she felt inside and that made him feel even more anxious. She knew that babies reacted to the emotional state of their caregivers, but she couldn't help it. Every time she looked into his eyes and remembered Carlos at that age, the emotions associated with her pain, hurt and loss would come flooding back and she couldn't hold back the tears. So mostly she just sang lullabies and rocked him to try to comfort him.

His demeanor was more like Luis J's when he was a baby – constantly needing attention – even though he was surely Carlos' son. There was no doubt about that now, although she had questioned it when she first learned about Luisa's pregnancy. "Mama's baby, Daddy's maybe." Her mother had always said that when she was growing up. Diane had hoped by having CJ in her life that it would ease some of her loss, but he couldn't do that because he was struggling with his own. He couldn't even begin to understand what had happened to his mother. Diane's heart ached for her son and her grandson because she wasn't sure she would ever have the strength to fill his void.

Luis came over nightly to spend time with CJ and speak to him in Spanish, letting him know who Diane was as well as himself. He told him the best he could that his Mommie and Papi had to go away but had sent them to care for their son. Careful not to overstep his boundaries, he supported Diane as she allowed. To his surprise and pleasure, she didn't make it difficult for him and, in fact, seemed to welcome his presence.

During this transition, David offered to keep Robert with him and this, too, was a relief to Diane. She didn't feel she could handle Robert's twenty questions right now or his need to be the center of attention. She was worried about how he would take to CJ since he never had to compete for his mother or David's attention. They weren't going to take him to the funeral, so staying with David before the time of their actual departure would make that transition even easier.

Then there was Chell. Diane noticed that she seemed withdrawn and quieter than normal. Since Diane's energy level was low and focused on CJ, she asked Luis to spend time with Chell during his visits to assess how she was coping with the loss. Magically, Diane finally accepted how much Chell longed for her father in her life. She clung to his every word, followed him around the house and sat so close to him she was almost sitting in his lap. She was like a love-starved child, even though Diane thought she and David had compensated for the absence of a male father figure. Clearly, she was out of tune with this child as well.

Last, but not least, was Luis J. She didn't see much of him since he was staying at Carlos' apartment, but she would call him occasionally to check on him and would get updates from Luis when he stopped by for his regularly scheduled visits.

Out of all of their children, she and Luis worried about the impact this was going to have on Luis J the most. It had become apparent that he had taken the individual strengths from both of them and he was definitely headstrong, but this was a blow directly to the heart and that organ heals slowly. Carlos had been a rock in his life for all of his life, especially once his parents had separated and ultimately divorced. They knew they would need to help Luis J and they hoped he would let them.

As the plane skidded to a halt on the runway, it sickened Diane to think that her first trip to her husband's – ex-husband's – homeland was to bury her son. She held CJ's hand to give him as much comfort as she was receiving as they walked down the airport aisles to baggage claim. As they turned the corner, Luis in the lead with Chell in hand, they saw NaNa, Angie and Bobby. A comforting smile appeared on NaNa's face as only a few words and lots of hugs were exchanged. Luis lingered in his mother's arms longer than anyone anticipated, rocking gently. It was so touching to see this grown man, physically towering over his mother, draw strength from her embrace. Diane wondered if he was breaking down until she saw his grip loosen and his mother release him.

She then turned toward Diane and opened her arms once again. The tears began to swell in Diane's eyes the way they did every time someone had that look of 'I'm so sorry for your loss.' So, she embraced her ex-mother-in-law briefly, for she couldn't help feeling she would have a breakdown in front of everyone in the airport and this was not the time or the place for anyone, especially CJ, to see that happen.

NaNa sensed that and quickly released Diane. Next she reached for CJ and he ran into her arms. He hugged her around the neck and wouldn't let go. It was more than anyone could bear, so Angie began rounding everyone up and making suggestions about who should ride with whom. Chell and Luis J would go with Bobby and Angie, while NaNa chauffeured everyone else.

Diane admired the countryside on the way to NaNa's as she sat quietly in the back seat with CJ, who had fallen asleep. Luis and his mother talked the entire ride. He hadn't been home in about three years and so they talked about politics and changes in the community and the rest of the family.

She told him that Antonio and Mary would be arriving later that evening and waited for some reaction from Luis, but he just nodded. She then mentioned Carlos' recent visit and how happy she had been to see him.

She said to Diane and her son, "It is sad, yes, that we must bury one so young, but be proud of the young man he had become. I admired his intelligence and focus on life when I heard him talk. He was so much like you, mijo, at that age, and he was unmistakably his own man."

Luis smiled at his mother's observation and Diane could swear he poked his chest out a little. She couldn't help but wish that she had seen that same man standing in front of her before he left. Oh, he was there… but she couldn't see him. She returned to looking at the village and tried to get lost in the images and sounds around her, for these thoughts of her short-sightedness were jabbing at her heart.

When they arrived at NaNa's home, Diane found it very comfortable and welcoming. Luis had shown her pictures and talked about it but it hadn't accurately depicted the love that poured out of every room. This woman had a calmness that surrounded her and was soothing to all who were blessed with her presence. You can't capture that in pictures.

NaNa had cooked and the aroma smelled of tradition. Neighbors who had stopped by to help serve the food greeted them. Everyone ate and talked around the table, in the living room and on the porch. Most of the conversations were slipping in and out of Spanish. Diane was surprised that it was coming back to her so quickly. She understood the gist of the conversations, but was unable to find the words to respond. It was alright with her though because she really didn't want to engage in any conversations right now. She was an introvert at heart and although she could make these situations seem natural to everyone around her, they did not know how much energy it actually took from her to fit in. And she knew she had to rebuild her strength for the days ahead. So, she just faded into the background during this gathering, smiling occasionally.

Once the kitchen was cleared, the family members gathered on the porch as the last of the guests left. Diane observed CJ's calmness around NaNa and knew it was from a place of familiarity. His maternal great grandparents thought it would be best for them to stay away today so as not to upset him when they had to leave without him. Diane knew they were missing him, though, and were looking forward to holding him once again. She was thankful they weren't contesting his custody. As he started to wind down, she scooped him up and began preparing him for bed.

Luis and NaNa remained seated in conversation as Bobby's car pulled into the yard. Luis stood and waited for them to approach. Mary was first to reach him, standing on tiptoe to hug him as best she could. Both of his sisters were short like his mother's side of the family, but today she seemed taller than he as his shoulders weren't as broad as usual. She had picked up a little weight but he was sure it was left over baby fat and today he found comfort in her arms, too.

The next person to approach the porch was Antonio, but Luis hardly recognized him. He was so pale and thin. He had probably lost about sixty pounds since the last time Luis had seen him. His face looked drawn and his eyes were blood shot. Luis was not prepared for this image of his brother, but before he could speak, his mother's words lobbed into the air.

"Ay Dios mío, what the hell is wrong with you? Antonio, are you sick? What's the matter?"

"Oh, that's how you greet your son? Is that the best you can say after all this time? Still the same mother. How are you?"

"Mijo, you have to know that we are concerned about you. You have lost so much weight."

"Yes and Mary found it," he responded, laughing.

He was the only one who found anything that resembled humor in that comment and in that moment. Everyone knew that Antonio's physical condition was a result of his alcoholism; they just didn't know until now just how bad it had gotten.

Luis moved toward his brother, but this action was met by Antonio stepping back and saying, "Hey, I was sorry to hear about your son. I came to pay my respects."

Those brief words established the level of engagement Antonio was willing or able to have at this time and for now Luis didn't push it. He glanced at his mother only to see her in deep thought, as she eyed her second born from head to toe.

"Now, who is this pretty thing? You must be Diane. I'm Antonio," he said, lifting her hand to kiss it as she rejoined them on the porch.

"Hi, Antonio. It's a pleasure to finally meet you," Diane responded, realizing that she had walked into the middle of something. Luis had made her aware of his issues with his brother and she could only assume they were continuing, although she had hoped he could find a way to be supportive to his older brother, at least for this trip.

"Luis, I don't know what the woman looks like that you're with now, but this one is smoking hot," Antonio said, eyeing Diane from head to toe.

"Pull up, Antonio, pull up," Luis responded, with the authority of an older brother, but also a man who was getting pissed off with his rudeness.

"No disrespect man. Just making an observation."

"Perhaps you should go inside and get something to eat since you don't seem to know what else to do with your mouth. Angie, fix your brother a plate. Bobby and Mary, too," NaNa interjected. She knew Antonio was headed toward a beat down if he kept pushing his brother.

"Of course. Come on guys," Angie replied, welcoming the chance to disperse the tension that was building up around them. Angie led the way as if they were guests, leaving Diane, Luis and NaNa on the porch.

"He reeked of alcohol. He probably drank the whole plane ride. I could smell it even though he didn't let me hug him," Luis said. He paused for a moment before continuing, "Mami, did you know it was this bad?"

"I had my suspicions. Camilla told me she saw him occasionally and there was always something going on with him. She just wasn't specific and I wish she would have been."

"He has to get help, Mami. If he doesn't, it's going to kill him." Turning toward Diane, he added, "Di, please accept my apology for his rude comments."

"No apology needed," Diane said, as she was able to catch up very quickly by just listening and knew his words were the effect of the alcohol.

"Luis, this time is for Carlos, but we will need to see what can be done for Antonio, if anything. Will you be able to help?"

"Of course, Mami. If he's willing and ready to accept it. That's the only way we will be able to help him."

Diane sat with them a little longer before saying her good nights. It was only eight-thirty, but she was exhausted and needed some quiet time. She found Chell in Angie's room listening to music and reading a book. She gave her some guidelines for the balance of the night and turned in.

Luis and NaNa sat on the porch, neither of them talking at the moment. They could hear Antonio snoring on the couch, belly full and the alcohol in full swing. Angie and Mary were sitting at the table getting caught up.

Bobby wandered onto the porch, bulldozing his way into their silence the way he used to do when they were kids. "I'm heading out. I told Luis J he could roll with me, if it's okay with you. I also invited him to stay with me 'cause it's crowded over here. Are you and Diane down with that?"

"Bobby, remember he's only seventeen."

"Mira, always the big brother. I got this," Bobby said, closing the car door. Bobby and Luis J had bonded right away. Bobby followed college basketball and had played in high school and college as well, so they were able to share information about their favorite teams, moves and players. It was this sort of exchange that Luis J had shared with Carlos.

From the time they left Bobby's apartment to the time they arrived at the club, his cell phone rang more times than Luis J could count. It was always a girl. Luis J was convinced he had made the right choice to stay with Bobby.

They hit a few spots that Bobby frequented and each one gave Luis J more insight into the life his uncle led. Bobby loved music, dancing and having fun, which he did with a diverse circle of friends. He was able to work the crowds and with his good looks had no problem attracting the ladies. In that way he was like Luis J; he had a way with women. He was smooth – giving compliments, buying drinks and commanding his space.

By default, Luis J was able to meet and entertain a few of the ladies himself since his Spanish was up to par, or so he thought. But to his surprise they all spoke to him in English. Bobby told him later it was because of his accent. They could tell he was Nuyorican. Luis J knew Carlos was laughing at him but he just shrugged his shoulders. He was glad Bobby didn't introduce him as his nephew as most of the women were in their twenties. Luis J met a few he could have easily taken to the next level had the circumstances been different, but he was pretty sure Bobby wouldn't give him that much leeway, at least not on the first day.

Bobby did allow him to drink a few cervezas though, mostly Medalia, because of the low alcohol content, but no tequila. Luis J didn't make a big deal about it because he knew this was exactly what he needed, time away from his family and the realities of why he was there in the first place. They hung out until about 3 a.m. and then finally crashed. He was "feeling no pain" as they say and fell asleep with none of his usual anxieties.

There wasn't much to do the next day; all the plans had been finalized before they left New York. Carlos' body was at the funeral home and they had elected to just have the wake an hour before the funeral to minimize the emotional highs and lows. Diane couldn't bring herself to go see him yet, so Luis and NaNa took care of the preview and approval.

While they were gone, Diane putzed around the house, occasionally chatting with Angie and Mary. People were still dropping by off and on, which required Angie to play hostess. Antonio had gotten up early that morning and left. He didn't exchange many words with his mother or brother. Diane could tell from the look on his face and the tone in his voice that Luis now had another person he was worried about, as if burying his son wasn't enough.

Several hours had gone by and Antonio still hadn't returned. Diane hoped that when he came back, he wasn't in the same condition as he had been the night before. She didn't need that drama on top of her parents' visit. They were due in around 4 p.m. and she was cautiously but optimistically looking forward to spending time with them, especially her sister Michelle. But Antonio's antics could send the whole experience spiraling. Her mother had no place for an alcoholic's performance.

When NaNa and Luis returned, they shared their pleasure of the job performed by the mortician. He had cared for Carlos as though he were his son. This was the same mortician who laid Luisandro to rest and helped the Rodriquez family many times over the years. He had a great respect for the family, and Carlos didn't have a hair out of place. Luis didn't share this, but when he saw Carlos, it looked like he was just sleeping and if he nudged him just a little, he would sit up and say, "No te preocupes."

NaNa noticed the far away look on her son's face, so she continued with the story. "We stopped by Luisa's grandparents' home to express our sympathies. Luis told me about your visit with her parents in the States. You'll be pleased to know that your interactions with the grandparents will be very different. They spoke very fondly of Carlos. Apparently, he really put on his Rodriquez charm, like his father and his grandfather, and they were so glad that he was there to step up and take on his responsibilities. You'll get to meet them tomorrow – they will be attending the funeral and then stopping by to spend time with CJ. I know how much he must miss them."

Diane was listening to the story but she was also distracted by the time. It was four-thirty and she hadn't heard from her parents yet. When her phone rang, she excused herself to answer it, anxious to hear they were on their way. But, to Diane's dismay, her mother informed her that they would be staying at a hotel downtown and once they were settled, if it wasn't too late, they would stop by that evening.

"But Mama, NaNa was expecting you guys over here for dinner. She's looking forward to seeing you. I'm sure you're tired, so why don't Luis and I come pick you up? That way you don't have to worry about finding a taxi and we can talk on the ride over here." Diane was asking for more time with her family, time she desperately wanted. "So, where are you staying?"

"Oh, dear, that's sweet but I don't want you to go out of your way. I know you have a lot to deal with," her mother replied. "We'll just take a cab. I don't want to add to your stress. Besides, I'm sure Luis has other things to do or people to spend time with. Didn't his GIRLFRIEND come with him? She won't take kindly to you whisking him off to pick up his ex-in-laws!"

Diane bit her bottom lip; she couldn't believe her mother had just thrown that in her face. The way she said "girlfriend" was meant to get under her skin. Did she have no empathy at all? Couldn't she let this rest, for just one day?

"She didn't come, Mother. So, really, it's not a problem."

"Honestly Diane, I'm really glad to hear that. She doesn't have a place here. But, we don't feel like waiting for you to drive over here and then waiting for you to take us back. We'll be fine."

Diane knew what her mother really meant was that she didn't feel like waiting. She wanted to maintain complete control over her actions and everyone else's while keeping Diane in her place. She smiled to herself, seeing herself reflected in the behavior. This way, her mother could come and go as she pleased and could minimize her interaction with Luis and anyone else she didn't feel like engaging.

It became clear to Diane now how much her mother still held a grudge against Luis, as though he had betrayed her as much as Diane. Even though they were burying his son too, she couldn't find forgiveness or compassion in her heart for him. Had her mother had her druthers twenty-plus years ago, she would have prevented their marriage, but she hadn't. She had not stood in the way of letting her make her own choice. In that way, they differed.

When that call ended, Luis J rang to tell her that he wouldn't be there until dinnertime. She didn't interrogate him too much as she knew he would be with Bobby and she could trust his instincts.

When Diane returned to the living room, NaNa was in the kitchen overseeing the cooking being performed by Angie, Mary and Chell, while CJ napped on the couch. Luis beckoned for Diane to escape to the fresh air they would find while sitting on the porch.

Sitting in the swing and knowing with whom she had just conversed, he asked Diane, "How are you holding up?"

"Barely. But hopefully it isn't showing. How about you?"

She had wanted to check in with him since he returned. She saw the pain in his face, even though he had been trying to hide it from her.

"It isn't showing; I just know you. I, on the other hand, am drawing my strength from my family and you," he offered, managing to find the semblance of a smile to ease her concern about him.

"I know you are worried about Antonio. Have you heard from him since this morning?" she continued.

"Antonio's situation is disturbing, but that isn't my focus right now. He called to tell Mami that he would be staying at our cousin's. He knew I would not allow him to act out, so for that I am grateful. I don't even know if he will be fit enough to attend the services. But at least he made the effort to come down."

"I can only imagine what you must be feeling. I'm here if you want to talk." She paused before shifting the subject slightly. "Your mother has been very sweet. She's treating me as though I am still her daughter-in-law. I can't tell you how much that means to me. She is so comforting in an unassuming way."

"In her heart, you still are. You're the mother of her grandchildren. That's all that matters to her. She loves you, Diane. And you have given her four beautiful ones. You know, she understood your pain. You women all stick together. My arm is still sore from where she punched me for hurting you," he chuckled, rubbing his shoulder as he recalled the conversation.

"For the record, she should have cracked you over the head. But it's the kind, loving woman that she is. I'm just sorry I made it so hard for her to really be a part of their lives."

Before Luis could respond, they both noticed a taxi pulling up in front of the house and watched as Diane's family emerged. They were early and Diane was thankful. She hoped they would bring her comfort and strength the way Luis' family had done for him. However, the way her mother stood and faced the house and then pursed her lips when she saw Diane and Luis sitting on the porch alone told Diane that her mother had left no room for comfort in the taxi.

Margaret gingerly embraced her daughter, shook Luis' hand as though they were meeting for the first time, and then waited on the porch to be escorted into the house. Since her actions set the tone, Diane's father followed in his wife's footsteps.

Michelle and Cindy weren't sure how to approach Diane either, so they, too, hugged their sister gingerly and then waited to enter the home.

Luis saw the disappointment all over Diane's face and in her posture so he took the lead saying, "Mama Margaret and Papa Ron, welcome to my mother's home. Please, make yourselves comfortable." Then turning to her sisters, he said, "Michelle, Cindy, how are you guys? It's been ages. You're looking well."

This kind of idle chitchat continued through the early evening and into dinner. The chemistry at the dinner table was very different from any of the previous nights – everyone was struggling to find the right thing to say.

Diane's mother's brief responses to questions and lack of engagement made it very clear that the only reason they were brought together this time was to mourn the passing of a child. Diane felt so awkward and embarrassed by her mother's behavior that she constantly struggled to introduce neutral topics that she hoped would gain some footing and compete with the clanging of forks against the plates.

Luis eventually became frustrated with the situation and stopped trying. Midway through dinner, Luis' cell rang and he excused himself to talk in private. When he returned to the table he told everyone that Luis J wasn't feeling well so they weren't going to come after all.

When Mama Margaret heard that news, she looked at Diane and asked, "You let your son give you that kind of excuse? Who's the parent?"

"Mama, please. He's grieving the loss of his brother. You know how close they were." Diane glanced over at Michelle as a memory of their childhood flashed before her. "We're all grieving, and none of us needs the tension this discussion will bring. So please, let it go."

Mama Margaret pursed her lips once again as she was too fit to be tied. So, she said nothing verbally, but her eyes let Diane know that she was not pleased with Diane's disrespectful tone or response.

Once the table was cleared and the coffee poured, Mama Margaret asked if someone would call them a cab. It seemed as though they all jumped for a phone or cell at the same time, but in actuality, it was only NaNa.

Retiring to the living room, they sipped their coffee, nibbled on dessert and watched the news in silence. Diane, whose seat was facing the driveway, was so relieved when the taxi pulled into the yard that she rose to her feet to announce its arrival. They bid their farewells and shared that they would be leaving right after the funeral.

Michelle looked at her sister for some sign that she wanted them to stay, but at this time, Diane could not make any gestures that indicated such. She wasn't able to, not any longer. She felt that her sisters and father had chosen their side and there was no place in their heart for her either.

Once the dust from the car speeding away settled, Diane collapsed into the seat on the porch. NaNa removed the coffee cup and handed her a mojito. She then motioned for Luis to give them some space.

The drink was refreshing. She had muddled the mint leaves just the way Diane liked them; she could rarely find a place that did it well. It was also just the right amount of rum. As she sipped it, she eventually found the words she had been searching for since Luis had left them alone.

"NaNa, I don't know where to begin. I did not expect that from my family. My mother was so rude. Had I known that she couldn't find warmth in her heart for me, for all of us in a situation like this, I would never have extended your invitation to them. Please forgive me."

"Diane, you are so sweet. Why are you asking for forgiveness?"

"I am so embarrassed by their behavior. None of you should have been subjected to that. And to act that way in front of the children. I was appalled."

"Mija, let me tell you something – you are not responsible for your parent's actions or your sisters'. They are all grown, as am I, and you don't have to protect me or ever apologize to me for other adults' actions. Your mother has never hidden how she really feels about my son but that does not translate to how I feel about you. She was disappointed with how your marriage affected your studies. I don't blame her for feeling that way. And she was even more disappointed that your marriage ended. Of course, she blames Luis, even though she may not have the full story. But he was the one who cheated and most people side with the person who was betrayed.

"But, my love for you is unconditional. I have loved you from the moment I met you. You were so good for Luis and he knew that. He still shares stories about your marriage with me. He used to call me and tell me how happy he was. Somehow, the two of you lost your way and that saddened me then and saddens me now. But I will never stop caring for you."

Diane didn't know Luis was still talking about their marriage with his mom. She figured he was now sharing Maria stories with her.

"I really appreciate that and feel the same way about you," Diane answered. "And I apologize for not allowing the children to have more involvement with you. I was just so angry. But this, losing Carlos, has made me see how precious time is. I can't go back, but I can begin now. I hope you will allow me to make that change."

"Diane, as a woman, a mother and a wife, I understood from the beginning. I was shocked and very disappointed with Luis' actions. I told him so many, many times. I wish you guys could have worked things out, but I know that sometimes it's difficult for a woman to forgive and even more so to forget. But, I pray that one day you will so you both can move on with your life. Anger and bitterness can't be good for your marriage with David either because of what it represents."

"What do you mean?"

"Feelings like that are fueled from smoldering embers of love, Diane. I'm sure David must be wondering why you're still living there, emotionally. But I don't want to overstep my boundaries. If you ever need anything or just want to talk, please feel free to call me." She reached out and touched her arm before continuing, "And don't be too hard on your mother; she has your best interest at heart. I'm sure you can appreciate where she's coming from."

Diane listened to her words about her feelings toward Luis, but she had to file them away. She couldn't embrace them right now. But she did have a response for her last comments about Ms. Margaret. "I don't think that's true. She has her best interests at heart. She is still so disappointed with me and my decision to get married instead of going to graduate school. Couple that with having four children and a failed marriage, well, she really doesn't have much to say to me or good to say about me."

"You're too close, you just can't see it. I shared that same message about you with Carlos when he was here. He responded the same way. But Diane, you have to find your own way. You have to stop living in your mother's and your sisters' shadows. Quite frankly, you shouldn't be living your life for your mother anymore anyway. And believe it or not, that's the path that Carlos had chosen. He knew that he had to begin living his life for him on his terms and that included Luisa and CJ. Now, you have a grandson who is depending on you to provide him love and guidance in the absence of his parents. And you have three other children who need you even more now to help them deal with this tragedy and the obstacles and challenges that lie ahead. And they will be numerous, even on a good day. Look for the beacon of light to show you the way. It's there; you are just having trouble seeing it through your inner turmoil."

Diane thought to herself, 'How wise and caring this woman is.' She was providing more support and comfort in this short conversation than her mother had in the last twenty years.

Luis emerged from the house and asked if he was interrupting. Receiving the invitation he was hoping for to join the women who brought him the most love and comfort in his life, he took a seat but kept his place to allow whatever was flowing between the two of them to keep going. He saw a calmness in Diane he hadn't seen in years and he was happy for her to have that moment. The three of them sat there for a while, drawing strength from one another in preparation for what they all knew would be the toughest day in a parent's life.

Chapter Twenty

The ceremony was beautiful. Luisa's grandparents and Aunt Carmen attended, which Diane and Luis greatly appreciated. CJ was so happy to see them and he clung tightly to all of them, especially his Tía. Diane wondered how CJ would react when it was time for them to leave again. She prayed he would be alright.

The eulogy was short as was his life. Luis said a few words, so did Diane's father, and of course, NaNa. As Diane and Luis expected, Luis J took it the hardest, which was evidenced by his decision to leave immediately after the service and not go to the burial site. And so some amount of Diane's tears were for Luis J.

It took all of Diane's strength to remain in an upright position when they lowered her son into the ground. She now had to accept that he was gone, that she would never look into his face and see that warm, loving smile. She had spent so much time being mad at him and arguing about his choices, but now she struggled to remember the origin of most of the arguments. Wasted moments. And now he lay in this final resting place, his body eventually to turn into ashes.

They had agreed to bury Carlos here, but as she watched them cover him with dirt, she was rethinking this choice because she wouldn't be able to visit with him. Everything would be left here, and all she would have from then on would be her memories and pictures. But Luis had wanted Carlos to be in the land that he had grown to love and where his father could watch over him. She felt she owed Luis that much after all the time she had stolen from him, from both of them. Luis put his arm around her waist and she was finally able to release all the bottled up pain like never before under his embrace.

Her face, flushed from the crying, revealed much. He shed a few tears, too, and they lingered together at the gravesite after everyone else left, still holding on to each other. They both remembered how happy "proud papa" was the day the nurse placed his first child, a son, into his arms. As the cars started pulling away from the grave site, they slowly walked away from their eldest child, leaving a piece of their heart buried six feet into the ground.

Luis paused to visit with his father and said a prayer, asking him to take care of his son. "I miss you, Papi. Please look after your grandson."

When the limo brought them back to NaNa's house, there were people in every space in the house. Music was blaring, people were dancing and the Bacardi was flowing. It was a real celebration of life. Diane appreciated the sentiment, but her heart could not embrace it. There were too many people and too many sympathetic comments. She whispered to Luis to take her away somewhere, anywhere. So they went for a walk along the beach and sat under the shade of a palm tree.

There was a cool breeze blowing and they watched the sun fade in and out of the clouds. She wondered if Carlos had spent his nights on the beach peering into the yonder and beyond. He had always loved the water, just like his father did.

"How did my life get so screwed up, Luis?" Diane asked, allowing herself to be vulnerable. Tears welled up in her eyes again. She wondered where they were coming from as she had cried buckets all morning.

"Your life isn't screwed up. We've had some challenges and will probably have a great deal more, but that's what makes us grow into good, decent people," he said, with that charismatic smile.

Diane returned the smile and wiped her tears with the handkerchief he offered her. "You're always so optimistic. And probably way too kind to me. I love that about you."

She paused there. She wondered where the word love came from. Then she remembered the words NaNa had shared with her last evening. And she continued, "I can't stop thinking about what Luis J said to me though, and I have to admit, he's right. I have caused a lot of pain for everyone, especially you and our two sons."

"Luis J was hurting. He not only lost his brother, but his best friend, too, and that's on top of everything else he has just gone through. You know kids usually strike out at their parents when they're hurting. Besides, he's transitioning now, becoming a young man. He's coming into his own. I always thought he would get there early. He's got that bit of old wisdom. Probably got those genes from me," Luis said confidently, but teasingly.

"Right. I know, I remember. But it's more than that. I'm just saying that Luis J is insightful. He can see; he's always been able to. Out of everyone, Luis J could always call me out. I didn't like it and overruled him because I am his mother, but he's got balls, Luis. He's right about all the time I took from you and Carlos, not to mention him, Chell and Robert. The years that I wouldn't let you be a part of their life. And now you can never regain that. It's a wonder you don't hate me," she stated, lowering her head. "Luis J's behavior is a result of my actions. When I'm hurt, I lash out and everyone around me is impacted."

Luis took Diane's left hand and rubbed the back of it. Her skin was so soft. "Luis J is a real deuce combination of us both, but I could never hate you, Di. I understand you better than you know. You were the love of my life."

Diane was surprised to hear him say that. She knew he loved her and that is what enabled him to deal with her all these years but to hear that she was the love of his life caused her to gasp. “I guess what I’m trying to say is I’d understand and not blame you if you did hate me. I sort of hate myself. I wish things had turned out differently.”

He leaned over and kissed her on the forehead. It was a gentle kiss, the kind you would place on the forehead of a child you loved with your whole heart. The kiss she placed on CJ’s forehead every morning.

After a few minutes of silence, he said, “I accept your apology. But don’t waste your energy on punishing yourself for long because we have a lot more work to do. Our children need us now more than ever.” Then he asked, “What are we going to do about CJ?”

“I honestly don’t know. I saw how happy he was with his great grandparents and aunt. It made me question if we are doing the right thing. What do you suggest?” She wanted his guidance with CJ. She welcomed it. She was about to be forty-three years old. The thought of starting over alone under these circumstances was paralyzing at times.

“How about we file for joint custody? We can get a nanny who is bilingual and she can stay with him at both locations.”

She thought to herself that the idea was a good one, with one exception. She still didn’t want Maria around her children and now it extended to her grandchild. But she didn’t want to make this about Maria. Not today. Not when they were taking steps toward mutual ground.

“I think having him go back and forth might be too confusing just now. He’s got to become familiar with what will be home to him, but you can come see him whenever you like. My apartment is small, but I think it would be good for Chell and Robert – especially Robert – to bond with him. Luis J too, once he moves back in.”

“You’re probably right, at least at first.” After a pause, he asked, “How are things with you and David? Will having another child there put more strain on your relationship?”

Diane wasn't sure how to answer that question. She had asked it of herself several times recently, especially after Carlos' death when the realization hit her of just how short life can be and nothing or no one can be taken for granted.

David had been such a good man to her and for her when she was at the lowest period of her life until now. But lately, they weren't able to connect on the level she had previously known with him. She was also getting concerned about these jealous, possessive traits he was exhibiting. Thankfully, he hadn't thrown up anything else during these circumstances, especially since she and Luis had exhibited so much closeness and were spending so much time together.

Still, that side of David concerned her a bit. She had never, ever wanted to hurt him. She did love him, but she always knew he deserved so much more than she was capable of giving him. He needed a woman who loved him, truly loved him, the way she had loved Luis.

She finally said, "Not good. We've been physically separated for three weeks now, but emotionally, it's been longer."

"I know he loves you and the kids. It takes a special man to step into a woman's life and help raise her children as his own. Don't take that for granted."

"Yes, you're right, and I haven't lost sight of that. He has been a rock for me and the kids. But because he's such a good man, he deserves more. Quite frankly, more than I may be able to give him."

"Diane, you're being way too hard on yourself about everything. I admire how you have managed your relationship, raised our children, continued your career and kept a loving home. It's difficult to do all that, especially the male part. David never had that honeymoon period of having you all to himself. He married you with a ready-made family and not one but four children, one of whom was a baby, and we both know how demanding that is!" He laughed, thinking of each of his children as babies.

Diane recognized the reflection and added, “Yes, that infant stage is the worst and most demanding. And you know what, Carlos was the easiest, remember?”

“Yes he was. I think it’s true what they say, that babies come here with the disposition imposed on them by the circumstances surrounding their conception and how the mother handles it.”

“Really, Luis? I never knew you to think like that or to indulge in old wives tales.”

“Oh, come on Diane, I’m Puerto Rican – we come from a long lineage of old wives’ tales!” Then he burst out laughing while Diane, amused, just looked at him hoping he hadn’t had a nervous breakdown. It was known to happen after tragedies such as the one they had just experienced. But then he stopped.

“Don’t you see? Carlos was like the beginning of our marriage; our love was so romantic. Then Luis J was conceived and it was still good, but we had barely gotten used to Carlos and the adjustment. You were still planning to go for your Master’s and were a bit miffed by the pregnancy, so Luis J was a little on the cranky side. When Chell came you were resigned and somewhat angry, and we know about the circumstances of Robert’s conception and birth all too well.”

“Yes, no need to rehash that. But I will say that Robert was easier, like Carlos, though he was moody.”

“Yes and you see, so were you. You became contemplative about the pregnancy. I thought it was a sign from God and embraced it immediately. Slowly you began to accept it and embrace it, too. We were good at the time, before…”

“Yes, we were really trying to bring back that initial love and commitment we enjoyed in the beginning of our marriage. And we were…until Maria,” Diane stammered.

"Don't. Really, don't. Let's not bring her into this conversation about our children," Luis said. "I was simply saying that it was a huge responsibility David took on when he married you. I know how difficult it was. But you are the one who needs to recognize that, acknowledge it and feel good that another man loved you that much that he was willing to do it."

All Diane could think in response was how she didn't feel very strong, especially not now. She had lost her eldest son long before today because of her stubbornness. She was frightened about the prospect of facing her second failed marriage. She really had no friends other than her sisters and even they had drifted apart; she had made David her "go to" everything. She had had friends at one time but she couldn't face them as a failure. A friend of hers once said, "After two, it's you." Perhaps she was right; the issues weren't with the men in her life, but with her. Perhaps her baggage was keeping her from having a meaningful, healthy relationship. They both loved her, that much she was sure of, but they were both dissatisfied with what she was willing or capable of reciprocating.

As she looked at all of the circles in her life, she had to accept that they had all shrunken. After divorcing Luis, their joint friends stopped calling because of the awkwardness around their loyalties. The age difference between her and David didn't really lend itself to making friends in his circle or hers. So she had to rely on her family when her ego would allow it. And now there was CJ. They were total strangers to one another, but he would need one-hundred-and-fifty percent from her and she would need to, want to give it. Not to even mention, of course, that his first language was Spanish; how would she cope with that?

It was too much to think about now. So she turned the focus toward Luis. "What about you? Wedding bells coming up?" she asked.

Luis turned away and looked out at the ocean. The tide was coming in so the waves were picking up height and strength. He thought about stripping and taking a dip and swimming as he had done often as a kid. He would allow the waves to soothe every inch of his body and calm his soul. He would love to have that feeling right now. It was as satisfying as making love. Well, almost.

"Wedding bells? No. I thought we weren't going to bring her into our discussion. But what made you ask?" Luis had taken note of Diane's demeanor and she seemed okay with discussing Maria so he had addressed her question.

"You've been together for a long time, so why not? I'm sure she's ready. If it were up to her, I'm certain you would have tied the knot the day after our divorce was final."

He wasn't going to get baited into that, but his mind did wander. He had never shared this with Diane and now wasn't the time, but she was a tough act to follow, even though she had her way. Luis hadn't met anyone like Diane before or since. Maria was in love with him and had been good for him for their season, but she was not the woman with whom he wanted to spend the rest of his life. People serve their time, but Maria was not the person who would grow old with him. It was about her view of life and people where they differed. They didn't share the same insight the way he and Diane had. Even in Diane's darkest moments, the core of who she was remained aligned with his. Luis chose to simply respond to Diane by saying, "I'd rather not bore you with the whys. Sorry."

Diane wondered what was behind that statement. Was he considering it but reluctant to share that with her today, given all she was already going through? Diane didn't know how she would deal with Maria as Luis' wife. It would clearly make Maria even more unbearable, if that was even possible. Maria was a pain in the ass, but Diane could dismiss her under the circumstances because she had no claim to the family. But marriage would change all of that, and with CJ, Maria could really stake her claim as the step-grandmother who spoke Spanish, knew Puerto Rico, and cooked foods for him. Diane tensed up and realized she'd have to cross that bridge – or blow it up – when ultimately faced with it.

Luis read Diane's body change, but said nothing. He chose to do no more than enjoy the moment, no matter how long or short. They sat there until the sun set, talking casually, until they thought it was probably time to return to NaNa's. To Diane's relief, just about everyone had left and they found Chell trying to rock CJ to sleep. He had had quite a day reuniting with Luisa's family and then being overwhelmed with all the comings and goings.

Diane took CJ from Chell, kissed her on the forehead, like Luis had kissed her earlier, and thanked her for stepping in. It made Diane think about what David had said when he was leaving, about how Chell was managing too many adult responsibilities. She held out her free arm and embraced Chell together with CJ and kissed her again, whispering at the top of her head, "I may not say it, but I appreciate you Chell, darling. I do."

Once CJ was asleep, Diane began packing before turning in for the night. She had had a long, emotionally draining day. She thought briefly about returning to New York and life after Carlos. It wasn't a thought she wanted to dwell on.

Standing on the porch, appreciating the cool that was now in the night air, Luis wrestled with the events of the day and the fact that his first born was now lying in the same graveyard as his father. He had wanted to talk to Luis J earlier in the evening, but Bobby wasn't answering his phone. NaNa told him that they had come by the house while he and Diane were out, but neither of them stayed long. They ate and made some excuse about the traffic on the weekends.

Luis turned over his thoughts about the impact of Carlos' death on their lives, too, but moreso on how Luis J would respond. He knew that something proactive had to be done.

That shifted his mind to his brother, Antonio, speaking of something that needed to be done. Antonio had missed the ceremony entirely, and Luis knew this was now weighing pretty heavily on his mother's mind. His cousin had shared that he left Antonio sleeping in the room. He had been out all night and stumbled in around six in the morning. Luis wondered if he would make his flight the next day. NaNa's hand on his shoulder both startled and calmed Luis as she began rubbing his back.

NaNa had aged beautifully. She was sixty-five years old, but looked like she was in her early fifties. She had always attributed it to "good genes" and her night cap. Family was the most important thing to her… and her heart ached for her first born.

Looking into Luis' eyes, as she had recently looked into his first-born's eyes only days ago, she said, "My heart aches for you, my son. Carlos was a great boy. No, a great young man. I'd really hoped that you'd be able to watch each of your children grow up, marry, have their own children and pursue their lives, as your father and I were thankful to have experienced with you and your siblings. It's so hard on a parent to bury their child, but in every life experience, there is a message."

Luis hugged her and without exchanging any words, she knew he was getting stronger. After a minute, they sat on the swinging bench. She reached for his hand and they intertwined fingers. It was the same practice he had taught to Diane to exhibit their connectedness. She finally said, "Your father would have been very proud of you today. You were strong for your family and that's the kind of man he was to us. I hope you still have those memories of him."

She paused as she reflected on the memories she held close to her heart of her Luisandro. "But now, it's just me and you. How are you, mijo?"

"Mami, I don't know how to answer that question. This has been the greatest challenge I've ever faced and sometimes I don't know if I have somehow brought this on myself. I am just as responsible for the time I missed with Carlos as Diane. I caused the pain in her heart that led to the anger and resentment. I will have to live with that for the rest of my life."

And he was living with it, every day. "But, for my short answer, the one I give everyone every day, I'm good."

"I see that because I know you. I have held my tongue about this thing with Maria because you are a grown man. But I have to tell you now at this juncture how very disappointed I am that you are still involved with her. I know I have said this to you already, but as I spend time with Diane, I still don't get why you even got involved in this affair. I'm not saying Diane's perfect, but she's good. She loves and cares deeply. Maria is all about Maria.

"And then once it happened, you and Diane didn't handle it like two mature adults. You struck out at each other and torpedoed your marriage and life together. I hope you can see now how it ultimately impacted your children's lives. You both allowed your blindness and selfish pride to come first, before your children's well being. I know that you're a man, and these things happen, but it's what you did about it afterwards that disappointed me. You let a woman – and I use that term loosely – come between you and your family. Your father and I always taught you to put family first. Neither of you really did that and that saddens me," NaNa said, patting her heart.

"I hope that starting from today, the two of you will figure out how to rectify that." After a pause, and no response from him, she continued. "You haven't said anything, but I assume you heard me."

"Yes, Mami, I heard you."

She and Luis had always had a stronger connection than she had with any of her other children. She had often told him that she loved each of her children and their unique personalities and strengths, but he was her kindred spirit. He was more like his father, wise beyond his years and always wanting to do the right thing.

"So what are your plans regarding Maria? Although, you probably don't think it's any of my business."

"My life with Maria has had its challenges lately, especially with Diane and the kids. But I don't have any plans beyond where we are right now."

"There's more to life than that, mijo. Don't you feel something is missing? Is she good for you? Does she mean you well? Is she good for your children, if God forbid something happened to Diane? You have done well with your career and I'm proud of you. You have bought a beautiful house, but do you have a home?"

"Mami, what are you getting at?" Luis asked, knowing on a deeper level exactly what his mother was saying. He had never thought about Maria as mothering his children, or how it would have made him feel knowing how Diane felt about it should something happen to her. It was a thought he never wanted to entertain. But that question, "Is she good for you?" really stood out. Had he confused great sex all these years with the substance of that question?

"Just this," his mother replied. "Life is too short for unresolved issues and not owning up to our true feelings. A relationship between a man and a woman is more than what goes on between the sheets. I know I don't have to remind you of that. Besides, I know what is in your heart…or should I say who. It's time for you to do something about that, one way or another. You're not being fair to anyone right now, including yourself, and as much as it pains me to say it, even Maria."

Luis could not believe that his pious mother had gone there, but indeed she had.

NaNa was not as direct as his generation would be; however, in the confinement of her proper way of speaking about such private matters, she had managed to convey exactly what she meant to say to him. And if Carlos' death taught him nothing else, he had learned exactly what she said, "Life is too short." He could not afford to waste time and continue to let it go by. They continued to sit in the swing, her hand in his, until she felt her presence had helped him and then she went to bed.

Luis continued sitting there thinking about how he had longed for a trip like this: Diane lying in his bed waiting for him to join her; his children asleep in the other rooms, exhausted from a day of touring the island and learning of their heritage; a life of opportunities awaiting all of them. He had always wanted to bring his family to Puerto Rico, but their finances had never been right. So, he would visit his mother and return to his homeland, alone. He had never even taken his children.

Now, the woman lying in his bed was no longer his wife and the last thing on her mind was waiting for him to join her. Losing Carlos to death was painful, but the idea that he may lose another – Luis J – to depression or some irrational behavior pained his heart even more. The last thing Luis wanted was for his son to follow in Antonio's footsteps, living life in a bottle. Luis knew he had to get a handle on the imbalance in his life and manage his truth. He needed to accept that he was a changed man, so he had to make changes and vowed that when he returned to New York, he would go about that.

Bobby dropped Luis J off at the airport just moments before the cutoff period for checking luggage. Luis shook his head at his little brother before hugging him. Everyone else was already at the gate. Luis J continued to have very little to say to anyone and sat off to himself. After all the rushing to get to the airport, they now learned that the flight home was going to be delayed two hours, so they sat in the airport trying to fill their time with games and other distractions.

By the time the airplane lifted off, everyone was even more drained and their patience with one another very short. They were not all able to sit together, so Chell sat next to Luis J, while Diane and Luis sat with CJ between them. CJ was exhausted, cranky and cried or whined for the first thirty minutes of the flight. This annoyed the rest of the passengers, but they became sympathetic when informed that his mother had died just a week ago.

When they finally got him to take a nap, Diane lay back in the chair and closed her eyes. Luis knew this was her way of self-preservation and didn't disturb her. Instead his thoughts went to Antonio. He had learned that Mary and Antonio made the flight and were on their way back to Chicago. This, at least, was some relief.

Mary had agreed to stop by and check on him as much as her life would allow given the children and distance they lived from one another. For now, that would have to be enough. Luis thumbed through a few pages of the Skyline magazine, glanced around to check on his family and then reclined the chair to get some rest.

When they landed, David was in the baggage claim area waiting to welcome his family back home. Luis J agreed to go home with his mother for the evening, for which Luis was thankful. As Luis watched his family, with whom he had just shared the most horrific yet intimate experience, walk away with another man, he felt a sense of loneliness that he hadn't been in touch with for a very long time.

They had spent almost a week together making decisions, enjoying each other's conversations and feeling like a complete unit. He had so enjoyed it, and he was damned if he was going to let that go. He was determined to correct and put things in order in his life so he could maintain that closeness with each of them.

Having made his way back to his own house, when Luis walked into the living room, he found Maria inside, excited to see him. She had prepared something quick, burgers and corn on the grill, but he was really too tired to eat.

As he put his bags down and headed for the cognac, Maria said, "I'm glad you're home. I really missed you. I wish I could have been with you through all of this."

"Maria, I know, but I'm really tired. I just came off a four-hour flight and I don't feel like talking."

"Of course. Why don't you take a hot shower and then maybe you will feel like eating a little."

"Thanks for understanding," Luis said as he headed to the bedroom, carrying his luggage with him. The beads of hot water covered every part of his body and he could feel the tension slowly begin to subside. He had been deep in thought most of the entire ride home and was taking it with him into the shower.

He heard the door open and felt the air on his wet body as Maria joined him. When she began rubbing his back and shoulder blades, he turned to face her. She was truly sexy and he found her body always so inviting. Tonight, right now, it was what he needed. He had slept with her the night after Carlos died, but he hadn't been in the mood since then.

But tonight, they embraced and he lifted her up so he could be inside of her. Wanting more room, he pushed her back against the shower door, forcing it open and they headed to the bed. He left the water running hoping it would wash his thoughts and emotions down the drain. He took her several times that night, each one more explosive than the previous until he finally succumbed to sleep.

Chapter Twenty One

Luis J shoved his damp uniform into his backpack after practice and headed toward the car. His mother had summoned him to the house without any indication of what she wanted. He assumed one of the questions would be about his progress with packing Carlos' things. Truthfully, it was going very slowly because every item he touched flooded him with memories of Carlos.

Flashbacks of them as kids playing; as adolescents when Carlos told him about sex, only later to learn that Carlos only knew from hearsay; images of Carlos showing him the moves on the court – now that was something he really knew about.

It all made Luis J smile. His parents had granted him the responsibility for deciding what to keep, what to donate and what to discard. All of Carlos' belongings were things that had characterized him as a man, and now Luis J's choices were fragmenting Carlos' essence into three piles. He had to reposition some items three or four times, trying to determine what should be in the "kept" pile and the "little CJ" pile.

Yes, he was pretty sure the status of his progress would be one of the first questions his mother would have, and then it would be followed by a series of others about school and his actions. The more he thought about what he was about to face, the more his anxiety built. He wasn't in the mood to deal with her without a little "help." If the traffic continued to be light, he would have just enough time to stop by the apartment and down a shot.

Dropping the backpack on the couch, he grabbed the bottle off the kitchen countertop. It actually took a couple of shots before he started feeling the numbness. Since that night with Maria, he had learned to let the tequila make it easier to go to sleep at night and get through the uncomfortable moments like the one surely waiting for him at the house.

When he stepped outside, the coolness in the air made him shiver. Zipping his jacket to shield the wind, he turned toward the subway stairs. He was feeling good, too good to get behind the wheel. As the train rocked his brain and the alcohol in his stomach, he let his mind drift back to practice.

Unfortunately, the trip to Puerto Rico had caused him to miss the first round basketball scouts and he wasn't sure how that would impact his recruitment and scholarship opportunities. On top of that, the team's winning streak had ended and he knew it had to do with his game. Since his return, his shots had been way off. He hadn't scored more than six points in the last two games combined. The shots would go up, but they weren't dead on. They were either too short or off to the right. His head just wasn't in the game. How could it be? He really was missing his brother. And then to compound things, when he had these slumps before, Carlos would snap him out of it. They would shoot some hoops and run some drills to help him get back in the groove.

Ugh, he couldn't think about this anymore. He could feel the tears forming and he was not about to go down like that on the subway. One more stop and he would be there. He closed his eyes tightly and listened to the screech of the train's brakes. They always made that noise when the train turned in the tunnels. Sometimes it was so loud that it was deafening and the lights would go out for a few seconds. He hoped that would happen now so the girl sitting next to him wouldn't see him brush the tears away.

When he got to his mother's around 6pm, the alcohol was in full swing. He took a seat at the table, exchanging the normal dialogue. His mother pushed a pile of envelopes so they were positioned right in front of him. It was information about the admission tests and some college brochures he had requested earlier in the fall. He thumbed through some of the contents until his stomach started growling and he started feeling a little light-headed.

When he drank on an empty stomach the effects were felt faster, which was fine when he was alone. But if he had to sober up, which he needed to do now, he would eat and the food would absorb the alcohol and reduce its impact. So he shared the college brochures with his mother hoping it would distract her and keep the conversation light while he made himself a plate. She had cooked one of his favorite meals, fried chicken wings, corn bread and greens. He filled the plate and sat back down. He swayed a little as he sat and he hoped that his mother didn't notice.

"Luis J, are you feeling alright?"

There wasn't much she missed so he quickly responded, "Yeah. Hey, thanks for telling me to come by tonight. I do miss your cooking. What do you think about the schools?"

His compliment made her smile. She had chosen these items as an olive branch. But as she watched him eat and observed his speech, she knew that he was drinking. "I hope you enjoy it. Luis J, what's going on? Are you sick? Your speech is a little slurred." Diane reached over the table to feel his forehead but he pulled away.

"Mami, stop. I'm not sick; I'm just really tired. I'm still recovering from Carlos – you know, the trip, the funeral, sleepless nights. Coach is pushing us really hard, too. We had drills for two hours after school. I'm just tired. As soon as I finish this, I better go," he said. He took a few more bites of food and began to rise.

"You're looking thinner, baby. Are you eating? You need to take care of yourself. You've got to keep your weight on for your game. Why don't you take some food with you?" Diane didn't wait for him to respond. She started putting food into Tupperware bowls and then everything into a bag. Handing it to him, she continued, "Will you be here this weekend? Chell, Robert, and I miss you. Maybe the four of us can do something on Saturday. Oh, and you really need to spend time with CJ so that he can get to know you. Carlos would want that."

"Where will CJ be on Saturday?" Luis J asked, choosing to ignore her comment about Carlos. No one knew Carlos better than he did and he didn't need her trying to guilt him into spending time with CJ. Luis J needed to practice his Spanish some more but when he was ready, he was planning to spend a lot of time with CJ.

"Your father will be here on Saturday to spend the day with him. CJ is really comfortable with him because he speaks to him in Spanish."

"I can imagine. How's David?" Luis J hoped this question would continue to deflect her attention away from him.

"He's fine. Chell and Robert are with him tonight."

"Are you guys going to get back together?"

"Honestly Luis J, I'm sad to say that I don't know." She looked down because she had wondered about this many times herself. Shrugging her shoulders, she asked, "So, what about this weekend, can you come?"

"I wish I could, but we're practicing this weekend, all day drills. I told you Coach has his foot on our back. Maybe in a couple of weeks."

Diane was disappointed with his answer. She wanted to see him again this weekend so she could evaluate just how much and just how often he was drinking. She wanted him close, if only to prevent him from indulging in alcohol.

"Luis J, I hope you know how much I love you and I'm sorry for any hurt I've caused you. Please know that I'm here for you, if you want to talk or need anything."

'Okay, here it comes, time to go,' Luis J thought. "Not now Mami. I gotta go. Tell Chell, Robert and CJ, I said hey." He grabbed another slice of cornbread, picked up the food and left. What did she think? Of course she had hurt him; that's what she does. He was so glad he wasn't living there now and couldn't begin to imagine what it was going to be like when he had to return at the end of the month. He ran down the stairs to catch the train.

Chapter Twenty Two

Each day, the pain lessened a tenth of an inch. They had been back for two weeks and Luis was ready to take the next move in his life. He dropped the keys on the table in the hallway and walked into the living room. Maria was sitting on the couch, her feet tucked under her, watching TV.

"How was your day?" she asked, moving over so he could sit next to her.

"A day," he answered, choosing to sit in the chair across from her instead of the seat she had created because he knew that he had been under her seductive spell all this time. Maria was a seductress of the worse kind. She had always deflected any real issues with wine and sex and like most men, he succumbed. But after his time spent with Diane and the talk with his mother, he had begun to think about all their questions concerning Maria.

She wondered why he was sitting so far from her. Usually at the end of "A Day," he couldn't get enough of her. "Need a massage or hot shower?" she asked, letting him know that she was ready to ease his tension.

"No, thanks." Luis knew that was coming and in the past, he would have played right along. He cleared his throat and began, "Actually, we need to talk."

Lifting the remote from her lap, she turned down the TV and shifted her position so that she was facing him. She wondered if something else was wrong with one of the kids or CJ. He was too calm for it to be about what happened between her and Luis J. But something was weighing on him. She apprehensively asked, "Is everything alright? The kids okay?"

"I'm good. The kids are fine."

'Alright, that's not it. Oh, I know. Finally, he's ready,' Maria thought. Losing Carlos must have been the turning point. A huge grin spread across her face and she said, "Yes."

Her grin was met by a frown of his brow and he asked, "Yes? Yes what?"

"Yes! Yes, I'll marry you, Poppie," Maria said, as if she needed to help him with his proposal. She had been waiting for this for such a long time.

"Slow down, Maria, this is not about marriage."

"Then what is it? You're worrying me. Did something else happen?"

She used the word worrying, but what she was actually feeling was irritated. She was starting to wonder if he was ever going to propose to her.

"I want you to know how much you have meant to me."

"I love you too, Poppie." 'Now we're getting somewhere,' she thought.

"That's just it, Maria. You love me. And just now you said, 'I love you too, Poppie,' when clearly I said, 'I want you to know how much you have meant to me.' You always do that. You interpret what I say and what anyone else says to you as you wish to hear it. I used to think you were doing it to be defiant, but there's no way you didn't just understand what I said. I've been thinking a lot lately about our interactions, how we as a man and a woman interact," Luis said, carefully. To him, Maria seemed to be listening as if she was perplexed, yet somewhat pissed.

He continued, "I know that there isn't anything you wouldn't do for me, and I appreciate that. I really do. But I have to be honest with you… and more importantly, myself. Maria, when Carlos died, something in me was awakened. It was a pain I was suppressing for years about being separated from my children and the emptiness I feel in my life. I'm so happy I got to spend a year with Carlos, but that doesn't even begin to make up for all the other years I missed."

"Hello, that's Diane's fault, not mine. I've always been supportive. I agree that you should enjoy your children as well. I've tried to give you some suggestions for dealing with her craziness – and quite frankly, her selfishness – but you never want to stand up to her, your 'fragile Diane.'"

"Are you really that blind? This situation that I'm in right now regarding my children is not Diane's fault or yours. It's mine. I was the one who was unfaithful to my wife. I was the one who sent our marriage into a downward spiral. I was the one who took away her safe world when she was most vulnerable and shattered her dreams. She was pregnant with the child that was conceived on a night that I hadn't even planned to share with her when you announced our affair. She almost lost our son and so she retaliated the only way she knew how."

Luis could still see Diane doubled over in pain and Maria standing in the doorway, looking triumphant and not acknowledging Diane's condition. He continued, "I still have three children and now a grandson who is parentless, so I plan to be a part of their lives."

'So now he's growing a conscience.' She still didn't know where he was going with this conversation so she asked, "So, why don't you ask Diane for joint custody? Surely she has to be more open to it now." While she waited for his response, she thought, 'There he goes again, defending his precious Diane.' Maria wondered if Luis ever defended her to Diane the way she always had to listen to his defense of her.

"Maria, yes, yes, yes! You always attack Diane and then talk about joint custody. How on earth could you co-parent my children when you don't show any respect for their mother? I accept my responsibility for my part in this mess, but do you? You've always held this self-righteous attitude as if you did nothing and do nothing. And I let you because I've been pussy whipped."

Maria snapped her head to the side and looked at him like he had just called her a whore. But what she was really concerned about was if he was finally seeing through her facade.

"Yes, I said it. And it's true. I'm no punk, but I succumbed to the only way you could manage me and make me feel good, to forget momentarily about what really mattered in my life. You never once apologized for causing Diane the stress that caused her premature labor that almost cost us Robert's life. I knew why you had come. Diane had told me. But with time, we got past that and were making progress. You knew it. And you just could not have that. No, you had to manipulate the situation like some soap opera affair. Even though she and I were separated, we were working through it. Our marriage was healing. Then you went and told her that I was seeing you, that I chose you. You did that and that's when she stopped me from seeing my children. I never brought it up to you because I was caught between a rock and a hard place."

"Luis, don't blame me for Diane's insecurities. She came with that. You told me about it, remember? Besides, I was fighting for the man I loved and I deserved better than stealing a few hours here and there. I wanted more."

"Maria, Maria, Maria, see that's what I'm talking about. You have these stories in your head that you act out and believe are true. You don't get to determine what I deserve or decide what is best for me. But that's exactly what you did both times you confronted Diane about us.

But again, I am to blame. What I don't quite get about me though, is why I accepted you after all that you had done. I just recently learned about the second call you made to Diane, but I did know that you had basically blackmailed me into staying away from my wife because you threatened to share information about our affair with the college board, knowing that it would ruin my chances for tenure and my career. That, Maria, is not love."

"Oh Poppie," she said, leaning forward and about to rise from the sofa.

Luis said, "Stop, stay right where you are. Why do you do that? Sex is not the answer to everything. You use your body like it will solve world hunger. Some topics have to be discussed. This is one of those topics. So you stay right where you are. I don't want your distractions right now."

He waited for Maria to sit back before continuing. "I'm just saying that I must have been depressed and found solace in the comfort of the familiar and the sex. I had never thought about it until just recently. I'm looking at Luis J and I am concerned about how he's handling Carlos' death. He's highly sexed and I think that he's seeking to numb his pain through sexual relations."

'If you only knew,' Maria thought to herself. She then asked, cautiously, "Okay, but what has that got to do with us?"

"Well he's my son. I see the similarities now that I've had the opportunity to be around him more. He didn't even come to his brother's burial. Instead he hung out with my brother, who is still young and wild. He loves women and is loved by women, so I just know what Luis J was up to while he was down there. And he's not going to turn it off now that's he's back. He can't without help from me. I need to let him know that it doesn't dull the pain or stop the hurt."

Perturbed and perplexed by the conversation, Maria asked, "What are you talking about? Where, if anywhere, are you going with this, Luis?"

"As I said earlier, I have to be honest with you about my feelings. I care about you, but I'm not in love with you."

"Is that all? Mira, you've been through a major loss, Poppie. No parent is supposed to bury their child. Your emotions are raw. You just need some time, that's all. Give your heart some time to grieve and then you'll find your love for me again."

"That's the point. I can't, Maria, because I've never loved you. And I've never told you that I love you, either. Never. Haven't you ever wondered why? You're a beautiful woman, and you deserve someone who can return your love and make a home with you. It's not me. We were making love and it's been great between us that way, but after all this time, something has prevented me from being in love with you."

"Poppie, people have built relationships, hell marriages, on much less than what we have. Besides, I love you enough for the both of us. I don't want to be with anyone else. No one else understands me the way you do. No one else makes me feel the way you do," Maria said in her seductive voice.

"And that's a problem. You can't do double duty for love. Love between a man and a woman is a two-way street. You say that it's okay now, but at some point you will resent me for not giving you what you want, which is for me to love you. That's why you always turn what I say into 'I love you,' when I've never said I love you. One day you will want children of your own and I don't want any more. I want to focus my attention to doing right by the ones I already have."

Maria was furious. Of course she wanted children someday. She had never hid that from him, but he never once said he didn't want any more. Someone was putting this crap in his head. Someone was making him doubt his feelings for her and she knew exactly who was at the top of the list.

"Diane's behind this, isn't she? She's using your children to break us up."

"No, Diane has no idea what I'm feeling. This is between you and me. It has nothing to do with Diane, and don't you pull one of your phone calls to her, not this time," he said, getting up from the chair and walking to the bar to pour a cognac.

"Oh, please. If I want to call her I will; I always do. But I thought you said you were going to be honest about your feelings. You're still in love with her."

There, she said it. She suspected all along that he was still holding some torch for Diane, but Maria honestly thought that she was putting it out. "That's what this is all about. I see it when you look at her, when you talk about her. And now that she has thrown David out like yesterday's garbage, do you honestly think you will have another chance? Guess again, honey. It will never work for a hundred reasons, but mostly because women like Diane will never forgive you. She can't. And even if she found some way to let you back into her life, she will never be able to trust you again. Believe me, I've seen it too many times. And you would be miserable because you would constantly have to prove your innocence and worthiness to Queen Diane."

Luis smirked and said, "There you are! The real Maria, always on the offensive. You are something else. Truth is, how I feel about Diane is not your concern. What is your concern is that I want to be free to do whatever I want, which isn't to spend the rest of my life with you. Do you comprehend that? Do I need to repeat it?"

Luis watched her eyes well up and he delivered his next words with a hint of softness. "Maria, I'm not trying to hurt you, but I need for you to hear me."

Like a mouse trapped on sticky paper, Maria wiggled and tugged to save her relationship, falling back on what had worked for her since she was a teenager. "Poppie, come on, give us another chance. We have had some great times together, in and out of bed. I have felt the passion in your heart; it was unbelievable the night you came back from Puerto Rico. Maybe you just need time for your head to catch up."

She stood up and started moving toward him. This time, she was not taking no for an answer. She began removing her strap. She would draw him onto the paper with her and he would be trapped once again.

"Maria, please don't. I told you before that sex can't solve this. Yes, we've had wonderful sex. That's why I've stayed, why I was first attracted to you. You're very sexual and sensual. You were initially drawn to me, I guess, because I was older or perhaps because I was your mentor and professor. But the moment you found out I was married, you turned on your seductive switch. And you are good at it. And I was a willing participant. Because of the problems in my marriage, I played right along with you. But getting me into bed is not the answer anymore. I've let that happen in the past and it has probably given you the wrong impression about my feelings. Love is not to be confused with sex. I won't do that anymore. It's over. We're over. I hope you won't make this any more difficult than it already is. I'll help you find a place to stay and you can take whatever furniture you need. I'll also pay for a hotel room until you can find a place."

He was surprised, yet thankful, that she didn't say anything. He was hopeful that he really got through to her and that she was going to accept his decision. He added, "I'm sorry if I've disappointed you, but this is best, for both of us. In time, you'll see."

Maria was standing directly in front of Luis now and could see in his eyes, for the first time, what had always been there: an emptiness.

He was looking back at her, but he wasn't looking at her. As much as she had tried, she never had him. He was always just outside of her reach.

The only words she could utter now were, "You asshole. That's it? Just pack my shit and go? You've been fucking me this whole time while it was convenient and met some need you had, but now that it's time for you to commit, you're standing there telling me to move out of our home?"

"I'm asking you to move out of my house. It was never our home. You just lived here."

The rage reached its peak inside of her and she pulled back and slapped him.

Luis waited for the tingling to subside before responding. "I'll give you that one."

Maria responded by pulling her arm back to land another blow, but Luis caught her by the wrist. "Maria, I'm not going to let you make this ugly. You know I have limits. I advise you not to cross them. Now, you can stay tonight if you want. I'll give you the bed and sleep on the couch."

Pointing her finger at him, she interrupted with, "Do you think I would spend one more night in YOUR house? I'm leaving here tonight. I don't need your handouts. I'm more than capable of taking care of myself." She had done it from a very early age and this situation was no different.

"Maria, I know that. I just wanted to help you transition. We've shared a lot of time together and that means something."

Maria picked up her purse, slipped into her shoes, grabbed her jacket and headed for the door. "You aren't acting like we've shared anything together. But you will realize what you're losing one day."

"Actually, I finally do. I'm very clear about this. Call me to make arrangements to get your things by next Wednesday. That gives you seven days. Leave your keys on the table by the door. I'll lock it after you leave. Good bye."

Maria sat behind the steering wheel of her Corvette, the engine running, and realized she had nowhere to go, or at least no where she felt she could go and save face. She had been telling her girlfriends that Luis was going to pop the question soon. Clearly, she had not seen this coming. They had been warning her for years that she should make him choose but they didn't know him the way she did.

'That arrogant son-of-a-bitch,' she thought, 'I gave him my best years. How could it be ending, especially like this?' She revved the engine loud enough for him to hear it, put it in drive, and pulled off. She only glanced in the mirror once to see the house getting smaller as she accelerated, but feeling her desire for vengeance growing.

'He has no idea what I'm really capable of.' Parking the car and entering the building, she knocked on the door and waited. To her relief, she heard movement behind the door and a voice say, "One minute."

Luis J opened the door, wearing jeans and no shirt. "Maria? What the hell are you doing here?"

"May I come in?" She walked past him into the apartment and removed her coat without waiting for a response. He closed the door and followed her into the living room.

"What's going on? Has something happened to Papi?"

"You could say that." She sat down on the couch, remembering the last time she was in the apartment. "Your father broke up with me tonight."

"What? Why? Did he find out…?"

"No. No, he didn't find out. It's really complicated, but he was pretty clear; it's over. He put me out, took my keys and said that I could pick up my things later. So I'm going to be moving out."

"Maria, I don't know what to say. But honestly you must have known this was going to happen eventually."

"Why would you say that? Well, it doesn't matter anymore. It's over." After a pause, she said, "I have a favor to ask."

"What?"

"May I sleep on your couch for a couple of days, until I can find a place?"

"Seriously? Why would you want to stay here? Don't you have somewhere else you can go?"

"No, I don't. Most of my friends are your Dad's friends so I can't ask them. It would be really awkward. I promise you I won't get in your way. Like I said, it's just for a few days. Besides, wouldn't you like the company?" Maria said, appealing to Luis J's sensibilities.

After thinking about her situation, the time of night and the fact that she had been thrown out, he said, "Alright. But this remains between us. You can take the bedroom. I'll sleep on the couch."

"I don't want to put you out of the bed."

"It's no problem. I've been sleeping on the couch most nights anyway. The TV's in here."

She smiled at the vision of his 6'4" frame sleeping on the pullout when there was a queen-sized bed in the bedroom. "I really appreciate this. I'll give you some money for expenses."

"Oh, don't worry about that. Can I get you anything?"

"One of your tee shirts would be nice. I'm kinda traveling light," she smiled, holding up her purse.

Luis J gave her a tee shirt from Carlos' drawer and she turned in for the night. He couldn't believe Papi had finally ended it with her, but in some ways, he was relieved. At least now it would never be because he had slept with Maria. She had said it was complicated so he wondered if his mother had anything to do with the breakup. He wouldn't put it past her. She enjoyed inflicting misery on others. If her relationship with David was over, perhaps she teased Papi with the possibility of their reconcilement.

Then Luis J wondered if his dad somehow sensed Maria's infidelity. They say women know, but is that true of men, as well? Surely he would know if Dany had slept with anyone else. Once again, Luis J regretted sleeping with Maria because now she could hold that over his head. The last thing he wanted to do was give her the upper hand. He had heard countless stories from Carlos about Maria's manipulative ways.

Perhaps he should have told her to go to a hotel. Well, hopefully, she would only be there for the few days as she had promised. He was enjoying his privacy and now it was being invaded. And he didn't know if having her sleeping in the next room was a good idea. Luis J drained the corner of his beer and turned off the light. He needed to go to sleep.

He awoke to the sound of pots and the aroma of coffee. "Damn, Carlos?" he called out, half groggy.

"Luis J, wake up. It's me, Maria. I'm sorry about the noise. I'm not surprised you're still sleeping, considering how many bottles are on the counter. How many of these did you drink last night?" she asked. She couldn't help but be reminded of what Luis had said about his and Luis J's similarities regarding handling stress.

"Just one. I need to get a recycle bag, so for now I just leave them on the counter. What are you making?" Luis J asked, changing the subject. The truth was, he really didn't know how many he drank last night. By the time Maria got there, he had had at least two Bud Lights and a shot of tequila.

"An omelet and some toast. I don't really have many choices," she said. "I'll stop by the store today after work. Aren't you late for school? Winter break hasn't started yet, has it?"

The way his head was spinning, there was no way he could handle classes today. "I'm not feeling well. I think I picked up a bug from Robert, so I'm just gonna lay low today. What are your plans?"

"I'm going to wait for your father to leave the house and then pick up some things." She had left the key on the table by the door, per his instruction, but she had a spare. She assumed he would change the locks soon so she was determined to move her things out today. She had reserved a van for rent that would hold everything. She did not want to have to rely on Luis or have to ask him for permission to get what belonged to her, and perhaps a few more items. Besides, she did not take well to his deadline, or having to make an appointment to move her things.

"Do you need help?" Luis J asked, reluctantly. Regardless of what he thought about her, his parents had raised him to be chivalrous.

"Thanks, but I've got it covered. Besides, you said you needed to rest."

"Well, call me when you're downstairs and I'll come down to help you."

"Deal. Now, come have some breakfast."

After Maria left, Luis J put his plate in the sink and lay back down on the couch. He was just dozing off when his cell rang. He answered it before he realized he hadn't checked the caller-ID.

"Luis J? Where are you?"

"Mami, um, I'm not feeling well, so I stayed home."

"How long have you been sick?"

"Just this morning."

"Then why haven't you gone to school since Monday?"

"I was at school. I was just late a few days."

"I'm on my way over there."

"No. I'm fine; you don't need to come over here." That was the last thing he needed.

"Your school called and said you haven't been there all week. Today is Thursday. What's going on with you?"

"I missed yesterday and today. Why are they making a federal case out of it? I'll be there tomorrow."

"Luis J, I want to see you. Do you understand? You come home, tonight."

"Mami, I told you I wasn't feeling well. You don't want me spreading my germs to Robert or CJ. I'll stop by tomorrow after practice."

"Okay, that's a thought if you're sick, Luis J. But I will see you tomorrow. Please don't disappoint me. If I learn that you are lying, it won't be pretty." Diane ended the call not waiting for a response.

Luis J pressed the end button on the phone. He wished his mother would just leave him alone. He wasn't really missing anything in class right now. Most of the teachers were coasting into winter break. He thought about drinking a beer but unfortunately, he had finished the last one last night. Carlos had stocked up for the holiday season, but now there wasn't anything left except the tequila, and even that was running low. He threw back a shot and then returned to the spot on the couch. He wondered how much time he had before Maria would be back.

On the third ring, Luis answered. "Diane?"

"Yes. Do you have a few minutes?"

"I have quite a few minutes. My next class isn't until two. How can I help?"

"Is it obvious? Can we meet for lunch?"

"Sure." He gave her the directions and headed to the campus.

On Thursday mornings, he had office hours for students and graded papers. He didn't have any appointments today so he looked at the stack of papers on his desk, not sure which session he should start grading first. His first-year graduate class was a good place to begin. He started reading the first paragraph of one of his brightest students, but he still found his mind wandering.

The drama with Maria last night had left him unable to sleep and he found his concentration still being affected. Now this call from Diane. He wondered what it was that she wanted to talk about. If Maria had called her pulling her old tricks, he'd…no he couldn't think about that.

Closing the paper and putting it back on the pile, he headed to the restaurant early. Perhaps a change of scenery and some fresh air would clear his head. Luis requested a table that allowed him to watch the door but was in the corner. He wasn't in the mood to have idle chitchat with any of his colleagues or the students. As Diane approached, he arose. Her face looked strained but she was dressed in a blue suit. The skirt and jacket accentuated her waist and hips and was very flattering. She had on a little makeup and her hair was pulled back into a ponytail.

"You look worried. Have a seat," he said, kissing her on the cheek.

"I'm fine and thanks for agreeing to meet with me."

"No thanks necessary." Luis waited for her to begin.

"Yes they are. Really, thank you for taking time out of your day. I have been so uncooperative over the years and now here we are talking about our children."

Luis didn't see that coming so he leaned in to listen intently. Diane continued, "It's about Luis J. I'm concerned about him." She brought him up to speed regarding the school's call, her call to Luis J earlier, and his excuses. "I think he's drinking and God I hope that's all. When he came over the other day, his speech was slurred and his eyes looked glassy. He was unsteady; he could have fallen, but he didn't. Have you spoken with him?"

"No, I haven't, although I have been worried about him, too. He hasn't really grieved, Diane. I think he's using alcohol and maybe sex to numb his pain. Maybe we should go see him this evening."

"He asked me not to come over. He said he would come by tomorrow after school. I want to keep my promise to him. I'm trying not to screw this up."

"Then I'll go by. I didn't make that promise."

"No. I want to trust him on this, but do you think you could be there when he comes tomorrow? I would like to get your assessment and help on how to handle this. One thing I know for sure Luis, I'm no substitute for a man, for a father."

Luis smiled, saying, "I'll be there. We'll do it your way, but you need to stop putting yourself down. And no, you're definitely no man."

Diane smiled shyly, then responded with, "Why Luis Sr., is that a back-handed compliment?" She didn't give him time to respond. She didn't need to. He got that "hand in the cookie jar" look on his face and that was all the answer she needed. "But honestly I don't know how to stop beating myself up. I feel so guilty because I am guilty."

"Diane you're not guilty. Yes, you are responsible for your actions. We all are. But we have to accept that and then face the pied piper for our actions." Taking Diane's hand, he asked, "How can I help, my Di?"

Diane felt butterflies in her stomach. His voice was so comforting and she didn't realize how much she missed that. "I don't know. I've had better days. I don't get much sleep. CJ is still crying at night. He's still so confused. I know we said we would keep him, but I wonder if we should have considered what was best for him. My Spanish is coming back, but at two-thirty in the morning, it doesn't come naturally. So I find myself just holding him and humming. Sometimes I feel so helpless. Then there's Chell. She is very distant, too. She loves CJ and is able to calm him down much faster than I am. But she misses Luis

J something awful and doesn't understand why he hasn't moved back home yet. Robert is the only one who hasn't really been affected by all of this. He knows Carlos is in heaven, watching over him, and that satisfies him. David has spent a lot of time with him and that has helped." Diane said this before she realized how it might hurt Luis, but she couldn't take it back.

He shifted in the seat and then asked, "So, how are things with you guys? Is it getting better?"

"No, it's the same. David's found an apartment and will be moving in at the end of the month."

"I'm sorry. I know how difficult this must be for you. For both of you."

"Yes it is, but this is for the best. At least now we're able to get along better this way."

"I hope you guys can work it out. I know he loves you. As for Chell, maybe if I spend some time with her…" Diane's posture changed and Luis prepared himself for her refusal.

"That's a good idea. She is happier when you're around. When would be good for you?"

He smiled and for the first time in a long time after a question put to Diane about seeing his children was answered in the affirmative, he felt a sense of hope. "How about Sunday?"

"Are you still taking CJ on Saturday?"

"Yes."

"Doesn't that tie up your whole weekend?"

"It does, but it's no problem. I want my time with Chell to be focused on Chell. I could take her shopping or to the movies."

"Well, if you're sure. Why don't you tell her tomorrow? It should come from you." They continued chatting through lunch until Diane realized it was time for her meeting and had to excuse herself from the excitement of their lunch conversation.

"Diane, try not to worry yourself senseless. We're going to need all your good sense if we're to help Luis J and Chell. We will get through this, I promise." She smiled, but Luis knew she was still very worried.

Chapter Twenty Three

It was six in the evening and Luis J still had not arrived. He was usually there by five-thirty after practice. Diane had checked with the school earlier and they confirmed his attendance for the day so he had at least kept that promise.

David had already picked up Robert for the weekend and CJ was still out with the nanny so it was just Chell and Diane. They were sitting on the couch watching television together. It was a rare moment for them since CJ came to live with them so Diane stayed there, despite the dishes in the sink calling her name or the basket full of clothes that needed washing. Chell was leaning on her and Diane was stroking her hair. Everything else could wait. The calm was ultimately interrupted by a knock on the door.

Chell leaped off the couch and ran to the door. Without saying a word, she ran into her father's arms. Luis hugged his daughter, leaned in and kissed her on the top of her head and breathed in the scent of her shampoo. It was the same that her mother used. She remained in his arms.

"Let him in honey," Diane said, shaking her head at Chell.

Chell grabbed Luis' arm and escorted him to the sofa. They sat down next to Diane, Chell in the middle with her head on her dad's shoulder and her legs across her mother's, as though she was trying to tie them together. After a few moments, Luis asked, "Where's Luis J?"

"Not here. I was just about to call him." As Diane extracted her body from her daughter's grasp, she moved to the kitchen to call her son. While the phone rang, she watched Luis return all of his attention to his daughter, listening to her excitement about the day and telling her of his plans for the two of them on Sunday. Diane closed her eyes and sighed.

"He didn't answer the land line at Carlos' apartment or his cell. What should we do?"

"Mami, what's wrong?"

"Your father and I need to talk to Luis J, that's all."

"Is he in trouble?" Chell now directed her question to her father.

"It's nothing for you to worry about. We just need to talk to him, like your mother said," Luis responded.

Chell returned to her position on her father's chest and continued watching TV until she received a phone call and excused herself to her room. By six-forty-five, they were pretty sure Luis J wasn't coming.

"I'll stop by his place on my way home. If he's there, we'll talk. If not, I'll leave him a note and try again in the morning, on my way over here." Luis said, reaching for the door. But he had to move back as it opened.

"Mr. Rodriquez, good evening. Mrs. Anderson, we're home," the nanny said, returning with CJ.

Luis had secured a bilingual nanny, Rosie, to help with CJ. Rosie came during the week in the morning and stayed until six-thirty. She fed and cared for CJ and was working with him on his English. She also accompanied CJ whenever he visited his grandfather so there would be continuity in his life. Diane was so appreciative of her assistance. Today, Rosie had taken CJ out around five-thirty for an evening playdate at the children's center. CJ was exhausted and falling asleep in her arms.

Carlos had surprised them all by leaving a $500,000 life insurance policy naming his mother, father, Luis J, Chell, Robert, Luisa and CJ as beneficiaries. Diane was a little disappointed that David had not been included, but it was reflective of their relationship. Apparently, Carlos had taken it out when he began working at FedEx two years earlier. When they informed FedEx of his passing, the insurance company had called and told them about the policy.

Luis and Diane had met with the insurance company handlers and thought it best to set the children's money up as living trust funds for each, with themselves as the executors. They allocated Luisa's portion to CJ and set up a trust for him as well. They did not share this with the children or anyone else because the timing was not good. Thankfully, the money made it possible to hire Rosie, comfortably.

Luis reached for CJ and gave him a big hug, greeted him in Spanish, and held him up high playfully over his head the way he used to do his children. This made CJ giggle, and in his face Diane could see Carlos' warm loving smile. 'That smile, that smile,' she thought. Thank God for that smile; it inspired her the same as when it was on Carlos' face. She felt it was a gift of a second chance from Carlos and it warmed her heart. Even in loss, there was gain. She was being given a second chance to do right by Luis and she would this time.

Once Luis had absorbed the love he needed, he handed him back to Rosie, kissing him goodnight. But these actions had the same impact on CJ as it used to on Carlos and Luis J, and now CJ was all stimulated and ready to go another hour. Rosie was not amused because she needed to give him a bath and get him into his PJs. Diane looked away as she fought back tears.

"Chell, I'm leaving. I'll see you tomorrow."

"Bye, Papi," she called from her room.

Diane had just settled down and was getting ready for bed when the phone rang. It was Luis calling to let her know that Luis J was not at Carlos' apartment, or he wasn't answering.

Unfortunately, he no longer had a key because Carlos had given it to Luis J. Luis left a note for him though under the door saying he would be back early Saturday morning. After hearing his update, Diane hoped that her son wasn't in any serious trouble.

Luis J was driving around, avoiding going home to Carlos' apartment and confronting his mother. His cell phone rang several times but he ignored it. He now used it to call Danielle.

"L?"

"Who else?"

"What are you doing calling me? Are you alright?"

"I need to see you."

"What? Are you crazy? You know we can't see each other. Besides, your actions in school have made it pretty clear to me that you're still mad at me and don't want to see me."

"I think I was valid in feeling that way then, don't you? You betrayed me, but I'm over that now. I really need to see you tonight."

They had avoided each other since the arrangement, but she remained very much a part of his thoughts. He still had feelings for her and knew she felt the same way, or at least he hoped she did. He would catch her watching him when he was on the court and smiling when he stole a ball or made the play just like she used to, like nothing had changed.

"L, this can't be a good idea. My mother and your lawyer were pretty clear." She was blaming them for her rationale, but the truth was that she really just didn't trust herself around him. She had missed him so much. She surely would succumb to his touch. Besides, she had wanted to reach out to him when Carlos died. She knew how much he had to be struggling with the loss. All she wanted to do was hug him and provide some comfort.

"I just want to talk to you, that's all. If you can't come out, I'll find someone old enough to be with me."

"Luis J, that's not fair. I'm just looking out for you and protecting myself."

"I don't need you to look out for me. You know what, forget it. I'm sorry I called."

"L, wait. Is there somewhere safe we can meet? We can't afford to be seen by anyone."

"I know just the place. I'll pick you up, back door, in about fifteen minutes," Luis J offered, before entering the expressway that would take him back to Brooklyn. He was glad she had given in. She would be the first and only girl to be in Carlos' apartment since he passed. It just didn't feel right having anyone over there, but Danielle was different. Being with her there wouldn't be disrespectful to his memory. He had talked to Maria earlier and she told him that she wouldn't be there this evening. She didn't give him a lot of explanation and he didn't ask; he was looking forward to having the place to himself once again.

At the light before Dany's apartment, Luis J reached behind the passenger's seat and pushed the bag containing a six-pack of Bud Light and a bottle of tequila under the seat. During one of his visits, Carlos had introduced him to Jerry, who worked at the corner liquor store. Jerry's father owned the store and Jerry would sell the alcohol to Carlos under the table, even though he was underage. Jerry did this to repay Carlos for helping him study for the GED. When he heard about Carlos' passing, Jerry was sympathetic to Luis J's loss and told him he could buy whatever he wanted whenever he was on duty. He couldn't wait to get to the house and have a drink.

When he pulled around back, there stood Dany in the eave of the doorway. She pulled the hood over her head, ran to the car and jumped into the front seat. As soon as she closed the door, he could smell her perfume and his mind drifted to the last time they had been together.

He winked at her and then backed out of the driveway heading to the apartment.

"L, is everything cool?"

"It's just great. How about with you?" he asked, so cooly.

"It's alright, but I must admit I was surprised to get your call."

"That's good. I always like to keep you on your toes. Besides, I'm tired of people trying to tell me what I should and shouldn't do. Now I'm gonna do what I want to do. Want a beer?"

"A beer? How did you get beer?" asked Dany, shocked that he'd asked her and more so that he even had beer.

"Yes, beer. It doesn't matter how I got it. Do you want one?"

"I can't believe you're drinking."

"Well, I'm not using it for gasoline," he replied, pulling a can out of the bag, popping the top and taking a long swallow. It was still cold and felt good going down.

"L, you really shouldn't be drinking. Coach would bench you for sure. And you really shouldn't be drinking and driving. That's just crazy."

"I got it under control. Just sit back and relax." Luis J didn't want her drilling him. He just wanted her to comfort him.

Dany watched him draining the bottle and thought about asking him to pull over. The last thing they needed was to be stopped by the police. "Where are we going?"

"To paradise. Trust me."

He turned up the Latin music he had been listening to as they drove to the apartment in silence. The songs were on a tape that Carlos had made of his favorites. There were slow songs and jams of some of Puerto Rico's rising artists. He let the tunes soothe his mind and prepare his body for what he hoped was about to happen with Dany.

When Luis J didn't consume anymore, Dany figured everything

would be alright. Hopefully, they weren't far from wherever they were headed.

"Come on into paradise."

He placed the keys on the coffee table and turned on the kitchen lights. Maria had straightened up and cooked dinner. He was appreciative, as he hadn't thought about getting any food.

"Hungry?"

"No, thanks."

"Suit yourself." He made a plate of spaghetti and while it warmed in the microwave, he grabbed another bottle of beer.

Dany stood in the doorway of the kitchen, watching him before asking, "L, what is going on with you?"

"What?"

"Why am I here? What did you want to see me about? And why are you drinking so much?"

"Be patient baby. Why don't you turn on the radio?"

She looked around the room because she had no idea where the radio was located. He knew she had never been there. She assumed it was Carlos' apartment, but since they hadn't talked in weeks, she had no idea what was going on in his life. When she saw a few female clothes laying on the back of the couch, she stopped her search and asked, "Where is the radio? Whose place is this anyway? Whose things are those?"

"Why do you care? Are you jealous?"

"No, it's not like we're a couple anymore." Truth was, it was all of that; she was curious and a tad bit jealous.

"Then why did you ask?"

"You know what, I don't need this crap. It was a mistake for me to agree to meet you. I thought you were grieving since you lost your brother and I thought I could help a friend. After all, we have shared a lot. But I can see you're not yourself. I'm gonna go." Grabbing her jacket, she headed toward the door.

"Dany, wait," he said, moving toward her and taking her arm. "Come on, sit down. I'm sorry. I was being an asshole. This is Carlos' place. I'm packing up his things. Those clothes don't belong to anyone special. Come on, please?"

She followed him to the couch and they sat down. Putting his arm around her shoulder, he leaned his head back and closed his eyes. "I really miss my brother. I never imagined he would be dead. I feel so alone. And I can't talk to anybody about it. But I feel comfortable with you."

"I know you do. It killed me when I heard about what had happened. It was so sad. I wanted to call you, but I didn't think you would talk to me."

"Of course I would have talked to you, Dany. I would have welcomed it. It's so hard to believe that he left me."

Dany removed her hand from his grasp and hugged him briefly.

"Baby, when my grandfather died, my grandmother told me he would always be with me, in my heart and my mind. The same is true for Carlos. I know he's still with you. And Luis J, he didn't leave you. He died."

"I know, but he's gone just the same. Nothing has been going right for me, until now." Placing his arm around her neck, he pulled her to him and kissed her, gently at first, as he wasn't sure how she would respond. When she didn't pull back, he moved closer, completely enveloping her body. "I want to be with you," he whispered, continuing to kiss her face and lips.

"L, I don't think that's a good idea," she said, even though her body was saying yes. She smelled the beer on his breath and she didn't like it.

"Who will know? I'll get you home before your mom gets home."

"That's what got us into trouble before."

Luis J laughed, "Yeah but I won't be in your bed."

"Do you forgive me for everything?"

"There's nothing to forgive." He hadn't been with anyone for about a week and tonight he wanted to find comfort from a girl instead of the alcohol. A special girl and not just for sex. He had never really stopped caring for Dany. In fact, some of the craziness in his life was due to his not being able to talk to and share with her the way he used to before that fateful night.

Putting on a condom before entering her, Luis J took his time to pleasure Dany so she would enjoy the experience. The way her body was responding to his caresses confirmed for him that she hadn't been with anyone either. She was still his. It was the first time they could lavish in total abandonment, free of fear of her mother's intrusion. "I miss you so much, L." He kissed her and became aroused again. She was so good.

At seven-fifteen in the morning, the alarm rang and they started getting ready to leave. Dany had told him that her mother and sister were out of town for the weekend, so Dany could stay without worrying about her mother's wrath. Luis J's head was throbbing from the beers, but he knew he had to ignore it so he could get her back home before her mom's check-in phone call.

"Hey, did you see this note?" Dany asked, picking it up off the floor near the door.

"No. Let me see it." He remembered that he hadn't turned on the hall light when they entered the apartment last night. The note read:

Luis J,

We missed you at your mother's last night. We need to talk to you. I will be by around eight in the morning. Please wait for me.

Love, Papi

"Oh shit, we have to get out of here. Are you ready?"

"Almost, what's wrong?"

"My father is on his way over here. I wish I had seen this last night. Hurry up!"

"Alright, I am."

They locked the door and pushed the button for the elevator. When the door opened, there stood Papi.

"Luis J, where are you going? Didn't you get my note?"

"Yes, Papi, but I didn't see it until this morning. I have to run a quick errand right now, so this really isn't a good time."

Luis looked at his son and then the young lady who was standing slightly behind him.

"Who is she?"

Luis J turned and looked at Dany, as if he needed to see who his father was referencing. "Her? Oh, she's just a friend."

"Does this friend have a name?"

"Of course she does. She goes to my school."

Luis turned to the young lady since he wasn't getting a proper response from his son and introduced himself.

"Good morning. I'm Luis Rodriquez, Luis J's father. And you are?"

"Hello, Mr. Rodriquez, it's nice to meet you."

"What is your name, young lady?" Luis was now tired of playing this game. He had his suspicions about who she was, but he needed to hear it from one of them.

Looking down, Dany responded ever so softly, "Danielle. My name is Danielle."

"Danielle? Danielle what?" He directed the question toward her, but his eyes shifted to his son.

Still avoiding his eyes, she blurted out, "Danielle Webber."

"Luis J, after all that we have all been through? I can't believe this!

Man, what exactly is going on with you? Are you trying to ruin your life?"

"Papi, don't blow this out of proportion. It's not what you think. I just need to take her home right now and then I'll meet you at Mami's. I promise."

"Hell no. We're going to discuss this now!"

"Papi, I can't. I have to get her home before eight-thirty."

"So then it is what I think. You're trying to get her home before her mother discovers she's been out all night. Dios mío. I don't believe you. Let's go. I'll drive."

Danielle sat quietly in the front seat, except for giving Luis directions to her house, and so did Luis J in the back.

"Would one of you please explain to me what the hell you were thinking?"

"Papi, it's no big deal."

"Really? And I suppose both of you have forgotten how we resolved the problem you and your mother created for him?" Luis asked, pointing at Luis J. "Have both of you forgotten the terms of the agreement?"

Neither of them responded. "I know you heard me ask a question. One or both of you need to say something."

"Papi, look, I missed her and she agreed to meet me last night. It was the first time. She would not have told her mother." He reached for her shoulder from the back and she instinctively reached for his hand.

"And why would this time be different? I'm sure you never expected her to fabricate that story about you the first time, either. Young lady, regardless of how you feel about Luis J, you have to stay away from him. This will not end well for either of you."

"Papi, no disrespect, but you have no right to interfere."

"Bullshit! You don't have the right to disrespect every adult who stood up on your behalf. I have every right, as your father and as the person who worked to clean up the mess caused by you, this young lady, and her family."

"But…"

"Not another word Luis J. You and I will talk later. Now, Danielle, you must abide by the terms of the agreement and stay away from Luis J. If I find out you agreed to see him again, my attorney will contact your mother to begin filing charges against her. Am I clear?"

Their beautiful evening was being tainted by this morning's events, but she had no choice but to say, "Yes, sir." She understood where his anger was coming from and she was truly sorry.

"Good. And to make sure, I'm going to have my lawyer contact your mother and give her a warning."

"Mr. Rodriquez, I swear to you I will never tell anyone about seeing Luis J last night. Please don't tell my mother. I wanted to see him because of his loss, your loss. I know Luis J so well and I knew he needed me. Whenever he was down, we'd always talk and work through things. I am truly sorry about Carlos and our decision to be together last night, but you don't have to tell my mother. I was trying to be there for your son when he needed me."

"Yes, thank you for your sentiment and for comforting him, but you could have done that over the phone. You didn't need to spend the night with him. How can I trust you, or you either for that matter, Luis J, since both of you violated the terms of the agreement?"

"Mr. Rodriquez, please, there must be another way. Do you want me to put something in writing? You can't tell my mom," Danielle said, pleading, "Please."

"I don't see one. I'm sorry. The fact that you are still that afraid of her reinforces my concerns. She could take this as an opportunity to bring legal action against Luis J."

Luis hoped that this would not be the outcome, but Mrs. Webber had shown her true colors to them already. As an afterthought, he asked, "Did you guys at least have protected sex?"

"Yes, Papi, damn."

"Watch your mouth, Luis J, watch your mouth. Danielle, I wish things could have been different and that we had met under better circumstances. You seem like a very nice young lady. I hope that things work out for you." Luis pulled up in front of her building and waited for her to exit the vehicle.

"Bye, L," Danielle stated, releasing his hand and exiting the car. As she walked to the doorway, she never looked back. Luis recognized their emotional connection for one another, but it was a recipe for disaster given her mother's vindictiveness.

Luis J could only imagine how she was feeling and hoped he could convince his father not to tell her mother or his mother about their getting together.

As they headed toward their next destination, Papi asked, "Would you explain to me what's going on with you? You won't talk to anybody but Dany apparently and God knows we've all tried. We thought leaving you to yourself would give you the space you needed to grieve. But son, this is suicidal behavior you're exhibiting."

"I made a mistake."

"This isn't the only 'mistake' you've made lately. Talk to me son. What's going on?"

"So, now all of a sudden you're concerned? Where were you when I needed to talk to my father? Where were you when Carlos comforted me every night, after you left? You can't just step back into my life and assume the father role."

"I can understand how you feel."

"No, you can't. It was horrible thinking that you didn't care enough to be there for me. I grew to hate you and it's not easy to just turn that off."

"You're right. I probably can't know how that must have felt to you because my father was in my life and you didn't have the benefit of knowing the full story. I just meant I understood. Carlos and I had this same conversation when he came to live with me. That wasn't easy and he was very angry, but we were able to talk through it and he found his love for me again. You have to understand that it was not my choice. I wanted to be in your life."

"Good for you and Carlos, but don't count on that happening with me overnight."

"Luis J, don't forget your place, I am your father. Honestly, I don't expect anything, but I do hope we can find some common ground. You came to me when this Dany business broke and asked for my help. So why all of a sudden are you against us getting to know each other? I thought you were looking forward to it. You know, I wish to God I could change some of the choices I made in my life, but I can't. They are what make me the man I am today. I have learned from them, as will you from yours.

"I would trade places with Carlos in a minute, but that's not possible. I know how close the two of you were and you have to miss him terribly, but you're doing some really messed up things that are going to affect the rest of your life and those are the things we need to talk about. Those are the things Carlos would talk to you about if he were here."

"I told you before, I have my life under control."

"Then why are you skipping school, missing meetings with your mother, not going to practice, having sex with the one person you're legally not supposed to be having sex with…and drinking?"

"I'm not drinking."

"The hell you're not! Yes, you are. One thing you should learn about alcohol: if you drink enough of it, it can be smelled on your body the next morning, regardless of your hygiene. It comes out through your pores. I can still smell it on you."

These words reminded Luis of his encounter with Antonio. The only difference was, Antonio was not trying to hide it.

"I just had a little last night with Danielle, that's all."

"Luis J, you're only seventeen; you shouldn't be drinking at all. And you're an athlete with a chance to play in college and maybe go pro. I thought you were serious about ball. Your mother told me you were high when you came by last Monday and I know you were drinking with Bobby in Puerto Rico. And don't think I haven't noticed that you didn't address the other items I mentioned."

"I'm not an alcoholic. I just had a few drinks. It's no big deal. I quit smoking cold turkey; I can stop drinking whenever I want." As he said this, he had to admit a shot of tequila would be good right about now.

"Luis J, I didn't say you were an alcoholic but again, you are under age and not legally permitted to drink under any circumstances. I won't even ask you right now where or how you are getting the liquor. But I will find out."

"Are you through lecturing me?"

"This is hardly a lecture. Son, I know that you're depressed about Carlos' death and you have every right to be. You're trying to cope. These things are part of finding out what works and what doesn't when dealing with our emotions, especially loss. But the problem with drugs and alcohol is that they are addictive. You can become dependent on them before you realize it. It can happen to anyone."

"I feel like sh…crap, okay? I wish you all would leave me alone. I can only stay in Carlos' apartment another week and it sickens me to think I have to go back home. There's no privacy there and Mami is always riding my back. Now that David's moved out, she'll be taking her frustrations out on me."

"Your mother wouldn't do that. That's not the person she is."

"You don't know what kind of person she is. You get to come and go, so you don't have to deal with the craziness."

"We're all a little crazy right now." They both chuckled and then Luis added, "But if you don't go back there, where would you like to go?"

"Anywhere but there."

"Listen, if you agree to talk to me, I mean really talk to me, about what's troubling you, how you feel, just like we're doing right now, then maybe I have an alternative. You say there's no privacy. I get that. So let's keep talking and see if we can agree to a plan of action to address your future. I might just have one."

"And what would that be?" Luis J didn't know why his father thought he was just going to open up to him, but he was willing to play along.

"You can come and stay with me for a while."

"Right. Mami will NEVER agree to that."

"I believe her main reason for saying no before was Maria. That's not an issue anymore."

"Why not?" Luis J asked. Perhaps now he would get an additional explanation.

"We broke up a few days ago. She's moved out."

"Where is she staying?" Luis J found a little humor in already knowing the answer to that question and he wondered how his father would respond.

"I don't know. I haven't been able to talk to her."

"Don't you care?"

"Of course I do. I want her to be comfortable, but she won't answer her cell or return my calls, so you know, what can I do?"

"I take it that it wasn't her idea."

"Not exactly. I actually did what is best for her and for me. In the long run, it wouldn't have worked."

Luis J smiled internally, recalling how he knew that when he and Carlos first went to their home for dinner. "When did you realize that?"

"I think I have known all along, but I didn't want to admit it. She'll be fine. She's strong."

"Does Mami know?"

"No."

"Why not? I'm sure that will be music to her ears. Maybe you two can get back together. After all, she's dumped David. I have an idea, you and Mami can get together and Maria and David can hook up."

"I told you already to watch your mouth, son. I won't have you saying whatever comes to your mind. I can't control your thoughts and don't want to. But you will learn what's appropriate and what isn't. Put that shit in check, man."

Luis J sat back and looked out the window. He hadn't gone up against his father and he didn't want to test him. Besides, his father wasn't the root of his anger and frustration. "I didn't want to have this conversation anyway. Why don't you drop me off and I'll take the bus back to the apartment?"

"Because that doesn't solve anything. Besides, we're almost there." The two of them drove the rest of the way in silence, much to Luis' dismay.

Chell greeted them and hugged her big brother for an extended amount of time. It reminded Luis of the greeting he had received the night before. The three of them waited in the living room until Diane could finish dressing and packing CJ's things.

"Luis J, when are you moving back home?" Chell asked.

"I don't know. Papi, I need some fresh air. I'll be on the balcony."

Luis didn't respond, he just nodded his head. He knew his son could interpret the unspoken words.

Leaving Chell in the living room, he stepped out onto the balcony. He was really not up for this conversation.

"Luis J, hey, what up man?"

"Hey, Derrick, you got it." Luis J shook hands with Derrick and shoulder bumped. Derrick lived in the apartment down the hall from them. He was about twenty-five and well known in the neighborhood. Rumor was, he was a hustler and had a few ladies working for him, but the police could never gather any evidence on him.

"Where you been, man? I usually see you walking your brother to the bus stop in the morning."

"Staying at Carlos' place."

"Yeah, I heard about that. You know your brother was down with me, right? My regrets."

"Thanks. Hey, you got any brew in your apartment?"

"Damn, it's kinda early for that, man."

"That's a matter of opinion."

He chuckled. "True. I just didn't know you drank. Carlos was always bragging about your hoop skills. But, no I don't have any beer. But I could hook you up with something a little stronger."

Luis J didn't know Carlos was bragging about him. He was always on his case and criticizing his game. The emptiness that Dany had been able to fill a little last night was slowly opening again and he wanted desperately to maintain what he had. So he asked, "Like what?"

"Come to my apartment. I'll take care of you."

Luis J could hear Carlos in his head so he said, "You know what, I can't, my parents are sweatin' me. But thanks anyway."

"Well, you know where to find me if you change your mind. Later."

"Yeah, see ya."

Just as Derrick closed the door to his apartment, Chell opened theirs and joined him on the balcony.

"Where are you going?" Luis J asked.

"To Michele's. Are you gonna be here for a while?"

"I hope not."

"What's wrong with you?"

"Nada. Life is just grand. You better get out of here before they chain you to your bed."

"What are you talking about?"

"Forget it."

"You know, you act like you're the only one who lost Carlos, but you're not. I miss him; hell, we all do, just like you do. And even more, I miss you because you're still alive. Carlos died and he's not coming back. We all have to get used to that. I miss talking to you. It's not the same without you here and you act like I'm the enemy just because you're mad at Mami. I can't believe you are abandoning me like this." She turned and headed for the elevator.

Luis J's eyes followed her and he thought to himself, 'What does she know, spoiled brat?' But he had heard her. Abandonment was what his anger was all about. His pain was not like anyone else's. He walked back into the apartment to find his mother and father talking at the table.

"So have the two of you already discussed and determined my fate?"

"No, we were waiting for you."

"Wow, that's new, Mami." Luis J saw his father shift from one leg to the other and knew he needed to tone it down some.

"Luis J, we are here because we know that you are still mourning the loss of Carlos. We all are. We just want to help you get through this. We know how hard this has been on you and it won't get better unless you face your sadness and we all talk about what we've lost," Diane stated.

"Why do you think I haven't dealt with it?"

"Because your actions indicate otherwise," Luis replied. "You have not made the best choices lately, and sooner or later things are going to get out of hand."

"Thanks for that vote of confidence. But I'm fine. I don't need to talk about anything except where I want to live."

"Excuse me?" Mami's eyes shifted to Papi's.

"I don't want to stay here any longer. I'm almost eighteen, and I need my own space. I really don't want to have to share a room with a six-year-old and eventually a two-year-old. I need privacy. I've been saying this for a long time now. But you haven't been listening."

"I am planning for us to move, Luis J, now that CJ is here, but it has to be planned out. It won't be tomorrow. I know it must be hard sometimes, but I really don't have any other options today," Diane responded.

She looked at Luis and prayed that he'd continue to abide by their agreement not to tell the children of their newly acquired trusts. That's all they needed with Luis J in this state of mind. They had agreed that they could not access their money until they had completed college, or at age thirty they would begin receiving a monthly allowance. Each child had received $100,000, as did CJ after they combined Luisa's portion. That left $100,000 for Diane and Luis to split. She was so thankful because she really needed that money, especially now.

"I know, but I have an option. Let me keep Carlos' apartment. I can get a job after school and that would cover my expenses if you guys could just pay the rent."

"Are you kidding us right now? Your behavior of late does not warrant our support of that idea," Papi responded. "You have not exhibited mature or responsible behavior or decision making that would indicate to us that you could be trusted that way."

"That's your opinion."

"No, that's fact. Do I need to recall the examples for you? And who are you to act so disrespectfully and then turn around in the same breath and ask for a favor such as this?"

Luis J knew this included the latest Dany incident, so he retreated a little more. Even though he had no desire to continue the conversation any further, he asked, "Then what else can be done? I don't want to live here any more. No offense, Mami."

"Diane, I offered to let him come and live with me. He can use my extra room, but there are going to be some stipulations, if you agree."

"I told you before I didn't think that was a good idea."

"What'd I tell you she'd say, Papi? Oh, newsflash, Mami, Papi and Maria have split up. She's moved out, so you don't have to worry about her negative influence over me."

Diane must have misunderstood Luis J. Could it be? "When did that happen?" she asked Luis.

"Earlier this week," Papi offered.

"But is the breakup temporary?" Mami continued with her interrogation.

"No."

"So, does that mean I can go, Mami?" Luis J asked, even though he wasn't sure if he would be jumping out of the frying pan into the fire living with Papi. At least he knew how to maneuver around his mother.

"It means that you need to determine if you can abide by my stipulations. If not, you will have to move back here until your mother can finalize her arrangements," Papi said.

"It seems I don't have much of a choice." 'Frying pan, fire, see what I mean?' Luis J thought.

"What does that mean?" Papi asked.

"It means I have to agree to your 'house rules.' But I do plan to stay in the apartment until the end of the lease."

"No. You need to finish packing whatever's left and be ready to move out by tomorrow."

"That's not fair. You both said I could finish out the lease."

"We made that agreement with someone we thought would behave responsibly."

"Give me a break, Papi. I'm out of school now for winter break and I was going to finish packing Carlos' things and make arrangements to drop stuff off at the Salvation Army next week."

"You can do that without living there."

"Why pay for the final week and no one's staying there? It's just one week. I won't disappoint you, I promise."

"You can stay tonight and tomorrow night. You have to be at my house Monday morning. I'll be by to pick up you and Carlos' things. And son, the rent was paid by Carlos a month ago."

"I know that. I'm just saying it's a waste of money to pay for the month and not have someone there the whole time. It's not like they're going to give you a refund. Besides, I can't get everything packed in just two days."

"Then I'll come over and help you," Papi offered.

"No. Fine, I'll get it done. I want to do it. I think it will help me process everything. Can I go now?"

"One more thing, driving the car is now off limits. I'll be over to pick it up this afternoon. Diane, do you want to drive it?"

"No. No."

"Then I'll park it in my garage."

"Why can't I keep the car?" 'They are completely paralyzing me,' Luis J thought. 'What I did with Dany wasn't that bad. Damn.'

"Same rationale. You'll have to earn the right to drive it again."

"Anything else, or can I go now?"

"I don't have anything. Diane?"

Diane was so relieved that Luis was handling this situation. She was not really prepared for any of Luis J's combative comments or defiant position. She would not have known how or where to begin to address his requests.

She finally said, "Only that we love you and are trying to do what's best for you. And that I don't understand all this hostility towards us when we've agreed to almost everything you've asked and still you're angry."

"I'm not angry. I'm just ready to go. May I leave?"

"One more thing, Luis J," Papi said, sternly. "You have to stop drinking. If we find out that you're still doing it, all bets are off, and I mean all are off…and there will be severe consequences. Understood?"

"Yes."

"Good, then I'll drive you back to the apartment."

"No thanks. I have a few errands to run, so I'll just take the subway."

Once Luis J was gone, Luis told Diane, "So, that didn't quite go the way I had planned or hoped. What did you think?"

"I think you handled things well, Luis. He's very bitter about Carlos and he's still mad at me, so he's striking out at both of us."

"I know. And newsflash," – he paused for effect – "he's angry with me too. You should've heard our conversation in the car. But I would be really worried if he didn't express some kind of emotion. We're just going to have to be patient and consistent."

After a pause, Diane asked, "So you and Maria really called it quits?"

"Yes."

That was music to her ears. That little home wrecker was out on the streets, finally. She had to know more, so she continued carefully so as to not show too much excitement over his long-awaited common sense kicking in. "So why did she end it, if I may ask?"

"You may, and she didn't; I did."

"Why?" Diane asked before she had time to assess whether she should. Now she was getting to the good stuff and it was hard to maintain a concerned look on her face when inside she was doing a happy dance. In Puerto Rico, she wondered if Luis was sparing her feelings when she asked him about an impending marriage. Turns out, he really wasn't. This was such a relief. 'Bring it on, Maria. I'm ready for you now.'

"Diane, we weren't right for each other. I wasn't happy, and eventually she wouldn't have been, either. It took this tragedy to wake me up and realize what I was sacrificing. I didn't want to continue that way."

"Change is challenging. Will you be alright?"

"Yes, I will. Now, when will CJ be ready?"

"About fifteen more minutes. He's still napping. Are you taking him out or will you stay here?"

"I was thinking about taking him to Leaps and Bounds. The kids used to love that place. Would you like to come? They have great pizza," he said, sarcastically. It was great pizza if you were under the age of ten.

"Thanks for the invite, but I think I'll stay here. We had pizza a couple of days already this week so go easy on that with him. I haven't felt much like cooking. Also, Chell has introduced him to his sweet tooth, against my wishes, so please don't encourage that too much either."

The look on Luis' face told her that she was giving him way too much guidance. After all, he wasn't a novice with children. So she adjusted her response with, "Besides, I want to be here when Chell gets home."

Luis admired how this woman loved with all of her heart and was such a natural caregiver. This made him wonder what natural instincts

Maria would exhibit when and if she ever had children. Well, she was out of his life now so he would never know. He eventually responded, “Sure, I understand. Maybe next time.”

‘Maybe,’ Diane thought, although she almost said yes this time. It would have been nice to spend the afternoon with him.

CHAPTER TWENTY FOUR

24

"Hey, Luis J, great news," Maria exclaimed, entering the apartment with her arms full of groceries.

"That makes for one of us," he responded, getting up to help her with the bags.

"I found a really nice apartment and I can move in on Monday. I love it. It's conveniently located and I got a really good deal. The owner had to evict the previous tenant and was glad to get a new one with great credit so soon. Isn't that great?"

"Yeah, terrific."

"What's wrong?" she asked, starting to put the groceries away.

Luis J didn't know where to begin and then he was pretty sure she wouldn't care anyway, but he started with, "I can't stay here any longer. They're not giving me the space I need and it's pissing me off."

She looked at him and slowly started smiling to herself. She couldn't believe how easy they were making this for her. They were literally doing all of the work to allow her to hook Luis J and all she had to do now was reel him in.

She had known about the apartment for a few days but needed time to get under Luis J's skin. She had observed him watching her when she walked around the place in her loosely tied bathrobe or wore one of Carlos' oversized shirts. But she had to guide him carefully. He was apprehensive about her actions and motives. He was an insightful young man.

So she said, "Luis J, I honestly don't understand why they can't see the man standing in front of me. You have been living here almost a month, taking care of things just as they asked. Besides, with CJ at the apartment, you won't have any privacy at all. That's just ridiculous for them to even think that's a good idea."

'Man, now see, that's what I've been telling them. Does she really get me?' he wondered. "Well, it's not that bad at least. They're making me move in with Papi. He's going to pick me up on Monday. But it still doesn't give me any freedom."

"I get it. You've enjoyed coming and going as you please. You haven't had to abide by your parent's strict rules. And don't get it twisted – Carlos loved staying with us, but I was there and could buffer him from your father's mandates. That's not the case now."

"Well, they're my parents so I have to accept it. It's not like a have a choice."

Hook, line and sinker. She stopped what she was doing and joined Luis J on the couch. Touching his leg, innocently, she said, "Maybe you do. Why don't you move in with me?"

"Move in with you?"

"Think about it, I have a two bedroom. I was going to set one up as an office, but you can stay there until you figure things out or find another option."

'What the fuck? Was she really offering him a way out?' He could hardly believe his ears, but with Maria there might be conditions, so he asked, "Are you serious? No strings attached?"

"Yes, Luis J, I'm serious. No strings. It would be my pleasure to help."

"So, I have to ask, what's the catch? There's got to be something. Does this have anything to do with that night?"

"No catch. I was there for you that night and you were there for me when I had nowhere else to turn. I'll never forget that and I owe you. Besides, I like your company," she added, with just the right amount of playfulness in her tone.

"So you're saying I can stay with you and you won't crowd me. I can have guests and come and go as I please."

"I won't crowd you. You can have guests, but not overnight, and you need to let me know in advance, of course."

"I don't have much money to contribute. It's hard to get a decent job after school during basketball season, but I'm sure I can find something on the weekends."

"Whatever you can when you can. I wasn't expecting that."

Luis J couldn't see any reason why he shouldn't say yes. Hell, this would be his first step to claiming his independence. He needed this. It was what he was asking of his parents by extending Carlos' lease, but they couldn't accept that. So he said, "Agreed. This is so *kewl* Maria, thanks."

As he waited for her response, a mischievous grin spread across Luis J's face as he thought, 'Won't that really screw with them? Both my parents will have cardiac arrests since they thought Maria was out of their lives for good. Technically she is, but now I'll be in hers.'

“My pleasure,” Maria replied. She was also grinning mischievously as she imagined the look on Luis’ face when she would share this with him on Monday. Luis would learn who he was dealing with and that she knew how to get even. He would regret tossing her aside the way he did, and one way or another, he would be held accountable for her pain.

Luis apparently was mistaking her love for him for weakness. Maria was many things, but weak was not on any of her lists, she had removed weakness years ago. Luis should have known that about her. But he would learn it now once the next few weeks were behind them. And, as for his poor weak darling Diane, she was hoping this would kill her. Yep, she was winning. Once again, Maria was taking in another one of Diane’s men, delivering what she was apparently incapable of providing.

Chapter Twenty Five

As Luis drove to his son's apartment on Monday morning, he recalled how much he had enjoyed the weekend. This would be it, the closure they needed for Carlos. Picking up his things and Luis J to begin anew.

He relished his time with CJ and looked forward to more opportunities like that. He hoped that Diane felt the same way. He hoped that maybe, this time, he could play a major role in this child's life and make up for the time he missed with Carlos, with Luis J, with all of them.

Luis' time with Chell was equally special, different, but special. He was able to gain insight into the young lady maturing in front of him. He really hadn't had a sense for her likes and dislikes, including clothes, music and school subjects, but after the weekend, he had a new appreciation for her preferences. So did his wallet, as a number of "designer this" and "latest fashion that" were apparently missing from her wardrobe and found their way into the shopping bags he ended up carrying.

It was also healing for them, as Chell was very blunt with him regarding her understanding of why he had left. "I can appreciate your wanting to spend time with me today, but is that because you spent time with CJ yesterday? If so, you don't have to do that. I understand he's your grandson and important to you," Chell had told him.

Luis had been both shocked and saddened by her comment. He wanted desperately to set the record straight with his sweet Chell. "Your mother was upset with me when we separated and then divorced. But Chell, what happened to our marriage had NOTHING to do with you or your brothers. What goes on between adults sometimes gets in the way, but it should never impact the children. But in our case, it did. We lost our way and couldn't get back on track, until now.

"Unfortunately, these things happen sometimes in marriages. My relationship with Maria did not meet your mother's approval, so you were not able to come visit me, nor me you. There are many more reasons for our breakdown in communication, but what's important is we are in agreement now. Know that I love you so much, Chell, and I have missed your growing up these past years. I hope this weekend is the beginning of a new relationship. We can't make up for the time we lost, but we can build a relationship experiencing the future together."

Chell began crying and nodded her head. "I love you, too, Papi. I always have. I've missed you and our family so much. David was really nice, but I'm glad you and Mami fixed things so we can spend more time together." She hugged him and he felt a huge weight lifted from his shoulders.

The drive to Carlos' to get Luis J was taking longer than Luis had planned, which surprised him given that the schools were already closed for winter break. He tried to call Luis J to let him know that he was running late, but he didn't answer either phone. Luis found himself hoping that his son wasn't going to disappoint him again.

Finally reaching Carlos' apartment, Luis knocked and waited patiently for some noise from behind the door, something to confirm that his son was in fact at home and they would be getting off to a good start. Luis finally heard the latch turn and the door opened. But he had to lower his eyes considerably to focus on the person opening the door – down to 5'4" to be exact.

"Good morning, Luis."

Luis was shocked initially and then pissed to see Maria standing there. He blurted out, "What the fuck are you doing here?"

"It's nice to see you, too, darling. Do you want to come in?" Maria answered, hoping she was infuriating Luis with every word she uttered.

"Maria, I ask you again, what are you doing here and where is Luis J?"

"He's in the bedroom getting dressed. We're running a little behind this morning. As for what I'm doing here, since you and I broke up, what I do, why I do, and where I do, are all no longer your concern."

"When I find you with my son at eight o'clock in the morning, it does become my concern. Maria, I swear I hope you aren't trying to use my son to get back at me. He's not a pawn in any sick game you might be playing. I knew I was right about what I finally recognized and admitted much too late about you. Our relationship is over and my son – as a matter of fact, all of my children – are off limits!"

"Oh Luis, you are so arrogant. Do you really think everything revolves around you?"

Luis didn't answer her question. Instead he looked around the apartment, trying to analyze the clues strewn about the room. The placement of clothes, the lighting, dishes, everything and anything that would give him an inkling of what exactly she was up to. All the while, his rage gage was rising. If she had in any way at all poisoned Luis J, he had no idea what he'd do. But Luis maintained his cool and his sense of authority. He didn't want to give her the satisfaction of knowing just how off guard he was feeling.

Maria, knowing him relatively well, asked, "Luis, are you looking for something? Do you have a burning question you want to ask?"

Instead of answering, he grabbed her by the arm and pulled her into him. "Don't play games with me, Maria. What are you up to?"

"Nothing. Now let go of me. Unless you want to play," she stated, flirtatiously, as she managed to pull away from him and move toward the kitchen. Just as she did, Luis J entered the living room from the bedroom.

"Luis J, what's going on here? And why is it that I keep finding you in situations that I have to ask that question?" Luis' tone demanded answers.

"Nothing, Papi. Maria needed a place to stay when you put her out, so I told her she could stay here."

"Maria, I told you I would have paid for a hotel. This isn't appropriate, not at all!"

"Why not? For your inquiring mind, I slept in the bedroom and Luis J slept on the couch. It's not our fault you think so little of your son…or are you projecting?" Maria looked at Luis J and winked.

"My feelings for and about my son are none of your damn business. Do you think this is funny? It isn't. Do I need to remind you that he's a minor? No matter, because this arrangement, whatever it is or isn't, ends today. I'm here to help Luis J move out. You can live out the lease if you still don't have anywhere to go. After that, you will be considered a trespassing vagrant and the landlord's problem at that point."

"I told you when I left that I didn't need your help and now I don't need your afterthought help either. I have a place. I'm moving into it this afternoon."

Ignoring Maria's response as he had had enough of her, Papi directed his next statement to Luis J. "We need to get going. Are you ready? Is everything packed?"

"Oh, Poppie," Maria said, using the same cadence she did when they were making love, "You didn't give me a chance to finish sharing our news. There's been a change of plans, Luis. Luis J is going to move in with me, into my apartment. He's not going with you today."

"What did you say?"

"Try to keep up here, please. Luis J is moving in with me, entiendes?"

"Maria, this has nothing to do with you. No te metas en esta situación."

"Oh, but it's too late for that. Your son needs a place to stay and I'm going to give it to him. You and Diane are treating him like a child. He is hardly that. You won't let him be a man. I get it and I get him."

"Luis J, leave Maria and me alone. We need to talk."

"Why? This involves me, too," Luis J responded. He liked how Maria was referring to him as a man.

"I'm not going to tell you again. Go in the room and close the door. Now!" Luis said, as his body braced itself in a don't-try-me stance and the authoritative voice that he rarely used kicked in. It was the voice that let everyone know he was very serious when he spoke.

"It's alright, Luis J. Let me talk with your father," Maria said, feeling the power of her position behind her. Luis J had spoken up and that was all she needed to know. She could handle his father.

Luis took note of this and wondered why she felt she could take that position with Luis J. Something was clearly going on and it made Luis very uncomfortable, especially when Luis J responded to her direction rather than his and retreated to the bedroom.

"Maria, you will not use my son to get back at me. Who do you think you are? You have no authority here. He's still under age and can be ordered by the court to return to the custody of his mother." Luis was quick to point that out.

"I'm not using Luis J. Now, he may be using me because he doesn't want to stay with you or Diane. He told me what was going on and how you guys are treating him. I have the room so I offered him a place; it was the least I could do for him, considering his generosity to me."

"You see, that's what I'm talking about. What generosity? It didn't cost him anything. This is his dead brother's apartment that was paid for in advance. He's simply living out the lease now because we thought giving him the space and task of packing up would help him through the grieving process.

"Obviously you could care less. You know what we are all going through. He needs his family right now and we need him on point. And in addition to all of that, this is a very important year for him, academically and with basketball. Is any of this resonating with you?"

Maria rolled her eyes at him without responding. Why on earth did he think she wanted to be pulled into this drama? He had yet to say anything that she didn't already know; she just didn't give a shit.

Tired of waiting for acknowledgement, Luis continued, "So, he's going to move in with me where I can provide the guidance he needs, and away from you and the games you like to play. I know the trouble you're capable of making, but I'm not the same love-starved man suffering from guilt you seduced and lured into your self-centered, hedonistic lair. All your tricks and schemes won't work because I finally see you. I see through everything that you do. I hoped it wouldn't come to this when we ended the relationship; I hoped that we could part civilly.

"I've always seen your potential, but you are so busy being competitive with the wrong people that you will never win. You may win a few battles, but the war you will lose. And so I'm warning you, don't stand in the way of me or my family. You claim you love me and my children, but these actions don't reflect that. So what do you want from me, Maria? And be very clear."

"First of all, I'm not taking advantage of Luis J. I told you that I'm treating him like an adult and giving him options. I'm letting him make decisions. I see a man, not a boy. This we both know isn't something Diane is capable of doing or seeing. She didn't do it with you, Carlos or Luis J."

Luis scowled and straightened his back. "Luis J is hardly a man. He's a young man, a teenage boy, but he isn't prepared for what you're offering him." Elevating his voice for impact, Luis said, "Listen, you don't want to cross me. It will not be pleasant, trust me. In all the years we spent together, I never had to show you that side of me. Don't make me now."

Maria was getting fed up with his threats and the accusations being hurled at her. She thought, 'He's the one who doesn't have a clue about me. He really doesn't know me at all.' Then, calmly but purposefully, she said, "Luis, you really shouldn't threaten a lady. It isn't the least bit becoming of a man. Now, he's chosen to live with me and there isn't anything you or Diane can do about it.

"Even if you do file for some injunction or whatever, it will be short-lived because Luis J will be eighteen soon. Once that happens, neither you nor Diane will be able to control his actions. Let's face it, she ran him away just like she did the others, including you. It's apparently what she does to men. Some women are just like that. And for God's sake, please don't start defending her to me; that is one thing I don't have to listen to anymore. But I'm sure you remember that, with me, a little bit of kindness goes a long way."

Luis was no longer able to control his emotions and he moved toward her just as Luis J opened the door. Without taking his eyes off Maria, Luis said to his son, "Did I call you out here? We're still talking. Get back in that room."

"But Papi, I can hear you guys yelling from in there. All of this is not that serious. I told you I didn't want to move back home and you and Mami refused to let me stay here. I know you don't believe I'm capable of taking care of myself, so this is the next best thing. Why can't you be down with that?"

"Luis Rodriquez Jr., what the hell do you know about what's best for you? Need I take you down memory lane, once again, about the countless ways you have demonstrated your inability to be on your own? Hell, we gave you the chance to show us on a silver platter and you screwed it up. But even staying here was not on your own accord, but on the back of your brother. He worked and paid for this apartment, not you. So now what, Maria is going to be your guardian, your provider? That's not the actions of a man." Luis finished his point, raising his voice once again.

"I'm not taking a handout from Maria. I told you how I felt on Saturday and based on our conversation today, right now, I don't see how I can live with you. It's clear we don't have anywhere near the kind of relationship that is needed for us to live together. I'm not at the same place Carlos was when he moved in with you."

Just saying his name made Luis J choke up. "Look, I'm planning to get a job and help pay my way. Why can't you give me another chance to prove to you that I can handle this? Why won't you let me prove to you that I am a man?"

"Listen to yourself, son. Just listen to how crazy you actually sound. First of all, Carlos would be the first to tell you this was no easy life. He wanted to go back to school and was preparing to do that. He'd want better for you. And secondly, you're not a man. By law, you have more than three years to have that title bestowed upon you, but even being 21 doesn't automatically make someone a man.

"That little incident with Dany and Friday night's hookup with her show that you just don't get it! How does your lame explanation for moving in with Maria, who you really just met as a teenager a month ago, even make any sense? You claim you don't have a relationship with me, but my blood runs through your veins and you don't even know her! Boy, you sound insane.

"I see right through your game. You want to live where you think you have no rules, but let me remind you of this – life has rules, and they are unforgiving, son, as you will soon find out."

Looking at his son and then shifting his glare to Maria, he said, "I'm going to back down, as you wish. You may lie in this bed you have made." Luis' temper was getting the best of him so he chose to stop it there before he said or did something that would alienate his son even further. He also didn't want to give Maria any more leverage against him or with Luis J.

"You mean I can go with her? You're not going to stop me?"

Luis chuckled. "Those questions right there show that you are still a child. You just stood there professing what you were going to do and in the end you knew I had to approve. So yes, you can go with her. Sometimes we have to fall down before we can see the bumps in the road that are clear to the person who has already traveled it.

"But know this, the law says that your mother is still legally responsible for you until you are 18. Make sure your actions don't cause trouble for her, let alone you. See to it that you give me a call every evening at 6:30. And I'm telling both of you, this is far from being settled. You also better stay in touch with your mother, support your brother and sister, and stay off the booze. Am I clear?"

"Yes." Luis J was relieved that he was finally getting what he had asked for. But at the same time, he heard his father's warnings and wouldn't take them lightly. He had already gotten a glimpse of Maria.

"It better be. And before you leave here, make sure you finish what you were sent over here to do so we can get Carlos' deposit back and not have any issues with the landlord. Do not disappoint me." Luis shot one final contemptuous glance at Maria before leaving the apartment.

He sat in the car for a minute, trying to gather his thoughts, but more so struggling to get control over his anger. He really couldn't believe

Maria would go to such lengths. He knew she was manipulative; hell, that's what ultimately caused the end of his marriage. But this? So Diane was right to think of Maria as she had all this time.

Although this move could drive a wedge between him and his son that might never be repaired, he was equally concerned with how Diane would react to the news. He had to tell her because he didn't want Maria dropping this bombshell in Diane's face, which had been her previous M.O.

With this one action, Maria could completely destroy all of the positive momentum he had been gaining with Diane and his children. Maria was threatening the thing that meant the most to Luis, his children, once again, and clearly she knew exactly what she was doing. He had never hidden those feelings from Maria. He had actually thought that her support of his feelings was one of the things that had attracted him to her in the first place and kept them together as long as it did. How could he have been so wrong about her?

Luis and Diane's interaction with one another had diminished to a functional level at best. She had scheduled a job interview on a day that the boys were in school and Luis was off. Unbeknownst to Diane, however, Luis had actually switched his schedule with a colleague and was dressing to go into the office. After exhausting her short list of options, Diane was unable to find a baby sitter for Chell. So she insisted that Luis take her with him to campus. He agreed because he was beyond tired of Diane's complaining, but he had no idea how this was supposed to work. In addition to the classes he had to teach, he also had office hours.

He brought tons of toys to distract Chell and miraculously managed through the first two classes. But now it was time for his first graduate student appointment and Chell was starting to get restless, as most children do when confined to a small space.

When Maria Diaz knocked on the door for their session, she immediately knew Luis' hands were full, as papers were strewn across the floor and Chell was just starting to color in a textbook. She smiled and picked up Chell. Luis and Maria didn't even have to exchange any words because she knew what he needed; it was the same way he and Diane used to be able to finish each other's sentences.

Chell was bonding with Maria as she held her, rubbed her back and connected over toys. In a matter of minutes, Chell had gone from a child being on the edge of a meltdown to one who was happy and content. Maria smiled when she noticed the relief in Luis' body, so she offered to reschedule her appointment and take Chell off his hands for the rest of the day. His problem had been resolved and he was thankful for that. So Maria's charm with Chell had killed two birds with one stone.

When they returned, Maria and Chell were a sight. There were ice cream and grass stains on Maria's neatly ironed shorts and Chell's clothes. All Luis could do was laugh and Maria eventually joined him. Maria had lost the battle with Chell, but she had cracked the door with Luis.

"Oh Maria, I don't know what to say. What can I ever do to repay you?" Luis had asked.

"Well, let me see. How about dinner, tonight?" Maria responded. She had been admiring him for some time, but didn't think she had a way in, until now.

That wasn't exactly what he was expecting her to say. However, what she suggested sounded like fun and the two of them did enjoy talking to each other. It seemed all very innocent. "Tonight isn't good, but how about Saturday?"

"You're on."

"Your choice, and send me the bill from the cleaners."

"Oh, don't worry, I will. Can you pick me up around seven?"

"That should be okay, but I'd rather you meet me. Call me once you pick the location," Luis said, removing Chell's slumbering body from Maria's arms. "And, thank you again."

The rest of that week was similar to the previous ones. Diane was complaining about everything: how much time Luis was spending at work, how much time he wasn't spending at home, and, of course, their finances. What she didn't understand was that they were all related. Luis was working long hours and volunteering to work on committees to secure his tenured position. That appointment would increase his income so he could give her the things she deserved and so she could stay home with their children until an appropriate age.

On Friday evening, Diane informed Luis that she had gotten a job. He was pissed. He didn't really think she would go through with it when he had been very clear about his expectations. In his mind, he was supposed to be the provider for his family and she was basically telling him she didn't believe in him anymore.

After arguing for a couple of hours, Diane retreated to their bedroom and Luis reached out to Maria to confirm their dinner outing. He was looking forward to an outlet from the toxins in his home and all the arguments.

On Saturday, he told Diane he had a late meeting with a colleague and would be out for a while. As he valet parked, he recalled his conversation with Maria. He had explained to her that since they still had a student/instructor relationship, they could not create any situations that would lead to innuendos about their interactions. So, it was best that they just meet at the Seafood Wharf Restaurant. It was a place on the lower east side that she frequented for home cooked food, but quite a way from her home. Therefore, Luis did agree to drop her off so she wouldn't have to be on the E train late at night.

Over dinner, they enjoyed lively conversations for hours. Luis found it so easy to talk to her about his goals and interests and to impress her with his accomplishments. She was good at stroking his ego, too, which was being bruised and battered at the moment by Diane.

Once they left the restaurant, they walked along the pier. The fall air was cool, so Luis gave Maria his jacket. They stopped and sat on a bench to watch the few remaining yachts and sailboats coasting along, trying to get the most out of the weather before it turned against them and forced the boats into hibernation.

"Wouldn't it be nice to be out there on the water, listening to some soft music, feeling the rocking of the waves? Close your eyes for a minute and imagine being there with me," Maria suggested.

Again, Luis was startled by her comment. She knew that he was married and had children. But she was definitely trying to "play" with him, that he knew. He had observed her aggressive manner in the classroom with some of her male classmates, but now he was on the receiving end of it. Surprisingly, though, it made her even more attractive to him. She was beautiful, smart, stacked, sexy as hell, and knew what she wanted.

Listening to her humming and the water hitting against the pier was quite relaxing. It reminded Luis of being at home in Puerto Rico as a youth. He would sit on the beach at night for hours, staring at the stars and dreaming of what life would be like as an adult. And here he was an adult thinking about life as a youth. Too funny!

"Would you put your arms around me? I'm still cold," Maria asked, moving closer to him.

Luis was reluctant at first, but convinced himself that it was just another completely innocent request. He placed his arm around her and she laid her head on his shoulder. She felt good, smelled good, felt soft and very inviting. He heard a child crying and it reminded him of his own children…and wife. It pulled him back into reality and he removed his arm.

Maria noticed the change in his demeanor and assumed guilt was invading her space and challenging her position. She regrouped and said, "Thank you for dinner, Luis, it was very nice." She knew this would be a neutral comment.

"You're welcome," he responded to the younger woman with whom he was out on a date. She was his graduate student. He knew he shouldn't be there, feeling the way he was, but there was something about Maria that was intoxicating. He needed to be very careful, especially with the problems in his marriage. That much he knew for sure.

"What are you thinking about?" Maria asked, trying to invade his thoughts.

"Life." That was all he could share with her at this point. If she only knew the affect she was having on him. He was starting to imagine things about her that would ultimately cause both of them a lot of problems.

"That's pretty broad," she giggled. She wanted to keep him talking. It would be one way for her to keep him there, to get to know him in a more intimate setting, and more importantly, to ascertain what he was feeling about her.

"Yes, it is…and that's all I'm willing to share right now. Let's just enjoy the beautiful scene you created for me." Luis hoped she wouldn't push it and he really was enjoying their time together. Right now, that's what he wanted to cling to.

Maria returned her head to his chest and began humming once again. Her scent and body kept hitting him with a good sensation and Luis just wanted to embrace this peace and harmony; it was something he used to get from Diane, but hadn't in a long time. They sat there until the warmth from the day's sunlight was completely removed by the chill of the night, making Maria shiver.

As he felt her body shiver, repeatedly, Luis apologized for his selfishness and suggested it was time to go. He was reluctant to leave the calmness behind, but reality was calling for him on the other side of town.

He drove Maria to her apartment and found himself standing in her foyer as she waited for the door to close, shutting out the cold, before removing his jacket and returning it to him. They lingered in the hallway for a few minutes. He continued to work hard at ignoring her obvious attraction for him, telling himself it was wrong for a thousand reasons, but somehow tonight he couldn't think of one. Still, he said, "I better go."

"Sure you can't stay for a night cap?" she asked in a sultry voice, batting her eyes slowly.

"Thanks, but it's getting late and I have a ways to drive. Thank you for a wonderful evening. I'll see you next week."

"Goodnight, Luis," she said, disappointed but not defeated.

After that night, Luis found himself over the next several weeks making excuses to spend time with her: lunch, office discussions, early dinners, and each time convincing himself it was to help her with her studies and that there wasn't anything else to it.

One afternoon, Maria made her move. Setting her trap, she said, "Luis, I want to repay you for all of the time you've made for me lately."

"Oh, that's not necessary. I've enjoyed it."

"I have, too, but I feel like it has all been one-sided. So, I hope you will allow me to fix you and your family a nice home-cooked meal. That is, if you would allow them to spend time with me."

"Of course I would. That would be nice. The kids don't get to experience that side of their heritage very often. I would appreciate that. However, I insist you let me help you prepare it."

"No argument there. When would be good for you?"

"Saturday?"

"Do you need to check with Diane first?"

"No, it's no problem. She will likely appreciate the free time."

"Okay, then it's done. Come by around 4, if you can, that way we can eat by 7:30, before it gets too late for them."

"Do I need to bring anything?"

"Just an apron. I'll have all the ingredients," she concluded, smiling as she walked out of his office.

Luis smiled at the thought of wearing an apron. That was a vision she would never see. Before Luis could tell Diane about his plans for the kids, Diane announced that she needed to visit her parents on the weekend.

"Are your parents' having health issues?"

"No. I'm not going because of them; I'm going because of you. I can't stand how we are, not speaking to each other, not interacting with each other. I'm so unhappy and lonely. I miss you. I miss us."

"I miss you, too, baby," Luis responded.

"Then what are we doing? Why are we at each other like this? Maybe we should go see someone to help us. Like a counselor," Diane suggested. She missed her husband's arms around her and she really missed making love to him. Lately, he was really tired or preoccupied and not interested in being with her in that way.

"Counseling? For what, Diane? We both know how this can be solved, but you're too selfish to do the right thing."

"I'm too selfish? What about you, Luis? This is exactly what I'm tired of. It's always me who is to blame. You can't just put this on me. It takes both of us. I need a break from this and more importantly, you. I'm leaving Friday night and I'm taking the kids. We'll be back on Sunday night."

"Give your parents my regards," Luis said, sarcastically, before returning to read the papers he had to grade. Diane rolled her eyes, poured a glass of Pinot Noir and went to bed.

Sitting there with his papers and cognac, Luis accepted that he could use the break as much as she could. He was more than tired of the tension between them. He called Maria to cancel, but she insisted they still have dinner. She suggested that he could just bring the food home for the children to eat upon their return. He agreed.

During the day on Saturday, Luis called over to his in-laws to see how his family was doing. He had missed the kids the night before and, quite frankly, he missed Diane, too. It had been years since he was alone in the house and he didn't like that feeling at all. He talked to the boys first and heard all about the fun they were having, but Carlos didn't mince words and told his father he was ready to come home. He couldn't understand why his father hadn't come with them. Luis chose to keep his response simple: a work assignment had kept him from going with them. This seemed to appease Carlos for the moment. When he asked to speak to Diane, he heard his mother-in-law tell the boys it was time to eat and to hang up the phone. Of course, they complied.

As Luis sat with the receiver in his hand, waiting to hear the dial tone signifying they were gone, it amplified his desire to get out of the house and away from the reminders of how dysfunctional his marriage had become. So, he grabbed his jacket and set out to Maria's a little early, hoping she would be home.

She lived in a small, two-bedroom apartment in Spanish Harlem. The ride uptown was a little slow because it was Saturday afternoon and the street markets on Lexington Avenue always attracted diverse crowds looking for a bargain. Luis navigated around all the people and the traffic until he found a parking spot at the end of her block.

When he entered the apartment, the aromas awakened his taste buds and stirred his memory of times when he snuck samples of his mother's cooking out of the pots on her stove. He walked into the living room, which was decorated in the flavor of Puerto Rico, with bright red colors throughout the apartment. It was very compact. Even the kitchen was small, basically a walk in and back out. But it was the perfect size for Maria's small frame.

Luis' attention was captured by the autographed poster of Santana on the wall. Maria told him the story of how she had met the guitarist backstage after a concert and got him to sign the poster. He was one of Luis' favorite artists. He owned every album Santana recorded. So Maria placed a tape of his greatest hits in the player and turned the volume to a level that would allow them to enjoy the sounds but still converse.

As Luis waited for his cooking assignment, he noted that she really hadn't left much for him to do. So he opened the wine and lit the candles. At different times, he pushed back on the thoughts that screamed, 'This is more than dinner, dude!' Maria had prepared red snapper, squid salad and plantains. He sneaked a taste and was impressed with the flavor. It was really good. He had no idea she was such a good cook.

Nothing got past Maria and she noticed Luis' delight in her food, so she took the opportunity to share a sensual moment. She picked up a plantain and hand fed him. The intimacy of the act went straight to Luis' head.

"Maria, that was great! Gracias. Now, it's time for the dishes."

"No, I hate doing dishes. Just leave them. Maybe my fairy godmother will grant me a wish and make them go away," Maria said, laughing.

"Very funny. ¡Vamos! I'll help you."

Luis was drying the last pot and singing Santana's song *Oye Como Va* when he felt wetness on his back. He turned to see what was going on and saw Maria holding the hose with the nozzle pointed straight at him.

"Don't even think about it!"

It seemed that was the challenge she was waiting to hear. Luis grabbed the hose from her and she took off running from the kitchen into the living room. One game led to an intimate other and soon Luis found himself locked in an embrace and returning Maria's kiss. Once he did, she pulled away from him.

"I shouldn't have done that, Luis," she breathed against his cheek. "Forgive me. I know you're having a tough time in your marriage. I don't want to make it any harder."

Her words made him want her more and inflamed his desire. All he wanted was to forget about that tonight. He'd deal with it Sunday evening. He pulled her to him and they kissed and caressed each other like new lovers hungry for the other. He stayed with her that night, making love several times. Each time was like a new adventure; new positions, different positions, tasting new flesh, breathing in new scents and listening to new sounds of lovemaking. It was great and he knew it wouldn't be the last time.

They continued to find ways to be together – afternoons, weekends, and educational conferences – while he and Diane continued to drift apart. If Diane suspected anything, she never let on. But once she did and everything was out in the open, those indiscretions with Maria cost Luis his children and his marriage.

Now, once again, Maria had found a way to disturb the flow of things and make him continue to pay. Parking the car and entering the house, he checked the answering machine. There were two messages: one from Diane, hoping to talk to Luis J, the other from the attorney. He assumed there would be similar messages on his cellphone once he recharged the dead battery. He returned the easier conversation of the two. The attorney told Luis that the meeting with Danielle and her mother was scheduled for the following week. He kept the subject of the meeting vague so as not to tip her off, but it apparently was enough for her to agree to meet with him.

Luis still wasn't ready to talk to Diane. He knew that conversation would be a difficult one, so he ate and checked the mail, trying to choose his words carefully in preparation for the call.

"Di, it's me, Luis. Before you ask anything, I have something to tell you."

"Oh no. What's wrong now?"

"Luis J is not here. Things didn't go as planned."

"Why not? What happened? Where is he?"

Luis tried to tell the story with the least amount of emotion possible. He knew this would not sit well with Diane.

"What the hell are you talking about Luis? Are they sleeping together?"

"No. I hope I didn't imply that."

"How do you know that?"

"Maria wouldn't do that. She's just trying to get back at me." However, as he said that, he remembered thinking how odd that interaction was between Maria and Luis J. He had taken direction from her so easily and that was so unlike his cocky son.

"What better way than to seduce your son? She has been nothing but trouble since she came into our lives, Luis. She's not going to stop now, especially since you left her. I won't let her ruin his life."

"Neither will I, but we have to handle this situation carefully. If we push too hard, she'll have even more power over him. She's a grown woman and artful about how she handles a man."

Diane rolled her eyes, "You're telling me. Honestly, that's what I'm afraid of. Luis J is a horny, immature, hurt boy. What better prize for Maria? I'm actually surprised she hasn't called to gloat. She's always loved rubbing my nose in her self-imposed triumphs."

"She hasn't because I warned her not to. This is aimed at me, Diane, and I'm sorry. I'll handle Maria. She knows she can only push me so far. I really am sorry about this. But I won't let her linger."

"Luis you think this is about you. It's never been about you. Or me, for that matter. It's always been about her. Her need to control, to be in control. And she will call me. She can't help herself. So, we'll work through it, together. We'll figure out how to stop her from taking our son down."

Luis liked the sound of that. Together. It was going to take that and more to stop this woman, but there was nothing like the love of a mother defending her babies. 'Look out Maria,' he thought, 'Diane's gearing up for a fight.' And Luis was well aware of what that looked like. This time he would be standing next to her, though, as they fought to save their son and their family.

The next morning, Diane called Maria. She had a few choice words for this woman who was providing a place for her underage son. There were a lot of things about this situation that Diane didn't like because at the base of everything, Diane didn't trust Maria, not one bit.

When Maria answered, she said quite smugly, "Oh, I see you couldn't wait. I was going to call to tell you that your son is safe."

Ignoring her, Diane kept the conversation on point. There were four things she wanted to convey and hoped that she could get them across without losing control. She told Maria that this arrangement was not authorized by either parent and if they chose to, they could involve child protective services. Secondly, Maria was putting Luis J at risk with school and basketball because of the distance he now had to travel to get to school. Thirdly, she tried to appeal to her adult side by reminding her of the great loss Luis J had just suffered stating that he was very emotionally vulnerable and in need of the right kind of attention, perhaps even professional care. And finally, if she as much as touched her son in a familiar way, she'd put her ass in jail for child molestation so fast, she wouldn't see it coming. To Diane's dismay, Maria responded exactly as she anticipated.

"Diane, you can't stand the fact that Luis J came to me for comfort and now you're trying to guilt me into putting him out. You created this train wreck and I'm doing my best to help a man through a very difficult time, just like I did for your ex-husband. I don't treat him like a child and he respects that. Perhaps you should take a page out of my notebook. And I can't believe you are threatening to call the authorities. Do you really want that level of exposure tuned toward you? They would do a complete investigation of your home to determine why he's living here in the first place. You have more to lose here than I do. What if they determine your home isn't fit to raise Michelle and Robert, let alone CJ? I would strongly suggest you reevaluate your position before you call me again."

"Maria, I am going to resolve this situation and Luis J will leave you once he realizes what a manipulative, uncaring, selfish bitch you really are, just like Luis finally did. And one more thing, Luis J is the one child of ours that is most like me, so he will see through you if he hasn't already. He's just so overcome by grief right now that he's been blindsided by your bullshit talk. But he will wake up."

"Goodbye Diane," Maria said, ending the call and thinking, 'We'll see about that.'

Chapter Twenty Six

Luis J was really enjoying staying at Maria's place. She was cool and treated him like a man, but he really liked that he had free reign and could bring friends over to his new place. It was really *kewl* when Maria was there. Maine teased him about sleeping so close to her, but not being able to hit it. Luis J usually just laughed it off because he actually already had hit it, and if he wanted her again he was pretty sure he could have her. She had given him enough clues. 'After all, she wasn't with Papi anymore. Who would it hurt?'

Luis J spoke to Papi every night, as required, but the conversations were usually brief. He saw his mother at Christmas as she insisted he spend the day with the family.

Needless to say, Christmas dinner had been an interesting evening, with the Rodriquez and Anderson families under the same roof, sitting at the same table. It was worse for David than for Luis J's father, because he was Diane's most recent outcast. However, David handled the situation well, claiming his seat at the head of the table and saying the prayer. Luis J watched as these two men jockeyed for his mother's attention. He couldn't believe how much they both obviously loved her and he couldn't help but wonder why. By seven that evening, Luis J had had enough and was ready to go. Since David had also reached his level of tolerance and patience with the situation, he announced he was ready to leave, too, and offered to give Luis J a ride.

Once in the car, Luis J initiated the conversation. "What an evening, huh?"

Taking the high road, David said, "It was nice."

"Whatever. So are you and Mami over?" Luis J pushed.

David wasn't sure what Luis J was looking for, so he responded cautiously. Perhaps he could get some insight from his stepson. "I don't know. What did she tell you?"

"I haven't asked in a while, but I wouldn't give up if I were you." Luis J knew that David still loved his mother, but he honestly didn't know how his mother felt about David…or his father. However, Luis J had noticed that his mother and father had been spending a lot of time together since their return from the funeral, partly because of their joint custody of CJ. But at times they seemed quite comfortable with each other. If this had happened years ago, Luis J would be praying for his parents to get back together. Now, he wasn't sure it was the right thing for either man. Besides, the more Luis J was able to keep David talking about his relationship with his mother, the less David would interrogate him.

"Sometimes things aren't that simple." After a brief pause, and in an effort to change the subject, David asked, "So how long are you planning to stay at Maria's?"

Luis J rolled his eyes. He wasn't successful diverting the conversation. He was in awe of the control his mother had over these men. She hadn't asked him a thing about his living situation, but Luis J knew she had put David up to it. He answered with as little information as possible.

"Until…I don't have a timeframe. You ask because...?"

"Do you know how much this is hurting your mother?"

"I'm not trying to hurt her. I'm just tired of living my life the way she wants me to, and from where I sit, you should be, too."

"You know, you have a really smart-ass mouth and I don't like it. Clean up your act Luis J, before you get into trouble that you can't get out of and it's too late."

Thankfully, it was time for Luis J to get out of the car. He was planning to take the subway from this point. "There's the David I remember. The one that slammed me into the wall. The one that made Carlos move out. Newsflash – you don't know anything about me, so you can keep your opinions and advice to yourself. Thanks for the ride," he snapped in his overbearing tone as he closed the car door.

Since then, Luis J hadn't talked to his mother, primarily because she hadn't called him and, of course, he had no intention of calling her. He definitely didn't want to hear her lectures. His thoughts were interrupted when Maria called out to him.

"Hey Luis J, what are you doing tonight?" Maria asked, hoping he wasn't planning on going out or entertaining anyone. She had spent Christmas alone for the first time since she and Luis had officially become a couple. Her head was full of memories of the past and it made her angry to think that he was spending the holiday with his new-old family. It was three days before New Year's Eve and she had no intention of spending that holiday with resentment and regrets.

"Not much; probably try to catch up with Maine. What about you?"

"I was thinking about going to the movies. Wanna come?"

He hadn't been out with her like that before and thought it might be nice. Besides, her company would be a whole lot more interesting than Maine's. "Sure. To see what?"

"How about a chick flick?"

"You gotta be kidding. What about Denzel's new action movie?"

"You won't get any argument from me about Denzel. Let's go."

"What time is the next show?"

"Who cares? I'll teach you my favorite trick."

They grabbed their coats and she took his hand and pulled him out of the apartment, which was located in Park Slope. It was a section of Brooklyn that was turning into the new, hip, yuppie area. It was specifically designed to attract the savvy urban dwellers, edgy but not bohemian, with very sophisticated upwardly mobile game changers and Luis J was in awe of the vast difference to his neighborhood. You could see downtown Manhattan from the rooftop of the building, which was pretty awesome. They took the subway downtown to the movie theater and then stopped in front of the listing of movies and times. Luis J stood slightly behind Maria, admiring her figure. She was really "thick."

Since he didn't want to bring just anyone to her place and people were on winter break, it limited his hookups. This made her even more enticing, especially when he thought about that night.

Maria selected a movie that was just starting and they watched that until it was time for the Denzel movie to start. Then when the Denzel movie ended, they went to a third movie. They watched that movie until the point where they left the first movie. When the first movie ended, Maria headed toward the door.

"But what about the end of the third movie?" Luis J asked, completely confused by all of this.

"Oh, we'll save that for next weekend. Want some ice cream?"

"No. What I really want is a drink. It's Friday night. Can't we have one?"

"Did you keep your promise to me?"

"Yeah. I haven't had any all week." Of course, Luis J chose not to tell her about the reefer he had smoked instead.

"Alright, but just beer. No shots."

"Deal."

There was a liquor store near the subway stop by their crib. They bought a six-pack of Heineken, went back to the apartment and sat on the roof. Luis J drank beer and they laughed and talked about the movies they had just seen. They even speculated on how the third one would end and made a bet on whose ending was right. The winner would be responsible for dinner next week.

Luis J couldn't imagine cooking so he thought if he did lose, he'd have to order carryout. Then he heard Maria speaking to him.

"Luis J, I have to tell you something."

Luis J noticed her mood shift and wondered what was going on. "What, some other trick?"

"Not exactly." Without pause, she continued, "I'm pregnant."

Luis J's movement stopped as though he were on the court trying to avoid a pick and roll. Did he hear her right? He didn't respond because he wasn't sure what to say. Instead he waited to see what she was going to say next.

"Did you hear me? I'm pregnant."

"Okay. So you're sure?"

"Yes."

"Does Papi know?"

"No."

"Are you going to tell him?" Luis J was asking questions that he thought were appropriate since he didn't know what else to do.

"No."

"Why not? It may change things between the two of you."

"I don't see that as a possibility."

"You never know. He loves children, you know that, and he would want to participate in the raising of this child since he missed so much time being in our lives as kids."

"I'm not so sure he would, especially when he finds out it's yours."

Now, Luis J was stunned. Did he just hear her correctly? How was that possible?

"What? Did you just say the baby is mine?"

"Yes. I didn't expect us to sleep together that night…and if you remember, we didn't use anything."

"Maria, are you kidding me? I mean this is a joke, right? You're a grown woman. How did this happen? I can't believe this." Luis J sat back on the bench and took a long drink of the beer. At this point, he was wishing he had something much stronger. "Don't take this the wrong way, but how do you know it's not my father's?"

"I can understand why you would question me. I'm not offended. Your father and I never had unprotected sex."

"What? Then why the hell did you have unprotected sex with me?"

"If you recall, it wasn't planned. It just happened. I thought I had calculated correctly. Sometimes, a woman's body can't be trusted."

"Maria, this is too deep. What are you going to do? How could you let this happen? I just assumed you were on the pill. Why aren't you?"

"Whoa, slow down, Luis J. You're asking way too many questions and not giving me a chance to respond. First of all, I am going to have this baby. I know this is a lot to lay on you and you can decide how much you want to be involved or not. I'll understand."

Thoroughly dismayed, Luis J said, "I'm not ready for this. I dodged this bullet once already with Dany. Now I'm facing it again with you, my father's old girlfriend – and need I remind you, you weren't his ex back when we had sex. I can't imagine having this kind of responsibility. I'm only 17. Why don't you just have an abortion? You're young, you can have another baby later."

"Oh, now you want to throw up the age factor? That's what your parents are always saying about you. But I've treated you like you asked to be treated, like a man, and now you throw in the underage card? I'm not having an abortion because I want this baby. I think it's a special gift from a night when we were all in such pain. A gift from Carlos, almost."

Luis J sat with his hands on his forehead. "Oh no, don't you dare bring Carlos into this shit! Don't try to use Carlos for your seduction. You said, 'Let me help you ease the pain.' And the next thing I knew you were all over me. I was drunk and you knew it. You took advantage of me. Seriously. I know Carlos would not have done this to me. No, he already knew about having a baby too young – so forget that crap.

"And what am I going to say to my parents? Papi's going to assume the baby is his. I didn't think I would ever have to tell him what happened between us because I thought you had it covered. He'll be so hurt. Hell, he's going to be pissed at both of us; he'll kill us!"

Luis J paused and thought before saying, "Maria…what if you just don't tell him? I mean you're no longer together so your business is your business."

"Now how realistic is that, Luis J? Your father is quick; he'll put two and two together. Luis will be shocked, but he'll get over it. Besides, what better way to show him how much of a man you really are? If that's what you want to be. But, like I told you, I don't expect or need anything from you. I'm more than capable of raising him or her on my own."

"I don't know what to say, Maria. You seem to have thought this all out to your benefit. So what's up with that? If you and Papi never had unprotected sex, why did you think it was okay to have unprotected sex with me? I'm screwed, Papi's screwed, and my mother is screwed. You win. And that's what you want."

Luis J shook his head imagining how Carlos must have felt when Luisa told him she was pregnant. The difference was that they were dating and he had feelings for her. This was literally a one-night stand with an older woman whom he was now certain was a conniving sex fiend. He thought Cassie was bad, but she was not even in the same league as Maria. She had set him up and done it beautifully.

He wondered how long she had known she was pregnant. He had had several of those kinds of quickies, but he had ALWAYS made sure he was covered. There were too many diseases floating around out there and he didn't want any of that. He knew Maria was clean so he didn't worry about that part of it, but he had also assumed she was on the pill. Honestly, he didn't even think about any of it that night. He had been so delirious with pain and the shock that his brother was dying. Now, he knew that that had been a huge mistake, and now, he really just didn't know what to say.

"I don't know what to say, Maria."

"You could say congratulations. That would be appropriate."

Luis J laughed, "Are you kidding me? No, I'm not going to congratulate you. I'm sick about this. Happiness about this is not even close to what I'm feeling. But I'm sure you didn't expect for it to be. Are you really sure about this? How far along are you?"

"Yes I'm sure. This is no joke, Luis J. I'm due in August. Deal with it."

Luis J felt like he was in one of the movies they had just seen and he needed to get out of the celluloid and back to his reality of happy-go-lucky-future-NBA-star. "Look, I really need to get out of here for a while. I'm sure you understand. This was not news I expected or wanted to hear. Can I use your car?"

"Nope, you just drank two beers. I'm going back downstairs into the house. When you get back, the door will be open if you want to talk some more. And Luis J, perhaps it will help if you remember that all things happen for a reason."

Maria was hoping he would have taken the news a little better, but it didn't matter. She had already made up her mind about this child. And yes, he was right. She had won. But what she had really wanted, counted on, was to have him side with her.

Now, that would have been pure unadulterated victory…when Diane saw them standing together – the future parents of her second grandchild. They would all have to continue with her in their lives. She had promised Luis that he wouldn't get rid of her that easily. That would be the best part – seeing that sick expression on his face. Then she threw back her head and laughed.

Luis J couldn't believe what Maria had just laid on him. His whole life was in a tailspin, again, right in front of his eyes. He wondered what Maria would have done if she were still with Papi? He knew that she would never have divulged their indiscretion. She would have found a way to have unprotected sex with his father, or she would have blamed it on faulty protection. But she would never have told him; this he knew. So it was about getting her vindictive payback. And he was caught in the crossfire. No, he was more like the sacrificial lamb.

He wondered what his father was going to say when he told him. What was it he had already said, "Son life has its own rules and they are unforgiving." This was really a mess. Luis J had impregnated his father's ex-girlfriend, the woman who was responsible for breaking up his parents' marriage, the woman his mother hated with all her heart. This same woman was now going to have his parents' grandbaby.

As he walked down the street, Luis J remembered that in a few days, they would be celebrating the New Year. But in light of all the recent events, he wasn't in the mood to celebrate anything. He would be beginning a new year without Carlos.

He kept walking down one block and up another, not even realizing that he didn't really have anywhere to go. He recognized the Latino cuisine restaurant, Miti Miti, and wondered if they sold tequila. He could use a few shots. But he was underage. Yeah he was a man alright.

No job, no money, no place of his own. His mind drifted back to Carlos and he really wished his brother were there. He wanted to talk to him probably for the 50th time that week.

But if Carlos were still alive, he wouldn't be talking about a baby on the way with Maria. No, they'd be talking about his game. "Damn it, Carlos, why did you leave me?"

Luis J sat on a bench in the city park and rolled a joint. Inhaling deeply, he was desperate to find the comfort that smoking cigarettes used to give him. The night air and the walking had sobered him and all he wanted was to feel numb again. It was becoming harder and harder lately and he found himself needing more to acquire the buzz. His father's warning about the addictiveness of drugs and alcohol came to mind, but it didn't take hold.

The park was virtually empty and Luis J welcomed the silence. Being honest with himself, he knew he wasn't ready to become a father, emotionally or financially. He wasn't mature or responsible enough to be a father and this pierced his core; he didn't want to be a father, but from the look of things, that didn't matter. Like his father said, "Life has its own rules."

Maria was an interesting woman. She was definitely beautiful, sexy and funny. But she was not the person he would have selected to be the mother of his baby. As much as he didn't want any part of this, he had to acknowledge how much Maria was willing to do to provide him with alternative living arrangements and if she was carrying his child, he wouldn't have that child feel abandoned by his father the way he had felt by his. Carlos had taught him many things, but this was his most recent lesson.

Still, he had school to think about. His game, his future prospects of playing pro ball, had it all been for naught? And he knew that Carlos had regretted not going to college. These new circumstances complicated everything for Luis J, but there was no going back.

He breathed the last drag in deeply, filling his lungs and holding it. He knocked off the end and put what was left into his wallet. It was getting late and although the neighborhood was improving, he didn't want to ask for trouble, so he started walking back to the apartment.

Though the lights were off, he saw that Maria's door was open, as she had promised. He walked into her bedroom and sat on the edge of the bed. It was firm and he could smell her fragrance in the air. She looked up at him and he could see that she had been crying. He had said some pretty tough things to her and he didn't mean to hurt her in that way. He lay down next to her, pulled her into his arms and held her until she fell asleep.

He slid out of the bed and returned to his room. Lying there in the dark, Luis J realized what a mess he had made of things and he wasn't sure how he was going to fare with this latest calamity. Damn if this wasn't some storyline from those crazy daytime television soap operas. This was some crazy shit and he didn't have anyone he could talk to about it. Not one damn person, especially not Dany.

Luis called Luis J the next morning to ask if they could meet. He wanted to talk to his son and see how he was really doing without the excitement of the holidays or the distraction of the family dynamics. Luis J agreed to meet him at 4 p.m., but he was really getting tired of being summoned like a child. Especially now, since he was apparently about to have one of his own. Yet wasn't that what he had just told Maria, "I'm too young for this?"

But there are different degrees of being a man. Having a child is on a whole other level, for which he was unprepared. He still hadn't warmed up to the idea, but if nothing else, it would surely bring things to a head with his parents. If his mother didn't kill him, they would clearly have to acknowledge his physical maturity now.

"Luis J, are you going out?"

"Yea, I'm meeting my dad, but I won't be gone long."

"It's alright. I'm not going anywhere. You need to talk to your father, but please don't tell him about the baby. I'm not ready to share that with anyone else yet. I hope you understand."

Luis J couldn't agree with her more, but not for the same reasons; he was pretty sure about that. "Will you be alright alone? I mean are you having any issues with the pregnancy?"

She touched her stomach before responding, "I'm having a little morning sickness, but that's normal. And I don't have a lot of energy. I'll probably just have a milkshake for dinner and go to bed. I don't feel like cooking," Maria said.

"Maybe I shouldn't go."

"Don't be silly. I'll be fine."

As per usual, she had set him up; Maria set up anyone she targeted by making them believe it was about them. That's how she had lured Luis J's father. He had always thought she was concerned about him, his well being, and his emotions, when it was always about her getting what she wanted.

She saw the forlorn look on Luis J's face and knew he was softening up to the idea of her, him and the baby. He was too much like his father and brother before him to walk away. Yes, that was the Rodriquez men's Achilles heel.

"Alright, but I probably won't be too long. I'll bring you back something to eat. You have to take care of yourself; after all, you're carrying my baby."

There, he said it! He let her know that he would do the right thing by her. He wouldn't walk out on her the way his father had on them. 'Gotcha Luis J!' Maria thought and then smiled to herself.

When Luis arrived at four to pick up his son, he found to his surprise

Maria and Luis J sitting on the couch. He really hadn't expected Maria to be there. Man, she had the audacity to wave her intentions right in front of him. He knew it then. She was going after his boy. He acknowledged her and then hoped Luis J was ready to leave. He had to get through to his son before it was too late. Diane had been right to worry. Luis J was a horny teenager, in way over his head, living with a seasoned, sexy lioness.

Luis J stood and grabbed his jacket. The tension in the room was suffocating. Luis J projected his feelings and imagined that Maria was feeling awkward as she sat across from her ex-lover of six years, pregnant with his son's child. Luis J even felt weird facing his father for the first time after learning of his impending parenthood. It was worse than facing him after having had sex with her. That had been painful enough, but this felt like betrayal of the worst kind. "Maria, I'll see you when I get back." Maria touched her abdomen quickly and then slid her hand down before saying, "I'll be here."

Luis frowned as he observed the interaction between the two of them. His radar alarm was going off full blast. Something was odd about the exchange of looks and the apparent hidden message. He couldn't put his finger on it, but it was ominous and made him even more uncomfortable. It wasn't quite sexual tension, but it was intimate, a familiarity.

As they drove to the restaurant, Luis contemplated how and where to begin the conversation with Luis J. He wanted to know how he was really adjusting to his new circumstance. Once they ordered, Luis asked, "Are you still convinced this is the best solution for you?"

Luis J was walled up, with his defenses on high intensity. He answered, "Yes, I am and I would appreciate it if you don't sweat me about it."

Luis couldn't leave it there, noting that tone again. He was worried about his son on many levels and this living situation was not headed in a direction that Luis J should be going. Luis had fallen prey to Maria's ways and he would be damned if he let it happen to his son. Besides, he desperately wanted to gain his son's trust and begin to rebuild a relationship. He was hopeful that this would happen like it did with Carlos.

But first things came first, and after his son's defiant statement, Luis had to lay down a stern and firm, "Check your tone, young man."

Luis J wasn't expecting that from his father, but thought, 'At least he referred to me as a man.' "Sorry Papi, I'm just stressed. So much has happened so quickly. One minute I'm happy with my girlfriend and basketball is on fire. Then I have a fight with David, then accused of beating and raping Dany and expelled from school. Next I'm reunited with you and get to know Maria, against Mami's better wishes, and learn that she was part of the reason for you and Mami's break up; I learn that Mami hasn't been forthcoming about why you hadn't come around; tension grows between Mami and me; then I learn that Carlos has a son and I'm an uncle; that Mami was the reason why Carlos never saw his son, who was living in Puerto Rico. David moves out, Carlos goes to see his son and boom he and Luisa are dead and we have his son.

"It's a lot, Papi. I'm just trying to hang. If I'm sensitive about Maria it's because that night I left the hospital, she was really there for me. She helped me through the pain I was feeling. I was so broken up inside. I just couldn't face that Carlos was dying. I couldn't. She helped me. That's all I'm sayin'."

Luis listened carefully and was learning how to discern his son's voice tone distinctions. He hated that he had missed all that growing up. He still didn't have a handle on all of the nuances. He knew that all that Luis J had said was true, yet he knew that there was more than that.

"Son, I know Maria very well. She's very smart and is very manipulative. Be careful."

"What does that mean?" Luis J shot back, feeling annoyed by the constant Maria bashing. Hell, if she were that bad, why had he been with her for all of those years? But then again, he knew why. She was explosive sexually and was unashamed of being sexual. Even though their intimacy had been alcohol induced and didn't last that long, he knew enough about women to know that she knew her way around a man and he remembered how very wet she had been. He didn't even have to spend time with the foreplay. Oh she was enticing, alright. He didn't hear all that his father had said, but he did hear his last words.

"You have to admit, the timing of all of this seems a bit staged," Luis had said. "Isn't it obvious she's out to get back at me for ending our relationship? I wouldn't put it past her to use you as a pawn to do that, you know, take advantage of the situation."

'Now that's really egotistical of Papi,' Luis J thought to himself. Hell, he had to know that Maria was the type of woman who went after what she wanted. Maybe it was about Papi. But one thing was for sure, it wasn't Papi's baby she was carrying and if it was revenge she was after, he was a pawn that had been played very effectively. Still, he'd have to acknowledge that the baby was his once Maria made the announcement.

"And I'm too young and stupid to recognize that, right?" Luis J countered to his father. He was getting frustrated with this whole conversation and frustrated with his father's notion of him and sudden disapproval of Maria. He was now regretting his decision to meet him. He wondered if the rest of the conversation would be like this – blocking and tackling – because football wasn't really his game.

Luis was tiptoeing in murky waters. He knew this conversation was going to escalate, so he tried to bring it back down by lowering his voice. "That's not what I'm saying, but let's face it, she has a lot more experience at this than you."

"More experience at what? How would you know how much experience I have at anything? Besides, no one's perfect, not even you."

"Luis J, I'm not trying to turn this into an argument or a test of wills. Listen, what happened between your mother and me is done. It can't be undone. But I'm talking about now, right now, and where we go from here, in particular you. We are two days away from a new year. I don't want us to carry this strain in our relationship, this distance with us, into the new year.

"You have to remember that the choices you make now will determine what your life will look like five, ten, twenty years from now. Believe me, I'm speaking from first-hand experience. I mean you're right, I'm far from perfect. But because I've made mistakes I can speak to this. You don't want to do anything rash that can ruin your future, mijo, I'm telling you.

"You're vulnerable right now. I know you are almost eighteen, but I would hope you would realize that above all else, I have your best interests front and center in my life. They guide everything I do. They made me agree to stay out of your life back then and they make me ask you these questions now. There are things about women like Maria that you may not be aware of and I want to help prepare you for them."

"You're a little late for that," Luis J said, pushing the food around on his plate.

"What do you mean? What's happened? Have the two of you been intimate?" Luis asked the question, but he wasn't sure he was really prepared for the answer or what to do with it if it was yes. This was Diane's biggest fear and although he played it down with Diane, he knew this was a real threat to his son.

"Just forget it, Papi," Luis J said, remembering his promise to Maria.

"That's not an answer to my question. Are you sleeping with her?" Luis asked the question again, praying that the response would be no. He knew his son was promiscuous and Maria was very seductive. The two of them in that apartment, day in and day out, was a recipe for disaster.

"No. Now can we just finish eating so I can get back home?" Luis J was annoyed by the questions and in reality he wasn't lying; he had fucked Maria, but they weren't sleeping together.

"Luis J, one day you will see what I am talking about and when you do, you can come to me and I will welcome you with open arms. You don't ever have to feel ashamed or think that I will stand on ceremony with you. I just pray it doesn't take you long to see what is right in front of your face. If you're done eating, I'll take you back…home."

Chapter Twenty Seven

Luis was disappointed with the outcome of his conversation with his son and knew he had to talk to the woman who had the power over him, Maria. The more he played back the afternoon and the interaction between Maria and Luis J, the more uncomfortable he became. He knew that there was more to his son's over-exaggerated agitation. Maria had agreed to meet with him the next day and he wondered if Luis J would be there since they were still on break.

When Maria opened the door, Luis addressed her head on with, "Where's my son?"

"I asked him to run a few errands for me. He should be back in about an hour."

"Good, I'm glad he isn't here. It will give us the privacy we need to settle some things. But hear me now, Maria. Stop playing with my son. I mean it. He's not your boy toy or anything else. I don't know what you're up to, but I do know it's no good and I pray that I'm not too late."

"Oooh, Poppie, you sound worried. Haven't seen you like this in a while. So what's wrong now? Things not working out like you wanted them? Anyway, we've settled things as far as I'm concerned and I've already moved on. Haven't you?" Maria asked, sarcastically.

Luis grabbed Maria by the arms. "Stop playing games with me. I mean it, Maria. Do you understand me? Do not use my son to get back at me or Diane. What happened between us happened between *us*. They are not a part of that."

"I wouldn't do that if I were you; you don't want to hurt me," she said as she tried to pull away from his grasp. "You don't want Luis J to return to learn that you have abused a woman half your size."

Luis did not loosen his grip; in fact he tightened it. He continued, "Maria, you need to make some excuse for Luis J to move out. I don't want him here. He doesn't need to be here. He has a drinking problem and he's suffering from the loss of his brother. The combination can escalate and spin out of control. His mother and I want him to get help.

"Can't you find it in your heart to do the right thing? He needs guidance right now to help him through this phase and get him back on track. He's only seventeen, for God's sake, or have you lost all of your good sense?"

"Did you and Diane rehearse those lines? She practically said the same thing to me. Besides, why don't you guys think I can't serve that role? After all, I helped you, didn't I? Now let go of me."

"Maria, this is not the same, and you know it. Damn it, I thought you cared about him, even if you don't care about me anymore. Do you really want to see him destroy his life?"

"Of course not, and that's not what I'm doing. We have been there for each other; I was there for him the night Carlos died and you were attending to your precious Diane; and he has been there for me ever since you threw me out with nowhere to go."

"I'm glad he was empathetic enough to give you a place to stay, as inappropriate as it was for you to even ask him and even more inappropriate that you made your apartment available to him. But remember, he was staying in Carlos' apartment where the rent was already paid for a month. Clearly he's not mature enough to take care of himself or recognize what's best for himself. He's not making good choices right now and is acting more like a teenage boy than he ever has. What about that is appealing to you?"

"He's hardly a boy," Maria said, smiling. "And I'm still waiting for you to let me go!"

"Maria, so help me God…"

"So help you God, what?! Are you threatening to go from restraining me to hitting me or something?"

"Oh, no. I would never hit you, but I can make your life very uncomfortable."

"Why would you want to do that? I think that would just drive a bigger wedge between you and your son. Besides, I have some news that you should be delighted to hear."

His grip loosened after that comment just enough that she was finally able to pull away from him. Maria moved to the other side of the room so Luis wouldn't be able to reclaim his hold as quickly should he decide to try it again. She sat down on the couch, facing him.

"The only news I want to hear from you is how you plan to convince my son to move out," Luis bluffed. He knew that whatever Maria was about to say was not going to be something he wanted to hear.

"Oh, I think you want this news. Consider it a late Christmas present, Luis."

"What is it?"

"I just thought you should know."

"Maria, this is getting old. You have about three seconds."

"I'm going to have a baby."

Luis had quickly tried to imagine the drama she would be unfolding for him: some new lover, money he owed her, some fabricated story. But not this.

"What? Are you really expecting me to believe that? What do you think this stunt will accomplish?"

"Oh, it's no stunt. I'm pregnant and I'm due in August."

"So you were cheating on me? Then I guess my timing was perfect in letting you walk because there is no way in hell you're going to try and saddle me with someone else's baby."

"Au contraire, Poppie. Remember the night after Carlos' death? You were so distraught. And then again, your first night back from Puerto Rico? How good the shower felt? Well, I thought I would do like Diane and 'forget' to use my diaphragm. And we both know how powerful your sperm are, Luis! They are dead on," she said, smiling triumphantly.

She could see the wind being sucked right out of him. There would be no easy path back to Diane. Not now, not ever, once she caught wind of this.

Luis stood there in the middle of the floor, hoping that this was some cruel joke, but in fact he did remember those nights and he hadn't been concerned about making sure things were in order either time. He hadn't imagined Maria would betray him in such a way. He had made it very clear to her from the beginning that they would not be having any children unless they were united in marriage.

"What's the matter, Poppie, cat got your tongue?"

"Are you sure?"

"Why do men always ask that question?" Maria asked, only half-mockingly. "Yes, I'm sure, Luis. Congratulations, dear."

"What are you planning to do?"

"Have it, of course. What did you think? You know I've always wanted to have a baby and yet you denied me all those years we were together. So now, once again, you will not be involved in raising your child."

Luis let out a non-humorous laugh and shook his head. "Diane was so right about you. You are a selfish, spiteful, master manipulator, focused on achieving your own ends. Damn everyone and anyone else. You can turn on all the charm and seem totally supportive – all just to get what you want.

"Well it's not working this time, Maria. This won't change things between us. Our relationship is over. And if you think keeping the child from me will hurt me, you'll be sadly mistaken. I have learned from my experience with Diane and I won't stand for that with you. Our relationship is very different and I will fight you for joint custody."

Maria was caught off guard by Luis' cold response. She had expected a rebuttal about keeping the child from him, but she got no rile from him. Instead he manned up and insulted her intellect. So she responded with, "I know that, and I resent your implying that I thought it would." Now Maria was smiling inside because she was leading him right down the alternate path she had planned for him.

"I don't need your money, Luis, and I haven't determined how much, or even if I want you to contribute to this baby's life at all. Didn't Diane refuse your money? And she did just fine, with what, four of your children by herself, not just one little baby."

"If you don't want me to contribute financially to the upbringing of this child, that's okay. I'll just cover their expenses when he or she is with me. You will not dictate anything to me about this child. Of that, I am clear."

Maria was causing the rage to build inside of Luis once again, the way she seemed to be able to do quite often recently, and he knew he needed to leave. He was also mad at himself for continually giving her the upper hand all those years.

"Maria, for now, this conversation is over. And given your situation, I would think you would want Luis J out of your life now more than ever. Wait…he already knows doesn't he? That's what you guys were alluding to when I picked him up yesterday. Well, now that I know, he doesn't have to be your caregiver. That's not his responsibility because I'm the baby's father. I'll let him know that I have this covered. Tell Luis J I'll call him later."

"I'll give him your love," Maria said coyly, not even looking at Luis and waiting to hear the door close. She locked the door behind him and returned to the couch. She touched her stomach and smiled. She could not have planned this better if she tried. This would really put them all on a crash course and all she had to do now was wait to see who would be standing when the dust settled. This would torpedo any chance of Diane getting back with Luis and if nothing else was gained, she would find comfort in that. Yes, she was still in the driver's seat and it felt good.

As Luis walked to the car, his head was full of outrage. He had always made sure she was protected, but the night after Carlos died and when he got back from Puerto Rico, he honestly hadn't thought about it. He had wanted to get lost in passion and Maria had been the person to fulfill that desire.

"Papi? Papi?" Luis J called to his father, wondering what was wrong with him when he didn't respond.

Luis was so engrossed in his thoughts, he hadn't heard his son calling him. He tried to regroup so Luis J wouldn't be able to determine what he was feeling. The thoughts that were floating around in his head, crashing like cymbals, made his head hurt.

"Papi, I called your name a couple of times. Did you just get here?"

"No."

"Have you been inside?"

"Yes."

"What's wrong with you?"

"We need to talk, son."

Luis J didn't really want to hear anything else about this situation, but knew he couldn't dismiss his father that easily. "Let's go inside."

"No," Luis said quickly, holding his hand up. "I would prefer to go somewhere private. Drop off your things and let's just go get some coffee."

Luis J quickly went up and dropped his packages off in the apartment, told Maria he was grabbing some quick coffee with his Dad whom he'd just run into, then came back downstairs and hopped into Luis' car.

The drive to the coffee shop was short and Luis used this time to calm himself and gather his thoughts. After ordering two cups of coffee and returning to the car, Luis J spoke first. "So what's up? I hope this isn't a continuation of yesterday's conversation."

"Of course it is, in addition to some news that I've just received."

Luis J interjected, "I actually have some news for you that will hopefully put this dialogue to bed for good. Maria's pregnant."

"I know. She just told me."

"She told you?"

"Yes."

"And you're not angry about it?"

"I was at first, but I didn't do what I was supposed to do. This is what I've been talking to you about for the past few months. Even the best of intentions can screw you up."

"Wow. I thought you would be really mad."

"Maria and I have been through a lot and we'll work this out. But this is even more reason for you to move out and stay with me. You don't need those distractions from your schoolwork or basketball. Things have finally come to a head and you can move on with your life. I assume you feel some obligation because you didn't know how I would respond, but it's not your cross to bear."

"Wait now, Papi; I'm confused. You still think I can move on with my life even though Maria is pregnant?"

"Sure, why not? What does one have to do with the other?"

"Because I can't turn my back on this child."

"Luis J, what the hell are you talking about? Slow down. Now I'm confused. Why would you have any responsibility for my child?"

"Your child?"

"Yes. That's what she told me. Do you know something else? I know you guys were being coy about this yesterday."

"Papi, it's not your baby," Luis J said, lowering his eyes. "It's mine."

"WHAT? What the f...what do you mean, Luis J? You said you weren't sleeping with her!"

"I wasn't."

"So, what the hell are you saying? Based on when she said she's due, this happened in November."

"The night Carlos died, remember I told you how upset I was? I wanted to get away from the hospital so Maria drove me to Carlos' apartment. I started drinking, beer at first, and then shots of tequila. We both were. Then your call came and something in me just snapped. She was holding me and well...Papi, I'm sorry. I never meant for it to happen and it hasn't since. I wanted to tell you, but she said it was better not to."

"I can't believe this. That's what you meant about her being there for you. You betrayed my trust by lying to me when I asked you the nature of your relationship. You denied sleeping with her. I warned you about Maria's manipulation."

"Papi, honestly, I have regretted it ever since, but then you broke up with her."

"And you said, 'What the hell? They're not together anymore, so why not?' What are you going to do, set up house?"

"It wasn't like that. I was just crashing until I got my stuff together. I just found out a couple of days ago."

"So why do you think it's your baby?"

"Because we had unprotected sex and she told me you guys never did."

"She's lying."

"No, she isn't."

"Luis J, she just stood in the living room and told me the baby was mine. That's what I was thinking about when you walked up. I was stunned and couldn't believe my ears. She was very clear. Even told me that she'd decide whether or not I could be involved in the child's life."

"That's not possible, Papi."

"Yes, it is. Trust me."

"I don't believe you. Why would she lie to me about that?"

"Because that's who Maria is, son. She slept with you one night and me the next. She knew you had unprotected sex so she knew she needed to cover her bases. Can't you see what she's doing? She's trying to make us fight over her. How do we even know she's pregnant? She could be making it all up.

"But one other thing – I told her that it would not change anything between her and me. I'm done. It's over. This is not about possession. I don't care who she moves on with. It just can't be you because she doesn't mean you any good, mijo. I'm just warning you."

"If she is so bad, why did you even let her into your life? You spent all that time with her, but do you really know her? If what you are saying is true, why did you have unprotected sex with her? You should have seen that coming. I know it's possible that that baby she's having is mine and until we know for sure, I'm not leaving her." He opened the car door and began walking back towards Maria's apartment – his apartment.

Luis called out, "Luis J wait, let's confront her together." But Luis J kept walking, so Luis just sat there, not knowing what to say or do. Maria had been true to form and Luis J was verbalizing all the questions and thoughts that were bouncing around in his head.

Once again, Maria had found a way to interfere with his future plans to reunite his family. Because as soon as Diane found out about this latest act of vengeance, she would retaliate in the only way she knew how and the manner to which she had become most accustomed: banning Luis from her life and the kids' lives forever. Luis wondered how one woman could create so much damage.

He recalled what his mother had said and knew that he had done the right thing to end his relationship with Maria, but pain and weakness had led him once again into her clutches. He wasn't even sure now whose baby she was carrying. If they had both been with her during the same time frame, how could she even know?

Maria was either having his child…or his grandchild…or no child at all. Two of those scenarios would be disastrous. God forgive him, but Luis thought it would be best if this was a cruel lie and there was no pregnancy at all. There was already CJ to raise. The timing was so wrong and a child with Maria would be disastrous and highly volatile, 24/7. Luis grunted at the thought before heading to his next destination.

When Luis J entered the apartment, he found Maria watching TV in the living room. He took a moment to assess her mood, and his own.

"Back so soon?"

"It wasn't a pleasant conversation, but then you knew it wouldn't be. Why did you tell Papi about the baby? You said you wanted to wait..."

"I never said that."

"Yes you did. And on top of that, you told me you guys never had unprotected sex."

"We didn't."

"Then why did he say you did?"

"I don't know, Luis J. I told him I was pregnant and he started telling me how he would help support me and I told him I didn't need his money. He's just trying to cause trouble between us so you'll move out and have to move in with him. Can't you see that?"

"Did you tell him the baby was mine?"

"No. I thought we should do that together. I'm sorry if he jumped to the wrong conclusion. What happened?"

"He kept going on and on about me starting over and moving on with my life and I finally blurted out you were pregnant. That's when he told me you told him he was the father."

"Luis J, I never told him that. This is your baby I'm carrying. You believe me, don't you?" Maria asked, sweetly, intending to wrap Luis J a little tighter around her finger.

"I don't know what to believe. I'm still not sure what is going on here, Maria. I don't want you talking to my father alone anymore. I want to be there to hear everything that he has to say to you and you to him."

"Of course, if you think that's best. I just don't want you to be hurt. I know how your father can be."

"Oh, I'm sure." Even though he didn't stop when his father suggested they talk to her together, he didn't think it was a bad idea. He just wasn't ready to have that confrontation with her yet because if she was lying, he would most definitely have to move out and his options for housing were still very limited.

"Come here." She reached for Luis J, but he didn't move.

"Come here," she repeated.

Luis J had to determine if he wanted to sleep with Maria again because he knew that's where this was headed. He was so angry about the whole situation – his father, his mother, Dany, all of it.

He knew Maria would make him feel good. She hadn't exerted any effort that first night and he climaxed quickly. Today there would be no rush. No guilt. Just sex. 'And now Papi knows we had sex, so what the hell,' he thought. So Luis J gave in and walked over to her, ready.

She kissed him passionately and he felt his body responding. They made love right there in the living room and then again in the bedroom. The reckless abandon was new to Luis J. Never before had he had such freedom. He was hooked simply by the idea of exploring his fantasies. It certainly beat sharing a room with a six-year-old and sneaking into Dany's bedroom on tiptoe. He had loved the uninhibited moans and sensuous sounds Maria had yielded. There was no fear of waking up a little sister or concern that someone might return home and catch them. Oh, he was free at last!

Later that evening, Luis J called Dany to end things with her for good. As his father had said, the New Year was only two days away and he owed Dany that much – a fresh, clean start.

Dany was surprised to get the call, but happy to hear his voice. She had really missed him. "L, I know I've hurt you badly and caused a lot of problems for you, but do you think you can forgive me?"

"Sure, Dany, I forgive you."

"Great! Does that mean we can get back together?"

"You're really special to me Dany, and had you asked me that before Carlos' death, I would have been elated. But it's too late for that now. So much has changed. Anyway what about your mother and how you're so afraid of her?"

"What? Oh, we can get around that. I'm learning how to check my mother now. I threatened to report child abuse and my sister sided with me on that one because she hates the beatings, too. So there isn't anything standing in our way now. So why can't we just start over?"

"We just can't; too much has transpired. I'm so sorry, baby."

"Is there someone else?" Dany asked, with grave disappointment in her voice.

"Sort of."

"Are you serious about her?"

"It's really complicated."

"Were those her things at your brother's?"

"Yeah."

"So, are you living together? Who is it?"

"It isn't anyone from school."

"Are you living with her?" she repeated. She had to know what was going on with him.

"Yeah."

"Wow. Well, I guess I was wrong about us. Does she know you had sex with me last week?"

"That doesn't matter and I won't go there with you."

"Why not? You went there with me last week. You can't be that serious about her."

"She's pregnant."

"Ohhhh. Pregnant? With your baby?"

"Yeah."

"Really? Well, L, you hit a home run this time. And you had the nerve to be giving me all that shit when we thought I might be pregnant? I thought I was the only one you went bareback with. Do I need to go get tested now? Were you sleeping with both of us at the same time? How far along is she? You know, my girls told me you were sleeping around, but I didn't believe them. I believed you when you said I was your baby. What's her name? Is it that slut from Brownsville, Cassie?"

"Look, Dany, I'm not going to play twenty questions with you. I know this must be hurtful and I never intended to hurt you. It's not black and white. I wasn't with her when I was with you. You were special to me. I just called to tell you myself so you wouldn't hear it from someone else. We both know how rumors spread at that school. I'm sure this is a lot for you, but you did lie on me and almost cost me my future. If we were still together, none of this would have happened."

"A lot for me? It should be too much for you. Listen to yourself. This baby is costing you any future you could have. Haven't we seen this a million times? We used to talk about it. Why is she having the baby anyway? Does she think you are going to stop sleeping around just because she's pregnant? If she cared anything about you, Luis J, she wouldn't have a baby right now. She'd want you to be all that you can be."

"Dany, come on. You aren't saying anything I haven't thought. Look, I'm hanging up now. I'll see you in school after the break. I do wish you a Happy New Year," he said in an effort to get off the phone because she had said things that rang true and he knew it.

"Not if I see you first," she said, before ending the call.

Luis J had mixed feelings about ending it with Dany, but he knew he couldn't continue to see her and live with Maria. He thought about all the times he had found comfort in Dany's arms or in just hearing her voice. There was no question that they were compatible and more so, he really liked her. If he had taken time to be honest with himself, he and Dany were on track, before the accusation of abuse and rape, to become long term. He was definitely going to miss that.

But at least Maria was willing to provide some of that physical comfort for him. He rubbed his groin as the memories were heading toward his penis. So maybe it would be okay for him after all to move on. Besides, he was about to become a father. Still, he heard echoes of

Dany's questions and a point very well made: "Why is she having the baby anyway? If she cared anything about you, Luis J, she wouldn't have a baby right now. She'd want you to be all that you can be." And then there was his father's comments and caution about her. Could both of them be wrong about Maria? He didn't know, but he would eventually get to the bottom of this.

CHAPTER TWENTY EIGHT

It was New Year's Eve. Luis J hadn't seen his father since the day they found out about Maria's pregnancy. He still complied with the nightly phone calls, but it was no more than checking the box as far as he was concerned. Luis had convinced Maria to confirm her pregnancy, but she refused to do anything about determining the paternity. She told him she was worried about the impact on the fetus at such an early stage.

Diane was still unaware of Maria's condition but Luis knew she needed to be told sooner rather than later. To Luis' surprise and adulation, Diane had invited him over for a New Year's Eve champagne toast that evening. He didn't want to read too much into the invitation, but he hoped it was an indication of changes the New Year would bring for the two of them. However, he knew he couldn't go into the New Year with any unfinished business between them either.

Diane had fixed the foods they had once enjoyed together as a family. It was a special dinner they would have before waiting for the ball to drop. She had prepared sautéed shrimp, steamed crab legs and a garden fresh salad. It was fun having to help Chell and CJ crack the shells and it made him laugh when Chell imitated what Carlos used to say when their father pulled the meat from the leg.

"Papi, do you remember, he would look at it and say, 'Is that all?'"

Luis and Diane laughed so hard tears rolled down their cheeks as they watched Chell imitate the look on Carlos' face before pushing the food into her mouth.

Diane hadn't continued this practice with David. She had preserved this memory and Luis was touched by that sentiment. The only thing missing was Robert. He was spending the night with David, but maybe one day he would join them in this ritual.

After they cleaned up the kitchen, gave CJ a bath and dressed him for bed, Diane told Chell they could sit up in her room to watch the ball drop on TV. She knew CJ would be asleep long before that happened. Chell wasn't interested, so she retired to her room and closed the door.

Diane and Luis kicked back on the couch with two glasses and a bottle of champagne, strawberries and chocolate. They didn't wait for midnight to begin drinking and savoring the taste of aged French grapes. Sitting together as the television provided background chatter, they talked about the children and more specifically CJ, and managed to share laughter. Diane told him about CJ's progress and exclaimed her joy that he was gradually becoming comfortable with them and was exhibiting less sleepless nights than he had initially. She was very relieved and thankful for that.

"And how about you?" Luis asked, stroking her arm.

Diane noted the liberty that Luis had taken, but she did not mind and answered, "Oh, I'm getting better. Each day is easier than the day before. I miss Carlos terribly. Even though things weren't the best between us, we at least were communicating more. I still can't believe he's gone, but CJ has really helped me to redirect my pain and transform it into love for him. He's so much like Carlos," she said, sighing. "And, I miss Luis J. I'm still so worried about him. I catch Chell on the phone with him sometimes, but he never asks to speak to me. He seems so distant. Have you seen him lately?"

"Yes. I saw him a couple of days ago."

"How was he? Relieved, I'm sure, about the whole Danielle craziness. Do you think they'll start seeing each other again? Could you tell if he's still drinking?"

"I couldn't tell, but he probably is."

"Do you think he's becoming an alcoholic?"

"I honestly don't know, Diane. I worry about that because of Antonio. Addiction can be hereditary. As far as Danielle is concerned, I can't say. He's not sharing much with me right now. We're not in a good space."

"But I thought you guys were doing okay, that he was at least talking to you."

"I don't know how to tell you this. I don't even know if I'm the one who should," Luis said, putting a little distance between them and placing his glass on the coffee table.

"Now what?"

"The situation with Maria is more complicated than I thought. I completely underestimated her. She has managed to create a scenario that has driven Luis J away from me and quite frankly, when you hear it, you, too, will probably refuse to talk to or associate with me. I curse the day I ever met Maria, let alone let her into our lives."

"Well, that makes two of us. But, oh no, don't tell me; he's sleeping with her, right?" Diane phrased it as if to say, 'I warned you,' but she didn't say it. Her worst fears were being realized. She knew Luis J would not be able to resist that wench. But there was no misplaced anger directed at Luis.

"Right now, I wish that was the extent of it," he said, gearing up to break the news.

Diane waited for the next words to come out of his mouth. Her eyes searched the curves of his lips in anticipation of what he was about to say next. He looked tired, defeated almost, and this worried Diane even more.

"She's pregnant."

"Who's pregnant? Pregnant. How is that even possible? They've only been living together for what, two or three weeks." When he didn't respond, it became clear to her and she continued, "Oh my God, is it yours?"

"I honestly don't know." He reached for her hand to hold it while he gave her the rest of the details. When she didn't pull away, he felt some relief that she wasn't shutting down or shutting him out. At least not yet.

"Go on."

"Suffice it to say, Carlos' death sent both of us, Luis J and me, into a downward spiral and Maria, doing what she does best, comforted both of us."

Diane removed her hand from Luis', stood up and walked away from him toward the kitchen. "She's good. That lying sack of shit is good. After all she has already put me through, after all we have just lost, now this. Well, congratulations, Maria." Diane raised her glass as though she, too, were in the room.

"Diane, please don't let her win. I can only imagine what you're feeling. But don't you see, she's hoping this will rip the entire family apart. I saw it; I finally saw her for all that she is. She intentionally created a scenario to destroy all possibility of us ever being a family again. She's counting on you throwing me out. Please, please don't give her that satisfaction."

"I'm listening."

"I met with Luis J a few days ago because I wanted to clear the air and create an opening for us to start fresh in the New Year. When I picked him up, I had a strange feeling that something was up because of the odd intimacy they shared. It didn't seem sexual then, but more like they shared a secret. We talked that night, but I didn't make much progress, so I called Maria and asked if we could talk. I told her that she had to tell Luis J to move out because it was not good for him to be there.

"After I told her that his life was hanging in the rafters, she lowered the boom with the gloom of her pregnancy. She told me it was mine; even quoted the date she purposely did not take precaution. She also said she wasn't sure if she'd let me be involved in the child's life. I told her that it changed nothing between us, that I am not in the mood for any of her emotional blackmail or bullshit. I was so angry that I left.

"I was still sitting in the car stewing when Luis J approached me. We went for coffee so that we could talk. We got to the subject of Maria's pregnancy and it became clear he was under the impression it was his child because that's what she had told him. He chose to believe her over me, and he said that I was motivated to lie about who the father was because I wanted to create a reason for him to move out. She set us up knowing that his youth and hot temper would set him off. She literally laughed in my face when we were talking about the baby. Now I know why. And further, she's filling his head with the idea that he's a man while staying at her apartment and contributing nothing," Luis said, shaking his head, which was held down. He was so embarrassed by all of this.

"It seems like all I've done lately is apologize to you and I'm sure you must be tired of hearing it. Someday, somehow, I will make this up to you. I promise, Di."

"This is a lot to handle," she replied, with her back to him, still drinking her champagne.

Reluctantly he responded, "Maybe I should go."

She turned and faced him. "No. Stay. I'm finished letting Maria dangle my emotions on a string. She may have the upper hand at the moment, but she won't for long." Raising her glass to Luis now, she said, "Here's to a Happy New Year."

"Happy New Year, Di!" Luis responded, somewhat joyfully because it had gone much better than he had ever imagined. Diane wasn't exploding. She was still looking at how they could work through this together. Yes, things were looking up. A happy new year may still be ahead. They finished the bottle of champagne, but they didn't talk anymore about Maria, the baby or Luis J. They just watched the ball drop and reminisced about previous New Year's Eves. When he finally left, it was about one-thirty.

The next morning, New Year's Day, Diane wanted to have some quiet time before CJ got up, so she arose around seven, grabbed her robe and headed to the kitchen to brew a cup of Maxwell House. Her head was a little fuzzy from the champagne, so she knew she needed at least a cup to get her day started. As she sat at the table, enjoying the smell and taste of the coffee with a hint of sprinkled cinnamon just the way she liked it, her mind drifted to the news Luis had shared with her.

Maria was pregnant and either he or Luis J was the father. Now that was really a story for the soaps! Her first inclination was to go right over there and demand that Luis J move out, but she realized at this point it was obviously too late for that. No matter how hard she had tried, both of her sons ended up choosing paths that were so far away from the goals she had set for them and, for that matter, as she was from the goals she had set for herself.

She thought, 'I'm separated from yet another husband and Luis J is sleeping with his father's ex-girlfriend. Yuck! I suppose it is par for the course, though; after all, I haven't met any of the goals my parents set for me.'

When the phone rang, she answered it quickly to keep from waking the children. She wondered who could be calling so early at the start of the new year. To her surprise, it was her mother. They hadn't spoken since the funeral and Diane was determined not to let her mother get under her skin on New Year's Day. Her father had cautioned them from a very young age that whatever you do or however you feel on New Year's Day would be the actions and emotions you experienced for the entire year. So Diane chose her tone and words carefully, trying to keep the exchange to a pleasant chitchat until finally the reason for her mother's call was made clear.

"I wanted to let you know that I am coming to visit with you for a few days."

After a pause, Diane responded, "Is everything alright? Is something going on with you and Daddy?"

"Yes, of course. That's a silly question. What on earth would be wrong with your father and me after all these years? Anyway, I just thought you and I could spend some time together. I want to spend some time with my great-grandson. There really wasn't an opportunity for that when we were in Puerto Rico."

"Honestly, Mama, although I can appreciate that, I'm not sure this is the best time. A lot is going on here. We're all still adjusting to Carlos' death and adapting to a new child in the household."

"Then now is the best time. Besides, I've already bought my ticket. I'll be there tomorrow and I'll be staying with you. I'll sleep in your room since David isn't there."

'Stay calm, stay calm,' Diane thought to herself. "Mama, how could you already have a ticket and you didn't even talk to me to see if this was a good time? Well, it isn't, I really need this time for myself. CJ is just starting to get used to us and his surroundings. I don't want to derail that."

"Nonsense. I knew you wouldn't have anything going on. Your house is full now and you don't have any help. I'll come and give you some help. I know you need it. It will also give us some time to talk and you'll feel better by the time I leave, sweetheart. Don't worry about picking me up; I'll just get a cab to your house. I should be there around six. Please make something for dinner that I like. I don't want pizza or anything like that."

"Fine, but since this is my home, I will decide where my guests will sleep, even if you are my mother."

"Oh. Well, excuse me. We'll figure it out tomorrow. Take care, sweetheart. Happy New Year! I'll see you tomorrow."

Diane listened to the silence on the other end of the phone until she heard the clicking sound and then the dial tone. She turned the phone off, but continued to stare at it, waiting for it to ring again and for her mother to say, "Just kidding!" Why did she just allow herself to be backed into this corner? Yet again, she couldn't and didn't stand up to her mother. 'You would think after all these years and all this pain and disappointment, I could keep her from interfering in my life.'

She could take a few pointers from Luis J. Boy, he had come out swinging and all she could do was take it. The truth hit you like that. It didn't feel good, but she was so glad that he had hit her with the reality. Somehow, over the next few days, she wondered if she could find the ability to come out swinging like her son.

"Mama, I've finally selected the school I want to attend. It's in Chicago," Diane said, waving the application and feeling proud of the results of her in-depth research.

"Chicago? What on earth is in Chicago?"

"Mama, you're funny. This school has a really good business program and I've heard really good things about it."

"Which school, Diane?" Mama asked with that, 'I'm feeling annoyed with you right now' tone.

"Mundelein," Diane replied, feeling less confident than she did when she entered the room.

"Mundelein? College? For undergrad? No dear, we decided on Emory."

"We didn't decide on Emory, Mama; that's where you think I should go," Diane said, starting to play with her hair. She had worn it loose today because it had been picture day at school, but she was starting to feel uncomfortable and playing with her hair was calming.

"Yes, I do and you know I have more experience with this than you do. After all, your two older sisters both went to fine schools that I selected, and they are now positioned to attend excellent graduate schools. You know how important it is to get a good foundation."

"Mama, I know Michelle and Cindy have done well, but I have done a lot of research and I think I would be happier in Chicago," she said, laying down her spreadsheets and the literature.

"Happier? Happier? What does that have to do with making the right decision about school?"

"Well, I just mean that I think the curriculum and environment will be better suited to my goals and interests. See, I have it all here."

"Dear, that's because you can't see the big picture. Your father and I have worked very hard to give you girls a nice home and a good education. All three of you are very bright and you know I have told you I expect to have three doctorate degrees to hang on my wall. Now, Emory will get you headed in the right direction."

"But…"

"No buts, sweetheart; get the paperwork for Emory – it's in my bedroom on the nightstand – and let's get started on the application so we can get it in the mail. You may even be able to get an early acceptance.

I'm so proud of you," she exclaimed, as she headed toward the kitchen.

Diane just stood there with all of her research, feeling dismissed. She pulled all of the ringlets that had brought her compliments all day away from her face and restrained them with a ponytail holder. If she couldn't be free and flowing, then neither could her hair.

As Diane returned to the present, she found herself pulling on her hair and searching her wrist for a ponytail holder just like that day. She was feeling that same helpless emotion all over again. It seemed like it was just yesterday.

When Chell emerged from her room, she was full of questions. She wanted to know how long Papi had stayed after the ball dropped; what they had talked about; when he was coming back; did they have fun together. Once she completed that series of questions, she moved on to who was on the phone. Chell was elated to learn it was her grandmother and was now looking forward to seeing Grandma Margaret again.

Chell grabbed a breakfast bar and went back down the hall toward her room, humming some song Diane had heard her sing in the car the other day. She wished she could be as optimistic.

Mama arrived the next day, as promised, promptly at 5:55 p.m., with two suitcases.

"Hello, dear; have Luis Jr. come help me with these things."

"Hello, Mama. He isn't here. I'll get them. This is what I meant. This is not a good time."

"Isn't it time for dinner? Doesn't he know he is supposed to be ready to sit at the table at six? Where is he?"

"I told you he's not here. Come in and have a seat. How was your trip?"

She looked around the room and perched on the edge of the couch. "So where are the children?"

"Chell is at a neighbor's. Robert should be here shortly; he's with David. I'll get CJ."

"Wait one minute. Where is Luis Jr.?"

"Mama, you just got here. Can we just enjoy each other's company for a few minutes before you start giving me the third degree?" Diane asked, as she headed toward her room to get CJ. Standing up in his playpen, he reached for her. She picked him up and held him close. She just needed to find some comfort in his arms before facing her mother's wrath again.

"CJ, here is your great grandmother. What do you want him to call you, Mama?"

"Great Grandma."

Diane laughed. "That's a mouthful. He's just starting to learn some English, but it's slow. How about Gee Gee or NaNa M?"

"Please. I never thought you would encourage your children to call me anything like that. I taught you girls to say Grandma Irene and Grandma Betty."

"But NaNa is common in Puerto Rico for grandmothers. It's a term of endearment."

"Yes, well, your children are not in Puerto Rico, honey. Carlos Jr. will eventually learn to say Great Grandma." She stood up from the couch, reached for him and took him out of Diane's arms. "He really does look like his father, doesn't he? Just like Carlos did at this age."

Diane's first thought was voiced out loud before she realized it. "How long will you be staying? And yes, he does look like Carlos. Just looking at him has helped me with my grief."

"I'm not sure how long I'll be here. Your father's leaving for a business trip and will be gone for a week. I thought this would be a good time to be here to help you."

Diane didn't respond. She didn't want to know what Mama thought she needed help with. She watched her hold CJ for a few minutes and then put him on the floor, returning to the edge of the couch again. Diane instinctively looked behind her to see if there was something keeping her mother from becoming comfortable on the couch. As Diane moved closer to see, the door opened and David and Robert came in.

"Grandma, hi."

"Hi, Robert, come give Grandma a kiss," she said, not moving from the edge of the seat.

Robert rushed over to her and planted a kiss on her cheek. He then placed his arms around her neck to embrace her the way he did his mother.

"Oh, not too tight honey," Mama said, pulling his arms away and encouraging him to sit on the couch next to her. CJ stood and pulled Robert to sit on the floor with him instead to play.

"Hello, Mama Margaret. What a surprise to see you. I didn't know you were coming. You look great," David said, as he leaned over and kissed her cheek.

"So do you, David; keeping yourself up I see," Mama said, glancing at her daughter in contrast before continuing. "We missed you at the funeral, but I understand someone had to stay with Robert."

David blushed from the compliment and said, "Oh, yeah, just keeping myself up a little. And yes, we thought attending the funeral would have been too much for the little man. How's Dad? Did he come with you?"

"He's fine. He's heading out of town on a business trip. Come, have a seat. Can you stay for dinner? I asked Diane to cook something decent."

David looked at Diane for some indication of how he should respond. Seeing none, he answered, "Actually, Robert and I have eaten and I'm sure you ladies have a lot to talk about." Then redirecting his attention, he said, "Robert, come give me a hug."

Robert hugged his father and then returned to a spot on the floor with CJ. David picked up CJ, gave him a hug and kiss, and returned him to Robert's attention.

"Okay, I'm out of here. Diane, I'll call you tomorrow. I'd like to pick up CJ and Robert and keep them for the weekend, if that's okay."

"Let's talk tomorrow," Diane responded, a little annoyed that David hadn't defended her against her mother's comment about her cooking. But David didn't push it and bid everyone farewell.

Once dinner was consumed, homework was checked and the kids were tucked in, Diane sat on the couch and exhaled. Her mother was watching TV, but turned down the volume so they could talk.

"So, Diane, how are you really?"

"Oh, I guess I'm fairing Mama. It's just me now as a single parent and CJ is a handful. It's been a while since I had a two-year-old to manage on my own, but I'm handling it."

"It doesn't look that way from here. You look exhausted. Almost as bad as you did when Luis left you."

"Well, that certainly makes me feel better," Diane said, rolling her eyes.

"That's why I came; I figured you needed help. I could see signs of it at the funeral and quite honestly, even before that. Child, what are you doing with your life? You had a good man who came here, married you with four kids, and was raising them as his own. I can see how much he cares for these children. He's even welcomed Carlos Jr., as if he were his grandson. Why are you throwing all of that away?"

"Mama, I'm tired and I really don't want to discuss this right now. Besides what goes on between a man and a woman is between them. That's our business and I am not going to discuss the particulars with you. I will tell you that we are doing what we feel is best for us right now."

"I'm sorry you don't want to discuss this, because we are going to discuss this. I'm going to help you see straight before I leave here. Now, why are you and David separated?"

Diane knew her mother would not leave it alone until she agreed to discuss it, so she began. "Mama, things are different. The circumstances that brought us together don't have enough adhesion left to keep us from drifting apart. It's that simple. We have had a lot of family issues this past year that have put the relationship under a magnifying glass and it has been a real strain."

"And what role has Luis played in all of this?"

"I didn't say Luis had anything to do with this."

"Oh please, Diane, Luis has everything to do with the problems in your life, starting with the day you decided to marry him."

"Mama, please, must we rehash this opinion of yours? And yes, David is a good man. He has loved me and my children; that is fact. I appreciate that. I will always be grateful to him. But it's not enough."

"What else are you looking for? Your father was a good provider for me and the three of you children. There wasn't anything he wouldn't do if I asked him. He respects me and will always be there for me. That is the kind of man David is. When you married him, I thanked God because I knew he would help you with your kids. When he looks at you, it's with love and admiration. What more do you want? So what is the problem?"

"Mama, your relationship with Daddy obviously met your needs and you have managed to make your marriage work. I'm happy for you, I really am. But my needs are different. I need more."

"What more do you need, Diane? He makes good money and one day, you'll be able to buy a small house."

"No, he makes decent money. But you just don't understand. You asked and I answered. I need more. That's my business. End of conversation."

Mama's raised eyebrows seemed to imply "now don't get smart little girl," but instead she said, "Yes, I do understand. You want Luis back in your life. That's what Chell told me. She also said he's been coming over here quite often to spend time with Carlos Jr. and her. She told me he was here for New Year's Eve. I can't believe you are going to let a good man like David go, to get back in bed with that…"

"Mama, stop it. You are now overstepping your boundaries. You will not disrespect me or the father of my children."

"Why not? He disrespects you, living with that slut and creeping over here. I raised you to have more respect for yourself than that."

"Oh my God, I'm not doing anything with Luis. And if we were, it would be my business, my mistakes to make, as you would say. But honestly, he's not disrespecting me because he and Maria aren't together anymore."

"Oh! Oh! Now I see. So you think it's over between them and you can get him back; move into that house he bought. Don't be a fool. Once a man strays, he will do it again. You can't trust him."

"Well, mother, it seems that you've written the screenplay and have it all figured out. You've cast me in a role, but you don't have a clue what is going on in my life. If you must know, my decision regarding David has nothing to do with Luis. I realize that I thought I loved David because I needed him and he was there for me. He was the prince that saved the damsel in distress. I needed him at a time in my life when I felt really low and alone. He filled a huge void and made me feel good about myself. I mistook that for love, but he deserves more from life than that."

"So this is about love and passion? What did love and passion do for your marriage to Luis? Let me tell you what it did. It brought you four children. It kept you from getting your Master's degree, let alone your doctorate. It has you living in an apartment that is too small for your family, while Luis lives in a house. It hasn't allowed you to achieve any of your goals. And to top it all off, your dead oldest son has fathered a child that you are now left raising."

Diane looked at her mother and grimaced, struggling to just get some inkling of the nerve Luis J had.

"You think you have all the answers, don't you?" Diane finally blurted out. "You have no idea who I really am or anything about me or what I want or need. I never wanted a doctorate anyway. That was all about you. Didn't you tell me, 'I expect to have three doctorate degrees to hang on my wall?' This has never been about me or my sisters. It's just about making you look good, the mother who raised her girls to be successful."

Mama fidgeted a little, seeming somewhat uncomfortable. "Don't be ridiculous. Look how successful your sisters are. They stayed focused and achieved their goals. They didn't fall in love and let some man derail them. They followed my guidance to a tee and it's worked for them."

"That's great. They're perfect, or so you think. Mama, you may not understand this, but I truly loved Luis. He was kind and gentle and listened to me. He cared about what I wanted and how I felt. We loved each other deeply."

"Love, love, love. You don't love David. You loved Luis. When will you learn to leave love alone? If he loved you so much, why did he have an affair? Why did he walk away from you and the four kids he fathered?"

"Yes, Luis had an affair. Oh, bring out the firing squad because he's the only man on the face of this earth who has done that. Besides, like I told you before, you don't know the whole story. Luis isn't the bad guy all by himself."

"You are still starry-eyed when it comes to him! I can't believe that, after all these years. You are still in love with him. How on earth will love help you in this situation you're in? It won't...because at the end of the day, it has nothing to do with life and raising children. Look around you, Diane. Go ahead, look and see what love has given you. You better wake up before it's too late."

"Wow. So, that's your advice? Seriously? Do you love Daddy? Does he love you? Do you even know what I'm talking about?"

"Yes, Diane, I know what you're talking about. And I'm telling you to forget about love and deal with reality. You are almost in your mid-forties. If you don't make this work with David, who in the world do you think will want you? Luis? His interest is purely one of competition. He wants to see if he can win you over from David. And trust me, once you let him, he'll drop you and move on to someone else. He's living the carefree life now. Why would he come back to this?" she asked, pointing to the bottle on the table and toys on the floor. "No, David is the key to some kind of future for you, not Luis."

Diane sat there realizing that her mother would never see her life through her eyes. And as much as she disliked it, when her mother did it to her, for the first time she recognized she had been raising her children the same way. She could see herself, the mirror image of her mother, sitting across from Carlos and demanding that he live his life the way she had wanted him to. Tears came to her eyes.

"And don't you dare start crying and feeling sorry for yourself. I can't stand it when you do that. It doesn't solve anything," Mama stated while glancing at her watch. "It's ten-thirty. Where is Luis Jr.? Where is that boy? Doesn't he have a curfew? He hasn't even called."

Diane pulled her hair out of the ponytail, and then rebound it, tighter than before. Nothing would be allowed to flow tonight; every strand must be bound. She finished this action before responding, "Well, you might as well know, Luis J isn't living here right now. But before you start on me about that, too, I have it under control."

"What? What do you mean, Diane? Where is he? Don't tell me he's living with Luis?"

"He's staying with a friend for a little while. It's crowded here with Robert and CJ sleeping in the same room with him." She didn't like lying to her mother, but it wasn't that far from the truth. No, Maria was no friend, but the room was crowded. Besides, she was desperate to have some control over the conversation. Her mother had just stripped her naked.

"Really? What friend does he have who is old enough, let alone responsible enough, to give him a place to stay?"

"Mama, please, I can raise my children. I'm not going to discuss this with you any further."

"It doesn't look that way from where I'm sitting," Mama said, sitting erect with her arms crossed.

"Then maybe you should sit somewhere else."

"What did you say?" Mama asked, shocked and surprised.

"Never mind. It's late and I'm tired. CJ doesn't sleep through the night, so why don't you stay in Luis J's room, with Robert. I'll see you in the morning."

Diane didn't wait for her mother to reply; she walked to her bedroom and closed the door. She found a little comfort in that she had at least stuck to her guns about being queen of her own home. The nerve of her mother thinking that she could come into her home, wreak havoc and tell her where people would sleep. Ugh! She lifted CJ's sleeping body from the crib and laid him in the bed next to her. He squirmed a little and put his thumb in his mouth.

"Carlos, forgive me," Diane whispered, as she clung to his son. "I promise you, I won't make the same mistake with your son."

Margaret was still sitting on the couch. She was so disappointed with Diane's decisions. Even now, she was still floundering in her life.

How had this happened to her youngest child?

Margaret Miller was born and raised in Roanoke, Virginia. Her parents had been landowners and raised livestock and grew crops like tobacco and soybeans for their livelihood. The money they raised was used to send their five children to college. All five of them graduated from Howard University, and Margaret with honors. She was the middle child and, her mother often said, the most determined. She had majored in English and began teaching at a public school in the D.C. area, where she met Ron Johnson.

He was an administrator for the school and was in awe of the control and respect she commanded from her students and colleagues. Ron had asked Margaret out several times, but she always had some reason for not accepting. He refused to let that deter him. He became more and more creative with his approaches until she finally agreed to a double date with a few of her colleagues. They had gone to a movie and then out to dinner.

At the end of the evening, to Margaret's surprise, she found herself enjoying Ron's company. He was actually quite charming and very attentive. At school, she had observed him on several occasions and noticed that he always seemed to be so quiet and subdued that she thought him to be a bookworm. He also wasn't very strong physically and she worried that he wouldn't be able to defend her, if it ever came to that.

But that night, he showed her a different side. He listened to her dreams and encouraged her to pursue them. He was also very kind, meeting all of her expectations, such as opening doors, pulling out chairs, and paying all of the expenses. What she ultimately determined was that this man was someone with whom she could partner and achieve great success. They continued dating for about a year before she finally accepted his proposal.

They had a small wedding because she wanted to use the money they had saved to buy a home. Once they were settled, she began working toward her dream, to get a doctorate from Howard University. She would be the first in her family and she knew with a supportive man behind her, it could happen.

But halfway into her second semester, the first of three children was born. She completed that semester and applied for a leave. Once the child was a year old, she applied for a substitute teaching position to rebuild their finances. She took an evening class to keep her skills sharp and to keep from falling too far behind her schedule. However, two years later, she was pregnant with her second child. They were using spermicidal foam, but it was not one-hundred percent effective.

Now she had a newborn and a three-year-old, so teaching was no longer an option. Instead, she offered to tutor the neighborhood children, which brought in a little money to offset their expenses. They had also begun experimenting with different brands of foam and other techniques that kept her from getting pregnant, and for that she was thankful. By the time her second child, Michelle was four, Margaret dusted off her books and reapplied to school. Ron fully supported her, taking on a second job on the weekend, helping with the children and not bothering her with things he could handle.

Margaret was so excited about being able to return to school. She was way off schedule, but that didn't matter; she could double up and close some of the gap if she put her mind to it. Imagine her surprise when she found out she was pregnant with her third child. It was a blow to her ego from which she was never able to recover.

Margaret withdrew for the final time, sold her textbooks and accepted that it was just not meant to be. No matter how hard she had tried, she was not able to control the distractions in her life. She thought that marrying Ron would help her excel because she would have someone who could support her financially, but in fact, it had done just the opposite. She vowed then that she would not allow her children to suffer the same fate.

The day after she gave birth to her third child, Diane, she embraced her new mission: to educate each of her daughters and hang their Master's degrees, and hopefully at least one doctorate, on her wall. She was not particularly happy that she had all girls, as she knew that they could very easily suffer the same fate that she had. She wondered if God was testing her yet again to see if she could keep her three daughters from succumbing to things that distract women.

Her oldest daughter, Cindy, followed in Margaret's footsteps and went to Howard for undergraduate and graduate school. Only upon completion of her Master's degree did Margaret allow her to date exclusively. Within six months, Cindy was engaged to a Morehouse man who was then a medical student at Howard. Margaret approved of this union because he was focused on his career and would soon be an intern, allowing little time for or interest in children for several years. Additionally, he would eventually have the money to allow Cindy to go to school full time and obtain her doctorate. Her plan was working just as she had scripted. Because it worked with Cindy, Margaret used the model again to keep the other two girls on the right path.

Michelle proved to be more of a challenge than Cindy. She was much more independent and opinionated. Margaret had to work extra hard to keep Michelle focused on studies. Margaret found that incentives usually worked nicely while Michelle was in high school: a new pair of jeans, a certain pair of sneakers, a new purse. Once Michelle made it to college, she was on autopilot. She wanted the degree because she had to be as good, if not better than Cindy. Michelle graduated summa cum laude from George Washington University and applied to law school at Howard. She ultimately met her husband in the courtroom when they were on opposite sides of a case. She eventually received her JD.

Last, but not least, was Diane, the starry-eyed daydreamer. Diane was the sensitive one who would cry if you looked at her the wrong way. Margaret knew early on that this child would be the one to cause her the most trouble. Diane had that innocence about her that attracted men. She also didn't realize how attractive she was and that, too, attracted men. Margaret would constantly talk to Diane about being focused, not losing sight of the prize. Diane was forbidden to participate in any after school activities, especially ones involving boys. When it came time to go off to college, Margaret had to be much more involved in choosing the college than she had been with the other two. Margaret wanted this child to go to a very strong academic school so she wouldn't have time for socializing. She also didn't want Diane to be anywhere where there would be a large population of Black men. Margaret would have insisted that Diane go to an all-female school, but they had a tendency to be magnets to the all-male schools nearby.

The first three years of Diane's academic experience were spot on. She was getting A's and B's and was on the Dean's List. Margaret encouraged this and knew that she had made the right choice by sending Diane to Emory. It wasn't until her senior year that Margaret noticed Diane slacking off. Her workload wasn't heavy because she had finished all of her major courses and actually had enough to graduate a semester early. But, instead of doing so, as Margaret had insisted, Diane elected to take a few human-interest classes. She felt that would round out her degree and would prove useful in a corporate environment. She also didn't want to work at the bank anymore, again as Margaret had planned to help fill Diane's down time.

Diane just wanted to enjoy some free time before starting graduate school. As a result, she started hanging out with some graduate students at a nearby college and as Margaret assumed, it brought trouble. She could still remember the day Diane called to tell her that she had met some man from Georgia State and they were talking about marriage. Margaret was stunned, yet on some level, she expected it. Margaret wasted no time telling her daughter that she was NOT going to give her permission for them to get engaged. She reminded Diane that the rule was to complete her graduate studies, like both Cindy and Michelle had, before getting engaged.

But when Diane brought Luis Rodriquez home for the Easter holiday, Margaret could see that her daughter was already smitten. She had fallen hard for this Afro-Latino man and Margaret had completely lost control. At least he had completed graduate school and he said he would encourage Diane to continue her studies.

Margaret recognized that similar offer of help from her own experience. She was sure that he meant it, but Luis was a ladies man and she could see that he and Diane had already been intimate. She certainly understood why. He was charming, with nice manners, and he certainly respected women. He opened doors, pulled the chair from the table, carried their bags and spoke respectfully. In some ways, he reminded Margaret of Ron. She could also see how much Diane was in love with this man and based on her upbringing, that was a disaster waiting to happen.

Not only did they get engaged, but they married right after Diane graduated from college. Margaret never really blessed the union because they had defied her wishes and wasn't at all surprised when it turned out the way it did.

News that Diane was pregnant broke her heart. In her mind, Diane was on the path to repeat the same life she had led. Margaret knew her daughter would never go back to school and complete her studies. Instead, Diane would now be tied to that man forever, just as she had been tied to Ron Johnson. Margaret knew they would never be able to provide for their children the way she and Ron had, not with how money was currently valued, and she knew that it wouldn't be long before Diane was overwhelmed with raising the children.

Then one day, Diane told her mother about David. He had been a blessing. He loved Diane, but was much more even keeled, willing to help raise Luis' four children and be a good, hard-working provider. Margaret could tell that David could handle Diane as long as Luis stayed out of the way. The way Luis had broken Diane's heart, Margaret didn't think that keeping him away would be difficult. But now, here they were, with Luis trying to worm his way back into her daughter's life. No, absolutely not. That simply was not an option.

The next morning, Diane and her mother barely said two words to each other over breakfast. Chell and Robert went to the park with CJ and the babysitter and they would be gone for a while. This was the time Diane needed to try and regain some footing with her mother. So she began with an act of kindness.

"Mama, is there anything you would like to do today? This is my last day off before returning to work and we could go for lunch or something if you like."

"Diane, I thought I was clear last night. I'm not here on a vacation. First, I want to see my grandson. Where is he living?"

Okay, that didn't work, so back to defense. "I'll call him and have him come by tonight for dinner around five."

"Why can't I go over there?"

"Because it isn't an option."

"Um…alright. I do have a few errands to run, but I'll be back later this afternoon, long before he gets here. When I get back, we can talk about the kids."

Ignoring that comment, Diane asked, "Where're you going, Mama?"

"To take care of a few things," she said, rising from the table and putting her dishes in the sink.

"That's very vague. I know you don't know your way around the city that well, so I'll go with you then."

"That's not necessary. I'll take a cab. Besides, you need to use this time alone to begin to clear your head – straighten up and then clean up this apartment. And please spend some time on yourself. Make yourself look decent girl! I'll be fine."

As Diane went to her bedroom for privacy to place the call to her son, she wondered why she had an uneasy feeling about her mother's errands. Diane told Luis J of his grandmother's visit and desire to see him for dinner.

"I guess. I need to talk to Maria first."

"I'm sure you know it's not a good idea to bring her with you."

"I know. Does Grandma know?"

"No, I didn't tell your grandmother that you're living with Maria. I don't think she's ready for that information and I certainly don't need to hear her opinion on that."

"Fine, but sooner or later she's gonna have to be told. And there's some information I need to share with you, too."

"About the pregnancy? I already know."

"Papi told you? When?"

"New Year's Eve."

"He had no right. He has nothing to do with this."

"Luis J, for God's sake, grow up. We're your parents; we are involved whether you like it or not. Technically, we could be legally libel for neglect of a minor. You are still under age and we allowed you to live alone at your brother's house where the conception technically occurred. You better remember to be respectful because if we want we can charge Maria with child molestation. But we haven't because we're trying to be sensitive and work through this with you. I don't want to make the same mistakes I made with Carlos. But Luis J, don't push me.

You must be respectful to both your father and me. And finally, until the paternity is determined, we won't know the extent of your involvement. You hear me?"

Stunned by his mother's calm delivery of information that in the past would have had her screaming and delivered with ultimatums and threats, Luis J answered in a calm voice as well. "Yeah I hear you, but I'm the father. Maria already confirmed that. Papi is lying about fathering this child."

"Honey, your father never said he fathered the child. He said that Maria told him that. He was just as shocked when she told him she was pregnant. He was more shocked when she told him that she had not taken precautions. He's really hurt by this confusion she's caused and the rift between the two of you as a result. Mostly he's worried about you. Maria is a grown-ass woman and she can fend for herself."

"Oh, so Maria is the liar? What makes you so sure about that?"

"Are you really asking me that question after all that woman has done to this family? You know what she is capable of and you know who she is. You're just so mad and hurt right now, she looks like the good guy to you."

Diane paused and remembered that her mother was in the other room and, unfortunately, the walls were thin. So she softly continued, "Sweetheart, please, we really shouldn't be having this conversation on the phone. I really just wanted to ask you to come see your grandmother. I don't want to argue with you. Some women like to play games. Maria is one of those women. She's playing with your emotions the same way she did with your father. He has lived with her for longer than you've been grown. He knows her now; he finally sees what she's capable of, but you, you're just getting a taste of her and I know it feels good to you. I know she's turning you out, making you feel like more of a man than any of those other girls have. She knew she could.

"But seriously Luis J, I thought you were the one most like me, who could see past her scheming, conniving ways. As a matter of fact, I told her so when she told me that she'd take you away from me just like she took your father and Carlos. And I said, 'Don't be fooled by Luis J's youth. He can see through your bull shit.' She laughed at me. But I know deep in my heart that you can."

Luis J let the words ring inside his head, forming all kinds of images that he processed before saying, "Really? You think I'm the most like you, huh? Well, we'll see. Anyway, I'll stop by around five, but I can't stay long."

He was sitting on his bed when the call came in and he remained there as he thought about her points. He had never heard that comparison before. He wasn't sure how he felt about it, but he had always admired his mother's "sixth sense" and ability to read people, and he was pretty good at it, too. He could see Maria moving around in the kitchen from where he was perched and he began looking at her through a clearer lens.

Once outside, Margaret hailed a cab and headed to the restaurant where Luis had agreed to meet her. It took a minute for her eyes to adjust, but she found him sitting in a booth by the window. He rose as she approached. Mama smiled to herself, 'Always the gentleman.'

"Mama Margaret, it's good to see you. How are you?"

Not bothering with politeness, she started right in. "I didn't say anything to you in Puerto Rico because of the occasion, but it is no longer appropriate for you to address me that way."

"I'm sorry, I didn't know you felt like that. We are still so connected."

"But it isn't appropriate; that's what David calls me now."

"You're right. He does call you that, but it's a title of respect. Elders are referred to as such in my native tradition. We do share blood through my children, but if it makes you uncomfortable, I will stop. Please, have a seat."

She removed her coat and sat down.

"You look well. How is…Mr. Johnson?"

"We're fine, just very concerned about Diane."

"As am I."

"Really? We don't feel she is making the best decisions right now. Losing Carlos and having to take on the responsibility of his son have her making really poor choices."

Luis leaned back in the chair and waited for her to continue. The waitress came to see if they were eating, but they both just asked for coffee.

"Now, where was I? Anyway, I think she needs help getting control of her life and that's why I am in town for a few weeks. I will be staying to put things in order."

"How does Di feel about this?"

"Diane doesn't know how she feels about anything. Don't you see that when you're there? Which is quite frequently, from what I've been told."

"Honestly, no, I don't. She had it hard at first, all of us did, and it's understandable. She lost her first born. However, she's very strong and determined. She just needs our support, not our interference."

"She doesn't need your support, Luis. You're not her husband anymore, David is. He is the one to supply the support you think she needs. But David can't do that because you are in the way. I thought you agreed to stay out of those children's lives? You are using this tragedy and your grandson to ruin Diane's marriage and ultimately hurt her again. Well, I won't sit by this time and watch you destroy her life again or those children's."

"I'm not the cause of any problems Diane may be having in her marriage. It started long before Carlos died and I resent your statement about me taking advantage of my son's tragic accident. Diane has realized how painful it has been for everyone by denying my involvement in our children's lives; mostly because our sons voiced it, as did David. We have worked through that and found a solution that has made everyone feel better."

"I doubt if everyone is feeling better. Besides, your presence certainly must confuse Robert. David is his father, you know."

"David has raised him yes, but one day he will learn that I am his father."

"Hopefully, we are many, many years away from that revelation. That boy is growing up nicely under David's parenting; let's leave well enough alone."

Luis cleared his throat and exclaimed, "You know, I don't mean any disrespect, but you are really extending yourself into my business and, frankly, I won't tolerate it."

"Yes I am and I make no apologies for it. I'm a parent who sets goals for her children and then lays the foundation to help them achieve them. My two oldest children did just that. Unfortunately, Diane got confused about her 'feelings' and you clearly took advantage of that, just like you are doing now, showing up New Year's Eve."

"I was invited."

"And you should have said no. You knew it had nothing to do with the children. But no, you have her on the ropes, telling her you aren't with that girl anymore, as if that matters, being sweet and attentive. Well, I won't let you bring her down again."

"Mrs. Johnson, a lot of – most of – what goes on between Diane and me is none of your concern. It wasn't when we were married and it isn't now. Besides, when was the last time you looked at your daughter? I mean really looked at her. Or listened to her, really listened to her? She's a woman. She is more than capable of running her life. I will regret to the day I die having hurt Diane. I really loved her, but we all make mistakes and at the time she couldn't forgive me. And quite honestly, part of that is your fault."

"My fault? Now you are blaming me for your indiscretions and failures?"

"No. I'm not blaming you for that. I take full responsibility for my actions. But, I am saying that Diane was very concerned about failing you and disappointing you. She wanted so badly to be able to show you that she could achieve the goals you had set for her. She hoped that together, she and I could be successful in your eyes, like her sisters. When I let her down, she felt that the only option she had was to find someone else to help her attain those goals. I couldn't see that then, but I do now."

"Too little, too late. Diane is still that starry-eyed girl she was when she was growing up. The only person who has ever been able to ground her is me, and that is why I am here. And hopefully, I can try to salvage Luis Jr. and Chell."

"You are Diane's mother and only she can set those boundaries with you. But Luis J and Chell are off-limits to your interference. They are my children, and Diane and I will determine what is best for them. Besides, they don't need salvaging; they're going to be alright."

"Now who's not in touch with reality? Your son isn't even living at home, for God's sake. He is only seventeen. He should still be under Diane's roof."

"He's just trying to find some independence. Diane and I have that under control."

"Hardly. Who is he living with anyway?"

"A friend."

"Which friend?"

"It isn't anyone you would know and it's none of your business."

"Well, I never. You and Diane are both avoiding this subject and I am going to find out why!"

"Mrs. Johnson, I'm telling you, don't go meddling in business that's not yours. We know what is best for our children, so let us work it out. Would you have allowed your mother to interfere with the raising of your girls?"

That threw Margaret off kilter and made her pull back a little. She knew Luis already knew the answer to his question, so she ignored him and let him have that one. "Fine, I'll get Diane to see things my way and then she can affect the change on 'your children.'"

Luis rose and placed the money for their coffees on the table. "If there is nothing else, I'll be leaving now. Oh and one more thing…stop trying to live vicariously through your daughters. You will be rewarded far greater if you let Diane live her life, the way she chooses."

Not to be outdone, Mama Margaret said with authority, "Just one last thing, Luis. Arrange to see the children outside of Diane and David's home from now on, and minimize, drastically, your interaction with her. If you care about her at all, you will do that and allow her to get back with David and keep you out of her veins."

Without responding, Luis buttoned his overcoat and strolled out of the restaurant onto the street. It took a moment for his eyes to adjust to the light and his ears to the normal sounds on the streets of New York City. As he stood there, he thought to himself, 'If Diane ever needed me, she certainly needs me now.' No wonder she had been so frail when they first met. That woman was a sheer bully. When he turned and headed toward the parked car, his cell phone rang.

"Papi, it's me, Luis J."

"Son, it's good to hear from you. I'm glad you called. How are things?"

"I didn't call you for idle chitchat. Mami told me that you told her about Maria. You had no right."

"Luis J, I'm a little tired of you talking about who has no right and that you're not a child and all the other childish crap you've been spewing lately. Wake up. You're seventeen, under age, no job, no high school diploma, living with an older woman who happens to be my ex-lover and who's pregnant by one of us. Stop bitching about who did what to you and man up!

"Yeah, I told her. So what? I told her because you and I both know Maria was just waiting for the right moment to drop a dime to your mother. If you have big cojones now, why didn't you call your mother and tell her? You knew she would try to split your head open, that's why. Men face their shit regardless of the outcome."

'What the hell? First Mommy, now him. Everybody is growing balls today. What's going on?' Luis J thought, but still he held his own and stuck to his position. "I was planning to tell her. You didn't give me enough time. But it's over with now."

"Oh no, it's not over. It's just beginning and you better hold on for the ride of your life. I don't care about Maria anymore, but like I told you before, I do care about you. You think you know who you're with, but you don't. Be careful son, be careful, because you're way out of your league."

"I heard you the first time you said that. Why can't you understand that I can't leave her now since she's pregnant? I told you I won't walk away from that child."

"Son, you still don't even know if it's your child and she won't take a paternity test, so she has both of us dangling on a string for the next seven or eight months. But now while we're dangling, we can work together to make sure that when she cuts the string – because, trust me, she is going to cut it – we will both land on our two feet when we fall or we can fight each other and not see it coming, which is what she plans. Think about that for a while and let me know which one you choose. I have to go, but I look forward to your answer."

As Luis J ended the call, he surmised that today was his day for lifelong lessons, analogies and things to ponder. It was not going to be a restful night, he knew that already.

"What a day. Between Diane's mother and Luis J, I am ready for that cognac," Luis proclaimed after he disconnected from the call and started the ignition for his drive home.

Chapter Twenty Nine

Diane noticed that when her mother returned, she seemed happier. She was carrying a few bags, but clearly the elation wasn't from shopping. There was a lightness in her body's movement that wasn't there earlier that morning. Diane couldn't figure out what was behind this change in her mother's behavior, so she asked, "Did you take care of all your errands? You seem much calmer than you were earlier today."

"Yes, I certainly did," Margaret said, smiling to herself. She had been quite triumphant with her first assignment, but she wasn't ready to share the details with Diane yet, so instead she asked, "Is dinner ready?"

"Just about. Luis J is here already," Diane responded, still taking note of her mother's demeanor. There was definitely something going on with her, but she couldn't put her finger on. Diane now turned her attention to her son and, projecting her voice slightly to reach the back of the apartment, she called out, "Luis J, your grandma is here."

He emerged from Diane's bedroom where he had been spending time with CJ and walked up to his grandmother for the traditional greeting: a kissed planted gingerly on her check followed by a brief embrace. It was delivered exactly the way Grandma Margaret had taught the children to do years ago and Diane observed her teaching the technique to Robert and CJ when she arrived yesterday.

This show of affection was so contradictory to Diane's hugs and kisses, which were full of love and intended to uplift the person on the receiving end of her affections. Diane remembered thinking that when she became a parent, her children would know how much they were loved in many ways, but definitely by the way she embraced them.

"My goodness. Look how you have grown. I didn't have a chance to interact with you at the funeral. You weren't around the family very much. But I can see you are definitely filling out," Margaret said, admiring her grandson's features. He was certainly handsome like his father and she hoped this was not going to his head. Raising boys was tricky and from her perspective, Diane wasn't doing such a good job with Luis J either. She was pretty sure these living arrangements had something to do with the opposite sex and she was determined to get to the bottom of that story before she left. With a smile on her face, she continued, "You are looking more and more like your grandfather."

"Really? Everybody always says I look just like Papi."

"No. I don't see him in you at all. You are much more like your mother's side of the family. You have your grandfather's build, tall and lean. Anyway, I'm glad you were able to join us for dinner. I have to tell you I was surprised that we had to invite you over here to spend time with your grandmother," she said, aiming a critical eye directly at Diane, but continuing to engage in her conversation with Luis J. "You know I have a ton of questions for you and you know where I'm going to start, don't you? How is school?"

"K, I guess."

"What kind of answer is that? And when did you start speaking in broken English? Dare I ask about your GPA?"

"It's alright. I'm a little above a 3.0."

"A little above a 3.0? Is that all? What happened? You had a 3.5 your sophomore year."

"Well, in case you haven't noticed, there's been a lot going on here lately." Luis J had to look to see if his mother was throwing her voice across the room somehow because for a second he couldn't tell which one of them was speaking.

"Luis J," Diane interjected, still cutting up the vegetables for the salad.

Margaret raised her hand to her daughter to stop her interference and said, "It's okay Diane, let the boy speak his mind. Go ahead."

"There's been a lot to contend with around here lately and it's affected some of my course work. But a 3.0 isn't a bad GPA, especially when you combine it with my basketball skills. I'm the team captain and usually score the most points on the team."

"I see. So what universities are you considering?"

"UCLA and UConn are at the top of the list."

"UCLA and UConn; why those two?"

"B-ball Grandma, that's why," he said, using his hands to imitate throwing and sinking a shot before continuing. "They have some of the best records and I know I could get some floor time my freshman year because of my outside shot."

"I see. And what do you plan to study?"

"I'm thinking engineering. You know how much I love math."

"Yes, I do. So, when will you be finalizing your list?"

Luis J reflected on the question and then his current situation. If Maria was carrying his child, UConn and UCLA would no longer be an option. So his response to her question was, "I'm not sure. I have other things to consider now."

Diane stopped her chopping and shot a glance at Luis J to get his attention. He was tiptoeing into territory that was supposed to be off limits right now to her mother. She had been very clear with him about that. She prayed that her mother wouldn't pick up on his comment.

"What are you talking about? What other things? There is nothing more important than setting your goals and achieving them. Look at your aunts."

"I just mean that your life doesn't always happen according to plan." He thought about his father's constant warnings lately.

"That's true. But you still have to have a plan. If you don't you will drift through life making one bad decision after another. So, don't wait too long to figure it out. At your age, it should be pretty simple. It's not like you have any other things to consider. Decide soon before you find your life completely derailed. Trust me, when that happens you usually don't recover," Margaret stated, again, looking at her daughter.

"Yes, Grandma Margaret."

"Good. Now, on to the next situation that's very troubling to me. Who is this friend you are living with?"

"Mama please, it feels like you're giving him the third degree. He's doing alright in school and I'll be here to help him with school choices when the time comes," Diane said, shielding her son from her mother's wrath. If he answered that question, all hell would break loose.

"Alright, dinner's ready, so let's eat." Projecting her voice once again, she called out, "Chell, bring the boys, it's time to eat." Diane was so relieved when her mother didn't push for an answer and allowed them to avoid the land mines. Additionally, she was thankful the conversation around the dinner table enabled Luis J to avoid talking about his potential impending fatherhood, too. When he finally said his goodbyes, Diane exhaled and felt the knot in her stomach subsiding a little. Crisis avoided, as well as criticism of her parenting skills.

Once the children were settled, mother and daughter found themselves on the couch once again. Diane was enjoying a glass of Merlot until she heard that tone in her mother's voice.

"Diane, he's a good boy, but I'm worried about his values. I don't think he is as grounded as he needs to be."

"Really, Mama, you're questioning his values? There isn't anything wrong with his values. Why would you even say that? Of all my children, he's the most like me. I know he'll be just fine once he gets over the hurdles he's dealing with right now."

Margaret chuckled. "The most like you? Well in that case, you definitely better keep your eye on him. You haven't done the best job raising these boys, Diane. Look what happened to Carlos at this age and he was such a bright boy. I told you I was concerned about him way before he moved out of your home. And as I suspected, he strayed away from the solid home values your father and I instilled in you girls and gravitated toward his father's, experimenting with sex at such an early age. I told you to watch him, but you were so distracted by what Luis was doing..."

"What are you talking about? By the time that happened, Luis and I were already divorced. They weren't even interacting with their father at that point. And Carlos' values were admirable. Yes, he was experimenting with sex, that's what teenagers do, but it wasn't because he didn't have values. If anything, he was missing his father's guidance. Carlos needed a man to provide the insight that I couldn't as a woman and David didn't because of their relationship."

"Is that how you see it? You obviously have a short memory. Who's the father of that two-year-old in your room? Who didn't go to college even though they had all kinds of scholarships?"

"Mama, I'm just saying that Carlos wasn't a problem and neither is Luis J. Am I the perfect mother? No. There, I said it. Are you happy now?"

"Diane, you are still so disconnected from reality. Carlos left your house to live with his father and his mistress and you allowed him to do that. Now Luis Jr., is living God-knows-where and you are allowing that. So, am I disappointed with your parenting skills? I think you already know the answer to that."

"Okay, Mother. You are the perfect parent. I, once again, have disappointed you. But I am not going to sit here in my house and let you put my life under a microscope."

"I have no intentions of doing that. I already have set things in motion that should get you back on track. I told you that's why I was coming here."

"Excuse me? What does that mean? What are you talking about?" Diane lifted her glass of Merlot and took a long drink. At this point, she wished she was drinking from the bottle.

"After our talk last night, I got a better sense of what was going on here and what you were really dealing with. I now know that I need to stay here as long as it takes until you and David are back together. Your sisters have agreed to loan you the money to buy a house. Now I don't want you guys to be in too much debt, so it won't be nearly as large as theirs or mine, but you'll have more room. This way, Luis Jr. can move back home, where he belongs. He and Chell need their own rooms and way more guidance and discipline than you are giving either of them now, but I'll take care of that. David is doing a fine job with Robert. That just leaves Carlos Jr. and I assume you can handle him. You have a long runway with him so you will have the time you need to learn from your mistakes."

"What the …"

"I'm not done sweetheart, and watch your mouth. I'll find a decent night school for you here so you can finish your masters. I don't know if getting your doctorate is still doable given how far off track you are, but we can make that assessment once you finish. I don't know if you have the finances, but maybe your job will cover some of the expenses. Your major was finance, right? Now, as for your ex-husband. I have already talked to him, which was very interesting, and …"

"Whoa. Stop right there. You talked to Luis? When?" Diane inquired, rising to her feet.

Watching her daughter jump to her feet, but not surprised by her reaction, Margaret continued, "This afternoon. I called him early this morning and he agreed to meet with me."

"Who gave you permission to do that?"

"You did when I saw how messed up your life was."

Ignoring her assessment, but appalled by her behavior, Diane demanded, "What did you say to him, Mama?"

"Don't raise your voice, Diane; you'll wake the children."

"I don't care if I wake the neighbors at the end of the hall! What did you say to him? I don't believe you had the nerve to interfere in my life like that."

"I don't know why not? I've always been the same person. There isn't anything I wouldn't do for my family. I basically told him to remain out of your life so you can get back together with David. David and I are meeting tomorrow."

"The hell you are."

"Diane, your mouth. Since when do you curse around me?"

"Mama, you had no right to meet with Luis about what is our business and you certainly are not going to meet with David to discuss anything with him. Who do you think you are? For that matter, who do you think I am, some child still living under your roof? The nerve!"

"Your life is a total disaster, dear. Don't you see that? I am just trying to get you back on track. You have never been able to take charge of things and get them accomplished without me. I have always been your backbone."

Diane looked at her mother sitting on the couch, proud of her actions. It made Diane feel ill. "Mama, actually I can see for the first time in my life. I went from your control to Luis' and then David's. I've never been in a position where I could make my own decisions, right or wrong. I've always felt that I couldn't stand on my own two feet, but it is way past time for me to take control of my life."

"Honey, some people can do that; it's a gift. I have it, your sisters have it, but you are more like your father. That's why you need me."

"No, I don't. Not that way, not any longer. Instead of helping me, you have stifled me. You have kept me from growing into a woman. I have to do this myself."

"Don't be silly. Why do you think you can handle things all of a sudden when you haven't been able to thus far? You said yourself you have let someone else control you all of your life. Now maybe I should have talked to you about some of these things first, but I felt it would be better to just give you the solutions.

"You don't have to worry; Luis completely understood. I don't think he will make it too difficult for you – you know, he'll call first before coming over and take the children somewhere else so you don't have to see him. I think he wants what's best for you. Only time will tell though about that. But, if you're really ready to start taking control of your life, you will insist he comply with that." Margaret knew this was a bit of a stretch, but she thought she would offer this as an olive branch to womanhood.

"And how long has this so-called plan been in progress?"

"Ever since the funeral; we all saw how dysfunctional your family was. Heavens, your husband didn't even come with you. He allowed some other man to be by your side. But, no matter. David doesn't know how to handle you yet, but I'll help him."

"You're not listening to me. I told you I don't need your help with David or Luis or my children. For once would you please hear me? What I need is for you and my sisters to mind your own damn business and run your own lives. Stay the hell out of my life."

"Diane! If your family can't be there for you, who on earth do you think will be? You just need some time to realize that this is the best way for you and your children. You owe them a chance to better themselves and you are not prepared to do that yourself. I know you wouldn't deny your children a chance at a successful future. Would you? I know you wouldn't put your needs ahead of theirs. I didn't do it for the three of you. I always put you first."

After a brief pause, she continued, "Diane, you know I'm right. In no time, you'll be thanking me. But more importantly, you'll be in a better place. Whew, I'm exhausted. I know I've given you a lot to think about so I'm going to turn in and give you some time to yourself. Goodnight dear." Margaret rose from the couch and walked away from Diane, who was left standing in the middle of the floor fuming.

Margaret walked into the bathroom and closed the door. She needed a moment to settle her nerves. She had never seen this Diane before. She clearly had an opinion tonight and wasn't shy or apprehensive about expressing it. Margaret had only wanted what was best for all of her children, especially her youngest child. When Diane gave birth to her fourth child and then divorced Luis, she was so disappointed. And then Diane had refused to allow any of them to help her. Margaret had planned a different path for her children than she had fallen into and the other two girls had made it, but Diane had steered way off course and Margaret feared she would never find her way back. That's why she was here. She had to do something before it was too late.

Margaret thought of her own life and how it compared to her youngest. She refused to lose Diane to failed dreams. She had to help her achieve some of those goals that had meaning, like obtaining her masters and having a successful second marriage. It was imperative. Margaret knew Diane had failed with Luis and Carlos, but there was hope for success with David and Luis J. And with her help Diane would be triumphant.

Diane sat back down on the couch, senseless, numb, not sure where she could go to get away from there, but she knew she had to leave. She finished the wine, gathered her things, woke Chell and told her she was going out for a little while. Once Chell was settled in Diane's bed so she could hear CJ if he woke up, Diane eased out and headed to the street. She hailed a taxi and gave him the address of her destination. The taxi smelled like a familiar perfume and she wondered what that woman's life was like and whether she was running away from or toward something.

She recalled the words exchanged with her mother and the hurt it had brought her. Why couldn't her mother accept her for who she was? Why did she think she still needed fixing? She had borne four children, buried one, and lost the love of her life. No one else in her family with their degrees and big houses had to manage through that level of pain. Her mother was as suffocating now as she had been twenty-five years ago. Diane knew now that she should never have allowed her mother to come.

When the taxi finally stopped, she was in front of Luis' house. His car was in the driveway and the lights were on. She sat there for a minute, trying to determine why she had gone there; maybe it was because they had both suffered the sting of Margaret Johnson that day, or maybe it was because she hoped he would be able to provide her some comfort and rebuild a little of her confidence. It had taken quite a beating the past hour.

When Luis opened the door, he smiled that warm, comforting smile and opened his arms. She instinctively walked right into them, feeling his strength flow from his body into hers and refilling her energy. She was so glad that he was still able to do that for her. She had missed it so much. After a moment, he led her inside and closed the door.

"Have a seat. Would you like a drink?"

"No, thanks. I've already had two glasses of wine. I should have called first; are you busy?"

Smiling, he said, "You probably should have called since you took a cab without knowing if I was here. But no, I'm not busy, I was just reading. And, I'm glad you felt you could come here."

They sat on the couch and she moved close enough to him that she could lay her head on his shoulder. He placed his arm around her and they sat there in silence for an hour. The only sound was from the *Bose* changer. Luis was listening to some light smooth jazz by George Benson, Marion Meadows and Najee. Thank goodness, it was the perfect mood for what she was feeling. Diane remembered how it used to be when Luis knew exactly what she needed. He wasn't letting her down tonight and she was grateful.

When she was ready, she started with, "I don't know what to say about Mama, except I'm sorry. I had no idea what she was planning. If I had, I would have tried to stop her, warn you, or at least insist that she allow me to come with her. Was it awful?"

"My mother told you when we were at her home that you're not responsible for other adult's actions. And honestly, I wasn't surprised by anything she said. She means well, but her execution needs a lot of work!" Then he laughed his full hearty laugh.

Those words brought a smile to Diane's face, the first one all day. And his laughter always made her heart happy. She told him the details about her discussion with her mother and how it made her feel.

"I tried to defend my actions but honestly, she is making me question them. Am I really screwing up our children's lives that badly? Are they suffering because of me?"

"Diane, I know this: whatever choices you made, they were well meaning. It doesn't mean that you didn't make mistakes. All parents do. But I have never seen a woman love their children more than you. You have always put their needs ahead of yours. Just like your mother claims about herself. Like her, you sacrificed your advanced degrees, your dreams, to give them a good beginning in life."

As Luis said that, it hit her in a peculiar way. She sat with those words for a minute and he gave her time to reflect before continuing. He was on a roll. "How do you think I was able to back away from being involved in their lives, as much as I didn't want to? I could see how well you were raising them and how much David cared about them. That gave me some peace of mind."

Diane smiled and then shared with him how those words had affected her. "You are amazing. I shut you out of your children's lives and you sit here trying to help me feel like a good parent. What the hell is wrong with me? I don't know where to go from here. My mother is driving me crazy in my own home. Who does that?"

"What do you want to do?"

"Scream!!!"

"Go ahead. But then what?"

"You're right. Then what? I need to make some major decisions regarding my life and my future and I need to assess what the children need. I would welcome your help with that."

"What about your mother?"

"I don't know."

"If you don't address that, things will continue as they are."

"But how can I? What should I say?"

"Diane, you know what you need to do. You just have to do it."

"You know me so well."

"No, I don't. If I did, we would still be married. I failed you and I'm…"

Diane put her hand over his mouth. "Enough apologizing. I have to own my role in our marriage's issues. But that is in the past. Let's leave it there. Remember, we toasted to the New Year and new beginnings."

And they laughed together this time. Then he took her hand and kissed the inside of her palm ever so gently. She placed that same palm on his face and looked deep into his eyes. He had seen that look enough to know what she wanted. Smiling, he kissed her lips passionately. She responded and he could tell that there wouldn't be anything to stop them. He wanted her. He had since the night he watched her sleeping in his bed in San Juan.

But, instead, he said, "Diane, you feel so good, and it's been a while. I've desired you for a long time, but you're hurting and have been through a lot. I wouldn't want you to have any regrets if we crossed that boundary. When and if you feel this way again, I want it to be beautiful. Hopefully, you will."

"What can I say, but thank you?"

"Believe me, it's my head talking right now. Listen, if you want to stay here, you can have my bed."

"Thanks, but I need to go home. I have to start facing the music. Besides I don't think I could face my mother if she knew I had stayed out all night." They both burst into laughter.

Luis stopped laughing first and returned to the subject at hand, "I can see in your face that you're ready to take this on and I'm here for you if you need it. But I don't want you to take a taxi at this time of night. Do you want me to drop you off, or you could take Carlos' car. It's still in the garage. Has the alcohol worn off?"

"Yes. I forgot about the car. I'll take it. I don't want to make you come out and I could use it now that David has moved out. Thank you, again, for listening. I really appreciate it."

"My heart is always open. I mean my door." He kissed her again before walking her to the car and getting her on her way.

When Mama came out of the room the next morning, dressed and ready to meet David, Diane stopped her. "Mama, I cancelled your appointment with David. You will not be meeting with him."

"What did you do that for? I have to start working on this right away. It takes time to find a house and then close on it."

"There isn't going to be a discussion between you and David. Michelle and Cindy aren't going to buy me a house, big, small or otherwise. I have already talked to them. When and if I'm ready to buy a house, it will be on my terms."

"Haven't you heard a word I have said since I came here?"

"Every single one, believe me. And, although I appreciate your opinion, I don't agree with it. I am a grown woman. I will make mistakes, but they are mine to make. They are my stripes to earn."

"Where did you go last night?"

"To clear my head and clear a path toward my direction. And what I realized is there is a difference between you being there for me and trying to control my life. You are doing, and always have done, the latter. Now it's time for me to end your interference. Face it Mama, I'm not the woman you envisioned and tried to mold me to be, but I am a woman. I have not turned out to be your third shining star and I have agonized over that for a very long time. But it doesn't mean I'm a failure. I finally accept that I have a different path to follow, but I can still be successful.

"Unfortunately, I forced my views on my children the same as you did on me, but they are strong-willed and hot-headed, so they rebelled. So if I've failed my children, it's because I patterned my child-rearing skills after you. I'm not going to do that anymore. I'm going to learn from how I feel every time you do it to me and change how I interact with my children and grandson. Now, thank you for what you consider an offer of assistance, but quite frankly, I don't need it and I don't want it. I'm going to be all right based on my standards and those are the ones I'm using from now on.

"I am grateful to you for helping to clear things up for me. Now, you are welcome to stay here and spend time with your grandchildren, as a grandmother, but if you insist on trying to interfere in my life, I will call the airline and book a flight for you that leaves this afternoon. Which will it be?"

Mama Margaret shrugged her shoulders and said, "Hmmh." She then headed to the room, thinking quietly to herself, 'Could it be that my daughter has finally come of age?' Margaret stayed for just a couple more days, keeping her place and spending most of the time with the children. She also quietly observed her daughter, Diane, and saw a much more confident woman than when she arrived. This allowed Mama Margaret to leave with a clear conscious, at least for the time being.

Diane had found a desire to reorganize the loose ends in her life. One requiring immediate attention was her marriage. She called David to arrange time for them to talk at his new place. She felt this was a good next step.

Chapter Thirty

Diane walked around David's apartment, impressed with his attempts to make it comfortable and like home. He had decorated it nicely. It reminded her of their home. The colors and patterns were very similar. This brought a smile to her face. He had selected a place that would accommodate and be familiar to the kids on the weekends when they stayed with him. This man had been so good to her and her children, even during the separation.

"David, my goodness, you have been a savior in my life. I didn't drown because of your love and strength. You are such a decent man and you deserve to have that love and tenderness returned tenfold. I haven't done that for you and I apologize."

"You need not apologize. I married you because I loved you and I believed we could make things work, and we have. And we can continue to."

Diane paused a minute before addressing David's expressed desire. She was about to change his life and didn't want to appear anxious to do that to him. "Can we?"

"Yes. If we believe in each other; if you believe in me."

"David, that's such a romantic notion, but I have to first learn to believe in myself. I need to find my inner strength and let that be my pillar. I have spent most of my life finding it in others. I can't do that anymore."

"Then let me help you."

"Did you just hear me? That's exactly what I can't do. Not anymore. My mother, Luis, you, have all been rescuers, saving me from something. I appreciate your willingness, but I have to learn how to help myself."

"I hear what you're saying, Diane, but everyone needs help every now and then. There's nothing wrong with that."

"That's true, but that's not the kind of help I'm talking about."

"So, while you're going through this, what does that mean about us and our family?"

This question reminded her of her previous choice to exclude Luis from her children's lives. She would not do that again. "Regardless of what happens between you and me, I deprived my children of their father once and I won't do that again. They will always be your children. That is, if you still want to be a part of their lives."

"Of course I do, why wouldn't I? I love our children. I will always be involved in their lives, especially Robert's."

"You know that someday Robert will have to be told the truth, don't you? It will be difficult for him, but one day he will need to know his biological father."

"I know, but not now. He's already dealing with a lot with the separation and Carlos. As his parents, we need to minimize the changes in his life."

"I agree."

"So, if you're feeling that way about Robert then you must be softening about Luis. Are you?"

"What do you mean?"

"I asked you once before if you were still in love with him and you told me no. Has that changed? You're not that angry with him anymore."

Again, Diane found herself pausing before her response. His statement reminded her of NaNa's about love and hate. She wondered now, though, just how to answer his question and how truthful she could or should be with him. So she said, "Quite honestly, I am feeling differently toward Luis. I haven't sorted through all of it yet. My emotions have been on a roller coaster ride lately between Luis J's behavior, Carlos and Luisa's death, responsibility of a grandbaby, and so much more."

"Yes baby, it has been a rough ride. That's why I think you need to take your time before finalizing any plans. But know this, I haven't given up on you or us. But I won't wait forever." Without warning he reached for his wife and pulled her to him. His hold was firm and the meaning was clear.

"David, I'm not sure this is a good idea," Diane whispered, looking up at him; his eyes were saying everything on his mind.

"Diane, please, I really want to be with you. After all, we are still married. Haven't you missed me?"

"I have David, but I don't want to complicate things any more than they already are."

Without saying a word, he kissed her lips, softly at first and then with more passion. She found herself responding to his touch, wanting more, the way she had felt that night when she was with Luis…only, the butterflies were missing. He led her into his room and maneuvered her onto the bed. Her mind was racing, was she really going to allow this to happen?

"David…"

He covered her mouth with his. His body moved on top of her and she could feel the excitement in his every muscle and the firmness growing inside his pants. She wanted him, too. It had really been a while now that she had been caressed, since before Christmas, and Luis' kiss and embrace had sparked something in her that was still burning.

She released herself and they made love. Afterward, they lay there in each other's arms. Diane felt physically relieved, but now she was dealing with the emotional guilt. She found herself searching for words to say when David broke the silence.

"Woman, you are incredible. I've always enjoyed making love to you." Rubbing her shoulder, he continued, "I know that we can work this out Diane, but you have to want to as well. It takes two."

"Do you?"

"Yes. I love you, even more than the day we married. That much affection and respect cannot be changed overnight."

"I've never doubted that, David. But our problems run deeper than that. Love is powerful, but it can't solve everything. Sometimes I think it just makes things more complicated."

Diane was saddened by having to say those words. She had always believed that love could solve any problem…until Maria entered her life. But that was a woman she didn't want to think about while lying in bed with David. She turned to get up, but David grabbed her arm.

"David, I have to go. I need to get back home. We shouldn't have..."

"Hey baby, that was damn good. For you, too; I could tell by the way your body responded that you missed me. You missed my good lovemaking. I know just where to touch you. I know just how to make you wet and arch to my stroke."

David had taken her and given her something to miss in that empty bed tonight. He had given her 100 percent of his attention before getting his. There was nothing wrong about that.

Diane couldn't deny what he was saying. He had made her feel good. She had missed that comfort, but it was all physical. Just thinking about his caresses and penetration was making her wet again, so when he pulled her back she went with it.

After their second round, as David slept, Diane slowly moved out of the bed and into the bathroom. It was five o'clock and she had told the nanny that she would be back in a couple of hours; that was nearly three hours ago. She showered and dressed, trying not to wake him.

It felt good being with David, it always had; it was one of the strengths and part of the glue of their relationship. But she knew that nothing had changed and at some point, she would have to address the issues that concerned her. He was going to be hurt by her and this made her sad. She had been making love with him, but her mind was thinking about Luis' touch, his smile and his embrace. She didn't want to hurt David but that's exactly where she was headed.

When Diane opened the door to her apartment, she saw Rosie sitting on the couch while CJ and Robert played at her feet. Her body language told Diane she was more than ready to leave. She had small children of her own and liked to get home by seven so she could tuck them in to bed. She lived in Spanish Harlem and it took her about forty-five minutes to get there. Diane gave Rosie some extra money for her troubles and apologized profusely. As Rosie prepared to leave, she told Diane that there had been two calls: Mr. Rodriquez and Luis J. They both wanted her to call them.

Diane spent some time with her younger boys before calling either of the Rodriquez men. Robert was in his own world playing. She was always amazed at how he could retreat into this world and occupy himself for hours. This was usually the trait exhibited by an only child. Diane assumed it was due to the age and gender difference between him and Chell. CJ, however, stood and came to Diane for his hug whenever she came home. CJ was so affectionate and loving, and he brought such joy into Diane's life, just like Carlos used to do until the arguments started.

"Robert, where's Chell?"

"I don't know. She left a while ago. What's for dinner?"

"Give Mommie a minute and I'll fix something for you."

"Is Daddy coming tonight like he said?"

Diane had completely forgotten that David was planning to take the boys tonight. They had made arrangements earlier in the week. "I think so. I'll call him after you guys finish eating and you can ask him."

"No, call him now. I want to know if he's still coming."

"Okay, buddy." Diane didn't really like his tone, but elected to be a little more lenient given David's recent absence from Robert's life. She put CJ down and reached for the phone. "I'll dial and then you can talk to him."

"No, Mommie. You talk to him. I'm still playing." The phone was already ringing by the time Robert came to this conclusion.

"Hey baby. Why didn't you wake me before you left? I was going to take you home."

"I had to get back, and I have Carlos' car now anyway. Besides, I hadn't planned on being out so long. I told you Rosie was here waiting."

"No problem. I was in a deep sleep of passion; I doubt that you would've been able to wake me anyway," he chuckled. But after a brief pause, he said, "Ummm, I didn't realize you had Carlos' car. When did you get it?"

Diane chose not to respond to either statement. "So, are you still going to pick up the boys?"

"Absolutely. As soon as I shower, I'll be over. You know, since it's getting late, maybe I could just stay with you and get up early in the morning and take the boys out."

"No, David," Diane shot back.

"But…"

"No. Either pick them up tonight or wait until in the morning. I don't want to confuse Robert." Diane hoped that was a reason that David would be willing to accept.

"You're right. But he doesn't have to know. I could sneak in and get up early as if I came in the morning, eh?" After a pause with no response, he said, "I really enjoyed this afternoon; it was great. Didn't you?"

"Yes. It was very nice. You're sweet, and apparently a little slick. How did you come up with that sneak-in, rise-early proposal? David, if I didn't know better, I'd think you've been tippin' with a married woman," Diane said, teasingly, to take off the edge of her rejection.

"Hey, me and Mrs., Mrs. Anderson…I hope you recognize the song. And as for today, sweet is not the adjective I was looking for, but it'll do for starters."

"David seriously, CJ sleeps in the room with me. That's not very romantic. And Robert sometimes gets up and comes to join me. I think it's because of CJ. He gets a little jealous sometimes. You know how you boys can be, right? Anyway, back to the issue at hand, what're you going to do about the boys?"

"Well, you just resolved that, so I'll pick them up in an hour. Can you have them ready?"

"Of course David. See you in a while." Hating to think that he was feeling rejected, she didn't wait for his response. She hung up and then turned her attention to their son.

"Robert, your Dad will pick you guys up in an hour. Go wash your hands and take CJ with you. Then come sit down and eat."

Picking up the phone, she dialed Luis J. The number he had left was the home number, so Diane geared up for Maria's craziness. "May I speak to Luis J, please?"

"Diane?"

"Yes. Is Luis J there? He called me and I'm returning his call."

"He isn't here, but I'm fine thanks. Actually, I guess I should say we're fine. By the way, do you know that I'm pregnant? Luis is going to be a father."

Diane's impatience with Maria's continued immature antics was wearing on her nerves. She purposefully said Luis is going to be a father, trying to play with their names.

"First of all, Maria, I didn't inquire about your wellbeing. I don't give a damn how you are. I mean, honestly, you are just confirming that you are the two-bit tramp I always knew you were. I know you don't have any idea who fathered your baby. But if it was Luis J, I'll have the proof I need to press charges and throw your ass in prison. And believe me, I'm praying that it's his just to get you out of our lives once and for all. So, enjoy what you think is a triumph while it lasts."

Diane hung up the phone and thought to herself, 'She's putting the noose around her own neck and I can't wait to tighten it and see her change colors!' She laughed to herself and thought, 'I guess that surprised the hell out of her when I said I'm praying that it's Luis J's. She wasn't expecting that.' Next Diane called Luis J's cell.

"Yeah, Mami, what's up?"

"I got your message to call you, so since I'm returning your call, you tell me what's up. Although, it is good to hear from you, honey."

"Thanks. I just wanted to know if I had any mail. I forgot to ask you the other day when I came by. I'm expecting my SAT scores."

"You do have some mail, but I haven't looked through it. Hold on." Diane placed the plates in front of the boys and began cutting CJ's chicken. She leafed through the mail in the tray she had purchased for Luis J, anticipating that he would start receiving communications from colleges. Rifling through the envelopes, she found several items and knew she would need to go through them and create some sort of filing system.

As she searched through envelops and brochures, she could hear music playing in the background and wondered where her son was at this time of night. He should be home, sitting at the table eating with the boys. But at least he wasn't with Maria. She just hoped he wasn't with some other girl getting into some more trouble.

She found the SAT scores he was looking for and announced, "It looks like you did very well. Of course your math is really high and your verbal isn't far behind. That's great! You know, we need to talk about college soon. There are a number of things you should be planning now and working on. I would like to offer my assistance."

"Yeah, but a lot is going to depend on Maria and the baby."

"Of course we have to consider that, but I'm sure Maria would not stand in the way of your education and future."

"Of course she wouldn't. Why would you even say that?"

"I didn't mean anything by it. Why are you being so defensive?"

"Sorry, it's just that I have a lot on my mind."

"You keep saying that, but you won't tell me what. Is it something you can share with me?" Diane hoped she could find an opening in his armor that would allow her to gain some footing.

"Not really. I'll get back to you on the college discussion. Thanks for offering to help."

"Sure. You don't have to thank me. I want to help in any way I can. The timing of Maria's pregnancy isn't the best, but if it's your child, we can work together to make the best of it. I'm here for you; remember that. Bye, sweetie." Diane held the cradle of the phone as though somehow her son would feel the caressing.

"Mommie, I'm finished. Is Daddy coming?" Robert asked, bringing her attention back to this son.

"Yes, honey. Go pack some things so you'll be ready when he gets here," Diane instructed Robert as if he really could pack.

As she cleared the table and began stacking the dishes into the washer, Diane wondered where Chell was. She had literally forgotten about her daughter with all that had transpired since her arrival. She would start making phone calls to locate Chell as soon as she finished. And she had to call Luis back too.

As she reached for the phone, through the door walked Chell, followed by David. They were busy chatting and didn't notice the frown on Diane's face.

"Hi, Mami. What's for dinner?" Chell asked, as if all was well.

"First of all, where've you been? I haven't heard from you all evening. You didn't ask me or tell me you were going out." Diane also took this opportunity to observe her daughter's outfit. The skirt Chell was wearing was shorter than it was when they bought it from the store. It had been pulled up and rolled up around her waist.

"I went to the mall with Stacie and Renee. I told Robert to tell you."

"Robert is hardly responsible for relaying your messages to me, young lady. Why didn't you tell Rosie? Better still, why didn't you call me or leave me a note?"

"I did. I called your cell, but you didn't answer. I left you a message. When you didn't call back, I figured it was okay."

"I'll give you that," Diane said, realizing that when Chell called, she must have been physically occupied with David. "But don't assume I've given you permission until you hear it from my lips from now on, understood? Who took you?"

Chell nodded her head yes and answered, "Stacie's brother."

"Stacie's brother? How old is he? And does he have a name?"

"Mami, stop trippin'. He's only eighteen."

"Eighteen? Never again! Do you understand me? And don't talk to me like you're talking to one of your friends."

"What? Why not?"

"Because I'm your mother and because he's too old for you to be hanging out with him. And because he's a 'him.' Understand?"

"David, tell Mami that this is no big deal. I know how to take care of myself. I didn't do anything wrong."

"Chell, I agree with your mother. You are not of age to be out with boys unchaperoned."

"Oh, give me a break. I'm almost fifteen. I'll be able to get my permit pretty soon. You guys have got to stop treating me like a kid."

"We aren't doing that. We're trying to protect you. There's a training process that produces maturity and you're in it. You're not even halfway through it," David responded. He was hoping to diffuse the situation because he could tell Diane was gearing up for a war by her stance and the look on her face. And if she started to tie her hair back, he knew the gloves were about to come off.

"Enough discussion, Chell. Never again. Do you understand me?"

"Whatever." She headed toward her room.

"Come back here. Don't respond to me that way. You remember at all times that I am your mother. You do not, not ever, speak to me like that. Am I clear? After you eat, clean up the kitchen."

Chell didn't respond and continued to walk toward her room.

"Did you hear me, young lady?"

"The whole neighborhood heard you," Chell said, just before closing her bedroom door.

"Girl, I will slap the taste out of your mouth. Get your butt back in here right now!" Diane yelled after her.

"I'm going to change my clothes. You told me not to eat and clean in my good clothes. Are you changing your mind about that?"

"No. But hurry up!" Diane then turned to David and said, "What am I going to do with that girl? I'm obviously not spending enough time with her or paying enough attention. Did you see how short her skirt was? And who the you-know-what is this boy she's hanging out with? I've been so focused on CJ and Luis J that I haven't been in tune with what she's doing or with whom. I didn't know she was hanging out with Stacie either. I don't really like her family's values."

"But you do like yours, right?"

"What?"

"Do you believe you have instilled the right values into Chell? If so, you have to trust that she'll abide by them. You aren't going to be able to shelter her all the time. Besides, she's simply feeling her surge of growth and sensing some semblance of maturity. She's taken on a lot lately."

"I guess. And I know you're right about Chell taking on a lot lately. I really want to correct that, but it's just been us here."

"Come here."

"David..."

"Come here."

Diane walked over to him, feeling somewhat hesitant. He kissed her on the cheek. "You are doing a fabulous job raising the kids. I'm a witness. I know what you've done, even if it doesn't seem like it. Children have to make mistakes – that's what bucking their parents' rules is all about. It's all part of growing up. Besides, no parent is perfect."

"Thanks," Diane responded, even though she didn't agree with his assessment. She felt that emotions were likely influencing that compliment. Based on her daughter's recent poor choice, she was sure that there was more to it than bucking the rules. Girls operate a little differently than boys. And Chell was being led by emotion. She had been so focused on Luis J, CJ, and her own issues that she had neglected her fragile, vulnerable fourteen-year-old daughter.

"Hi, Daddy. Can we go now?" Robert asked, coming out of his room and carrying a bag with a few clothes and a stuffed animal inside.

"Hey, big guy. Almost. Is CJ ready?"

"Why does he always have to go? He's not your son. I'm tired of him." Robert sat down on the couch in a pout and crossed his arms.

It reminded Diane of Luis J's behavior at that age. Here was another kid rebelling against the circumstances that confronted him. He was yet another smart mouth child under her roof. "Robert…"

"Diane, let me," David interjected. He picked Robert up and sat him on his lap on the couch. He talked to him for a while and before long Robert jumped down and ran down the hall, calling CJ.

"What did you say to him?"

"Just a conversation between a father and his son."

"Now CJ, you have to call me Uncle Robert," Diane heard Robert tell his nephew. "Can you say that? Daddy said it may be too much for you right now, so you can just say Unc. Can you say Unc?"

"Unc."

"That's right. Now, let's go. Daddy, we're ready."

"Give me a minute, son. I want to say goodnight to your mom."

Diane looked at David and smiled. He was so good with Robert. It was times like these that she welcomed his manly support and help with managing all of the hardheaded personalities to whom she had given birth. It would be nice if that was enough to welcome his return to their home, but that by itself was not going to solve anything in their relationship.

"What did Luis want?" David asked as he approached his wife and noticed the note on the counter. Diane frowned in response to his question, but didn't utter a response.

"What does he want?" David asked again, pointing to the note.

"I don't know; I haven't had the opportunity to call him back yet."

When David didn't respond, Diane said, "David, come on now, don't go there. Have a nice time with the boys and I'll see you tomorrow."

He pulled her close and kissed her on the lips, as if to make a point, as if to mark his territory. Then he released her and said, "You can't blame me for being a little jealous. So I thought I'd leave you something to remember when you talk to him."

"David, I've never given you a reason to be jealous of Luis and I don't plan to now."

"Oh really? You've never not given me one. Can you honestly say that you love me the same way you loved him?"

"David, I know you did not just ask me that question! Of course I loved you. I still love you. Let's just leave it at that, please."

Observing and listening to his parents, Robert was quick to speak out: "Mommie, Daddy, don't fight!"

David reached down, scooped him up, and said, "Son we're not fighting. We're just talking."

Diane and David looked at each other and knew that they had to be more conscious of their interaction in front of the children, who were all ears.

"Good night Robert, CJ. I love you guys."

David put Robert down, grabbed CJ's hand, and mouthed, "I love you" to Diane as they left.

"Good night Mommie."

"Nite Nite NaNa."

David winked at Diane as he closed the door behind them. She sat on the couch to gather her thoughts. This afternoon, as good as it was, was a mistake. Even though they were still married and she had enjoyed the way it made her feel, it was sending David mixed signals. She understood now what Luis had meant the other night. She was glad he hadn't given in to the familiar. It would have been very easy, but the guilt would have weighed so heavily on her afterwards.

She didn't want to break her vows, but she was definitely finding herself attracted to Luis again. Perhaps David was right by asking her if she loved him as much as she had loved Luis. But at any rate, David was misinterpreting their actions that afternoon and she was going to have to be more careful going forward.

"Mami? Mami? Pick up the phone; it's Papi," Chell called out, breaking Diane's introspection. She had been in such deep thought she hadn't even realized the phone was ringing. She picked up the extension.

"Hey Di, I hope you're doing alright. Did you get my messages?" Luis said in a serious tone that suggested something was up.

"Messages? Rosie told me you called once. And I was intending to call you back, but trust me, so much has been going on since the time I walked in the door until I just closed it behind David and the boys."

"I left another message on your cell."

"I haven't checked my cell. What's going on?" Diane asked, wondering if her battery was dead given all the calls she had obviously missed that afternoon, from Chell and from Luis, and who knows whom else.

"I saw Luis J earlier today and he didn't look well at all. His eyes were bloodshot and his speech was slurred."

"What! Where was he?

"At their apartment. I stopped by to see how he was, and to see if he needed anything. Apparently, he'd been drinking for several hours."

"I just talked to him. He called to see if his SAT scores had come yet. His speech wasn't slurred, but he wasn't at home. Wherever he was, there was music playing in the background." She thought back, wondering if she had missed that he was slurring or ignored it out of denial.

"Anyway, he did well enough that we can be proud of his scores. Especially his math. But tell me about your conversation. What did he say?" Diane was searching for some good in the situation. Just when she thought things might be progressing, here's this news. She swore deep in her soul then and there that before this was over she'd make Maria pay for every second of discontent she'd caused her family.

"Not too much. He was a little hostile and I didn't want to make things any worse between us, so I just left. How did he sound to you?"

Diane paused for a moment to replay the conversation in her head. "Honestly, there was so much going on around here that I didn't notice it at the time. But now that you mention it, maybe he was talking slower than normal and his diction seemed a little off."

"Di, until now I didn't think his drinking was that serious, that it was how he chose to grieve, but maybe we made a mistake to think that it would get better with time. When he first started smoking cigarettes, we should have known that was a sign of a problem. Like I said before, he may have a predisposition to addiction, like my brother. Can we meet tonight to talk about it?"

"Of course, Luis. There isn't anything I wouldn't do to help my son. Just when I think we're making strides and things are settling down, something else rears its ugly head. Some new damn problem." After she was done wallowing, she asked, "Where do you want to meet?"

"I was going to just come over there since I know you can't leave the boys."

"Didn't you hear me say they're with…David. In the meantime, Chell's grounded, so she's in her room."

"What did she do?"

"She's fourteen going on thirty-one, or so she thinks. Maybe we could meet somewhere for drinks and dessert. I just ate dinner."

"That sounds great. But I'm not in the mood for crowds. Would you feel comfortable meeting me somewhere?"

After a brief pause and allowing her head time to catch up with the conversation, she responded, "Sure, I guess that would be okay. I'm going to ask Mrs. Davis to check in on Chell until I get back. What's the address?" When she finished writing, she asked, "Luis, where is this?"

"Someplace I want you to see."

Those were the last words they shared before she prepared to leave. While she waited at the front desk for Luis to respond to the doorman's call, she looked around the lobby of the complex. It was beautiful. The marble floor was shiny enough for her to see herself. The flowers were freshly cut and the aroma filled the air as though it were a spring day. The waterfall sounded so relaxing, she found herself drifting into a place of serenity.

"Wow, you look great."

She was so enthralled with the ambiance that she hadn't noticed Luis' arrival. She instinctively touched her hair and then found herself blushing to his comment, especially because she had just thrown on a casual St. John sweater and skirt set from one of her favorite consignment shops. "Thanks. What's going on? Why are we here?"

"I'm sub-letting a condo here while I do some renovations on my house. I'm thinking about maybe buying something like this as income property. There's so much construction going on over on the west side. What do you think?"

"Not a bad idea. It's beautiful and it would be a great investment. What are you doing to your home?" Fumigating all signs of Maria, she hoped.

"It has too many memories that I'd rather not be reminded of, so I'm ready to make new ones. I'm going to redo the kitchen and upgrade the bathrooms. I've also hired a decorator and we're going to upgrade the flooring throughout and add new paint. It'll probably take a few months. Come on."

She let him take her hand and lead her through the corridors toward the elevators. She had seen these new high-rise buildings springing up in Manhattan but knew that something like this was nowhere in her future given her family dynamics. Besides, she was a house, yard and picket fence kind of girl. But tonight, she could live vicariously through Luis. The doors leading to his tower were about twelve feet tall and were opened by a button on the wall.

"Did you have any trouble finding it?"

"No. I've driven by here before, but never had a reason to stop. How did you find out about it?"

"A colleague at the university is going on sabbatical to Europe and asked me if I was interested in house sitting. The timing couldn't have been better. 'Thank God for knowing what we need and when we need it,' as my mother would say. I'm slowly moving in. Here, this is it," Luis said, opening the door.

The view was breathtaking. They were on the 30th floor facing the Hudson River and all she could see were thousands of stars against the backdrop of the night sky.

"Oh, my God, how beautiful. It's absolutely gorgeous! It's a wonder you leave this place in the morning to go to work. I would spend every waking moment in here and never venture outside again."

"You know, that would be easy if I were independently wealthy, but I haven't mastered that yet. So, I get up every day, drag myself to work and look forward to enjoying it at night. Would you like a tour?"

He led her through the rooms; it was hard to believe the size of the unit given that it was in Manhattan. It had to be about twelve-hundred square feet, spread across two floors. The master bedroom was on the second floor, with a private sitting area, balcony and huge bathroom.

When they returned to the living room, Luis asked, "Would you like a glass of wine?"

"Sure. Luis, this is really 'off the hook' as Chell used to say. Are you really thinking about buying a place like this?"

"I'm not absolutely sure yet. The location is perfect and because we're on the river's edge, there'll never be any construction to block the view. It's nice, but I don't want to rush into anything since I'm not sure where my life is headed." Luis knew in his heart that he would walk away from this unit in a heartbeat if he were given the chance to reconnect with Di and the children.

"Good luck with it all," Di encouraged. "You deserve some happiness." Sitting down on the couch, she lifted her glass in a toast. "To you and your new memories."

He lifted his glass in agreement. Sitting next to her, Luis began telling her of his visit with Luis J and his observations since Carlos' death.

"What do you think we should do? I could talk to his counselor and teachers at school. We need to find out how serious this is. Do you think he's doing drugs, too?"

"It's hard to tell. His red eyes may indicate marijuana use, but I can't be sure. I don't believe he's doing anything hard yet. But we must intervene." They continued to discuss the nature of their intervention and concluded they would have to talk to Maria.

"Above all else, I have to believe she cares about Luis J's well-being," said Luis. "He won't be much good to her if he is the father, if he has a drinking problem. I'm going to arrange to meet her Monday."

"Here?"

"No, at her office."

"Has she been here?"

"No. She hasn't been invited. She doesn't know what's going on in my life anymore. And I want to keep it that way. With the exception of the child she is carrying, I'm done with her."

Diane felt some comfort in knowing that, for once, she shared a new memory with Luis that was all hers and one for the future. A smile came to her face. Then she spoke, "Seriously Luis, why would you think that she has Luis J's best interest in mind when she's done what she's done and allows him to destroy his life? If you ask me, it's all part of her horrible scheme."

"Diane, my dearest, I can only pray that you're wrong. But if you're right, Maria better start doing some praying for herself because I swear I will kill that woman."

Diane smiled again and took Luis' hand and said, "I understand the emotion – trust me I've thought about it myself – but if you do that, surely you'll go to prison and then who will raise your children and grandchildren? So let's stay calm and focused. Besides, I have something waiting for her. Don't worry, she will not get away with her conniving ways."

"Let's connect on Monday after we've had our meetings."

Diane had enough of these thoughts and didn't feel like talking about it anymore. It was becoming much too aggravating. She stood and walked to the window, wanting to get lost in this moment in time — freeze the calmness, lock out the world.

"Ready for your dessert?"

"Not really, but I will take another glass of wine. Did you bake something?"

"All afternoon," Luis replied, chuckling.

Diane stood there, motionless, not wanting to move. Luis handed her the refilled glass, without disturbing her perfect scene. He stood behind her and she could feel the heat emanating from his body. It was so quiet that she couldn't tell if she was hearing her heartbeat or his. She leaned back onto his chest and closed her eyes. He didn't move, other than to shift his stance to accommodate her weight. She slowed her breathing to match his and at that moment, the two of them were like one, just like old times before the kids.

"I hope you don't mind my leaning on you."

"Are you? I hadn't noticed," he said.

She took another sip of wine, sat the glass down and returned to her place of serenity.

"Luis?"

"Uh huh."

"How do you feel about me?"

"What do you mean?"

"How do you feel about me?"

"I feel good about you. Can't you tell?"

She smiled as he shifted his body closer, pressing his erection into her. "That's how your body feels, but what about your mind?"

"Aw, the mind, that's way ahead of the body. My body is actually trying to catch up." He smiled and placed his arms around her.

Diane acknowledged just how good he felt to her, so strong, so inviting. Once again, she wanted him, then and there, but she had just said to herself that she wouldn't betray her vows.

"Why are you asking these questions?"

"I don't know. Caught up in the moment I guess."

"Is that all? I was hoping it was more."

She turned abruptly to look at him and they lost their balance and tumbled to the floor. They both started laughing and couldn't stop. Thankfully, there were pillows strewn on the floor that cushioned their fall.

"I'm so sorry. I didn't realize I would make you lose your balance."

"See what happens when you disturb the natural flow of events."

"I suppose."

She started to stand and he stopped her. "You didn't answer my question."

"I did. I said I was caught up in the moment."

"And I said, was that all, right before you made us fall."

"Oh, yeah, that question. You didn't hurt anything did you?"

"No, and stop avoiding the question."

"Luis, I don't know what to say. I don't know why I asked you those questions. I don't know what I expected you to say. I'm not really sure why I'm here."

"I am. You're here because I asked you to come and you accepted. You're here because you feel sorry for me."

"Sorry for you? I don't feel sorry for you."

"Then what do you feel?"

"Confused. I'm confused about how I feel about you, about us."

"That's fair and understandable. And it tells me there's still hope."

"I better go."

"No, not yet. Besides, I didn't answer your question either. I feel the same way about you right now as I did the day I first saw you. You take my breath away. I enjoy your company and I find myself looking forward to the next time I get to see you."

"Do you? So do I."

"Then don't leave. I would love it if you could stay a little longer. We don't have to talk about this anymore if you don't want to. We can just go back to sitting – not standing! – with each other."

"You're so funny. I didn't mean to make you fall."

"I know, I'm just teasing. So will you stay a little longer?"

"Yes. I will call Chell and I'll check in with Mrs. Davis, too. If everything is alright, I'll stay."

Luis smiled and she moved their wine glasses closer to where they were sitting on the floor. After her assurance that Chell was still at home, she sat back down and they found a position that afforded both of them comfort. Luis turned on Pat Metheny and together they sat in silence listening to the smooth sounds. The next thing that registered for Diane was the smell of coffee. She sat up and looked around the room.

"Good morning."

"Morning? What time is it!"

"About eight-thirty. I didn't have the heart to wake you."

"What happened? I don't remember lying down and falling asleep."

"Actually, I guess we were more relaxed than we thought. We both fell asleep. I woke up around midnight. I figured it was too late for you to go home so I called Chell and let her know. Then I got us a blanket and just laid down next to you."

"Are you sure she's fine? She was home alone all night."

"Yes, she's fine. I talked to her again this morning. She actually got a kick out of it."

"I bet she did. You know she tells Mama about us. She's the one that told her about your house visits." Diane howled with laughter. "I can just imagine the look on Mama's face when she hears about this one! Is the coffee ready?"

Luis laughed heartily as well, then paused before speaking, "Yes. And so is breakfast. I remembered I still owed you something to eat. I put some towels on the sink. Hurry up so your food doesn't get cold."

She moved toward the bathroom, her head still a little foggy, but feeling rested. Luis used to cook breakfast for her on Saturday mornings when they first got married. It was her morning to lounge in bed and be pampered. That was usually followed by some kick-ass sex. Yep, she still had those memories.

She was so relaxed with him last night, apparently more than she had realized. She couldn't even remember falling asleep. 'Wow,' she thought. 'What a difference I feel in Luis' presence. It makes all the difference in the world.'

"Breakfast was great, and so was last night," Diane commented as she finished eating the last piece of bacon and scrambled eggs.

"No regrets?"

"No. I really enjoyed the view."

"And?"

"And, what?"

"Funny."

"And your company. Thanks."

"No problem. However, I reserve the right to repeat this invitation and you have to promise not to make me fall and not to fall asleep on me."

"Deal. I better go. David will be bringing the boys home soon and Robert will not understand why I'm not there."

"I'll walk you out."

As Diane drove home, she recalled the events of yesterday. What a lot to sort out. "Chell, I'm home," she called out as she closed the door behind her.

"Home from where exactly?" David asked.

Diane jumped, startled by this unexpected voice. "David, you're early. How did the evening go with the kids?"

"You didn't answer my question. Where're you coming from, Diane?"

"I was out," she said, unbuttoning her coat and dropping her keys on the table.

"Out where, Diane? Or should I guess?"

"Don't do this."

"You slept in my bed yesterday, made love to me twice, and then you crawled into bed with Luis!"

"David, keep your voice down. This is hardly the time or place to have this discussion."

David said to Chell, who was in earshot, "Your mother and I are going out onto the porch. Watch the boys." Then he grabbed Diane's arm and led her out onto the porch.

"Let go of me, David. You're hurting my arm. Besides, I just got home and I want to check on the kids. This conversation can wait."

"No. It can't. Did you spend the night with Luis?"

She rolled her eyes and sucked her teeth without responding.

"Answer me, damn it!"

Alarmed by the tone in David's voice, she said, "No. No. I did not spend the night with Luis. I went there to talk to him about Luis J's drinking problem and some other issues that you're not aware of. It got late and I fell asleep on the floor. Nothing happened."

"Are you sure?"

"Yes, David, I am sure. Now can we drop it? See, this is one of the issues that concerns me. When did you become so overly possessive and distrusting of me? I am not comfortable with this." David's actions reminded her of when he seemed to have lost control and hit Luis J that morning.

"Did you want something to happen?"

"Okay, now this is getting ridiculous. I'm going inside. When you cool off, you can come in." Diane left him standing on the porch and walked back into the apartment, glad he did not force her to answer that question and didn't stop her. At that point it was irrelevant. What he was missing was how she felt with him.

31 Chapter Thirty One

Diane entered Ms. Jones' office and observed right away how neat it was. Her degrees and certificates were prominently displayed on the wall. She had a Master's in Academic Counseling from NYU. It reminded Diane of her mother's wall of degrees and triggered a reminder of how she herself had fallen short of the goal.

She brushed aside these emotional triggers of memories of her failures because her focus was on her son and how this counselor would hopefully enlighten her regarding their options. Ms. Jones was probably in her mid-fifties, with soft brown highlights in her hair to camouflage the greying.

When Diane approached her desk, she looked up over her glasses and pointed to a chair. Diane had prayed last night that Ms. Jones would be angel-sent and would aid in rescuing Luis J, who was teetering dangerously close to the edge of a cliff. Diane had pulled him back herself countless times when his daredevil behavior presented itself: pulling him back when leaning too far out the window, slowing him down when riding too fast on the bicycle. However, this addiction, this illness, was well out of her reach.

"Mrs. Anderson, first of all, I want you to know that we are committed to helping you get some answers and assisting your son in every way."

Diane nodded and took out her portfolio to record the information.

"I have talked to Luis Jr.'s teachers and his coach. Our records indicate that there have been a number of unexcused absences recently. I have been observing him in class since this was brought to my attention and I have to tell you, some days he's sharp and responsive, others he's very disconnected, asking for passes to the restroom that last until the end of the period. I have his mid-semester grades here and as you can see they're dropping in every class except math, and every teacher has expressed a genuine concern about his performance. I know I don't have to tell you how critical this year is if he is planning to attend college. We have sent several notices home, but never received a response. Did you receive them?"

"No. I did not. Did you call?"

"Yes we did. A woman answered but when she told us she wasn't you, we did not leave any messages."

Diane knew that it must have been Rosie. She wished they had said something to her, as Rosie always made sure she received her messages. But that didn't explain what happened to the notices. She would have to talk to Ms. Chell about this when she got home.

"Anyway, I was relieved when you finally called and requested this appointment. After my evaluation, with no response from you, the next step was to engage child welfare services."

Diane let those words settle in her brain. That was the last thing they needed when trying to get permanent custody of CJ. Ms. Jones was still talking and Diane returned her attention to the conversation at hand.

"We all know how well Luis Jr. plays basketball. He and the team have done well for the school. However, the coach has reported observations similar to mine. Luis Jr. is about to be benched for the remainder of the season. The coach has a very strict policy around attendance, drug use and performance."

"We know that he is drinking. We just don't know how much and how often. What else have your observations told you?" Diane asked.

"Mrs. Anderson, we know for sure he is using alcohol. There are days we can smell it on him. We also know he is using marijuana…for the same reason. My question to you is where is he getting access to this? Do you have alcohol in your home? Is he out late, unsupervised?"

Diane wasn't surprised, but hearing it from a person of authority made her suspicions real. She suddenly felt like a frail parent again. Yet she kept her composure and began her address to the question.

"Ms. Jones, in light of all that has happened recently since my eldest son Carlos' death in November, things have been challenging. He and Luis J were very close and he has not taken his death well at all. In fact, I think he is in denial and his indulging in alcohol and marijuana is his way of trying to numb himself. But we both know that only leads to exactly where he's headed…addiction. At the moment, he's living with a friend since we inherited the custody of our grandchild, Luis J's nephew, which has made our living space cramped.

"We thought it would help to give Luis J the space he needs now because before all of this happened, he shared a room with his little brother. He needed his space and his distance. So we don't see him often."

Diane paused for a moment, as this little white lie was going to give her just enough wiggle room to avoid any further external investigations. For now. But she knew that they were on a very short leash.

She continued, "His father and I have observed some alarming behavior in the past few weeks when he does stop by the house or when we go to see him. When we've confronted him he's always had a quick answer and explanation. But he's been like that all his life. He'd try and explain things away with basketball drills or a heavy load of homework. He'll sometimes even admit that he has a lot on his mind concerning his brother's passing, but we can't get him to share anything beyond that, nor can we get him to accept any responsibility for anything else. He flat out denies drinking even though we have seen the signs, and that's why I'm here. What can you recommend?"

"First, I would like to express my condolences for your loss. The whole school was in shock when they learned about the accident. Carlos was well-liked and respected here. I am deeply sorry about that. With a loss like this, I often recommend you consider family counseling, as these life-changing events can often affect everyone in the household. I seem to recall from Luis Jr.'s records that he has a younger sister who will be attending this school next year as well. It's just a suggestion.

"Anyway, as I mentioned before, every faculty member I have spoken to, and most of the administration, really respect Luis Jr. Quite honestly, that's one of the reasons he hasn't been suspended yet. You and your husband have done a great job raising him. He's mannerable, respectful and his behavior is appropriate. A number of the students on the team look up to him. He's often viewed as a role model for the ninth graders interested in basketball. I just thought you should know that we have observed that about him and your son Carlos. So please do not blame yourself for where we are right now."

Diane sighed and took a deep breath as she nodded in appreciation. It was as if Ms. Jones was reading her mind, or at a minimum, her body language. She also made a note about Chell in her portfolio, as she honestly didn't know how this was impacting her.

Ms. Jones continued, once those words of comfort and recognition had gently placed a band-aid on Diane's discomfort. "Given where we are now, since he is clearly in denial, I would suggest we consider something like an intervention meeting. Are you familiar with that process?"

"Yes. I have heard of it, but I haven't participated in one."

"It is a forum where we would bring together members of his family, select friends, and Coach Watson – people who love him and know him. It should be people whom he trusts and that won't judge him or make him defensive. The sessions can be as long as an hour and as short as the recipient will allow. We would each take turns telling Luis Jr. what we have observed about his behavior and let him know how concerned we are for him. The intent would be to create a safe space for him to open up and talk about what's going on. If that happens, then we may be able to get him the help that he needs."

Diane listened to this professional talking about her son as though he were some drug addict on the street. Those words of comfort she gave out earlier were not enough to even begin to cover the open wound that was bleeding now, with implied words like failure, incompetent, worst parent ever. She finally managed to say, "I can't believe this is happening. How did I let it get to this point?"

"Mrs. Anderson, I have these types of discussions with parents more often than I care to count. In each situation, every one, parents like you who are caring, nurturing, responsible and intelligent, ask that same question. I have to tell you that even in the best of situations, this can happen. Alcoholism and drug abuse are the most common problems our teenagers face when it comes to coping. Most often, they want to avoid facing the pain or disappointment that life throws at them. Adults mimic this behavior as well. It's only the ones with addictive behavior who find themselves unable to function in life. However, with the right support and therapy, he will get better, but we have to act now. Would you be open to the intervention forum?"

"Yes, of course."

"Good. You will need to identify a list of four to five participants. Remember the types of individuals I mentioned to you earlier.

Our school has an affiliation with a program at the Bronx teen center. I called them and set up a tentative appointment with the coordinator. Can you be available tomorrow morning?"

"Tomorrow?" Diane was quickly checking her mental calendar and wondering if Luis could make something on that short of a notice. But she knew he would do anything he needed to for his son. So she continued, "Yes, we can be ready. I'll call you later this afternoon to confirm, if that's not too late."

"That will be fine. I've shared a lot of information with you today. I also have some brochures to give you. If you have any additional questions or would like a referral to a family counselor, please don't hesitate to call me. I really do want to be a resource for you and to help Luis Jr. Take care and I'll wait for your call."

As Diane drove back to her office, she called Luis to brief him regarding her meeting with Ms. Jones and to see if he would be able to participate in the intervention. Once that was confirmed, she wished him well as he was about to enter Maria's office; they both knew it would not be a pleasant exchange.

Maria had agreed to meet with Luis even though she really wasn't in the mood to have another confrontation about the baby. But he had promised her it had nothing to do with that. This piqued her interest though, as she then wondered if it was about Luis J again. That topic was becoming equally as boring to her and she was almost at the point of asking Luis J when he would be able to find his own place.

Her thoughts were interrupted by the intercom and her assistant's voice, "Ms. Diaz, Mr. Rodriquez is here to see you."

"Thank you, Lori. Please have him wait a few minutes while I prepare." Maria had a light schedule that day, but she found pleasure in making Luis wait. She sat in her office drinking a cup of coffee, flipping through some magazines on her desk, and looking at her calendar for the next day. She was about to make a few phone calls to the research and accounting departments when Lori chimed in again.

"Ms. Diaz, I'm sorry to bother you again, but Mr. Rodriquez would like to know how much longer you'll be. I didn't see any conflicts on your calendar, so I told him I would check with you."

'That Lori, always so efficient,' Maria thought. But today she wished Lori would mind her own business. But Maria replied courteously with, "I have some personal conflicts, Lori, but you can have him come in now."

Luis strolled into the room and stopped in front of her desk. He paused just long enough before sitting in the chair across the table from her to let her know that he meant business.

When he sat down, he acknowledged to himself that he had never visited Maria at her office, so he took a moment to observe her command of the room as she sat behind the oversized desk. She had on a two-tone suit, which was a little snug around her breasts. He could tell her body was already adjusting to the child she carried in her womb. Her hair was shorter. She had cut it to sit just above her neckline and it actually looked very cute on her.

He remembered when she landed the job with MetLife, working in the research and development department, responsible for writing grant proposals. Her style of writing had always been one of her academic strengths and was serving her well in this position. The plaques she had received were prominently mounted on her wall. He remembered when they had been given to her. He had been happy to know that she was doing well. He always knew she would excel. Even now he didn't wish her any ill will. He just wanted her out of his life, especially his son's life, and were it not for this child she was carrying, they would be close to making that happen. But right now, today, he needed her help.

"Luis. Were you waiting long?" Maria asked with mock concern, knowing that she had made him wait twenty minutes for no reason. She observed his handsomeness and how good he looked casually dressed in gray flannel slacks topped with a long sleeve black cashmere polo shirt. The turned up collar framed his beautiful face and highlighted his light brown eyes. She hadn't decided who was better looking, Luis or Luis J, but one thing was certain, Luis was without question a MAN. His recent declaration had made him even sexier than before. And she still wanted him.

"I know you're busy and your time is precious, Maria. Thank you for agreeing to see me away from the apartment. How are you feeling?"

"Do you really care?"

"Yes. After all, you're either having my child or my grandchild; you know me."

"Is that supposed to be a dig at me? The doctors told me to avoid stress and you told me this wasn't about the baby, so what do you want, Luis?"

"You're right. No Maria, it wasn't a dig, just the truth. I came to talk to you about Luis J. We want to determine how to help him. I stopped by your apartment on Friday and he was there. He seemed very agitated. His speech was slurred and his eyes were red. So you have to know that he's drinking and or doing drugs."

"Who are 'we'?"

"Out of everything I just said, you focus on one word?" After a brief sigh, he continued, "We are Luis J's family. His mother and me. Now, please tell me what you've observed."

Maria curled up her lip with that, 'Argh, Diane…' look before responding, "Yeah, he drinks occasionally. I haven't noticed it being abusive. I haven't seen him taking drugs, but I may have smelled weed a few times."

"He's not eighteen yet. He's not supposed to be drinking period. Have you said anything to him about it?"

"I told him that he can't use drugs in our home. He drinks beer, but usually nothing heavier than that."

"That you're aware of."

"I think I would smell it on his breath at night," she smiled, waiting for a reaction from Luis.

"There are some drinks that don't fall into that category," he said unperturbed, not taking the bait. "Look, I'd like to think that you would want to help Luis J, and since he's living with you at the moment, you're in the best position to influence him. Will you?"

"I am helping him. I'm giving him an alternative to living with you and his possessive mother. That alone keeps him grounded. I won't treat him like a child. I'm not going to take on the role of his parent."

"I'm not asking you to. Would you just promise to call me if you notice anything out of the ordinary? And, please don't enable him in this. Instead, use your influence to inspire him to his greater qualities since he believes he's going to be a father. And if he is, I would think you would want him to be a role model for your baby."

"I'll do what's right, Luis. After all, like you said, you or Luis J is the father of my unborn baby." Most of the time this was said to be hurtful, but this time the words settled in for her. She thought about the man she loved standing in front of her and his son, who was like a mirror image.

In that moment she realized that she was using Luis J as a surrogate for his father, and said, "Look, I care very deeply for Luis J. He really reminds me a lot of you. Well, in some ways," she said, with that Cheshire cat grin. "I have been keeping an eye on him. I'll do what I can. Is there anything else? I'm pretty busy at the moment." When he didn't respond, she added, "You owe me, Luis; don't forget that. And you can be sure, I will collect."

"Maria, what I owe you, I'm not sure you want to collect. But thank you for agreeing to do what's right. Have a nice day," he said as he rose and strolled out of the office the same way he had entered.

Diane and Luis had agreed to meet that evening for dinner in a little quiet bistro near her midtown office to talk about the next steps regarding their son's future. She had made arrangements for the kids and was already there when he arrived. She began by filling him in on the rest of the details regarding her discussion with Luis J's counselor and that she had confirmed the intervention meeting with the counselor. They were about to discuss who should attend when Diane's cell phone rang.

She excused herself and answered it. "Hey David, what's up?"

"I called the house and Rosie told me you were out. Where are you?"

"Excuse me?"

"I said, where are you?"

"I'm having dinner. Why?"

"With whom?"

Diane rolled her eyes before she saw that Luis was staring right at her. She had to shut this down, so she said, "David, this is not a good time. I'll call you when I get home."

"Are you with Luis again?"

"Look, I do not have to indulge your twenty-nine questions. Please don't make me remind you of our current circumstances right now." Breathing deeply, she then said, "Good bye, David," and hung up the phone without answering his question or allowing him to respond.

"Is there a problem?" Luis asked, pushing the food around his plate instead of looking at her. He wanted to give her some wiggle room to respond as she felt she wanted to, although he knew that it was David she had just shut down and he had to smile to himself as he recognized the actions of a man trying to stake his claim. Luis had made a vow to himself that he was not going to add to the problems in their marriage, but if David opened the door, he would definitely walk through it.

"No, not really. Anyway, who should we ask to attend?" Diane asked, shifting topics.

"Obviously the three of us and the coach, I guess."

"I'm not so sure David should be there," Diane said, thinking about the criteria Ms. Jones had given her. Especially the part about anyone who would be judgmental and David certainly was, which antagonized Luis J. Therefore, he would not be invited to the session. She could envision David picking at her, Luis and Luis J the entire time.

With Diane providing that crack, Luis peeked inside. "I haven't wanted to pry, but how are things with you guys?"

"David was at the apartment to drop off the boys when I got home that morning after falling asleep at your house and he's been analyzing my every move since. Chell told him I spent the night with you – out of the mouths of babes, huh – so he's not handling it well."

"Did you tell him it was totally innocent? Even though I didn't want it to be," Luis said, with a smile meant only for her.

"Cute. That kind of response I don't need anywhere near Chell or David," she said chuckling, but at the same time taking note of his comment. "I gave him some mixed signals and now I'm paying for it. I'll talk to him this weekend and work it out."

"I'm sure you will," Luis replied, offering words of encouragement. He knew exactly what "mixed signals" she was referring to. She had slept with David but was now worried about how he was interpreting her emotions. That's exactly why he didn't allow them to be together. But Luis didn't want Diane because she was love-starved. He wanted her to be with him with a clear head, body and soul.

Once they were set regarding the actions required for the intervention, Luis briefly shared Maria's observations and then they put a pin in it.

They were ready for tomorrow. They ordered after dinner drinks. Diane had an Irish coffee and of course, Luis had his cognac. As they enjoyed this icing on the evening, they also recognized that they felt a little lighter than they did when they arrived.

As she sipped on her coffee, hands hugging the warmth of the mug, Diane studied Luis' face, his inviting smile, and enjoyed his sense of humor, which all reminded her of the man she once loved.

Luis paid the check and then walked Diane to her car. They stood by the door for a moment as awkward with each other as a couple on their first date until Diane finally ended the awkwardness with a kiss on his cheek. As she drove away, she saw that he was still standing on the sidewalk watching her. What he didn't know was that he had given her enough to carry her over for the night and well into the next day. Tiny butterflies flickered in her stomach and a smile embraced her face. Yes, she loved that man!

When Diane arrived home and put the key in the lock, the door was pulled opened and Diane almost fell. Standing on the other side was David. He looked menacing to her and she wondered if that's how he had looked that morning when Luis J walked through the door.

"David, what on earth are you doing here? Did something happen with the kids?"

"What do you think I'm doing here? No, nothing's wrong with the kids. We need to talk."

Relieved, Diane tried to move pass him to enter her home as she responded, "That's true, but it's late and I'm tired. Besides, you didn't tell me you were coming over. You shouldn't just show up."

"Oh, so now I have to ask for permission to come home?" he asked, blocking her movement further into the apartment.

"Yes. You moved out, remember? You forfeited your come-and-go-as-you-like rights. Technically, this is no longer your residence.

You have your own apartment, in your name. Look, I don't want to fight. David, sit down, please."

These words seemed to have an impact on him and he moved to the side. Diane closed the door, removed her coat and made a quick inventory of the house. She heard the TV in Chell's room and knew she was safe in her room. Robert's door was closed and she could see the nightlight under the door, so the boys were asleep. With that confirmation, she turned her attention to David. He was perched on the edge of the sofa and watching her every move.

He started the conversation with, "Diane, was the other day a dream? Didn't we make love? Didn't that mean anything to you? How could you have left my arms and gone to Luis? And if that night truly was innocent, then why were you with him again tonight?"

"David, I don't really owe you an explanation, but I'll give you one. First of all, I am finally doing what you advised me to do a long time ago, to allow Luis to participate in his children's lives. Luis J is having a serious problem with alcohol and drugs. Luis and I have been meeting to discuss some preventative actions. I have not slept with him. We fell asleep on the floor that night because we were both exhausted."

"Both of you slept together, on the floor, huh? How did that happen exactly?"

"David, I'm not going to give you a play by play. Don't do this; please don't let your imagination get ahead of you. It just so happened that we sat on the floor and the next thing I knew, I was waking up. If you recall, I was exhausted that day when I left your apartment."

Ignoring that statement, David continued, "Were you drinking?"

"Yes, I had had a glass of wine to relax me, but what difference does that make?"

"A lot. It means you were in a comfortable enough position to fall asleep."

"David, I didn't intend to make love to you last week, but we did. The moment was perfect and we fell into one another's arms. And that's okay; we are married. I needed it and so did you."

"You're damn straight we're still married. I may have moved out, but I'm still faithful."

Diane continued, not responding to David's accusation masked in his declaration. "Now I'm concerned about how you're interpreting those actions. For goodness sakes, look at the way you're acting right now. And it didn't just happen – your behavior has escalated over the past few weeks and I'm uncomfortable with it. I don't like this aggressiveness you're displaying."

"Well, are you sorry we made love now? Because you weren't that afternoon! I know how much you enjoyed it and I know you weren't faking it. And if I'm aggressive, it's because I don't like hearing that another man is sleeping with my wife and wining and dining her. I hate that you feel you have to turn to Luis for comfort and guidance. Yes, I said you shouldn't shut him out of the kids' lives, but I meant just that – the kids' lives. You don't need him in your life; you have me. The idea of you turning to Luis for comfort makes my blood boil," he ended, throwing one of her magazines against the wall.

"David, calm down. I wasn't faking anything. I said it was good. I meant that, but it doesn't solve our relationship issues. Our love-making has always been good. That's the least of our worries. But there are other things that concern me, that concern us, and good sex doesn't fix them. We aren't going to get back together just because we spent a few hours sweating sheets," Diane said, not responding to his comments about Luis.

"Sweating sheets? Is that supposed to be funny or sexy? I'm not sure which. But if you could just stay your ass away from Luis, maybe sweating sheets and leaning on me would be enough for us to get back together."

"Oh my God! Did you just curse at me?" Diane put her hand on her hip and pointed at him. "Don't you dare use curse words when you talk to me! Look, I need you to listen to me. You're so hung up on Luis that you apparently didn't hear anything I just said about Luis J. We're holding an intervention tomorrow for him, that's how serious this is, and you're drilling me about wine and dinner with this boy's father? Do you think that right now you could find some emotional support for me and allow us to talk about it after that meeting? I'm really tired and need to get my energy up to be ready for this."

David softened his tone. She needed him and that's what he wanted to hear. So he said, "Why didn't you tell me? What time? Where?"

"I don't have all the details yet. The school counselor suggested we keep the group small."

"Oh, okay. So let me guess, just you and Luis, right?"

"Yes. The counselor warned us to keep the group small. I'm sure you're supportive of that; after all, we're all trying to do what's best for Luis J, right? And just so you're clear, Luis did suggest we include you. But it is my choice that you not be there because it would be a distraction for Luis J." Diane was once again trying to calm David down by shifting the focus toward Luis J.

"Diane, of course I'm going to support Luis J in whatever way I can. I just don't want you to shut me out in favor of Luis. After we were together the other day, I realized how much I missed you. I want to move back here with you. I want us to go the distance on this and work on our marriage. We vowed 'til death do us part,' remember?"

"I hear everything about what you want, but I don't hear you asking me about what I want or need. And furthermore, the last thing that excites me is that you realized you missed me because of sex."

"Oh come on Diane! You know I didn't mean it like that. I can give you what you need. I know how. You know I do," he said, as he walked closer and filled her space.

She had to pause to breathe in deeply; his large frame always consumed her. "Then why are we separated? You still haven't addressed your possessiveness or aggression that I just told you make me feel uncomfortable. Where is it all coming from?" she asked, stepping back to claim her space. "Look, like I said, I have a lot of things on my mind and it's getting late. I need to make sure the kids are settled and I still have a few calls to make. I think it would be best for you to leave now."

'Ah, no,' David thought. 'She's not going to dismiss me like that. Not tonight, not ever.'

"I'm not leaving," he said. "I'm going to stay here tonight. I'll take you to the intervention meeting tomorrow, even if I can't attend. At least I will be there for you when you come out. Luis J needs to see that we are a united front. I think that some of his behavior is because I left. It's too much change all at once."

Diane listened and actually heard David. "Perhaps that is true regarding the impact of too much change," she acknowledged. "But David, for goodness sake, the real reason you want to take me is to control my interaction with Luis and that I will not allow!"

"Mommie, why are you yelling at Daddy?"

Diane turned to find Robert standing in the doorway. She had been trying to be mindful of their voice levels, but this last exchange was just too much for her. She was about to respond when David, once again, took the lead with him.

"Hey little man, we didn't mean to wake you. We're just a little upset about some grown-up things. Your mother and I love each other. Everything's alright. Go back to bed now and I'll be in to tuck you in soon. Tomorrow morning I'll get you ready for school."

"You're going to come back?" Robert asked, rubbing his eyes.

"I'm actually not going to leave. I'm going to stay here tonight. Now get back in bed."

"Yay! Good night, Daddy. See you in the morning."

David smiled as he saw how much joy this brought to his son. He returned to his conversation with Diane once Robert closed the door.

"I can't believe you just did that. What the hell do you think this is? You're treating me with the same disrespect as my mother and I will not tolerate that. I asked you to leave, now get out!"

"Diane, calm down. I don't know why I told him that. I was just trying to allay his fears. You didn't see the initial look on his face."

"I don't care what look he had on his face. I do not want you to spend the night. Now please, leave!"

"No, you listen. How dare you say that I only want to control you and Luis' interaction? Control is your game. I just want to support Luis J. And besides I can't leave, not now. I told Robert I was going to stay. I've never lied to him before and I'm not about to start now. He looks up to me. I know you want him to learn how to be a good and honest man."

"How convenient. You can stay, but you aren't sleeping in my bed."

"Oh, but that's exactly where I plan to sleep."

"You, my dear, are out of your mind," Diane said, leaving David standing alone as she headed toward her bedroom. The more she thought about David's actions, the more she realized she was seeing a side of him that she had never seen before. He was becoming very possessive, willful, intrusive, and controlling, much like her mother, and she didn't like it, not one bit. He was also displaying a mean streak, infused by jealousy, and honestly, that scared her a little.

Diane sat on the edge of her bed collecting her thoughts. She wondered, again, if they were doing the right thing regarding Luis J. What if this intervention succeeded in alienating him even more instead? Diane couldn't bear to think of her son feeling even more resentful toward her. She started to dial Luis' number when the door of the bedroom opened.

"What're you doing?"

"Making a phone call," she said, pointing to the receiver in her hand.

"When you're done, can we talk some more? I've been out there thinking."

"No, David. I'm talked out. When I finish these calls, I'm going to bed. I need to be fresh, have a clear head tomorrow. I already told you that."

"I get it. Alright, we'll talk tomorrow morning, after the kids have left for school."

David left the room, returning to the living room, but didn't close her door. Diane got off the bed and slammed it before making her call. CJ stirred in his crib and uttered a few groans. While the phone rang, she stood by his crib and rocked him gently.

"Hey, Di," Luis chirped. "Are we all set?"

She shared her recent doubts with him and waited for a response.

"I don't believe that," Luis said finally, a little more serious now. "Will he be defensive? I would expect that. Will he deny the allegations? Yes. But in the end, I have to believe we're doing the right thing. Many people try to quit on their own, but that rarely works. Luis J has to choose to stop himself, but he needs to know that we're there for him at the same time.

"And like the counselor told you, he also needs to work through his issues himself, and it's work that neither Maria, you, nor I can do for him. Diane, we're doing the right thing. This is our only alternative as I see it. If our relationship with him were better, maybe we could try another approach, but unfortunately, that's not the case. With any luck, after a while, things will improve. Hopefully."

"I'm so afraid of losing him."

"Yes, I know you are. So am I. But if we don't do something, we'll lose him anyway."

"You're right. Thanks for the reassurance."

"No problem, anytime. By the way, do you need a ride to the meeting or are you going to drive?"

"No, I'm okay, thanks."

"Sorry, I wasn't trying to push. I just thought maybe we could talk on the way."

"I know and I appreciate the offer, but thanks anyway. I better go. Goodnight."

"Okay. Hey, don't worry."

'Easier said than done,' she thought. Just as she was about to doze off, she felt David climb into the bed. She really wasn't ready for this fight, so she just got up and grabbed the blanket off the bed.

"Where are you going?"

"To sleep on the couch. I told you I was not sleeping with you."

"Fine, Diane, you stay. I'll sleep on the couch."

Diane was relieved and returned to the bed. She was exhausted and needed a good night's rest. The last thing she wanted was a horny estranged husband trying to collect on her wifely duties.

In the morning, David took Robert to the bus as he had promised and returned to find Diane sitting at the kitchen table drinking coffee. Damn, she looked sexy. He had always loved watching her. And when she was mad or slightly disturbed, her mouth did that thing that ripped through him and possessed his soul.

Aware of him watching her, Diane poured David a cup and thought about the points she wanted to make. Then she gestured for him to join her.

"David, I didn't want or feel like having a confrontation with you last night, and honestly, I don't have the energy to now. But, I really didn't appreciate the corner you backed me into. I hope that you never put me in that kind of situation again."

"I love you, Diane. I told you last night that I want us to get back together. I know that's what's best."

"Based on what, David? Some idea you have of what you think I need or what you think I don't need?"

"Both. We were good together for a number of years and I know we have many more great years ahead of us."

"Stop it, David, just stop it! Ever since that night I fell asleep at Luis', you've been acting strange. I've never known you to be possessive, but the stunts you pulled yesterday were unbelievable. First, you tracked me down at the restaurant, then you showed up here last night, trying to sleep in my bed like we were back together, and then you insisted on taking me to the meeting today. I can't live with anyone like that, let alone be married to them. Honestly, I feared that you might force yourself on me."

"Hey, I'm not behaving any way that isn't warranted. You're my wife, damn it, and it isn't acceptable for you to spend the night and have dinner with another man, not even your ex. I think you would agree with me if the situation were reversed. Hell, Luis just likes crossing the lines. He crossed them with Maria and now he's doing it with you and me. And frankly, I'm almost too insulted to dignify addressing the fact that you'd think I'd ever force you. I'm not that sort of man."

"But David, you said it yourself a few months ago – what kind of marriage do we have if we can't trust each other? And I'm saying that I didn't trust your behavior last night. As for my actions, nothing is normal anymore. Carlos' death changed all of that. Not to mention this baby of Maria's on the way."

"Uh, Diane, for clarity's sake, it's not you that I don't trust. I see how Luis looks at you. I know how much he wants you back, even though he's gone and knocked up Maria. I'm not just going to stand by and let him back into your life. You're still my wife, as of now, and I don't intend for that to change. I will do whatever I need to do to keep him away from you. Whatever."

There it was again, an even more intense anger than she had ever experienced from him before. Lowering her voice to regain control of the energy in the room, Diane said, "David, it's not up to you to determine what I do with my life. Where do you come off with that craziness? And further, Luis is not crossing any lines. He's always polite and considerate. In fact, he has more than once acknowledged the man that you have been in my life. He has even said that if he had not thought well of you, there was no way he could have left his kids under your authority."

"Well, that's good to hear. Still, what's crazy is you wanting to give Luis another chance. Don't you remember the pain he caused you? Can't you see that Maria isn't really out of his life? How can she be? She's having his child."

"We aren't sure whose child she's having. Luis J believes it's his."

"Luis J just wants to get back at his father. I don't believe the baby Maria is carrying is his, but I do believe it's Luis'. And that's what's going to cause you heartache once again. I won't stand by and let him do that to you this time. And one day soon, you'll thank me."

"This is incredible. That's what I'm talking about. David, you are not my father. You do not get to decide anything for me. I do that. I'm not going to allow you to dictate anything to me. I never told you I wanted to get back together with Luis. I had dinner with the father of my children, that's all. We have four children and a grandson. You can't expect me not to have some interaction with him. And David, if the child is his, they lived together common law for as long as we have been married. So if it is his child, so be it. I'm not as fragile as you seem to think I am. Luis will do right by Maria and the baby, but they won't get back together."

"'Some interaction,' as you put it, is different than having dinner and falling asleep in his arms. Did he tell you that? Diane, I am warning you. He will break your heart again. You'll see."

"That's it! Don't you see that you are acting like my mother, the big bad fairy who comes into my life uninvited, judges me and tries to make my choices, what I should do and what I shouldn't, and how? One of those in my life is more than enough. I didn't choose my mother, but I certainly didn't marry you for that kind of relationship.

"This discussion is over. I'm still your wife and as long as I am, I will honor our vows. But let's be clear where the boundaries are; you cannot dictate to me anything about my choices outside of that. What's more, my heart can only be broken if I hand it to someone and let them break it and I don't plan on doing that. No, I choose to manage my own heart. But David, more to the point, you moving back in here is not an option at this point. And based on our recent conversations, we are even farther away from it than I thought. I'm leaving now, so you have a nice day!" Diane opened the door, went outside and hailed a gypsy cab.

32
Chapter Thirty Two

As Diane rode to the Bronx center, she allowed her mind to replay the conversation with David. She couldn't understand why he chose this day and time to probe her on the state of their marriage when he knew she was about to confront her son about his addiction. Everything was at risk in her child's life. His whole future was up for grabs and she and Luis were doing everything they could to get him back on track. Why wasn't David able to put this boy, whom he helped to raise over the past six years, as a priority? When the taxi stopped in front of the center, Diane took a deep breath to calm her nerves before getting out. She had originally planned to drive but changed her mind after the talk with David. He had left her nerves on edge and the morning traffic would have driven her over the cliff for sure. She also prayed that the intervention would go well and that perhaps she, Luis J, and his father would be able to drive home together.

When she opened the big steel door to the center, she found Luis standing on the other side. He had gotten a haircut and was very clean-shaven. It looked nice on him. He stood there looking pensive until he caught her eye and his jaw relaxed and the wrinkles above his eyebrows began subsiding.

It was now his turn to observe Diane. She had sounded so worried last night. He hoped that she had been able to get some rest. But the half smile she gave him said she was still in that frail space this morning. He reached out to her and kissed her on the cheek.

Welcoming the affection, she said, "Good morning. Have you been here long?"

"No. About 15 minutes. I didn't know what to expect from the traffic so I gave myself a little extra time. What's your state this morning?"

"Oh Luis, I just pray this goes well. I am so apprehensive about doing this."

"I know exactly what you mean. But we can't get our hopes up too high. We don't know how the events or his reactions will unfold. Admitting addiction doesn't usually happen on the first confrontation. But if we can at least get him to stay and listen to what the counselors have to say, it will be a start," Luis said and then asked, "So, what else is on your mind?"

Diane thought for a few seconds before responding. She wasn't sure how much she wanted to share about her wacky morning with David. But then she acknowledged that Luis wouldn't stand in judgment of her like her mother and now David would, so she chose to be honest with him.

"No matter what I say, David thinks you and I are seeing each other romantically. He's so afraid of losing me that he's seeing signs of infidelity everywhere. He's been so jealous and possessive these past few days. At first it was just reading my messages, but now he's tracking me down. The behavior is getting completely out of hand and I told him so last night. What he doesn't realize is that he is pushing me away from, not towards, any reconciliation."

Luis thought to himself, so David was there with her last night. That would explain some of the tension he heard in her voice. He honestly didn't blame David for how he was feeling, but obviously David didn't know Diane as well as he should. Luis had learned first-hand that you couldn't make Diane do something by bullying her. It was too reminiscent of Mama Margaret and that was not good company to keep. But Luis chose to use this teachable moment as a chance to help her understand things from a man's perspective.

"And for good reason, Diane," he began. "As much as I hate saying this, he's doing exactly what any man would do who is fighting for his woman and his marriage. He knows how much we have shared and that the recent series of events have brought us together, and that since then we are growing closer. It's only natural for him to be suspicious. But he's fighting for who he loves. Don't be too hard on him for that. I told you before that I respect David. He's a good man. And I understand his fear of losing you. Hell, I lost you to the 80/20 rule."

"What's that?"

"You haven't heard of the 80/20 rule? As Chell would say, where have you been?" Luis said, chuckling. "It's somewhat of a long story and it looks like they're ready for us."

Diane appreciated his perspective and it gave her a chance to look at this a little differently, from David's point of view. "Okay, I'll ease up a little on him…but just a little," she teased. "I would tell him to thank you, but I suspect that would only cause another jealous outburst." Diane laughed, as she imagined him standing in her kitchen demanding to know how many times they made love before the intervention session began. She closed her eyes and shook her head to reboot her thoughts. "But right now, I just want to get mentally ready for this confrontation."

Luis reached over, hugged her and smiled. She had found tons of comfort just from his presence, but the embrace gave her just the additional dose she needed.

Ms. Jones opened the door and beckoned them to enter the room. She was dressed conservatively today in a navy blue Dana Buchman suit ensemble that reminded Diane of the Ellen Tracy suits she loved, but with more edge to it. It added to Ms. Jones' trust factor. As a banker, Diane recalled that they were encouraged to wear navy as the color of choice because it inspired trust. People wanted to feel they could trust the bank employees depositing, withdrawing or investing their money.

She smiled at Ms. Jones, who looked pleasant enough considering what they were about to do. Diane introduced her to Luis and watched the reaction on her face. She clearly found him attractive, too. Diane scowled a little, even though she had no claim to this man.

The conference room was filled with standard Lane line office furniture. There were a few tables that had all been pushed up against the walls, leaving room for six or seven chairs to form a semi-circle in the middle of the room, with one chair noting the center. The fabric on the chairs was a turquoise green, meant to be soothing and warm. There were two other men in the room who turned as Diane and Luis approached them.

Ms. Jones began, "Mr. Rodriquez, Mrs. Anderson, I was just informed that Luis Jr. is on his way with Coach Watson. They should be here in about 10 minutes. Obviously Luis Jr. doesn't know why he's coming here. So, while we wait, there are a few rules we want to go over with you. Are we waiting for anyone else? Will your husband be joining us?" she asked Diane.

"No."

"Or your wife?" she asked, directing the question to Luis.

Looking at Diane and smiling, he said, "No. Everyone's here, so we can get started."

Ms. Jones pulled on her suit jacket to adjust it and then proceeded to introduce the two men who were on staff at the center. One was Stan

Morales and the other, Terry Davidson. Stan was twenty-four and of mixed heritage like Luis J. His father was from the Dominican Republic and his mother was African American. He had graduated from Hunter College in New York City about two years ago and had been working at the center since then. Terry was eighteen. He was black and a product of a single parent upbringing. His father was raising him and his sister; their mother had died from a drug overdose. He was now interning at the center while attending college at night.

As they talked, Diane made observations of her own. They were both about Luis J's height and physical build, but Terry looked very thin. Much thinner than Diane would want her son to be. It reminded her of how Luis' brother looked when they saw him in Puerto Rico. She wondered how long Terry had been free of addiction.

Stan took the lead in the discussion and reviewed the guidelines for the meeting. They laid everything on the table to prepare Diane and Luis for the worst and when they were finished, Diane had to admit that, unfortunately, they had done a really good job at it. Her expectations were now very level set and she was no longer sure she wanted to go through with the session anymore.

Luis quickly noticed that look and said, preemptively, "Di, in for the penny, in for the pound."

They milled around the room, sipping on lukewarm coffee, waiting for their son's arrival. About ten minutes later than Ms. Jones had predicted, the door opened and Luis J walked in with Coach closely behind him.

Looking around the room and finally settling his eyes on his parents, Luis J asked in shock, "Mami, Papi, what are you doing here?"

Stan spoke before Luis J's parents forgot any of his instructions.

"Luis Jr., my name is Stan and this is Terry. Please come in and have a seat," Stan said, pointing to the chair in the center of the semi-circle.

Coach instinctively took a seat next to Diane. She wondered how many of these he had participated in and if that was his normal place in the room.

Without moving, Luis J watched Coach take his seat before asking, "What's going on here?" As he waited for a response, he looked at Coach, then back at his parents. Had everyone conspired to lie to him?

Diane fidgeted in her seat, fighting the urge to reach out to her son and reassure him that they were there to help him. But the counselor's instructions were very clear, so she stayed still and silent.

"Here, Luis Jr., please sit down," Stan repeated, having now walked over to Luis J and invaded his space. Stan clearly commanded the room and Diane recognized the calm yet firmness in his voice. It reminded her of how Luis used to talk to the boys. As a result, Luis J moved toward the chair, without taking his eyes off his parents. He was searching for answers in their faces and could identify none.

"Hey man, relax, we're here to help you," Terry chimed in. He was sitting to the right of Luis in the last chair.

"Help me? Help me with what? Mami, what's going on?"

Tears started forming in Diane's eyes, but she turned away from him and did not respond. Once again, he reminded her of when he was a child with no control over a situation but a desire to make you think he was in complete control.

"Luis J. May I call you that?" Stan began, but didn't wait for a response. He didn't need permission in this room. "The reason you're here is for us to let you know that these people – your father, mother, school counselor and coach – are all very concerned about you and your wellbeing. They came to us for assistance so that, in turn, we can help you."

"You still haven't told me what this is about. I don't have any problems. If somebody doesn't tell me something right now, I'm leaving."

"Do you know what addiction is?" Stan continued, ignoring the threat.

"Addiction? Of course I know what addiction is. I've seen people with addictions. Why are you asking about that?"

"I'm asking about that because we believe you have addictive behaviors. They first exhibited themselves with your cigarette smoking and now it would seem they have escalated to an abusive use of alcohol and drugs. Do you deny that?"

"Is that what this is about? I'm not an addict and I'm certainly not an alcoholic or drug addict. You're all wasting your time and mine. I'm leaving."

"No, Luis J, you're not. Not until you hear us out first. Once we have had our say, then we can talk about your next action this morning," Stan stated, quite firmly, standing just to the right of Luis J between him and the door.

Luis J pushed out his chest to show he was not weak or afraid to take him on should it be necessary and said, "Why should I?"

Stan smirked and said, "So you think you can take me? Guys twice your size have tried and failed. I think you should stay because your future depends on it, Luis J; because your family and coach are in for the long haul and if they are, you damn well should be willing to listen to why. Hey man, don't kid yourself; addiction is quite serious. I know, because I sat in that same position, in that same chair, myself six years ago…and it saved my life."

Stan proceeded to tell Luis J his story while everyone else listened. Stan hit "rock bottom" his senior year in high school. One weekend he consumed a pint of gin in a matter of three hours and after still not feeling the effects he wanted, he moved to scotch with beer chasers. When he woke up, he found himself in the hospital. They told him that his sister had found him passed out on the floor and called 911. He had been diagnosed with alcohol poisoning and other side effects.

When he was discharged from the hospital, instead of his family taking him home, they brought him to an intervention because they feared for his life. The participants at his session also included family and friends, and they each took turns telling him how his actions were impacting their lives. Stan said that most of the conversation he had dismissed because he, like Luis J, didn't think it was a problem. But when it was time for his sister, who was two years his junior, to share the impact of his addiction on her life, it became his sobering moment.

She told him that the night she found him unconscious, she took her first drink. She drank because she thought he was dead and she didn't want to live without him. He had been there for her through bullying, body image issues, and just provided overall guidance in her life. When she overheard the paramedics telling the dispatch officer that her brother's pulse was very weak, his blood pressure low and they weren't sure if he was going to make it, she just knew he was going to die. It was more pain than she could bear.

So, after they rolled Stan out on the stretcher, she knelt down and picked up one of the unfinished bottles, taking her first drink. She could still remember how it burned going down and how she could almost immediately feel a light-headedness. The second swallow went down a little easier and so did her body as it slid down to the floor. She was still crying, but it was more controllable as the effects of the alcohol entered her bloodstream. She didn't remember much after that, but when their parents returned from the hospital, they found her asleep on the floor, the nearly empty bottle next to her.

As she retold the story, Stan said the images of his sister lying on the floor from alcohol and fear for his life and the shock his parents must have felt finding her there was more sobering than any other story he heard that day during his intervention. He had driven his sixteen-year-old sister to take her first drink and to pass out. He knew how much she looked up to him and all she was doing was mimicking his behavior. But that life was not what he wanted for his sister and the only way to stop her was to get help himself.

In two months, Stan said he would be celebrating his sixth year of being clean and sober. When he graduated from college, he took the job at the center to help him maintain his sobriety, and also try to help other teens help themselves.

The images were painted very clearly on the walls of the room for everyone to see. Diane saw the paramedics, his body on the stretcher with tubes connected to him, and an oxygen mask on his face. It reminded her of when Carlos was in the hospital. Next she saw Stan's parents standing over their daughter holding their breath in hopes that she was just sleeping while feeling completely powerless to help either child. That child was only two years older than Chell.

All of this was hitting a little too close to Diane's heart and she put her hand over her mouth to keep from screaming. She looked at Luis J and he was looking down. She couldn't tell if there was any reaction to Stan's tragic story.

Stan sat down hard in his chair. He looked physically drained, very different than when they all first entered the room. Every time he had to relive that night, it was very emotionally difficult, but once he was done, every time, it made him a little stronger.

Next, Terry stood and moved closer to Luis J to share his story. It was equally compelling. Terry was only in his second year of sobriety.

He began drinking at fifteen and escalated to drugs six months later when the alcohol no longer gave him the buzz he craved.

He was ultimately kicked out of school because he was absent too many days and his grades were failing. Because of his mother's addiction and ultimate death, his father had a zero tolerance policy in their home. So Terry moved in with a friend. It was ideal because he no longer had to follow any rules or meet anyone else's expectations. He had total freedom and he loved it. But what he didn't realize was this freedom was actually the beginning of his downfall. His roommate was also an addict and was experimenting with even more vices than Terry. These vices were expensive, so Terry found himself having to sell drugs to fund his habits. There were a few dealers in his neighborhood and he hooked up with one who owned the most territory.

One day, when turning in his money, Terry was informed that his take was short. He couldn't for the life of him figure out why. He remembered counting and recounting the money after all of his sales. As he stood there emptying his pockets and counting his stash, he was joined by the supplier. This guy was about 6'3", 285 pounds and carried a nine millimeter as his firearm. He was a man of few words and nobody crossed him. Terry had heard countless stories of dealers coming up short either because they were sampling the product or just stealing the cash. Either way, it did not end well for them.

Terry tried to explain that he had all the money and that someone on the train must have picked his pocket, but honestly, he was so high he couldn't remember what had happened. The supplier and two of his crew circled him and the beating began. When Terry came to, he was in the hospital. He had been kicked and beaten before being shot three times. The doctor told him that with the extent of his injuries and the location of the bullets, it was clearly a miracle he was still alive.

Terry knew he was being given a choice and it was time for him to choose wisely. If he returned to the streets, next time he probably wouldn't be as lucky. While he was recovering in physical rehab, he met some of the counselors from the center. They were there to conduct group sessions. Stan was a speaker at one of Terry's sessions, and he eventually became Terry's sponsor. Ironically, those beatings and bullets he took actually had saved his life.

Tears were steadily falling down Diane's cheeks by then. She looked at Luis J and prayed he was hearing what his future could be like if he did not wake up now, face his addiction, and make the choice to give up drinking and drugs.

It was time for Luis, Diane and Coach to try to reach Luis J. Luis began first.

"Luis J, do you know that every morning I am greeted by an unbearable pain before my feet hit the floor? It is the pain that took up residence in my heart the night Carlos died. Now, it would be easy for me to give in to that pain and turn to drugs, pills, alcohol, anything to numb it. But my parents taught me that how you handle pain defines the person you will become. It's easy to give in to difficult times in your life, but it is best to face these times with your feet firmly planted on the ground and maintain a forward momentum.

"When you drink and smoke marijuana, it alarms me because of your Uncle Antonio. You saw him at the funeral. He is not well. He is on the verge of losing everything in his life, including his life. He is very sick and it's from his addiction. I don't want to have to bury another child, Luis J. Please don't make me have to do that."

When it was clear that Luis was finished, Diane wiped the tears from her cheeks and said, "Luis J, I have made a lot of mistakes in my life, especially when I made the decision to keep your father away from all of you, but especially you. You and your father had such a close relationship and I just ripped it out of your arms and away from your reach. Then I pushed Carlos until the only option he felt he had was to move out. I have seen you struggling with these losses in your life, but I didn't step in to help you deal with them. Instead, I started pushing on you, driving you away from home and away from me.

"I should have noticed your addictive behavior when you started smoking, especially because you're a gifted athlete with a promising future and your smoking was compromising that. But I knew Carlos' moving out was emotionally difficult for you and honestly, I was relieved that you were only smoking. But now I see that it was just the start of a bigger addictive pattern. I am so worried about you, especially because you're not living at home and like Terry, you have no adult supervision."

This slipped out of Diane's mouth before she could stop it and she hoped that it wouldn't cause Luis J to put up a shield in defense of Maria. When he didn't say anything, she continued. "I, like your father, am so worried that something bad will happen to you. You could get into a car accident or worse. Can you imagine how Chell would feel if something happened to you, too?"

The last person to address Luis J was Coach. His conversation was very short and simple.

"Look Luis J, you are one of the most talented young men to come through this school since Carlos. I believe in you, support you; I know what you're capable of. Hell, you're one of the few great athletes that actually has a great academic record, too. But it's because I see that greatness in you that I am so disappointed in your recent life choices. First it was that thing with Danielle and now this. You are literally killing your future. It's a waste son, it's just a waste."

Luis J, who had been silent and still, shifted in the chair after hearing their experiences and perspectives, but still didn't make eye contact with anyone in the room. Instead, he stared into an emptiness that settled in his head. So the coach thought Carlos was talented, too. To be truthful, he heard them and yet it seemed like a dream. They all seemed so far away. Strange, but just then he wanted to talk to Dany. What did she think? Did she think he was an addict, too?

Diane in her head questioned the reason for Luis J's quiet demeanor. Had he slipped away into some shell and was staring into the abyss? Was he listening? Did he understand they were trying to save his life?

"Look, I don't need this. I don't want it. I'm not out of control like you guys were," Luis J finally said defensively, pointing to Stan and Terry. "I'm not drinking that much or that often. Sure I've missed a lot of school lately, but I've been sick. I've had this recurring stomach problem, that's all."

"The one where you throw up in the morning?" Terry asked.

"Something like that," Luis J replied, ignoring Terry's attempt to be witty. After all, what did he know, he was only a year or so older and was just getting started on this "recovery journey" thing.

"Oh, is that all. Most people call that H.O.," Stan added.

Luis J chuckled. He didn't expect to hear that.

"Oh, not the H.O. you're thinking about; I'm talking about hang over man; sometimes it's a precursor to alcohol poisoning and a sign of addiction. Denial is also one of the signs. Thinking you're in control of your use is another. Can you tell me when you had your last drink? What did you drink and how much?" Stan asked.

"Of course I can. It was about two weeks ago. I had a beer."

"That's a lie, Luis J. Your father told us you were drunk and possibly high on Friday. Did that skip your mind?" Terry asked.

Shocked again, Luis J defended himself, "I wasn't drunk, Papi. Why did you think I was?"

"Because you were. Your eyes were red, your speech was slurred, and the school records show you left early that day," Luis responded.

"I had something to do. It was an excused absence."

"Excused by whom? Your parents didn't excuse you; we at the school didn't excuse you," Ms. Jones interjected.

"Regardless, you didn't answer my question. Did you have a drink Friday?" Terry asked again.

"Maybe a beer, but I wasn't drunk."

"A beer. Are you sure it was just one beer? Maybe it was two or three. And you said you hadn't had a drink in a couple of weeks. Are you confused about what day it is?" Stan fired at Luis J.

"No. I made a mistake. Don't make a federal case out of it."

"Terry, I think he's getting mad. Are you getting mad Luis J?" Stan asked.

"Screw you man!" Luis J shrugged and dismissed them.

"You sound mad. The next thing would be for you to shut down. Is that where you're going next?"

Luis observed how much Luis J reminded him of himself when he was fed up. He recognized the behavior and knew it was going to take an act of God to get him to respond. The DNA was amazing. Just seeing his son this way made his heart ache. He hadn't been around to see himself reflected in him, but here it was. His mannerisms just warmed his heart even more. This son was the most like him, indeed. Luis wanted to speak, but followed protocol.

"Hey Luis J, are you ready to leave?"

"I've been ready to leave. You guys are all wrong."

"Okay man, you can leave. But you have to answer one question for me first," Stan said, standing up.

"What's that?"

"Do you wish you had a drink right now?"

Luis J didn't appear to be ready for that question and it took him a moment to respond.

"Come on, that wasn't a difficult question. Were you just thinking that you wish you had a drink right now?"

"No."

"You're a liar. I see all the signs, man; you can't fool me. You can't sit still, you keep licking your lips, and your palms are sweating. I've been there, man, and I know. That's what we're telling you Luis J – you can't run from the addiction. It will hunt you down like a rabid dog. You can't escape it. You have to face it if you want to beat it. Otherwise, it will destroy you. It'll kill you, man. Truth. Real talk."

Luis J didn't respond. He just sat back in the chair, dazed by all that was being said, but never changing his expression or composure.

"But hey, if you're ready to go, go. We're not gonna stop you. You have to make this decision for yourself."

Luis J was relieved and as he rose to leave, Stan continued with a few more remarks, "My card is on the table in the hall. Take it or leave it, it's up to you. But remember, you won't get too many more of these chances before you hit rock bottom like both of us. And you best believe there are hundreds of others who come to this center with a rock bottom story. Why don't you be smarter than them? Hell, smarter than me and Terry, and avoid the rock bottom experience."

Luis J walked out not knowing where he was going since he had gotten a ride from Coach. They all watched as he closed the door behind him. Diane broke down, crying uncontrollably, but was somehow able to whisper in between her sobs, "We failed. Now what?"

Luis pulled Diane out of the chair and held her.

"Mrs. Anderson, we didn't fail," Terry said. "Luis J isn't ready. He hasn't fallen far enough yet. Until that happens or he realizes how much danger he's in, we can only make ourselves available in case he reaches out."

"I'm sure he took my card. I'm sure he'll call. I just can't tell you when," Stan offered, trying to reassure her.

Luis thanked all of them and led Diane out of the conference room, his arm still around her.

"You tried to warn me, but I didn't want to believe you. I honestly thought he would hear the counselors, Coach and us, and be scared enough to seek help."

Luis pointed to the table and said, "Maybe he was. I saw myself in him today, Diane. He heard them. It was his pride, his manhood, that stopped him from admitting what he knows to be true. He didn't like that we had all ambushed him. I wouldn't have liked that either. But I would have appreciated the information and the insight. Come on, let's go get some lunch."

Diane noticed that Stan's card was missing from the table where Luis had pointed. Once she put on her coat, Luis returned his arm around her shoulders and they walked to the lobby.

"This is really hard, Luis, but I guess one thing I heard in there is that we have to take this one day at a time. But what about you? How are you doing with this?"

"I'm not sure. I'm worried about our son. I saw too much of me in there. I hadn't recognized our similarities. We all try to numb ourselves from pain. I chose sex, so did he in the beginning, but after Carlos' death he sought something that he could do all the time. It's a way to avoid the pain we feel."

Diane listened and said nothing as they headed to Luis' car to go get something to eat. Sitting in his car in the parking lot, David watched the two of them walk to Luis' car and Diane get in. He couldn't believe she didn't anticipate that he would come for her. Had he not told her that he would drive her in the first place? Surely she must have known that he wouldn't let her take a cab home as well, after the kind of emotional encounter he was sure the intervention would provide.

David looked at the flowers on the seat next to him and wondered why she was so drawn to that man. It was almost as if she had an addiction, too. After all Luis had done and continued to impose upon her, David could tell she was still in love with him. But he was not going to let Luis take Diane away from him; after all, what did love have to do with it? She just didn't see Luis the way he did, the way Mama Margaret did, too.

Mama Margaret had called David the morning she left and warned him about Luis. She had told him of Luis' renewed interest in Diane and Diane's weakness for him. Mama Margaret had told him how Luis was always finding ways to be with Diane. But David was not going to stand by and let him take away the love of his life. After all, Luis had lost his opportunity for Diane when he took up with Maria.

David sat there for a moment, deciding whether to go to his apartment or meet Diane at home. He elected to go back to his place; he didn't want to anger her any more than she already was about his behavior. How could he explain that he had let her mother get inside his head? Instead, he had to get into Diane's head somehow. But he needed a new strategy. This one wasn't working for him.

33 Chapter Thirty Three

Luis J slammed the door to the apartment and yelled out, "Maria?"

"I'm in the kitchen. How was your day, sweetie?" She asked the question, but already knew based on the tone in his voice.

"As if you don't know," he continued, joining her in the kitchen. She was standing at the sink with her back to him and he noticed that her hips seemed wider.

"What's wrong?" she asked, turning to face him.

"Why weren't you there?"

"There, where? What're you talking about?"

"Don't act like you don't know. I know you know. My parents scheduled an ambush today. They think I'm some kind of addict. It was insulting and I can't believe they embarrassed me like that in front of Coach, the school counselor and total strangers. Did you know about it?"

"What happened?"

"I just told you. The coach tricked me into going with him and when I walked into the room, there sat my parents, the school guidance counselor and two total losers. They went on and on about how they were strung out and tried to get me to admit I was. I told them to forget it and I left."

"Don't you think your parents are just worried about you?"

"I'm sure they are, but for all the wrong reasons. They just want to interfere in my life, find some reason for me to have to move back in with one of them and out of here. I'm not about to do that. They were treating me like a kid before; I can't even imagine what it would be like now if they think I'm drinking or doing drugs. I would be in total lockdown."

Maria smiled at his expressed resentment towards his parents and commitment to her, or at least to the option she was giving him. "Honey, I don't think you're an addict. You do like drinking, but it seems like you're in control of it to me. Aren't you?"

"Of course I am. My mother blows everything out of proportion. She doesn't accept that I'm almost 18 and with that adult title may also come the title of father. She's treating me the same way she did Carlos and look how that ended. She drove Papi away and David – but I'm going to stand up to her. I'm not going to retreat into some corner. She always complains about her mother controlling her life, but she has done the same damn thing to all of us."

"Luis J, baby, you're upset. Why don't we go sit down?"

"No, I don't want to talk about this anymore. I'm going out."

"Why don't you just stay in? We don't have to talk; we could just be with each other."

Luis J declined. As nice as the invitation sounded, his need for a drink was greater. He went to his room and closed the door. He grabbed the fifth of tequila he had hidden in the closet. It was almost empty. He drained the corner and tried to remember when he had bought it. It didn't matter; he would have to go by Derrick's to get some more. That was closer than going back to Carlos' neighborhood and less risky.

Maria let him drive her car so he took side streets to get to Derrick's as quickly as possible. He turned up the radio and rolled down the windows to drown out the throbbing that was building in his head and to give him some fresh air. The thirty-minute drive felt like ninety.

When he finally got to Derrick's, there were a few guys and girls sitting around in his living room. There were always people there. Some looked a little shady, but that was to be expected given Derrick's line of business.

"Listen, Derrick, I'm running low on my stash. Can you hook me up with a couple of fifths?"

"Already, man? What are you doing, partying every night?"

"Funny. But I do have a couple of friends who can really drain it, if you know what I mean. So, you got my back or what?"

"Of course…but you might want to try something a little stronger, bro. It can get you there faster and keep you there longer with fewer side effects. You interested?"

"No, man, 'quila is fine for me."

"Whatever, but I told you before, if you change your mind, you know where to find me." He reached inside the cabinet and handed Luis J a bag.

"You didn't have to go to the store?"

"Naw, man. I knew you would be by either today or tomorrow, based on how often you've been here over the past coupla weeks. I keep track of my client's addictions," Derrick said, laughing and handing him the brown bag.

Luis J froze for a moment. Did Derrick just call him a client and an addict? There it was…from someone who had no idea what he had just been through that morning. There was a mirror on the wall behind Derrick and Luis J looked at himself in the mirror. His external appearance looked the same, but something inside was changing.

When Derrick shook the bag, Luis J handed him the money and took it from him. "Thanks, man. I'm not expecting any buddies by, so this should last me for a while."

"Right, sure. I'll see you later this week, man," Derrick said, looking at the guys on the couch and laughing again.

Luis J clutched the neck of the bottle and shoved it inside his jacket. He opened the door and walked onto the balcony. He looked down into the yard to see if his brother's or David's car was in the parking lot. When he didn't see either, he thought about stopping by the apartment to spend time with Robert, CJ and Chell. He hadn't spent much time with them in several days and he was feeling it was long overdue. But he didn't turn in the direction of the apartment because he didn't want to risk running into his mother. Besides, he was still mad about the day's events.

Just standing there recalling them made him anxious. He pulled the bag from his jacket, opened the bottle and took the first swallow. It was soothing. He followed that with a second and then a third. He was returning the bag to its place inside his jacket when he felt someone touch his shoulder. He turned to see Chell standing directly behind him.

"Hey, big brother. I thought that was you. Are you coming by to visit us?"

"Hey, Chell, I just stopped by Derrick's to pick up something. Where you headed?"

"Home. Are you really gonna come all the way over here and not even stop by?"

"Yeah, unfortunately. I gotta run. I'll stop by some other time."

"Well, before you go, do you have a sec to talk?" Chell asked, looking down and using her foot to draw circles on the ground.

"Just a second. What's up?" Luis J was starting to feel the buzz from the alcohol so he didn't know how helpful he was going to be to his sister.

"Is it true that Maria's pregnant?"

"Yeah."

"And she doesn't know who the father is?"

"Who told you that?"

"I heard Mami talking on the phone. Is it true you might be the father?"

"Yeah, it's true. It's sorta complicated. Why?"

"Wow. Isn't she old enough to like be your mother?"

"Shut your mouth. You don't know anything about it and you shouldn't be eavesdropping on Mami's call. Look, I already told you I don't have a lot of time. Is that all you wanted?"

"Sort of. You know this is kinda weird, right? I mean you knocking up Papi's girlfriend."

"Chell, I don't need your smart-ass comments. I'm out," he shouted, walking past her and heading to the stairway.

"Luis J, wait. Please. I didn't mean anything by it. I'm not judging you or anything. I wasn't trying to piss you off."

When he didn't stop, she shouted after him, "Luis J, please!"

He stopped and turned around. "You didn't piss me off, Chell. It's getting late and I need to get back. I'll call you sometime this weekend."

"It can't wait that long. I don't have anyone to talk to. I always thought you would be there for me. I really need you."

Luis J walked back to his sister and looked down into her face. He saw how sad she looked and once again recognized how much she had been maturing. Luis J remembered how Carlos would always comment on how much he was spoiling her. But this wasn't a request from a spoiled child; it was from one who was in some kind of trouble.

He touched her shoulder and lowered his voice. "Hey, I am here for you. I'll always be here for you. I'm going through some tough times right now, but you can always call me if you need anything. I just can't be at the house when Mami's here, that's all. So, what's going on?"

"I may have a problem," she replied, returning to drawing circles on the ground with her foot.

"I'm listening. What kind of problem?" With the way his day had been progressing, he hoped the next words out of her mouth weren't addiction, alcohol or drugs. He didn't think he could take any more, not so subtle, coincidences.

"Now, don't get mad, alright?"

"About what?"

"I don't know if I should tell you. You have to promise not to tell Mami or Papi. Do you?"

"Chell, what is it? I'm not making any promises and you're still going to tell me. What?"

Looking down at her feet, which were no longer moving to form any pattern, she said, "I might be pregnant."

"What the hell? You have got to be kidding me right now!" Luis J was so shocked he almost dropped the bottle nestled inside his coat. He had to shift to keep it from crashing to the ground.

"I'm late. I've never been late before. I'm just not sure."

"Chell, you are not standing here telling me that you have been having sex! How the hell did that happen?"

Frowning up at him now, she said, "You, of all people, should know."

"Look little girl, you know exactly what I mean. Uggh, who have you been with?"

"Roger." The frown now softened and she repeated, shyly, "Roger."

"Roger? Who the hell is Roger?"

"My friend Stacie's brother."

"You mean Roger Winn?"

She nodded.

"Roger, who is on the basketball team with me? That asshole? What the hell are you doing going out with anyone, let alone someone four years older than you? Chell, damn…" Luis J was in complete disbelief.

"Luis J, he's really nice. He takes us to the mall and buys me stuff. He says I act older than most girls his age."

"Well, that's fucking good, because he isn't going to live long enough to sleep with anybody else!"

"Luis J, what do you mean?" she asked, alarmed by the anger in his tone.

"It means I'm gonna kick his ass! I know that low life MF and his ass is mine. He doesn't have your best interest anywhere on his moral barometer. And you may be pregnant? Girl, what the f… You shouldn't be sexually active yet anyway. What were you thinking?"

Now her tone matched his and she said, "I didn't tell you this for you to go after him or for you to lecture me. I really care about him. I don't want you to mess this up. I just need help figuring out what to do."

"Mess what up, Chell?" Luis J said, seething. "That asshole has about three girls he bangs regularly. You don't really think he's just with you, do you?"

"Yes he is. He broke it off with his other girlfriend."

"Really? And when did this happen?"

"He told me about two months ago."

Grabbing her by the arm and leading her away from the house, he continued, "Chell, we need to talk and we can't have this conversation in the hallway. Call Mami and tell her you're going to a friend's house to do your homework. I'll bring you back whenever she wants you to come home. Do you have anything you're supposed to be doing right now?"

"No. Rosie is with the boys."

"Good. Make the call from the car," he said, now pulling her behind him. He couldn't believe what he had just heard. He had just seen that

S.O.B. yesterday under the bleachers with some white chick. It was pretty clear what they were doing and now he learns that Roger has been banging his sister, too. And that asshole didn't even have the decency to wear a condom. If that were the case, it would be no big revelation if Chell was pregnant, and, if they were lucky, that would be the extent of it. He prayed that she hadn't contracted some disease. 'This is some bullshit,' he concluded.

When Chell finished the call, Luis J asked, "How long have you been seeing him?"

"About four months."

"Four months? And he told you two months ago that he broke up with his girlfriend…so there was overlap, and you were okay with that? How many times have you slept with him?"

"Well, I wasn't sleeping with him at first. We were just hanging out. I guess we made love about six or seven times starting about three months ago. That's why he said he was breaking it off with his girlfriend," she smiled, remembering how good it made her feel to know she had ended that relationship.

"My God, Chell! Made love? Is that what you think you were doing? Is that what you think he calls it? Girl, why didn't you talk to me about this first? You knew I knew him. That's why you have big brothers. To keep hard legs like that mofo in check." Luis J realized that he had said big brothers, plural, and it made his stomach hurt. Carlos was gone, so all Chell had now was him and he hadn't exactly been there for her.

"Talk to you about what? Besides, you haven't been around much lately."

"For starters, about making him use a glove? Do you know how many diseases are out here? You could contract something and ruin your whole life."

"The first time we did use a condom, but then he told me he didn't like how it felt. He told me all the big girls were on the pill and asked me if I was. It wasn't like I could ask Mami to put me on the pill, so I told him I was."

"Shit, Chell, what the hell were you thinking?"

"You and Dany had unprotected sex. Why is this different?"

"It was only that one time. And I know she isn't screwing the rest of the high school. Damn, I'm going to kill this mutha!" Luis J envisioned slamming Roger into the floor, lockers, walls, anything that would put him into a world of hurt. "So, how late are you?" he asked, calming down a bit.

"About two weeks."

"And you say you've never been late before?"

"No, not like this."

"Then we need to find out for sure. There's a drugstore on the corner. I'll give you some money to buy a test. See if you can find one that will give you the results right away."

Luis J waited in the car for his sister. The effects of the three swigs of alcohol were completely worn off. Conversations like this one can be sobering. This was really fucked up. How was he going to help Chell if she really was pregnant? Not to mention that their parents would probably jump off a cliff if they found out.

When Chell returned to the car, he drove her to his place so she could take the test. He knew Maria would be cool with it. They rode the rest of the way in silence. What a day this had been. But surprisingly, for the first time in a long time, Luis J didn't want a drink. He had to keep a clear head so he could help his little sister, who had crossed over into the land of adulthood in a big way.

When they entered the apartment, Luis J called out to Maria, as he had earlier that afternoon. She joined Luis J in the living room and was surprised to see Chell by his side. When he had left, he was so irate about the day's activities, the last place she thought he would end up would be home.

But this was supplying her access to yet another Rodriquez child! Maria smiled to herself as she waited for an explanation. But Luis J skipped the pleasantries and went straight to the reason Chell was there. Maria took Chell by the hand, led her to the bathroom and closed the door. It reminded her of when she had saved Luis that day from Chell's behavior in his office when she was a toddler.

Luis J was getting frustrated with how long it was taking. He had never had to experience this, so he had no idea what the procedure entailed. While he waited, his mind wandered to try and figure out how in the hell Chell had opportunities to meet with Roger, let alone screw him. His mother had kept him and Carlos under such tight reign. But how could he know; he wasn't at home to monitor Chell's actions and clearly his mother had way more to contend with now with less help. Everyone was so caught up in CJ getting settled, David moving out, and all in his business that Chell was left to handle her own pain. He finally heard the bathroom door open and the footsteps getting louder as they came back to the living room.

"It was negative," Maria stated. "It's negative, Luis J," she repeated when she noticed he was still staring at them.

"Thank God! Sweet Jesus," he blurted out. "Are you sure? Could there be any mistake? I mean, she said she's two weeks late."

"I know, but these tests are fairly reliable. If she hasn't started in a few days, though, she may need to go to a doctor because something else may be going on."

"Doctor? I can't go to the doctor," Chell said. "Mami would never understand. I'd be grounded for life."

"Honestly, you should be! You just dodged a bullet, little girl. I forbid you to see Roger. Do you understand me? From this day forward, he's dead to you, and I mean it, Chell; I'm not kidding!" Luis J informed her.

"Luis J, you can't tell me what to do. Besides, I told you we really care about each other."

"Really? You think so? Chell, I just saw Roger yesterday banging some chick under the bleachers at school. Does that sound like someone who cares about you? Does that sound like someone you want to be with? Not to mention you're not even fifteen. You shouldn't be having sex with anyone anyway."

"You're lying, Luis J. You just don't want me to be with him."

"I don't want you to be with anyone, Chell! Damn it girl, I was older than you the first time I had sex and I'm a guy! If you don't stop seeing him, I'll tell Mami and Papi. I swear I will."

"You have a lot of nerve! You were with Dany and other girls. Plus you hate Mami and Papi...and you would side with them against me? I can't believe you!"

"I don't hate them; I'm trying to do what's best for you. And you don't know anything about me and Dany, or me and anybody else. That's Roger in your ear. So listen up, Roger is going to dump you as soon as he finds out you're not on the pill or the excitement wears off. Believe me, I know what I'm talking about. He's playin' you, lil' sis. I've done it to a few girls myself, but not fourteen-year-olds."

"He's not you. He's kind and gentle to me. I don't know why I told you in the first place! I don't know why I thought you would be there for me now when you haven't been for a long time. I want to go home. Will you take me home now, please?"

"Chell, I do care about you. I love you. I just don't want anyone to hurt you." Luis J paused because he had heard those very words from his parents a lot lately and met them with the same attitude as he was receiving from his little sister. "I'll take you home, but you have to promise me you won't sleep with Roger, or anyone else for that matter, until we find out what's going on with your body. Will you do that for me?"

"Fine. I need to go now so I can do my homework."

"Is that a 'fine, I will not sleep with Roger or anyone else' response?"

"Yes! Now will you please take me back home? Thanks, Maria."

"Of course. I hope everything works out for you. And for the record, listen to your brother. He's right."

After dropping Chell off, Luis J headed back to the apartment in deep thought. Unfortunately, he didn't think he had really gotten through to his sister, so that only left one alternative and he would address it the first opportunity he had. He stopped in the park to find some calmness before going home. He just sat there with his thoughts, clear now for the first time in a long time because they weren't clouded by alcohol or weed. He had been so self-centered with his pain that he hadn't taken the time to consider the effect of his actions on everyone else, especially Chell.

She was in for a long road ahead of her, whether the test was accurate or not. She would never be the same after this. She had no idea how Roger trashed girls and labeled them as whores. She would have that reputation before she even walked through the door of the high school in the fall. And no matter what he did to Roger, it wouldn't change anything for Chell. He thought about Stan's story from earlier in the day. Stan's sister had suffered because of his actions and now Chell was suffering from his. But he was not going to let her down anymore. He headed back to Maria's so he could plan his course of action.

Chapter Thirty Four

Luis J walked up to his teammate in the locker room and pushed him from behind into the lockers.

"What the …" Roger turned his head slightly to see who was behind him and then said, "Luis J, get the hell off of me, man."

"You son of a bitch. I'm gonna kick your ass, right here." Luis J released him so he could turn and face him.

"What the hell is wrong with you, man?" Roger asked, brushing his shirt like he was removing any remaining signs of Luis J's grip.

"You know what's wrong with me and I'm warning you to stay the hell away from my little sister. Are we clear?"

"Man, she approached me. Get a grip."

"How about I get one around your neck? I don't care what she did. She's not old enough to be with you and you damn sure don't deserve her. Keep your hands off of her or answer to me," Luis J said, standing his ground and ready to knock Roger down.

"Hey bro, calm down. What the fuck?" Maine shouted, as he entered the locker room and placed a hand on Luis J's arm in a preventative action.

"Let go of me, Maine. This asshole is sleeping with my little sister. I'm not going to tolerate that shit."

"Fuck you, lil' man. I can do whatever I want with whoever I want. You don't control shit here. You better try to get your own house in order."

"What the hell is that supposed to mean?" Luis J redirected his attention from Maine back to Roger. Roger played forward, so he had a few inches and a few more pounds on Luis J, but to Luis J, Roger was the same size as "Mugsy," but with none of his skills or prowess.

"You drink like a fish and knocked up your Dad's girlfriend. Chell told me all about it." He stopped just long enough to entice the bystanders around the room to listen to the conversation. "You gotta lot of nerve trying to tell somebody about what's right. Now back the fuck up off me before I take you out."

Before Roger could finish the sentence, Luis J leaped forward, knocking Roger to the ground, and the brawl began. Arms and legs were flying, stools were being knocked over and Maine was doing his best to try to break it up without taking a blow. The rest of the team just circled as their bodies rolled around the floor, with some teammates adding fuel to the fire with taunts and comments.

"Break it up…do you hear me? Luis J, Roger, break it up!" Coach yelled at the two of them as he tried to pull Luis J off of Roger.

Once Coach was on the scene, some team members began pitching in to help break it up, while others left so as to not be affiliated with the fight at all. Once they were separated and standing on opposite sides of Coach's extended arms, he said, "What the hell is wrong with you guys? Don't we have a game in twenty minutes?" When he didn't get a response, he spoke again, "Somebody better tell me something, quick!"

"It was personal."

"It's always personal, Luis J. But not in my locker room. Alright, everyone else get into uniform and hit the court. I want ten laps from everyone because you all stood there and watched. Maine, you're excused from that, but then I want three-on-three drills. Move it! And tell those other cowards to join you. Just because they tried to slip out of here after the fact doesn't give them a pass. The two of you," he said, removing his hand from their chests and pointing his finger from side to side, "In my office, NOW!"

Luis J picked up his gym bag and threw it on the bench before following Roger and the coach to his office. Slamming his pad on the table, Coach started, "Sit down, both of you, and tell me what this is about. Roger, you start."

"Aw, this boy is trippin', Coach. Everyone knows he's stressed right now. I don't know what set him off this time. You've seen his game, or should I say, so-called game, lately. He's hyped about some stupid shit. I don't even know why he's still captain. He certainly doesn't deserve it."

"I know that's not the explanation you want to give me or the ploy you want to play," Coach said. "I know damn well there is more to this fight than that. Luis J, care to share your insights?"

"Coach, I didn't mean to start this in your locker room. Can we just suit up?"

"I'm tired of this shit. You both jeopardized the team's standing in the league because of your egos and all you say is, it's personal? Well, you're both benched for the next two games…and it's not personal. But I hope you guys realize how much your being benched will jeopardize our chances for playoffs. Now get out of here and if I hear about either of you touching the other again, whatsoever, you're off the team for the remainder of this year and half of next for you, Luis J. Think about that while you're sitting on the bench. Am I understood?"

Roger nodded, still pissed. If Luis J hadn't blindsided him, the rest of the team would have been watching a completely different fight. It was just like Luis J to take the coward's approach, attacking him from behind. Roger was sick of Luis J's so-called leadership role on the team. It was as if he could do no wrong in Coach's eyes.

'Oh, I won't touch him, but I will definitely make him hurt,' Roger thought as he stood there waiting for Luis J's response.

"Luis J?"

"Yeah, right, I got it," Luis J finally responded. He was still fuming and annoyed with how this was going down. He was also trying to ignore the pain in his side. Roger had managed to get off a sucker punch as Coach was separating them.

"Roger, go suit up and start the drills with the first string. I'll be out in a minute. And keep your mouth shut about this. I don't want that bullshit on my court. Luis J, wait here for a minute."

Roger made an off-hand salute to Coach before turning toward the door. Once they were alone, the coach turned his attention to Luis J. "Son, what's going on with you? First the smoking, the drinking and drugs. Now locker room brawls? Roger asked a damned good question a few minutes ago. So, what do you have to say for yourself?"

"There isn't anything to say. You guys have made up your mind about me, so what's there to talk about? Roger never wanted me to be Captain anyway. He's never hidden the fact that as a senior, he thought he deserved it."

"Listen, Luis J, that's Roger's issue. I have always had your back. I have gone to bat for you on several occasions when any other coach would have dropped you in a New York minute. I didn't because, like I told you yesterday morning, I see potential in you."

Coach paused to look at this young boy standing in front of him. He had a gift on the court. He was smooth with his movements, dribbling the ball low and in control and that awesome outside shot was spot on. He had an eye, too. He could see the play before it materialized and could adjust his game to make the steal or drive in for a layup. Coach didn't understand how someone with insight like that on the court could be letting life derail him so much off of it.

He finally continued, "Son, I know you're having a rough time; who wouldn't be with what you've gone through? But life is what you make of it, Luis J, and you aren't doing too good of a job at the moment. I want to help you out, but you've got to confide in me. I haven't noticed any signs of alcohol use, which is why you're still on the team. But I have witnessed behavioral changes, like you losing your cool. You're the team captain because you've always demonstrated a level head and sportsmanship. Did we make a mistake with that appointment? Because I'm starting to wonder if maybe we did. What are you going to do about where you are in your life? Did anything we said to you yesterday resonate? Did you call the counselor and ask for help?"

"No. I keep telling you guys I'm not an addict."

"Right," Coach said, disappointed. "Then, what's going on with you now? What was the fight about?"

"Nothing I can't handle."

"Really?" Coach shook his head. He wasn't getting through to this kid and it was pissing him off right about now, so he said, "Okay, then go home."

"What? Why?"

"I don't even want you on the court today. You aren't acting like a team captain and I don't like the effect it's having on the team. Did you happen to notice when you were out there with fists flying that the only person trying to stop the fight was Maine? That doesn't seem like a team behind their captain to me."

Coach was right. No one had cheered Luis J on. In fact, they were watching to see who was going to emerge victorious. He had even heard some of them yelling, "Kick his ass, Roger!" He didn't see who they were, but if he allowed his mind to recall the voices, he was pretty sure he would know exactly who they were. If that's what they wanted, then he would comply.

"Fine, you want me to quit?"

"No, I want you to be a man, damn it! I want you to start acting like the man you claim you are. What is it that you guys say, man up? That's what I recommend to you Luis J, before you can't."

Luis J thought this might be an opportunity to give Coach a view into his world. Perhaps if he understood some of what was going on, he would be more supportive of his actions in the locker room. Perhaps he would cut Roger from the team.

"You asked me before if I called the counselor and I said no. The reason I didn't is because I had a sobering enough conversation with my little sister. My fourteen-year-old sister told me last night that Roger has been sleeping with her for about three months. The reason she finally told me is because she thought she might be pregnant by him. She's all starry-eyed over him and he doesn't give a crap about her. Hell, he probably orchestrated this whole thing just to get back at me in some way. So yes, I tried to kick his ass today and I'm only sorry you broke it up before I could put a good hurtin' on him!"

Coach was twisting his mustache as he listened to the story. He said, "I see. So fighting with him like you're on some street corner is showing him that you're a man? Is it restoring your sister's honor? Is it doing anything meaningful? Allow me to respond – hell no! What you should be doing instead is talking to your sister and educating her on what is right and what she should be looking out for with guys like Roger. You should be talking to me and asking me to deal with Roger. Don't you get it? I have authority over him and I know what he values.

"Trust me, I understand your protective instincts. I have a younger sister, too. But the actions you took today can get you kicked out of school, for real this time, and could land you in jail if Roger chooses to press charges. There was a room full of people who saw you attack him first."

"I get that, but I'm dealing with a lot right now. You just don't have a clue."

"Then let me help you."

"Coach, I honestly wish you could, but you can't. It's just all too complicated. Thanks for the offer, though." Luis J wanted to share everything with Coach right then, but there wasn't enough time before tip-off and Coach had to be on the floor or the team would forfeit. "So, do you still want me off the court today?"

"Yes I do. But I want you at practice tomorrow with a clearer head than today. And Luis J, if you change your mind about talking, I'm here."

"I appreciate it, Coach," Luis J said before heading back to his locker. When he turned the corner to his aisle, he saw his backpack on the floor and a note stuck in the slates of his locker door. It read, "This isn't over." Luis J thought to himself, 'You're damn straight it ain't.'

As he approached the exit door to the building, heading for the subway, his phone rang. "Speak."

It was Chell. "Luis J, I can't believe you confronted Roger. I asked you not to do that. Now he's breaking up with me."

"Chell, give me a break. I told you last night that you aren't in a relationship and I am not about to allow him to continue to take advantage of you. Where are you anyway?"

"At home. We are in a relationship. Why can't you just accept that and stay out of my business? If we really break up, I'll never forgive you for this. Never!" she said, before ending the call.

Luis J exhaled hard and thought to himself, 'Not only will she forgive me, she'll actually thank me some day.' He pushed hard against the exit bar, throwing the door way back and then letting it slam behind him. As the lock reengaged, he envisioned Roger's neck just inside the doorframe. A smile came across his face.

Chell was so mad at Luis J. She had told him how she felt about Roger and begged him to stay out of it. When Roger called, he was furious. He called her "a little bitch." He had never said anything like that to her before. She had to speak to him and try to explain. When she called him back, it just went to his voicemail. She figured they were on the court and his phone was now off. So when she heard the beep, she said, "Roger, I'm really sorry my brother tripped on you. I don't know what's wrong with him. Please don't break up with me. I really enjoy being with you. Besides, he can't tell me who I can and can't be with. Call me back when you get this message. Good luck with your game."

Chell hung up the phone and headed to the kitchen. Her mother was sitting at the table reading the paper. The house was quiet for a change because the boys were out with Rosie. This was the perfect time to make the "ask."

"Mami, I haven't been to one of Luis J's games in a long time. Would it be okay with you if I went today?"

"Chell, I have a lot to do today, I can't stop and take you right now," Diane said, looking up from the paper.

"I know you're busy, but you don't have to take me. I know how to get there by bus. Besides, in the fall, I'll be going by myself anyway."

"That's true, but not at 4 in the afternoon. You know it still gets dark early. And since Luis J isn't living here right now, is he going to be able to bring you home?"

"Yeah, he'll bring me home," she said, even though she didn't want to spend any more time with him today, or tomorrow for that matter.

"Who else is going with you?"

"I'm going to meet some friends there. I'll be okay. You don't have to worry."

"Let me call Luis J just to make sure."

"You can't. He's already playing. Mami, I'm going to be fine."

Diane looked at her daughter and could see the maturity in her stance, but the baby features still in her face. But she was right, next year she would be making that trip on her own. So she said, "Alright, but you need to be back here right after the game. No exceptions. Tell Luis J to call me when you guys are on the way."

Chell kissed her cheek and grabbed her jacket and bus pass. As she rode the bus to Luis J's school, she thought about what she would say to Roger. The last thing she wanted was for him to think of her as a little girl instead of a teenage woman. He made her feel so special when they were together. She thought about the first time they were together; he had asked her to show him how much she cared about him.

They had just come back from the mall and he had parked his car across the street from where he lived. He had moved out of the apartment with Stacie and their parents and was living with some friend. He had asked her to show him a few times before, so she knew he meant for her to move to the back seat. She was sitting there admiring the bracelet he had bought for her from Claire's, her favorite store in the mall. They sold all kinds of cool stuff for her room, like silver jewelry and hair accessories. She had even gotten her ears pierced there when she was ten.

Usually, when they did this, they didn't talk to each other. They just kissed. He would put his tongue in her mouth, lick her breasts and then rub his thing. But this time before they started, Roger asked her if she knew how special she was to him. She remembered feeling butterflies in her stomach and licking her lips in preparation for his kiss. She nodded her head and smiled, not taking her eyes off the silver bracelet that had little blue stones of some kind. He reached over and pulled her to him so they could kiss. He slid his hand inside her shirt to caress her breasts.

She had liked it when he did that. She liked how it made her feel down below.

But this time what came next was different because he took her hand and placed it on his crotch. He placed his hand over hers and moved it back and forth to rub it. It wasn't long before she could feel his manhood growing inside the jeans. She had seen Robert and CJ's penises because she had given them baths, but somehow this was different; this was very different. It had made her feel a little uncomfortable and she tried to pull back, but Roger wouldn't allow her to remove her hand. He just kept using her hand to rub himself and his eyes were closed.

"Oh, girl, do you see how you make me feel when I'm with you? I can't control myself," he mumbled, his eyes still closed. He used his left hand to unbutton and unzip his pants and then guided her hand to remove his dick. She had never seen a penis stand straight up like that. It looked like an arrow and was really hard.

She thought that strange and asked him, "Why is it standing straight up like that?" Roger had laughed and said, "You really don't know? You did that, girl. You made it stand up like that. That's the power you have over me, my sweet thang. I can't control myself. It wants you. Chell, I want you." Chell wasn't sure what was going to happen next and she felt even more uncomfortable. She remembered thinking that she hoped no one would park next to them or see his dick standing up like that.

Roger told her that if she really cared about him the way he cared for her, the way he dreamed about her at night, she would let him be close to her. After all, he had saved up money to buy her the bracelet and treat her to Wendy's for lunch. She knew he was right, and besides, Stacie had told her that Roger had dumped other girlfriends because he was always doing things for them and they never showed him how they appreciated it. Chell did not want him to dump her, so she let him do what he wanted, even though she didn't know what was ahead for her. He used his hands on her private area, rubbing it and making her warm all over. Then, before she knew it, he had moved over her, put on a condom and his "thing" was in her. She made a fist with her hand to give her something else to focus on. It hurt so badly. She was letting him do "it" to her. He moved back and forth against her body, each movement becoming more and more forceful against her private place. It felt like he was trying to see just how far inside of her he would fit. Then, as quickly as he was hard, it was over. His body went limp and his breathing slowed. She remembered thinking that this wasn't at all like Sparkle and Stix's romantic experience in the movie "Sparkle." Sparkle seemed to enjoy it.

After a while, Roger rose and started putting himself together before saying, "Damn, girl, you were a virgin. You bled a little, but it's alright. It won't do anything to you. It was probably a little painful, but you were so good to me. I'm proud of you for being willing to bear the pain for me. Next time, it won't hurt so much."

When she didn't answer, he looked to see what she was doing. She was staring at the blood on his seat. "Hey, it's alright," he said, grabbing a towel off the floor and wiping the seat off. "Like I said, next time it won't hurt so much. Here, wipe in between your legs and put your panties back on," he offered, handing her the same towel. She looked at it and it was filthy. There were all kinds of stains on it. She declined and just put on her panties.

They got together again the following week, but it still hurt. He told her that sometimes the condom made it hurt more so they wouldn't use it anymore. Chell had mixed feelings about having sex with him, partly because it hurt, but mostly because she wasn't sure what it was doing to her body. She still didn't understand how that big "thing" fit inside of her body and when it did, what was it doing to her insides?

Especially now, because the pregnancy test said she wasn't pregnant, but her period still hadn't started. She had wanted to talk to someone about it, but who? She couldn't tell Stacie and she wasn't sure where to begin the conversation with Luis J, so she didn't speak to anyone about her concerns. And then, after each time, he would tell her she was the best girlfriend he had ever had and every now and then, he would treat her to something.

Now she was just looking forward to the day when it didn't hurt anymore and Luis J was not going to interfere with that. The bus dropped her off right in front of the school. It was about five-fifteen, so Chell ran into the gym to see if she could catch them returning from half-time. She looked for Roger on the court, but she didn't see him. She turned her eyes to the bench and there he was. He was sitting there, watching the game. He had on his long pants and didn't look like he had been sweating at all.

She had missed half-time, so she looked in the stands to see where she could sit and blend in. She then scanned the floor for Luis J. He wasn't anywhere to be seen. She wondered where he could be. Perhaps he was still in the locker room for some reason. She wondered if maybe he had been hurt. She hoped not.

"Hey, Chell. I thought that was you. How did you get here?"

Chell turned toward the voice to see Stacie. Smiling, she said, "Oh, hey Stacie. I took the bus. How are they doing?"

"They're winning, although I don't know how. They benched my brother because your brother jumped him. What's up with that?"

Chell lowered her head and said, "I don't know. Have you talked to Roger?"

"Not yet. But I know he's pissed. He's been pacing on the sidelines the whole game. So, why are you here?"

Chell looked over toward the bench and Roger was sitting quietly in his seat now. Maybe he was calming down. "I wanted to talk to him. But you know I used to come and watch Luis J all the time. He is still my brother and the team captain. I used to come to the games to see him long before I even knew Roger."

"You mean Carlos brought you to the games," she responded, giggling, before continuing, "Anyway, it isn't a good idea for you to speak to Roger right now, let alone try to see him. I've known my brother a lot longer than you have and I'm telling you to wait until he cools off. You don't want to ignite that temper," Stacie said, fanning her hand as though it were on fire.

"I'm not worried about that. Roger has never been mad at me. I just need to explain to him what happened."

"Suit yourself, but don't say I didn't warn you."

Chell took a seat in the row just above Stacie and Valerie. She didn't want to have her back to them with the way Stacie was acting; they might do something to try and embarrass her. Sometimes Stacie could be so mean to her and she didn't know why. Then she asked, "Hey, do you know where Luis J is?"

"Somebody said the coach sent him home; I guess because of the fight. Probably for the best. You haven't seen him playing lately. He misses more than he hits." She imitated Luis J taking a shot and started laughing again. "Anyway, I'll talk to you later. We gotta go," Stacie announced, rising from the bleachers and heading toward the door. Valerie rose and ran off behind her.

Chell now realized she had a big problem. She had told her mother that Luis J would bring her home. He wasn't there and so she would have to take the bus at night by herself, which would get her home really late. 'Oh God, Mami is going to be furious,' she mouthed. At this time of night, the bus schedule changed – they ran only once an hour and on a completely different route through some tough neighborhoods. This just reinforced that she had to straighten things out with Roger and get him to take her home.

After the game, she waited for him outside the locker room. There were about ten other girls waiting for the players as well. Some were cheerleaders. She hadn't thought about it until now, but maybe Dany was among them and she could ask her for a ride home if Roger wouldn't take her. She scanned the girls, but Dany was not among them. She figured that since Dany and Luis J had broken up, she probably didn't hang out anymore waiting for anyone. Chell observed that the girls were laughing and talking about fashion. Some seemed impatient as they waited for the guys. When the door finally opened, Roger was one of the first to come out. Since he didn't play, there wasn't much preparation required.

Chell smiled and opened her mouth to say hello when she heard instead from a girl just behind her.

"Hey, Baby. What's going on? Why didn't you play?"

Chell turned to see that the question was coming from one of those ten girls. Chell watched as she pushed past her and straight up to Roger. She looked older, definitely in high school, like she was about seventeen or eighteen. She was black, tall and thin, with long permed hair that had that cellophane shine. She was dressed in jeans and a very revealing button down shirt. She didn't look anything like Chell. She had a little accent though, like she was from the islands or something. Chell had a friend who was from Jamaica and this girl sounded a little like that.

"Long story," Roger responded, smiling at her. He was carrying his gym bag on his shoulder and had a water bottle in his hand.

"Roger?" Chell called out to him. She ultimately had to wave her hand to get his attention away from that girl.

When he finally saw her, the smile disappeared from his face and frown lines across his forehead replaced it before he asked, "What are you doing here?"

"I came to watch you play and I really need to talk to you," Chell replied, moving her way toward him through the clusters of people and conversations.

Roger stood his ground and waited for her to get close enough before he said, "We already talked. There isn't anything else to talk about."

"Who is she, Roger?" the girl asked, eyeing Chell up and down.

"She's a friend of my sister's," he said, rubbing the girl's arm with his eyes still on Chell.

"Seems like she thinks it's a little more than that to me," the girl said, now staring at Chell with that, 'Honey-this-is-my-man-so-back-the-hell-up' look on her face.

"Girl, quit trippin'. I'll meet you at the car," Roger said.

But the girl stood her ground because she did not want to leave the two of them together. Roger noticed this and then said, with a slightly raised voice, "I said, I'll meet you at the car. Why are you still standing here?"

The girl sucked her teeth and before heading for the door said, "Don't keep me waitin'."

Chell watched Roger eye the girl from head to toe, staring hard at her butt. "Oh sweet thang, I'm worth it." Roger's words trailed off into laughter as she walked away.

Chell's mouth fell open. 'Did he just say sweet thang to her? That's what he said to me,' she remembered. He always said that to her after he finished. Did that mean he was having sex with her, too? "Roger, who's that?" Chell asked.

"She's in my class. So, what else do you have to say to me?"

Chell didn't like the way he was talking to her or the implications made regarding her being his sister's friend. She was also pretty sure there was more to that girl than schoolbooks, but she tried to focus and say the right things. Plus, at least now they were alone, so she said softly, "I wanted to talk to you about Luis J. I heard he picked a fight with you. I never thought he would do that."

"Why did you even tell him what was going on between us?"

"I didn't, he overheard me talking to Stacie." This was obviously a lie, but she couldn't tell him the real story, not right now when he was so mad at her.

"Well, Chell, I don't have time for this shit. Your brother is crazy. I need a girl who doesn't need her big brother to run interference for her or get into shit that is none of his business. And you aren't that girl."

"Roger, please, I really care about you. You said you felt the same way. That hasn't changed, has it?" she asked, hoping that Luis J had called it wrong.

"Look, if I have to explain that, then I know you're as crazy as your brother. No, you aren't special anymore. Now go home; your mother's probably looking for you. Besides, I have someone waiting for me."

"But, Roger, I don't have a ride. Can you at least give me a ride home?"

"See, this is exactly the shit I'm talking about. You can't even drive. You're a liability. I'll ask a friend to drop you off if he has the time. Later." Then he walked off.

Chell just stood there as Roger walked out the door without even looking back. She couldn't believe he was dissing her like this. She had done everything he asked her to do and now he was telling her she wasn't special to him anymore. A few more minutes passed and the crowd was really starting to thin. She zipped her coat, looked at her watch and figured the next bus would be leaving soon. When she pushed open the door, a man was standing on the other side of it and startled her.

"Hey, you Chell?"

"Yeah," she answered, cautiously.

"Roger said you needed a ride."

"Yeah," Chell responded, still apprehensive since she had no idea who this guy was. She didn't recognize him, but he looked older, so she asked, "Who are you?"

"Do you need a ride or not? I don't have all day."

She looked around and he was the only person out there. It was dark everywhere except for small rays of light emanating from the headlights as the last few cars were leaving the parking lot. She looked at the bus shelter just in time to see the bus pulling away, loaded with people. She thought about going inside to call Luis J, but when she tried the door handle, it was locked. She turned back to face the guy, not sure of what to do, but apparently he was her only ticket home.

Her mother had warned her countless times about taking rides from strangers, but this was sort of different. At least Roger knew him and had asked him to take her home. So it must be okay. 'Maybe he isn't that mad at me,' she thought. Since she hadn't responded, the man was now walking away from her toward the parking lot.

"Wait, I'm coming," she called out, not wanting him to leave her there alone.

He was tall, a few inches taller than Luis J, and she wondered if he played on the team, too. "So do you know my brother?"

"Who's your brother?" he asked, opening his door and climbing in.

"Luis Rodriquez Jr. Most people call him Luis J," she answered, opening the passenger door and closing it behind her. The car was cleaner than Roger's. It didn't have an odor either. She looked in the back seat and didn't see a towel on the floor. This made her feel a little more at ease. She couldn't tell what color it was because it blended in with the dark of the night. The interior was black, though, and when he started the engine, the music came blaring out from the speakers all around her. He had been listening to WBLS and the music was so loud, he had to shout over it to answer her question.

"Yeah, I know him. If he hadn't started the fight with Roger, we could have won and he would have been here to take his little sister home instead of me. Luckily, it's not out of my way. Roger told me you live off Pitkin and Euclid. That right?"

"Yes," Chell yelled back. She also noted that he obviously wasn't a friend of Luis J's, so she thought it best to keep her responses short and questions infrequent. As she rode along in the passenger seat, she didn't recall seeing the driver on the court before but maybe he was just a spectator. He seemed a little older than Roger, but it could be the facial hair this guy had. When he turned his head to change lanes, she noticed the letter G outlined in the center of his head. She wondered what that stood for.

Since he was jamming to the music and not going to talk to her, she allowed her mind to wander and thought about that girl. Who could she have been? Roger took the girl somewhere and had left her to ride with Mr. G. She giggled to herself and then continued with her thoughts.

She had to figure out a way to reach Roger. It wasn't going to be easy, but she was not ready to end it with him. Caught up in her thoughts, Chell didn't even realize she was now in front of the yard just outside her apartment building. Once he pulled to the curb, Chell reached for the door, but Mr. G reached over, grabbed her by the left arm, and stopped her.

Turning the music down now, he said, "Now, I know you don't think you're just going to get out of this car without giving me something for the ride."

Chell was still able to open the door with her right hand and when she did, the overhead dome light came on and she could see him clearly now. He was staring at her with dark eyes, almost as dark as the interior of the car. He looked threatening to her and it frightened her. She finally managed to reply while trying to wrench free from his grip, "I don't have any money. I just have a bus pass. I'll ask Luis J to pay you."

"I don't want anything from Luis. I didn't give him a ride, I gave you one."

"But I told you, I don't have anything to give you."

"Oh, I think you do. Back seat, honey."

"What?"

He tightened his grip and raised his voice. It was deep and made her even more fearful. "I said back seat. You owe me and I intend to collect."

"But, I don't do that," Chell said, her voice cracking and her lip quivering.

"Bullshit, Roger told me you were good for it. He told me you put out. That's your payment."

"But, I'm not like that. Roger couldn't have told you that about me. I've only been with him. Let me give you something else; I'll give you my watch." Chell's trembling was now uncontrollable. Had Roger really told this man that about her? She was trying with all her might to get free of him, but he was holding fast. He let go of the steering wheel and was about to get a stronger hold on her when she pleaded with him, "Please, don't do this. I'm only fourteen."

"And? You're sleeping with Roger, right? I just want my share. Now you can get in the backseat on your own or you can take care of me from the front seat. Which will it be?"

Before she could respond, the passenger door was pulled out of her hand and was now wide open. When she turned to see who it was, she saw David.

"Chell? Get out here. Now," he stated, standing with his arms folded and his feet slightly apart.

Mr. G couldn't see the owner of this voice from where he was sitting, but he recognized the authority and released Chell before asking, "Who is that?"

"My Dad!" she exclaimed, pulling away from him and getting out of the car. She was so relieved.

"You caught a break…this time. Go on, get your ass out," he said, starting the ignition.

Once Chell had cleared the door and was standing next to David, he pointed to the car and asked, "Who the hell is that and what were you doing in his car?"

"It's okay, David, he gave me a ride home because Luis J wasn't at the game and I missed the bus."

Placing his hand on the door handle to brace himself, David leaned down so he could see the person sitting in the driver's seat and repeated his question.

The driver could now see the face and body of the voice and determined he wasn't up for this kind of confrontation, so he just said, "Hey, man, I just gave her a ride home. She was stranded at the school after the game."

"Really? And why is she shaking?"

"I don't know, cold I guess. My heat isn't working. Anyway, I need to go; would you please close my door?"

"Don't ever let me catch you near my daughter again. Do you understand me? And I have your license plate number, buddy; don't make me have to use it."

"You know, you could just say thanks. I could've left her ass at school."

"Don't be smart with me, boy. I know what was going on here and you should be glad I don't call the cops. How old are you anyway?"

"If you think you know so much, old man, maybe you should talk to your daughter. I think she needs to bring you up to date."

"You have something to tell me about my daughter, then be a man and get out of that car, asshole," David instructed him, while at the same time heading over to the driver's side. But as soon as he cleared the passenger's side back door, the car accelerated, burned rubber and pulled away. The door that Chell had struggled to get out of slammed shut from the motion.

David returned to the sidewalk where his daughter was standing and stopped in front of her to say, "Chell, what the hell were you doing sitting in the car with him?"

The words were drowned out by the crying that had started. She recognized just how close she had come to being raped, right in front of her own house, and the intensity of her crying increased.

David pulled her into his arms, holding her tightly and trying to calm her down. It reminded him of the countless times he had to be there for Diane like that. Once the crying subsided to a whimper, he asked her again, "Chell, who was that?"

In between gasps for air, she said, "I don't know."

"Excuse me?"

"I don't know."

"What do you mean you don't know? Were you really coming from the high school? How did you get there? Does your mother know you went there and didn't have a way home?"

David observed her before realizing he hadn't asked the most important question, "Did he hurt you?"

"No, he didn't, but it was because you saved me. How did you know I was in the car?"

"I was walking toward the building and I saw two people in the car. I didn't know it was you until you opened the door and the dome light let me see your face. When you didn't get out of the car, I knew something was wrong."

"Thank you David."

"You're welcome, but you are not out of trouble. Not by a long shot. For starters, why were you in the car with that jerk? So you don't know his name, but do you know him?"

"No, but he knows Luis J."

"But how'd you end up in the car with him?"

Chell sighed deeply. "Luis J didn't play today, but I didn't know he wasn't going to be there at the game. Then I missed the bus and the next one wasn't for an hour. I promised Mami I'd be home early. So my friend Stacie has a brother, but he couldn't bring me home either, so her brother asked this guy to drop me off."

"Chell, you know better than that. Why didn't you call your brother to come and get you? Or your mother or me for that matter?"

When the tears started again, David said, "Alright, young lady, let's go upstairs. You're going to have some explaining to do to your mother and me. Understand?"

"David, please don't tell Mami." Her worst fears were coming to light. Her mother would surely ground her because she wouldn't stop with the interrogation until she had all the facts. Facts that Chell had been hiding from her for the last few months would now be out in clear view. She wouldn't be able to avoid her mother's rapid fire. She had seen Carlos and Luis J experience it enough times to know she was in for a real ass kicking.

"Really, Chell? Don't even ask me that. Come on."

Chell followed David upstairs and they entered the apartment. He had called Diane earlier to tell her he wanted to talk and she told him to come by after the boys were put to bed. Diane was standing in the kitchen pouring a glass of red wine from the almost empty bottle on the countertop. David figured it was her Merlot. She had to be stewing by now because Luis J had Chell out so late and hadn't called. He knew Chell was in for a world of trouble, and almost felt a bit sorry for her considering the terrifying ordeal she had just fortunately escaped, but she had brought it on herself.

"It's about time you brought your ass in this house," Diane started, already in gale force form. "Where have you been and where is your brother? He didn't have the decency to walk you to the door and explain to me why the hell he had you out so late?"

"Diane, she's okay. Keep your voice down or you'll wake the boys," David said, trying to put her in check.

"What's going on, Chell? Where is Luis J?"

David motioned for Chell to sit on the couch and then he followed her. They removed their coats while sitting and waited for Diane to join them in the living room. David was using this tactic to get Diane to calm down and meet them in their space. Once she did, David said, "Chell, why don't you start from the beginning?"

"Mami, Luis J wasn't at the game and I didn't have a way to get home. A friend of Luis J's brought me home."

"Why wasn't Luis J at the game? Did you know he wasn't going to be there?"

"Coach benched him and he didn't stay. I didn't find out he wasn't there until I got there. I had just talked to him before I asked you if I could go."

"But I specifically asked you if he was there and you told me he was. You hadn't talked to him, had you?"

"Yes, I talked to him before I left, but he didn't tell me he wasn't going to be there. I swear."

"Uh, huh. But you didn't tell him that you were coming, or ask him to bring you home, so you lied. We'll talk about that later. Okay, so why didn't you leave as soon as you got there and realized he wasn't there? Better still, why didn't you call me and ask me to pick you up? Okay, so a friend of his brought you home. What friend?"

"He's on the team with Luis J."

"That tells me how Luis J knows him, it doesn't tell me who he is. What's his name?" Diane asked, reaching for the phone.

"Mami, who are you calling?"

"Luis J, I want to know what he knows about this boy. Hopefully he'll answer his phone now. I've been trying to reach him since 7:30 when you guys weren't here yet."

"Mami, don't embarrass me."

"Embarrass you? That's the least of your worries. This kid now knows where you live and that you're silly enough to get into a car with him. I want to know everything you know about him."

Chell looked down into her lap and the first teardrop hit the back of her hand before she mumbled, "I don't know anything about him, really."

"Excuse me? What did you just say? You have got to be kidding me! You got into a car with someone you don't know? That is just ridiculous. How many times have I told you about getting into cars with strangers? Chell, there's more to this story than you're telling me. Spill it. All of it, now!"

Chell didn't answer, primarily because she didn't know how.

"Chell, I swear, I will beat the crap out of you. Are you dating him?"

"No!"

"Then tell me what's going on little girl, because I am about two words away from knocking some sense back into your head!"

David watched Diane and wondered why she never spoke to Carlos or Luis J that way. She was always softer with them than he thought she should be. Chell was crying uncontrollably now and it was really bothering him to see her like that.

"Mami, do you promise you won't beat me?"

"No. I promise I won't kill you."

"Diane, calm down."

"Calm down?!"

"Yes, calm down and give her a second. Can't you see she's frightened by all of this?"

Diane wanted her to be frightened. She wanted her to realize how vulnerable she had been getting into a stranger's car. Decisions like that made for news headlines every day. She did not want this child to become another statistic. She was about to say the final two words when Chell cleared her throat enough to begin her story.

"I didn't know that Luis J wasn't going to be there. Honestly Mami. And once I found out, I just thought Stacie's brother would bring me home, but instead he asked this guy," Chell explained.

"I thought I told you to stay away from Stacie's brother in the first place!" Diane huffed, her anger building even more now because Chell felt that taking a ride with Stacie's brother was still an option.

"I know, but it was getting late and I didn't know who else I could ask. Stacie was there and I didn't think you would mind. Besides, you said you couldn't take me so I figured you couldn't pick me up."

Diane mulled over the words coming out of her daughter's mouth, but there were so many gaps in this story that they weren't painting any kind of outline on the canvas. "It's not adding up, Chell. It still doesn't make sense. There's more to this story and I want to hear it. First, you hide notes from Luis J's school and now this? Okay, you can tell me, or I can call Stacie's mother and find out what's going on."

"No, Mami, don't."

"Why not, Chell?"

"Because, it isn't Stacie's fault."

"Really? Well, I think this has something to do with Stacie's brother, if you ask me. Like I said before, you told me Luis J was going to bring you home; that's the only reason I agreed to let you go. If he wasn't there, that means you didn't tell him you were coming to his game. He would never have left the school if he knew you were on your way there. Am I getting warm?"

Chell didn't respond.

"No response, huh? Okay, let's call Luis J then."

"Mami, no."

Diane raised her hand to stop Chell's drawing of the story. Diane wanted a clear outline so she could begin filling in the shapes, colors and their shades. She wasn't going to get that from Chell, but she knew she could count on Luis J. 'He'll be just as mad when he finds out what she did and what happened to her,' Diane thought. When Luis J's phone started ringing, Diane pressed the speaker button.

"Speak."

"Luis J, it's your mother. I need to talk to you about Chell."

"What about her? Is she alright?"

"Now why would you ask that question? What do you know?"

"I talked to her earlier; I was just asking. What's wrong?" he asked, calmly.

"Chell went to your school this afternoon to watch your game, but you weren't there so she didn't have a way to get home. She ended up getting a ride from some guy who claims to be a friend of yours. What do you know about it?"

"Who's the guy?"

"I don't know. She didn't get his name."

"Can I speak to her?"

"Go ahead, you're already on speaker."

"Mami, come on, that's not necessary."

"Yes, it is. Go ahead, she can hear you."

"Hey, Chell. What did the dude look like?"

"Tall, thin, dark skinned. He drives a dark car and has a really deep voice. Oh yeah, he had a letter in the back of his head."

"A letter, what letter?"

"A capital 'G'."

"Oh, that's Jimmie Lane. They call him 'Goober' because of the 'G'."

"So you know him?" Diane asked.

"Yeah, but what was she doing getting a ride from him?"

"That's what we're trying to figure out. She said Stacie's brother wouldn't give her a ride." When Luis J didn't reply, Diane asked, "Luis J, did you hear me?"

"Chell, why didn't you tell me you were going to the game? I would have stayed there or told you not to go. And you need to stay away from Goober," Luis J added. "He's a…just stay away from him. Understand?"

"Fine."

"So Luis J, maybe you can tell us why Chell went to the school in the first place. She told me you were going to bring her home; that's the only reason I let her go. Did you tell her that you were going to be there?"

"I don't remember if I told her."

"Don't try and cover for her now," David added to the conversation. "It's only going to get her in even more trouble in the long run."

Luis J didn't know David was there. He was surprised to hear his voice. "I'm not, David. It's just that when we talked right before the game it was before I had decided to go home because I wasn't feelin' well."

"Then why would she have been there?"

"Chell needs to tell you that. I can't speak for her."

"Luis J, do you want to see your sister get in over her head? She's only fourteen and hanging out with boys your age, and in Stacie's brother's case, older. I'm sure I don't need to tell you that no good can come of that," Diane said, frustration in her tone.

"Mami, I understand, but Chell needs to tell you what's going on. I can't do that."

"Thanks a lot, Luis J, for confirming there's something for me to tell," Chell mumbled back.

"I love you, pumpkin," Luis J countered. "I will do whatever I can to protect you, but you have to tell them the whole story. All of it," he said, knowing that she would understand what he was referencing.

"Including the part about you getting into a fight and not being able to play today?" Chell continued, a woman scorned, but also trying to deflect the attention away from herself for a few minutes.

Diane shook her head when she heard about the fight, but her comment was not what Chell expected. "Don't try to make this about Luis J. This is about you."

Frustrated and defeated, Chell started painting Diane a clearer outline. "Alright, fine. I went to the school to see Stacie's brother. When I found out Luis J wasn't there, I just figured he would give me a ride home instead." She knew Luis J was on the other end of the phone fuming since she hadn't completely complied with his mandate. She thought that she would spare him from any further information by asking, "Mami, do we really need to do this with Luis J on the phone?"

"Oh, I don't see why not, especially just because you asked," Diane said. "Go on."

"That's it. He said he couldn't give me a ride and asked this guy, Goober, to do it."

"Chell, I'm tired of this! What's going on between you and Stacie's brother, and what the hell is his name? 'Cause I'm tired of saying 'Stacie's brother,' and I know you know."

Hesitating, Chell answered, "Roger," in a voice barely heard.

"Roger. Okay, when did it start? And how far has it gone?"

"Mami."

"Don't Mami me. How long and how far?"

"I don't have to answer that question."

"The hell you don't. I know something is going on with you. I can see little signs, but I haven't wanted to accept it."

"What signs? What are you talking about?" Chell asked, wondering if there was something that her mother could see in the way she walked now. Maybe his thrusting had made her hips wider. She had read something like that in a story in *Seventeen Magazine*.

"Let's try this one. I know you haven't had your period yet this month. How's that for starters? And I've noticed you taking showers at night."

"Oh God, did you just say that in front of David and Luis J?"

"Yes, I did. And since you didn't deny it and haven't asked me why you might be late since you have never been more than a day or two late, I have to suspect that you may already have the answer. So I have to ask, are you pregnant?"

Chell knew her mother watched everything, but even down to her period? But thankfully, she could respond "no" and give herself some more room to wiggle around in this conversation. "No." But she wasn't prepared for her mother's next comment, at all.

"So, you have been sexually active. You didn't say, 'Pregnant? I can't be pregnant.' Instead, you calmly, and almost triumphantly, said no. Sounds to me like you either had reason to check it out, or you're using protection. I can't believe my ears, Chell," Diane said quietly, full of so many emotions she couldn't even see straight.

Luis J spoke, "Mami, I'm gone. I can't contribute anything to this conversation."

"You knew about this and didn't tell me?" Now Diane had two foxes trapped in the hen house.

"Just talk to her and help her, Mami. I gotta go. Chell, call me if you want to talk. Remember what I told you, I'm here for you."

Diane pressed the speaker button to end the call. Then she poured the rest of the wine down the drain. She needed a clear head to have this discussion with her fourteen-year-old daughter.

David had wanted to talk to Diane, but recognized that tonight was not the night for that, so he told them he was leaving. Diane walked him to the door and they stood there for a second.

"Are you going to be alright?" he asked.

"Yeah. Thanks. I'll call you tomorrow once I find out what's going on. I'm sorry about our plans to talk. And David, thank you for being there for Chell. I really appreciate it."

"I've been trying to tell you, I'm here for you, for us; we're family."

She bid him good night and locked the door. She then turned to her baby girl and sat down on the couch next to her. Chell was calmer now and Diane had to find out what challenges may be lying ahead of them. She lightly put her hand on her daughter's knee and gently tapped as she said, "Alright, it's just you and me. I'm listening."

Chell looked up at her mother, her eyes now red and her lids puffy. "Mami, can you forgive me? I don't know how this got so out of control. I don't think I'm pregnant, I took a test, but I still haven't started."

"How many times have you had sex and with whom?"

"I don't know. Maybe four or five. It's only been one person, Roger — Stacie's brother."

Hearing his name made Diane cringe. "And you didn't use protection?"

"We did the first time, but, well it hurt so much, and he said it was because of the rubber. But even when we stopped using one it still hurt. Do you think something's wrong with me?"

Diane was fuming. She was angry at that lying punk, but more so at herself for not having had the sex conversation sooner with her daughter. "I don't know, Chell. When did you take the test?"

"Last night."

The details behind the how and where and when of taking the test didn't matter right now. Diane suspected Luis J was involved since he wasn't surprised by what was going on. The next priority had to be her child's wellbeing.

"Our bodies are very delicate, Michelle. Your body is still developing, which is why I told you to wait until you were older to have sex. It could be he was too big for you. Or he didn't take the time to make sure your body was prepared for him. You have to be lubricated so it doesn't hurt. But I honestly don't know. I'll make an appointment with my doctor and have her examine you."

Diane had planned to take Chell for a gyne appointment when she turned fifteen. It would give them the baseline they needed for her as she matured into a woman. Now, there would be no baseline. She prayed that it was an infection or something, nothing permanent or damaging to Chell's body, and not pregnancy.

This thought made her ask, "Why didn't you come to me before you did this? I know you read and you and I have talked about how dangerous unprotected sex is. I thought you and I had an understanding about this. I thought we could talk about anything. I told you months ago I didn't want you hanging out with Stacie's brother…Roger, now that he has a name. This is why. He's way too old for you for starters and I know he doesn't care about you."

"But he did Mami, until Luis J attacked him today. He was mad about that and that's why he didn't bring me home."

"And why do you think Luis J did that, because he thinks this is such a great guy? No, he was defending your honor and jeopardized his status on the team. I don't condone what Luis J did, but I sure as hell understand it. Roger knew you were there by yourself and he left you to fend for yourself? What guy who 'cares about you' does that? Don't you get it? That's who he is and Luis J knows it."

Chell knew her mother was right. Especially given what Goober had told her Roger said about her, that "she put out."

"Mami, I know you're disappointed in me. I'm sorry I let you down."

"I believe you. Yes, you have let me down, but more importantly, you have let yourself down. You have changed your whole life by your actions. You can never go back to being innocent." Diane paused for a moment thinking about Chell, who was no longer innocent but still very much a young girl, before asking, "Another thing, one last question – where did this sex take place?"

Chell wanted to fall on a knife and end it all right there. She was so embarrassed to say she was in the backseat of a car.

"I'm waiting."

Chell just fell on the knife. "In his car." And then she waited for what was coming next.

Diane wanted to throw up but instead just put her arms around her daughter and said, "Look, go get some rest and we'll take you to my doctor or the clinic tomorrow. And in the meantime, you will not be with Roger, or anyone else for that matter, until you are old enough to understand the emotions behind having sex and what you need to do to protect yourself. And for sure never in a car. Do you understand me?"

"Yes, Mami."

"I certainly hope so."

Diane poured herself another glass of wine, went to her room and sat on the bed. She had been able to transition CJ out of her room and in with Robert and she was thankful for that. She could now watch television or read before going to bed. But she did neither.

Instead she thought about what was waiting around the corner for her with yet one more of her children. She had no idea what was wrong with her baby girl, none whatsoever. And in these situations, time is not on your side. She thought she had been clear to Chell to stay away from that boy, Roger, but obviously Chell chose an even worse path. One that led right into his arms. Ugh, it made her sick to think about it.

But she had to face the fact that she had been so absorbed in the chaos in her life surrounding Luis, Carlos, CJ, Luis J, and now David that she had not given Chell the attention she needed. Instead, she was using the "fear of Diane" to try to control her, to scare her into doing the right thing. What she didn't realize was Chell was growing up and the control Diane used to have over her with threats and beatings was being replaced with starry-eyed feelings for boys. She thought about Luis J jumping Roger and although she would never admit it, she hoped he beat the shit out of him.

Diane was thankful that David had been there for Chell. She didn't know what he had seen and would have to ask him later, but he had probably saved Chell from an even worse situation. She was also thankful he didn't push her to still have that "talk" he wanted. He recognized this was far more important and left her to address it. It was a relief given all she had to deal with right now and reminiscent of the David she had loved.

Before turning in, she looked in on Robert and CJ and then Chell. She was asleep, curled up in a ball. Her frame was so small, so young and yet, possibly carrying a child. Diane thought to herself, 'Here lies another example of how I have failed my children.' And she could hear her mother now.

CHAPTER THIRTY FIVE

Diane called her office and told them she needed to take off a few hours in the morning. She hoped it wouldn't cause her any problems with her new supervisor but she had to be with her child. She had called her doctor's office and they didn't have any openings but said they would squeeze her in once Diane told them what was going on. Even though the waiting room was packed, they took in Chell right away to at least begin some lab work.

They returned to the waiting room and hadn't been there more than fifteen minutes when the nurse came to get them and informed them that the doctor had ordered an ultrasound. An orderly brought Chell a bottle of water and told her to drink all of it to make her bladder full. After a while, they took Chell to the other side of the floor for that screening. Diane waited outside the door and started to worry a little because of all the attention they were suddenly giving to her child, someone with whom they were not familiar, but fitting into Dr. Stevenson's schedule.

When Chell came out of the room, she still had on the hospital gown with a whimsical print that reminded Diane of Chell's childhood pajamas. 'Where did the time go?' she thought, as the nurse escorted them to an empty room. Chell sat on the examining table and Diane in the chair. She had been in these rooms tons of times before, but her place had always been where Chell was sitting.

There were a few quick knocks on the door before it opened and in walked Dr. Stevenson. She was short with a little pudginess around her mid-section, a remnant of the baby she had about a year ago. Obviously she had not worked off the excess weight. Diane assumed her schedule interfered with any desire to get back to her fighting weight. She had been Diane's doctor for the past ten years and had delivered Robert; all that time she had always been at her best physical form.

"Diane, it's good to see you." Without pausing for Diane's response, she continued, "I'm going to get right to the point," she said, putting her hand on Chell's leg. "Michelle is pregnant and there is a complication."

Diane's heart sank at hearing the word pregnant, but she was more concerned about the one that followed it in that sentence. "A complication? What kind of complication?" she asked nervously while wondering, 'Has this girl contracted a venereal disease as well?'

"It appears to be a tubal pregnancy," the doctor continued. "That is why she received the false negative results. Do you know what that means, Michelle?" the doctor asked, directing the question to her.

"Not really," Chell muttered in a child's muted voice, unable to look at her mother or the doctor, feeling very embarrassed.

"Let me explain it to you with these pictures," Dr. Stevenson said, as she started pointing at pictures of a woman's organs that were mounted on the wall. "Here's your womb. Here are your ovaries. These are your fallopian tubes. When you are fertile or able to conceive a baby, the egg travels down the fallopian tubes and lands in the womb. If the egg does not meet any sperm, it gets to the womb and dissolves. You then have your period to flush it out. But, when you have sex during the ovulation period and the sperm meets the egg, the egg gets fertilized. It starts to make an embryo right away, but it is still supposed to travel down the fallopian tubes to your womb and implant itself there. In your case, the embryo is stuck in your fallopian tubes and is growing there. That's why you haven't had your period. Your body is confused. Have you had any pain in your abdomen or felt any illness or nausea in the morning?"

"No. But how do we get it to move?" Chell asked.

"Well, we can't Chell. It doesn't really work like that. Sometimes, Mother Nature can correct these things, but most of the time, it doesn't happen that way," she answered, then addressed her next statement to Diane.

"Given Michelle's age, I would like to perform a procedure to correct this as soon as possible. I want to avoid any permanent damage to her body because she's so young and has never given birth."

"What procedure? An abortion?" Chell interjected, drawing the attention back to herself.

"Not quite. It is a little more complicated than that. You will have to stay in the hospital for a few days."

"Mami, I can't do that. I don't want to have an operation. I don't want to miss school; everyone's going to talk about me."

"Chell, I know this must be scary, so let's take it slowly. I'm going to step outside and talk to the doctor alone. We'll be back in a minute. Stay in the room. I'll be right back."

Dr. Stevenson loved technology and used it for all of her patients' records, so her office was not cluttered with a lot of paper and x-rays. Diane took a seat at her conference table before asking her question. "So, just how serious is this?"

"Not too dangerous because we caught it early," the doctor replied. "She is probably about six or seven weeks pregnant. If it had been later, it could have been much more dangerous. She should make a full recovery. Once this is over, she will need bed rest for a few days, like I said. And Diane, I would suggest we start her on the pill if she's going to continue to be sexually active."

"The pill? I don't think that's necessary. She has promised me not to see him again."

"I can't tell you how to raise your child, Diane, but if she were my daughter, I would do it purely from a precautionary standpoint. Look, I know that you don't want to encourage sexual activity, but let's face it — she should have used a condom. She didn't. Young girls, especially ones who are sexually active, can easily be misled. But certainly, it's your call. I also ran some tests for STDs. I won't have those results for a few days. Once I get them back, I'll get her on any medications she may need."

"Is there reason to think there might be? And when will you perform the procedure?"

"STD testing is standard. I especially want to test for the human papilloma virus, HPV. At her age, there is a huge risk of exposure. As for the procedure, I want to admit her now. The sooner the better. We will keep her under observation for a couple of hours and then perform the surgery this afternoon."

"How worried do I need to be?"

"Diane, this should be pretty routine, believe me. I won't know for sure until I get in there, but there isn't anything out of the ordinary that would make me think otherwise at this point. I've done plenty of procedures like this and I will take care of your daughter. I would tell you not to worry, but I know that you will anyway. Any further questions?"

Dr. Stevenson's voice was very caring and Diane appreciated that. She shook her head no, then said, "In my day, this was pretty darn serious. Has technology changed things that much?"

"Yes, actually. It's amazing what we can do now. A lot of these procedures aren't even invasive. Listen, this is going to impact my schedule today so let me get out of here. I'll have the nurse work with you to complete the paperwork and get her checked into the hospital. If you have any more questions, feel free to have them page me."

Diane left Dr. Stevenson's office feeling numb. Her baby, with a tubular pregnancy, was about to have surgery. She needed to call Luis and get him up to speed on the situation. He had a right to know. Once Diane was finished with the paperwork and Chell was settled into her room, she stepped into the hallway and called Luis. She found it so difficult to tell him what was going on with their daughter because once more she felt inadequate as a mother. Everything that she had done to keep him away from their children to assure that they'd be better backfired because of her choices. One by one, each child was stumbling and falling and she had missed all of the warning signs because she had focused more on her emotions tied to Luis.

When she finished telling him the story, he reassured her that Chell would be fine – after all, she came from good stock – and said he was on his way. Next she called David to repeat the story. She was so relieved when David said he would leave work early and stay with the boys so Rosie wouldn't have to work late. He also offered to come to the hospital, but she felt the boys needed him more than she did. Of course she didn't bother to mention that Luis was on his way. David was in a good place and she didn't want to say anything to change that.

By the time Luis arrived, Chell had drifted off to sleep. The nurse had started an IV and given her a little pain medicine that Dr. Stevenson ordered. Diane was reading a magazine while she waited. She was sitting in a chair next to the bed with her back to the door so she didn't see Luis walk in, but she heard his silky voice say, "How is she?"

Diane looked up and managed to allow a small smile to appear on her face. She didn't want him to worry more than he probably already had on the way there. In a soft voice she told him, "She's scared and so I am."

"How did this happen?"

"Oh Luis, puppy love. She fell for some older guy who plays on the team with Luis J. Girls her age are already vulnerable, but with all that's going on with us, our family, she was even more susceptible. I have been searching my brain trying to understand why I didn't see this coming. I obviously wasn't watching her closely enough. She and I have talked a little about sex and the responsibilities that come with it. I even told her if she felt she just had to, that she needed to take precaution. But, here we are. I thought she understood what I was explaining to her and that she knew better. Here again another one of our children has fallen down. I have been the worst mother to them. Each one has suffered as a result of my choices."

Diane brushed away a tear from her cheek knowing she didn't deserve the empathy that tears often fostered. She had made this mess, so she had to own it. Every nasty bit of it.

Luis put his hand on her shoulder and said, "Di, you can't be with them 24/7. I know you taught her right from wrong. I know you would not have let this happen if you could have avoided it. But she's been through a lot, like the rest of us. Girls react differently to things than boys do."

"Apparently not; she turned to sex, too."

"But she didn't really turn to sex, it just ended up involving sex. She was looking for attention and affection. When I moved out and didn't have a paternal relationship with her, that started her down this path. Even though David was there, he wasn't her father. She was missing me. Then she lost Carlos and finally Luis J. She needed to know if it was because of her somehow. So she needed to find a guy who could give her what was created by our absences. This boy recognized her neediness and took advantage of it. When that need isn't there, then boys have to lure nice girls with gifts, dates and lies that she's special. Horny, teenage boys are the worse. We just have to do better in preparing our baby girl. We talked about this regarding Luis J, but I think now more than ever we should consider family counseling. I think it might help all of us."

Diane felt a little calmer by his observations. She loved her children so much and only tried to protect them, to give them a fair start in life. She wasn't doing so well with that goal.

"The doctor recommends we start her on birth control pills. I'm not so sure I want to do that because I don't want to give her a green light that it's okay now for her to have sex. What do you think?"

Luis moved closer to the bed to kiss his daughter before responding. "Diane, that may be sticking your head in the sand. She'll be fifteen next month. Like I said, she was looking for attention. Sex is just a symptom. I agree with the doctor. She should take the pills until we can work through what's bothering her. Can you support that?"

"I guess so. I never would have imagined we would be talking about tubal pregnancy and sexual promiscuity regarding Chell, at least not at this age." She paused as she watched him gently rubbing Chell's forehead. "Luis, I can't help but wonder why the hell I can't get this right. I mean, can't we just catch a break?"

"I know Diane, it's been a rough ride since Carlos' passing; one thing after another. It's not what we're doing, but what we've done. This is all a culmination of life choices and mixed messages. I know it seems unbearable, but I assure you that we will get through it. The one good thing is that we're finally a family going through it together."

Diane heard him and knew he was right, as terrible as it all seemed. She wondered where she would be were it not for marrying David when she was at her lowest, or repairing her relationship with Luis after they lost Carlos. She would be going through all of this alone. It would have killed her. She just knew it.

She relaxed as the two of them sat with Chell until it was time for the surgery. Diane saw how vulnerable and fragile she looked lying there covered by the white sheet and thin blanket. Diane hadn't been in a hospital since the night Carlos died. She shivered at the memory and Luis thought she might be cold. He reached out to embrace her and shelter her from the coolness in the hospital room. She welcomed his touch and prayed that he would one day forgive her for ruining their children's lives.

Around three-thirty, the team wheeled Chell to the surgical floor. Diane and Luis were told they could stay in her room because that's where she would be returned after post op treatment. They engaged in small talk until Diane dosed off in the chair. Luis sat on the foot of the bed, reading. That's where they were when Dr. Stevenson entered the room.

"Mr. Rodriquez, it's nice to see you." The greeting made Luis smile because she had remembered him after all this time and because Diane apparently hadn't trashed him with her.

Diane stirred and then set up when she heard the talking. It took her a minute to regain her composure and remember why she was there. Dr. Stevenson waited for Diane's consciousness to return and began, "The procedure went well and Michelle's going to be just fine. She does not have any damage to her fallopian tubes. Youth was on her side. She's in post op on a pain medication drip and will be given antibiotics. It will make her very drowsy, so she'll be out of it for a few hours. As I said, we'll keep her in the hospital until tomorrow and then you can take her home. She will need bed rest for two days or so and then she can move around, but be careful that she does not overdo it. I want her to stay out of school for a week. I'll have a prescription for you for the birth control if you agree with my recommendation for her to take the pill."

When Diane nodded, Dr. Stevenson continued, "Good. I really do believe that is the right choice. I will also have her on some mild pain medication and antibiotics to fight off any infections. The note for school will simply allude to a virus. They don't need all of the details. And by the way, her time off would be a good time to revisit that sex talk. Do you have any questions?"

Neither Diane nor Luis said anything, so Dr. Stevenson continued, "We will start her on the pill tomorrow before she is released. If you prefer, I can talk to her about it as doctor to patient."

Both Diane and Luis simply nodded, so the doctor continued, "We'll also schedule her checkup to make sure she's healing and to assess any side effects of the pill. As you remember, we may have to play around with them to find the best one for her. I think a low dose will work, but we'll talk about that tomorrow, with Michelle, during her discharge. Michelle will have to be responsible for taking the birth control and needs to understand what the pill does and doesn't do. Like it won't protect her from venereal disease. I know this is a lot to absorb, but I'm here for the whole ride."

She put a hand on Diane's shoulder. Diane smiled and said, "Thank you, Dr. Stevenson, for taking care of my baby...better than me."

"You're welcome but please don't say that. As parents, all we strive to do is our best. And even with our best, things happen. So don't beat yourself up. She will learn a lot from you based on how you handle what happens next. How you help her get through this will teach her quite a bit about how to handle adversity in our lives. We all go through it, but it's what we learn from it that counts. Now, go home and get some rest. You both look exhausted. She's in our hands tonight. There isn't anything you can do for her but sit here and watch her sleep, or go home and come back refreshed and clear headed tomorrow. Besides, if you stay any longer, your names will be added to the bill," she said chuckling, as she walked briskly away down the hallway.

Luis smiled. He could see why Diane still saw Dr. Stevenson. She cared about her patients and that was a trait one wanted in a physician. "Come on, Di, she's right. I'll take you to get a bite and then I'll take you home."

"Thanks, but my car is here. Besides, I need to be alone for a while."

"No, the last thing you need is to be alone and beating yourself up. Leave your car in the garage and come over to my place for a little while. You said David has the boys, right?"

"Yes, but I don't know if I should go with you."

"Why not?"

Diane could think of a ton of reasons why she shouldn't go with him, but her need not to go home just at that moment was stronger. "You know what, you're right. I'm not ready to go home yet. I can't be a mother right now."

"You've had a long, stressful day. You can take a long hot shower and lay down for a while. I'll get you something to eat and you can let me pamper you for a few hours. When you're ready, I'll bring you back here so you can get your car and drive home. Come on."

It sounded wonderful so Diane didn't fight him; instead she took his hand and walked to the car. They drove to Luis' condo with very little conversation between them, yet all that had been said lingered in the air. Diane was so tired of having these traumatic events popping up in her life, uninvited and certainly unwanted. She had sacrificed so much and fought so hard to give her children a good life. But the more she fought, the more roadblocks she ran into. The pain in her heart launched the tears that rolled down her cheeks when she blinked. She turned toward the window so she could brush them away without drawing attention to herself. But Luis was so in tune with her, he reached out his hand, palm up, fingers spread as he had done for years when he knew that words wouldn't bring her comfort. Diane slid her fingers in-between his and they closed around each other's. They stayed connected like that until they reached the condo.

Luis led her into the bedroom and handed her some towels. He turned on the shower and left her to get settled. She removed her clothes, laying them on the sitting chair in the bedroom and stepped into the master bathroom inside the waiting shower. It was an oversized tub with the nozzle mounted up high and set to pulsating. Diane stood in the middle of the stream so the beads of water could mix with the salt in the tears that were streaming down her cheeks now. She was crying for her fourteen-year-old daughter who was experiencing things adult women face. She was crying for her seventeen-year-old child who was battling with some form of addiction. She was crying for Carlos who was lying six feet below and never going to be able to raise his son. She was crying for Luis, whose heart was so big he still could care for the woman who ripped his children out of his arms six years ago and stood at the root of every bad act that was happening to them.

The stream of water was so strong it was starting to make Diane's muscles ache, but she didn't move. She couldn't because she hoped the water was somehow cleansing her, that perhaps when she emerged from the shower, she would have washed away all of the hurt and bad luck that was hovering over them and better moments would lie ahead.

When she finally came out, her skin wrinkled and hair soaked, she slid into Luis' robe, which was on the back of the door and smelled of him. She wrapped it tightly around her body as though it was his arms. When she opened the bathroom door, the steam was sucked into the bedroom and dissipated quickly, leaving little evidence of its existence. She hoped that it pulled her bad mojo with it. Luis had turned the sheets back and the lights off so the only light in the room was from the few candles strategically placed so she could find her way to the bed.

There was a glass of red wine that she assumed was Merlot, but when she sipped it, the body was different. She took another sip and shook her head as her palette reminded her of its origin, Argentina. It was a Malbec. It was one of her favorite wines, but she didn't buy it often because it could be a little pricey. She took another sip before sitting on the bed. She was feeling a little calmer and as she sat there, she could hear the smooth jazz radio station playing Roy Ayers' song *Everybody Loves The Sunshine*. She was just crawling into the bed when she heard Luis climbing the stairs to his bedroom. The smooth coolness of the four-hundred thread count sheets comforted her body.

"Can I get you anything?" Luis asked, standing in the doorway, glad she was finally in the bed.

Diane pointed to the wine, gave him a thumbs up, and smiled. He looked back at her and winked. That mere act of familiarity, once again brought tears to her eyes. "God, Luis, you have done so much already. What more could I possibly ask of you?"

"You could let me hold you, with your permission. May I?"

She smiled and gave a slight head nod. That was something she could always use.

He lay down on top of the covers, next to her, and slowly placed his arms around her. He snuggled close and could smell the scent of the soap on her body. He closed his eyes and remembered how soft her skin felt.

With his eyes still closed, he said, "Di, no one can control what happens to their children. We try to protect them as best we can from the harsh realities of life, but most of the time, it's out of our control. All we can do is try to prepare them for what lies ahead so that they know how to react and hopefully bounce back with minimal scars. If you think back on your life, you will see the pitfalls you had, the impact it had on your life and how it shaped the woman you are today. A beautiful, sensitive, caring woman."

"But all three of our children have had some unbelievably tough times so early in their lives. I know some parents who have raised children that have never had any issues. My record sucks right now and I'm almost afraid to think about what lies ahead for the last two kids under my roof. My mother told me I wasn't doing a good job with them and it turns out she's right."

"Diane Rodri…Anderson, that is so far from the truth that you need the Golden Gate Bridge to get from where you are to that statement you just made," he said, chuckling. "I honestly hope you don't really believe that. Your mother was not perfect by any dictionary definition. She was way too controlling and it was to a fault, especially where you're concerned. She has fueled your insecurity and caused you to have self-doubt. No good parent does that to a child."

"That's the only side of my mother I can ever remember. I'm lying here now trying to figure out how I am going to tell her about Chell's missteps, let alone Luis J's. I would keep it from her, but she may be a great-grandmother, again. I'm sure that will make her day."

"I wish you could see yourself the way I see you. You have grown so much since we met and even more since we divorced. Clearly our divorce has had a negative impact on the boys and now Chell, but they aren't in any trouble that can't be corrected. NaNa says, 'What doesn't kill you makes you stronger.' I know that has been true for me."

"Luis, it wasn't the divorce, it was me. I had the negative impact on the kids. It was a result of my choices, my behavior and my parenting skills. I have to own that. Chell had surgery this afternoon because of how I handled the divorce, not because we got a divorce. I am starting to see things much clearer now. I just wish it wasn't at the expense of the children's and your wellbeing, physically and emotionally."

Diane just wanted to put all of this out of her mind for a while. She wanted to feel good and there was one way she knew to capture that blissfulness. "Oh Luis, I want to feel good tonight. I want to make you feel good. Would you do that? Would you allow me to at least do that for you?"

"Di…"

"No, don't talk me out of it this time. I remember how good you made me feel. I want to feel that way again. I need to feel that way right now."

Luis held her tighter and said, "Oh, sweetheart, you're hurting. I don't want to compound that. Besides, you're still married to David. You're able to keep him grounded because you can honestly say that you are not cheating on him. This isn't you. You don't break your vows."

Ignoring his words of wisdom, she asked, "Aren't you still attracted to me?"

"You know that I am. I always have been. You are my addiction and I don't know why you keep testing me. Sooner or later I'm going to give in," he said, smiling.

"Make it sooner. Make it now."

He exhaled deeply. He wanted her. He knew he could make her feel good for this moment, but he also knew it wasn't what was best for either of them. "Di, I don't want to be the cause or source of any more pain in your life."

"You won't be."

"I've wanted to be with you for months. I can't believe you're lying in my bed right now with no clothes on and I'm on top of the blanket. I need to have my head examined," Luis said, still holding her, his eyes closed once again.

"So, stop talking and kiss me and then let me examine your head."

He chuckled at the pun and lifted his head. She raised hers so they could exchange a passionate kiss. But instead, Luis kissed her on the forehead.

"We can't do this. Just let me hold you until you fall asleep. I'll wake you up in a couple of hours and we can go back to the hospital."

Diane exhaled because she knew he was right. So she turned off the ringer on her phone, closed her eyes, and felt safe in the arms of her first love. He was never forceful and that comforted her. She slept in his arms and he in hers for about two hours.

When they finally returned to the hospital to retrieve Di's car, they stopped on the floor for one last check on Chell and found David there. Diane felt a sudden tinge of apprehensiveness, wondering if something had gone wrong with her daughter. She walked straight toward David, but before she could inquire about Chell, he demanded, "Where the hell have you been?"

"David, lower your voice. We took a break for a little while. What're you doing here?" Diane asked.

"The hospital called. Chell's fever spiked and they wanted someone to be here. They said that you and Luis had left and you weren't answering your phone. Why did you leave her alone?"

Diane tried to peer around his frame, which was blocking the path to Chell's room, to make sure her baby was okay. "I didn't. She was fine when we left. Dr. Stevenson told us she would sleep through the night. In fact she urged us to go home. Is Chell alright? What's wrong? And where are the boys? You didn't bring them here, did you?"

"No, I took them to Marvin's house and then came over here immediately. The doctor is in with her now so I don't have an update yet. And what about you? Where did you go? Where's your cell?" David asked, looking at Luis in disgust.

"David, I took Di to my place so she could shower, freshen herself and rest. I live really close to here. She was exhausted. I'm sure you can appreciate that."

"I wasn't talking to you, Luis. And no, I don't appreciate that. Would you if she were still your wife?"

Diane's calmness remained intact in spite of David's insinuations and she said, "David, can we talk about this later? Here comes a doctor."

"Good evening, Doctor. What can you tell us about our daughter?" Luis asked, purposefully saying "our" while standing next to Diane. He was beyond annoyed with David's confrontation with Diane after he had just spent the last several hours trying to calm her down. It was obvious that he was emotionally over-the-top by the way he was behaving. Luis noticed the vein in his neck pulsating and the beads of sweat on his forehead when the hospital's temperature was probably not even sixty-five degrees. David was being reckless exhibiting this possessive behavior and Luis knew that it was going to drive Diane right into his arms, exactly where David did not want her to be.

"I checked her vitals, increased her antibiotics and we will continue to monitor her. Sometimes people run a fever after surgery. It's the body's way of fighting back, but we don't anticipate any further issues," the doctor replied.

Luis observed how very young this doctor was. It reminded him of the doctor who first reported Carlos' condition to them. He wondered if the night shift was reserved for the interns and residents. It was a perfect training ground, but he didn't want them learning on his sweet Chell. Luis had just witnessed the artistry of Dr. Stevenson and by comparison, this young doctor before him was green, very green. So the next set of questions he asked were designed to shed some insight into this doctor's familiarity with the case.

"Dr. Stevenson told us that Chell was already on an antibiotic. Which one was she on and why didn't that work? What did you change it to and did you consult Dr. Stevenson to confirm it was best for a young teenager?"

Familiar with these lines of questioning, the doctor smiled and said, "Mr. Rodriquez, I have completely reviewed your daughter's charts and I am very familiar with her case. I should also let you know that I was in the operating room assisting Dr. Stevenson this afternoon with Chell's procedure and I am one of her residents. The reason this happened is that sometimes we develop a resistance to antibiotics when they are prescribed too frequently over a period of time. When that happens, they don't work as well. As you can imagine, there's a list of them for us to choose from. Look, trust me, I have your daughter's best interests as a top priority this evening. She's in the best care."

He stopped, pulled on the stethoscope that was dangling from his neck, and waited to see if there were any other questions or challenges to his capabilities. Assuming the silence meant they were satisfied with his explanation, he said, "Now, all three of you are welcome to stay, but we're going to keep Michelle sedated for the rest of the night. She won't even know you're here. As Dr. Stevenson suggested earlier, you guys should go home and get some rest. We will definitely call you if anything changes. Good night to you all."

The doctor shook their hands and headed off down the hallway to check on his next patient. Luis' concerns had been put to bed – the young man was impressive and was on his way to becoming a good doctor.

David was first to break the silence. "Diane, come on, I'll take you home. Since Luis lives so close by, there's no need for him to be inconvenienced any longer."

Diane rolled her eyes. "Thank you for coming to the hospital to check on Chell, David. I have my car, so I don't need a ride. But will you keep the boys tonight? I just want to go home and get some rest."

David was suspicious of her motives until Luis spoke, "Di, I could take the boys. It would give both of you a break."

"How the hell is that supposed to work?" David shot back. "It's not surprising, though, coming from you Luis, since you took a long break. Man, Robert doesn't even know who the hell you are. Besides, I don't need a break from my children."

Not appreciative of David's snide remarks, Luis only coolly noted them, but didn't respond for Diane's sake. He merely nodded okay.

"David, can you please stop cursing? Geez, we are in a hospital." She didn't know where this foul-mouthed behavior was coming from but it was yet another change she did not like. "So can you just keep them?" she asked.

"Of course I can keep them. I just think it would be better for them to be in their own bed and they also need to see you."

"I can't, David. I can't be responsible for them tonight. I'm not in a nurturing mood. Please, just do this without giving me a lot of grief about it."

"Sure, absolutely. So what type of mood are you in exactly?" He had a ton of other interpretations of her mood that he wanted to share, but he didn't want to push her any further. Not right now.

Ignoring the dig, but satisfied with his response to keep the boys, Diane then turned to Luis and said in a warmer tone, "Luis, thank you for the offer. I really appreciate it, but we do need to minimize the amount of change we expose them to tonight. I hope you understand." She wanted this man to know how much he had given her this evening without causing David to go any further off the deep end.

Continuing to "cockblock", David interjected, "Let me walk you to your car. It's late and sometimes those garages can be a haven for bad types."

Seeing right through him, Diane said, "Thanks for the offer, but I'll be fine. I really just want to be alone. Good night." Both of the men in her life watched as she walked away.

Without taking his eyes off Diane, David asked, "So what exactly happened tonight between you and my wife?" He made sure to place the same heavy emphasis on "my wife" as Luis had previously placed on "our child."

But Luis was no longer watching Diane. Instead, he was facing David and staring him down, waiting for him to turn toward him. When he finally did, Luis responded, "Nothing, David. Diane is a beautiful woman who's going through some very difficult times. We all are, but she doesn't need either of us piling on. When you attack her like that, it makes her feel like a failure."

"That's not what I asked you, Luis. What happened between you two that has her wanting to be left alone? What is she so upset about that she doesn't even want the boys?"

"I don't know what you're implying, man, but I already told you what happened. She went to my place, took a shower and slept. When she woke up, we came back over here. End of story."

David knew there was more to it than Luis was saying. There was a coolness that Diane had given him and he knew it was being fueled by something. "I don't trust you, Luis. You like drama and sleeping with another man's wife, or cheating on your own, obviously gives you a rise. But I won't allow you to pull my Diane back into your crazy life."

"Well, that's not up to you, now is it, David? If Di needs me, whether she's yours or not, I will be there for her. If you have a problem with that, that's just too damn bad. I haven't interfered with your relationship with my children in all the time you've been together. I've respected you and never questioned your love for them or Diane. And I don't interfere with how you're raising Robert now, even though you have no legal rights to him. He may call you Daddy, but his last name is still Rodriquez, so don't push me, man. I'm happy they have you in their lives, but Di is allowing me to reconnect with them and I have no intentions of letting you or anyone else interfere with that. And for the record, I've never slept with another man's wife. But what about you, did you sleep with Diane before our divorce was final?"

Disarmed a bit by Luis' question and declaration, David ignored the implications and said, "Look, man to man, just keep your damn hands, and everything else, off my wife."

"David, I won't sully Diane's vows and neither will she, but if you aren't able to keep her, it won't be my fault. You just keep on falsely accusing her and belittling her and the door will be wide open. And believe me, if it ever opens again, I'm walking in and locking it behind me." And with that, Luis headed down the hallway to check on his daughter.

David watched as Luis walked away. He had to fight every urge to tackle him from behind and take him to the floor. But instead he thought, 'He is so fucking arrogant. If it ever opens again, he's walking in. Hell, he's the one trying to kick it down. It's so obvious he can't wait to get Diane into bed, try to reclaim his position in her life, pick up where they left off. Well, not in this lifetime, son.'

But he had to get Diane to see through Luis' bullshit. He had to soil that armor that Luis was working so hard to clean up. David climbed into his car and steered it carefully out of the garage. Once on the street and with a clear cellphone signal, he dialed his mother-in-law and waited for her to answer the phone.

"Mama Margaret, good evening, it's David. I know it's late, but do you have a few minutes?"

"Yes, it is late," Diane's mother replied. "It must be almost 9:30, but I can talk for a few minutes. What can I do for you?"

"I'm just leaving the hospital."

"The hospital? At this time of night? What's happened now? Is it you?"

"No, no, it's not me."

"Then who? Oh, Lord. Is it Diane?"

"No, but she's barely hanging in there. I don't know how to tell you this, but it's about Chell."

"What's wrong with Chell?" Mama Margaret asked, preparing for the worst. This was her only granddaughter. She closed her eyes and mumbled a quick prayer while she waited.

"She was pregnant. There were complications and they had to perform surgery on her today."

"Pregnant! Oh no. Not my sweet Chell, too? I told Diane she needed to get better control over those children. She is damaging each and every one of them. She's my only mistake and for the life of me I can't see what I did wrong with her." She paused for a moment to quickly rewind and fast-forward through Diane's childhood and upbringing before continuing.

"You know what? You should have never moved out. You should have stood your ground and got her to see things your way. She needs that discipline and that control, always has. And now that we know, so do her children, apparently. They are all over the map, looking for love in all the wrong places. Umph, umph, umph! I don't know what to say. Is Michelle going to be alright? Will there be any permanent damage?"

"She's resting. I just left her. The doctors say she should make a full recovery."

"Thank goodness for that. Did Diane stay with her tonight? I can't bear the thought of her being alone."

"No, they told all of us to go home and come back in the morning."

"All of us? So I guess Luis was there, too?"

"Of course. But that's understandable."

"I suppose. But son, thank you for telling me. I know she would have tried to hide it."

"I just thought you should know, but you can't let her know I told you. It'll cause all kind of problems for me."

"I know, dear. She'll be looking for someone to blame and you'll be it…when we all know who is really to blame. How are the other kids?"

"Robert and CJ are fine. I've continued to be involved in their lives. I love them and they need the consistency. Luis J, on the other hand, I don't know what to say about him."

"Now, that's a topic I want information about. What's really going on there, David? Couldn't get a straight answer from Diane. I know she's hiding something from me about him, too."

David smiled because he was getting exactly what he wanted. He was setting Diane up for an ambush from her mother and then he would be the one to come in and save her, build her back up. He just had to make sure Mama Margaret didn't name him as her source.

"I really shouldn't be the one to tell you. Why don't you ask her? She's going to be home alone tonight; I'm keeping the boys. Maybe she'll be more willing to talk about it with you now. Mama Margaret, I'm really worried about her. She's making some very questionable decisions. Like tonight, the hospital couldn't find her when Chell's fever spiked so they called me. I give you one guess as to why she didn't answer the phone."

"Don't tell me she was with Luis."

"Sorry to say, that's exactly where she was. They gave me some story about her only taking a shower and napping because he lives close to the hospital. But I don't trust him and I know you don't either. I know he's taking advantage of Diane's insecurities and vulnerabilities. She's so susceptible right now."

"Oh, you can bet he is…and he's smooth about it, too. Oh, David, I'm so sorry. I raised her better than that. It's that Luis. He gets into her head and turns those brains into mush with his bedroom voice. Son, you have got to stake your place in her life and you have to move quickly. Now would be a good time. I know she's feeling defeated with this, her third child, suffering from her poor child rearing. I'll do whatever I can, you know that, to help you get back into her life before she completely ruins everything – including those kids – trying to get back with Luis," Mama Margaret concluded, sucking her teeth.

"Mama Margaret, thank you so much for your support."

"I wouldn't have it any other way, David. Give her a call in the morning and see if she is more receptive."

"Right. But remember, she can't know that we've talked. Good night, and thanks again."

David ended the call knowing that he had been disloyal to Diane, but he had nowhere else to turn. He was losing his grip on his wife and he had no idea what to do to stop it. He tried to figure out what had changed and why she was so different.

He had to acknowledge that Luis had never been a threat before because he hadn't been a part of their lives. He was on the outside and that's where Diane wanted to keep him. He was banned from her heart and her kids. That made it easy then for David to suggest that Luis have a relationship with his children because he knew that Diane would never allow it. But now, she was walking, no running, into Luis' arms and it was torturing him. He wondered if Diane even realized how much she was affecting him, threatening him almost. He never liked being backed into a corner.

Diane had not long laid down, her head buried in the pillow, when the phone rang. She thought for a moment of letting it go to voicemail, but considered that it might be the hospital again so she answered the ringing.

"Hello."

"Diane. It's your mother."

There was that voice. Now she wished she had Caller ID and she had countless reasons for buying that phone feature lately. But staying calm, she said, "Hi, Mama. It's kinda late for you. Are you guys alright?"

"We're fine, but you sound exhausted. Is everything alright?" Mama Margaret asked, laying the foundation for the ambush.

"Yes, but it's been an incredibly long day. As a matter of fact I was just hitting the hay. I'm tired."

"This early? You don't usually go to bed until well after 11. How are the kids?"

"They're fine. They're with David."

"Michelle, too?"

"What? No. Look Mama, if this isn't urgent, can I call you back tomorrow? I'm really tired."

"Yes, you keep saying that. What's really going on Diane? I can hear in your voice that something's not right. Is Chell asleep? She's usually the first one to answer the phone. Why didn't she answer the phone?"

"She would have, but she isn't here. She's spending the night away from home. Speaking of going to bed early, why are you still awake? You usually turn in by 10 yourself." Diane wanted to make sure they were both really alright before she politely excused herself and ended the call. She was not ready to relay any information about Chell to her mother. Not yet.

"Diane, you can't distract me that easily. Why is Chell spending the night at a friend's? Oh goodness, what has happened now? I know you, something's wrong."

"Oh, for goodness sake, Mama, can't you leave well enough alone? Good night!" Diane exclaimed and hung up the phone.

Of course Mama Margaret called right back, but Diane refused to answer it. It rang again and again but she still didn't answer it. When it started ringing for the fourth time, she grabbed the receiver.

"Mama, this is ridiculous. It's way past your bedtime. Would you please just leave me alone?"

"I want to know what's going on. You might as well tell me. Has Luis Jr. moved back in yet? You still haven't told me where he's living. Or does this mood have something to do with Luis? Has he broken your heart again? Well, say something…or I'll make another trip back there and stay until I find out myself."

"You think so? And stay where exactly? You would not be welcome here with that attitude." Diane heard her mother gasp as she continued, "Why can't you respect my position as an adult woman and accept yours now as grandmother? I make the decisions in my house for my family like you did when we were young and living in your house. Your mother wasn't sniffing around inserting herself into your marriage or how you were raising your children and I'm not going to allow you to do that to me. You are my mother and I love you, but you don't control my life. I don't have to tell you what's going on with me, my children, my husband, or my ex, unless I choose to. And right now, I choose not to. Please don't call here any more tonight or tomorrow until you're ready to accept my terms. I need to get some rest, so I'm hanging up now. Good night."

Unable to let it go, Mama Margaret had to trump Diane. "Diane, I already know about Michelle. You really screwed up this time. I told you to keep an eye on her when I was there. You were so busy kicking me out, you didn't listen. Now you have another mess on your hands. David told me all about it."

"You're right about one thing – this situation is on my hands, Mama, not yours. And it's not a mess; it is life. Life is messy. You should know; you gave birth to three children. So look, don't try to turn your interference and intimidation on me. It does not work anymore. And why am I not surprised to hear that your dear sweet David has been talking to you behind my back? I should have known that you were in his ear and he in yours."

Realizing her slip, Mama Margaret stressed, "Diane, it doesn't matter who told me. You're missing the point. Besides, he's just worried about you; so am I," Mama Margaret interjected, still trying to move the focus from David. Diane had pushed her so far she had blurted it out without considering the implications to him that would surely be coming. She had never seen Diane have such an opinion or position before. Diane had started exhibiting this behavior during Mama Margaret's visit and apparently it had been building steam and gaining momentum. But she didn't approve of this defiant attitude and she had every intention of letting her baby child know.

"Mama, it does matter. And this has backfired for David because you just made things worse between us. This is a marriage between David and me. You are not married to us. I am taking care of my life and my family and I would appreciate it if you stayed out of it."

"I can't stay out of it. Those are my grandchildren's lives you're ruining. If you want to ruin your life, going back to Luis, so be it. But I think you should let Michelle come live with your Dad and me. I can keep an eye on her better than you, apparently, and make sure she gets refocused on school and not those crazy boys. None of you were sidetracked because I had you on a plan…until you met that Luis."

Diane chuckled and said, "Mama, you must be kidding. I would never agree to that. That's all my poor baby needs is to think that I abandoned her so she can be ambushed by your heavy-handed, insensitive self. Never! I don't need your help with Chell or any of my other children and I don't want your help. I've told you before and I'm telling you again, I'm perfectly capable of raising my children on my own."

"Really? Are you sure about that? Are you proud of what you have done so far?"

"Yes I am, because I'm doing it my way. Bumps, bruises, successes, everything my way."

"You better get your act together Diane, before child protective services gets wind of this and comes a-knocking. They don't like bumps and bruises on children. You're treading on thin ice, my dear, thin ice."

"Are you threatening to report me?"

"Oh I wouldn't do it. You've made it clear that I should mind my own business, but you do have neighbors and the school officials watching everything. And any impropriety will have to be reported. I'm just trying to give you an alternative, at least for Chell, to a foster home."

"First of all, the school and neighbors have no idea about Chell's condition, so if I do hear from them, I will know that it came from either you or David. And I am warning you now, if you even think about doing anything to cause any more complications in our lives, you will find out just how much I've changed. I mean it Mama, step back and step off!"

Diane paused to maintain her focus and then said, "You can't bully me or make me feel inferior anymore. I have moved to a new place in my life and there's no room in it for the woman who raised me. Your time for beating me down has expired and there are no options to renew. I don't want to shut you out of my life, but I will before I allow you to try to make me live in that world again. And I will never let you do that to my children. So, I'm done talking tonight. I'm going to hang up and

I hope you make the right choice to determine if we will have any kind of relationship at all. Good night, mother."

Diane didn't give her mother a chance to say another word. She pressed the off button and returned it to the cradle. She was so proud of herself. She had finally stood up to her mother and it felt good. Really good! She could finally breathe a full deep breath and not feel like her lungs weren't fully expanded. The knot in her stomach that had taken up residence twenty-five years ago was loosening. She didn't even jump when the phone rang again about fifteen minutes later. She was ready for anything Margaret Johnson had been practicing for the last fourteen minutes.

"Mama, I just need to hear one word out of your mouth and that will determine if I hang up on you for the last time in my life."

"Whoa! Diane, it's me, Michelle."

"Oh, sorry, girl."

"Well, now I see why Mama called me. She told me what was going on with you and the children, but she didn't tell me about your tongue. Are you alright? How are the kids?"

"I'm fine for the first time in a long time. I am praying that Chell will make a full recovery. And Luis J is still acting out his mourning for Carlos, but I am hopeful that he will turn the corner, too. But I really don't want to talk to you about this. I have had enough of Mama's interference."

"Diane, I'm your sister. I love you. I didn't call to judge you or instruct you on what to do. I called to support you. I just want to see if I can help. I am not Mama."

"Really? It's funny I never hear from you until I'm on my back with my belly exposed."

"Is that how you feel?"

"Yes, it is."

"You know, you could call me sometimes. You could let me know what's going on with you. Our lack of communication has been your choice, little sister. I'm just following your lead."

"So I should reach out to you and what, have you share everything with Mama? Give her the 4-1-1 she needs to try to paint me as a total failure?"

"Wow, I had no idea you thought so little of our relationship."

"I don't know why not. When was the last time we talked, Carlos' funeral?"

"Yes. And I'm sorry about my behavior at the funeral, but I wasn't getting a vibe from you that would indicate the door was open. And then when I saw you and Luis, it made me feel guilty about my role in your divorce. But afterwards since the funeral, I have called you a few times. You weren't home. I talked to Chell. I guess she didn't tell you."

"No, she didn't. So, what do you want from tonight's call?" Diane chose to be forward because she was not going to allow Mama another avenue into her life. She had given her the only two options she had and using Michelle to gain access was not one of them.

"I'm just offering you my help, a sisterly ear, or shoulder to lean on if you should need one. If you want you can use it now or you can save it for another day. I won't pressure you. But know that it takes two to have a relationship and you've done a great job shutting some of us out. Good-night, baby girl."

Diane hadn't heard that title in a long time. It was one only Michelle used as a term of endearment. As Diane remembered the closeness they once shared, a different emotion entered her and she said, "Michelle, wait. I could use someone to talk to who isn't going to judge me. Can you be that person?"

"Anytime you need it," Michelle responded, happy to be asked.

Diane thought about how that used to be true. "What makes tonight different, Michelle? I once thought we were thick as thieves, that there wasn't anything we couldn't share. But you betrayed me once before, so why should I believe this will be different?"

"You're right. I did. But Diane, that was a long time ago. I thought I was doing what was in your best interest. I know now that I should have kept my place and let you deal with the issues in your marriage. I regret the day I betrayed you to Mama and told her about Luis' infidelity. I will never know how much that impacted your decision to divorce him instead of working it out. I truly regret that choice I made. I don't know what else I can say to convince you I've learned my lesson and can be your confidant again."

"But surely you can understand why I would be hesitant now. I called you that night in confidence. I needed your support and I told you not to tell anyone. But you did. Why?"

"Mostly because I didn't know how to help you and thought Mama would. Hell, she's the one that's been married forever. She really does love you, despite some of the things she does and the ways she does them. But I didn't think she would lash out like that at Luis, and certainly did not think she would suggest that you divorce him. But you know, you're her child, just like Chell is yours. Mama's way of protecting you may not be right, but she only thought she was doing what was best for you. All I can tell you this time is, I've learned my lesson and I would like the opportunity to prove it to you, to really be supportive of you, if you need it."

With that, Diane's barriers came tumbling down and she told Michelle about everything. She talked about her thoughts about her marriage, where it was heading, and why David's betrayal and new aggressive behavior was pushing him out of her life. About her self-doubts about her parenting, Luis, and the emotions that were being rekindled. About Luis J and his addiction. About the child Maria was carrying that could be Luis' or Luis J's. About Chell. And lastly, about her mother, their mother, who was making her feel completely inadequate and not worthy of having the title of mother. It was a cleansing that Diane had longed for but didn't know of anyone with whom she could trust to share her emotional content and allow her some release.

"So, what do you suggest I do with my life?" she asked, hoping her sister had a magic potion for her to consume.

"Exhale and inhale and then swallow your pride," was the potion that her sister offered.

"What do you mean?"

"You have always been harder on yourself than you need to be. You always think you have to solve everything on your own. No one expects you to be perfect...except you."

"Mama does and she takes every opportunity she can to show me that I'm not."

"Diane, newsflash, you're grown. Mama only has as much control as you give her. Don't you think she tries to insert herself into my life? I have to constantly remind her to back off. You need to do the same thing, and based on how you answered the phone just now, you're starting to figure that out."

Diane laughed. "If only she would listen to me. In her eyes, I failed and you haven't. You delivered your Master's to her. I did not. She just tries to marginalize me every chance she gets. She even goes behind my back and talks to my husband and my ex. Who does that? In fact, I am certain she orchestrated David's dependence on her. Bet. She's convinced he's the answer to all of my troubles and that she has answers for him to help our marriage."

"Diane, you have to stop empowering her. You have a number of decisions to make about your life, but you don't need to make them all at once. Your priority right now is Chell. Being there for her is what's most important. Luis J is almost eighteen. He needs to be held accountable for where he puts his dick and all his other foolishness. He knows what alcoholism can do to him and his future. He's seen his uncle and knows what addiction does. What person who claims to truly be an athlete is addicted to drugs…other than steroids?"

They both laughed heartily, and for Diane, it was a much needed release. Michelle continued, "You should let me have fifteen minutes with his smart ass. And Maria is due for an ass whupping, too. Once she drops that baby, you just say when. You remember Tonya, don't you?" They both laughed again as they recalled the times when Michelle would have to remind Tonya, the neighborhood bully, not to mess with her little sister.

"But seriously, as far as Maria is concerned, if that wench, and I use the term loosely, is carrying my nephew's child, Luis J is just going to have to step up, man up, and be responsible for that as well. You can't solve all of your children's problems, Diane. Doesn't that remind you of someone else we know? And you have to know that even she's not perfect."

"I know. You're right and I hate to see that in myself."

"Hell, there you go again. You know Mama never got her Master's either, but she had planned to. So how the hell can you let her make you feel small?"

"Oh yeah, I forgot that she had planned to get her Master's, but she got married and then we came."

"Bingo!"

They both laughed and then were silent.

"Diane, search your heart and your mind. You have always been more in tune with your inner self than anyone I know. Don't let anyone destroy that about you. It is one of the things that makes you unique. When you find that, you will know what to do about David and Luis."

Those words were similar to the ones Luis had said to her the night she escaped from her mother's wrath. She let them settle inside her tonight. There was space for them now.

Michelle knew Diane was processing, so she waited a few minutes before continuing, "Listen, lie down and get some rest. You need to be strong when you go back to the hospital and see my namesake. Give her my love and tell her I want to come and see her soon. And one last thing baby girl, if you want to fall in love with Luis again or acknowledge that you never stopped loving him, that's your business."

"Whoa, where did that come from?"

"Darling, I am your sister. I may not have talked to you in a while, but I know you…and I see everything. I saw you guys in Puerto Rico. I watched him admiring you. It was very lovingly. And I know how much you both loved, and if I were to guess, still love each other. It's just my opinion, but only you can live your life. That's what you have to remember. And you need to tell Mama that again because I suspect you have said that before. But she's a little hardheaded and can be unreasonable sometimes, so repetition works best with her. Okay sweetie, good night. If I can help in anyway, please call me."

"I will. And thank you for listening."

"You're welcome. That's what big sisters are for…or so they tell me. Good night, Diane."

Diane lay there in the dark for a few minutes listening to the music from the clock radio. It was the same station Luis was listening to earlier and they were playing Roy Ayers' *Everybody Loves The Sunshine* again. It reminded her of Luis' warmth, his smell, his love, and that was the last thing she remembered before drifting off to sleep.

Chapter Thirty Six

Somewhere in Diane's subconscious, she finally realized the ringing was not part of her dream, but reality. She rolled over just in time to catch it before it went to voicemail.

"Hello," she responded, in a sleepy voice.

"Good morning, Diane. Did I wake you?" David answered back, with a morning gaiety.

Looking at the clock and trying to focus her eyes, she responded, "Yeah. Is it really eight-thirty?"

"Yes. I was calling to see if you wanted me to pick you up and take you to the hospital."

"No, David, that won't be necessary. I got it," she said, stretching and focusing on relieving the kink in her back. Then she asked, "How are the boys?"

"They're fine. I let them stay at Marvin's since they were already asleep when I left the hospital. And, it's no bother to pick you up. I can be there by the time you're dressed."

Diane really didn't feel like being with David today because she knew he was the reason she didn't sleep well last night. She recalled her conversation with Michelle and how she inspired and encouraged her. She felt good. She had really missed how she and Michelle used to talk like that about everything; Diane could only hope that last night was a new beginning for both of them.

"Baby, are you still there?"

David's voice brought her back to the moment. "David, I know you talked to my mother last night. Why did you do that? What on earth did you hope to gain from that betrayal?"

"What are you talking about?" David asked, frantically hoping Mama Margaret hadn't completely divulged the crux of their conversation.

"My mother called me after I got home last night and knew about Chell. She told me you called and told her about it. Why would you do that? Why would you give her that ammunition to come full blast, guns-a-blazing at me?"

Backed into a corner, David had to think quickly. Realizing the jig was up and that admission was the best course of action, he said, "Yes, I told her."

"I know that you told her," Diane countered quickly. "I ask again, why would you do that, exactly?" She was wide awake now, "woke" and ready for some answers.

"Because I knew she would have to be told eventually and I thought you would appreciate my doing it and bearing the brunt of her comments," David skillfully lied.

Diane chuckled and rolled onto her side. She saw the sun was shining through the slats in the blinds and knew the rays would soon warm the hardwood floors by her side of the bed. She liked to feel that on the balls of her feet when she sat on the edge of the bed. It was soothing to her, but she didn't get the chance to enjoy it often because of work and the kids. But today she didn't have either and could enjoy that sensation if David didn't ruin it for her.

"Did you really think that telling her would spare me any humiliation and criticism?" Diane asked, playing along with his lie. "Come on, you know my mother better than that. I can't believe that's the only reason you told her. What's really going on David?"

"Well, she gave it to me pretty good last night," David persisted along his chosen path. "She even questioned my parenting skills. Told me I shouldn't have moved out because boys would know that there wasn't a man in the house anymore and make Chell their prey. Honestly, by the time she was done, I didn't think there was anything left for her to ridicule either of us about. So what did she say to you?"

David was taking great liberties with the truth, but given how he was blindsided by Diane's knowledge of events, he had no choice. He made a mental note to speak to Mama Margaret about their so-called agreement.

"What didn't she say, would be an easier question to answer. David, you keep reminding me that we're married. That means you and me. My mother is not in this marriage. And every time she pushes her way in or you invite her in, she only manages to make things worse between us. I am not a child for you or her to manage or chastise. Please don't ever interfere like that again, certainly without talking to me about it first. Like I said, I can't believe that you told her thinking that I'd appreciate it.

"But last night, I wasn't the usual wreck I am when I hung up the phone with her. It was hard, but I managed to stand my ground. But still, I probably would have been up all night if not for the phone call that followed hers."

"Let me guess, it was from your precious savior?"

"No, it was not Luis," she replied, sighing heavily. "But, honestly, what would have been the problem with him calling me and then helping me get through a rough situation? One that you created, by the way. It's not like I wanted to call you."

"You can't be serious? For starters, for the hundredth time, he isn't your husband anymore. And yeah, you should have called me, if only to clear the air, if it meant you would have been able to sleep."

"Oh, I was just too angry and had nothing nice to say to you at the time, buddy. I know Luis is not my husband, but we were married long enough to have four children and now a grandchild, maybe two, together. And now we have rekindled our friendship that began before you and I were married. You're going to have to accept the fact that he's going to always have a place in my life."

"It's the kind of place in your life that I'm questioning, Diane. A working relationship with Luis is what I wanted in the beginning, but you were so against it. Now that we're going through a rough patch, you want to befriend him and open up to him. That allows him entry into our family and gives him the green light to try to place dibbs on you. It seems to me that he's in our marriage. And, what about all the hurt he caused with Maria? Are you really willing to just forgive and forget?"

Diane was really shocked and looked at the phone as though she could see David on the other end before she spoke. "David, this is the 'you' I don't know. You just said that you had pushed me to have a relationship with him as my children's father for years. Now, it's a problem. Am I willing to forgive and forget? Didn't you marry someone who you thought was compassionate and loving? Don't you want me to be that way? I will never forget what Luis did, but it was not to me. He did what he did to fulfill his needs. I was hurt by it, yes. His actions affected our relationship in a way that neither of us planned for, but we were both at fault for our relationship getting to that point.

"So yes, David, if I'm going to have some semblance of a healthy life, I have to forgive him and move on. I can't harbor this resentment any longer. It's self-destructive. You've been telling me that for years. So I would think you would be happy I'm finally listening to you."

"Okay, that's fair. I'm good with that. But see here, I don't like what else I see. The closeness, the bonding between you and Luis is not just about parenting. I'm not accusing you, but I sure in hell am pointing the finger at him. I have eyes. I can see."

"You have eyes, but you aren't seeing what's right in front of you. Luis won't be the cause of our marriage failing. It will be because of stunts like the one you orchestrated last night. Those will put an end to our marriage."

"So you can forgive and forget how Luis trampled all over your heart, but if for God's sake I talk to your mother, that's grounds for ending our marriage?"

"Yes, it could be! And I don't get why you can't see that. Listen, the morning is getting away from me and I need to get to the hospital. I'll call you later."

"You're right; it is. I'll meet you at the hospital. Bye."

Diane threw the sheets back and laid there for a minute. When she did finally lift her head off the pillow, followed by the rest of her body, she climbed out on David's side. When she arrived at the hospital, David was already there. He kissed her on the cheek, but when she didn't respond, he moved to the side and allowed her to enter the room.

Chell looked healthy. She was awake and watching television. A big grin came across her face and she lingered in her mother's arms. Diane stayed with her until lunchtime and then, recognizing she hadn't eaten anything at all, she left the room to find a candy machine. David was sitting on a chair in the hallway, waiting for her.

"May I take you to lunch? You must be starving by now," he asked, looking for some wiggle room.

"Sure. We need to finish our conversation from this morning anyway. I'll let Chell know we'll be back in a couple of hours."

They found a sandwich shop that wasn't too crowded and ordered. Diane had a cup of cream of chicken soup and a half-sandwich of turkey. She hadn't been able to work out much lately, so she had started watching her caloric intake. Her jeans felt a little tight when she put them on this morning. David had ordered a roast beef, chips and a large soda, his usual. She watched him as he scarfed down the first half of his sandwich before she began.

"What do you want from me, David? I don't have all the answers. I'm still working through it all. I'm taking one day at a time. And each day has been filled with one surprise after another. I can hardly catch my breath sometimes. And your aligning with my mother to ambush me doesn't help either of us."

"All throughout our conversations lately, there has been one common thread and that is Luis. He's invaded our life more than your mother has, and guess who's letting him in? You, Diane. You say this marriage is between me and you but lately, it's been Luis in the middle. So, I want you to be honest with me – and more importantly, yourself – when I ask you this question. Are you in love with him again?"

Diane stopped sipping on her soup and placed the spoon on the saucer before responding, "You asked me to be honest with myself. I also have to be honest with you; you deserve that. Well, here goes. I'm not sure how I feel about Luis. We have been spending a lot of time together as you pointed out. We've been working through resolutions to problems with the children, parenting issues, and it feels comfortable. It's reminding me of the relationship we used to have. So am I falling in love with him again? I don't know. All I know is that at one time I was very much in love with him. He was my first love, my first lover, and he is the father of my children. His affair hurt me to the core. It broke me. I went from love to hate. I thought that it was the only way I could move on. But now I know differently."

She stopped and took another sip of her soup. She knew she wouldn't want it once it got cold and she had to put something in her stomach. Returning the spoon to the side of the saucer, she continued, "David, I know this is not what you wanted to hear and you may be mad at me for saying it, but you did ask me to tell you the truth. Now, having said that, I must tell you that I will not be unfaithful to you. But you have to stop pushing me to make a decision or you might not like the decision I make."

There, she said it. It was out in the open and they could deal with it in their marriage and try to figure things out.

"Wow. Okay. Well, I asked for the truth. As bitter as it is to swallow, I think I have a better understanding. That bond exists because of the children, so I know what we need to do."

"And just what would that be, given I just revealed to you how I'm feeling and nothing can be changed about my children's DNA?"

"Let's have a child of our own."

"Excuse me?" Diane couldn't believe her ears. Perhaps she really hadn't left the hospital. Instead, she had crawled into the bed with Chell and was now dreaming.

"A child of our own might help make things better between us. You are always talking about the bond and the closeness because of the children. Perhaps that's the missing element in our marriage. Besides, you didn't say that you no longer loved me. And you know I've wanted one for a few years now, but I didn't press you about it because of the stress you were experiencing with Carlos and Luis J. But things have changed now and I think the timing is right. Hell, it couldn't be better."

Shaking her head in disbelief and pushing the cup of soup away because her appetite was now completely gone, Diane leaned back from the table and crossed her arms before asking, "David, are you living in the same relationship that I am? In the same world, for that matter? There isn't one reason I can think of for bringing a child into this world now, under these circumstances. Not one. Not to mention that I already have a baby living under my roof that I have to raise. I can't even imagine what that would look like. Why would you want to complicate our lives like that?"

"I don't look at a child that we would bring into this world as a complication. It would be a child that represents our love. You heard Luis last night. It's only a matter of time before he inserts himself into Robert's life and that will change my relationship with him forever. A child of our own would be just that. Our child."

"Honestly, David, I don't agree. Ordinarily, a child is a gift, but I am talking about a life where I would have to raise CJ, Robert and a newborn. It was tough when I had my four children and I was a lot younger then; I can't even wrap my head around this scenario. Don't you see that?"

Diane's mind wandered and she recalled that she was just looking at the want ads because she was considering hiring a housekeeper, too, now that she had money to do that, thanks to Carlos. She hadn't shared any of that though with David and she had no plans to tell him. Since she didn't know where their marriage was heading, she didn't see the need to give him too much information just yet.

So she explained further the real reason there would be no baby conceived. "Besides, your idea won't work anyway, so it doesn't matter. I can't have any more children David; I had my tubes tied."

David slammed the glass on the table and the soda bounced against the sides and onto the floor near their table. The cashier looked at them for a moment and then went back to checking out the patrons.

"You did what? When?"

"Lower your voice. I said I had my tubes tied right after Robert's first birthday. I knew my marriage was over and I didn't see any reason not to have the procedure. I have always gotten pregnant when I didn't plan for it and I couldn't risk that happening to me again."

"But you never told me that – before or after we got married. Didn't you think that was information I was entitled to know? We were already talking by then. You knew how I felt about you, that I was falling in love with you. At a minimum, you could have consulted me at that time."

"In hindsight, yes David, I should have told you before I accepted your marriage proposal. But I was so messed up mentally, I couldn't bear the thought of you leaving me, too. So I kept it a secret from you. But one thing I knew for sure – I didn't want to have any more children. I couldn't manage the four I had and since I didn't know where my future was leading me next, I made a choice that I felt was best for me. And then when you and I got married and you told me you would help raise my children as though they were your own, I honestly thought it would be alright."

Still in disbelief, David continued trying to suppress his rising anger. This chick had gone behind his back and taken away his chances of having a child. And on top of that, she had kept that secret from him for the last five years. He never realized how secretive and selfish she could be. Perhaps he was right to believe there were other secrets she was keeping from him.

He finally managed to say, "I don't even know you anymore. This marriage has been a sham. Your love for me was not enough to respect me or trust me with your feelings and your concerns. Yes I told you I would love your children as my own – I have and I do – but I also told you how much I wanted a child of my own. A child with you. Now, today, you tell me that will never happen, never had a chance of happening, because of a choice you made before we even got married. It was best for you…and to hell with what David wants!"

"David, look, I know you feel betrayed. I can completely understand if you are mad as hell at me. I should not have kept this from you. I should have told you long before now. But our marriage has not been a sham. I do respect and trust you; I just didn't know how to tell you about this. Once I started down the path of omission, it was hard to find a way off of it. Maybe one day you'll understand."

David didn't respond. It was now his turn to be silent on the other end as he suffered this blatant betrayal of his love, loyalty, commitment and trust. He wasn't mad, he was livid.

As Diane sat across the table from him, imagining what he was thinking and feeling, she took an inventory of her own emotions. She was sad that she had destroyed his dream of having a child with her. She was ashamed of having kept this lie between them every time he asked her to make love without protection.

He would ask about her ovulation cycle and then make love to her three and four times during that period, hoping she would tell him a few weeks later that they had conceived a child. She would go along, but knew there was no way that would ever happen and she would have to try to block out the disappointment on his face when he saw the empty tampon wrapper in the garbage.

And, finally, she felt relieved. Relieved that the secret was finally out and that maybe it would help him see that there wasn't enough left for them to rebuild this marriage.

Still dumbfounded and irate, David sat back in his chair and looked at her straight on before saying, "Diane, I can't believe you took away my chances to have a child. All those times I waited to hear those words out of your mouth…I guess you would have let me wait until the day I died. You had me wondering if I was firing blanks. I was going to have my sperm count tested because we knew the problem wasn't with you. And you sit across from me at this table and tell me so cavalierly that you can't have any more children."

"You're right. That was very selfish of me. I was in protection mode by any means necessary and all the while hurting you. But David, you're young. I can't have children, but there are tons of women out there who can. You don't have to let that dream die."

"Do you hear yourself? Are you suggesting I have a child with someone else, like a surrogate? Or are you suggesting I follow Luis' journey and have an affair? You don't think anymore of yourself than to put up with that kind of behavior from your husband?"

"No, I wasn't implying either of those, David. I was saying that I would understand if you wanted to end the marriage and find someone who could give you a child. I mean, given the state of our relationship, we both have to admit we aren't moving closer together. We are actually moving further apart. You betrayed me last night and I kept a secret from you before we even got married. What kind of foundation are we standing on here? Certainly not one strong enough to weather this storm. Wouldn't you agree?"

David managed a sinister chuckle that sent chills down Diane's spine. She watched his body as every muscle seemed to be protruding from it, like the body of a weight lifter. She looked around the room to see how many patrons were left and if they would be shocked by his next action. He was liable to throw something and accidentally hit someone. Most customers, it seemed, had taken their meals to go; there were only a few sipping coffee near the door.

"Oh, and wouldn't that just make things so easy for you? And to think that you're now trying to use my conversation with Mama Margaret as an excuse for what you really want to do anyway. Hey, my 'betrayal' last night doesn't even begin to compare to what you did. Your actions all those years ago and the deception you continued throughout our entire marriage are far more damaging to this relationship than a call I made to your mother looking for help to better understand you. You could have told me about this a thousand times, Diane, and you never did. There were countless times you could have said, 'David, yes, I'm ovulating, but we'll never have a child. It's not possible' before today.

"You talk about trust, but you don't even know what that means. You don't know what trust looks like in a relationship because your ex treated you like shit. And why today, Diane? What drove the big revelation today?"

"I don't know," she said, but in her mind, Diane did know that she wanted him to feel betrayal, as she had last night. "Maybe because of the pain Chell is going through. Maybe because of the hurt and betrayal I felt last night when Mama called. All of those things made me realize that we have been broken for some time," she said, as she remembered laying in Luis' arms and how she had wanted to be with him.

Nodding his head up and down, David said, "These things are bad, really bad, but that doesn't mean we can't fix them. I meant it when I signed on for better or worse. I am willing to forgive you, but it might take some time. I think I've earned the right for you to give me time to do that. And given your actions, I know you couldn't possibly think I don't deserve forgiveness. So no, I'm not throwing in the towel on this marriage. I'm in for the long haul and you damn well better be, too." 'She must think I'm crazy if I'm going to let Luis win. I will never let Luis have her,' he thought.

Diane heard David, but she didn't agree with him at all. Yes, she could forgive him. Honestly, she wanted to thank him because that call from her mother last night had changed everything for her. But the truth was that the fire and passion she felt for Luis was not what she felt for David. Sitting right there in the café, she had made up her mind. Her feelings for David weren't even as warm as the cup of lukewarm soup sitting in front of her. There wasn't anything left to this marriage and she couldn't stay in it any longer just because David had been there for her.

Actually, she was surprised that he hadn't made the first move. It was probably his pride. But it no longer mattered. She knew what she wanted; it was very clear to her. But David's explosive anger that she had been observing over the last thirty minutes made her cautious about telling him any more bad news today. She would wait until the circumstances were more conducive to tell him that he should move on with his life, with no regrets, as she planned to do with hers.

"David, I am truly sorry that I have hurt you so deeply. That was never my intent. You are a good man; hell, you're a great man, and I love you for all that you've done for me. I will never forget it."

After a moment, she switched subjects, "Look, I came to the hospital to be with Chell and it's almost time for rounds. I don't want to miss the doctor because I need to know how she's really doing." Pushing back from the table and standing, she said, "Thank you for lunch. If you don't mind, I would like to spend some time alone with Chell so we can talk mother to daughter. Would you please allow us to have that space? I'll call you when I'm on my way home and will stop by to pick up the boys. Thank you for keeping them."

"Fuck you, Diane," David spewed, very matter of factly.

She turned away from the table and headed back to the hospital with no intent of addressing him further. As she recalled the conversations from this morning and over lunch, she had to acknowledge that David was not going to be the one to end the marriage. She even understood his last dismissal of her. However, he had made his position regarding their marriage very clear. Some part of her wondered if it was because he loved her so much or if he just didn't want to lose her to Luis. She had just admitted that she had married David because she didn't want to lose him.

She also knew that she wasn't being as honest with herself as she needed to be. She was not feeling David, that was true, but she was very much falling back in love with Luis. Her heart didn't belong to David anymore, that much was certain. And if she really allowed herself to be honest, she never loved him the way she had loved, still loved, Luis anyway. So, at a minimum, she had to take action that would be fair to herself, David and the kids.

Diane pushed all of those thoughts to the back of her mind when she returned to Chell's room. She looked at Chell, who was lying in bed after having surgery to remove a fetus from her fallopian tubes, as her priority. She would turn all of her attention toward her and be the mother Chell needed her to be, nurturing, caring, loving and supportive. And once she was physically stronger, they would begin the journey toward Chell's emotional recovery and healing.

Chapter Thirty Seven

37

Chell was released from the hospital two days after the procedure and spent a week at home. She was on a few different medications but regaining her strength and Diane was grateful. She had made arrangements to secure Chell's homework so she wouldn't fall too far behind, but now she was back in school and things were slowly returning to a familiar routine.

Diane was feeling a little better about the direction her life was moving in since she took the time to recalibrate her feelings and connect with her emotions. Her initial conversation and the subsequent ones with her sister were really helping her refocus and gain some momentum in dealing with their mother. Diane greatly appreciated her sister's friendship and caring spirit. Michelle mostly just listened as Diane shared milestones, breakthroughs, strategies and plans, and only offered an opinion or advice when asked. Apparently, she had kept her word because Diane had not heard from their mother directly. She had called to talk to Chell and see how she was feeling, but there was little to no conversation between them. For now, Diane accepted that. It was giving her the space she needed to get grounded and stronger.

As for David, he had been keeping his distance. He was still spending time with the boys, but his interaction with Diane was on an "as needed" basis. Diane wasn't sure how to interpret that, but like her mother's actions, this too was giving her space. She had not shared her revelation with Luis, but continued to advocate and encourage his growing involvement with their children.

This Saturday morning, Diane was sipping her coffee. Today's added spice was vanilla. She had tried it one morning at Choc-Full-of-Nuts while on her way to the office and liked the new taste buds it had awakened on her tongue. She bought a bottle so that she could have it with her coffee whenever she desired.

She stopped reading the paper and stared outside. It had been raining all night and was continuing into the day. The forecast called for heavy rain later in the afternoon. Diane pulled the robe around her, trying to keep the warmth from escaping. It was going to be one of those chilly days. She had just finished her cup when the phone rang. To her dismay, it was Stacie calling for Chell.

"Chell, would you come here for a minute please?" Diane called out.

Chell had eaten a while ago and retreated to her room. When she emerged, Diane saw she was still in her pajamas. Diane covered the mouthpiece and said to her, "It's Stacie. Do you know what she wants? Do you even want to talk to her?"

"No, Mami, I don't know what she wants. I've seen her in school since I've returned, but the friendship hasn't been the same."

"Well, I could tell her you're not available if you like, or do you want to take it?"

"No, it's alright. I'll talk to her."

"Now, remember I…"

"I know, Mami," Chell said, sucking her teeth and putting her hand on her hip. "You don't have to remind me every day. I'll take it in my room."

Diane was disturbed by this call. She wondered if Stacie was a front just to get Chell on the phone when the person she was really going to talk to was Roger. As Chell picked up the extension, Diane kept the phone to her ear long enough to hear Stacie's voice, which eased her worry just a little, then returned the phone to the cradle to respect her daughter's privacy.

Diane had tried talking to Chell the week she returned to school, but she wasn't getting very far. Every attempt was met with a similar reaction like she had just received. When she discussed it with Luis, they agreed to accelerate their plans to find a family therapist. Diane was working with her insurance company to understand options. In the interim, Luis was being very supportive and loving to Chell, giving her tons of attention. At the end of the day, Diane prayed that Chell's experiences had taught her to select her friends more carefully and make her choices more wisely.

After a few minutes, Chell returned to the kitchen and asked Diane, "May I go out for a while?"

"Why? Where are you trying to go and with whom?"

"A few of the girls want to go to the mall. I haven't been able to do anything since the operation. I would really like to go out and just have a little fun."

"Which girls?"

"Jessie, Missy and Stacie."

"How are you getting there?"

"The bus."

"Chell, I hope you haven't forgotten our conversations, as one-sided as they've been. I sure hope that you have learned from your previous choices and remember them when faced with future forks in the road."

"Yes, Mami, I remember and yes I've learned. May I go?"

"I'm telling you now, I am not crazy about this, but I will let you go. I have to learn to trust you again. Please don't make me regret it. When you girls are ready to come home, call me and I'll come and pick you up. You can take my cellphone."

"We aren't going to be gone that long, so we'll just take the bus back. I'm going to be fine. Don't worry."

"But Chell, I do worry. These are the same girls that you went off with and ended up riding home alone with some stranger who tried to molest you. Now I'm telling you to take my cell and call me if you need me."

Oh yeah about that, she had never corrected her story about going to the school alone and not with her girlfriend that fateful day when Roger threw her to that horrible Goober. Not wanting to fight with her mother about it any longer, Chell took the phone and headed to her room to get ready. Once outside, she saw the girls standing under the eave of the entrance to the other building's door and ran to join them. She hadn't told anyone other than Stacie about the pregnancy because she was hoping to keep it a secret. The only reason she told Stacie was because Stacie had guessed since she was out of school for a week. After that, Stacie seemed to be a little nicer to her although she didn't really understand why. "Hey, girls, what's up?"

"Not much. How are you feeling?" Stacie asked.

"I'm cool. So, which mall are we going to?"

"Is your mom still trippin'?" Stacie questioned again.

Chell had never noticed before how much she sounded like Roger at times. They had that same raspy voice and could be condescending. This was one of those times.

Chell didn't appreciate Stacie talking about her mother in that tone, but she stayed composed and answered, "Sometimes, but it's cool; it's her way of showing her concern for me. Hey, the bus is coming, we better cross the street." The rain had let up a little so they could make their way to the bus shelter without getting too wet. Chell's hair was thick and long, hanging down her back. It was a sandy color brown, a cross between her mother's hair and NaNa's. But when it got wet it would frizz up and be really hard to comb.

"Girl, we aren't taking the bus. Roger and Goober are going to drive us. Come on."

Chell froze in her tracks and turned toward Stacie. "I can't go with them. I told my mom we were taking the bus."

"And have it take us an hour to get there? No thanks. Besides, not everyone has that good hair," Stacie said, flinging one of Chell's ponytails and chuckling. "Come on, he's not mad at you anymore. They're just going to drop us off and then we'll take the bus back…so you didn't really lie to your mom."

Chell moved her head away from Stacie's hand and frowned at her. She was back to being mean again and Chell didn't like it. "But I don't like hanging around with Goober and I can't go against my mom."

"Since when?"

"Stacie, would you guys come on. I don't have all day," Roger called from the car.

"Chell, it's okay, trust me," Jessie added. Reluctantly, Chell followed them to the car.

Roger was standing by the car as they approached and said, "Hey, Chell. Long time no see. Where've you been?"

"I was sick."

"Uh huh. Stacie, you guys ride with Goober. Chell and I need to talk."

"Damn Roger. Goober's so fussy about his car and he always plays his weird music so loud. Why can't we just ride with you?"

"Get your ass in his car or stay your ass at home. Your choice," he threw back at her before getting into his car.

Chell waited to see what her friends were going to do. When they turned and walked in Goober's direction, she opened the door of Roger's car and climbed in, hearing Stacie tell her brother, "You are such an ass sometimes."

Chell was relieved that she would not have to ride with Goober and relieved that Stacie had not set her up. But she also acknowledged that Roger was an ass towards all females, even his sister, so how could she expect any more? She hadn't talked to Roger since the basketball game two weeks ago, and the incident with Goober. She wondered what he wanted to talk to her about and felt those butterflies in her stomach again.

Once they were on the expressway, he asked, "So is it true you were pregnant?"

"What?"

"You heard me. Were you pregnant?"

Lowering her head, she responded, "Yes. Did Stacie tell you?"

"Why wouldn't she? Was it mine?"

Looking up at him in shock, she replied, "Of course. I haven't been with anyone else."

"So, what happened?"

"It wasn't in the right place, so they had to remove it."

"I thought you told me you were on the pill. Did you think I wouldn't find out you lied to me?"

"No, but I am now."

"And what's that supposed to mean to me?"

"I just thought you should know. Are you still seeing that girl you were with the night of the game?"

"I wasn't seeing her."

"But, she acted like…"

"You see, that's what I mean. No one determines who I'm with except me."

"So, are we still going to be together?"

"I don't know. Why should I want to be with you? Your brother is an asshole and I don't want to have to hurt him. You're just too high maintenance."

"My brother doesn't control my life. I can see whoever I want," Chell said, before analyzing her current choices. She was violating everything she had just promised her mother she had learned. She was in the car with Roger, not on the bus, and if this went wrong in any way, she'd never gain her mother's trust again. But, oh those butterflies!

"You know, you can prove that to me by being with Goober."

"What are you talking about, being with Goober?"

"Why am I having to repeat myself today? If you can prove to me that you can date Goober for a couple of weeks and not have that crazy brother of yours find out, then maybe we can be together."

"Yuck. I don't like him. He's a pig. He tried to force me to have sex with him that night you asked him to give me a ride home. If my father hadn't seen me, I think he would have raped me. Why would you have someone like that give me a ride home anyway?"

Roger smirked, "He told me about that. First your brother, then your father. You see, there's too much bullshit with you, and your little pussy isn't worth it."

"Roger? Oh my God. How could you say that to me?" The tears were burning in the corner of her eyes. Suddenly Luis J's words came back to her, "He doesn't deserve you. He doesn't really like you."

"Chell, Chell, Chell. Don't you get it? I never cared about you. I was tired of your arrogant ass brother walking around thinking he was some shit. He doesn't deserve to be team captain. He's not even a senior. He took that away from me and I was determined to get him back. And then I remembered you and how much he was always trying to keep you away from the guys on the team. You were a fine, sexy little thing with such innocence. It was a bonus to find out that you were a virgin, too! Wooh hoo! I don't get many of those anymore. All of these girls throw their pussy around like it's nothing special, which is fine by me. Anyway, little girl, I've hurt your brother enough and I'm just waiting for him to retaliate. And when he does, Coach will kick him off the team and I'll be in my rightful position, even if it is only for a couple of months."

Chell was listening, paralyzed. Did he really just say he had used her all this time to get at Luis J? That nothing between them was real? She was starting to feel sick to her stomach and the butterflies disappeared.

"But Roger, you said you cared about me. What are you saying?"

"I think I was clear. This was all a plan and Stacie helped me from the beginning. She doesn't like you as much as I don't like your brother. So now, our plan is complete and you are no longer needed." He slowed the car and pulled over onto the shoulder.

"What're you doing?"

"Puttin' you the fuck out."

"Putting me out? In the rain? On the side of the road?"

"Yep. And do me a favor, call your brother and tell him everything I told you and exactly what I did to you. Then I'll be waiting for his sorry ass. Now get out."

Chell opened her door and climbed out, but before she shut the door, she said, "You know what? I lied to my mother and snuck around to be with you, but Roger, you are an asshole. I couldn't see it because of how you were treating me, but now that I know the whole story, I understand exactly what my family was trying to tell me. I am going to tell my brother and my father and you're the one who's going to be a sorry ass."

"Fuck you and your family. They can't do shit to me. Now close my goddamn door or I'm gonna slap the shit out of you."

'No one has ever talked to me like that. Not my mother, my brothers, my father, no one,' Chell thought, as Roger's words cut through her soul – but only for a moment because in her mind now he was the devil.

As soon as she closed the door, Roger peeled off, splashing water on Chell and drenching her coat. Shortly after that, Goober pulled up, with a smirk planted firmly on his face.

"Need a ride?"

"No."

"Sure?"

She didn't respond. She may have been stupid the first time, but there was no way she was about to get in a car with him, even if she had to walk home.

"Suit yourself." He laughed as he, too, pulled away.

No one was even in his car, not her friends. They were all in on it. Stacie, Jessie and Missy had all faked her out. They had set her up. What had Roger said, "Stacie hates you as much as I hate Luis J?" Well, that explained a lot about all of them. Chell stood there for a moment in the rain as the cars sped pass her. She wasn't even sure where she was. She walked for a while to see if she could determine the closest exit. The wind had picked up and she was walking right into the rain. It took her about 15 minutes to get to the next sign. By now, she was drenched. She took out the cell phone and called Luis J. He picked up on the third ring.

"Speak."

She hadn't talked to him much since the night he told on her. She had been so mad at him. Now, with tears rolling down her check, she realized how wrong she had been.

"Mami, is that you?"

"No, it's me, Luis J. Chell."

"Oh, hey. What's up?"

Through lots of sobbing, she was able to give him enough information for him to come and pick her up. By the time Luis J arrived, Chell was drenched and shivering. He didn't say much to her. He just turned on the heater and gave her his jacket to replace the one she was wearing. The look on Luis J's face was blank and he asked Chell to tell him the whole story. When she finished, he reached out and hugged her.

"Luis J, I thought he cared about me. I never thought it was all a plan to get back at you. You were right all along. He didn't care and he didn't deserve me. I was so stupid."

"Roger and Goober are punks. I'm so sorry, Chell. You didn't deserve to be brought into this bullshit. How would he have liked it if I did that shit to his conniving little sister?"

"It wouldn't matter. He wouldn't care. He doesn't care about her like you care about me," Chell interjected, as she thought about how Roger had really treated her. He had handed her a dirty, bloody towel to use to clean her private place; taken her in the back seat of his car like some whore; and bought her one cheap gift. The bracelet broke two weeks after he gave it to her. She had wanted to have a boyfriend on the basketball team and feel important, like Dany felt being Luis J's girl. But clearly Roger was nothing like her brother. Even with all their issues, Luis J always treated Dany well; he never cursed at her or mis-treated her. Roger wasn't worth her time and certainly didn't deserve her love and respect.

"I knew he was pissed off and didn't like me, but I had no idea he would take it out on you. I'm so sorry Chell. I really am. If I had known or even had a clue, I would have confronted him on this shit a long time ago. You just got caught in the middle. That's why I was telling you it was too soon for you to be sexually active. You deserve someone who is going to treat you with dignity and respect."

"So now what? I don't want you to go after him. I'm afraid he might do something to you."

"Let me think. Is Mami home?"

"Yes."

"I'm going to take you home. I'll stay with you so you can tell her what happened. Then we'll figure out where to go from there."

Chell hugged Luis J tightly. She had so missed her big brother and she was so glad to have him back. Although, she knew what he had done before to Roger and she could only imagine what he was feeling now. This made her really worry about him.

When they arrived and Chell opened the door, Diane sank into the chair.

"What the hell happened?" she screamed, looking at her child who was still wet. This child who had just had surgery two weeks ago.

Luis, who had been in Robert's room playing with CJ, came running into the living room, carrying him.

"Chell, are you alright?" Luis asked, shocked at the sight of his drenched daughter.

"Mami, Papi, she's alright. We'll both tell you what happened, but she needs to get out of these clothes."

Diane smiled at her son's paternal instincts; it made her think he'd actually be a good father. She said, "Yes, of course. Take off your coat and shoes and go take a warm shower, honey. Not hot, just warm. I'll bring you a change of clothes." Diane searched Luis J's face for answers and she wanted tons of them.

Once she got Chell in the shower, Diane joined the family in the living room. CJ was entertaining himself with the TV and a toy truck Luis had just bought for him. The two men were now sitting on the couch and Luis was listening intently to his son.

"Luis J?" Diane interrupted.

"Mami, it's a long story and Chell really needs to tell it to you. She's been burnt again by Roger. But don't be angry with her."

"I knew it! That little Stacie was a ploy to get her out of this house. I knew it."

"Yes, that's true. But Chell didn't know anything about it. Really, let's wait until she comes out."

"I'm not waiting for anything," Diane said, putting on her coat and looking for some shoes.

"Di, calm down. Anything you are thinking about doing won't have a good outcome. If I thought it would, we wouldn't have been sitting here when you came out of the bathroom. We'd be gone already!" When she didn't stop her forward motion, Luis stood and grabbed her. "Baby, please. I need you to trust me on this."

Luis J's ears perked up. Did his father just call his mother baby? What the…was going on here? He would table it for now because first things first, but he would get back to that with his mother at the first opportunity after they took care of this business.

Diane finally stopped her forward movement and said, "Alright, fine."

"You were going to feed CJ. Do you want me to do it instead and you and Luis J can continue talking?" Luis volunteered.

Diane nodded. She placed her coat on the back of the couch and sat down in the chair opposite her son. Reaching for his hand, she said, "Thank you for being there for her. For bringing her home."

"Sure. In some ways, this is all my fault."

"Honey, how could this be your fault?"

Luis J shared the part of the story that explained Roger's plan. He watched as his mother clinched her fists and fought back tears.

"Are you telling me that this boy did that to your sister to get back at you over some position on the basketball team?"

"Yes. I knew he was pissed, but I never would have imagined he would stoop this low. If I did, I would have just given up the position immediately. I never intended for any harm to come to Chell over b-ball."

"Oh Luis J, I know you love your sister. And I don't blame you for what happened. None of us do. I'm just shocked that kids can think like that. It's beyond cruel what they did."

Luis J looked at his mom and then his dad to see if he shared the same sentiment. This was a relief to Luis J, but he still felt responsible in some way for what had happened to his sister. He also knew that if he had been living at home, he could have helped keep an eye on her. He might have seen her sneaking around with Roger and put a stop to it before it got too far. Hell, she might have even talked to him about her actions before she took them. But that was all water under the bridge now. They had to move forward from here. But one thing was certain in Luis J's mind – he would never let her down again.

Chell finally joined them in the living room. Everyone could tell she had been crying because her eyes were red. Her hair was pulled back into a ponytail and Diane shuddered. She did not want this to emotionally damage her child any more than it had already.

They sat and talked for about an hour. Chell told them everything, pausing at times to get hugs from each of them before continuing. Even CJ hugged her and told her to not cry. It touched Diane's heart because it felt as though Carlos was there with them during this family meeting.

"I know what we are going to do," Luis said, once all the facts had been laid out on the table. Everyone waited to hear what he was about to say.

"First, we are going to file charges. Endangering the life of a minor by leaving you on the side of the road…and statutory rape, to be precise."

"But he didn't rape me," Chell said, feeling embarrassed by the whole experience.

"Not technically, baby, but you are fourteen. You're too young to consent to having sex with someone four years older than you. Besides, there's no love story that can conjure up any sympathy. Roger said so himself. It was a conspiracy to anger your brother, provoke him and cause him to lose his team captain position."

"Oh yeah, I remember when we were at the attorney's office and he talked about cases of statutory rape with high school boys. He told us that if found guilty, you could go to jail. Roger's eighteen!" Luis J added, a huge grin growing across his face.

"Do you think that's a good idea?" Diane asked. "Won't it just provoke him even more? What if he tries to go after Luis J?"

"Mami, I can take care of myself."

"I don't doubt that, but remember, he's trying to get you kicked out of school. You can't fight with him."

"I'm not going to go after him. I'll call Coach and tell him because he asked me to come to him if I had any more trouble with Roger."

"Good son. I know it's a risk, Di, but we have to take it. Roger needs to be punished for his actions and the legal system is the only avenue we have for that. I think this is our best course of action."

The room turned very quiet as each person examined what the potential outcome of this decision might be. But it was almost simultaneous when each one said, "Yes, let's do it."

Luis instructed Luis J to make his call to Coach, not to confront Roger, and for everyone to keep this confidential until he could meet with the attorney to chart the best course of action. He would let them know on Monday the next steps.

Luis J thought the plan was a good one and couldn't wait to see Roger and hopefully, Goober too, behind bars. That would truly make his day. He put in a call to the coach, who was elated that Luis J had made a wise, mature choice. "Son, I believe you're back on the path to greatness," he had said.

After talking to Coach, Luis J stayed for dinner because he wanted to continue to be there for his sister. The conversation now was lighter and he cracked a few jokes to make them all laugh. He hadn't spent that much time with his family this way in a long time and it felt right. He even stayed long enough to play with CJ. His parents were washing dishes together, laughing and talking. They were working together as a family. It reminded him of how they had done that for him when they held the intervention meeting. Today he got a glimpse of what it was like when you worried about someone's wellbeing and he understood why they were so concerned about his drinking.

Once Maria has his child, he would have that same desire to protect them from hurt and harm. He looked at his watch and saw it was getting late. He hadn't heard from Maria since he left and he had her car. He kissed his mother, hugged his sister, scooped up CJ, and embraced his father before heading back to the apartment. He promised Chell he would call her the next day and he had every intention of keeping that promise.

When Luis J got back to the condo, he found Maria sitting on the couch. He told her what happened and what they were planning. Maria listened intently and found herself a little envious of Chell. Maria didn't have a brother to protect her honor the way Luis J was prepared to do so for her. Hell, she didn't even have a man willing to do that for her the way Luis always did for Diane.

The baby moved and she shifted in her seat. Maria looked at the young man sitting across from her and noticed a difference. He was more mature. He was coming into his own. She was proud of him, but she didn't like the fact that they were all banding together around this. Especially since it seemed like the family wounds she had planted and nurtured between Luis J and his father were healing. She was hoping to keep them at odds for at least a little while longer, but it would be hard if they bonded over Chell's unfortunate experience. Well, she was pretty sure this baby would still be a way to keep the wedge in place. She patted her stomach as the baby moved again, causing a little discomfort this time.

Luis J saw her touching her stomach and asked, "How's the baby?"

"Moving a lot lately."

"Does it hurt?"

"No. Just feels weird. Do you want to feel it?"

"No, that's okay. So, what are you looking at?"

"Just some pictures of me when I was a teenager."

"Really, let me see. What were they wearing back then?" Luis J asked, laughing as he moved to sit on the couch next to her. Together they thumbed through the photos.

"Who is this?"

"My mother."

"She's pretty. You look like her. Where does she live? Have you told her about the pregnancy?"

"She and I haven't talked in years. She sent a message to me by my cousin to indicate her disapproval of my living arrangements with your father."

"Yeah. The older generation can be like that sometimes. But once she finds out about the baby, don't you think her feelings would change? She would be a grandmother." As Luis J asked that question, he remembered Carlos' situation and how his mother had reacted and she wasn't even of the same generation as Maria's mom.

"Did it for your mother when Carlos had CJ?" Maria asked, knowing that a response wasn't required because they both already knew the answer. As she sat there looking at the pictures, she started to remember what had ruined their mother and daughter bond.

Maria's parents were both from Puerto Rico. Anna lived alone because her parents were killed in an automobile accident a month before she graduated from high school. They had left enough money in their account to enable Anna to stay in the home and take care of herself until she obtained her college degree.

Anna chose a university near her hometown in San Juan that enabled her to also work in the local hospital. She was responsible for feeding the patients and reading to the children. The children's ward was her favorite. She marveled at how those children were facing chronic illnesses, but never lived as though tomorrow would be their last day. They were full of hope and were fearless and it reminded her that although she was left to fend for herself, she had her whole life ahead and had to make the best of every day.

When Anna graduated from college with a bachelor's degree in nursing, she was hired into a full-time position in the obstetrics ward at the hospital. This was an opportunity for her to help children from the moment they took their first breath. The doctors often told her she was a natural.

One afternoon on her way home from work, Anna stopped for a bite to eat at the diner in the hospital basement. There was a guy that frequented the cafeteria whom she had seen for about a month. He always ate dinner alone. She had found out that he worked in the X-Ray lab. She thought he was really cute and he appeared friendly; he always smiled when he saw her. That afternoon she had garnered the nerve to ask him to join her for dinner if he was there. He was! She asked and he accepted her invitation.

His name was Juan Cortano. He was from Humacao, which was on the other side of the island. Juan was the oldest of eight and had come to San Juan to work so he could help his family. He had two jobs, one at the hospital and the other with a delivery service. He was renting a room with a family not far from town. He would eat dinner there and then catch a nap in the on-call room between jobs.

A month passed and Juan and Anna shared dinner together three to four evenings each week. One evening, Anna broke their routine by inviting Juan to her house for a special dinner and a bed with fresh, clean sheets. He was very appreciative and it quickly became their new ritual.

Juan admired her home. It was spacious, clean and quiet. It was very different than the home he grew up in and especially the place where he was currently renting a room. Anna's home was also in town, which made it a convenient location for his commute to work. A huge smile broke across his face the day Anna gave him a key and asked him to move in. It was an act that solidified their friendship. She was no longer alone in that great big house and that made Anna very happy.

Their friendship continued to grow over the months and then it happened. One evening Anna saw him through a different lens. He had just finished eating dinner and was drinking a glass of ice-cold water, sitting on the couch. It was very hot and he didn't have on a shirt. Anna's interest suddenly piqued as she stared at the sweating glass and his sweaty body. She had never seen him without a shirt but she could tell by the way his shirts outlined his body that he was physically fit. His night job was labor intensive and contributed to the rippling muscles across his chest.

As he drank the water, the condensation from the glass dripped from off the bottom and landed on his chest. It traveled down the creases and pooled in the area of his belly button. He looked so sexy to her. She had never been sexually active but had talked about it with her coworker Carmen whenever they saw the radiologist and anesthesiologist. They were the only two unmarried doctors on the day shift and she and

Carmen would fantasize about their bodies and what a sexual experience would be like.

Tonight, Anna wondered what it would be like with Juan. She wondered if he even thought of her in that way. After all, he had never made advances towards her. She picked up her own glass of water and crossed the room to sit down next to him. He was used to that because the best breeze could be felt from that spot on the couch, so he slid over to accommodate her. But this time she sat closer to him, very close.

Juan didn't move until he felt the warmth of her leg against his and could smell her natural body scent emanating from her skin. He turned his head to search her face for an interpretation of her flirtation and what he found in her eyes was a sexual invitation he had never received before.

He reached for her, but did it slowly to see if he was reading the cues as she intended them. When she didn't pull away, he took her. She was soft and sweet and he filled her body with his hotness. That night was followed by countless others, equally as sultry as the first.

When Anna's period was six weeks late, she knew she was facing another new experience. There was a life growing in her womb. Her body was already changing to accommodate it: her breasts were tender and fuller, and her behind more round as her pelvis shifted to support the impending additional weight. Juan had planted his seed in her, entrusting her body to nourish it and love it. When they made love the night she discovered she was pregnant, her increased wetness made Juan come quickly. Her whole body loved him and she wanted him to know. As he lay there, surprised by how different she felt and unsure as to why, he said, "I didn't expect that."

She smiled and kissed him before saying, "You could feel it, too?"

"Yes. You were wetter and hotter than you've ever been and I couldn't control myself. But give me a few minutes and I'll be ready to please you," he said, as he was already getting aroused from just thinking about the sensations he had just felt.

"Juan, you have already pleased me. I don't need anything else," she said, feeling content.

"What caused that? What did you do differently?" he asked, wanting her to do it every time from now on.

"I'm carrying your child. It's growing inside of me and my body is responding to your love," Anna said proudly, awaiting words of elation and love to leave his lips. She wondered if those words would be, "I love you," or "You have made me the happiest man."

But a frown started creasing her forehead as he was taking longer than she had anticipated. Then she began smiling because perhaps he was about to ask for her hand in marriage. Her body shuddered in anticipation, the same way it did the first night he made love to her. But the response she finally received caused her to gasp. He was not happy. He didn't want children right now.

"Anna, I care for you, but I don't love you. Not the way a man should love a woman if they are going to have a family together."

He then pleaded with her to terminate the pregnancy so they could go back to enjoying the life they had built together before this mistake. Anna was as still and cold as one of the statues standing in the front of her yard. He was asking her to choose between the child they had created and the life they were leading but promising her nothing in return.

She had been alone for so long after her parents' death and until he had come into her life that she knew one thing for certain, that she didn't ever want to be alone again. So, she chose the first gift he had ever given to her – the child, whom she would love and raise and who would never hurt her so deeply.

This left Juan with one option, to move out and find another room to rent somewhere in town. And he wasted no time, rising from the bed right then, packing his things and sleeping on the couch.

Anna laid in the bed that still smelled of him and curled up into a ball. She gently rubbed her stomach as tears rolled down her cheek and landed on the pillow. She would protect her baby tonight and always from the pain men could inflict upon you.

Their child grew inside Anna and she prepared for its arrival. She and Juan would still see each other in the cafeteria and around the hospital, but words were never shared between them. She often wondered how he could watch her belly become larger every day and not want to inquire about their child. The coldness he displayed was so foreign and outside of her realm of comprehension that it broke her heart every time.

Then one day, he was gone – poof! Gone. No warning, no goodbye, no forwarding address, no nothing. He wasn't in the cafeteria; he wasn't walking around the halls; he just wasn't. After the baby was born, she received a letter from Juan. The postmark was from Humacao. She put Maria to bed and sat on the couch in that same spot where it all began and paused before opening the letter, noting the increased palpations of her heart and the tightness of her stomach. Perhaps he had a change of heart and was writing to tell her of his impending arrival. She held her breath in hopeful anticipation before sliding her finger under the flap and unfolding the paper that read:

My Dearest Anna,

I heard you had the baby. I hope that everything went well. I hope you received the same care and nurturing that you give to your patients. I am writing this letter to help you understand my choice. What I didn't tell you when we met was I was already engaged to be married. The love of my life was back in Humacao waiting for me to save enough money to buy her a home so we could start our life together. I never expected our friendship to evolve into a sexual relationship and certainly not to create a child. I never intended to hurt you in this way. You were such *a generous and caring woman and I will never forget that. However, the child and you have no place in my future. Don't try to contact me or share any information with the child about me. I have enclosed $500. It's the most I could spare. I wish you and the baby well.*

Juan

Anna gasped and the letter with the money fell from her hands. Unbeknownst to her she was in shock. Her heart pounded faster and harder. He had used her and now wanted to sweep her and his baby under some rug in San Juan. They deserved better than that.

She rose from the couch and stood in front of the fireplace, the fire now mostly embers. Anna was still steaming, but as she watched the fire burn out, her hurt seemed to die along with it. She picked up the letter and tossed it and the money into the fireplace, which caused the dying fire to burst into a roaring flame. She watched as it burnt brightly and pieces of the paper floated in the air until it eventually went back to smoldering. It was exactly how her relationship with Juan had been.

In that moment, she shut down her heart and dismissed the sweet, loving and idealistic person she used to be, and vowed never to open her heart again. She turned away from what was left incinerating in the pit and went to bed. She had closed her heart, but it was without accepting any responsibility for her choices in their interaction.

Anna was enamored with her little bundle of joy that looked like a miniature her. As Maria grew up, she and Anna were inseparable except when Anna went to work. She intentionally treated Maria like a princess. She wanted her baby to feel loved.

Anna never treated her like a baby and, in fact, needed her to be very independent at a very young age. Maria was cooking for herself by the time she was seven-years-old. She was sometimes left at home alone at night, while her mother took night classes to become a midwife. Maria would entertain herself reading fantasy stories and developed a very active imagination. When Maria turned fourteen, she finally asked her mother why she didn't have a father. Anna didn't realize that her response would be detrimental to the bond they had shared over the years and influence how Maria viewed men.

"You have a father, Maria. How else would you be here? He's not part of our lives because he didn't tell me he was already engaged when he slept with me and got me pregnant. He told me to never look for him because there was no room in his life or his heart for us. So my dear, learn this lesson and learn it now – men will use you, if you don't use them first. They can't be trusted, but they can be manipulated. I gave your father my heart, handed it to him on a silver platter, and he loved it while it served him. Then it was over because you were growing inside me. When you're older, I'll tell you more. So, mija, forget about the man who gave you life and accept things as they are between us. After all, I have always been there for you and always will be. We don't need a man in our lives."

Maria didn't fully understand all that her mother had said, but she did comprehend that her father didn't want her. In all her stories the prince and princess had lived happily ever after. So her mother must have done something to run her father away from her. And worse, something that made him not love her. Now she was curious. She wanted to learn what attracted men and then what would keep them in your life.

A year later, Anna made two announcements: she received her license to practice as a mid-wife, and she was engaged to be married. Maria was shocked by the second announcement. Her mother had been dating several men over the past five years, more than Maria could even count, but no one seemed like the marrying kind. A number of them were married men with families of their own. Maria would see them in church on Sundays or in restaurants during the week with their families, after having watched them leave her mother's bedroom the night before.

They would smile sheepishly at Maria as they moved closer to their wives as though they were worried she would reveal their secret.

When she asked her mother why she was marrying, the response she received was, "I'm tired of playing with those men. You can't build a life with a married man and I'm ready to do that now. I want someone to call my own. I want someone who will be faithful to me, not like those men I was with or your father. Jorge loves me. He wants to be with me. He would never betray our marriage."

"But Momma, do you love him?"

"I do, but not the same way he loves me. It's better when a man loves you more. Then you have the upper hand. They will never stray if they love you more than you love them."

So Anna married Jorge. He was about 30 at the time, ten years younger than Anna and fourteen years older than Maria. He was a quiet man and didn't challenge Anna about anything. Maria could see what her mother was talking about. He really did love her mother.

But Maria didn't like the dynamics in the household now. Her mother never seemed to have much time for her anymore while being a wife and fulfilling her career dreams. It had been the two of them all her life and now she was being made to share her mother. So Maria acted out her displeasure in the only way she knew how, by being defiant. She challenged her mother at every turn. She was determined to do whatever she could to make this man go away regardless of how much he claimed he loved her mother.

Jorge often tried to run interference between them. He didn't like how they argued and how this upset his wife. Maria would try to encourage Jorge to see things from her perspective sometimes, pointing out how insensitive her mother was when it came to things Maria wanted or needed. He would try to smooth things between them, which Anna hated, as somewhere in her skewed mind it was viewed as an act of betrayal.

Over time the breakdown in communication between Anna and Maria escalated. Outsiders who didn't know them before could only see the growing anger of a daughter towards her mother. The only solace Anna seemed to get some days was when she was traveling. As her midwife reputation grew, she received requests from all over the northern section of the island. Sometimes, she would be gone for days at a time, leaving Maria and Jorge at home alone to fend for themselves.

Before one trip to deliver a baby, Maria and her mother had a blowout argument about Kenny. Kenny was Maria's current boyfriend and Anna was insisting that Maria stop seeing him. Maria wondered how her mother felt she was qualified to choose whom she dated, given her history. But Anna didn't like Kenny because he was too old for Maria. He was almost the same age as Jorge and Maria was only eighteen then.

But Anna also didn't want Kenny with her child because she had heard he was married. Maria denied this accusation, even though she, too, had heard this about Kenny. She had never been to his home so she really didn't know and to be honest, didn't care. Anna did not want Maria to repeat her mistake with a man who was already spoken for, so she threatened to confront Kenny if Maria didn't stop seeing him.

That infuriated Maria. She couldn't believe her mother was turning against her. Maria agreed to abide by her mother's wishes, but this disloyalty was not going without retaliation.

When Jorge came home from work that evening, he ate the dinner Maria had cooked and enjoyed the mojito she had made especially for him. He was completely unaware of the argument that had ensued earlier between his wife and stepdaughter or the events about to come.

"Maria, you are a really good cook," Jorge innocently complimented. "You're really growing up to be quite a young lady. You continue to impress me with your skills. We're going to miss you when you leave for school."

"Why, thank you, Jorge. Wait until you see what I made for dessert."

She refilled his glass from the pitcher of mojitos she had mixed earlier and encouraged him to relax on the sofa. While he sat there enjoying the libations, Maria excused herself. When she returned to the living room, she was wearing comfortable, revealing clothing. She took a seat in the chair across from him.

"What's for dessert?" Jorge asked, sipping on his drink and noticing Maria's change of clothes.

"How about me?" she said softly.

Wondering how many mojitos she had consumed and thinking it must be affecting the way her brain was interpreting his question, he asked her again, "No, I said, what's for dessert? You just mentioned you had something special. You for dessert is not an answer to that question."

"Isn't it? I see how you look at me, Jorge. I know you have feelings for me. A woman can tell. Besides, my mom's always traveling and leaving you alone. If I were your wife, I wouldn't leave you for a day, let alone a week."

Feeling suddenly quite uncomfortable with this dialogue, Jorge loosened his tie and took another drink before responding. "It doesn't bother me. She's living her dream. I'm proud of her. And, I don't look at you in that way. You are my stepdaughter."

"Come on, Jorge," Maria said, slowing opening her legs and shifting her body so that all that could be seen was even more revealing. "You're curious. I know that you think about me like that. You're always siding with me when she and I argue. It's only a matter of time before you get tired of her, just like my Dad did."

Placing the glass on the table and averting his eyes from Maria, he said, "Uh, we need to end this conversation. It's not an appropriate one for you and me to have."

"Isn't it? I know I can make you..."

He now stood up, as he could feel his body responding to the sensuousness in her voice. "Maria, stop it. I know you and your mother have been at odds with each other, but we're not going to complicate things in this way. Now, your mother will be back tomorrow, so I suggest you take a shower and go do your homework. And this conversation right here, it never took place."

"You're making a mistake. You really don't want to pass this up," Maria said, as she rose from the couch and ran her hands down her body, slowing them as she caressed her ample breasts. Kenny had rubbed them this way and become erect almost immediately. They always ended up making love once he touched her body and smelled her scent. She could easily get him to cancel his plans with his wife just to spend more time with her.

"Jorge, give me a chance to show you, Poppie..." Maria started unbuttoning her shirt and moving toward him. To her surprise, he didn't move. Was he really going to be that easy? She pushed him back onto the couch and climbed onto his lap. She straddled his legs, and leaned in to kiss him.

"Maria..."

She stopped his words with her lips. It only took a few seconds before he started to respond. She was a beautiful young woman and few men could resist her advances. Jorge was no different, even if he was her stepfather. She knew that her likeness to her mother made Jorge imagine Anna in her youth and Maria used it to her advantage. It was working. Maria had learned how to entice men by watching her mother. Anna could get them to do all kinds of things for her and her daughter by using her body, not as a prostitute would, but as a woman who understood the power she had in her beauty and the results it could bring.

Tonight, Maria was using that same charm on her stepfather. Before he knew it, he had been swept up in her seduction and they made love on the couch and then again in Maria's bedroom. To Maria, Jorge was sexy and somewhat pleasing to her. But it wasn't the emotional or physical content Maria was aiming for; she was on a mission.

In the quiet of the night and the darkness of the room, Jorge, lying on his back with one arm under his head, spoke as if an alarm had sounded somewhere, catching him dead to rights. He said, "I can't believe I allowed this to happen."

"The first time or the second?" Maria asked, giggling.

"This isn't funny, Maria. Do you realize what we just did? Do you know how hurt your mother will be? This can never happen again and you can never tell her. Promise me that! It wasn't my intention, but you were so inviting and I was weak. You hit a nerve when you mentioned how much your mother leaves me alone. But it was wrong. I do not want to hurt her or you. I love your mother. This cannot happen ever again. And you cannot tell your mother. Do you promise?" he asked, repeating it for himself to emphasize his seriousness.

Annoyed by his sanctimonious words, Maria said, "Wow, Jorge, how quickly you changed emotions – from passion to cowardice in sixty seconds. That must be a record."

"Maria, I'm not saying this because I'm a coward. If your mother finds out, she will be devastated. That's why I don't want you to tell her. That's why we can't do this again. I love your mother and I have never been unfaithful to her before today."

"And?" Maria asked, getting even more annoyed with him.

"And, I don't ever plan to do this again."

"Jorge, please! I never asked you to fuck me, did I? You could have pushed me off you. You didn't even put up a fight. And you claim you love her?"

"It was something about the way you moved. Your smell was intoxicating…no mesmerizing, even familiar. It was as if you conjured up your mother, only a younger version. I didn't want to take you, but my body was on auto pilot."

Even now he was remembering how she felt and how she moved. She was hot and he wondered if she was even aware of it. He had never been with anyone like her before. As he laid there, he wondered how he would be able to live under the same roof with her now, sleep in the room across the hall from her and not think about her sexually. Not want her again.

Maria moved and allowed the sheets to expose her breasts as she leaned over his body to turn on the light. As she did, she lingered for a moment as if trying to find the light's button, allowing her nipple to touch his chest and her thigh to lean against his. Jorge's yearning began turning to lust and hunger for her young, firm body again. He wanted to push her away, but he couldn't; so instead he asked, "What're you doing?"

"I'm trying to reach the light so I can turn it on. I can't seem to quite reach it. Maybe you could try? Can you feel it?" she asked, not moving her body from touching his as she could see the outline of his penis getting hard again under the sheet.

Instead of reaching for the light, he reached around her small waist and pulled her frame on top of him. This was about to be the third time. She was facing him now and he was moving his hand to find her opening. Before he entered her, she said, "Jorge, I don't…"

He pulled her to him and found her mouth wet, as he knew her lips below would be. The way she felt inside was her poison. He kissed her firmly and slid inside. Maria smiled to herself for she had him just where she wanted. He was easier than she had imagined. What was it her mother had said about his infidelity?

They continued to sleep with each other for two months, mostly while her mother was out of town, but sometimes within hours of her returning home from bringing a new life into the world. It was thrilling and exciting to Maria knowing that Jorge had been inside of her only minutes sometimes before her mother's return. And then she would hear her mother beg him to make love to her and he wasn't able to because Maria was in his head. For Maria, he was a means to an end, the end being her mother's unhappiness.

For Jorge, Maria appealed to his kinky side, an enjoyable one, but one nonetheless. He had tamed the freak and put it to sleep when he met Anna because he knew he wanted more from life. He wanted to spend the rest of his life with her. But Maria had awakened that beast and now he could not, he did not want to, re-cage it.

One particular Thursday evening, Maria initiated the tryst. They usually took turns depending on the mood between them. But Maria didn't anticipate Jorge's response this night.

"I don't think this is a good idea. I'm not sure when your mother is due back."

Starting to kiss him, she said, "Don't you think I checked on that? It's okay."

That was all Jorge needed to hear. He began unbuttoning and then lifting her dress, feeling the warmth of her round butt. She didn't have on any underwear and this excited him even more. He was about to pull her closer when she stopped him, saying, "Let's take a bath together first."

"Why?" he asked, his eyes closed, already anticipating the excitement ahead.

"I just thought it might be fun; something different. Let's be clean and wet. What's wrong with that?"

"I feel awkward doing that in your Mother's and my bathroom and yours isn't large enough. Besides, we don't need to do anything different. You're already exciting enough."

"Then let's stay out here in the living room. I'm tired of using my room."

"Fine," he said, anything to get her to stop talking and allow him to feel that wetness.

They had both just climaxed when the front door opened and in the doorway stood Anna. She dropped her bag to the floor and her mouth fell open as she blinked several times to clear up her vision. There on the floor was her daughter's naked body lying next to her husband's, the condom still drooping vulgarly on his limp penis.

Anna screamed out in pain, "Ay Dios mío! Maria, what the hell are you doing?"

Maria smiled as she sat propped up on her elbows to see her mother standing in the doorway. The taxi driver was just behind her carrying her suitcase. Jorge leaped up and quickly began reaching for his clothes. They were strewn all over the living room floor and furniture.

"Anna, it's not what you think!" he exclaimed.

"The hell it isn't!" she said, before turning to the taxi driver and handing him the payment. "You may leave my bag there, thank you." He took the money, but didn't take his eyes off Maria's body. Anna had to push him out the door, slamming it behind him, before returning to the two people who had just betrayed her in the worst way.

Once the driver was out, Maria slowly moved to gather her clothing. Slipping her dress over her head, she waited for the next words from her mother or Jorge.

"Jorge, how could you? She's my daughter, your stepdaughter. I thought you loved me? Loved her?"

Buttoning his pants and zipping them, he said, "I do love you, Anna. Look, let me explain." Then turning to Maria, he said, "Would you give us a minute?"

"No, I won't, actually. I want to hear exactly how you plan to explain this to her. After all, I never once had to twist your arm."

"Did you just say you never once had to twist his arm? So this isn't even the first time?" Anna was feeling sick to her stomach, as the situation called to life all those old suppressed memories of Juan kindled inside her. She wanted to burst aflame. She couldn't tell if it was from the smell of their pheromones lingering in the air, suffocating her, or the thoughts of them fucking each other all over this house that was supposed to be her "home sweet home."

Not responding to his wife, Jorge continued pleading with Maria for privacy to explain things and to think clearly. He couldn't do that as long as she remained in the room.

"Maria, I'm not asking you, I'm telling you! Now please, let me speak to your mother in private."

"Why should I leave? I have the right to stay here. When you started fucking me, you made this about the three of us. You shared the wetness of mother and daughter."

At that, Anna slapped Maria. She couldn't believe the nastiness coming out of her daughter's mouth. There was something so very carnal about the way she said it and it disturbed her. She watched as Maria rubbed the area of her smacked cheek, knowing it must be stinging, but she didn't let on her concern.

How could she have raised this child to be so cold and heartless? Then the memory of the letter flashed across her mind. It was obvious Maria had inherited that coldness from her father, the one she never met.

The thought made Anna raise her hand to slap Maria again, but Jorge stopped her.

"Anna, don't. You're mad at me; don't take this out on Maria."

"I'm not mad. I'm furious! With both of you. I know that she seduced you, Jorge. Inside, she's an angry little girl because her father left. But you, you are supposed to be the adult. But even knowing all that, I still can't believe my own flesh and blood stooped so low," Anna stated, glaring at her daughter before continuing. "After all I've done to show you love, to make certain that you never felt alone in this world, all I've done to prepare you for life. And this is what you do? Who are you?"

Maria couldn't wait to tell her mother what had been on her mind since she put her plan into motion. "I don't know why you're so surprised, mother dear. All these years I watched you do this to other men's wives. I watched you manipulate them into getting what you wanted. I wanted to seduce him, and I did, because I can. I wanted you to know that I was listening when you told me about men and what to expect from them. And I wanted to prove to you that Jorge was no different. Your precious Jorge who would never betray you – I wanted to show you that given the opportunity, he would screw another woman no matter how much he claimed he loved you."

Anna shook her head in disbelief, feeling the pain from her daughter's words jabbing her heart. "And why was it so important for you to prove me wrong about Jorge and right about men, for God's sake, Maria?"

"Because you brought him into this house with us when we didn't need anyone. We were fine all by ourselves. So I figured I needed to remind you of what you taught me when I asked you about my father. Do you remember mother? You said, 'Men will use you if you don't use them first. They can't be trusted, but they can be manipulated.' I wanted to see the look on your face when I proved you right. You forgot and I needed to remind you. Now it can go back to being just the two of us.

Won't that be better?"

Jorge was stunned. He had been a pawn in some sick game of Maria's and now he had been completely exposed. He looked at Anna and she was looking down, but she wasn't crying. Perhaps that was a good sign, so he spoke up.

"Maria, you don't know what you're saying. You don't know anything about me or my love for your mother. I gave into your temptations and I see now it was all some sick game to you. You even orchestrated tonight to have your mother find out in this horrible way. Every time I tried to stop, you turned up the flames and drew me in like a moth to a flame. I had no defense against you."

Anna looked at her husband, smirked ever so slightly, and said, "Jorge, is that really the explanation you want to use? You were defenseless against an eighteen-year-old? If so, you are not the man I thought I married. If you sullied our vows with my daughter, you have no honor at all. Perhaps she was your target all along. Was she?"

"No, of course not. I fell in love with you."

"So how did this happen?" Anna asked.

"Weren't you listening? She seduced me as part of a plan! Look, I've been an asshole. I never meant for you to get hurt, Anna. She's young, sexy, looks like you and she's manipulative. She came on to me; she aroused me. You weren't here, and it happened. It shouldn't have, but it did. But I promise you, I will never touch her again."

"It's too late, Jorge. It's too late. I thought you were different, but as Maria proved, it was all in my head. Pack your things and move out of my home, tonight. I'll be in touch with you regarding the divorce."

"Anna, you don't mean that. I know you are hurt, but we can get through this." He paused and then said, "I don't care what you say, I really loved you, I still do love you."

"No, Jorge, we won't get through this. Our marriage is over," Anna said, turning her back to him, pushing out the hurt and filling her heart with emptiness.

Jorge watched his love treat him as a stranger and he still couldn't believe that she wasn't crying. Didn't all women cry when their hearts were broken in love affairs? He wondered what that meant. When she didn't budge, he headed toward their bedroom. As he passed Maria, all he could do was shake his head in disbelief. She had been a seductive snake and was proud of it. She had definitely played him. Psycho bitch.

Maria stared right back at him, but she did feel a little sorry for him. She knew that he loved his wife and was innocent in this discovery, but in war there were always casualties.

When the two of them were finally alone after Jorge left, Anna turned her attention to her daughter. "So, do you feel victorious now? Did you accomplish what you wanted? I should have known there was a reason you asked me to come home tonight instead of tomorrow. I was just as helpful to you as he was – a lamb being led to slaughter in creating this scenario. I hope that it was worth it to you."

Anna didn't wait for a response. She just turned away from this woman standing in front of her and headed for the door. She didn't want to breathe in the smell of betrayal any longer.

"Mommie…"

Anna stopped and waited to see what words would be thrown at her back.

"It was!" Maria commented, laughing. "Welcome home."

Finished with her reverie and returning her mental focus to the living room with Luis J, Maria reflected on how she had refined her ability to seduce men over the years. There had been many she left pining for her through college and then on into graduate school until she met Luis. He was a challenge for her and she welcomed it. There was something about him that was intoxicating and for the first time, the roles were reversed. He was having the same impact on her that she usually caused to others.

But she eventually drew him in and away from his wife, too, ultimately destroying his marriage the same way she had destroyed her mother's. But this was different because she really liked Luis and had wanted him for herself. She was certain the baby she was carrying was his and once born, she would have some piece of him forever. No matter what, Luis wouldn't abandon her and this child the same way her father had abandoned her.

"No, Luis J, I'm pretty sure she won't care," Maria responded to Luis J's supposition about her mother changing because of her pregnancy.

"Well, I'm sure my mother won't have that reaction. She's learned from interfering in Carlos' life. But don't get me wrong, I don't imagine her wanting to come over here with open arms to spend time with you, even if it is her grandchild."

Luis J chuckled at the image of them all sipping coffee at the table before continuing. "She can be a piece of work sometimes, but then we both know that you have contributed to some of that behavior," Luis J claimed, thinking of the countless examples of his mother's comments about Maria.

"Was that supposed to be funny?" Maria asked. She did not need him defending his mother's honor, too. She didn't have the stomach for it.

"No, not at all. Before Carlos died, we had time to talk about you, Papi and Mami. He told me all about your role in our parents' divorce. And even though Carlos was able to forgive you, you don't get a pass with me that easily. But you are carrying my child, so we'll all have to put that in the past and find a way to get along. But this toying with my mother like she's your prey and taunting her has to stop. This child will not be raised in that kind of environment and drama, whether it's mine or Papi's. I have seen and experienced firsthand what happens when parents are dysfunctional and angry," he stated, adamantly.

Now Maria was enraged. She had let him live there and now he was giving her his opinion on how she should behave and questioning the paternity of the baby. Who does this little boy think he is, talking to her in that way? But she thought carefully about her next move and how to respond before saying, "Luis J, I told you that this is your baby. What are you talking about?"

"Maria, I'm not that naïve. Even though you claim you never had unprotected sex with Papi, it seems very suspect that the first time you and I sleep together, you have unprotected sex with me. It all seems a little too convenient, don't you think? Especially now that you and my dad are no longer together.

"But I couldn't see clearly then. I was susceptible to your claim because I was so confused emotionally over Carlos' death. I was drinking tequila and smoking weed to drown out my pain and I was mad as hell at my parents. Your condition was a perfect assist and the ball sailed in, nothing but net. Or so I thought. But when Chell told me about all this shit with Roger, I had to clear my head so I could be there for her. Hell, I shouldn't have been drinking in the first place. You shouldn't have enabled me, let alone allowed it in your presence.

"When my parents saw how bad I was, they pulled out all the stops. That intervention set me on the right path and showed me how much they really cared about my wellbeing, no matter what. And then I saw it again when they banded together to help Chell. They love us and they loved Carlos. My mother may go about things like a bull in a china shop, but she's learning from her mistakes, too. So, I've worked through all of that anger and I'm working on repairing my relationship with them. Blood is blood, family is everything, and as far as that baby you're carrying, I won't allow it to suffer from our craziness. We will all do right by that baby, regardless of the paternity."

Once again, Maria was stunned by his response. He had matured from all of this pain. She had underestimated him. What had Diane said, "He was the most like her?" But she still needed him to get back at Luis and to stop this so-called banding together that was occurring. The only way to do that was to continue to convince Luis J that the baby was his.

"Wow, you've said a mouthful. But the one thing I need for you to know is that this baby I am carrying is yours, Luis J. I swear."

Luis J shook his head from side to side as he looked at the woman sitting next to him. With a clearer, sober head now, his thinking was, 'Why would my father lie about sleeping with her bareback? He wouldn't need to. And it's quite clear that he's trying to get back with Mami, so he wouldn't hide anything from her either, and she's cool with it. Yeah, Maria, I got your number.' But he simply said, "Okay, Maria. Since you swear."

"Thank you for believing me. And, you're right, Luis J, a toxic environment is not good for children. So I will do my part to keep the peace. I'm so glad you haven't turned your back on me or this child the way your father has. He hasn't called or anything to check on us." Maria leaned over to kiss him, but Luis J pulled away.

"I know you said you didn't want to feel the baby, but give me your hand." When he didn't retract it, she placed it on her stomach. "Do you feel that? Wait a second. There. Do you feel that?"

"Yeah. Wow, that's cool! She's moving. Interesting," replied Luis J.

"Isn't it?"

"Yeah, that, but I was talking about your comment just now about Papi. About how he's deserted you and the baby and not checking up on you. Why do you care… if it's not his baby?"

Had she just said that out loud? All of his sharing had taken her off her "A" game. She had slipped and said too much. "Well, you were just saying how he was being there for you and I didn't see him calling to check on me. After all, it is possible this could be his baby, even though we never had unprotected sex. Mistakes do happen."

What was she doing? Why was she saying these things to make him question the paternity? She needed him to continue playing the game. But by the change in his posture, she could tell that she was losing her hold. She had to move him away from those thoughts and back to the baby. She would use the baby's welfare to draw him back in.

"You just said she. Why did you say that?"

"I don't know. It's a feeling I have. I think it's a girl." He could still see her moving around in Maria's stomach.

"I think it's a girl, too."

"Why?"

"Because she moves every time she hears your voice. Just like she's doing now."

"Oh...okay," he said, sarcastically.

"No, I'm serious," Maria said, as she began weaving a new net for him. "So what do you think we should name her?" And just like that she had maneuvered him from one line of dialog to another.

"I don't know. I just figured you would name her," he said. He replaced his hand upon her abdomen so he could feel the movement. There was a baby living in there. Maybe his.

"Something sweet and gentle; that's the kind of child she's going to be. I think she's going to look just like me," Maria said, followed up by a look of sweet invitation on her face.

"Yeah, and she could be just like my mother!" They both laughed. "I'm heading to bed, Maria. I'll see you in the morning." He removed his hand and headed to his room, leaving Maria sitting on the couch alone.

He wasn't drawn to her the way she had anticipated and she was now left considering her options. She was losing ground with this Rodriquez man, too, and that was clearly not the game plan.

Chapter Thirty Eight

Luis J saw Roger and Goober as soon as he got to school Monday morning. They watched him approaching and increased the volume of their voices to make sure he would hear their exchange. They were talking about some young thing they had left on the side of the road in the rain and wondered how long it took her to walk back home.

Luis J knew they were baiting him and he bit his bottom lip as he walked past them toward the locker room. His non-response forced them to escalate their voices and their laughter. They wanted him to react; that had been the plan from the beginning. They slapped hands with each other and then broke out in laughter. Luis J could hear them talk about the naivety of that piece of ass, who probably wasn't foreign to street walking anyway.

Luis J had his first real experience of counting to one-hundred to keep from bashing their heads into the concrete. He focused his energy on the color orange as he let the gym door slam behind him. Orange would soon be Roger and Goober's new color of clothing if all went as planned and they found themselves in lockup. This is what he was focused on as he approached his locker, so much so that he almost missed the note that was tacked to the locker door.

It was from Coach. He suited up and reported to the office as instructed. He found Coach sitting at his desk reviewing plays. As Luis J approached the desk, Coach leaned back in the chair, closed the playbook, and gestured with his chin for him to sit.

Once he was seated, Coach began, "Luis, I know you just walked past Goober and Roger and the fact that you don't have any bruises on you and security isn't standing in my office right now, I know you took the high road. Thank you for doing that. It shows great restraint and maturity. I know they did not make that pathway an easy one."

Coach paused to let Luis J soak in the complimentary feelings. "I also wanted to thank you for confiding in me regarding your sister's abuse. You did the right thing bringing this to me. I have already met with the principal and guidance counselor about both of those guys. There's still a few i's that need to be dotted, but they will likely be suspended, pending investigation, by the end of the day.

"Of course, this will have a rippling effect on the team and as their captain I have to ask if you are up for the battle that might ensue?"

Luis J knew exactly what Coach was referencing. He was inquiring about his drinking and drugs, but he hadn't had a drink since the night Chell first told him about Roger. Oh, he had thought about it, especially after Roger stranded her on the side of the road, but once again, that evening Chell needed him and he wasn't going to let her down anymore.

When Luis J didn't respond, Coach filled the silence with the rest of his thoughts. "So, does your silence mean that you aren't ready? Because there's no place for you here if that's your answer."

"Coach, I'm going to be the captain you need me to be and the one I want to be. Just like I'm here to be the brother my sister needs me to be. I will call the guys from the intervention and get some help. I don't think it will take much, but I know I can't assume that I can do this on my own. Thank you for all your patience with me. I know I've been a pain in your…well, you know." Luis J nodded his head as a sign of affirmation of his words.

"I believe you, Luis J. The look in your eyes tells me you're serious. But don't underestimate the road that lies ahead. You are going to hear all kinds of things and be provoked by Roger's crew, but you have to remember the end game. And if you need to be reminded, you know where to find me."

"Thanks Coach." Luis J extended his hand and they shook. "I'm going to shoot a few hoops before first period. I'll see you later this afternoon."

Coach watched his star player walk out the door and exhaled. He hoped that he wouldn't lose his way again.

Chapter Thirty Nine

When Luis J ran out of the locker room and onto the court for their scrimmage, he noticed right away that his team was split into two groups. He took note of who was in each one and recognized that the lines had been drawn. They were all looking toward the sidelines and Luis J followed their gaze. Just off to the left of the court was a scene he had been looking forward to observing since Friday.

There were three policemen talking to Coach and the school principal while Roger and Goober stood next to them in handcuffs. Apparently the attorney had acted swiftly in securing the warrant for their arrests. As the officers concluded their interaction with the school officials, they placed a hand on Goober's and Roger's shoulders and led them out of the gymnasium.

Luis J wished he had taken a photo to share with Chell, but knew it wouldn't be necessary as he had a million shots of the image in his mind. The principal left the gym and Coach returned to a seat on the bench, his eyes on his team. Luis J squared his shoulders, walked right up to the two groups and stood in the middle. He cleared his throat and said, "Well, I know the rumors are running fast right now, faster than some of you guys do when you're on the court," he chuckled, hoping to add a little levity to the mood.

When no one joined him, Luis J stiffened his lip and continued, "Look, I can't give you any specifics about what is going down, but I will tell you that very soon all will be revealed and you will either agree with my actions or, at a minimum, at least understand them. I also need to say that I know I haven't been the team captain that all of you have deserved because I was not handling the loss of my brother's death very well. And for that I apologize to each of you and to Coach."

Luis J shot a glance in his direction. He was still sitting on the bench watching to see how Luis J was going to manage things. He was close enough that he could hear the dialogue and nodded his head as a gesture of acceptance.

Luis J nodded back and continued addressing his teammates. "So, we have a choice today. We can pull together and play this game as a team or we can let this divide us and jeopardize all of the hard work we have put into this year. What will it be?" Luis J extended his arm, palm down and waited.

Most of the team had always admired him, but had been thoroughly disappointed by his most recent behavior on and off the court. They had secretly been waiting for the Luis J they knew as their captain to come back to them. One by one, starting with Maine, his teammates followed suit, one hand on top of the other, and the scrimmage began.

40
Chapter Fourty

Luis J stopped by his mother's after the scrimmage to see Chell and to share the good news. It was a bonus when he discovered that his father was also there. Now they could all share in this triumph together. Luis J saw the three of them in an assembly line. His mother was washing, Chell was in the middle drying, and his father was trying to figure out where to put the dishes. He hadn't been too successful, as they were piling up on the countertop in front of him. Luis J chuckled as he greeted the boys, who were eating ice cream at the kitchen table and playing with some action figure toy he didn't recognize.

Luis J headed to the bathroom to wash his hands before pitching in to help his father. The kitchen scene looked like the cover of a Hallmark card and this made Luis J wonder if his mother would be making an announcement sometime soon.

Within minutes they were done and Diane took the boys for their bath, leaving Luis to talk to his older children. He shared with them the outcome of the attorney's investigation and why the police were able to act so quickly. Apparently, the District Attorney was already working on filing a case against Goober and Roger. There had been other girls who had made allegations against them, but unfortunately, the girls were too old to prosecute Roger and Goober for statutory rape.

Chell's case, though, gave them what they needed and the other girls' allegations would be used to show a pattern of behavior. They also assumed there were other underage girls who might come forward when they learned of Chell's bravery. Luis J contributed to the story by providing a frame-by-frame replay of what he had witnessed and the closure he experienced in the end.

"So, it's finally over?" Chell asked, looking at her father for confirmation.

"Well, there still has to be a trial, but it's going to be an easier case to prosecute because it didn't just happen to you. You will still have to testify if those jerks don't plead guilty, but you don't have to worry, we'll be with you every step of the way. Right, mijo?" Luis asked his son, wanting him to realize that Chell would need all of them.

"Every step, Shortie. We'll all be with you," Luis J added, gently punching her arm.

"But what about Stacie and the other girls? What's going to happen to them?" Chell continued, sharing the thoughts that were swimming around in her head.

"Not surprising you should ask. They are actually going to be charged with conspiracy to endanger the life of a minor, with a few other charges for Ms. Stacie. They won't have to go to jail, but Stacie will likely have to serve some time in a juvenile facility. The others will probably get off with probation. Alright?"

Chell nodded. At least Stacie would have to pay. But she still worried about the kind of reception she would receive from others at school. She knew there was no way that what had happened to her wasn't already common knowledge in her class and she was equally sure Stacie's posse would still find ways to make her life miserable.

Luis J noticed the blank stare on her face and knew from his own experience what she was thinking, so he said, "Hey, Shortie, I know you must be worried about how this is all going to play out tomorrow when you get to school. I had the same concerns today when the arrest went down and the team was literally divided on the court. But you have nothing to be ashamed of or to feel bad about. This was all a game to Roger, a really sick one, and it finally caught up with him. If anyone bothers you, just let me know. I could even take you to school in the morning if you think that will help. I would be willing to do that and more to help you get through this." Luis J couldn't bear the thought of his sister suffering anymore and was prepared to take on the whole eighth-grade class of piss-ass little girls if he had to.

Luis started to respond, but held back to allow Chell to speak, "No, Luis J, I don't want you to do that. It will only make things worse. Thankfully, this is our last week of school before spring break. I just need to make it to Friday."

She sighed as sadness, anger and resentment settled in her stomach. She wondered when she would feel better and could get back to a normal life. "If it's okay, I'm going to go to my room and get ready for bed," she stated, pushing back from the table.

Luis opened his arms to invite her to feel his love and strength. She laid her head on his chest and closed her eyes so tightly she was seeing spots. Pulling away from him, gently, she mumbled, "Good night."

But Luis held on for an extra second, looked gently into her eyes, and said, "Chell, Luis J is right. Roger's sister was acting in cahoots with him and she's probably done it before also. She will be held accountable for what she's done. They left you with a boy that cared nothing about you on the side of the road. He could have really done you harm. Keep that in mind."

"Yes, Papi, I get it."

Luis J and Papi watched her retreat to her room and close the door behind her. Luis J asked his father, "Do you think she will come through this alright? I'm really worried about her."

"Yes, she will, because we will see to it that she does. I meant what I said earlier, she will need all of us. Are you up for the task?"

This was the second time today he had been asked that question. He smiled a bit and answered his father with the same level of commitment. "I know I have let you guys down and disappointed you these past few months, in a number of ways. But I'm ready to do what I need to, including getting the help for my drinking, so I can help Chell heal. I don't want her to turn to alcohol or drugs the way I did to ease her pain."

Luis nodded his head in agreement and was impressed with his son's insightfulness. Still, he had to provide clarity. "Son, I hear you and I am grateful, but you might be taking on a bit much if you think it's your responsibility to help Chell heal. Your responsibility is to heal yourself. Chell has to heal herself. All we can do for loved ones is to be there for one another."

Luis J did not speak, but he understood clearly what his father conveyed. He had just recently chosen life for himself and now it was Chell's turn. He'd have to give her that space and let her choose on her own time.

Silently, Luis was prayerful that Luis J would stand behind his words. He needed him to because he didn't want him to suffer his brother, Antonio's, fate. He hadn't shared this news with any of them, but he had received word from Chicago that Antonio was very ill. He had been hospitalized and diagnosed with cirrhosis of the liver. His mother had arrived in Chicago that morning, but had suggested to her oldest son that he stay in New York with his family.

He could still remember the love, and the wise and caring words she imparted to him, "Mijo, Antonio chose this path years ago and now he has to finish the journey. I will go and be with my son. But your children are suffering and they need their father. You must show them how much they mean to you. You must find a way to give them whatever they're craving so they don't follow in Antonio's footsteps. You and Diane must work together to find a way to reach them. That is where you are needed now, not in Chicago." And she was right. He was glad he had stayed.

He would call and check on his younger brother in the morning, but tonight it was all about his family. A family he was once again able to love and support. He and Luis J continued talking a while longer before his son bid his farewell and headed home to Maria.

With the boys tucked in bed and Chell in her room resting comfortably, Diane joined Luis on the couch. He kissed her gently on the top of her head once she curled up next to him and laid her head on his shoulder like old times.

"Luis, I wanted to give you and Luis J some time to talk. Was it my imagination or wishful thinking that he sounded better? Stronger even?"

"No, it wasn't. I experienced it, too. We really connected tonight like father and son. It was amazing and long overdue. Thank you for giving us some privacy, but more importantly Diane, you need to know that Luis J stepped up to the plate. He admitted that he had been difficult and that he has a drinking problem. He said he's going to seek counseling," Luis said, feeling contented as he recalled the interaction between them. It had reminded him of the early stages of his reconnecting with Carlos.

"I'm happy for you. Both of you. And yes, that is great news! Our son just may be growing up," Diane replied, before lifting her head to continue her statement. She wanted to face him.

"I've been thinking. I believe we are finally moving our family into a good space and I'm so thankful for that. But we can't all successfully get there without addressing one important element. It's time to tell Robert the truth. I've been thinking about this for some time and although I felt justified at the time, what I did was wrong. And once I set the story in motion, it was hard to rectify or retract it. But what I am realizing now is my lies and half-truths have laid a foundation for some of what we have been experiencing. I don't want Robert to find out about who you really are at a time in his life where he might not be able to handle it and turn to drugs or alcohol or worse. We need to tell him now, while he is still young and we can help him understand what it means and then move beyond it."

Diane saw the smile on Luis' face and it made her happy, but she had to slow him down because she knew he would head to Robert's room tonight and wake him with the announcement.

"Now, we will have some ground work to do. I need to tell David about this action first. I don't want him to feel like I'm minimizing, negating or negatively impacting the bond they share. Secondly, you will need to spend more time with Robert. He needs to observe you interacting with Chell, CJ and me. He needs to see how much you love them and get to know the wonderful father you are. I also want him to see how you interact with me so he won't be worried about me. If your schedule permits, perhaps we could start this weekend with a family outing. What do you think?"

Luis leaned over and kissed Di on the cheek. "What an amazing evening. First my son talks to me, I mean really talks to me. Something he hasn't done in years. Chell spoke what was on her mind and then did the right thing. Now you tell me I can fulfill my role of father to Robert. I'm speechless. You are amazing."

"No, Luis, I'm not. But I'm trying to get back to a good place with you and our children. I'm trying to rebuild my life and carefully correct the problems I created. I'm working on helping this family heal. When I get there, then you can say I'm amazing!" They both laughed and then he hugged her. It was a familiar hug and it felt good to both of them. When he released her, she introduced her next topic.

"Next week is spring break for Chell and I'm worried about leaving her home all day unsupervised. I can't take any more time off work. Although my office has been understanding to this point, they have expressed some small concern about my commitment to the role. What's your schedule like?"

"Um, mine's tight next week, too. We're having midterms. I can't take any time off either and she really can't come to campus with me. She'd be bored and that can breed other behaviors and potential trouble. So, I agree with you. Have you thought about what we could do?"

"I was going to ask Michelle and Steve if they could keep her. She has more flexibility with her job since she's one of the partners. And it's just them and that dog, Scooter or Scooper, or something like that. It would give Chell a change of scenery and time to get stronger emotionally. You know how much Michelle loves her. And she's actually mentioned recently that she'd like Chell to spend time with her."

"Di, you don't have to convince me; I think it's a great idea. But when she gets back, will you have resolved everything related to the family therapy sessions?"

Diane nodded her head. "Yes. And, I know this family outing trip doesn't replace that at all, but thanks for supporting the idea. I know my family hasn't always treated you well." She specifically recalled the last time her mother was in town. "I'll call Michelle tomorrow and see if she can pick Chell up on Sunday."

They made plans for Saturday that included a trip to a Delaware beach. It was a little far, but the weather was supposed to be warmer and at least they could picnic even if they couldn't get into the water. They covered a few more logistics and then Luis left since they both had early starts to their day.

Diane leaned against the door, looking forward to the trip like a teenager anticipating their first date and feeling good about her help in reconnecting father and son. Using her foot, she pushed her body off the door, turned off the lights, made one final check on the kids and turned in. Lying on top of the cool sheets, her mind drifted into the evening's experience and the high emotions they all shared. As a family, they had worked together to punish those no-good boys and get them out of Luis J and Chell's life; next would be the evil girls who helped with the plot. And, they had fun planning for the future. For the first time in a long time she felt that they might all finally be on the path to recovery and happier times.

Chapter Fourty One

41

Luis knocked on Diane's door around seven, Saturday morning. He had rented an SVU so they had a car large enough to accommodate all of them, the picnic basket, cooler, chairs, stroller and blankets. It took them about an hour to load the car, which required several trips. But by nine, the boys were dressed and the ladies were ready to go. Robert was so excited he had hardly slept the night before. He had never been to the beach, but Chell had told him about all the sand and water he would see and the castles they would build. So last night, he woke up every two to three hours to ask if it was morning yet.

Now that the trip was a reality, Diane found herself feeling a little anxious because she wasn't sure just how Robert would interact with Luis. Even more concerning to her was how she would answer any targeted questions he might ask about Luis' identity. Robert knew he was Carlos, Chell and Luis J's father, but he hadn't connected the dots to his paternity. There was something to be said about a young, easily directed mind.

Diane turned to check on the occupants of the back seat and at the moment, Robert was being fully entertained by his Power Ranger action hero and that was the extent of his world. CJ was sitting in a car seat comfortably between Chell and Robert and playing quietly. She could tell from the length of time between blinks he would be asleep shortly.

Her last check was of Chell. She had on her CD player and Diane knew it wouldn't be long before she would join CJ in la-la land. She was always lulled to sleep when riding in the back seat.

Returning her attention to the front seat, Diane and Luis started chatting. They shared stories about his students and his interest in pursuing the Department Chair's position, and her new boss and how her responsibilities were changing. When they weren't talking, they were listening to WBLS playing the oldies. They played a game to see who could recall what they were doing when those songs were hits. Diane was winning or Luis was letting her win, but either way, they were having fun.

It was so comfortable that it reminded Diane of the many trips they had taken like this when Carlos and Luis J were younger. They loved the beach, especially the ones along the Delaware coast, because they were usually cleaner, the sand whiter and the water less rough. But when they only had a few hours or just wanted to find some relief from the hot New York City concrete, they would settle for either Rockaway or Rye beach.

Since the divorce, though, Diane hadn't been to this beach or any other. David didn't really like the beach. He didn't like the whole sand experience. And it was too much for her to try to do a beach outing alone. When Carlos and Luis J were older and could have helped her with Robert and Chell, they always had something else going on most weekends, usually something sports related. Diane eventually stopped thinking about the beach altogether.

Luis pulled into the parking lot and turned off the engine. Diane opened her door and inhaled. She loved the smell of the beach. She glanced around and was happy to see that not much had changed over the years. There were more vendors and stores along the boardwalk, but the beach had been well maintained.

She couldn't wait to introduce this to Robert and reintroduce it to Chell. She felt comforted by the thought that CJ might feel like he was actually back in a familiar surrounding since he had been growing up in and around the water in Puerto Rico. She couldn't wait to feel the sand between her toes so she gently nudged Chell to wake her so she could keep an eye on the sleeping boys.

Then Luis and Diane began unpacking the car and scouting out a location. They didn't have to walk too far before they found the perfect area. It had some shade and a few picnic tables. It was also close enough to the water that they would be able to hear the waves, but not too close that it posed a risk for the boys. It was a little cooler than had been forecast, so Diane predicted there would be no swimming today, at least not for her.

Once they had settled in at their ideal little spot, Diane returned to the car to get the boys and Chell. But as soon as she was in earshot, she heard Chell fussing. 'Ugh,' Diane thought. She had hoped they would all get along for at least thirty minutes and enjoy the beauty of their surroundings. She opened the front door and said, "Chell, what's wrong?"

"Mami, Robert is so spoiled. He gets on my nerves. He doesn't want CJ to play with his stupid truck and he hasn't even played with that thing for months," Chell said, snatching it from his hand.

"That's not true. Mommie, tell her that's not true. Give it back to me. Daddy bought it for me, not CJ," Robert said in his defense, trying to retrieve his property.

"Nobody said he didn't," Chell said, moving it from his reach.

"Chell, stop teasing him. I told you that you have to redirect him. When you bully him like that, it just antagonizes him and we don't want to teach him to do that to CJ, right?" Diane said calmly, now trying to redirect Chell.

"Whatever," she said, sticking out her tongue at Robert, who was still trying to grab the truck from her extended arm.

Contrary to what Diane really wanted to do, she lowered her voice and said, "Chell, please, not today. I know I explained to you how important this trip is for Papi. They need to have a positive experience with each other."

Diane had explained to Chell multiple times during the week their plan to tell Robert the truth about Papi, but that they first had to build a bridge slowly and carefully to make it easier for Robert to accept him.

"Oh Mami, why are we even going through this charade? It's not that complicated," Chell fussed. Turning her attention back to Robert, she tossed the truck on the seat next to him and yelled, "Robert, stop crying…you are such a baby!"

"Chell, enough. You are not his parent. Take the diaper bag and CJ to your father and ask him to come join me. And as you walk over there, check your attitude, please. Thank you!" Diane instructed, throwing in a little sarcasm before redirecting her attention to Robert.

"Robert, really, is all this necessary?"

"Mami, do you see how you baby him? He makes me sick," Chell mumbled as she unbuckled CJ and lifted him out of his car seat. By now, tears were starting to well up in CJ's eyes.

"Don't cry CJ. You don't want that broken down truck anyway. When I get my allowance, I'm going to buy you a bigger, better truck. It'll make noise and everything and then we'll see who we allow to play with it."

"Chell? I'm about two movements away from your behind."

"I'm going…"

Diane shook her head as she watched the two of them headed toward Luis, leaving her with Robert who was now a complete wreck.

Retrieving his truck from the seat and examining it, he managed to say, "Mommie, I don't want to stay here. It's not going to be any fun. And why couldn't Daddy come with us? Chell doesn't yell at me when Daddy's here."

"Robert, I told you that Daddy had plans today. You'll see him tonight. But for now you have to stop crying and being so selfish. CJ doesn't have as many toys as you, so you have to share. That's what we do in this house. As for Chell, she isn't feeling well, so you have to excuse her. But she shouldn't yell at you or tease you. I'll remind her of how we're supposed to treat each other."

By now, Luis had surmised what had happened and was waiting patiently for an opportunity to engage with them. "Diane, is everything alright?"

"Yes, Chell and Robert had a difference of opinion, but everything's fine now. Right, Robert?"

"No. I can't tell if my truck is broken. Chell said it was broken. Is it, Mommie?" he asked, extending his arm for her to examine it.

Luis saw an opportunity, so he reached out his hand instead, offering to examine the toy. Neither of Robert's parents was prepared for his reaction.

Pulling the truck away from Luis, he yelled, "No, you can't look at it! My daddy bought this for me. Only my daddy can fix it."

Luis stayed composed and said, "And it's a nice truck. I was just going to look at it for you and make sure everything was working."

"I said, no!" Robert responded, kicking the back of the driver's seat.

"Robert Rodriquez, stop it this instant!" Diane barked. "You know better than to talk to adults that way. Do I need to help remind you of your manners?" Diane had her "I mean business, boy!" tone in full gear.

Instead of giving Luis the truck, he threw it on the floor and folded his arms. Diane was appalled. She shuddered because the behavior reminded her of David's as of late and she was absolutely not going to have Robert mimicking that dysfunctional mess. So she slapped his leg and said, "Pick it up and hand it to him. Right now! And say I'm sorry!"

Through sniffles and tears, Robert did as instructed. Diane continued, "You better check yourself, little boy, and keep your mouth shut for a few minutes or you will get a punishment that you will never forget."

Diane could only imagine how those words dug into Luis' heart, because it had the same effect on hers. Robert was only seven but his words and actions were deliberate and intended to be spiteful. Not only was he mimicking David's behavior, but she could also see herself in him, the side of herself that emerged when she was hurt and self-preservation kicked in. But she did not want Robert to embrace those traits from either of them. So she had to find a way to nip that in the bud, immediately.

Robert was familiar with that look she shot him and knew she meant business, so he picked up the toy and handed it to Luis. He examined it all over and then reassured Robert that it was in fine working order. But, he also told him that if it would make him feel better, he should also have his father look at it, too.

Diane helped Robert get out of the car and the three of them headed to the picnic site. Robert trailed slightly behind, carrying the truck and the Power Ranger. Every now and then, Diane heard him sniffling and muttering. She could only imagine what he was saying about her, but if he didn't stop soon, she was going to pull his pants down and spank that behind, family bonding or no family bonding, right there on the beach.

She was glad she had scheduled the family therapy appointment and had been debating whether or not Robert should attend. The therapist had suggested they all attend, but she was still on the fence about Robert. After today's behavior and the impending truth he would eventually be told, she no longer questioned it. He was already harboring quite a bit of resentment because of CJ's arrival and then her and David's separation. Once they told him about Luis, she was pretty sure there would be even more emotional baggage for them to address. But for the next few hours, she just wanted to enjoy her trip to the beach and hoped her children would allow her that.

After they ate, Luis took CJ and Chell down to the ocean and played games with them in the sand. But Robert didn't go. Instead he sat next to his mother sulking. Luis tried everything he could think of to break the ice, but Robert was determined not to be accommodating under any circumstances.

When Chell and Luis returned from their last excursion, Chell was wet from the waist down and laughing from ear to ear. "Papi, that was so much fun! Mami, did you see us jumping the waves near the shore?"

"Yes, sweetie, but promise me you won't do that by yourself. Your Dad is a really good swimmer and can protect you. We need to get you back into swimming class so you can strengthen your skills."

"Oh geez. Do you honestly have to put a damper on everything?"

"Chell, that's not what she was doing. She was just warning you of how dangerous the ocean can be. That's what parents are supposed to do, try their best to protect you from getting hurt," Luis said.

"Oh well, it's too late for that," Chell said, sucking her teeth. She had been hurt, badly.

"Mija, you've been sort of harsh today. I'm going to need you to tone that down."

"Have I? Well, at least I'm not ruining the day like Robert is with his sulking and whining. You've tried everything to get him to get out of that mood and he hasn't even tried to meet you halfway. And all of this over some stupid toy?"

Luis looked at Robert and as Chell surmised, he hadn't moved one inch from that spot since they finished eating. But singling him out was not the right way to deal with his behavior, so instead Luis said, "No one is ruining the day. Aren't you having fun? I know I am. CJ, are you having fun?" Luis asked, raising him over his head and causing the sand from his body and feet to go flying everywhere.

Diane put her hand up to shield herself and said, "Luis, stop, he's full of sand!"

Luis started laughing and swung him up again. "CJ, did NaNa just get her hair done? Is that why she hasn't gotten in the water?"

"Dunk her, Papi, dunk her," Chell chanted.

Diane didn't know if Chell was saying that because she thought it would be fun or if she actually would derive pleasure out of seeing her mother drenched. But Diane wasn't the least bit concerned because she knew Luis didn't dare get her hair wet. Well, at least she hoped he remembered the golden rule about her hair, so she stood up and started backing away while cautioning him, "Luis, don't even think about it."

As Luis started moving toward her, Chell started laughing, but Robert jumped down from his stationary spot and ran to stand between his mother and Luis, yelling, "Stop it! Don't hurt my Mommie! I'm gonna tell my Daddy if you hurt my Mommie!"

"Robert, he's just playing," Diane said, now laughing, too. She remembered when Luis used to threaten to dunk her in the water all the time, but he knew she didn't swim well and would never have done it.

"No he's not, and I'm going to call my Daddy, right now. He'll be mad at you and make you stop."

"Robert, for goodness sakes, David is not your Daddy. Papi is!" Chell blurted. "Don't you get it?"

"Chell!" Luis yelled, stopping in his tracks and turning toward her. He was hoping to silence her by just calling her name. But she ignored him and continued to unwrap the truth like it was Robert's Christmas gift that she had been appointed to open for him.

"Why do you think I and Luis J call him Papi? Even Carlos called him that. Papi's our father, not David. You don't have David's last name. Your last name is Rodriquez, like mine and like his. He's your father," Chell said, pointing to Luis.

Robert's lip began quivering and his eyes filled with tears. "That's a story. Mommie, Chell's telling stories." Robert turned to look at who she was pointing at, but then quickly turned his head away. "That's not my father. He's not my father. Mommie, I wanna go home. I told you I didn't want to stay."

Luis snatched Chell by the arm and pulled her away from them. His step was brisk and her short legs had to trot to keep up. They walked far enough away that they were able to have a private conversation, but close enough that he could keep an eye on the scene unfolding in front of him, a scene his daughter had spitefully orchestrated.

They stopped in front of a bench, where Luis pushed her lightly and Chell plopped down. He stood to the side of her and propped his leg up on the bench next to her.

"Chell, what on earth was that all about? Why did you do that? Who gave you the right to pull the foundation out from under Robert like that? Can you imagine what he must be thinking and feeling? What possessed you to do that to your little brother?"

Chell looked down at her feet. She began making circles in the sand with her toe before she finally said, "I don't know. I'm just so tired of him acting like a baby. CJ acts more mature than Robert and they're five years apart. And then to have him stand there and threaten to tell David, his daddy, on you just made me sick. I hate how he treats you like some stranger. Carlos used to talk about that and I didn't get it back then, but I do now."

"But this isn't about you. Your mother and I put him on this path and your mother and I should be the ones who take him off. We're not perfect. We made a ton of mistakes regarding you guys, but we're trying to put things back on track on our timeline and in our way, in a way that minimizes the hurt. And you just come along and screw all that up."

Luis stopped for a moment to calm himself and glanced over to see what progress, if any, Diane was making in calming Robert down. The boy was sprawled in the sand, feet flying, and Diane was trying to strap CJ into the stroller so she would have both hands free to contend with Robert. Without redirecting his eyes to Chell, he said, "Look at him. Do you think you helped make him behave better? Do you think he is eager to get to know his father now?"

Chell looked at her little brother and then back at her father. Her heart began breaking. "Oh, Papi, I don't know what's wrong with me," she cried, tears rolling down her cheek. "I was so angry with Robert for being mean to CJ because it reminded me of how cruel Stacie was to me. I just couldn't control my temper."

"Chell, I have an idea of how difficult this has been for you, but only an idea. You haven't shared much with me about your feelings or thoughts. But I will tell you that when we face our demons, it takes away their power. When we let others help and support us, it lets us heal. Would you allow me to do that?"

"You want to know how I feel? I feel stupid and gullible. Like a fool. I don't know why I fell for Roger. I don't know what I was thinking when I got into Goober's car. I'm talking about how immature Robert is, but what I should be doing is looking in the mirror. I know you must be mad at me and totally disappointed in me," she said, lowering her head again and returning to making circles in the sand. She had buried half of her foot and could feel the dampness of the sand around her toes. She found it soothing.

"Chell, let me explain something to you. Teenage boys have one thing on their mind. Well, maybe two, but one dominates and that is,

'Who is going to be the next girl I can screw?' They focus all of their energy on accomplishing that goal. Sometimes they do it in a respectful manner, but most of the time it's an 'in-and-out,' literally. They look for the path of least resistance. They will say and do almost anything to get it. So, teenage girls, like you, need to be aware of this and choose their path wisely. If you are not ready to enter into that kind of sexual exchange with a boy, then you should let him know and not feel bad, at all, about saying no. And if you say no, they should accept that and never, ever, force themselves on you. Roger and Goober were wrong on so many levels, but you have to own that you put yourself into that compromising situation.

"When parents give you the third degree, it's for your protection. They want to know where you're going and who's going to be there so they can ascertain if you are exposing yourself to danger. Why? Because often we've been there and in some cases done that and we are able to see warning signs that you can't."

He paused to once again check on Diane. She was now holding Robert in her arms and was rocking him gently. "Does any of this make sense to you?"

Chell listened to her father and now understood the message her mother had tried to convey when she drilled her about where she was going and who was going to be there. She was even starting to understand now that Roger had lied to her about his feelings and she had fallen for it, completely. She hadn't stopped to analyze anything about his pursuit or her reasons for sleeping with him. Then, to make matters worse, she had allowed herself to get pregnant and could only imagine what her life would have been like had she given birth to a child. Yes, Papi was right, she had lied herself right into the arms of a vulture and he had tried to destroy her and her brother's future.

"Papi, I hear you. I see what you mean and I see what I did wrong."

"Can you? Do you? Because you need to know that there are going to be plenty of guys who are going to want to be with you, physically. You are a beautiful young girl and very smart. But you will have to decide who is worthy of being with you. And honestly, as young as you are, you should wait until you are physically and emotionally ready and can make the best choice. Your body is still maturing. You have to give it time to finish developing. And with that will come an emotional maturity. When that happens you won't be in some dirty backseat of a car. And the guy won't put you in harm's way. Instead, when you meet the right person, you will know and it will be special."

Chell watched her father's look soften as though he were having a pleasant memory, so she asked, "Is that how you and Mami felt about each other when you first hooked up?"

Luis laughed. He wasn't sure if he should divulge to her that they slept together before they got married but perhaps she would learn from this honesty, so he replied, "Yes, it is. But your mother and I dated for a long time before we took things to that level of intimacy. She wanted to be sure about me and I respected that and I didn't pressure her in any way. I was your mom's first."

"Papi, do you still love her?"

Luis should not have been surprised by this question, especially not from Chell. She was usually very observant with things, much like his mother. So he chose the words he used very carefully to give her the truth, but not be misleading. "Mija, your mother and I will always be connected because of the life experiences and children we share. When you have that much history, it's hard to stop caring about someone."

"But do you love her?"

Even with all that strategy, Chell was not going to let him punt. So he said, "Yes, I do."

She smiled and said, "I knew it. Then why aren't you guys back together? I bet she still loves you, too."

"Unfortunately, it's not that simple."

"NaNa says the truth is always simple."

Luis had heard his mother say that a thousand times and here his daughter was repeating it right back to him. He looked at Chell and it was like NaNa was sitting next to him, like she was on the porch at home, staring into his eyes and seeing exactly what his heart was feeling. Perhaps she was right, but he had to be sure. He did not want to move too quickly and cause pain for anyone or lose the reconnection that seemed to be happening naturally.

"Anyway, I want you to know that I will be here for you as you work through this. I will listen and answer any questions you might have. I love you and I know you will be alright once you heal." He leaned down, hugged her and kissed her on the forehead.

"Now, we should probably head back so you can apologize to your mother and your brother and then we'll start packing the car so we can head home."

Chell pulled her foot, which was fully covered in sand, out from under it and shook it off. Standing up and taking her father's hand, they started back toward their site.

Diane had watched Luis pulling Chell behind him and couldn't remember him ever being that upset with her before. She had really crossed the line this time and that rarely visible Luis temper was going to let her have it. She directed her attention toward Robert, who was lying on the ground kicking and crying like a child going through the terrible twos, though he would be turning eight soon. He was clearly being overly dramatic. It wasn't like Chell had told him David was dead, but Diane knew she had to meet him where he was, so she strapped CJ into the stroller and then picked Robert up off the ground. Holding him tightly so he would feel loved and secure, she finally got him to stop squirming and settle down. When the sniffling subsided, she slowed her rocking and starting talking to him.

"Robert, I know what Chell just told you is a surprise, so let me explain it to you. A long time ago, I was married to Papi. He and I had three children and I was pregnant with you. Sometimes grownups have fights and disagreements and find that they can't fix it or move beyond it. That's what happened to Papi and me. But when it did, I was very mad at him so I didn't let him see you. After a while, I married David and he loved you like his own child so I let you call him Daddy. It was wrong of me to do that because it has confused you. I didn't tell you that you actually had two daddies. One who created you like mommies and daddies do and one who was helping to raise you. That's what Chell told you today. I'm sorry if the news hurt you. It should not have been shared with you like that. Actually, David and I were going to tell you together this week. Do you understand? At least a little?"

Diane paused to let his seven-year-old brain process the information. While she did, she glanced over at Luis and Chell to see how they seemed to be reacting with one another. When she witnessed Chell nodding her head, she felt some sense of relief. As long as she was being responsive and listening, they hadn't lost her yet.

"So, I have two daddies?"

"Yes, you're very fortunate to have two daddies who love you very much and would do anything for you. So with time, you'll get to know Papi just like Carlos did, and Luis J and Chell do, and you'll love him, too. But you will always be able to call David, 'Daddy.'" When it seemed like he was ready to get up and return to his world of life's simple things, she gave him a kiss and let him go. It went better than she had anticipated, as least for now. The only problem she could foresee was how David would react when she gave him the news that she was forced to tell Robert without him. She shrugged her shoulders and grabbed a bottle of water for the boys and herself. One bridge at a time, she thought, remembering Michelle's advice.

As Chell and Luis approached the rest of the family, Diane saw that they were holding hands. Robert watched Luis out of the side of his eye and then slowly approached him, handing him the truck. Luis smiled, that warm loving smile Diane had fallen in love with years ago, and took the truck from Robert. The two of them started talking about David and when he had given Robert the truck. 'That was a good place to start,' Diane thought.

Chell then walked up to her mother and hugged her, whispering an apology. Diane welcomed it and together they sat on the bench to watch the interaction between father and son while CJ slept. Before long, Luis and Diane began packing and Chell took the boys closer to the water where the sand was softer and they could build castles. Diane and Luis watched them as they walked away, brother on one side and nephew on the other.

Diane asked, "So, what did she say? Were you able to reach her?"

Luis summarized their conversation and how he hoped he had reached her. But he suggested they continue their conversations with her. Diane should share a woman's perspective and he and Luis J should continue to provide the man's. Once that topic was complete, he listened to the recap of Diane's "Hail Mary" with Robert. To his relief, she had divulged it all and Robert hadn't gone running to the car or the police. It explained Robert's gesture and their interaction.

As they continued talking, they began repacking the car in preparation for the ride home. With everything and everyone onboard and fast asleep, Luis headed back to the city. The truth was finally out. The way it had occurred wasn't ideal, but at least now they could begin to build something from these blocks.

Chapter Fourty Two

42

Diane looked at her watch and it was four-o-clock in the afternoon. She had helped Chell pack in preparation for her stay with Michelle and Steve and they had pulled out about half an hour ago, heading back to Jersey. Diane had enjoyed yesterday's outing, despite some of the hiccups, and now she had the house to herself and it was the perfect culmination to a nice weekend.

While she waited for David to bring the boys home, she grabbed a stack of her *Soap Opera Digest* magazines and piled them on the table in front of her. She had started watching soaps years ago when the children were all babies and had never stopped. With all of the meetings and arrangements lately, she had fallen way behind in her ABC soaps. When that happened, she relied on the magazine's recaps.

It wasn't her favorite way to catch up because the synopsis was told from the editor's point of view and was written with the intent of having the reader react to the characters in a certain way. Additionally, Diane found that the coverage was rarely of her favorite characters. But, when you were weeks behind, it was better than nothing.

She was just getting into the third week's episode summary when there was a knock at the door. When she opened it expecting the boys, there stood David, alone. Before she got a chance to say hello, come in, he walked in past her. She could smell alcohol on him as he placed a kiss on her cheek and took a seat on the couch. This bothered her. They had an agreement that they would not drink and drive with the kids in the car.

"Where are the boys?" she asked, looking in the hallway to see if they were playing a game of hide and seek with her.

"They're at Marvin's," he responded, admiring her outfit. She had on a light blue pencil skirt and a white polo shirt that fit snugly against her breasts. "We need to talk."

This furthered annoyed Diane because she had wanted to get the boys to bed early and then turn in herself in preparation for the work week ahead. They were involved in a conversion and she already knew the days would be long. Now she was realizing that not only did David leave the boys at Marvin's, but based on his level of intoxication, she would have to be the one to pick them up. She was not looking forward to that because of the distance and the traffic on the expressway on Sunday afternoons.

"David, I wish you had brought the boys home even if you wanted to talk. They've had a long weekend." She was so annoyed with him right now she found herself rolling her eyes the way Chell did to her. Then she figured, the sooner they started talking, the sooner they would be done and she could be on her way. "What do you want to talk about?"

"Just, why the hell you can't do one damn thing the way I ask you to do it."

"What are you talking about? What did I do wrong in your eyes now?"

"Why did you tell Robert about Luis when I asked you to allow us do that together?"

'Ugh,' Diane thought. She had meant to call him last night and tell him what had happened. But she was exhausted by the time they got home, unpacked the car, put everything away and then started their normal evening routine. She was going to call him before she fell asleep, but Chell asked if she could sleep in her room and watch TV with her. Unfortunately, before Diane knew it, the television was watching both of them.

"David, let me explain, that was not my intent, at all. Chell is still reeling from the Roger/Goober mess and she just hit a limit yesterday and blurted it out. Once she did, I had to explain it to Robert. I had planned to call you and give you the heads up last night, but the night got away from me."

"I just bet it did…but we'll get back to that. And don't you dare blame this on Chell. You didn't have to tell him, no matter what she said. You could have continued to perpetrate the lie a few more days. So why didn't you?"

"I didn't think it was best for him. You weren't there. He was becoming unhinged. I just knew I wouldn't have a good explanation or earn any respect if I stood there and lied to his face yesterday and then turned around and told him the truth a few days later. I'm pretty sure you would have done the same thing, so I hope you can understand why I didn't lie."

"I don't understand shit, Diane. Not one goddamn thing!" he said, slamming his fist on the table and shifting the magazines slightly. "You told him because you saw it as a way to endear yourself to Luis. Didn't you?"

When faced with the choice of protecting David or protecting herself, she had taken the path of least resistance by not lying to Robert and having that backfire on her days later. The same way her mother had done to him. When Diane was beginning to figure out who had told Mama Margaret about Chell, Mama Margaret had thrown David to the wolves to maintain her relationship with her daughter, even though Mama Margaret had pledged her loyalty to him. And in the process, she had torpedoed David's relationship with Diane.

It was Mama Margaret's fault Diane was so mad at him. It was her meddling that was driving Diane away from him and toward Luis. And when David had confronted Mama Margaret about it, she told him she did what she thought was best at the time. It sounded just like the explanation Diane was hiding behind right now. Neither of them had stood behind their word and he was not going to continue to do things the way they wanted to anymore. He pounded his fist in anger once again.

Diane jumped from the loudness of his fist hitting the table. "What are you talking about David? That is absolutely not why I did it. Honestly, it was all about Robert and what was best for him," she answered quickly. She could tell his anger was escalating and she was trying to diffuse it as best she could.

David rose from the couch and moved toward her, saying, "I am not going to let you make me look like a fool. Are you fucking him? Is that how the night got away from you? And don't lie to me. I know you are. I see it all over your body." The way she was standing, the softness in her face and her hair. She was wearing it down and in soft curls. She hardly ever wore it like that in the five years they were married. It was usually in a ponytail even though he liked it loose. For the last few weeks, it was free flowing. 'Now, why is that?' he wondered.

Diane felt her anxiety building in concert with his anger because his behavior was very unsettling. She assumed it was being fueled by the alcohol and that was a dangerous combination. She wanted to put some distance between them so she walked around the back of the couch and sat near the end before responding softly, hoping to help lower his level of aggravation. "David, do you hear yourself? I need you to calm down."

He watched her breasts rise and lower according to the increase in the frequency of her breaths. He was looking at her legs, the firmness in her calves, and remembering how good she always felt to him. David thought, 'Yeah, I'm pretty sure something is going on with that asshole Luis. Men can tell when other men are sniffing around their stuff.'

Diane was searching her mind to find a way to reach him. She had to make sure he knew that she had not betrayed him. She pulled on her skirt to make sure it wasn't bunched up under her. It was a cotton blend and wrinkled easily. She had meant to smooth it out before she sat down. She hated ironing and seldom wore the skirt but it was cute on her and matched her mood when she woke up that morning, carefree and happy.

Then he saw it. It was very subtle, but she did it. She pulled on her skirt to pull it down. Was she really trying to cover up her stuff from him, her husband? Oh, Luis had done more than sniff it, he had touched it, and David was not going down like that. And as unpredictable as a lightning strike, his mind shifted and the rage took over. He picked up the magazines and threw them against the wall. They scattered all about and Diane jumped again. He didn't care. He wanted her to know who was in control and that he knew she was lying. She had already proven she was good at keeping secrets.

"You are not going to make a fool out of me, damn it! I won't allow that."

Diane stood and started to back away from him. As soon as she started moving, David grabbed her arm, keeping her within his reach. She wrenched from the pain and tried to free herself, saying, "David, you're hurting me. Please let me go. What are you doing?"

David was on autopilot now and nothing was registering. He began dragging her down the hallway toward the bedroom. Diane bent her knees to try and stop the forward motion, but he was too strong for her. Her mind was racing, looking for anyway to get away from his grasp. As he pulled her past Chell's bedroom door, she reached for the doorframe and held on. But he just pried her fingers loose and now had both of her arms by the wrist. Was he really about to do to her what he had saved Chell from just a few short weeks ago?

Once in the bedroom, he pushed her onto the bed and straddled her with his body, continuing to hold her arms over her head. She was kicking her legs and trying to free her hands, but his grip was firm and his body dead weight on top of her. He bent down to kiss her mouth and she shook her head to keep him from landing on her lips. But that didn't deter him; he let the kisses land wherever they could. She could feel him getting hard and he took one hand and started unzipping his pants. She pleaded with him as tears formed in her eyes, "David, stop it. Please, don't do this!"

"Shut up Diane. If you want to give your stuff away so freely, then I'm going to make sure I get mine. After all, you are my wife and I'm entitled to it."

"David it's me, Diane. Do you hear me? This isn't you. It's the alcohol. Stop and think for a minute. David!"

Her words were battling against David's sense of right and wrong, but they were being overpowered just like her body was. The words were colliding into each other, but wrong was winning and the others began retreating. So did Diane. She stopped fighting him and just laid still. She didn't want him to physically hurt her. When she did, David released her hands and was fully engaged. It took him longer than usual to climax, but when his rhythm finally slowed she knew that he finally did. She could feel his heart racing, the same way hers had earlier, but for completely different reasons. When that too slowed, she pushed against him and he rolled off her onto the bed.

She laid next to him for a minute, on what used to be his side of the bed, before she rose. With her back to him, she pulled her skirt down and touched her hair ever so gently. She then turned to face him. He was lying on his back with his eyes closed. She looked directly at him and said, "I hope you enjoyed that because it will be the last goddamn time you touch me. You just killed what was left of our marriage in the bed we shared as husband and wife for five years. Look at the bruises on my arms and my thighs."

When he didn't open his eyes, she raised her voice and turned her arms and hands palm up. "Look at them David!" When he finally did, she said, "You did that to me. You just raped the woman you claim to love. I could have you arrested for what you just did…but I won't. Because the next time you hear from me, it will be through my attorney and you will accept whatever terms I request."

She lowered her arms and briskly brushed away the lingering wetness on her cheeks. "Now, I'm going to take a shower. Have Marvin bring my boys home within the hour. Call in advance from now on to make arrangements to pick them up because I will be nowhere around when you come. And get up and get the hell out of my house."

Diane turned away from him, walked into the bathroom and gently closed the door. She didn't even lock it because she had the power now. She looked at her image in the mirror and observed the wrinkled skirt and disheveled hair. She had just had it done on Friday. She had spent time in the mirror just this morning admiring how it looked. It was healthier than it had been in years. She slipped out of her clothes, turned on the shower and waited for it to get hot. When it was, she stepped in and allowed the water to wash every visible sign and smell of her ex-husband from every inch of her body. They were done.

CHAPTER FOURTY THREE

43

Diane was sitting at the kitchen table with her check list. She had made quite a bit of progress on it during the week. She had contacted an attorney and started the divorce proceedings. The attorney had tried to convince Diane to file for a legal separation first, but Diane ensured her that was no longer necessary. She had already outlined the settlement she wanted. They would split everything they had 50/50 with the exception of the proceeds from Carlos' insurance coverage. Luckily, she had placed it into a trust in the children's names, so legally, David was not entitled to any of it. The attorney had also drafted a preliminary visitation schedule. Given that Robert was not biologically his son, joint custody was not an issue for the judge to rule on.

The next item on her list was to secure a realtor. Diane wanted to move into a house. She chose a location that would afford a good education for the kids, but not add too much time to her commute to work. She wanted a place large enough to accommodate the boys, Chell and Luis J, should he chose to move back home at some point. And there would also be room for his child, if it turned out that way. She wanted him to be able to spend as much time as possible with his child and be a good father to him or her.

A move would also allow Chell to go to a new school district and have a fresh start. Therefore, it was Diane's intent to be in their new home by the first of August. She had gone out with the realtor on Saturday and found a few promising prospects, so she was confident that her date was doable

She and Luis had discussed the immediate future, with a focus on the children. They were in alignment around the approach to use with Robert, and the boys were actually with him for the weekend. She had talked to Robert a few times on the phone and he was adjusting well. She was very thankful for that.

She had also scheduled their first series of appointments with the therapist. They would occur during the week, with one on the weekend.

That left only one item on the list she hadn't touched, but she would address that one today. Diane glanced at her watch in anticipation of Chell's arrival. She and her aunt Michelle were due back any minute. She had really missed her daughter, but hoped it had been fun for her. When she walked in grinning from ear to ear, Diane was comforted. She hadn't seen that Chell in a very long time and she had missed her.

When Chell burst in the house, she gave her mother a big hug followed by a complete rundown of her last week: the trip to Uncle Steve, the Judge's, courtroom where he had allowed her to bang the gavel a few times; working in Michelle's office a few days and helping her with filing; and having the responsibility of walking Scooter twice a day. All of these experiences had made the week fun.

She just couldn't stop talking about the people, the things she had done and the one-on-one time she had shared with Auntie Michelle. Diane was so thankful to her sister and brother-in-law for providing her child a loving environment. They ate the sandwiches Diane had made and then Chell bounced down the hall to her room.

"Can you stay for a little while?" Diane asked her sister with a warm, welcoming smile.

"Sure. The traffic shouldn't be too bad. Did you enjoy your week?" Michelle asked, before pointing to the paper on the table. "I see you are making lists. I recognize that Diane; that's the one on a mission," Michelle noted, smiling at her baby sister.

"I did. It was very cathartic for me in a number of ways."

"So, have you made any decisions about your marriage and Luis?"

"Wow, straight to the point, I see, Attorney Grant." Diane wasn't sure where to begin, so she thought she would start with the lowest point and work forward. She hadn't shared with anyone the violation she had suffered by her husband's hands, but she did today. She chose words that found a way to convey her anger, resentment and ultimate closure. Once she stopped, Michelle didn't say anything. Instead, she just gave her sister the kind of hug that soothes the soul and heals wounds. That was all Diane needed before she continued sharing her other accomplishments and plans. She was moving her life forward and that was bringing her great comfort.

"Diane, I'm so proud of you. You have really found yourself. I'm just sorry that David violated you like that. You didn't deserve it. Mama's precious David. Isn't that ironic? Are you going to tell her?"

"Probably…but only so she won't meddle in any of my future plans. David isn't a bad person. I grew up and he couldn't handle it. He became possessive and then jealous the closer Luis and I became. I wish him well though." After a brief pause of reflection, Diane continued, "There is one favor I have to ask of you. It's regarding Chell."

"You know that's my heart. What do you need?"

"I don't want her hanging around here all summer with nothing to do and no one to watch her. I'm worried that no good will come of it.

I was wondering if she could stay with you and Steve. I'll contribute toward her expenses, of course."

"Do you think she will want to come with us for the whole summer? You know she'll miss you and the boys, of course. She has really grown attached to CJ. I know you're trying to do what's best for her, but are you sure this is it?"

"Did you see that happy little girl who bounced in here? That's the Chell I raised. That's the Chell who has been missing for quite some time. I can't provide her the love and care she needs to get stronger right now. I need to find my way first and this will give me the time to do that as well. I want to create a home that is loving for all of the children under my roof, but especially for Chell. One where she can find the same safe haven she experienced at your home this past week. This summer break will give me that time. We'll come visit her on the weekends, including Luis."

"Well, it might be a little tight if the two of you aren't willing to share the same bed," Michelle stated, with a huge grin spreading across her face.

The Grant home was really nice. They had a four-bedroom house with a finished basement. There was plenty of room for guests or family members to have their own space. When they first moved into the home, it was in anticipation of two children. But after Michelle's third miscarriage, they resigned themselves to the fact that she was not able to carry a child to full term. They had considered adopting at one time, but Steve's career was taking off so they put that on the back burner and focused on enjoying life with one another. They traveled all over the world and didn't want for any material things.

So Diane responded, "Girl, with all that room you have, I can't see why that would be a problem. But, by this summer, we just might be!" They both chuckled and slapped five.

"Diane, I would be happy to take her, but let me check with Steve first. We were planning a trip this summer to the Dominican Republic, but she can certainly come with us. You have plenty of time to make sure she has her passport. It will be tons of fun."

The sisters continued talking about choices and life's lessons before Michelle announced it was time for her to head back to Jersey. As she closed the door behind herself, she smiled because she was leaving behind a stronger black woman who was working to find her new center of gravity. Her baby sister was going to be just fine. She smiled to herself because, ordinarily, she couldn't wait to tell her mother, but not this time.

44 CHAPTER FOURTY FOUR

Luis J was almost home. He was returning from their third family therapy session and was in a good place with the open dialogue and honesty that was being shared by everyone. The topic of Maria hadn't surfaced yet and he wasn't sure how things would progress once it did, but the therapist had instructed all of them to trust the process. He pulled into the parking spot and grabbed his phone on the third ring. "Speak."

"Luis J?"

He wondered if his mind was playing tricks on him. He pulled the phone away from his ear to check the display, but the number was blocked. "Yeah, who's this?"

"It's Dany," she said and then paused, nervously awaiting his response.

"Hey, Dany! How are you?" Luis J said slowly, articulating each word. He was apprehensive about the call, but pleasantly surprised to hear her voice. They hadn't spoken since the day he told her about his living arrangements with Maria. He had seen her around school and, of course, at the ball games, but they had respected each other's space. He often wondered if she had hooked up with anyone else. As pretty as she was, he was certain someone had asked her out by now, but he hadn't seen any evidence of it.

"I'm doing well. I just wanted to call because I heard about what happened to Chell and I wanted to say how horrible I felt about that. I never liked Goober or Roger. Roger used to tell me that I was too good for you and he was the one who eventually told me you were cheating on me. He tried to hit on me a few times, but I always shut him down."

"Dany, why didn't you tell me? I would have confronted him about it," Luis J said, surmising that Dany was part of Roger's plan to destroy him, too.

"Because I knew that's what you would do and I didn't want you to get into any trouble. Roger is an asshole and I knew how to handle him. I could see right through his BS. But anyway, he got what he deserved, finally. I just wish I knew he was going after Chell. I could have protected her from him."

She paused for a moment to connect with her feelings. Since she had learned about Chell, she had sat her sister Steph down and had a long talk with her about boys. She wanted to protect her sister from any experience like Chell's.

"Luis J, I know how close you and Chell are, but sometimes a girl needs to talk to another girl. So I just wanted to tell you that if she wants to talk, she can call me. I always liked her. She's a sweet girl."

Luis J was now realizing that Roger had also broken one of the team's unwritten codes of conduct: Don't mess with someone else's girl. Dany was absolutely right not to have told him because he would have ripped Roger's head off his shoulders for sure. And now, he was touched by Dany's offer. As he listened to her, it reminded him of the countless conversations they used to have and how she would always be willing to be his sounding board and often his voice of reason, like Carlos had been for years. He had lost that.

He realized now that their breakup had also contributed to his turning to alcohol and drugs. Not only had he lost his brother, but his girl, too, all within a few weeks of each other. It was just too hard to face, so he found another way to dull the pain. But Dany's reaching out to him now highlighted her genuineness. She was still the same thoughtful girl he had fallen for two years ago and he missed her. He wondered if they would ever be able to rekindle their friendship, or even something more.

"Thanks Dany. I'll tell her. I really appreciate your willingness to help. Especially given all that you and I have gone through."

"I still care about you, Luis J. I never meant to hurt you. I hope you believe that."

"Hey, that's what I was just going to say to you. I never meant to hurt you either and I never stopped caring about you."

After a brief pause, she asked, "Are you still living with your baby's mama?"

'Oh well, that was short lived,' Luis J thought. He was pretty sure the awkwardness would return once he answered that question. He wished she had kept the high road.

"I'm still living with a friend. Things have changed since we last spoke. It's complicated and I would prefer not to go into it right now. I hope you understand and that it doesn't change the honesty we just shared with each other."

Dany had heard that he was living with some grown-ass woman, but she wasn't sure of the extent of their connection. She noticed that he didn't say girlfriend, which was different than the last time they had talked about it. She shrugged her shoulders and said, "Sure. Well, I have to go. Remember to give Chell my message. I'll talk to you later."

"I hope so. Take care," Luis J added. He wanted to say more but it wasn't the right time, so he just left it there. Perhaps he would have another opportunity since she had said, "I'll talk to you later."

When he walked into the apartment, he found Maria lying on the couch. She looked flush and was holding her stomach.

"Maria, are you alright?"

"No. I'm not feeling well. I was in the kitchen and became really lightheaded. Then I started having cramps. I tried to get to my phone to call you, but I couldn't make it any further than the couch. I had just laid down right before you walked in."

Luis J walked over to her and felt her forehead. She didn't seem to have a fever, but she wasn't looking herself at all. "What do you want me to do?"

"I think I need to go to the hospital. Something's not right."

Based on Maria's tone, Luis J knew there was a sense of urgency. Ironically he was in the same position Maria had been seven years ago when she had watched his mother suffering with her pregnancy with Robert, based on what Carlos had shared with him. He didn't know what Maria had thought then but he grabbed her jacket, helped her stand and took her to the car. She was moaning and breathing heavily the entire ride to the ER. When he finally pulled in front of the doors, he jumped out and motioned to an attendant, who was smoking a cigarette on the bench.

"She's pregnant and cramping. Also very flushed," Luis J summarized quickly.

The attendant crushed the butt on the floor and grabbed a nearby wheelchair. Once he had Maria in tow, Luis J headed to the parking garage. By the time he returned to the ER, Maria had already been triaged and was under the doctor's care. The nurse directed him to the waiting room until further notice. While he sat there, unsure of what was happening or going to happen, he called his father to give him an update.

Since Luis' condo wasn't too far away, he told Luis J he was on his way to be with both of them. Luis J thumbed through the magazines as he awaited his father's arrival and some word on Maria's condition. The former happened first. Father and son hugged, Luis J gave him a more detailed explanation, and then they both waited for an update. When the nurse finally returned, she was only able to provide a brief synopsis of what was happening with Maria.

"Ms. Diaz gave me permission to talk to Luis Rodriquez. Which one of you is he?"

"We both are, actually. I'm senior and he's junior."

"Oh, she didn't specify, so I'll share this with both of you. She is being examined by the doctors, an obstetrician and a neonatologist. We've determined that her blood pressure is very elevated and she's also in premature labor. The doctors are discussing the best course of action. Once I have any additional information, I'll come back and let you know."

"It's way too early for the baby to be born. She's only 6 months. What are you doing to stop the labor?" Luis asked, very familiar with this process and the implications of a birth at this stage of gestation.

"As I said, the doctor is still examining her and assessing the best course of action. That's all I have for now," the nurse repeated, before retreating back down the hallway to Maria's room. All they could do at this point was wait and see. Luis said a prayer and acknowledged that they likely had a long night ahead of them.

When the nurse reentered the room, she found Maria still awake and watching all of the machines to which she was connected. There was a fetal heart monitor registering the baby's vitals, a blood pressure cup that inflated on her arm every ten minutes or so, and an IV. In an attempt to redirect her attention, the nurse said, "Ms. Diaz, I gave them an update as you asked."

Maria nodded. She was still feeling lightheaded, but she wondered who the nurse was referring to with the term "them." Returning her attention to the activity in the room, she could tell from all of the scurrying that her condition was serious. She had been trying to be patient, waiting for someone to give her an update, but her patience was now worn thin and she said to the people in the room, "Excuse me. Would someone please tell me what's going on?"

"Ms. Diaz, my name is Dr. Taylor. I am the obstetrician on call. We've paged your doctor and she is on the way, but I'll tell you what's going on. I am concerned about your blood pressure. We have already sent for your records, but did your OB-Gyne ever tell you that you had preeclampsia?"

"No. Never. What does that even mean?" Maria shot back, looking for as much clarification as possible.

"Your blood pressure is extremely elevated. It's 140 over 100. This can happen sometimes during pregnancy. We're going to start you on some medication to help lower it, but you are also in premature labor. That requires us to pick the right combination of medications. We really want you to keep the baby in utero for at least another four to six weeks. However, in case the medication doesn't work or your condition worsens, I've asked Dr. Brown to examine you and your blood work as well. He is the neonatologist."

Dr. Brown now moved closer to Maria's bed to talk to her. "Ms. Diaz, I'm running some tests now and will know more about your baby's health and viability shortly. Once I've finished that, we'll talk in more detail. I know you must have a lot of questions, but for now, I want you to rest and focus on keeping your baby nestled inside of you. That's the best thing you can do for your child. We'll be back shortly." Dr. Brown rubbed her shoulder and then they stepped out of the room.

"Nurse, is Luis J able to come in here with me?" Maria asked. She was so scared and worried she knew she didn't want to be alone. She started patting her stomach and then stopped. For the first time, she realized that she always patted it. She never rubbed it like she had seen countless women do. The way Diane had rubbed her stomach the day she went into premature labor. She now took her hand and rubbed her tummy gently, lovingly, connecting with the life that was growing inside of her. When she did, the contractions subsided a little.

"Sure, I'll get him." The nurse assumed since she said Luis J, she must be referring to the younger one. She finished adjusting the IV drip, checked her blood pressure reading, and then headed to the hallway. She found the two men in deep conversation.

"Excuse me. Ms. Diaz is asking for Luis J. Would you care to follow me?" she asked, leading the way to the room. But when she turned around, she saw that he wasn't following her. He was still in conversation with his father. "When you're ready, we're in room 1111," she said, returning to complete the doctor's orders for Ms. Diaz.

"Papi, she asked for me because she doesn't know you're here. You two were together for a long time. If anyone can provide her comfort through this, it would be you, not me. I think you should go and be with her. She must be freaking out."

"But mijo, this might be your child. Don't you want to be there in case it is born early?"

"Papi, I honestly don't think she's carrying my baby. It just doesn't feel like it's mine. That probably sounds crazy, but…"

"Actually, it doesn't. I know exactly what you mean. Maria has been playing games with us and our emotions for months now, but I believe she already knows whose baby she's carrying. That child, like you and me, has been a pawn Maria has been using for some outcome she hopes will make her happy. Sadly, I think it may all be blowing up in her face now," Luis concluded.

He had had time lately to think back on Maria's actions and he did remember that she hadn't used the diaphragm two times: the night after Carlos' death and the night he had returned from San Juan. Every other time in their sexual history, the diaphragm was in place because he would feel it after he entered her. Those two particular nights, he was in so much pain, he just wanted her warmth and comfort and he never suspected she would be so manipulative as to have unprotected sex while she was ovulating. Little did he know then that she was just being Maria and weaving a net of chaos and confusion. Using his pain and loss to create a life with a man she knew didn't love her was classic Maria. She could foresee, better than both of them, that Carlos' loss would change everything between him and Diane, and she was not about to be left with the short stick.

"Luis J, this is probably going to sound like a weird question, especially coming from your father, but do you remember feeling anything inside of her when you had sex that night? It would have felt like a condom, but on the inside."

Luis J thought back to that night, to the good and the bad, before responding, "Now that you mention it, I do. I remember thinking it felt like I was rubbing against something. Was she wearing a diaphragm?"

Luis J had never slept bareback with anyone except Dany, and all of the other girls he had sex with were on the pill even when he used a condom. So he didn't know how a diaphragm actually felt, but in retrospect, he was pretty sure that's what she had used.

"Yes, I believe she was," Luis opined. "So unless the diaphragm wasn't working, which is possible, I don't think the baby is yours."

"Wow, Mami was right about Maria all along. She is something else. No offense, Papi, but how in the…I mean, how did you get mixed up with her in the first place?"

"Remember what I told you some time ago? Your choices determine your consequences. I have been living with mine for over five years. We'll talk some more about this, but for now, there's a woman on the other side of that door who is sick and needs support and help so I'm going to be there for her, in spite of her manipulation. Are you going to hang around? You can if you want to."

"Naw. I'm heading home. Call me when you know something." Luis J stood and embraced his father. "Tell Maria I said good luck." And with that, Luis J left the hospital.

When Luis entered the room, the image he saw was sobering, but he squared his shoulders and strolled over to Maria's bedside. Her eyes were closed and her hand was moving in a circular motion on her abdomen. He touched her arm and she turned her head in his direction. He met her stare with a warm, comforting smile and a few humorous comments.

"So I see you couldn't wait to become a mother after all. And you almost have the whole hospital waiting on you hand and foot. How are you feeling?"

Maria was surprised to see Luis standing there, but honestly she was thankful. She reached out her hand and he held it with a sense of strength and care.

"I'm scared, Luis. They haven't given me much information but I can tell by the whispers and the attention that this is serious."

"Hey, one step at a time. We just need to wait and see what the tests show. If it's alright with you, I'd like to stay."

She nodded her head. She had envisioned all kinds of scenarios when it was time to give birth, but none of them even remotely resembled this one. She was so deep in thought that she didn't notice that Dr. Brown and Dr. Taylor had returned.

"Ms. Diaz, we have the results of your tests and are ready to discuss our plans with you," Dr. Taylor began. "Is it alright to talk in front of this gentleman?"

Maria quickly introduced them and then said, "Yes, you can go ahead."

"We have started giving you a medication to lower your blood pressure and we should start to see it come down pretty quickly. However, we have determined that the baby is in distress. We will not be able to stop the contractions. Dr. Brown will share with you what implications that will have on your baby."

Stepping closer to the bed, he started, "Ms. Diaz, do you know the sex of the baby?"

"No." She and Luis J had guessed it was a girl, but she hadn't even gotten to the point of asking her doctor to perform that test. She had been trying to avoid any tests that might prematurely reveal the paternity to either of them, although she already knew. She had known all along. 'How ironic,' she thought, 'that she just used the word prematurely.'

"This discussion might be easier if I told you the sex. Is that alright with you?"

"Sure, yes. Just tell me what's going on." At this point, everything else was a much lower priority.

"I'm not going to sugarcoat this. Your baby is very premature. Her lungs are not fully developed and she is in distress with every contraction that you are having. I'm recommending that we do a cesarean as soon as possible. I've already assembled the team in the OR and they're waiting for us."

So they had been right; it was a girl and now her daughter needed her to do what was best for her. "No. You said I needed to keep her inside of me for four to six more weeks. How can delivering her now be what's best for her?"

"Yes, we did say that originally, but I'm telling you that with the results of your tests, that's no longer an option. We need to deliver her now so we can try to help her from outside your womb. If you take note of the monitor, every time you have a contraction, her heart rate lowers. She won't survive in utero four more hours, let alone four more weeks."

'There was no sugar coating in that comment at all,' Luis thought. The doctor was being very direct about their options. He just hoped that Maria would grasp the severity and do what was best for their daughter. He was about to offer his point of view when she suddenly started shaking. Immediately, the doctors began attending to her and the nurse escorted him from the room. As he was leaving, he heard one of them say, "She's seizing. Her pressure's too high. We have to get her to the OR, stat."

Luis found a seat in a chair near the door. He removed his phone to call Diane, but it was already ringing.

"Luis, it's me, Diane. Luis J called and told me what's going on. He told me everything. How are you doing with all of this?"

"It's pretty crazy right now. They just took her up to do an emergency cesarean. It's not looking very good. She was seizing. Honestly, I'm worried about both of them. She's having a girl."

Diane could hear the distress in his voice. "Do you want company? I could come over and be with you."

"That's a really generous offer considering who we're talking about, but I don't want you to leave the kids. Thanks, but just talking to you on the phone is helpful."

And that's what they did. Luis continued sharing his observations and concerns and with each one, Diane offered loving, supportive comments. About an hour later, the nurse offered an update and he gave her his undivided attention, ending the call with Diane.

"Maria is in post-op. Her pressure is now back to normal and there doesn't appear to be any lingering side effects. The baby has been delivered and is now in the neonatal ICU. Dr. Brown will provide an update to both of you as soon as Maria is taken to her room. Follow me, please." The nurse escorted Luis to Maria's room, where he waited for her.

It was two hours later before Maria was brought to the room and was conscious enough to receive any updates. Luis had tried to see Baby Girl Diaz, as the nurse had called her, but she was not stable enough yet and he had to wait. He sat in the chair next to Maria's bed and watched her dozing off and on. It made him flashback to Robert's premature birth where, no thanks to Maria, they had a similar scare. But fortunately, Robert was developed enough to do well outside of the womb.

Dr. Parker visited first to share an update regarding Maria's health. "Your vitals are good. You're going to have some soreness in your abdomen from the surgery, but everything should heal nicely and you'll be able to still wear a bikini," he said, smiling. "The nurses will be by shortly to get you on your feet tonight. You should experience normal bleeding, but if anything appears to be out of the norm, let us know immediately. You will likely be here for a couple of days so we can monitor your blood pressure, but I'm really not expecting there to be any issues. Do you have any questions about your body or your health?"

"Not at the moment. I'm more concerned about my daughter."

Dr. Brown took his cue and began, "Ms. Diaz and Mr. Rodriquez, I'm sorry to say I don't have good news for you. Baby Girl Diaz is in trauma. We are doing everything we can for her. We're trying desperately to stabilize her small body – she's only a pound and six ounces – but we're facing an uphill battle. The next twenty-four hours will be critical and so we are monitoring her very closely. She is intubated and in an incubator. I wish I could give you more to hold onto, but I want you to know how serious her condition really is."

Maria bit her bottom lip to keep from crying hysterically. He had just told her that her daughter might not make it through the night. She looked at Luis to see his reaction. He was probably hoping she would die so he could go back to his precious Diane and not have to be bothered with her and their baby anymore. Even Luis J had already left her without so much as a "goodbye" after all she had done for him. Well, she didn't need them. She and her daughter would be just fine without either of them. "I want to see her."

"Ms. Diaz, that's not possible right now. We have her in isolation and only essential personnel will be allowed in there tonight. Unless something changes, you should be able to see her in the morning. Do either of you have any other questions?"

"Is she in any pain or distress? We don't want her to suffer," Luis stated.

"She isn't in any pain. I promise you that." Dr. Brown waited for a few minutes and then both doctors retreated, bidding them goodnight.

"Maria, I..."

"Don't say a damn word. You never wanted this baby anyway. She was an inconvenience at best. I don't even know why you're here."

"You don't have any idea how I feel right now. You dangled this pregnancy around our necks to cause all kinds of turmoil and not once did I wish ill for you or that baby. Not one damn time. And if you think I did or do, you don't know me at all," Luis responded.

It was the second time he made that revelation. In fact, he had already told Maria that same thing a few months ago. He thought she had understood him, better than Diane, which is why they hooked up at first. But what she really knew was how to please him, physically, and stroke his ego. That was what she was good at, but when it was time to address adult challenges, she was not the one to stand next to him and help figure things out. She was not the one who was a rock in good times and bad. It was Diane...and always had been. So, no, she didn't know him. How could she?

Given that, Luis continued, "Now, you've been through a horrific night and your hormones are off balance, so I suggest you get some rest and I'll be back in the morning. Because, at the end of the day, that baby is my daughter and she is lying in that incubator fighting for her life. She is going to need both of her parents to help her through this. I'll be back around 9 a.m. Good night, Maria."

Before she could say anything, Luis grabbed his coat from the back of the chair and walked out. He was done playing Maria's games. All of her manipulations and backhanded, conniving ways had no place in his life anymore.

Maria watched him walk out and turned up her nose. Oh, she knew him. She knew exactly what he was planning and she was going to find some way to stop that reconciliation. She pressed the button to dispense more morphine and waited to fall asleep.

45
Chapter Fourty Five

The next morning, Maria and Luis were taken to the Neonatal ICU. In one section of the room was an incubator that their daughter had slept in the night before, clinging to life. They were dressed in hospital gowns, gloves and shoe covers, and wore masks over their mouths. Her immune system was very fragile and could not have any germs introduced in her environment.

Maria sat in the wheelchair and slowly reached her hand inside the incubator's cutout. The baby was so small it was almost covered by Maria's hand. Her eyes were shut and they could barely see her face because of the tubes, lines and IVs. Maria still managed to find a small area of exposed skin and she rubbed it gently through the glove.

Luis stood slightly behind her, shaking his head. He had never seen a baby that size and it brought tears to his eyes. It didn't seem like this was best for this child, any child. He remembered the doctor's guarantee about her not experiencing any pain, but standing there witnessing what she had gone through to get all of this equipment connected to her made him question that response.

He reached out and rubbed Maria's shoulders. He wondered how she was handling all of this. She hadn't said much to him since he arrived so he broke the silence, "Maria, we need to name her. Did you have one in mind?"

Maria didn't stop rubbing her, but responded to the question. "Gabriella. I like Gabriella, with two l's." She looked up at the nurse who was attending to the machines and said, "What do we need to do to change the tag to Gabriella Diaz? I want all of you to call her Gabriella and stop saying Baby Girl Diaz. Please." It was important for her daughter to have a name. Maria wanted them to connect with her as a person, not just another preemie.

Her mother had told her stories about premature babies and that was one fact she had remembered: when they had a name, it seemed everyone worked harder to save their life.

The nurse nodded her head and told her what was required to make the change. She handed Luis a marker and he crossed out "Baby Girl" and replaced it with "Gabriella."

When the nurse moved, she motioned to Luis that he could sit on the other side and he did. He, too, reached in, carefully, to touch his daughter. He said a prayer over her and then just sat next to her quietly. This routine continued for two days. They would sit by Gabriella's side and wait to see if there was any improvement. They were allowed to stay with her for thirty-minute intervals. In between that time, there were routines the nurses had to follow to keep her vitals as stable as possible.

Dr. Brown had shared that Gabriella was holding her own, but she wasn't improving the way he would like to see. Maria elected to only embrace the first half of his sentence, "She was holding her own."

Luis watched Maria become more and more attached to Gabriella. She was becoming a mother right in front of his eyes and he had mixed emotions about that. If Gabriella lived, Maria was showing him how much she loved her. But if Gabriella died, Maria would be devastated. It was a tough situation for her and there wasn't anything he could do to help her or prepare her.

No one could have prepared him for losing Carlos; it was the biggest loss he had ever experienced and he would have to live with it for the rest of his life. He and Diane had talked about that last night. She had called to check on him and he invited her over to have dinner at his place. Luis recalled the evening as he sat there.

Diane had started, "Luis, I know this must be so difficult for you. My heart goes out to you and Maria. I wouldn't wish this on anyone, not even her," she added, trying to introduce a little humor. When she saw him smile, she continued, "I just want you to know that I am here for you. No matter what, you can count on me. And, if you and Maria will allow it, I'd like to come and see Gabriella. She's our children's sister, your daughter, and sort of my ex-stepdaughter. Let me know when and if an opportunity presents itself for you to broach the subject with Maria. But only if it doesn't add any stress to her or you."

"Diane, that is so gracious of you," Luis had responded. "Your heart is so big and forgiving. It means a lot to me that you would open it to my daughter with Maria. But I have to ask, is there still any room in your heart for me, too?" He froze as he waited for the answer.

She had already told him that David wasn't contesting the divorce and that it would be final within a few months. She had also been making all kinds of plans to move on with her life and he wondered if there was a place for him, or if there was still too much hurt.

"Luis, you never left my heart. I compartmentalized my feelings for you because it made it easier for me to deal with the hurt and the loss, but they were always there. I love you. I never stopped loving you. But I don't want us to rush into anything. You have to focus on Gabriella right now and then you will have to work out custody arrangements with Maria. Those discussions will likely go better if we aren't rubbing her nose in our happiness. I also have some personal accomplishments to make and I need to do that to ensure I am whole before we become a couple again. I know that's a long answer to your question and may have been more than you asked…but you opened the door!" she said, laughing.

He had opened the door and she had waltzed in. He took her into his arms and they made love, for the first time in a long, long time. It was as he had remembered, but it was also different. She was different. She was a woman now, in the true sense of the word, and he was a man and that's what they experienced. Diane didn't spend the night, though, because, as she had said, they were going to take things slowly. He had laid in the bed still able to smell her scent, remembering her touch, and he eventually drifted off to sleep.

Luis' attention was snapped back into the hospital room with Maria when the monitor alarm sounded. He stood up and the room was full of nurses and doctors within seconds. He and Maria were ushered out into the hallway.

"Luis, what's happening? What's wrong with Gabriella?" Maria screamed, moving into his arms. He held her without saying a word and they waited just outside the door for some explanation. One by one, the crowd in the room thinned out, but no one said a word to them until finally Dr. Brown's resident joined them in the hallway.

He walked up to them and cleared his throat before speaking. Luis could tell that the news wasn't good, so he increased his hold on Maria and they waited for him to begin.

"Ms. Diaz and Mr. Rodriquez, Gabriella's condition has worsened. She has had a stroke."

"A stroke? That's not possible. Babies can't have strokes. You must be mistaken!" Maria barked at him. "Where's Dr. Brown? He has been with Gabriella since she was born. He knows what's best for my daughter."

"I know he has and so have I. It's his day off or he would have been here. I just talked to him before I came out here to talk to you."

Luis adjusted his hold around Maria and felt her muscles relax a little. He then asked the doctor to continue.

"Babies can have strokes and Gabriella has just had one. I'm sorry. She is no longer showing any signs of brain activity. She's gone. The only thing keeping her alive are the machines. We tried to save her. I hope you know that, but as Dr. Brown said from the beginning, it was an uphill battle. She just wasn't strong enough."

"I don't believe you. She was just fine. I have been here every day and she's been getting stronger. She even gained a few ounces. I want to see her. Now!" Maria demanded, pushing her way into the room and changing into fresh coverings.

Once again, Luis had lost a child, both in such tragic and sudden ways. He hoped that he would never have to experience a loss like that again. "Thank you Doctor for taking care of our Gabriella for the few short days she was on this earth. What happens now?"

"As I said, she is being kept alive by the machines. I know you haven't had the chance to hold her, so if you'd like, we can disconnect her and put her in your arms until she takes her final breath. I don't think it will be long. But legally, Ms. Diaz has to make that call. She is the only one with the rights to do that. I'm going to leave the two of you to discuss it and then just let us know what you decide. If she were my daughter, I would want to hold her through this transition. Again, we're sorry we couldn't do more." The doctor touched Luis' shoulder and then walked away.

'He's right,' Luis thought. He did want to hold her. He did not want her to die alone in the belly of some machine. He reentered the room and redressed also. Maria was in her usual spot rubbing Gabriella. Luis noticed that she was very still. He watched her chest rise and fall in synchronization with the machine and it was so painful for him. But the doctor had been clear, it was Maria's choice. He just hoped she would do the right thing.

"Luis I'm being punished. I have caused so much pain and hurt in your life, Diane's life, and my mother's that now it's my turn."

"Now you know it doesn't work like that, Maria. You are not being punished."

"Yes, I am. I conceived this baby to drive a permanent wedge between you and Diane. I could see the two of you pulling together and I didn't want to lose you. So I did what I do best, I got you to make love to me when I knew I was ovulating. So you see, she was not conceived out of love. I was just being manipulative the same way I have been for most of my life."

She paused a moment and brushed a tear from her cheek. "You know, I realized the other night that I had never talked to her like she was my child when I was carrying her. I talked at her, about how she was going to make you pay. I even used this baby to try and destroy any chances of a reconciliation between you and Luis J."

Maria stopped talking to Luis and began talking to Gabriella. "Gabriella, I'm sorry I didn't show you how much you meant to me. I didn't love you the way a mother is supposed to love their child, the way I have seen mothers willing to lose their life for their child. If I could breathe life into you right now and take your place, I would. Mami loves you, dearest."

She kissed her fingertips and placed them softly on Gabriella's forehead before saying, "Luis, I don't want to make her suffer any more. I need to do what's best for her for the first time in her sweet, brief life. Would you please find out how I can hold her? I want to hold her."

Luis smiled and kissed the top of Maria's head before beckoning for the nurse. They had to leave the room while the staff removed

Gabriella from the machines. While they waited, Maria said, "I get it now. I understand the pain you felt when Diane kept you from your kids because of me. I understand why she was always trying to protect them the best way she could because she didn't want anything bad to happen to them. I even understand why my mother did what she did to provide for me the best way she knew how. It was never about the sex and manipulation for her…but that's what I thought it was about and that's how I lived my life. Luis, I hope one day you will forgive me. I cost you so much and it was not even for the right reasons. It was about winning. But now I know what it really feels like to lose and to love."

The nurse opened the door and they went back into the room. One of the nurses was holding Gabriella and sitting in a rocking chair. She stood and waited for Maria to sit. Once she did, Gabriella was placed in her arms. She looked even smaller now outside of her mechanical environment. Maria held her gently and whispered to her, words meant to be heard only by her child.

"My sweet Gabriella. I am ready to set you free. You have served your purpose, but it wasn't the one I had in mind. You have changed my life and I will be a better person for it. I promise you." Maria then motioned to Luis. "Would you like to hold your daughter?" She wanted to make that proclamation as well before Gabriella died.

Luis leaned down and whispered a prayer over his Gabriella as she lay nestled in Maria's arms and then he kissed her gently on the forehead. He lingered there for a moment so he could remember her features. Then he retreated to the corner, stifling a tear, and continued watching Maria as she rocked back and forth, humming to their child. There was a calmness over her that Luis had never seen before. She seemed to finally be at peace with life.

Gabriella clung to life for an hour before she took her final breath. Maria swore that she smiled right before that, as though she felt she had accomplished her mission and was happy for the woman staring down at her. The nurse removed her lifeless body from Maria's arms and she and Luis walked into the hallway, leaving their daughter behind. The next time they would see her would be at her funeral. Maria kissed Luis on the cheek and left him standing in the hallway. There was nothing more to say to him today.

46 Chapter Fourty Six

When Maria opened the door to her apartment, the numbness hit her. She had left her baby in the hospital for the last time and would never be able to hold or see her again. She placed the keys on the table and took note of the suitcases in the hallway. She smiled to herself; it was a fitting end to her day. She entered the living room and took a seat across from Luis J.

"I'm sorry about Gabriella. I know you must be feeling really bad."

"Thanks."

"I'm sure you saw the suitcases in the hallway. I'm moving out tonight. I honestly should never have moved in here in the first place. It's time for me to get on with my life."

"I see. Where are you going?"

"I'm moving back home. I need to be there for Chell and I want to be there for my family. I need to help raise CJ. Carlos would have wanted me to do that," Luis J said, smiling fondly at his brother's memory.

After the revelation of Maria's manipulations, he had called his mother to see if he could move back home. She had told him of her plans to buy a house and that she would be delighted to have him come back home. The conversation with her was different. She was less stressed out and they had an exchange of information, not the dictatorial discussions they used to have. Diane acknowledged that Luis J was not the little boy who had moved out anymore. He was a young man and she expected him to behave in that manner.

That was the acknowledgement he was seeking, but he was also ready to accept that she had his best interest at heart and he had to respect and appreciate that. He was going home and it felt good. He had been Maria's pawn long enough.

"I know what you did Maria, how you tried to use my sister – not my daughter – to drive me away from Papi."

"Luis J, I want you to know that I didn't plan to sleep with you. I honestly was trying to help you through a tough time that night and it was the only way I could think of. It wasn't until after that, when I found out I was pregnant, that I used that night for my own personal reasons. I'm sorry I did that and I hope you will forgive me one day. I never meant to hurt you."

"I don't have any hard feelings about it," Luis J replied earnestly. "In fact, I wish you all the best. I hope you can find whatever it is you're looking for and stop trying to hurt other people. I hope that you can see now that all you really end up doing is hurting yourself. Take care, Maria. I'm out." And he turned away from her, picked up his suitcases, and left Maria's lies and deceptions behind him.

Maria sat on the couch, by herself, and cried like a baby. She cried for Gabriella and she cried for herself. She had been broken and misguided and all of that had led her down this destructive path. Now she was alone and she had to embrace why. She had made so many mistakes, but she hadn't learned from any of them until now. "I'll make you proud of me, Gabriella. You'll see," Maria said, as she rose from the sofa, took her medicine and went to bed.

Chapter Fourty Seven

Maria and Luis stood at their daughter's gravesite. They had determined that it wasn't a good idea for the kids to attend since they had recently experienced Carlos' loss and there were so many secrets and half-truths regarding Gabriella that it wouldn't really leave anyone in a good place.

Just before exiting the grave, Maria said to Luis, "I apologize for everything I did under the guise of love. I didn't know what love was until I held Gabriella in my arms." She was now looking at the small grave. "Oh, I saw it in your eyes and heard it in your voice whenever you talked about Diane and your children, but I didn't understand it. So it frustrated me and it infuriated me because I never saw it in your eyes when you looked at me or heard it in your voice when you talked to me."

Maria exhaled and could relate to the expression that hindsight is 20/20. "If I had been a friend to you back then, which is what you needed when you and Diane were having problems, you guys would never have divorced and your children would not have suffered so without their father in their life. But I didn't care about that. And when you asked me to move out and I knew it was because you wanted Diane back, I couldn't handle it. So I set the wheels in motion – 'Operation Make You Pay' for choosing Diane over me.

"It was wrong, selfish and spiteful, but I couldn't see anything but envy. And then it was a miracle. I was pregnant and had been given the best pawn in the whole world. But those toxic thoughts and actions are what contributed to us standing here in front of our daughter's grave instead of standing beside her crib. And for that, I apologize to both of you." Again, she paused. She wanted him to hear the sincerity in her voice. She needed for him to believe her.

"Thank you, Maria, for your honesty."

"Too little, too late. But I am leaving town. I'm going to move to California and try to get a fresh start on life. Besides, if I'm not around, you and Diane can truly move on with yours. You love her and she loves you. She was angry, but that fire for you was always there, which is why her marriage with David was doomed from the start. I hope you're able to work things out and reunite. You both deserve to be happy and I wish you well. I really do." She stood on tippytoe and he bent down slightly and she kissed him on the cheek. "Goodbye Luis."

"Good luck, Maria. I wish you well."

She smiled and then left him standing at the grave as she walked towards what she hoped would be the start of a richer, more meaningful life. Maria took out her cell phone and dialed a number she hadn't in years, "Mami? Yes, it's Maria..."

Luis stood there and watched Maria walk out of his life much more calmly than how she had entered it. It was really over now and he, too, could move on. The engagement ring he had brought for Diane was in his pocket. It was a two-carat, emerald-cut, diamond beauty.

Luis had sold his house and made a nice profit from it. When they were first married, he was barely able to buy a ring, but this time, he wanted everything to be different. That was one of the reasons he had chosen the emerald cut. It was unique and special – that was what she was to him, and that's what this marriage would be for both of them, this time.

Of course he knew the road would be bumpy at times; all relationships have their ups and downs. Their children were still healing and their grandson would eventually understand what had really happened to his parents and they would have to help him embrace that. But, as long as they were standing side by side, listening to each other, loving each other and having fun, they would be much stronger in this marriage.

And he, too, was a different man. Luis had loved and lost the most precious thing in his life and it had hurt him to his core. He had always been prideful and his father would tell him, repeatedly, "Mijo, pride goes before the fall." Back then, Luis had no idea what that meant, but he did now. He was not willing to compromise and give Diane what she desperately needed. She wanted them to have more than his salary afforded at the time, especially given that they had three children, but he saw it as an attack on his pride, not the pure reasons Diane intended.

It was true that she was wrestling with her own demons, but he hadn't been able to see the big picture either. His manhood, his pride, was threatened and that was not an option. So he fell…and he fell hard. He lost everything.

But now Luis had learned from his mistakes and was a better, caring, more insightful man for it. He was waiting for the right moment and then he would propose to his Di again and they would begin a "new" life as Mr. and Mrs. Rodriquez.

CHAPTER FOURTY EIGHT

48

Diane had wanted to go to the funeral with Luis, but when they talked about it, they felt it best that she and the kids remain detached. She was looking forward to having dinner with him later that evening. Luis J was back home and the house was full of life. She would laugh every time she watched Luis J take a brush and show CJ how to manage his hair. He was trying to mimic Carlos' obsession with his waves, but CJ's hair texture was completely different. The more he brushed it, the more static it built up and would not lie down. Diane chuckled, but she didn't interfere. That was for them to experience and hopefully, eventually, figure out.

She hadn't talked to her mother yet to bring her up to date on all that had happened these last few weeks, so she took this moment to step out onto the porch and dial her number. Diane had only planned to engage in a one-way conversation where she would give as much information as she felt she wanted to share and then conclude the call. But her mother was surprisingly easy to talk to, so they did. She told her about the rape, her divorce, Maria's baby, and Luis J returning home.

She also told her about her rekindled feelings for Luis. "Now Mama, I know you don't approve of my love for Luis, but I'm not seeking your approval this time. I love him and he loves me. We're going to take it slow, but we're going to be remarried. It would be nice if you gave us your blessings, but it's not going to make me change my mind if you don't."

"Diane, first of all, I have to apologize," her mother began. "I should never have interfered in your marriages, either of them. I am appalled by David's behavior. I talked to him that day and I may have helped set him off. I will have to live with the fact that I may have had a role in his snapping. I only wanted what was best for you, but I went about it the wrong way. I see that now, just like you see how you could have handled your interactions with Carlos and Luis J differently. I'm going to learn from you, but you may have to be a little patient with me. It's a new job description. It takes a long time to teach an old dog new tricks," she said, laughing that hearty laugh Diane hadn't heard in years.

"I may have to be reminded myself sometimes, Mama," Diane said, laughing with her and finally acknowledging that she had been more like her mother than her sisters all along.

"Diane, it wasn't that I didn't like Luis. I just knew how much you loved him and I was worried that you would be hurt. I respect the man that he has grown into and I'm glad you have found your way back to each other."

"Thank you for that, Mama. It means a lot. And for the record, you didn't cause David to violate me. He was building up to something like that for a long time. I don't harbor any ill feelings towards him or you."

Diane paused and then closing that book, continued, "Mama, I'm going back to school. I'm going to get my Master's. Why don't you enroll with me and we could graduate together? If you need some money, I can probably help pay for it. And I know Michelle and Cindy would help, too. After all, you sacrificed your career for us, so it would only be appropriate, now that we're grown, to help you achieve your dream. I know there's space on that wall for your degree, too. But I have to tell you, I'm keeping mine for my own wall!"

Mama Margaret patted her heart, exhaled and smiled. She was overcome with emotion and had to hold back her tears. Her baby had grown up and was in control of her life. That was all she ever wanted for her. "You're on, Missy," Margaret said, voice quivering. "You're on."

Diane ended the call, walked back into the kitchen, and saw Luis J applying water to CJ's hair. She just shook her head and went to her room to get dressed for her date.

49
Chapter Fourty Nine

Luis J sat on the edge of his bed and reflected on the changes that had occurred over the last year. There had been a lot of closure as well as new beginnings for the Rodriquez family. He was now a freshman in college at UConn, with a full basketball scholarship. He was second string, but confident that he would be with the starting team by his sophomore year. That was aggressive thinking, but he knew he had skills. Of course, he was majoring in math. He was thinking about engineering or business as his ultimate direction, but he had time for choosing that path.

He and Dany had reconnected during his senior year and that made him happy. They had a special bond that he would always treasure. She was now attending Virginia Tech as a pre-med major. They were only able to see each other during the holiday breaks, but they still found time to talk at least once a week and share updates on the milestones in their lives. He had finally learned how to harness his raging hormones and redirect them to his b-ball game and applied discipline. He wasn't spilling his seed recklessly like he had in high school.

Chell was healing, too. She ended up applying to The Putney School and was accepted. Turned out, Auntie Michelle knew someone in admissions and pulled a few strings to have her application considered after the normal deadlines. They were so impressed with her grades and poise, they extended her an offer and a pretty decent scholarship. She was settled on campus and getting acclimated to being away from home. The family was proud of how well she was doing, academically and socially. Luis J did remind her though that, if necessary, he would be on her campus in a heartbeat to keep an eye on her. He also reminded her that the guys who were interested in her better bench press more than his 250. They had laughed about it but she knew he had her back if she needed him.

The boys were adjusting well to the changes in their lives and to each other. Robert was still able to spend time with David some holidays and for two weeks in the summer. David had moved to Atlanta where he worked for a different bank and was doing well. Luis J's mother told him about a letter she had received from David. She didn't go into specifics but she said it had brought her closure.

Luis J's mother and his grandmother were now both enrolled in a Master's program and were on target to graduate in about six months. He was proud of both of them. The three of them were all involved in a one-hundred-dollar bet driven by grades. Whoever had the highest GPA at the end of the school year would win the pot. So far, his grandmother was winning, but he still had a semester to go.

His relationship with his father was now on solid ground. They had buried all of the past and held a mutual respect and admiration for one another. His father had applied for the Department Chair's position and got it. He was doing very well at the university and Luis J was happy for him.

Papi had also told Luis J that he was going to remarry his mother and asked him to be his best man. Luis J agreed, with one stipulation – that this had to be the last time. No more do-overs. Luis had laughed and said, “Until death do us part…for real this time!”

Luis J checked his ball schedule, which was mounted on his table, to confirm tomorrow’s opponent. It was Yale, the second time they were playing Yale this semester. They had lost the first game, so they had to win tomorrow to preserve their standing. “March Madness” rankings were contingent upon this game. He had heard from his UConn coach that he might actually get some court time tomorrow if there was a large enough lead. If that were the case, he knew he had to be on his game, so he turned off the lights. It was eleven-o-clock and he was exhausted. He laid down and that was his last thought of the day. That and a message to Carlos, “Hey big bro, make sure you’re watching the game tomorrow man.”

EDITOR'S NOTE

Cover Designer Renne Rhae is not present
to see or celebrate the final presentation of her work
as she passed August 6, 2018, but her memory will
live on through her wonderful works.
We miss her.

THE JOURNEY

Seventeen years is one year less than it takes for a child to become a voting adult. It is also how long it took me to give birth to my first novel, Leave Love Alone. I started writing to fill my time and to occupy my mind when I was on disability leave because I longed for a way to just get lost in a world that I could create and have total control over. I didn't have any thoughts about it becoming a published piece of work. When I was a teenager, I used to write short stories and hold my sisters and friends captive to the character's daily experiences. And as I wrote *Leave Love Alone*, I envisioned having the same outcome and that would be sufficient and fulfilling.

Every day, I would write a paragraph, a chapter or sometimes just a few thoughts. The words would flow from my head to hand to the paper as though the character was living inside my head and pushing me to write faster so he or she could share his or her experiences with me. I "finished" the story in a year, printed it and handed it to my husband, James, an avid reader. It wasn't quite the same as reading to my audience as I did when I was younger but I still enjoyed watching him laugh, tear up and get angry at various points in the story. When I saw a reaction, I would interrupt his reading to ask, "Where are you now? What's happening?"
He would answer me and then go back to reading. When he finished, he looked at me and said, "You have something special here." He began talking about the story to his family and friends, one of whom was Kai EL' Zabar, a writer, editor and publisher. That's when my journey from a story teller to a writer really began.

Kai read the story and agreed with James, I had a unique writing style and interesting storyline but it wasn't a novel. It needed character and storyline development so that they each had unique voices, mannerisms and would ultimately arc. She wanted the story to be framed from a richly contextual foundation and suggested that I study the cities in which the story takes place – to look at them the same way as people with personalities and distinctions different from the other. So I was also guided to research Puerto Rico if the story was going to talk about the heritage, countryside and its people, I had to know and be familiar with them. In other words, I wasn't finished.

For the next three years, I worked on Kai's various suggestions. I visited Puerto Rico several times, studying the history, learning about the culture and embracing their individuality and uniqueness. The story evolved, the characters became individuals and the number of pages increased significantly. I can hear Kai saying, "Let the characters talk to you. They will tell the story." And the characters spoke. I went from hearing one character's voice tell the story, to hearing the voices of each character and what they had to contribute to the evolution of what is now a novel.

The next review with Kai resulted in her seeing the growth and that was pleasing but I still had more work to do. Every other weekend, for a year, I would read the story to her, paying attention to how they spoke, ensuring each character's uniqueness was being heard through the words and descriptions of their surroundings. We both agreed, there was still more work required and the journey continued.

It's been seventeen years from the time I wrote words on a paper to get to this moment where you are reading this section in my published novel. Kai has reminded me on several occasions what I will share with you: it took the renown and highly respected poet, Maya Angelou, sixteen years to write a poem. I didn't understand it then as I do now. It has been a journey and I have learned and grown so much as a person, a writer and an author. I hope you enjoyed the story as much as I enjoyed writing it. I am working on my second novel whose main character will be a person of color, who holds an executive-level position in corporate America. I can't say when it will be published as I have also learned that novels are born when the characters finish telling their story and say, "Now, we're ready!"

— Viola Maxwell-Thompson

ABOUT THE AUTHOR

Viola Maxwell-Thompson is a new author who enjoys breathing life into her fictional characters and sharing their experiences with the readers. Her story lines are told from various points of view and explore emotions like love, fear, anger and sadness.

In addition to being an author, Ms. Maxwell-Thompson is the President and CEO of IT Senior Management Forum (ITSMF), a national organization committed to increasing the representation of black professionals in the technology industry. Their members, who are CIOs and other senior-level technology executives, are from Fortune 500 companies, the public sector, Academia and privately-owned technology companies. She has drawn on her vast experience in program management and career training to transform ITSMF into a professional development organization with the fiscal soundness and practices to prepare the next generation of black technology leaders for the executive suite.

Prior to joining ITSMF, Ms. Thompson was a partner with Ernst & Young, LLC's, where she specialized in organizational development, process re-engineering and technology deployment.

Ms. Thompson is often featured in the media for her expert insights on a variety of business topics, including diversity and the retention of executives; work-life balance issues; and career management as a female executive of color.

As a graduate of Lake Forest College and a native New Yorker, she taps into her life experiences to fuel her creativity and contribute to the development of her current and future story lines.

75520729R10428

Made in the USA
Columbia, SC
19 September 2019